APEX MAGAZINE

2021

ALSO BY JASON SIZEMORE & LESLEY CONNER

DO NOT GO QUIETLY: AN ANTHOLOGY OF VICTORY IN DEFIANCE

THE BEST OF APEX MAGAZINE: VOLUME ONE

APEX MAGAZINE (APEX-MAGAZINE.COM)

BY JASON SIZEMORE

FOR EXPOSURE: THE LIFE & TIMES OF A SMALL PRESS PUBLISHER

APEX MAGAZINE

2021

EDITED BY
JASON SIZEMORE & LESLEY CONNER

APEX BOOK COMPANY
LEXINGTON, KY

Apex Publications, LLC
ApexBookCompany.com

ISBN (pbk): 978-1-955765-06-0
ISBN (epub): 978-1-955765-07-7

FIRST EDITION: OCTOBER 2022

A BRIEF HISTORY OF APEX MAGAZINE WRITTEN IN THIRD PERSON

In the fall of 2004, Jason Sizemore worked for the Risk Management division of the Lexington-Fayette County Urban Government. While insurance and mitigating risk are important tools for governing, the job was without an ounce of creativity and personal agency. Jason decided to look into various creative outlets.

At the time, he had met Christopher Rowe and Gwenda Bond, local genre authors. They ran a small saddle-stitch weird fiction journal called *Say...?* Jason loved the journal and the DIY nature of printed zines. He decided he would improve his editing skills, and when he felt they were sufficient, he would launch his own zine.

In the spring of 2005, the first issue of *Apex Science Fiction & Horror Digest* was released. It featured original fiction by Philip K. Dick winner MM Buckner, Lawrence Schoen, and one of Lavie Tidhar's earliest published stories. The issue was well-received, and by the third issue, Apex had landed a distribution deal to be carried in 1,200 bookstores.

While Jason had discovered an innate ability to edit, his small business skills were far more dubious. The company accrued a large amount of debt to meet the increasing orders from the distributor. One of the zine's distributors went bankrupt, leaving Apex holding an empty bag that should have been filled with nearly $10,000.

After twelve issues, *Apex Science Fiction & Horror Digest* ended its three-year run. The combination of ill-intentioned business partners and the incoming ebook tide convinced Sizemore that it was time to approach the zine world with a new strategy. He took a year off to pay down some company debt and to learn about online publishing.

In 2009, he rebranded the zine to the much easier-to-say *Apex Magazine*. Because of a new day job that required far more of his attention, he decided early in the creation of the new zine to hire someone to function as editor-in-chief. A talented young writer named Catherynne M. Valente expressed interest in the job. She was hired, and Apex was off to another great start.

Sizemore's and Valente's vision for the publication matched, and soon *Apex Magazine* made a name for its daring short fiction choices. Valente, in response to an ongoing hate campaign against people of the Muslim faith, created an issue focused entirely on Muslim genre writers.

Unfortunately for Apex, Cat Valente's prodigious talents as an editor were only surpassed by her skill with the written word. Her writing career had taken off in tandem with her editing run. After two years with Apex, she resigned.

Before she left, she recommended an up-and-coming editor named Lynne M. Thomas to step in her shoes. Lynne and her partner, Michael Damian Thomas, led *Apex Magazine* to a successful run that included three straight years of Hugo Award nominations for Best Semiprozine. They eventually left Apex to start their own publication, the highly successful *Uncanny Magazine*.

Following Lynne and Michael's run, Apex turned to another relatively new editor in the field: Sigrid Ellis. Most notable under Sigrid's run was the publication of the instant classic "Jackalope Wives" by Ursula Vernon.

During this time, Jason's career as a software developer grew unfulfilling ... again. He once more took over as *Apex Magazine's* editor-in-chief. The publication grew in popularity and has placed stories on the Hugo and Nebula ballots nearly every year.

In 2019, Jason had a serious health issue that required immediate attention. Its sudden onset and severity excluded the possibility of finding an editor to take over, even temporarily. So, after ten years and 120 issues, the magazine went on hiatus.

In the vernacular of online zines, "going on hiatus" is usually code for "That's it, folks, we're folding." However, Jason had plans to bring *Apex Magazine* back when he became healthy enough to do so. After four major surgeries and a dozen smaller procedures, the time was right for a return.

Apex Magazine made a triumphant return in January 2021. The publication has returned without missing a beat, placing stories on several award ballots, most notably "Mr. Death" by Alix E. Harrow. In the summer of 2022, Sizemore promoted his long-time managing editor, Lesley Conner, to co-editor-in-chief.

In September 2022, *Apex Magazine* won the prestigious British Fantasy Award for Best Magazine/Periodical.

What does the future hold in store for *Apex Magazine*? More awesome cross-genre short fiction, of course! And thought-provoking essays. And interviews with writers. And amazing podcast episodes. We are a full-service zine.

To the readers who have followed us from day one in 2005 to our new fans in 2022, Apex thanks you for supporting our little production. It feels great to be back in print with this anthology, and we hope you enjoy it as much as we loved finding these stories to share with you.

Jason Sizemore
Lexington, KY
September 2022

CONTENTS

CONTENTS, CONT.

ROOT ROT

FARGO TBAKHI

By the time I hear that my brother is looking for me, and has somehow scraped together enough credit to get on a commercial flight to New Tel Aviv, and that he's also brought his three-year-old daughter on her first interplanetary trip, my insides are already rotten. Can't get to the doctor without citizen papers, but I know. I can feel it. Lungs, liver, stomach, whatever—they're done for. Most days I wake up, bleed, drink, bleed, and pass out. I am fucked beyond any reasonable doubt.

When the two OSPs are finished beating the shit out of me outside Farah's (only place in the Arab Quarter with a liquor license which means what's happening currently, a beating that is, happens less frequently than if I was drinking somewhere else) one of them checks for warrants. I'm swaying like something in the breeze though the provisional government never fixed the generators so there isn't any breeze this part of the planet. Sometimes I blow in my own face just to remember what wind felt like.

"Hey, you got a brother?"

Word drops into me. Shakes me up bad to hear it and for a second I almost don't process what it means. Then I do and want to die. I spit out some blood and nod.

"Posted a bulletin. Yesterday looks like. Asks if anyone's seen you. Want me to forward your location?"

I try to think and then try not to think, and for a second I am really still, and then that second is one of the worst things I've felt in years, so I stay quiet and make a gesture like I'm going to hit the OSPs and they start in again and, later, when they've gone and I get feeling back in my body and start to register the pain, I go back inside and then I pray and then I don't look at anybody and then I drink until I pass out.

When I start wishing I was dead I know it's morning. I spend a few minutes trying to work out where I am. Still at Farah's maybe. In prison maybe. In the street probably. As long I'm not at the house. Take a few minutes and press at my body. Feet. Stomach. Throat. Eyeballs. Thighs. Feel like crying but don't.

My fingers are crusted with blood, and I think one might be broken. For a second, I think the blood might be dirt, that red Mars soil, and I get confused and think maybe I've still got a job, maybe it's years ago and I've just been dreaming all of this pain, and maybe I'm still handsome and unbroken, maybe Farah and I are still in love and I can still make something grow, I can still get my fingers in the dirt and hear it, and then I shift slightly and get a bomb's worth of pain from my ribs and my vision blurs blue and when it clears I know the soil is blood. I know where I am and who and why.

I turn over and make myself puke, and it's that familiar yellow color with a little bit of blood threading through it like embroidery. Try and see my face in it but can't. I'm sure if I could I'd look worse than dead. Skin pale and covered in bruises, my hair falling out, a few teeth gone in the back and I swear I'm getting shorter too. Maybe if I just lay here for a while nothing will happen and then I can start drinking again.

"Get up."

Maybe not. Guess I'm at Farah's. He kicks me in the ribs and cusses me out until I sit up.

"Hi," I say. Voice sounds like a bad engine and I know my breath is probably toxic. I'm struck by the hugeness of how unwantable I am. Farah used to think I was pretty when I was clean. I used to think so too. Well, nothing's inevitable but change and skyscrapers as they say.

Farah's just standing there and his arms are folded across his chest. I want to lick it like some wounded animal, him or me I don't know but there's some combination of animal and wound. "Hi," I say again.

"You can't come back in here."

When Farah and I were together we used to draw on each other's chests little maps. Plots of land we wanted to live on, spots on Mars we'd go and build our freedom. He would laugh and then when things got bad he wouldn't laugh so much. But the ones I drew on his chest were so real to me. I never laughed.

"I'm okay, I just need to rest today. I'll be okay. I won't come back tonight, I'll go somewhere else and cool off and come back tomorrow."

"You can't come back in here, ever."

Really detailed mine were with all the land sectioned off into what types of plants I was going to have and then I'd get so excited to tell him how I'd figured what they needed from Mars soil and sun and air and he would listen and smile or listen and look so sad when things changed and I did too.

"Okay."

"You haven't paid your tab in months. And when you get in fights outside it's bad for business. Offworld Settlement Palmach fuckers are over here constantly for you and no one wants to deal with that."

Farah was the one who was waiting for me outside Ansar VI when I got out but I didn't know what to say and neither did he so we didn't. And he took me back to the bar and poured when I asked and that's it and that's where we've been since.

"It's bad for business. And it's bad for me. They'll take the liquor license and maybe my papers too. And I don't want to ever look at you again."

I sit there like a puddle and try not to think. If I keep my eyes focused on the puke I won't let what's happening in. It'll stay out so I can move and breathe some. I stare at the little thread of blood in the bile and in the corner of my eye I see Farah start to go and the desperation in me rears up.

"Fathi's here," I say.

He stops and I can see he's being really careful with what's on his face. Blank like a stone wall.

"He's looking for me. OSPs told me last night. Please don't do this."

"Maybe you should see him."

"Don't want to see him. Please. I love you."

"Fuck you."

"Okay."

"You owe me too much for that. Just too much."

"Okay."

We both shut up and I know that we might not ever stop shutting up now. That we might be shut and closed forever and no openness ever coming back. Every day there are moments like this when whatever might have been waiting for me in the future just goes away, I can feel it just burning up. I wish I could stop drinking. No, I don't. I wish I'd never come to this planet. No, I don't.

"I'm going to code the bar's door against your breath until you settle the tab. Maybe Fathi can help you. I don't know. I don't think I can anymore. If I ever could. I'm sorry."

Yes, I do.

"Please. I can't pay. I don't have anything left."

Farah and I touching the dirt before this was New Tel Aviv when it was still new. Holding seeds. Playing with gravity and dreaming of freedom. Kissing. The way I could make him laugh like the sun was out and we could photosynthesize.

"You could always sell it. You know somebody in the city will pay good money."

It. Flash of red. Memory. Dirt. Petals. Whatever.

"Don't have it. Confiscated. All gone," I lie.

Farah shakes his head, really tired-seeming. Looks like he's going to say something, maybe argue, push me to do what I should, but he doesn't. I think I'm glad about that but I'm not really sure. It's a long time before he talks again.

"Either pay your debts or don't come in here again."

"Okay," I say. He reaches out and puts his fingers on my knee and I remember how much he used to like touching it, how he liked to feel where it'd been broken and reset. We hold still like that for too long so I say "Can I have one more drink, just to get me going, for today?"

For a second his face looks like it's got something like pity on it, and for that I'm grateful. It's all I ever want.

I get out and sun hits me like a missile, and if anyone outside is looking at me with any kind of anything on their face I don't know it, I can't see anything at all.

Getting to the other side of the Arab Quarter means going through the New Tel Aviv settlement civic center but I really don't have a choice if I want to get some cash and keep drinking. If I had better papers and hadn't been in prison I could drink somewhere anonymous and illegal and maybe fade away but oh well. Walking to the delineation gate I stop by the dried-out water tanker (left over from when we were still trying to fully terraform the Quarter when any of us thought this could be home) to visit the cat. She came up on the second or third rocket from somebody's alleyway in Khalil and when things were good she was adored and we joked about making her mayor. Then we all got fucked and she did too. Once the settlements got on the Mars train and surrounded what we had we were all panicking and trying to stay free and in the panic, nobody took her with them. Now she's forgotten like me. Like all of us I guess, but me especially I like to think. I check on her when I'm sober enough to remember.

I crouch, eye the underside of the tanker. She's there looking like I feel. We look at each other for a while and eventually I reach out my hand to try and pet her. Too far back and I'm stretching to just get a scratch, something to let her know I'm here. No luck. Oh well. Yank my hand back out and go to look at her again but she's gone. I stay down there for a moment because it's cool and my head hurts. The space where she was, where my hand couldn't reach.

Closer to the delineation gate I find some kid selling flasks. I manage to convince her to take some synth watermelon seeds I found in my pockets for a flask of arak which is all I can afford since nobody drinks it anymore. It does the trick and soon I'm numb again. The thing about drinking a lot is that there's nothing meaningful about it. Just fucks you up and you're not in the world anymore and there's no past or future really just one foot in front of the other if you can manage that. And sometimes you can still kind of experience what's around you only it's not as intense on a personal level. Like now, when the arak's fuzzed me up, the settlement drones flashing hasbara holograms aren't so annoying. They're kind of like insects that aren't biting. Just something to look at with corpse eyes.

At the gate, the guard asks where I'm going and checks my papers, which are shit, obviously. I say I'm just going across to the other side of the Quarter and I'm sticking out my arm before he's even finished looking. Window opens and the little mechanical arm comes out to stick my vein. Once they've got the liter of my blood they approve a fifteen-minute pass to get through to the settlement. The blood loss and the arak have really messed me up but I think I can manage getting to the next gate into the Quarter in time. They're usually pretty good about getting the blood back in once you're there depending on the line, though once or twice I've gotten someone else's liter. Probably healthier than whatever I've got going on, probably might have saved my life. I don't know.

The settlement civic center looks the same as always. Clean and stupid. The glass looks terrible and it never lasts. And they've ruined all the landscape work they made us do in Ansar too, synthetic olive trees on every fucking corner like a postcard. And the synth poppies look as sad as I knew they would. I stop and bend down to feel them, the sickly genetic smell. None of the settlers know how to grow anything real here and none of the Palestinians have the resources even if they did know which they don't.

Before the settlements when this was just empty planet it was so possible, just crammed to the brim with possible. It was going to be free and we were going to learn the land and find God again and all that bullshit. I believed it so deeply I left everything behind on Earth. The people who couldn't leave I cursed and tore from my heart. I was stupid and I thought things would be different. And when the settlers followed and they liked the wide open planet so much they left the old land behind, they declared any flora from Earth contraband and put me away. Now we've got a provisional government I don't know or care about and my brother's been living in Reunified Palestine for years while I drink myself to death, which reminds me my brother is here for me, and I want to just pull up everything with roots on this fucking planet, just salt the ground and then salt myself too. But I've only got a few minutes before the blood loss passes me out so there's no time for being angry or anything else.

At the other delineation gate, there's a protest on the Arab side. They're holding signs in Arabic I can't read. Somebody took down one of the hasbara drones and they're passing it around like a football though it doesn't really roll. People are dancing and something's on fire. I don't know what they want, not sure I can even guess anymore. Some days I'm sad about losing the language, but most days I don't mind it. Ansar policy is to reprogram prisoner consciousness with Hebrew once they wipe the Arabic which serves me fine. I like not understanding things.

The blood bot gives me my liter back and I stand a little straighter. I'm looking at the faces of all the Arabs through the light-meshed gate and I hear myself thinking they're idiots, they're evil, we ought to just shut up and die and float out into space, cold and empty as every day here, all we deserve. Sometimes I don't know what's my voice and what's the guards at Ansar VI and what's the drones and what's the drink and what's Farah and what's God. All I know is when the protesters make space for me to stumble through their anger, when they touch me and tell me to join them, I loathe, I loathe every cell on my body that feels and I loathe every second I'm breathing and the pit opens up in me and I want something more and I don't know what it is. So I push them away and while they're yelling and spitting at me *collaborator coward fucking drunk* I drain the last of the arak and I say thank you to the drone when it passes out an Arab in front of me and I can pocket a few loose coins that spill out from her hands like petals.

When I get to Abu Khaled's he's curled up on the floor and I can tell he's soiled himself. Touch his forehead and it's hot as an iron. Probably he'll last a few more days and then go. I wonder if he has papers for the house or if it'll go to the settlers. Last place I ever felt decent was in this front room of his—curled up a lot like he is now and crying nonstop while I tried to dry out for the first time in years. His hands on my head. His hands. Remembering feels terrible so I dig a nail into my palm until the pain brings me dull again. I need to get him stable and then ask for some cash. That's it. That's all.

I get his pants the rest of the way off and drag him into the tiny bathroom and into the tub. While I rinse him off and he's groaning, eyes floating open-closed like a camera shutter, I look at him. Skin used to be brown but now it's some sick grey blue. Bruises everywhere. So thin you could think he was just pastry.

When I'd stumbled in, that night I was trying to be good, he was patient. I cried and he just sat there and touched me, just a little, just to show he was there, and eventually, I slept, and the next day he fed me and we didn't say anything to each other since he only spoke Arabic and I didn't. I was close to dead from trying to stop drinking cold, but he kept me alive and I got back to normal. I'd hated him for how kind he was and how it made me feel okay for a moment so one night I drank enough so that I knew I'd do something cruel, and I did, and so I left and knew that it was my fault that I was leaving, which was right. After that, I didn't see him again, but I went back once, late at night when I knew he was asleep, and I worked for hours until the sun was just coming up, sweating and freezing and pissed myself but couldn't stop until it was right, until I'd made him these long wooden planters with bell peppers growing in them, real ones, part of the stash of seeds I'd hidden, or at least I hoped they were growing, but they were definitely there. I felt good, so I went and loitered near the border fence until the OSP spotted me and did what they do, and I fell unconscious feeling nothing.

Now he's shivering in the tub all wet. It takes me a while to get him out and into the bedroom because I'm starting to shake from not drinking since the arak a few hours ago. The room is nearly empty. Only things around are socks and his paintings and cigarette butts. Get him on the bed and pull the sheet over him and it pretty quickly gets soaked in his sweat and a little after it's got some of mine on it too. Abu Khaled is shaking and I'm shaking and I can't think straight, and I'm trying to ask him how he is, or if he can hear me, or if he has any money he can spare, but I can't get the Arabic out though I really try and remember. So for a few minutes, the two of us are just making sounds at each other, groaning a little like birds. He starts to sound like he's in a lot more pain, and I don't know what to do or say so I start crying and just touching him, his head, his neck, the soles of his feet, shoulders, stomach, just putting my hands on him the way I would put them on soil, just getting to know what it is. He starts trying to say something, and I'm listening harder than I ever have.

"Law samaht," he's saying, over and over, "law samaht, law samaht." I don't know what he means except that his voice sounds like he needs something. And I'm remembering what he did and what I've done and didn't do, and I can't fucking understand what he's saying and I'm a sorry excuse for flesh so I take some deep breaths and I leave him there crying out like I was an angel who turned away. And in the front room, I find a few crumpled-up shekels and stuff them in my pockets. Hold down some puke and try to stop shaking. Hear him still in the room saying what he's saying, needing what he's needing, and I walk out and I shut the door, and in the yard the wooden planters are empty.

Next morning I've got a few ribs broken. Last night I took Abu Khaled's money and went to a bar in the civic center. Wasn't enough money to settle my tab at Farah's, so I figured it was worth it and besides some settlers might beat me bad enough that I'd be passed out until my brother's gone back to Earth. No such luck obviously as I'm awake now. Neighborhood drone picked me up walking toward the bar and put me on the municipal timeline, so some settlers came by and I hit one of them kind of half-hearted but enough to get beat. It felt alright. I actually think one of them might have served as a guard at Ansar VI, but I couldn't be sure, passed out too quick, and besides, I can't remember much from those days. This morning the money's gone and I still haven't had a drink, so things are pretty bad. Can't even puke. Can still feel my insides breaking down. I'm willing them on.

Out of options, so I get up from the civic center street and limp through the delineation gate. Nothing left to do but go to the house. My head is killing me and something in my side is aching, in addition to the broken ribs. Maybe they're poking some organ, something fragile in there, just puncturing it with every step I take back toward the house. Or maybe that's just all my fuckups talking.

The breath scanner at the front door is busted, stripped for parts by someone since I've been here last, so I muscle down the door and get inside. Most of the inside's been stripped too. I stopped caring about it a long time ago so I let it happen, even encouraged it sometimes. Not much left inside the wooden walls, most of it synth wood but a few planks here and there are real that I brought with me on the first rocket. Standing inside it's still, empty like the remnants of a ghost. A reminder of what gets left when I try, which is nothing. A wave of something hits me and I feel sick, really sick, a new level of pain and nausea. Get on my knees to wait for the puke to come.

I know what to do in my throat to coax it out and I do, little burps and swallowing, and soon enough there's a new puddle of bile on the floor, some arak smell, and more blood than usual. Something in me knows there can't be much of this left. I rest my forehead on the floor. Red dirt tracked in by looters mixes a little with my sweat and I rub it around a little: Mars makeup. Almost pretty again. Don't want to get my head up from the floor or open my eyes so I crawl with my forehead pressed to the synth wood floor like some protracted migratory prayer. Feel my way around to the little closet I used to keep seeds in. Check first for the liquor compartment—found, broken, and emptied. I figured as much. But I reach behind and underneath and open up the second compartment, the one nobody knows about, not even Farah when we shared this place as lovers and comrades and fools. Eyes closed I'm fumbling around in the dark trying to find the last part of the person I was and then I do. I stay still for a little, and feel the blood pump in my body and around my rotten organs and through to my bruised and broken and reset arms and into my fingers and then somehow a little bit into the soil that my fingers are feeling, and through the soil into the roots of the last real poppy on Mars, the last remnant of the place I thought this planet could be.

When they took me to Ansar I'd already started drinking. Already just a shadow and welcomed the Palmach vehicles, the shackles. Farah already gone even when he was with me, the country on Earth already reunified, free. I knew I'd missed whatever a person's life could be that was good. The ship had flown. I gave up everything and let myself conceive of the life held in the imagination of Ansar VI and that was all. But still, I kept this plant. Sometimes, in that sweet spot when the drink loosens my mind but doesn't wipe it, I remember the little poppy and get wistful, swear to myself I'll find a piece of land for my own and get things going, start over, eke out home through the sweat and the tears, and then I take another drink and it all just seems too hard so I let go again. But here it still is, rare as all hell, almost impossible to keep alive on this planet. My last resort.

My hand still stuck in the compartment and illuminated by the artificial sunlight bulb I installed, the misters come on. Wet fingers, a little caked up blood or dirt washing off, and when the sound is done I can hear somebody behind me in the room. I try to yank my hand out and turn around and get up off the ground all at once and do none of them, somehow end up hitting the ground face first. When I can open my eyes and lift up my head a little some things swim into view, two pairs of feet, one big, one heartbreaking small, and I know.

"Hi, Fathi," I say, trying to push up onto my hands and knees but not quite getting there. Suddenly my arms feel like spun sugar. Nobody says anything while I keep trying to get up, scoot over to the wall, and sort of push up against it to get some leverage. Eventually I give up and stay on the ground. I shut my eyes and move my face so they're pointed where I know Fathi's face will be and then I open them and I keep them trained only on his face. I can't look at her. I don't want to see how she's seeing.

Fathi looks older but then he always did. People always used to guess he was the older one of us and sometimes I thought they were right. I was born first but Fathi was born smart. Born good maybe. He's dressed in nice jeans and a yellow collared shirt and I start counting the hairs in his beard to avoid looking at her.

"I'm here to take you home."

Looking right in his eyes I try to smile a little. "Like that British song. Remember that? *Pack your things I've come to take you home.* Something like that right? Only I don't have anything to pack."

"Farah told me you're sick. Dying."

Fucking Farah.

"*Solsbury Hill*, that was it. Gabriel. You remember? Every time we'd play it Dad would tell us Peter Gabriel was pro-Palestine. Remember?"

"I don't want you to die."

My eyes are locked on Fathi's face like a leech but I can hear her breathing, I can feel her here with us seeing me and I don't know why these memories are coming to me now but I need Fathi to remember them with me. I know I smell like alcohol and blood, probably other things more vile and sick, but he's looking at me without any pity, without any anger even, and for once I let myself sit in that non-judgment, in that love, and I don't run away this time.

"Do you remember that? Fathi? The song?"

"I remember that. Of course, I do." His eyes are soft and blue. I can feel one of my ribs poking into my skin and I wonder if it's bleeding but I can't look down to check because I might see her. "It's been a long time, habibi."

"Yeah." My mouth feels like brick and dust. "How have you been?"

"Good. Things are good."

Fathi used to cover for me when I came home late back on Earth. When the soldiers were looking for me after throwing rocks. When our parents were looking for me after the boys. Fathi was my anchor and I've only been able to drift so long because I didn't have him here with me.

"You know things are different now, back home. There's a place for you there."

"I don't know. I don't know about that."

"I do."

Fathi and I playing football. Trying cigarettes together. The way he held me when my heart got broken. The way his face looked when I left him in the morning, asleep like an angel, and I took my bag of seeds and crawled through miles of tunnels to get to the rocket and held Farah's hand while we sobbed and the land got smaller and smaller and then gone.

"I left. I gave it up. It doesn't want me back."

"It doesn't want you dead either."

"I left you there. I left you all alone and I went away."

"Yeah, you did. So you're a piece of shit. What else is new."

Even sick as I am Fathi gets a laugh out of me. But the laugh hurts my ribs which reminds me I've got ribs which reminds me I'm a person and so on. I try to avoid thinking those things because they hurt so I say something to get this to stop.

"I'm glad I left. And I'm glad I didn't take you with me." I don't feel anything when I say it, because I'm staring at the corner of Fathi's mouth and praying he'll get hurt and leave. I don't want to do this. Fathi's eyes I can't read and he comes forward, leans down to me, and touches my forehead. Like some insect landing on a bloom. I'm blinking hard and he's wiping off the sweat from my brow. Fathi speaks softly to me while he holds my hand.

"I will forgive you no matter how hard you try to stop me. B'hebbek. Remember? B'hebbek. You can still come home."

The Arabic doesn't process in my brain but it does somewhere else. And I know he's telling the truth. His mouth is in that little curve it makes when he's being sincere. It used to make me annoyed that his body was bad at lying and mine was too good. I want to shake him and tell him to lie for both our sakes, for her sake.

"I don't have papers. They've got me on no-transport. There's no point in trying."

"One of the port employees agreed to get you off planet. They'll get you papers and a ticket on our return flight and you can live with us. You can come home."

"How much?"

"Sixty-five thousand."

His words are sieving through me like water, and the drink-guards-God-me voice is saying *You could get that for the poppy, easy. This is it. This is the moment. This is your soil telling you to come back. This is goodness finally coming to meet you where you are.* Trying my hardest to listen. To believe that this is my voice and that it's telling the truth.

"I'll try to get the money."

When I let myself say that my eyes almost waver, almost drop down to meet her gaze and let her see me. But I don't. Fathi looks down at her, and then at me, and his eyes get harder, sadder. I watch the muscles in his arm tighten, relax, tighten.

"The flight leaves at 11. Meet us there."

He turns to leave, tugging at his daughter's little arm so gently, just the way I used to tug at his when we were kids.

"Fathi?"

He stops and looks back.

"How's the soil?" I say. He smiles.

"Lush," he says. "Waiting for you." Between the three of us, Fathi and his daughter and me, something almost begins to grow, something almost claws its way to taking hold. I close my eyes, and as they leave the little one says "Buh-bye" but I hear it for a moment as "alive."

Alive.

Now everything's a blur. The blood bot a blur. The still-raging protest a blur. Hasbara drones projecting blurs as I get close to the Import/Export and Contraband Office in the civic center, hands obsessively going to the little package of soil and life hidden in my crotch, making sure it's still there and I didn't break it. Now the IEC guard checking my papers and getting ready to jail me. Now whispering into their ear what I have and who I need to see. Now the higher up. Now the little room and the surveillance bots blanked for a few minutes. Now I'm taking out the poppy and now the higher up's eyes going wide and now "Name your price" and now I hear somebody's voice saying "Sixty-five thousand" and now one of the times I can't hear if it's me or God or drink or death or love but now the cash in a discreet little tote bag and now the leaving my hand and now the last chance I had at what I'd dreamed of gone into the hands of a bureaucrat who'd sell it for more than I'd ever dare to dream. But, now, I don't care. I have what I came for. I know where I'm going. And all the way back through the civic center it's like I'm floating like the gravity's gone out again though it hasn't. And I get my rotten blood back and I keep walking and as I walk I'm shedding so much weight: the poppy, Ansar, the drones and the blood bots, the IEC, the beatings and the OSP, the settlers, Abu Khaled, the protest, the Quarter, hope, home, hope. And then I get where I'm going. And I'm silent as I push over the tote bag of money. And I speak in the voice of somebody too stupid and too wrong to do any different and I want to say so many things but instead I say "This covers the tab and then some. I'm going to sit here and drink and I don't want you to ever try and stop me" and Farah looks at me like the way you look at something that's not there anymore, like the way you look at where a plant used to be or a vase or a building, and then something in his eyes changes and he pours me something clear and unknowable and that's the end of it, and I drink until I can barely speak, and then when I'm ready I go to the port.

Can barely stand. Make it to the viewing section and find the hole Farah and I hacked into the lightmesh fence years ago. Sneak through and collapse onto the bit of shadow on the edge of the takeoff platforms and find the one rocket gearing up for a launch. Where Fathi is. Where she is.

Pain in my back and in my stomach. I don't care. I take a swig from whatever I brought from Farah's and things quiet down. Just my rot and the settlement's rot and the planet's rot all communing, all sharing a body. I'm blissful knowing I did exactly what everybody with any sense thought I would do. I'm already somewhere floating outside anyone's jurisdiction. And then I look over at the rocket and my eyes roam to one of the windows and there she is.

It's too late to look away, I've already seen her and I swear she's seen me even though I know that's not possible, I'm too far away and it's dark. But I believe we're looking at each other. She's plain looking and sweet, a brown curtain of hair and her eyes like two onion bulbs, little I mean, and light. If anything was left of my heart she would break it. I can't remember her name, if anybody ever told me in the letters to Ansar or on the bulletin or maybe Fathi said it or fuck maybe she told me herself once but I can't remember. The ship's starting to lift off and I send my soul with it. I touch my empty knee and I whisper like she can hear me.

I tell her they're right about me. They always were. I'm bad and I'm a criminal and a threat and I tell her it's okay, that she doesn't have to be that way, that people disappear from your life and you can forget who they were or what they did to you or what they looked like drunk, I tell her she's home and she should know that she's home, that her dad is good how I'm not, I tell her that God loves her and the land loves her and I tell her that poppies need lots of sun and not too much water and she just has to care for them until they're gone, and I tell her that they self-seed so beautifully that she'll forget about them for years and then, so suddenly, like heartbreak or hope or pain, just so fucking quick, they'll come back, and she won't even remember they were ever so far gone.

LESLEY CONNER

Occasionally, I will read a story in the slush pile that is so good, that it ruins the rest of the day for me. I can't read any more slush because I'm comparing every story to this magical experience I had. I can't edit because my brain keeps yanking me back to the story, turning it slowly so I can inspect it from every angle. The only thing I can do is gush about the story to the Apex slush team and hope that Jason loves the story as much as I do. "Root Rot" by Fargo Tbakhi is one of these stories. The moment I finished it, I was breathless. I knew we had a truly exceptional story, and I wanted to buy it for the magazine now, now, now!! But that's not how our process works and I had to wait.

While waiting for Jason to read it, most of our slush readers read "Root Rot" and a buzz was building about how much we all loved the story. For the first time in my experience with Apex, we had a situation where if Jason didn't love this story as much as the rest of the Apex team, I was worried our slush readers might revolt. They loved this story! They wanted this story! This was an Apex story! Luckily for Jason, he loved it as much as we all did and it was one of the first stories bought for the 2021 year.

YOUR OWN UNDOING

P H LEE

While you're washing the floors (he does love to make you wash the floors, doesn't he?) down on your hands and knees with cold, soapy water soaking your pants, I come to you in the form of a gray-striped cat.

You look at me and you don't recognize me.

It hurts that you don't recognize me, your own familiar that you made from a part of your own soul, but there are more important things for us to deal with right now. I push through the hurt and speak to you, saying, "This is not a story you are reading. This is actually happening, and it's actually happening to you."

You don't believe me. You probably think that me speaking to you is just a narrative device. Regardless, you go right on washing the floors like he told you to this morning.

You think that you're reading a story, that you're not actually down on your hands and knees, washing the floors like a servant in your own academy-by-the-sea. You're imagining that there's an entire world out there, a whole life full of cars and taxes and international commodities markets and who-knows-what else.

But there isn't. That whole world, that whole life, is an illusion.

This is real.

This is not a story. This is a curse.

At night, while you are standing up in a closet not sleeping (you don't sleep anymore), just standing up in a closet like a disused mop, I come to you in the form of a housefly.

You look at me and you recognize me from the last scene. It still hurts me that you don't remember, but at least it's a start.

I land inside your ear, my forelegs dipping into your earwax, and whisper to you, telling you what happened. Because you imagine that this is a story you are reading, I tell it to you as if it were a story.

Once upon a time, you were a scholar and a sorcerer. People came from each and every land to wait at the hundred steps of your academy-by-the-sea, to pay or promise or beg to study with you, even for an hour, even for a day. Most of them left disappointed, back to their petty tricks as conjurers and illusionists. You would choose a lucky few—and how you loved to choose!—to take as your students, to train in names and numbers, in magnets and multitudes, in all the subtle forces of the world. Years later, they would go out from your academy-by-the-sea as great sorcerers, becoming heroes or tyrants or sages, famous or infamous, but always your disciples, spreading further, always further, the glory of your name.

He was there one day, among all the other hopefuls on the hundred steps of your academy. He was poor and scared and young and hungry. Did you first notice him because he was beautiful? Or did you already see his power, boiling thick like tar inside of his heart? I cannot say, and I dare not guess, even though I am a part of your own soul. But I do know this: You stopped and looked at him. Then he met your eyes and your whole body shuddered.

You asked his name.

"I don't have a name."

You welcomed him and you named him Shazhiji and he bowed his beautiful head and he smiled.

Did you know, even then, how dangerous he was? You must have seen at least a hint of it. But you took him as your student anyway. Did you think that you could contain his power? Did you think that you could master it? Or did you convince yourself that it did not matter, because he was young, because he was untrained, because he was beautiful?

Only you know the answers to these questions. Even I, a part of your own soul, cannot answer them for you. But I suppose that it does not matter now. You took him in, you took him as your student, you trained him and guided him and gave him every answer to your own undoing.

While you are washing his students' dishes, your arms deep in scalding water, hands chapped and red and raw from the rough brushes and rougher soaps, I come to you in the form of a black and white rat.

It was hard for him to get you to wash the dishes. Washing dishes is complicated and boring, both of which present unique difficulties to his particular holds over you.

Because you will only do as you were told, a complicated process requires him to give you a very specific set of nested instructions. Often, he lacks the patience to formulate your instructions correctly, and you're left alone for hours, motionless, dishes undone, your arms cooking in the water.

But as bad as the complexity is, the boredom is worse. Because you think that this is just a story you are reading, if it gets boring, you'll just skip ahead. When you do skip ahead in the story, your entire body goes limp and falls on to the floor along with any dishes you were holding.

Still, despite these problems, he makes you wash the students' dishes every night. You break a lot of bowls, and you have the cuts to show for it.

"Who are you?" you ask me. You recognize me easily now. "Why do you keep insisting this isn't a story?"

"Because it isn't," I say. "Because it is a curse."

"I don't know what that means," you say, as I run along your shoulder and hide in the armpit of your shirt.

"I'll tell you," I say. I still remember your magic.

You cannot control someone's mind with magic. This is not because of any particular law or because of any romantic capacity of the soul. It is simply rooted in the relationship of magic with the physical world.

You can control a living body with magic. But you cannot control it well. Bodies are subtle things and not at all suited to the gross motions of a magic spell. If you move a body with magic, you will sprain its ligaments, break its bones, bruise its muscles and bleed its veins. Perhaps you care about this, perhaps you do not, but regardless, it is true.

The brain is, of course, simply a hunk of water and meat, as prone to magic as anything else. But a brain is even more subtle than a body. Try to force it with magic, and all you'll do is cause a stroke or, if your control is particularly precise and subtle, a seizure.

All of these techniques are largely useless for any degree of subtlety or control. Better, and easier, to animate the dead, or the cold waters, or a pile of stones. Better still to study prophecy or will or fireworking—skills that any wizard might need.

You told him this—Shazhiji—when he came to you in that early purple evening with his beautiful body and said that he wanted to learn to control minds. You told him this, all clearly, each part each, explaining when he did not understand. Did you know, then, that you were only teaching him your weaknesses? Did you still think that, because you named him your student, his power was yours to control?

"Still," he said. "Still I want to learn."

Because he was beautiful, you did not deny him. Because he was beautiful, you let him study whatever he wanted. Because he was beautiful, you sowed in him the seeds of your own undoing.

While you are on your knees, eyes streaming tears, bowing at the foot of his great seat, when he has long since left, and it is the middle of the night and still you knock your head, again and again, the impact ringing through your skull with each "I'm sorry," I came to you in the form of a guardian dog.

"That is your seat," I say. "You carved it with a word from a single block of granite."

"I'm sorry," you say, but you have nothing to apologize for.

I lick your face, but you don't stop. Why should you stop? To you, this is only a story you are reading.

"Do you remember me now?" I ask, although I know that you do not. "Do you remember the familiar you grew from the seed of your own soul?"

"I'm sorry," you say, and knock your head again.

"Don't be sorry," I say. "I still remember, and I am a part of you, just as you are a part of me."

"I'm sorry," but I've already begun.

There was no academy-by-sea when you first came here, young and hungry and mourning. There were no hundred steps, no great white doors, no towers, no libraries hidden or overt. There was simply a cruel old woman who everyone hated, living alone with her magic on the cliffs-beside-the-sea. But she saw you and, even starving, even untrained, even half-mad with grief, she saw your power and craved it for her own.

I will not tell you what she did to you, then, when you did not have the power to fight back. Your life—this story—is miserable enough without it. But one day by the sea you found a smooth round stone. You held it and you felt the weight of the sea inside it and it seemed to you as small as a world and as large as alone. You wanted to take it back with you, to have it but more to have something that wasn't hers, that was yours, that she could not demand and could not destroy.

But as soon as you had the thought, you knew that she would never allow you to have anything, even something as simple as a stone. You knew, so you hid your stone in a sea cave, and every night when the sky was at its thickest you would pick your way down the cliffs to the cave and hold the stone in your hands and tell it all your secrets and cry it all your tears. You would tell it about your family, about the sins you'd done unknowing, about the anger of her fists and the chill of her hand across your back in the middle of the night.

You didn't realize it, but I was already growing then, out of all those bits of your soul too jagged for you to hold. I grew and grew until that stone my egg was too small to hold me, until one night you came down, and instead of your familiar stone, there was me, your familiar, amidst the broken rocks in the form of a sand crab. You knew me right away. You laughed, and I scuttled up your leg and across your shoulders, and we danced like that, me a crab and you still a child, until the moon had sunk beneath the edge of the sea.

You did not know, then, nor did I, that we already held the key to our liberation. That I was a part of you, your familiar, a part of you deeper than your body, deeper than your power, deeper even than the name she gave you. I am the part of you that she could never break.

When I come to you in the form of a night bird, you are alone in the round room on top of the tower, with the window that looks out over the ocean, breaking your own fingers, one at a time. He told you to do it, of course. Whether he was angry at some imagined slight or simply cruel, I cannot say. Right now, you are holding your left index finger in between the thumb and forefinger of your right hand. Your pointer and middle fingers are already broken. Your pointer finger has swollen black and purple, and your middle finger, still red, is on its way.

We are alone in the room. At first, he was with you. He thought that it would be exciting to watch you break your own fingers. But after you broke your left pointer finger, he gasped, and threw up, and ran out of the room.

But he told you that you were breaking your fingers, one at a time. So you are breaking your fingers, one at a time.

I cry out to you, but you don't respond. You press harder, as hard as you can. The middle joint of your left index finger gives way with a sharp, wet noise. It is extraordinarily painful, but worse than that, it feels wrong, nauseous, some thing out of place. Your own body. Your own body. You take a moment to lean to the side and vomit onto the floor.

You don't mind, though, because you imagine that this isn't really happening to you. You imagine that this is a story you are reading. It isn't.

"You have to stop this," I tell you. "Someday soon he will have learned all he can from you. He will grow tired of torturing you. And when that happens, unless you stop this, he's going to kill you."

"It doesn't matter," you tell me, gripping your left pinky finger. "This is just a story that I'm reading. It's already halfway done. And then I'll finish it, and I'll never have to think about it again."

"You need to understand," I say, but you don't understand. The lower joint of your left pinky gives way, and you hold the upper two joints in your hand. You can feel the bone grating against itself in a series of sharp pain pain pain. One part against another.

Your own body.

You look down at your fingers at odd angles, your ruined hand, swelling through purple into black. You look at me.

"How did this happen?" you ask, and I tell you.

In the middle of a black night Shazhiji came to you. You opened your door for him, of course you did, to look at his beautiful face in the light of your old lamp wick.

"I have found it," he said, his face grinning, wild like a mountain cat is fierce. He had not slept, his hair plastered all down with summer sweat, all excited shakes, but still beautiful, still.

"You've found what?" you asked. When you took his face in your hand to calm him, he stopped.

"I will tell you," he said. "I will tell you a story."

Master, he began, you were right. I spent months searching through all the libraries—yes, even the ones you think you've hidden from us—in your academy-by-the-sea, reading motion and physic and all manner of neuromancy, and there was nothing. A brain is a brain, whatever electric within it thinks and feels and knows is all well beyond the knowing of greater mages than you or even I.

You should have known then. You should have stopped him. But it was already too late.

Still, he continued, the problem ate at me. What matters a sorcerer if not for power? And what matters power if not the mastery of other men? To gain even a respect, to gain even a mastery, that is the work of a lifetime, and most lifetimes insufficient to even that. So much better—yes?—if they can be mine to take.

Conquered by my failures, I took to wandering long days outside the academy-by-the-sea, and in those wanderings I came across an illusionist, working his cinemas in that parliament of hovels that passes for a village beneath the academy-by-the-sea. All around him, children crowded—and men and women too, I'm sure—each one enraptured by the sound and the fury. As I watched them, it occurred to me that they were very much ensorcelled, and not by the naive illusion, but instead by the story of it. They were not confused, but they thought it real nonetheless, because they wanted it to be.

This is not the power of illusion, although illusion is its media. This is the power of want. This is the power of a story.

He paused and met your eyes, and your whole body shuddered.

But that, he concluded, is not quite the whole of it. The trick is an illusion, yes—to think that mere illusion was the key!—but the illusion is not the story. No, the illusion is everything that is not the story.

Because you think this is a story, you will do just as it says. Because it is only a story. Because you have decided that it does not matter, and that is what matters most of all.

Look, even now: You think that this is a narrative device when it is, in truth, a cage that binds you whole.

By the time you knew it, it was already too late. You were lost in that first moment when he began his story and held you within it.

"Get down on your knees," he said, "and beg for my forgiveness."

You got down on your knees, nightgown riding up, stones pressing hard and sharp against your knees. You hit your forehand on the rock, again and again. You begged for his forgiveness.

"I do not forgive you," he said, his right foot pressing just beneath your skull, "and I will never call you Master again."

When you are already halfway in the water, when the waves and ice lap against your shins and knees, I come to you in the form of a great white bear.

"Stop," I say.

This morning, he told you to walk into the sea.

You keep walking, dragging your broken body slow step by slow step. You look down at your hands, black and cracked. There's the smell of salt and gangrene.

I push my snout against you. You try to walk around me, but you're too weak to think. You fall face-first onto the wet rocks. I nose you over so you don't drown in the salt sea or the blood of your broken nose.

I speak to you, and I tell you what you must do.

You must look at yourself, I say, you must look at your hands and your face and your pride and your entire self.

"I don't want to do that," you begin to say, but you choke on blood and bile in your throat.

Because I am a part of you, though, I know what you were going to say. "I don't want to do that," you were going to say, "because this is just a story that I'm reading, and besides, it's almost over. Why should I think about myself? Why should I think about what's happened to me, about my hands and my face and my pride and my entire self?"

You must think about it, I say, because when you do, you will realize what has happened. You will realize what he's done to you. Still, trapped, you will take a step forward, and then another.

But then you will feel, again, within you, the roots of your power, even now, waist deep in ice and brine. You will plunge your hands into the water, drawing the very life of the sea where your ancestors lived before the dawn of time when the waters of heaven and earth were undivided. You will call the brine to you as blood, and guided by all your names and all your knowings, by the whole of your magic, your hands will knit themselves together, will return that rot to the sea and take in exchange all life and strength and power. You will squeeze your hands shut, and then, laughing, you will splash yourself with the water and rub the ice along your body, all shocked and real and true, the wounds closing behind them, your face, let the tide take all the bruises and your broken body and your broken mind.

You will stand, then, your full height and call to you all your names and servants, magnetics and electrics, and you will stride forth from the sea in the fullness of your power, towards your academy-by-the-sea, to find it waiting for you, oh yes, your academy-by-the-sea has been waiting for you, despairing for you, mourning for you. Hark! How the crowds part before you, the master. Hark! How the great white doors open at your slightest touch. Hark! How the students he corrupted cower at your mighty name. Hark! Your academy-by-the sea will be yours once more, as it always was and ever shall.

You will go, then, to where he holds court of toadies and apprentices; you will stand before him, still dripping from the sea, whole and unbent, no story to trap you now, all ablaze with your own name. Even then he will, surely, draw up his power against you, for he has learned from you all these months of his domination, all the secrets you held yourself and all the names you never spoke, for fear you might be overthrown. He has power, yes he has power, but this will not be a duel of sorcerers.

Instead of all the spells, instead of all the incantations, you will instead reach out, looking at his face, wondering how you ever found it beautiful. You will reach out, with your whole and perfect hands, and you will take hold of his name, Shazhiji, the name you gave him, and in front of all his apprentices, right before the fullness of his power, you will break his name to powder at your touch.

After that, it will not matter. After that, he will already be lost, not only to you, who was his master but the magic and time and history and anything of note. No more will be the glory of his name. No more will be the treacheries he told.

You will do all that. You will do all that and you will do so much more, the rest of your magic and life and time. You will do all that, but only if you

Stop reading this story. You must stop reading this story. To defeat him, to save yourself, you must stop reading, right now, and turn away. This story will not save you. It contains only your undoing.

To defeat him, to save yourself, you must write your own ending.

JASON SIZEMORE

The key to pulling off a story like this comes down to immersion. Is the reader so involved in the story that they inhabit the "you" of the piece. P H Lee understands that you do this the same way when you're telling a story in a more traditional point-of-view: provide the reader with details, setting, and questions that drives them to continue reading.

The use of structural repetition along with the anthropomorphic versions of the familiars effectively grounds you in the story and makes the stakes of your survival feel even higher. Just outstanding writing through this whole piece.

LOVE, THAT HUNGRY THING

CASSANDRA KHAW

"Sister," pants the white fox as it dangles upside-down from the railing, its tail like a question mark, its grin like something the devil had won from Saint Peter. "You're getting *soft*."

I pinch my midriff and shrug, winking an eye. "I've been busy."

"No, no, no." It chortles, all teeth and the sly red hint of a tongue. The parent-god themself speaks only in keigo, but their messengers won't abide such formality. Over the years, I've heard these foxes converse in Louisiana creole, gossip like gang-bangers fresh from Peckham, even debate in Bislama. Today, however, this fox's all Brooklyn, every diphthong authentically and anachronistically New York, New York. A taunt. That version of Gotham is long dead, black-blue with bodies, and all that is left of that city is him. "That's not what I meant. Sister, don't play dumb with us. You know exactly what I'm talking about."

"Maybe, I do. Maybe, I don't." Sunlight knifes through the foliage. Post-apocalyptic anywhere has a tenderness to it and Tokyo is no different. Patches of the city still bleed, the psychic resonance of a million casualties deafens. But here, under the eaves of the shrine, jeweled with summer rain, it is beautiful. "Who knows?"

"You do, sister. But alright, I'll bite. I'll talk." And its smile lengthens into a warning. "You're getting soft. A decade ago, you wouldn't waste your wishes like this. But now? Now, you've gone and given up a proper promise, all for that little counterfeit fox of yours."

"Every fox is a fake next to you and yours," I soothe, the flattery half-ritual already.

"Riiiiiight." The god's emissary screams a laugh, and the cicadas cease their chorus, scandalized by the interruption. "Right, right, right. So tell me. Tell me what makes that pretty little fox-thing worthy of a borrowed boon, why don't you? Tell me and maybe I'll whisper this request into the right ears."

"Because his smile in the right light looks like another word for home," I say without recitation, with the ease of rote. When the fox cocks its head in reply, I continue, softer than before. "Because he cares so damn hard that I don't know what to do about it, sometimes, and the thought of him is an ache. Like coming home from the blizzard and letting your heartbeat thaw in hot water. That same kind of sweet, slow pain."

"And you'd be happy with such a simple thing?"

"Brother, I could build a life around that."

The white fox reverses the tilt of its sleek head. "But he won't build a future around you."

I smile, slightly forlorn. "Yeah, well, that's never been what's it about."

The gods woke as we fled the planet and boy, were they hungry.

To this day, deities remain a contentious topic despite how they've made themselves common on our ships, manifestations drawn from every version of themselves. For example: Odin, one-eyed and stentorian. Odin, as portrayed by Ian McShane a lifetime before, Odin as recognized in comic books, Odin as a roar of thunder. That sort of thing.

Mine called themselves Daji and declared themselves victorious over all other foxes. Daji, Dakini, even Reynault in France, who they assure me was once as numinous as them. At least, until they cracked Reynault open and supped on his marrow.

But we're digressing. Before, if their fiction is to be believed, they were happy to content themselves with glasses of alcohol, rice dressed with sweet soy and blanketed with fatty char siu. *Money*; always a favorite. The nights, however, have become as long as grief these days. The gods now require better nutrition and blood, as history endlessly repeats, fills that need like nothing else.

I found this out one night when I was desperate. When *he* was ill, writhing in sick bay. I offered a pour from my veins and Daji's messengers lapped it up, giggling like children throughout.

"Sister, he doesn't deserve you."

At that, I only dug deeper into the vein. "I know."

"Ama?"

I slide a look over my shoulder as Rita jogs into view, voluminous hair bramble-wild in the humidity. Sweat glistens along her jaw, drips; it gleams along the holocaust of her right cheek, the muscles wefted into something like rough wool, skin crocodilian where it isn't absent, flesh all pink. "Yeah. What's up?"

"I heard you talking—"

A shrug. I'm not a priestess. Not really. Daji isn't my god to hawk.

"I'm always talking to someone." I pinch the bridge of my nose, let go, a smile following after, a hound on the hunt. "Usually they're under the age of two and about ready to shit on my suit."

Rita gives one of her rare laughs, the sound of her voice precise, dangerous. Bad whiskey on a bleak night. Recruits get themselves killed over that noise; it's a lie that says everything's good, everything's safe, everything's alright, don't think too hard on any of this, don't think, just go. "Yeah. Sorry. We'd look into getting some help—"

The rain starts up again, machine-gun fire on the wooden roof. "Promises, promises."

"You could *teach* someone." Rita slants a reproving look, and I half-shrug into her admonishment, both shoulders going up, staying up. The white fox isn't anywhere to be seen and neither is the offering I'd brought, vacuum-packed and primly divided, each section labeled. Not one of Daji's menagerie has ever remarked on whether the gesture is appreciated, but since no disapproval has been expressed either, I'll continue my little courtesies. Gods are strange these days.

"I could."

"Why don't you?"

"Because you'd pitch me out of an airlock if I did."

Rita shakes her head. The light threads itself through her scars, transforms her skin into a mosaic. "Lies. I wouldn't have a cook if I did."

"I appreciate that you appreciate my functionalities. It says a lot about what you feel in regards to my personality."

"The less said about your character the better." Rita drags fingers through her curls, restless. I don't blame her. The pret—our word, a colloquialism, not the official epithet—gravitate towards biophysical activity, evidence of synaptic function. If someone told me a decade ago that this is what we'd be fighting, afterimages and psychic runoff, I'd have—no, I probably wouldn't have laughed. But there'd have been incredulity, skepticism.

"You know what I like about you? I always know where I stand with you." I let my shoulders drop, thumbs hooked through my belt loops. Civilian attire is always so risky, but I miss pockets, miss the convenience of draping fabric, the feel of cotton. The breeze snakes through the undergrowth, a faint rustling. A floral sweetness suffuses the air, luscious, nameless. Humanity's exodus catalyzed the parturition of a billion new species; bacterial and vegetal and animal, every phylum contributed offshoots to this new ecosystem.

"Careful." Her eyebrows go up. "Or I'll really jettison your ass."

I bark a laugh, avid and hungry. "Promises."

Rita's expression pares itself of playfulness. In its place, she installs a portraiture of the decorated commander: analytical, apathetic. "What *are* you doing here, Ama?"

A Cold War of ciphered expressions before I allow a smile to tender my submission, eyes lidded, a lie slotted into my smile. Rita sighs, compromises on pretending that whatever I'd say next is something approximating honest fact. "Just felt like—I don't know. Giving back a little." I palm an orange-red pillar, let my expression color sly. "The shrine was kind of enough to stay upright despite the end of the known world, so I figured it merited some gratitude in return."

"Uh-huh."

"Honestly," All teeth now, my grin. Gods are vectors of contagion, their idiosyncrasies breed like viruses, infect with impunity. All worship is a contract of sorts, tacit permission for the numinous to edit their flock. You can't help but evolve in their proximity. "What's wrong with a little prayer in our line of work?"

Her expression calcifies, a snarl coiling her ruined mien. "Everything."

We fled to the stars before Earth let out its last breath and drifted between galaxies for four hundred years, listening to the heartbeats of our ships. Fiction would have you think that such an enterprise would turn the species feral, but the truth is kinder. Humanity lost its fear of itself, shed its hate like a mouthful of rust. When you have nothing but each other, you learn to love your neighbor. You do that or you die.

"Not that again."

"Serotonergic activity increases the—"

I flap a hand. "I know, I know. You don't have to keep banging on about it."

"We've lost six already."

Eight, I think, not wanting to remind Rita of that cat's cradle of charred bodies I'd found on the riverbank in Seattle. Two new recruits who'd been separated, who did everything right but still died with their spines fused into a black rope of burnt muscle, teeth hard and small and commercial white, studding jawbones like bridges of charred fat.

Still, no reason to bring up the dead and even less purpose in bringing up guilt. Casualties are all part of the business.

I study Rita's features for a hard minute before I shrug, my apathy invoking a look of chagrin. She rakes a hand through her hair again, shakes out the curls. She'd been a girl once: soft, certain in the world's charity. And despite the banality of that revelation, its raw absurdity, it surprises me. I search her countenance, wondering if I could decode an image of that child from the wreckage of her face, some uncharacteristic vulnerability to suggest that Rita wasn't harvested from a cloning facility, full-grown, cynical from activation.

"What?" I say.

"Talk to me."

"What do you want me to say? I see trees of green, red roses too?" I enfold the world with a gesture. The rain maintains its desultory assault. The air thickens, a green sweetness on the tongue. Through the trees, I see the detritus of Tokyo, verdant, its skyscrapers excised of their original purpose, nothing more than trellises now, overrun with new life. "I see them all. Yeah, I—"

"That's not what I meant."

I cock my head. "Meaning only the slightest disrespect, Colonel, but if you're dissatisfied with me in any way, I invite you to file a fucking report. Otherwise, you don't have jurisdiction over what I do during my free time."

Rita's tongue laves across her mouth in a quick motion. Her fingers spasm into claws, then fists, squeezing shut. We'd sparred. Of us two, Rita is quicker, more practiced, but I've the advantage of density, my frame made to endure. "This is not about your performance."

"Then with even less respect than before, Colonel, I ask that you fuck off and let me do what I need to do."

"Fucking hell, Ama. Can't you—we're not fighting here. This isn't a war between the two of us. You and I? We're not enemies." Sentences like buckshot, violent.

"Nope." Deer, pelts red-brindled and muzzles tusked, spring from the undergrowth, and I pivot on a toe to watch as they bound across the road below, their bodies reflected in the dark glass of a shop front. Inside, mannequins like desiccated bodies, haute couture rotting into shreds. "Not enemies."

A sigh. "I know what you've been doing."

I slant a look across my shoulder, the horizon bleeding to dusk. A smile spills again into place as I dip my head, body tensed against the implied accusation. "And?"

"You're going to kill yourself this way."

"I'm careful," I say, carefully, picking my way through the sentence, eliding anything that may be construed as incriminating. Every marine is kitted with telemetric machinery, methods with which to conscript and transmit data: barometric pressure, atmospheric nuance, confession. "I'm a trained medic. I know the limits of the human body."

"You're an idiot."

"It's not your business anyway."

Implacable, Rita continues, pursues her interrogation without a pretext of courtesy. "Yes, it is. You're my friend, Ama. Like it or not, I care about you. And he doesn't—"

"Still not your business."

"Fuck me. Will you just listen?"

"Love makes you do stupid things, I guess. " Conversation, like everything else, is subject to weaponization. A pair of foxes skulk from the undergrowth, bleach-pale and too broad along the scapulae, almost primitive in the way they hulk. They bay like wolves, like women halfway to wolves, like things wilder than both, sublime in their lack of classification.

"What are you hoping to accomplish?"

"I don't know," I tell her with a frayed smile. "I'll let you know when I stop lying to myself."

I spoke to Daji. Once. When I represented an unprecedented novelty: a mercenary who would be a priestess, without training or even the excuse of familial affiliation, with nothing but audacity and avarice. They came to me in the ship's hold. A murmuration of porcelain foxes, hundreds strong, each as delicate as a child's phalange. When they spoke, it wasn't in chorus but in concert, their discourse Mozartian in its elegance. They sang and the ship sang with them, ecstatic, effusive.

"He will never give you what you want."

"Probably not," I told them. "But that's not the point."

"He won't love you back, you know? Not the way you want him to. Not the way you could be loved." Daji disclosed futures in potentia: a woman, black-haired and solemn, a ring on a pale finger; a man, gaunt, starved of ego; daughters without the preamble of romance: two adopted, a third hand-crafted by medical professionals. So much uncomplicated happiness, only a decision away from corporealization. All I needed to do was ask.

Gods are cruel that way.

I closed my eyes against the Technicolor possibilities, breathed out. "Maybe. But that's not what we're here to talk about."

"So, why?"

The answer's always inelegant, always has been inelegant. Without the framing of my private neurochemistry, without the context of love, its poetics, my response has never been anything but clumsy, sentimentality absent of sense. So I said nothing on the topic, instead deflected with a question. "What will it cost me?"

"What will what cost you?" Daji disseminated themself across the space, multiplying between seconds until the infrastructure swarmed with enameled bodies, their eyes a universe of unblinking stars.

"My wish."

"It depends on how much you want it."

My voice husked without intervention or irony. "Like air."

The quality of the light altered, became syrupy; halogen deepened to gold; the seconds slowed to something like honey; a meadow-sweet aftertaste of clover you could crunch between your molars. "Tell us again. Tell us what you want."

Their instruction turned in my breastbone like a key.

"Keep him safe," I said and the words had the suppleness of practice. They no longer hurt on exit. The yearning expanded in my breast. "No matter what, keep him safe, keep him safe."

"No matter what at all? No matter what I ask?"

"No matter what."

And Daji laughed like a thousand worlds ending at once.

"All this is for—"

"Yes."

"*Why.*"

I pinch my tongue between incisors, press down until the taste of rust steeps in my mouth. It isn't until a rill of wetness winds down my chin that I pause, thumbing at the blood. Swallow, smile. But the lie of nonchalance doesn't come easy this time and behind my ribs, my heart drums a dirge. Ten years of prayer, of consorting with spirits from a thousand light years away, all for someone who has never looked past next Wednesday. The irony is an incision, a cut in a lung, and when I breathe, it hurts.

But this story was never about me.

"I don't know what you're talking about."

"Ama." Rita thumbs the trigger of her ion pistol, then palms its grip in the next stroke. The rain recedes, seeps between the cobblestones and spreads into puddles, an upside-down window to the bruised-plum firmament, suddenly so very dark now, deepest indigo save for the gold lacquering the mountain line. I gaze out at Tokyo, the city inert and still. The air flexes. Somewhere, a fox screams. "Don't."

"Don't what?"

"Don't lie to me. Don't try to weasel out of this. Don't do this to—" Leather, petri-grown, sliding over leather. A motion in the periphery of my vision, gunmetal gleaming. "—*us.*"

I look back to her, the firearm in her grip, no threat as of yet but the nascent vow of one. Rita's expression is a reflection, familiar in a way that I wish it wasn't, that exhaustion intimate as a fillet of muscle from my thigh. I know that look. Worn and weighted down, weathered, weary, dragging regret like someone else's sins. Rita's spent forever trying to save me from myself. "Didn't know we were dating. I'd have dressed up for you more, otherwise."

Click. "Please don't make me do something I'd regret."

"Like what? Shoot me? Is that where you're going with that? Because we both know you're not supposed to pull out a gun unless you're planning to use it." I spread my arms, palms turned up. "No one is getting hurt by this."

"Except you."

"That's not your cross to bear." I take a step forward. "That's not your fucking business either."

Rita doesn't back down, only lowers the barrel so the muzzle aligns with my knee. Her expression is glacial, the look of someone who has brought more people out of this world than in. "Why do you owe him this? What the fuck did he do to deserve any of your consideration? This is a security risk."

"It wouldn't be if you didn't insist on hanging around."

"That isn't the point. This is still a security risk. A member of personnel—aka, you—is still at risk from these activities. And gods, I—I can't understand why you're taking these chances, why you're putting yourself in harm's way. Because as far as I can tell, this whole thing's been in his favor and all you're doing is bartering for scraps. Hell, does he even know you're doing this? That thing with the Daji shrines?"

"I've sent images."

"And what did he say?"

I grit my teeth. "He said he appreciated the sentiment."

There is no warning between the moment when Rita makes her decision and when she fires, the bolt cleaving through my augmentations, past bone, boiling synovial fluid to steam. The shot is precise, intense; it cauterizes the flesh as it passes. I collapse, panting, my vision haloed by magnesium flashes.

"The fuck did you do that for?"

"Daji needs a sacrifice, right? That's how it works?" Rita bends down, face frescoed with darkness. She unholsters a knife, small and primitive, slices a curl of fat from my thigh before rising to her feet. "A friendship's got to be worth its weight in something."

A buzzing noise suffuses the atmosphere, lower than the sound of cicadas, lower even than the hiss of old-fashioned television static; something that murmurs through the spine like the song of a million pale foxes. Through the torii gates, I see something move, a teardrop of a body uncurling, and it's anyone's guess if it is one of Daji's messengers or the pret come to feed, and if there is any difference between the two.

JASON SIZEMORE

Cassandra Khaw was selected for our inaugural "Commitment to Quality" group of writers that we promote in our annual funding Kickstarter. The author shows us again why they're one of our most frequent contributors.

When I'm looking for fiction, I crave stories that have a unique voice and unique imagination. While this might be the most gentle post-apocalyptic tale we've ever published, the story has enough playfulness to make it fit as an "Apex" story.

MR. DEATH

ALIX E. HARROW

I've ferried two hundred and twenty-one souls across the river of death, and I can already tell my two-hundred-and-twenty-second is going to be a real shitkicker. I know by the lightness of the manila folder in my hand, the preemptive pity in the courier's face as she gives it to me. I read the typewritten card paper-clipped to the front with my stomach tensed, braced for the sucker punch.

Name: Lawrence Harper
Address: 186 Grist Mill Road, Lisle NY, 13797
Time: Sunday, July 14th 2020, 2:08AM, EST
Cause: Cardiac arrest resulting from undiagnosed
long QT syndrome
Age: 30 months

Jesus Christ on his sacred red bicycle. He's two.

Two is, by break room consensus, the worst age for reaping. Their souls are still baby-soft and cottony, wholly innocent, but full of the subtleties and quirks that define their selfhood. They're balanced right at the teetering edge of themselves, so full of potential it makes your eyes water just to be near them.

Also, two-year-olds are contrarian bastards and it takes several hours and a family-size pack of M&Ms to coax them across the river.

These days, with the child mortality rate comfortably below 7 per 1,000 births, we don't process too many of the under-fives—some of the older reapers like to bitch about how we've got it soft, reminiscing about the good old days before seatbelt laws and vaccinations and the EPA--but six-point-six out of a thousand is still six-point-six too many. Every reaper hits one eventually.

This was my first, in my three years of reaping. I was starting to think somebody upstairs was looking out for me, shielding me in case one of the under-fives turned out to be a little boy with corn silk hair and dark eyes. In case I cracked like an egg and had to retire early.

Every new reaper is shielded, at least a little. The first dozen or so deaths we're assigned are generally people with one spiritual foot firmly in the grave: your stage-IV seventy-year-olds, your left behind spouses, your great-grandmothers who just overheard the term *assisted living* floating up the stairs.

There's something satisfying about those reapings. A routine heroism, like covering a shift for your hungover friend or shooing a trapped bird out the window. Those are the times it's easiest to believe my supervisor's speeches about the pristine order of the universe and the cyclical shape of time and the necessity of death.

(Some reapers dance around the word *death,* preferring verbs like *passing* or *ascending.* My supervisor—Raz, Reaper Recruitment Coordinator and Archangel of Secrets—believes euphemisms are a form of cowardice, and Raz doesn't recruit cowards).

But eventually you run out of easy deaths.

Eventually the courier slinks into the locker room and hands you a manila folder without quite meeting your eyes and you know you're in for it: newlyweds in car crashes; leukemia that was supposed to be in remission; restraining orders that didn't work. Or sometimes it seems fine—*88 years old, ischemic stroke, 4:12PM*—but when you arrive you find a soul so wasted and dim, so shriveled by bitterness and regret that you want to stop the clock and say: *Look, you've got a week. Try a new ice cream flavor. Listen to the Hamilton soundtrack. Call your son. Live, you damn fool.*

Except you don't because you can't, and because of the pristine order of the universe and the cyclical shape of time, et cetera. Instead you sit beside him and watch the plaque crumble from his carotid and drift sluggishly up to his cerebral artery. The fizz of electricity in his brain goes dark and the sour muck of his soul rises from his body, glaring. It's a long ride across the river that night.

So I don't come apart when I see little Lawrence Harper's name on that neatly-typed card, the curve of that 3 staring up at me like half a heart. I lay the folder in my scuffed briefcase—I was never a briefcase-carrier before, but fashion in the hereafter runs twenty to fifty years behind—and head out for 186 Grist Mill Road.

I already know how it will go: I will wait beside him in the night (does he have a bed shaped like a plastic race car like Ian did? Does he kick the blankets off his legs every night?) until 2:08AM, when the bird-wing flutter of his heart will go still. I will tuck his ghostly hand in mine as I lead him through the dark to the riverbank, and when we reach the other side I'll watch his soul disperse into the depthless firmament of the universe. It will be achingly sad but also kind of beautiful, and afterward I'll sit in the break room and drink burned coffee and cry. Leon might come by and give me the Circle of Life speech from *The Lion King* and we'll both laugh and he'll thump me on the shoulder and say *it's just the way it goes.*

And then tomorrow I'll open my next manila folder and do it again.

Not because I'm a heartless bastard; they don't recruit heartless bastards to comfort the dead and ferry their souls across the last river. They look for people whose hearts are vast and scarred, like old battlefields overgrown with poppies and saplings. People who know how to weep and keep working, who have lost everything except their compassion.

(The official recruitment policy is race and gender-neutral, but forty-something white males like me are a rarity. We are statistically less likely to experience shattering loss, and culturally permitted to become complete assholes when we do. We turn into addicts and drunks, bitter old men who shed a single, manly, redemptive tear at the end of the movie, while everybody else has to gather up the jagged edges of themselves and keep going).

Raz told me she also looks for people with kind eyes and a high tolerance for bureaucracy, who have never cheated at anything in their entire lives (poker, *Settlers of Catan,* marriage). "You can cheat a lot of shit," she says, "But not death."

Lawrence Harper doesn't have a race car bed, thank God. Instead he has a twin mattress on the floor of his parents' single-wide. He also has: a Spiderman blanket that smells like a thrift store, dusty and flowery; a plastic Buzz Lightyear clutched in one sweaty fist; reddish hair, skim milk skin; a heart that will fail in approximately eleven hours and twelve minutes; and a soul that shines like a comet streaking across the last midnight of summer.

Even for a two-year-old, it's a stunner of a soul, vibrant and hungry, bonfire bright. It's the kind of soul that might lead revolutions or write symphonies in an adult, but in a kid it mostly translates to trouble. I bet his parents spend a lot of time smiling fixedly at strangers as they haul him out of restaurants or pry him out of trees. I bet his grandma refers to him as "a handful" and refuses to babysit except in emergencies.

I bet they'll miss him like hell once he's gone.

That's what makes this job tough, of course. It's not the dead rejoining the limitless love of the universe; it's the ones they leave behind, who have to keep on trudging through the world beneath the burden of their terrible, limited love.

I settle cross-legged on the carpet, trying not to nudge the piled laundry or set off some battery-powered toy. Reapers have what the training manuals call "limited corporeal capacity," which means we can move stuff but not much, like when you're in a dream and your limbs are filled with wet sand and everything is impossibly, illogically heavy.

I figure most ghost stories are the result of clumsy reapers, although there are late night break room rumors of reapers who went rogue. Who abandoned the Department and haunted the living world until they faded into tattered wraiths. I don't know if I believe those stories, because A) what kind of asshole wants to spend eternity creeping around a Victorian mansion or an old psych ward, scaring teenagers, and B) Raz or one of the other archangels would atomize them so instantly and thoroughly there wouldn't be enough drifting motes of soulstuff left to tell a story about. Raz is the kind of sweet, middle-aged Black woman with whom you do not fuck.

I've never been tempted to do anything more than bum a cigarette or flick a light switch, myself. (Except the one time, right after my own funeral. I slunk back into my shitty, tobacco-stained apartment and took the only thing in it that I cared a damn about. But it wasn't a big deal and nobody saw.)

Lawrence stirs beneath his Spiderman blanket and sits up, his hair smeared sideways, his eyes blue, unfocused. His dad must hear the rustling on the baby monitor because he turns up two seconds later, a lanky, tired man in sweatpants. He drapes Lawrence casually over one shoulder and pads back down the hall, and for a moment I'm too choked with envy and pity to follow them. Envy because he's holding his son in his arms, sleep-soft and sweaty; pity because this is the last time.

By the time I make it out to the kitchen Lawrence is snapped into a plastic booster seat crunching off-brand Cheerios. He looks up as I enter and I figure it's nothing, just a coincidence, but then his eyes focus on me. Lawrence waves.

I've been seen before, but not often. For most people I'm a prickle at their hairline, a smudged not-quite-reflection in the mirror behind them, a strange and unwelcome awareness of their heartbeats in their ears. Reapers are the reason fewer people board doomed flights and good dogs sometimes bark at nothing.

But the way Lawrence is looking at me—head tilted, eyes flicking from briefcase to old-timey suit to beard stubble—I know he sees every single undead inch of me.

I wave back, awkwardly. He smiles. I press one finger to my lips. He copies me, then whispers "*SHHH*" so loudly that his dad laughs and shushes him back, and then they're drawn into a competitive shushing game that lasts through snack time and outside into the sweet fresh-clover smell of the July afternoon.

Their yard is several inches past overgrown and littered with sun-faded scraps of plastic. I don't feel the heat so much these days but I can tell from the wavy lines coming off the trailer that it's hotter than the hell that doesn't exist. Lawrence's dad settles into a busted lawn chair in the shade while his son wanders. I trail after him.

Lawrence picks up a stick and slashes invisible enemies, narrating a story that sounds like a combination of *Toy Story* and *Star Wars*. He tosses a tennis ball at the trailer for a while, apparently intrigued by the showers of rust that pour out from under the siding, then throws it, for no reason at all, to me.

And I catch it, like a dumbass. It strains against the insubstantial edges of my existence. Lawrence holds his arms out, waiting.

I can't quote the Book of Death line and verse the way Raz can, but I'm pretty sure there's a policy somewhere against playing catch in broad daylight with a doomed two-and-a-half-year-old, surrounded by the green hum of summer.

But like—fuck it. I toss the ball back. Lawrence misses it, because two-and-a-half-year-olds have the coordination of drunk bear cubs, but it doesn't matter. I am immediately promoted from boring stranger to Imaginary Friend and conscripted into a series of opaque games involving tennis balls and shrieking and running in circles around the trailer until even my death-cold skin is flushed and sweaty and my chest is aching, as if my heart is either mending or breaking.

By the time the game ends the sun is slanting pink and sideways and the world has softened like butter on the counter. Lawrence collapses backward onto the densest patch of clover and lies still for the first time since he woke up. I can see white streaks of cloud in his eyes and, if I squint, the red muscle of his heart contracting and releasing in that secret, imperfect rhythm. His soul blazes back at the sky, wide-open, a private infinity of possibility.

I wonder if Ian's reaper watched him like this, with something aching and tender lodged like a splinter behind their breastbone. I wonder if Ian's soul shone this brightly (I know it did). I wonder how it will feel to watch a soul like this disperse into the endless everything, scattered into a billion lonely atoms.

Raz was my reaper. She showed me my folder afterward and the card paper-clipped to it: *Sam Grayson, 44 years old, 11:19AM EST, respiratory failure resulting from small cell lung cancer.* The cancer came courtesy of a pack of Lucky Strikes a day for fifteen years or so; my personal fuck you to mortality after Ian.

I couldn't see her, but I could sort of sense her: a soft, amber gaze hovering at the edges of the hospital room, watching the labored rise and fall of my chest.

It's department policy to spend at least four hours prior to death with the soon-to-be-deceased. It's supposed to "forge emotional bonds between souls and reapers" and "encourage compassionate care"—the department has been working tirelessly and fruitlessly to combat the whole sweeping robes, menacing scythe stereotype—but Raz believes in a full twelve, even during busy weeks (flu epidemics, civil wars, the holidays).

So she sat at my bedside through the night and half a day until my clogged lungs bubbled into silence and my pulse stuttered and I drowned in carbon dioxide and cancer. I died thinking *fucking finally.*

I could see her, then: a brown-skinned woman somewhere between thirty and seventy wearing a white cable-knit sweater and comfortable Levi's.

She smiled—a professional smile, smoothed by centuries of use, but still somehow genuine—and launched into what I now recognize as a version of the same "welcome to the afterlife, kid" speech I've given two hundred and twenty-one times. It begins with some variation of "it's all right," which is an absolute lie and both of you know it, but which manages to imply that there's some sort of plan, a system in place, and usually buys you a few minutes to explain the rest.

It worked on me. I drifted, perfectly placid, as Raz explained that I was dead, and that we would shortly be stepping together into a vast and endless darkness, broken only by an even darker river, which she would guide me across. Then there was a lot of other stuff about how my soul would unravel and rejoin the spangled cosmos, and how the universe itself was love, which is all true but is still unforgivably hokey.

And then she paused and I had the feeling—even as machines beeped in ineffective alarm and my soul hovered above my body like steam above pasta water, milky and vaporous—that we were going off script.

She tilted her head, the gentle amber of her eyes sharpening. "Or," she began, and let me tell you the human brain is capable of a lot of wordless scenario-spinning in the infinite space following the word *or*. *Or* this isn't the end. *Or* this is a bad reaction to my meds and I'll wake up hungover but alive. *Or* I get a pair of feathered wings and I'll go soaring through the pearly gates and Ian will be waiting for me on a puff of cumulus, laughing his wild laugh, and these fifteen years of heartache will be wiped clean, set right, the moment my palm brushes the soft corn silk of his hair.

But she didn't say any of that. She handed me a cream-colored business card with my name embossed cleanly on the front—*Sam Grayson, Junior Reaper, Department of Death*—and offered me a job.

Just before dark, Lawrence's mom shows up in a puttering Corolla. She wears a red apron with Tractor Supply embroidered across the top and smells like rubber and chicken feed and the gray film of receipt paper, but Lawrence doesn't care: he practically teleports into her arms, face mashed against the stringy bone of her shoulder.

The Harpers clatter together into the trailer and start the dinnertime circus of bib and highchair, mac n' cheese and canned peas he won't eat, adult conversation slipped expertly between threats and pleas (*"if you spit your milk out one more time I'm taking it away—did you pay the gas bill?—two bites, baby, eat two bites of peas"*). His dad pulls on a polyester uniform and pours himself a thermos of burnt coffee. Before he leaves he kisses the back of his wife's neck and she tilts her head back, eyes closed.

I can see how tired they are, worn thin with work and worry. I can see how there's never quite enough money, how they rinse out Ziploc bags and resent the loss of milk-splattered macaroni. But I can see, too, that it's worth it. That they'll keep working and worrying and the impossible alchemy of love will turn never enough into plenty.

Except that, at 2:08 AM the following morning, their son's heart will stop and I will ferry his soul across the river and their lives will be permanently, irreparably fucked.

I want to leave. I want to step sideways out of the world and reappear back in the break room, smoke a stolen cigarette with Leon and forget all about the Harpers.

Except Lawrence would still die. Except there would be no friendly stranger waiting to take his hand and show him the way. He would wander alone into the darkness on the wrong side of the river and wisp away into nothing instead of everything.

So I stay. Raz doesn't recruit cowards or bastards, after all.

Lawrence's mom does bath and bedtime on her own while Lawrence chatters about Maui's magical fish hook and his big kid underwear and his new friend who's very tall and sad. She makes the right noises—*really? that's great sweetie!*—but she's not really listening, and I have a sudden, wild urge to shake her until her teeth rattle.

This is it! I want to say. *This is the conversation you will replay again and again for the rest of your life! You will wish you took his soft cheeks in your hands and looked into his eyes and said: I love you, Ian, and wherever you go a part of me will always follow, across that dark river and into black beyond, through every eternity.*

But I keep my fists balled in my pockets as she zips him into pajamas and plugs in his nightlight. Her last kiss is a routine brush of her lips across his forehead. "Night, love."

"Night, Mama."

The door clicks. He thrashes for a few minutes before falling abruptly and profoundly to sleep.

I watch the treacherous thump of his heart, counting out beats. I've watched enough heart failures and cardiac arrests to hear the fatal hitch in its rhythm, the tiny irregularity that will fail him when he needs it most. He's a brave kid—the kind who laughs at barking dogs and watches the garbage truck with an expression of aspirational awe—or he wouldn't have made it two and a half years without startling his heart into seizing.

But tonight something's going to scare him or thrill him. A nightmare, maybe, formless and childish, that will send his heart into an ungainly gallop. Then it will stumble. Then it will stop. His parents won't even know until they open his door in the morning, wondering why he's sleeping so late.

I see the nightmare arrive, drawing a line between the pale red of his brows. The line looks fresh somehow, like tracks in new snow, as if he'd never really frowned before. I watch his heart beat faster, *tut-tut-tut*. The delicate chambers pulse raggedly now, losing the rhythm they've practiced for thirty months. Thirty-nine months, I guess.

His heart seizes. The frown line deepens. His mouth opens as his pale skin goes from red to white to pearl-blue, and I see the first wisps of his soul rise like steam from his body.

I don't think. I don't debate or decide. I just—*do.*

I reach between his ribs and wrap my hand around his heart. It feels impossibly small against my hand, a hard apple plucked too early from the tree. I squeeze it as hard as I can with my fingers that don't exist and my fist that isn't there.

His heart shudders back to life like an engine on a cold morning. It flutters against my hand as the blue leaches out of his lips and his soul spools back into his body.

I sit beside him until dawn, watching the miraculous thud of his heart and thinking: *he's alive, he's alive* and also *oh, fuck.*

It's the failure to submit my Certification of Soul's Passage that gets me, of course. You can't forge them or fake them or forget them; when a soul disintegrates into the void it automatically generates a sheaf of papers in triplicate, signed with the last fading imprint of a soul as it leaves the world, and Lawrence Harper's soul is still very much in the world, tethered to his illegal heartbeat.

Raz finds me sitting on the pier, splashing my feet in the river of death. I'm half-expecting her to skip the small talk and go straight to the smiting but instead she sits beside me on the dry decking, the soft white of her sweater brushing against my shoulder.

She's quiet for a while. And then: "You know it doesn't work like this, Sam."

"Yeah," I say, because I do know, and what else am I going to say? That there was a beautiful boy and I didn't want him to die like my beautiful boy died? That I didn't want to ferry his soul to the far side of the river and watch it merge, however beautifully, with the infinite love of the universe? And P.S. *fuck* infinite love, give me the desperate, finite love of the living?

I don't say any of that, because I don't (quite) have a death wish.

Raz says, softly, "Would you like me to reassign him?"

Even burrowed deep in my doomed funk, I feel a flick of surprise. Deaths aren't reassigned, traded, escaped, called-out-sick-on, avoided, or skipped; your deaths are your deaths, no matter how grisly, and if you can't handle them you have a brief but blunt conversation with your supervisor after which no one ever sees you again. None of us know where you go, but it's unlikely that it's anywhere pleasant.

I look directly at Raz for the first time and find her face glowing with that terrible, bottomless compassion. She draws a Lucky Strike from her breast pocket and passes it over. She touches her fingertip to the end and it glows hot orange. "Do you still have the picture?"

I don't move. I don't breathe.

Raz knows. She knows that I flagrantly ignored the chapter in the Book of Death on Releasing Your Worldly Connections and Severing Familial Ties. She knows what I stole from my shitty apartment. She probably even knows that it's resting right now in my breast pocket, directly above my heart.

I swallow once, inhale smoke. "He was—he was a good kid."

"I know, Sam." Her voice is still so gentle. "And so is Lawrence, and it's bullshit that they have to die, but that's how it is. It's the ugly half-bargain of living, and it's our job to make it a little less ugly when we can." She pauses and adds practically, "And we can't save every cute kid. We can't cheat death."

But I think: *I did.* How long did I buy Lawrence? How much would I pay for another day, another hour with Ian?

I don't say anything. Her voice turns considerably less gentle. "That car was going eighty-five miles an hour when it hit the ice. There was nothing Leon could have done to stop it, no matter how many rules he broke."

Leon. I never knew who reaped Ian's soul and hadn't asked. Leon is a good dude—soft-spoken and big-hearted—but for a split second I want to drag him into the river with me and hold us both under until our second and final death closes above our heads.

"I'm going to ask you again: do you want me to reassign him?"

It's a kindness. A favor, and Raz doesn't really do favors. I am obscurely warmed and almost tempted to accept—but I don't want Lawrence reassigned. His death belongs to me. However many beats his heart had left, they are mine to witness.

"No. I've got it. Thanks."

Raz leans across me, plucks the still-lit cigarette from my fingertips and flicks it into the river. Her breath against my ear is sulfurous, too hot. "Then don't fuck it up this time."

She hands me a freshly printed card with Lawrence's name on it—July 28th, 5:22AM, cardiac arrest again—and vanishes.

I run my fingertip around the crisp edge of the card and realize I was wrong. It wasn't a kindness or a favor: it was a test.

It's July 28th and I'm in the back bedroom of the Harpers' damn trailer again, watching Lawrence's heart pump like a tiny red bellows in his chest.

Except this time I've had two weeks to anticipate it. Two weeks to sit in the break room refilling my coffee from the pot that never empties, feeling the time-softened folds of the Polaroid in my breast pocket, thinking about the order of the universe and the Circle of Motherfucking Life and things you can't cheat.

This time I know exactly what I'm going to do.

At 4:00 in the morning, one hour and twenty-two minutes before he's scheduled to die, I take Lawrence's hand. I stroke his forehead with barely-real knuckles and he half-wakes. He smiles a muzzy, sleepy smile and sinks back into sleep.

I keep holding his hand. I make sure that nightmare never comes.

At 5:23AM Lawrence's heart is still beating, red and wet and alive, and I'm smiling so hard I can feel my face splitting along the seams. I want to sing. I want to weep. I want to recite the poem I memorized in seventh grade because it was the shortest one on the list: *how do you like your blue-eyed boy/Mr. Death?*

I know I didn't cheat him, not really. Mr. Death always wins in the end. But maybe sometimes—if you're stubborn and sad and tired as fuck of the way things go—you can win a hand or two.

I stay with Lawrence til dawn, wondering idly if I should cut and run while I still can. It seems more important to stay, to watch the stubborn *thu-thump*ing of Lawrence's heart, the miraculous pooling of drool on his pillow. I should have spent more time watching Ian.

I feel it when she arrives: an abrupt rise in temperature, a whiff of brimstone. I look out the narrow window to see Raz standing in the yard like the end times, like vengeance in a cable-knit sweater. I look back at Lawrence one last time and am pleased to find I don't regret a single damn thing.

I slip through particle board and fiberglass and corrugated tin of the trailer wall and stroll to Raz with my hands in my pockets. I smile at her. It's not really the time for genial smiles—I'm about to be atomized or incinerated or disappeared, whatever the hell they do with reapers who fuck up—but I can't seem to stop.

Raz smiles back. "You idiot." Her eyes are still kind. Behind her I see the faint, fiery outline of wings.

I shrug.

Raz steps forward and reaches two fingers into my breast pocket. She withdraws the Polaroid, flesh-warm, and studies it for a long second. "I knew the second you went back for this that you wouldn't last," she sighs. "A reaper has to forsake his worldly attachments, relinquish his earthly loves."

"Yeah, but..." My eyes fall on the picture, upside-down: my son at four, caught at the apex of a swing that will never fall, his corn silk hair haloed by a summer dusk that will never end. Ephemeral. Everlasting.

I shrug again. "But *fuck* that, you know?"

Raz laughs. She tilts her head. "Tell me, Sam: What would you do if I left you here?"

"Left me?"

"Burned your records. Pretended you'd never worked for the Department of Death."

"I would stay." The answer comes easy and honest. "I'd watch over Lawrence, keep his heart beating another day, another hour, for as long as I can."

"Even if it meant you could never cross the river. Even if you would fade into nothing instead of rejoining the great everything."

Would I trade my eternity for one little boy and his tired parents? The infinite love of the universe for the fleeting, finite love of the living?

"Yes." It occurs to me what absolute horseshit it is that I spent the last thirteen years of my life on earth wanting to leave it and yet now, in death, I've found something worth staying for.

Raz nods, unsurprised. "That's what I thought." There's a wistful something in her eyes as she smiles at me. "You were a good reaper, Sam. Tough enough to do the work, soft enough to do it right—two hundred and twenty-one times. I'm sorry to lose you."

She sounds genuinely sorry for whatever it is she's about to do to me. I wonder idly if it will hurt.

"Could—could you assign Leon to this case, after I'm gone? He's a good guy. I want Lawrence to be with someone who—"

Raz is distracted, rooting in her jean pocket for something. "No."

"Why?"

"Because Lawrence Harper is no longer under the jurisdiction of the Department of Death." She hands me the thing from her pocket and adds, "And neither are you."

There's a silent rushing of wings, a flick of heat, and Raz is gone. I blink around the yard, empty except for the dew-pearled lawn chair, the scattered plastic toys, the precious trash of the living.

Then I look down at the cream-colored card in my hand: *Sam Grayson, Junior Guardian, Department of Life.*

JASON SIZEMORE

Alix E. Harrow's "Mr. Death" has become one of the most popular stories on our website. It's also been nominated for a host of awards for Best Short Fiction, winning several.

When Alix submitted "Mr. Death" as her "Commitment to Quality" story for the Apex Magazine 2021 Relaunch Kickstarter, she included a note in her cover letter that she feared her story wasn't any good. I hope she's feeling more confident about the story these days.

THE NIDDAH

ELANA GOMEL

I am not the woman I once was.

None of us are. Epidemics are the fire and we are the candle wax. When the fire burns out, we are melted and reshaped.

When I was in college, I read a book about the influence of the Black Death on the ecclesiastical art of Europe. Golden icons of the Madonna and the child before. Frescoes of dancing skeletons led by the grinning Death after. *The Danse Macabre.* As if they could possibly know …

But the bubonic plague had been eradicated decades before I was born, in that sunny interval between pandemics when science promised that the horrors of the past were … well, in the past. I grew up with vaccinations, and antibiotics, and the belief that every disease had a cure. I still remember the TV ads of my childhood where smiling couples lounging on the beach offered a medicine for bad mood, and loss of love, and unhappiness. At the time I watched them with detached curiosity because, of course, nothing like that could ever happen to me.

The cracks had been there all along, but the illusion collapsed on the eve of my departure to Berkeley for my senior year, when my mother announced that she and my father were divorcing. I yelled at her, accusing her of selfishness. Why would she do that to me? We were happy, weren't we? Every time this scene flashes before my eyes—which is every day—I feel a hot wave of shame like the first symptom of MHF. What I meant was that *I* was happy in the shelter of my deliberate ignorance about my parents' hollow relationship. And the worst thing was that I did not really care whether my father was around. I needed my mother, and I should have known she would be there for me, no matter what. But I was stung by what I perceived as her betrayal and I said cruel, stupid, unmeant things that buzzed in the charged air between us like a cloud of hornets.

That was the last time I had seen her. She moved back to the UK the next week—and disappeared, along with the entire population of that country.

"Gemma!"

My husband's voice. I winced. Nick does not often address me when I am in the niddah. It is considered bad form, and he is a stickler for propriety. When we met, I often joked that he was more British than me, even though he was born in Outer Richmond, a suburb of San Francisco, while my birth certificate said *London*. But the faint traces of my British accent had dissipated long ago, and nowadays I never brought up the subject of my foreign birth. There was a stigma attached to your origin in the graveyard of the world.

"What?" I stood, stretching my stiff muscles. We have a big house, so there was no need to make my niddah shelter so cramped. It was bad enough that it had to be windowless. But there were unspoken assumptions about how comfortable—or rather, uncomfortable—a woman had to be made during her dangerous time of impurity. And did I say Nick was a stickler for rules, especially unwritten ones?

"The police are here."

"Why?"

"They want to see you."

"What?!" It felt like I'd been punched in the face. I grabbed the edge of my narrow cot to steady myself. "They can't! I'm ..."

"I know what you are!" Nick growled from behind the locked door—the door that was always locked for five days every month and to which only he had the key. "But it is urgent. Put on your restraint!"

The golden era of global health was shattered by COVID-19. There had been epidemics before, of course, but since they had all taken place in the Third World, they did not disturb the placid assumption of the developed countries that the Danse Macabre of ages past had been stopped for good. Then the *coronavirus* had opened the door and ancient nightmares came pouring in. Even though a vaccine was soon mass-produced, the complacency was gone, never to return. There were some years of fragile and uncertain calm before the Kashmir *ebolavirus*. Before MHF, and my mother's disappearance. That was when I went to college, majoring in Art History but eyeing law school. Women could be lawyers at the time. Now, paradoxically, my formerly useless Art History degree brought in a trickle of income as I taught online courses to bored, secluded housewives.

I turned off my computer and stood in the dimly lit room, blinking like an owl about to venture into daylight. It was strange how quickly we adapted to the new conditions. Viruses are better teachers than Sunday schools or madrasas. What countless generations of misogyny could not accomplish, a pandemic did. I, who used to wear skinny jeans and a tank top everywhere, was now feverishly pulling on my veil, my arms snagging on the rough fabric.

The sack-like garment covered everything, but my face, pale and unwashed, remained exposed. It was like an inversion of one of my fondest memories. During COVID-19, people had to wear face masks. Every time we went out, my mother would put on her designer red mask and hand me an identical smaller one. She would kneel by my side and we would look together in the mirror: a woman and a girl, our red-veiled faces clustered together like a flower and a bud. It made me feel secure, that mask.

No mask could protect against Mutational Hemorrhaging Fever.

Nick knocked again, and I realized I did not have time to apply makeup. How long before they insisted that we should cover our faces, too, like the pious women had done in India and the Middle East for ages? I had seen those pictures in my studies: burkas, abayas, chadors ... Only eyes were showing and sometimes even they were shadowed by a net or a fold of gauze. To preserve female purity and chastity, they said. Women still covered up the old-fashioned way in Saudi Arabia—what was left of it.

I tugged down the black fabric that fell down onto my sneakers and grasping the ties, managed to manacle my own wrists. Some women also hobbled their ankles, but I refused to do so, much to Nick's displeasure. Speaking of which, I heard his impatient tapping on the door once again.

"Ready!" I yelled and the door opened.

I emerged into the crystalline light of Californian summer. Sitting in niddah, your time-sense is scrambled. Even though I knew it was 3PM, the glorious sunshine streaming through our glass wall caught me by surprise. My eyes watered, as I tried to make out the figures in the living room. They kept their distance from me, nobody more so than Nick who was standing by the open front door as if ready to bolt at the first inkling of danger. Ridiculous, of course: you could not outrun a virus. But I focused on the two people standing slightly closer. A man in a suit and a covered woman. She was not wearing her restraints—those were only for those few, like me, who, for whatever reason, had to break their niddah. But the veil had become compulsory for all females, even though there was no real reason for it.

The woman was older than me, with strong features and a dark complexion. In times past, we would call her East Asian. Now Asia was as remote as Mars.

I stood by the open door to my niddah quarters, feeling mildly agoraphobic. I saw that the man's hand was resting on his gun. There had been cases of women killed by vigilantes on the mere suspicion of being impure.

"Gemma Drennan?" the woman asked.

"That's my maiden name. I'm Gemma Russell now."

"Was your mother Nina Drennan?"

"Yes. What is this all about?"

"Your mother is alive," the woman said.

MHF ... A dry scientific nomenclature trying—and failing—to dispel the horror. They had more imagination in the Middle Ages, not afraid to call plagues by their proper names: the Black Death, St. Vitus Dance ... There had been some spooky labels circulating on social media at the beginning when the pandemic appeared to be just another flash-in-the-pan scare, jangling the planet's frayed nerves. The Scarlet Plague, the Bleeding Contagion, even the New Ebola. Only that last one had even a smidgeon of scientific validity. The virus that caused it was a mutation of the Ebola virus. Unfortunately, while the traditional Ebola had a vaccine, there was none for the Kashmir *ebolavirus* that caused MHF.

The first reports of a strange affliction coming from India were met with a heightened sense of foreboding—the aftereffects of COVD-19. But the reports were so bizarre that it took the medical community, still reeling from the *coronavirus*, a lot of time to figure out what was really going on. And when they did, it was too late.

MHF began with fever, fatigue, muscle ache: the generic symptoms of just about any disease. What happened next, however, was unique. Some people recovered. Some died of internal bleeding or raging fever that could not be brought down.

And some—very specifically—changed. *The Danse Macabre* coming back with a vengeance.

"What do you mean, my mother is alive?" I asked stupidly.

"We received an email from her," the woman said. "Addressed to USCIS. Asking that her American citizenship be reinstated, and she be issued a new passport."

United States Citizenship and Immigration Service. I was sure the agency had been disbanded. It was not like they had anything to do.

"But my mother was in London!"

"The email was sent from the American Embassy in London. What *used* to be the American Embassy."

MHF is spread by exposure to blood. The virus is in everybody by now. I had seen it swimming in my own blood—a spiky sphere like a miniature hedgehog. But it is dormant. It does nothing.

However, if exposed to even a small amount of someone else's fresh blood, whether via a scratch, transfusion, or absorbed through the skin, it wakes up. It takes you over.

And then you are either burning in fever, go into a coma, recover—or ...

Of course, the social consequences of that are incalculable. Crash victims are left to bleed on the pavement or dispatched with a sniper's bullet through the head—authorized by an act of Congress empowering sheriffs and cops to perform *sanitary triage*. Children are restrained to prevent them from scratching or injuring themselves until they are old enough to be shown videos of Dancers. Training by trauma. Transfusions are outlawed and so are most surgeries. Childbirth is attended by midwives in full protective gear who are either suicidal or saintly. And menstruating women are put in seclusion, away from their partners and families. The ancient tradition of niddah, a menstruating hut, has been resurrected.

The East Asian woman's name was Radha. She and I sat together at the kitchen table while the men—Nick and her partner—hovered uneasily in the background. It was not that women were less deadly to each other than we were to men. A drop of my blood on Radha and she would join the damned. But women trusted each other. And men no longer trusted us—if they ever did.

She showed me a printout of the email. It was an ordinary request for the reissue of a passport. It was as ancient and brittle in my hands as an object from the Titanic.

"Did you try to contact the Embassy?"

"Of course."

"And?"

"No answer."

Satellite pictures of London showed squares being reclaimed by weeds and Regent Park drowning in vines. The Thames flowed clear. There was movement in the countryside, but nobody was sure what it signified. All transatlantic flights and most domestic flights were grounded: too much danger of an accidental injury in a confined space where droplets of blood could travel from one passenger to another. MHF had neither cure nor vaccine.

"But there must be electricity in the Embassy if the computers are running! Wi-Fi, servers ..."

Radha shook her head.

"The email was not sent from there. We traced it. It was rerouted several times, sent from a private computer in Felton."

The name sounded familiar, but I could not place it. And suddenly it clicked.

Felton was a tiny town in the Santa Cruz Mountains, twenty miles away.

"Are you saying ...?"

"Yes, Gemma. Your mother is here."

The emergence from niddah involved humiliating tests to prove to your partner and the medical authorities online that you were no longer polluted. Normally I resented the tests. This time I went through the whole rigmarole absentmindedly, thinking of what Radha had said in that first meeting.

After the MHF's massive and simultaneous global outbreak, after the grounding of all flights, and the internet being flooded with terrible videos of Dancers, I desperately tried to reach my mother. My father had moved to a small town in Indiana that later became known as the Scarlet Ballroom. I knew he was dead, and it was a sort of detached comfort to me; we had never been close but at least I could bury him in my mind by delegating him to the precious memories of childhood. My mother, on the other hand ... I kept waking up at night and talking to her: apologizing, explaining, justifying myself. She did not know what was happening to me. She did not know I had married Nick after her disappearance. She had never met him. We had been dating for a couple of months when he proposed during the height of the pandemic. At the time, I saw it as proof of his devotion—he was willing to expose himself to the danger of blood contagion for my sake. Later I realized he had simply been prescient. The strict marriage rules of traditional societies that we, Westerners, had scoffed at for so long came into fashion as the dating scene dried up and Tinder went out of business. You could control and monitor your wife in a way you could not control and monitor a stranger.

"How did she come back?" I had asked Radha. "Are there flights between the US and Europe?"

"Actually, yes. Military, commercial, cargo. Life goes on."

"If you call it a life," I muttered.

Radha shrugged. There were dark circles under her dark eyes that made them appear larger. I noticed that she had applied some thick eyeliner and mauve lipstick. I liked it.

"Anyway," she continued, "these flights are strictly monitored. Your mother did not arrive on any of them."

"So?"

"So, either she slipped on the last passenger flight from Heathrow under an assumed name and has been living here ever since, or there are some unauthorized, unknown flights that have kept going. In any case, we need to find out."

"You are not really the police, are you?" I asked.

"No."

"The FBI?"

"What does it matter?"

"I want to know what law enforcement agency still employs women."

Radha smiled. Her teeth were a little too big, a smidgeon of lipstick on their whiteness.

My mother put on her makeup every day before going to the university, even when she was not teaching, only working in the lab. She taught me that beauty is a matter of self-respect.

Nick told me I was a good cook. He told me I would be a good mother. He never told me I was beautiful.

Recently he had started talking about *family purity*. He hinted that a face veil would be a great idea. I scoffed; he sulked.

He and Radha's unnamed partner were sitting in the kitchen and drinking beer. Nick did not offer us any.

"But why to write a letter to USCIS? This is ridiculous."

"Not unless she wanted to get in touch with you and didn't know how."

I frowned. This made sense. My mother did not know my marriage name. She did not know where I lived. There were still ways to find out such things but only if one was a real computer pro—an increasingly rare breed in these days of the dwindling and fragmented internet. My mother had been a biology professor; her knowledge of computers was no better than mine.

"OK, you found me. Now what?"

"We want you to meet her."

"Wearing a wire?" Recently I had become addicted to pre-pandemic thrillers. Their quaint plots of free-wheeling assassins, plane-hopping around the world, gave me a nostalgic thrill. Some of those assassins were female.

Radha smiled.

"Something like that."

"But why? If you know she is in Felton, why don't you just bring her out?"

"We don't know where she is. We hope she'll come out of hiding to meet you."

The protective suit I wore was incredibly awkward. I looked like a Michelin Man with a face shield.

Nick pointedly refused to see me off when the sleek, black car pulled into our driveway. He had threatened to prevent me from going, only to find out that he had no legal power to do so. Laws lagged behind the growing societal support of the purdah and the gynaeceum, so the pre-pandemic laws still gave legal autonomy to married women.

Radha was in the back seat of the car, driven by a glum-faced man who brought down the plexiglass partition the moment I stepped inside. I looked back at our large, glass-walled home, searching out the bricked-up window in the back—the window of my niddah room.

I fidgeted, trying to find comfort inside a suit whose rough seams chafed my inner thighs. The tiny recorder had been so cleverly concealed that even I did not know exactly where it was.

"How many are there?" I asked.

"About a hundred."

"All immune?" I asked incredulously. Some people *were* immune to MHF, but they were rare. Scientists still could not identify genetic markers for immunity. To have a whole colony of them would be astonishing.

Radha did not respond, staring fixedly ahead. I persisted.

"If my mother is immune, maybe I'm immune too."

The driver must have heard our conversation despite the plexiglass. He snorted.

Then it all clicked. The pieces of the puzzle shifted in my brain and suddenly everything became different—and dangerously clear.

"They are not immune," I said slowly. "They are Dancers. Felton is a Ballroom."

Such a fanciful name! But seals have their rookeries and gulls their colonies. Why not a ballroom?

Radha nodded.

"How is my mother surviving there?"

"This is what we want you to find out."

A suicide mission, in other words.

I jiggled the door handle. The door was locked, of course.

I lowered my hand and sat up as straight as the suit allowed. The pieces kept shifting in my brain, the skeins of knowledge and understanding, straightening out despite being constantly tangled by fear of the disease. Nick. The niddah room. The blinking screen of my computer, channels of information drying up, my life narrowing to a vanishing dot …

"I will find her," I said.

Something red flashed ahead, a gleam of scarlet disappearing into the woods so quickly that I could make out nothing. The driver swore and hit the brakes so hard that the car fishtailed, and Radha and I were thrown against our seatbelts.

"That's it!" the driver yelled. "I'm not going any further!"

Radha told him we needed to be closer.

"I'm not taking orders from bleeders!" he snarled.

"I will walk from here," I said.

The driver reluctantly unlocked the door. I pushed it open and clambered out.

Radha put a gun in my hand.

"You might need it," she said.

The driver snorted again but said nothing.

"Thank you," I told Radha.

She leaned close and whispered something so shocking that I was left wondering whether I had heard her correctly. As I walked along the grassy verge, heading into town, I still wondered.

When I was seven, I wandered into my mother's office. At first, I did not see her.

The computer was blinking on the desk but her ergonomic chair was empty.

She was curled on the floor, a pile of yellowing paperbacks in front of her. The smell of paper dust mingled with her Vetiver perfume. She beckoned to me without lifting her face from the disintegrating book she was reading. On the book's cover, a snarling, poorly drawn dinosaur stomped a car.

"A kaiju," she said. "Do you want me to read it to you?"

I made a face. I was not crazy about giant monsters. My father often made fun of the fact that my mother was a nerd, cramming her bookcases with old sci-fi paperbacks, dog-eared pages spreading the musty odor of old adventures, while I was partial to Disney princesses. We disregarded his jokes, and eventually he stopped making them.

"Mum," I said, "I want to study ballet."

Putting her paperback aside, she stood up in one graceful, fluid motion, her swanky blue dress, the color of her eyes, creased from sitting on the floor. She stretched her arms to me.

"I wanted to be a dancer too," she said. "But I was too tall. So, I became a biologist instead."

I cuddled up to her. She did not feel too tall to me—just right.

"Can I be a dancer?"

"You can be whatever you want, Gemma."

Now, twenty years later, it sounded like a curse.

Only women become Dancers.

Men get sick, infected by blood. They burn with fever, they recover, or they die. Women get sick, infected by blood. They burn with fever, they recover, some of them die. And some ... *change*.

The redwoods' feathered tops swayed gently in the cloudless sky. A bird chirped in the undergrowth. It was so peaceful that I stopped thinking about my mother, Nick, Radha's words. I was just enjoying a walk. It had been a long time since I had hiked or even walked on my own. Solitary women, even fully veiled, were often attacked.

The protective suit was heavy and uncomfortable. Leaning against a tree trunk, I unzipped the suit and stepped out. I was wearing a T-shirt and leggings underneath and for a moment I stood there, enjoying the warm caress of the verdant air on my face and arms. I left the suit behind, but I took Radha's gun.

When I turned around, a Dancer watched me no more than fifteen feet away.

The Kashmir *ebolavirus* rewires your DNA. All viruses do that but none other so radically. The end result, should the infected woman survive, is something inhuman.

The stick figure danced toward me on clawed feet. It resembled a giant praying mantis, a seven-foot-tall skeleton covered with incarnadine leathery skin. A Day of the Dead reveler bearing a skull-like mask marked by scarlet swirls. It was every nightmare that made you cry for mommy when you were a child.

The Dancer was mercury-swift and dragonfly-graceful as it navigated the forest floor, the long, thorny spurs on its back-bent ankles jutting and quivering. My mother, a biologist, would have been fascinated by its strange anatomy—the tapering thorax ending in the sexless bulge of a narrow abdomen, the still-human teeth set in a lipless mouth, the unnervingly mammalian eyes protruding from the bony, lidless sockets. She would have studied how the creature fed; followed the knots of its stringy musculature; puzzled over its strangely articulated bones. Perhaps she would have been able to answer the question that still baffled scientists: why did Dancers attack? Normally they kept away from people. Even though they were not supposed to retain any trace of human intelligence, they were wary of men with guns. But, occasionally, they would congregate in giant flocks and run through towns and cities, biting and scratching, spreading the infection through their diseased blood.

Maybe my mother did know; she was here, after all, and she was immune. I would ask her if I survived this encounter. Meanwhile, I was spellbound by the creature: the graceful fluidity of its movement; the many hues of scarlet, red, and crimson that dappled its hide; the white teeth in the skull-like face. It was as beautiful as it was abhorrent.

I drew my gun. The Dancer moved closer.

Radha's words rang in my ears.

I slipped the gun in my waistband and lifted my hands, palms up.

The consensus was that the extreme physical modifications induced by MHF damaged the brain, rendering Dancers mindless. Scientists claimed that Dancers' reactions were as reflexive as the contractions of a severed lizard tail.

The Dancer stopped, its head swaying hypnotically. Its forelimbs were no longer remotely human. Scissor-like with ragged edges, folded like the forelimbs of a praying mantis, they looked unsuitable for any activity I could imagine. But then I realized that what I took for sawtooth protrusions were actually folded fingers distributed in clumps along the entire length of the forearm. So, they could manipulate objects, after all. I felt inordinately pleased with myself for figuring out a tiny piece of the Dancer's biological puzzle. My mother would be proud.

The Dancer suddenly darted into a stand of tan oaks and disappeared within their dappled shade. I stood, shaking, before finally moving on.

Finding my way into Felton was not hard. I followed Route 17 along the verge of the woods. Soon enough, I found the abandoned gas station, pipes snaking on the splintered pavement. Clumps of weeds pushed through the cracks. Beyond it was Felton's downtown: a couple of mom-and-pop grocery stores, a tiny antiques mall, a church, and a café decorated with an inexpertly painted mural of a cluster of hands reaching up from the ground and the inscription "Together we rise" which struck me as unintentionally ominous. The stores were locked and shuttered. A dusty Ford Corolla rested in the middle of the sidewalk.

It was tranquil. I lifted my face to the sun, luxuriating in its warmth. The fear drained out of me like the blood I shed in my niddah.

I started down the street, trying to figure out where my mother could possibly be hiding. Probably not downtown. I knew there were secluded homes among the redwoods—Felton had been famous for its streak of surly independence. On the other hand, if she had deliberately sent the email to bring me here, surely, she would hang around.

A torrent of red, glistening bodies burst into the street. Their insectoid arms flailing, whipping around; their clawed feet drumming on the pavement; their heads bobbing on skinny necks, teeth bared, skeletal masks thrust forward ... It was not a dance but a stampede, an unstoppable wild charge, a frenzy. They would have trampled me, bitten me to pieces. I was too shocked to move.

Someone grasped a handful of my T-shirt and pulled me through a doorway. I fell onto the floor, gasping. I stood, frantically examining myself for open wounds. Public health requirements had trained us like Pavlovian dogs. I didn't see any blood, but that didn't mean I was safe.

I turned to face my savior.

The red leathery mask bobbed above my head.

I could have run away but the rest of them were outside, milling around, darting, pirouetting like a school of fish. Still, I could have pulled my gun, put a bullet in its head. Or, at least, screamed.

I did nothing. I waited as it studied me with its bright blue eyes. Its skin was soft and slightly wrinkled, the texture of human skin despite its lobster coloring.

It turned and went deeper into the house which, I realized, must have been a flower shop. Broken pots littered the floor. In the back, there was an office cubicle with some cabinets and a laptop on a desk. The laptop was plugged in and humming.

The Dancer stooped over the table and bent down, folded itself. It started typing with its distributed fingers.

"Gemma," the screen said.

My mother had never left the US.

She had given her passport to a friend who, naively, hoped that Europe would be safer. It did not matter; in those days of chaos nobody studied travel documents closely as immigration services collapsed with every other governmental agency. My mother had been staying with another female friend in Felton, unsure what to do. She wanted to be close to me, close to Berkeley where I studied at the time. But she knew how angry I was with her for breaking up what I, in my adolescent egotism, imagined to be our perfect family. So she waited and bided her time.

Her friend had her period. A tiny speck of blood on the washbasin, perhaps.

My mother became sick. Her friend took care of her for a while but when the terrible news took over the internet, she ran away, leaving my mother alone, shivering with bouts of fever that threatened to fry her brain. She survived the fever, the thirst, the shakes, the vomiting. But she was too weak to call 911. And when she managed to crawl out of bed, she had started to change.

"Does it really make you dance?" I asked her.

She nodded—such a human gesture. The spines on her backbone crackled as she leaned forward to type. Her anatomy was not suited for office equipment.

"Yes. It is a side effect," she typed. "Like St. Vitus Dance. Sydenham's chorea."

Neurological damage, in other words.

The Kashmir *ebolavirus* was not a benevolent intruder. The rewiring probably came with a host of problems I knew nothing about. Not to mention the strong possibility of death.

"Can you talk?" I asked hopefully, even though I knew she would have already if she could. She opened her mouth: her tongue was fused to the roof.

"So ... what are you?"

I hoped she would type:

I am superhuman. I am an alien life-form. I will take over and make the Earth into a paradise.

She typed nothing.

She was evolving. They all were, the Dancers. The virus had shaken the evolutionary mechanism loose and rattled the strands of DNA, and made ... this. A new species. Some of them were wild. Some of them were sick. Some of them were dying.

And some were becoming. Something new, something different. How could she possibly know what? Ask a tadpole how it feels to be a frog.

The blood that flowed from my mother to me and from her mother to her ... all the way back to the primordial ocean. Thalassa, the mother of all living.

In what was left of civilization, men were trying to dam the flow. Building barriers and partitions. Seclusion, separation, quarantine.

I remembered Radha's words:

They are going to put all women in the niddah. Permanently.

I wondered briefly if it had happened before, in the ancient sands of the Near East or in the Hindus Valley. The practice of seclusion must have come from somewhere.

But what difference did it make? I was here. With my mother.

"Mom ..." I said.

She lifted her inhuman limb and I could envision the flesh flowing, rearranging itself. She was a process, not the end result.

She picked up a shard of a broken flowerpot and dragged it along her forearm. A bead formed: red on red, almost invisible.

I touched my finger to it, feeling my mother's blood flow gently into my veins.

AUTHOR NOTES

My story "The Niddah" is inspired by two things: one shared with everyone; the other shared with no one. The first is the COVID pandemic. The second is my grief over my mother's untimely death which flared up again in 2021, ten years after she passed.

My mother Maya Kaganskaya was a distinguished writer, essayist, and dissident, and I am her only child. Grief is always private but in 2020-2021 when the story was written and published, the entire world knew fear and mourning as the pandemic was at its height. Lockdowns and quarantines brought back the dark history we thought we had left behind. And part of this history was blaming other humans for the disaster nature unleashed. In times of epidemics, women were always viewed with suspicion as a source of contagion and disease. The Niddah is the ancient ritual of locking away menstruating women because their bodies were seen as polluting and dangerous. In my story, the ritual is resurrected in a world where a new disease threatens to transform humanity into monsters.

And yet, the story is also optimistic, finding hope in what seems to be alienation and monstrosity. It is about embracing change. It is about freedom. And it is about the unbreakable bond between mother and daughter. My mother was the most fearless person I have ever known. This story is a tribute to her.

ALL I WANT FOR CHRISTMAS

CHARLES PAYSEUR

Holiday Horrors Flash Fiction Winner

Robby, seated in the living room on Christmas Eve night, recites The Rules to himself to the trembling grind of Daddy's snoring.

1. Santa visits every home on Christmas.

2. Santa enters through the chimney.
This seems to break Rule 1, but Mommy quickly amends.

2.1. Where there is no chimney, Santa makes one.
She shows him a clip from an old movie of a chimney growing from the middle of drywall, yawning open like a jolly, laughing mouth.

2.2. The chimney appears where the stockings are hung.
It must, because every year there was a present from Santa and a full stocking. Robby runs his hands over the wall where they pin their stockings, imagining. It shows no bruising, no sign of having been torn apart and restitched. Robby tugs sleeves down over scars. The wall is not flesh.

3. Santa gives what you want most.

Robby never argues, but it's wrong. Santa gives a new handheld, maybe clothes. This year will be different.

What he wants most is for Mommy and Patty, Mommy's secret friend, to take him to live in Florida like he heard them talk about. Florida, with the ocean and Disney and no trips to the ER for Mommy or Robby when Daddy's been drinking too much.

4. Santa won't come unless you're very, very quiet.

Quietly, he unpins the stockings from the wall. Quietly, he drapes them over Daddy's sleeping body. Quietly, he recites The Rules in his mind, and waits for Christmas.

AUTHOR NOTES

I wrote "All I Want for Christmas" specifically for the Holiday Horrors contest, so in some way, the inspiration was *Apex Magazine* itself. But I knew I had to focus in on one image that was going to really sell the horror of the piece, that was going to hopefully take the more "innocent" magic associated with Christmas and turn it into something else.

As I sat thinking about Christmas, I remembered the scene in *The Santa Clause* where a house doesn't have a chimney. So, the magic of Christmas makes a chimney for Santa to descend and deliver the presents, which seemed like a cheat in some ways but a necessary one in the face of so many people not having chimneys. It's an answer to a child's question, a "how" that gets hand-waived away.

This stuck with me, the hole opening in the wall. The story formed quickly, taking that idea and twisting it as much as I could, to turn that magic into layers of pain and dread. Of course, I made the mistake of forgetting what the word count limit was for the contest so I had to make it almost half as short as it was when I thought I was done. But then, that might have ultimately helped the piece as I had to think about how to convey as much impact in as small a space as possible.

GRAY SKIES, RED WINGS, BLUE LIPS, BLACK HEARTS

MERC FENN WOLFMOOR

A girl has lost her soul down deep in the City. It wandered away while she chipped out another grave in the catacomb brickyards. She set down her pickax, wiped grit from her cheek, and noticed how empty her body was. Looked down at her wrist and found it blank.

That's what she tells Redcap Kestrel as she sits cross-legged on the abandoned warehouse floor, well away from the grimy windows. The girl who lost her soul doesn't offer a name. Few people do in the City.

"You want me to find it?" Redcap Kestrel asks. She crouches at a right angle to the girl, not looking her in the face. It's for the girl's sake. No one likes to look at a half-alive thing for too long, lest you find yourself on the wrong side of dead.

"Yeah." The girl swallows. "If I go back to the yards, people are likely to try and take advantage."

Redcap Kestrel understands. The soulless are easy pickings in the City. It's all a matter of gradient. How much are you predator and how much are you preyed upon. It varies day to day, like most things in the City.

The girl fidgets, rubbing her wrist where the sin stretches raw and glossy like a burn. She doesn't quite turn her head; her gaze skips and skitters towards Redcap Kestrel, then away, away, away. "How much do you want?"

Rarely has Redcap Kestrel allowed visitors, rarer still does she listen to those who need help. She ticks through the old scraps in her head, remembering how conversations like this go.

"I'll take a promise," Redcap Kestrel says.

The girl's shoulders arch in defense. That's dangerous, offering or asking. Too many ways a bargain can go wrong. Everyone knows that.

"It's this." Redcap Kestrel doesn't have much of a voice to raise. It's all tatters and frayed strings in her throat. "When I get your soul back, promise me you'll wear a sleeve so it doesn't go wandering again."

The girl blinks. A sleeve does about as much good as a wish. And it's hardly a promise worth paying with. "That's it?"

Redcap Kestrel shrugs. "That's all."

The girl hesitates, because nothing in the City is that easy.

"See," Redcap Kestrel says, expending more voice and breath than she's got to spare, "you wouldn't take help for free, and I wouldn't give it. So that's the promise I want."

"That's really all?" the girl whispers.

Another shrug. Redcap Kestrel's arms are taut with muscle and her shoulders are sharp like metal wings. She's a half-alive thing, if one looks at her slantwise. She doesn't wear the guard uniform any longer; all the leather she dons, she tanned it herself. There's plenty of skin if you know where to look in the City.

In the silence bubbling up between her and the girl, Redcap Kestrel sees all the times gone by when she ignored the helpless, when the desperate crawled to her and she stepped on their throats. There's a lot of regret built into a hundred years of being half-alive. She's tired. And this is the first time anyone has been brave enough to ask her for help so directly. The girl knocked so loud on the warehouse door, it was either listen to her story or kill her so she'd quiet up. Redcap Kestrel hadn't been curious in a long while until the girl, and she wasn't yet hungry.

"All right." The girl exhales and blows away the silence and the memories trapped in it. "Deal."

Redcap Kestrel hops to her feet. "Good. Wait here." It's dangerous anywhere else, and she's got nothing worth the price of stealing. Meat and breath and bone are all that's worth anything in the City.

Redcap Kestrel lopes to the biggest window, glass tarred black and cracked with many a fist, and slips out into the streets. Her boots are worn thin save for the iron heels, hard enough to bruise a god. Her steps warn away the ones that fall into the predator shade, in that gradient that defines the City.

The thing about souls is that they don't wander off. Not unless a body is so broken-down that there are too many cracks to hold even breath inside. The girl isn't that far gone. She's still strong, still has grit, and still believes in a future.

So something stole her soul. Redcap Kestrel knows where to look for the things that steal and the things that kill. She lived among them for a long stretch during her existence in the City. She's haunted and hunted where the buildings crumble, where the damned weep, where the perpetual twilight hides worse monsters than her. It's like going back to the nightmares grown in a home you don't remember.

Up on the top of the horizon, the lights of the Prosperous Above shine. No one from the City is allowed past the Prosperous Gates. There are only rumors: clean water, food aplenty, fuel, medical care. It's said that behind the Prosperous Gates, the grief-eaters can't find you. A lot is said about the Prosperous Above.

Redcap Kestrel was Prosperous once, long ago, before she ripped the demon from her heart. She doesn't talk about that time. Her hands ache when she looks up every once in a while, and sees the Prosperous lights mocking the deeps of the City.

The light hurts her eyes, so she's stopped lifting her head up too far. There's no reason to look up when you know you'll never fly again.

Redcap Kestrel hasn't been to the Brittle Warrens in a decade. She lost most of her voice and part of her throat last time. This is the mulched, bog-deep heart of the City. There are things that creep under the salted earth; there are things that crawl through the long-dried gutters; and there are things that cry out, and the things that eat the criers.

She's not interested in those things. She's here to visit the most dangerous person she's ever known: Windchime Owl, first and last of their name.

It's not really *fear*, per se. Redcap Kestrel doesn't have much of that left. Really, she's hard pressed to decide if she feels much at all. This job she does for the girl, this is new, so it brings a spark of anticipation. It keeps her from thinking too much for a day, and that's a rare treat for a half-alive thing like her.

The slums are made from dilapidated stone and crusted darkness. The living scuttle close to walls and the dead haunt the narrow streets. The in-betweens are the ones you ought to heed. Redcap Kestrel walks as she always does: head tilted down, arms loose at her sides, her boot heels clicking. She skirts scummy puddles and mite-chewed corpses, steps over potholes lined with old teeth.

"Where you going, birdie?" calls a grief-eater from the broken curb. It's stick-like, hungry: long bony limbs canted at uncomfortable angles, a face that's just a wide, gaping hole rimmed in stretched flesh.

Redcap Kestrel glances at it sidelong. She still has her red cap: her skull shaved and tattooed scarlet with the litany of her oaths to the Gray Prince. She wears a hood sometimes—not now, she lost it somewhere she doesn't remember—but those who've survived long enough in the City recognize her by her gait alone.

"Going down," Redcap Kestrel says.

"I can ease your burdens." The grief-eater coos, extending a hand nicked with desperation bites. "It doesn't hurt. Let me have a taste."

"No," Redcap Kestrel says, because the grief-eaters always lie. She took one of them to her nest shortly after her fall. Asked it to eat away everything that hurt so she'd be numb. Grief-eaters are a misnomer. They only slake their hunger on the things you want to keep.

She let hers suck on her body and soul for days, even knowing what it was doing, until it tried to eat the memory of her oath-siblings from the Gray Prince's guard. Then she killed it.

This grief-eater is too starved to be a threat. It slumps back against a charred brick wall. There's so little in the City to feed anyone any longer.

Redcap Kestrel walks on.

Legend says that the City was built in a crater so wide it could hold an ocean. There are still stretches of empty rock far, far away, some wanderers claim, where the City hasn't bled. Redcap Kestrel doesn't believe those tales. The City is too vast. It'll have touched those crater edges and spilled over and swallowed whatever is beyond. The Prosperous Above is like the City's mirror, or maybe its heaven, just as vast and untouchable as the City.

So down she goes, deeper along broken streets, hopping from stairway to stairway as the City burrows itself forever lower, away from the Prosperous Above's sight. That doesn't mean it's all dark in the Warrens: the light here is soaked with bitterness and spite, a sharp incandescence that will betray you soon as not.

Shadowy things skulk and hiss at her, but they know better than to get too close. She has to eat and she's not particular about where her meals come from. Redcap Kestrel used to bask in the biggest light of all—a sun? a moon? hard to remember after so long—when she flew in the Prosperous Above. Darkness is easy. She knows the way into the pitted core of the Brittle Warrens; the City won't let her forget what hurts most.

And then, sudden like a burst eardrum, she's in front of Windchime Owl's palace. The gates are pieced together from bits of finery: quilt squares and finger bones, gold rings and predator teeth, glass fresco tiles and chunks of tanned hide. Basalt pillars and a center post hold up the weight, and a handful of still-living skins sway and shiver miserably, stretched wide with hooks and cord.

The gate guard, a tremulous shadow stolen from a body once human, bristles at her approach. "Do you have an appointment?"

Redcap Kestrel lifts her chin and tilts her head so the shadow can see her scalp. It flinches away and the gates groan wide.

The maze through the Warrens is nonsensical: mirrors and salt pillars, rusted ore and carved stone, all paths twisting in, out, around. Stairways lead nowhere and pits gape in the walls. She keeps her gaze averted from the darkness, where Windchime Owl's oldest secrets lie. She walks past a trio of lost souls, all scrabbling at a doorway upside down. Her heels click against mercury glass and she doesn't look at the visions the mirrored floor shows. She's not ready to go mad.

At last, at the deepest point in the Warrens, she reaches Windchime Owl.

They sit in a large nest made from fur and silk and lost ideas. They're wide at the shoulder, head crowned with a white mane of hair, their skin bleached from decades of shriveled light. They're every inch as terrible and beautiful as Redcap Kestrel remembers.

Redcap Kestrel inclines her chin, taking a breath.

"You're unexpected," Windchime Owl says, their hands never still as they roll marbles between their palms. "Then again, you've always been bold, Red'kes."

Redcap Kestrel shrugs. "You liked that once, Win'owl."

"So I did."

Redcap Kestrel had a name before she joined the Gray Prince's guard. It's been scrubbed away: excised when she had her scalp tattooed in the red cap of her fledge. All the guard were identified only by their caps. She had a hundred Redcap sisters, and a hundred Bluecap brothers. Windchime Owl had a name, too, but they've never shared it. They were here when the City rose, or so the hauntlings say, and they will be here when the City rots beyond saving.

Windchime Owl seems to be in a good mood, their latest meal still twitching at their feet. "What do you want, Red'kes?"

"Your insight," she says. "A girl lost her soul. I need to find it."

"Why?"

Redcap Kestrel expected this. It's no easier now than when she pondered it on her journey. Windchime Owl hates lies, even the slantwise half-truths and omissions that fuel the world. If Redcap Kestrel is anything but honest, Windchime Owl's wrath will engulf her, and she isn't certain she'd win a second fight. Her throat aches where Win'owl's talons cut her clean to spine.

"I needed help long ago," she says. "I should've asked."

The guard died because of her; all her siblings-in-wing. She lost her pride and her purpose, and she spurned her brother who fought to pull the demon out. Bluecap Shrike defied the Gray Prince, seeing through her, seeing what she had done, and she had refused to let him save her.

Redcap Kestrel spits the last of her words out, ashamed. "But I didn't."

Windchime Owl stretches, their body sinewy and fluid. Once upon an age, they were a Prince—or so the rumors say. A Violet Prince, with Greencaps and Goldcaps flying in formation at their sides. One story claims the Violet Prince forsook their duties and cast down their own legions, seeding the deeps with rage and loss. But it was so long ago, no one really remembers why. There are many stories forgotten in the City.

Windchime Owl hops from their nest and offers a talon-tipped hand to Redcap Kestrel. "Give me a piece of your skin, and I'll look for this lost-soul."

"For your collection?"

Windchime Owl sighs. "To taste. I miss your mouth."

Redcap Kestrel let the grief-eater suck away the affection she'd once had for Windchime Owl. They'd fought—and Win'owl had ripped out her throat—not because she wanted to leave, but because she'd wanted Windchime Owl to come with her. *Let's leave the City,* she said, *let us go Above. We can be Prosperous again. Together we can make the climb.* She was a fool. Windchime Owl kept the laws and held back the deeper things that churned under the Warrens; if they abandoned the City, it would sink forever beyond reach of the Prosperous Above. Win'owl nursed her into something less broken after she tore the demon from her heart, after she fell, and she'd repaid that poorly.

"Well?" Windchime Owl says.

"Agreed." Redcap Kestrel pulls a razor from her boot. She reaches back and cuts a strip of flesh from her skull, around the curve of bone, blood trickles down her nape. The air bites at raw nerves, and it's almost refreshing to feel again. She hands Windchime Owl her dripping skin, the piece where tattoos read: *and in the sky bright-burning.*

Windchime Owl inhales as they take the skin, then they swallow it in a single gulp. Redcap Kestrel feels the damp warmth of their throat, the pressure of muscle constricting and pulling her flesh deeper. She shivers, and so does Windchime Owl, as they both savor that moment of devouring.

Then the stinging pain and wetness on her neck jars Redcap Kestrel and she wipes clean her razor. "Uphold your word."

Windchime Owl's eyes glaze over, a white film on which flickers a thousand microscopic images. They are the City's pulse: nothing happens in these streets, in this air, in light or in shadow, that Windchime Owl doesn't know if they choose. They curl their bare toes into the earth and tip their head back, throat an arch of pale scarring.

"Oh," they say after a moment, and there's distinct ... sadness, a regretful lilt in their tone. "Red'kes, you won't like who took your girl's soul."

"Who?"

"Your brother."

Windchime Owl tells her she can find the thief in the Lovers Quarter. Redcap Kestrel hasn't felt shock in years. That electric moment, that impossible revelation, makes her breath catch.

And then cynicism, the fabric of reality, wraps about her once more. She has no brothers any longer. All her sibling-guards are dead.

Whoever this thief is, she will find it, kill it, and return the girl's soul. Another day will settle into calendar dust and blur into the palette of time. Nothing changes much in the City.

Your brother.

Windchime Owl can't lie, which is why they hate falsehood so fiercely. The words burr under Redcap Kestrel's ear, an itch she can't scratch.

She races back through the Warrens, an urgency she doesn't want to dissect burning her muscles. She must *hurry*. Souls don't keep long when stolen from bodies, and she's moved ponderously, deliberately, until now.

Running hurts and makes her think of the clouds.

She used to fly. As one of the Gray Prince's guard, she had wings of silk and steel and shadow, etched with scarlet spellwork. The magic came from the Gray Prince's blood: it flared brilliantly in the light, full of grandeur when she flew in formation. It skewered her enemies' gaze in battle and her wings pierced the sky like blades.

The Gray Prince was the first to die under her hand when the demon gnawed at her heart, and afterward, she cut off her wings and jumped into the City below. The demon kept her alive. The fall hurt.

She runs faster, now, her boots a staccato heartbeat on the streets. Her breath rattles in her throat, an enhanced pain that siphons away memories of the sky.

The Lovers Quarter is a killing ground.

Once, the Prosperous Above's light reached deep enough to kindle old spheres, globes of living silk that floated pale and luminescent over the park. Like moth-lures, the spheres promised tranquility and revealed only death. The Prosperous came down on moth-dust kites tethered Above to hunt the bedazzled City denizens, a sport that soon turned rancid. The Prosperous gutted the spheres for the light they didn't need, filled with arrogance as bright as Above.

So the shadow things and the hunter things and the mad things rose up and snipped the kite tethers. Without a way back, the Prosperous were trapped. The City things left Prosperous' bones stripped and glistening in the streets until all the ground was carpeted in calcium and splinters. The things that lived in the City caged the richest and most delicate trophies in blown glass, and the bones eventually stopped wailing.

Redcap Kestrel reaches the stones rimming the Lovers Quarter like islands from the floor of bones. She crouches, breathing ragged. The Lovers Quarter sank, like everything in the City does, until it is now a steep-walled pit with glass jars hung like lamps about the edges. She sees the thief ambling towards the lowest gouge of the quarter: the murky waters of the underground spring, thick with sulfur and despair.

It's human, skeletal, and wearing the scavenged blue rags of a guard uniform. A Bluecap's threads. That dishonor of her old life sparks her rage like kindling. She lunges across the street, toward the edge. The thief spins around and stares up at her.

Redcap Kestrel stills, cold and motionless as a fresco.

Below in the pit is the demon she ripped from her heart. It's latched onto Bluecap Shrike, clinging to the base of his skull.

Her oath-brother. One of the Gray Prince's Hawks: elite, proud, fearless. All dead now. Except her. She thought she was the last, when she watched Bluecap Shrike fall, broken-winged, into the Deathshead River so long ago.

Windchime Owl never lies.

Shrike was a Redcap, briefly, before he came out as a man. The tattoos on his scalp are more purple than blue, and it didn't matter, for the Bluecaps welcomed him. He was Redcap Kestrel's brother-in-arms, her closest friend, and he was her anchor when she flew too high on arrogance. He had never betrayed the Gray Prince. She hadn't let him save her.

And now he's here, possessed and dying, just as she once was, deep in the City.

He lifts his chin, staring up at her with glassy eyes. The demon's tendrils wrap his throat and dig into his ears. The demon is smarter now: it took his head instead of his heart, where it's harder to wrench loose.

Redcap Kestrel takes a breath, air hissing through her tattered throat. "We're not finished, demon."

She knows this wretched thing. It is jealousy and greed and dissatisfaction. It will never be sated. She let it into her heart when she thought it would please her Gray Prince: she thought it would make her faster, stronger, more brilliant than any of the other guards, and the Gray Prince would look on her with favor.

She knows now that they never saw her, nor any of their guard. All were all peripheral to the Gray Prince's own glory. Now she's a half-alive thing, and still has her red cap and disappointment takes a long time to die.

The demon wrenches its teeth from Bluecap Shrike, and her oath-brother collapses. His lips are already tinged drowning-gray. She doesn't let herself flinch.

The demon wriggles. *You came to us.*

"That's right," Redcap Kestrel says, extending her hand and clenching her fist in challenge. "You belong to me."

The demon flies at her, a spill of burned oil, once as addicting as poppy and as beautiful as obsidian and as tempting as forgiveness. It ripples with teeth and hook-tipped legs and it smells of decay. She dives down to meet it in mid-air. She has no wings, but she's never forgotten how to fall in the City.

The demon's greasy film bites down hard into her shoulder, coiling about her arm and neck. She carries it to the ground, landing hard on her back in the bones. She rolls, crunching brittle, bleached remains. The sound is like her heels: sharp and hard and echoing. The demon's teeth nick her collarbone.

It used to suck at the inside of her neck, sensuous, the stinging pain arousing as promises of glory. *She saw the Gray Prince embrace her, call her their favored, and her wings turned silver at their touch.*

Redcap Kestrel lurches to her feet. She pries one-handed at the demon, her left arm numbed by its venom. The demon grinds through muscle, down into her breast, seeking the heat in her ribs. It is so much smaller than she remembers. When she first found it, when it crawled from the edge of the City into the Prosperous Above, it was mighty as a Prince itself. An eagle made of inverse light. Now it scarce stretches the length of her arms spread wide.

It wants her heart, like it did before. It wants to fill her with its twisted dreams and promises of void. It wants to devour her like it does everything else, pressing visions into her eyes so she won't notice how weak she's become.

She senses where it's been. The demon, riding Bluecap Shrike, has preyed on the weary and made the poor hopeless. She tastes the dozen lives it has sucked dry since she drove it out.

If you had only kept us, there would be no need for such waste, the demon hums. *It is your fault we needed to feed so often. The blood is on your hands.*

She gasps, sinking to one knee. Faces blur like smoke before her, screaming, wailing, pleading, dying. Ten, then twenty, then—then Bluecap Strike, and after him, more and more and more and more, unless she accepts it back, unless she surrenders.

Together, they will grow strong. Together, she and her demon will feed on Windchime Owl and the haunts and the girls who work the brickyards and the children in the river-reeds, and the people who beg for crumbs and the grief-eaters who crumple in alleyways: all will welcome her devouring, for there is nothing left to live for in the City.

The girl's soul is but a morsel in the demon's belly; it is being digested with tantalizing slowness, and Redcap Kestrel can know that satiating fullness herself.

Let go, you need us, you want us, you are nothing without us. Let us in, and we will let you climb from this tomb, take your place Above!

No one escapes the City.

We can, the demon says.

"I'm too weak," she says. She isn't bound to absolute truth. "Share your feast … give me … strength …"

The demon undulates. It coughs up the girl's soul and Redcap Kestrel catches it, tucks it in her palm.

Then she stops fighting. The demon squirms and digs and she grits her teeth against the pain—so sharp and fresh—as it slithers fully into her body, worming through her meat, and at last: it sinks into her heart. Not just the muscle and fat and veins, but deeper, into her innermost self.

Its glee echoes through her like a cleaving knife, for now it can drain her like it has always wanted, revenge itself on her for disowning it. It will eat her heart and make her watch every delicious, spiteful bite—

Redcap Kestrel laughs. She throws her head back and her splintered laughter bounces from the glass orbs and the shattered bones in the Lovers' Garden.

Inside her, the demon screams in rage.

Her heart is empty, already hollowed out. And now the demon is trapped, nestled in emptiness, where it will wither and starve, and she laughs, she laughs, she laughs.

Her body remembers; her bones and her flesh and her blood all recall how they were sustained on the demon's vast, plentiful bounty. Meat doesn't *forget* in the City.

She's hungry, and with the girl's soul caught safely in her gloved palm, she has nothing else to eat except the squirming, wretched thing inside her heart. The demon shrieks, the demon flails, the demon is being devoured from within one spiteful, delicious bite at a time.

Redcap Kestrel's body contorts as it remembers how to feed. She arches her back, jaw locked. Only the wound in her shoulder offers escape.

The demon, shredded into fragments of what it was, makes one last desperate escape. It is scarce the size of a singular wrist bone. It drills up through its entry passage and writhes like a maggot, one broken hook-leg caught on her collarbone.

She grips the demon's slippery body. Her arm is not so numbed anymore, nurtured by the demon's sustenance. It writhes and thrashes, but she holds tight. She crushes it slow and methodical in her fist. Panicked, it squirts fresh memory at her.

Down deep in the City, a girl lost her soul. It was stolen in the night: cold hands choking her silent, greedy teeth sucking her wrist and yanking out her deepest self. She's ashamed that she didn't fight harder. Didn't leave more than a scrape of nails on the thief's arms. The girl cried. The thief was gone, leaving her gasping and hollowed out. The demon likes shame. So heavy and rancid, dripping thick into the heart, where it rots away the will to live.

Redcap Kestrel remembers shame, oh yes she does, the burning horror of her willing betrayal, the knife she slit the Gray Prince's throat with. Remember how their eyes met hers, so full of hatred? Or the shame as she burned the rookeries and let her brothers and her sisters drift on ash. Oh, that deep and abiding **shame** *that curdles her soul, the* **shame** *that will never let her forget what she has done—*

"You're too late for that," Redcap Kestrel tells the demon. "I don't need you any longer."

It squirms, spitting again into her eye.

It can find the others of her rookeries, the lost 'caps scattered through the city! It can—

—die. But not with her.

She lowers it to the ground and crushes it with her heel. Grinds her boot down until there is nothing left of the demon but a smear of discontent. It squeals and the City swallows its final cry. The demon is dead.

She allows herself one shuddering sigh and wipes her face. Her shoulder will heal. She's not as hungry as once she was.

Redcap Kestrel sprints across the pit to where Bluecap Shrike lies prone. He's half-alive, like she always is. His body is more bone strung together with stretched skin and fragile tendons. He's starving and he's alone, but he *lives*.

Redcap Kestrel kneels. She cups the back of his skull in her free palm, supporting his neck. Blood seeps between her fingers.

"Red'kes?"

She nods. "Hey, Bluetop."

"You ..." He coughs, a rasp-rattle of air in his lungs. "Look good."

Redcap Kestrel can't stop a twitch of a smile. "You don't."

"Harsh as always." His eyes roll back. "Why'd you come?"

She has no satisfactory answer. If she'd known he still lived, would she have sought him out? She's not much for what-ifs or probabilities. So long she's endured, a half-alive thing, day to day, carried along by apathy and stupor in the City.

"There's a girl," Redcap Kestrel says. "Needed someone to help her."

Bluecap Shrike's mouth quirks. He slides one hand atop hers behind his skull. "You would."

"Learned it from you." The wound across her scalp still aches, crusted in scabs. She matches him now. They used to compare scars and he won more often than she. Redcap Kestrel lifts him into her arms. "You never let go."

His head lolls onto her shoulder. "Not 'til you do."

Redcap Kestrel carries her oath-brother through the City, untiring. She ignores the begging of grief-eaters, the threats from those who remember the Gray Prince's guard, the offers to buy what's left of Bluecap Shrike for soup.

She lays him in her nest to sleep.

"Red'kes?"

"Here," she says.

She unfolds her old guard uniform from where it's collected dust, fabric that once wrapped her in glory. It's just a coat now. It'll keep him warm.

The lost girl is still where Redcap Kestrel left her. It's been a long time since someone genuinely surprised her.

"Didn't know where else was safe," the girl mumbles, hunch-shouldered and wary. Under the defensive cowl there's something else Redcap Kestrel hasn't seen in years: possibility.

The girl slept restlessly but safely, she says, and without dreams manifesting. This building is painted thick with Redcap Kestrel's viscera, one brush-full at a time. She's got her own nest and nightmares can't intrude. If you live this long in the City, it's because you learned how to survive.

"Don't lose it again," Redcap Kestrel says, and hands the girl back her soul.

The girl swallows it down and looks at her wrist, which glows again with the faint imprint of life. Her name's embedded in those lines and dots. Redcap Kestrel doesn't read it, though. If the girl wants her to know, the girl will share.

"Here," Redcap Kestrel says, offering the scrap of her jacket hem. Too much effort to sew it back on. And then, because she's still raw, and hasn't let herself scar, she adds, "If you need somewhere to stay, there's room here."

The girl nods. She wraps her wrist, and inhales like she hasn't breathed in days. "Thanks."

Redcap Kestrel shrugs, missing the weight of her wings. She limps to her nest, her heels dulled, and snuggles against her brother.

When Redcap Kestrel wakes again, Bluecap Shrike is drowsing by her side, and the girl hasn't gone. She's leaning on a shovel, her pickax slung over her shoulder. The coat hem is still bound tight about her wrist.

"I'll earn my keep," she says, chin thrust out. "I like it here better than the brickyards. This place could use some renovations."

Redcap Kestrel blinks. Bluetop will need his own nest when he's strong enough, and after that? Perhaps she'll try and think of a future. She could use some help, and the girl is offering.

Hope isn't as rare as it used to be, not even this deep in the City.

JASON SIZEMORE

This was the second story we've published by Merc Fenn Wolfmoor (the other being "The Gentleman of Chaos" in issue 87). Both are dark fantasies featuring a clever adventurer-type as the protagonist. There's a bit of hope among the dreariness at the end of both stories that I like. Check them out!

BAREFOOT AND MIDNIGHT

SHEREE RENÉE THOMAS

Three men emerged from darkness and walked to the edge of the wood, the scent of roses rising all around them. The moon hung like a broken jaw above the Memphis night. The schoolyard lay ahead, its wood fence disjointed and leaning. The fetid scent of wet grass, of mold and moss, floated on the evening wind from the bayou.

"You ready?" asked the first man, his face pockmarked, lips leering, eyes sullen.

"Light 'em up," replied the second. The third nodded his head and produced the gasoline.

They knew the children slept inside. No one had to tell them. The Freedmen's School in Gayoso's Flats was one of several humble buildings where the former slaves gathered to grasp what hope lay ahead for their futures. Most had no home but the damp, mosquito-infested fields surrounding the bayou. The school housed thirteen orphaned children, those who didn't even have a mother's lap to lay their little heads on.

When the fires calmed and the bright red embers turned to ash, when the city grieved and grieved until it couldn't grieve anymore, Dusa Dayan rose from the back pew of Beale Street First African Baptist Church and let the sounds of Doctor Watts' hymns usher her out the red door.

I heard the cry. I, I, I heard them cry.

The fire had burned the schoolhouse to the ground. All that remained were the crimson rose bushes. The roses, the first seeds the children had planted together. She could still see the faces of her students, not much younger than herself, their beautiful smiles, the lustrous brown skin, the determination in their eyes. She tried to make those memories replace the burnt, black splinters of bone that haunted her nights, the faces unrecognizable, lips pulled back in horror. And the cries that made her wake from sleep, her face covered in tears.

I heard the cry. I, I, I...

Hidden in darkness, donated evening meals still covered in her basket, Dusa had heard every scream.

And now, like a visit from a long-forgotten friend, the story her grandmother told her many years ago became Dusa's only thought.

There, under the roots of the Lynching Tree, were the remains of countless members of Dusa's kinfolk and others. Unfortunate souls singled out and taken away in the cover of night. Under the bloodstained boughs, innocents had dangled and danced, lifeless beneath the broad, twisting limbs. It was a dance no soul wished ever to witness, a struggle of spirit and flesh, of ropes and blades and fire, a litany to pain that you could never unsee.

In the darkness the mound looked too small, too well-shaped to be natural. Only visible to eyes who had seen hell and lived. Beneath the grass was the specter behind the stories, no one knew the origins of the legend, the haint whose soul was said to hover above Voodoo Fields.

Dusa placed her satchel on the dirt. She drew the hatchet from the twine at her waist and gripped a hardwood handle laced with ancient carvings. The tree loomed over the mound, casting shadows. The few surrounding weeds were scraggly, thick with drops of dew. The land around the tree was fallow, as if the blood-soaked earth refused to nourish natural life. Dusa circled the mound, hatchet in hand, then she hacked off a branch from the Lynching Tree. The wet blades of grass felt slick against her bare soles. The wind whipped and pricked at her naked flesh. Exposed to the biting night and all its appetites, she knew the few drops of blood would not be all of the sacrifice. When she took the branch from the tree where no leaves or blossoms grew, the ground grumbled and growled beneath her feet. Dusa held her breath.

Barefoot and covered only in the darkness that was midnight, she shivered. On bent knees, she dug her fingers into the grass, grasping at the moist earth, clutched cherry bark and broken twigs, her back arched in pain. She lifted a flask, sprinkled bathwater from a child who was not baptized. Behind her the creek murmured and whispered, a cool invitation to abandon her mission. She could toss all the gathered items in the creek's dark waters, leave the terrors behind her. She could forget the tree and the cursed land that surrounded it, walk back through the red doors of the church, and beg for forgiveness.

Dusa rose on one knee, flask in hand, praying that she had the strength to turn her back on the Lynching Tree, but a fire burned in her soul. The faith she once had was replaced with an unholy rage, an anger so hot, it incinerated all forgiveness. She willed her body to move. But the scent of roses, overpowering in the night, strengthened her resolve, holding her there.

The fires were started by those who hated the very idea that any of them were now free. White Memphis defined itself by the darkness it kept outside of Freedom's light, by the darkness that festered within. The Freedmen's School was the only home Dusa had ever known. Frozen in winter, smoldering in summer, she and her thirteen students had suffered and struggled together as one. The bite of skeetas, the occasional serpent intruder were all well worth it. She had watched them, ages eight to fourteen, come through the old pine doors, eyes glistening with want for knowledge. The confidence on their faces emerged like spring blossoms as they slowly moved from signing their names with an X to the new names they had chosen for themselves in freedom.

But Voodoo Fields was where the ancient spirit lay, waiting. When no earthly justice would bring stolen Black lives peace. Dusa dug up the earth, the raw scent filling the air. She sprinkled the soil with her tears and pulled the ragged mud doll from its dreamless slumber. Wrapped in tree roots, its garment was tattered. Whatever color or pattern it once held faded long ago. A dark, rust-colored stain covered the space where its heart once was. It had no head. Only a red ribbon where it should be. It had no limbs. No mouth or plump cheeks and belly to kiss and pinch.

Dusa held a rose petal for every child she lost in the fire. She pressed them into the freshly made mud she used to cover the old doll. The mud spread like a second skin, the old layers, hard and cracking. As she held the doll, she thought she heard it cry out, the sound like a newborn baby hungry for its mother's milk. She nearly dropped it, but fear made her hold fast, the scream stuck in her throat.

The Lynching Tree branch smelled of smoke, fear, and blood. Pain radiated through her palms as she worked to fashion two arms, two legs, and a fist full of dark, earthwormed-soil for a head. She sculpted the head as roundly as she could in the darkness, resisted the urge to abandon the writhing ball of rotten soil. As she worked the doll felt heavier in her hand, like the child she once bore and buried before its first spring.

She sang the song before she realized she knew the song. In a language neither she nor her mother's tongue had ever sung before. Words that came from no leatherbound hymnal. Words that were dark, mournful, dangerous. It was the same song her grandmother sang before the spirit doll had slain the men who hung her husband, the same song she sang, they say, when the black doll came for her, too.

Hear I. Hear I cry. Rend them, spin them, hear them crying.

Dusa placed her palm flesh over the hatchet's blade and sang until her voice grew hoarse from crying. Her elbows were steady but arms wobbly. Her knees had grown numb, but the sharp scent of sweat, burned flesh, and urine made her squeeze the blood more rapidly into the doll's primitive mouth. No eyes were carved into the mud. The spirit doll needed only blood and the ashes of the dead to see.

Eyes stinging, Dusa held the doll to her bosom. She rocked and stroked it as she had once rocked her own child. Lulled by her mother's voice, the infant girl had gone to sleep one cold wintry night, but the child never opened her eyes again. Dusa was thinking of the baby's warm, fat fingers when she felt the mud doll's head shift in her hand. More corpse than baby, the doll once cold and still, began to writhe and twist in her arms. The fat, sightless grubs and earthworms burying through its mud-bottom flesh. A rotten smell, like spoiled vegetables and dead leaves, filled the air. Strange roots burst from the doll's center. Dusa dropped it and scrambled to her feet.

Hear I! Hear I cry!

The bayou moved around her. The Lynching Tree leaned left, now right. Its greatest branches twisted, as if reaching for the spirit Dusa had released from its sleep. A howling wind moved across the black waters, spreading the sound of wailing and the scent of long dead things. A great sound, timber fall and cracked limbs, roots twisting over the sour earth joined the endless drone of cicadas resting on the bark of the Lynching Tree.

Rend them! Spin them!

Dusa did not recognize her voice but she knew the cracked notes that joined hers was the root child now fully grown. Sightless, the creature rose on driftwood legs, the rags left in a pile in the cursed soil, the mound exposed, an open wound. Its bulbous head blocked the moonlight. Dusa could not tear her eyes away from its pitiful face. Earthworms writhed across its muddy skin in shifting waves, like water. The stench of terror, of lives cut short from rage, greed, jealousy, and madness invaded all of her senses. Her voice now a whisper, but still she sang.

Hear them crying!

The mud doll towered over her, facing her as if awaiting instructions. *Cry!* Its voice growing stronger as the wind whipped bark from the Lynching Tree's limbs. *Cry! Hear I!*

Dusa raised her arm, the deep gash stung. She handed the hatchet to the spirit doll. The blood from her palms emblazing the carved symbols in the handle, bright red suns and comet tails in a script that appeared in frightful dreams.

Red blossoms burst from the spirit doll's chest, sprouted along its limbs and legs. Thorny vines twisted around its throat. Its rib cage was made of roots and twigs, splinters of charred bone, remnants of the Lynching Tree. It held the hatchet high and swung.

News of the vicious killings spread faster than the fires that had lit the city's nights.

For three whole days, white men's intestines hung from the Lynching Tree, the limbs heavy with the weight of strange fruit. To Dusa, the spilled guts looked like a string of bloody rubies and pearls. How beautiful they were, glistening in the sunlight. She wished she could wrap them around her throat like a necklace and dance. For three days she walked the streets of Memphis with the mud from the Lynching Tree dried on her feet, blood caked in the palm of her hand, a red ribbon tied around her throat. On the fourth day Dusa walked barefoot through the ashes of the fallen school.

The wound had not healed.

She plucked a rose from a bush and drifted down to the bayou in the same gown she'd worn since that first night beneath the Lynching Tree. The crimson ribbon unraveled around her throat, the jagged gash spilling fresh blood. Dusa's head wobbled on her neck like a strange, stringless puppet. The creek was placid, a black mirror, shimmering, calm. The dark water she touched was the last of what had passed and the first of what was to come. She washed mud from her fingernails, sprinkled the water over her eyes, a baptism, and waited for the doll to come for her, barefoot and midnight.

JASON SIZEMORE

"Barefoot and Midnight" is a story about wounds that do not heal and that's perfectly okay. Some wounds should never be forgotten.

This story came to my desk via our special fiction editor Maurice Broaddus. He usually includes a short paragraph covering the story's strengths and weaknesses when he sends a story for me to consider. With this particular submission, the only comment he included was "You'll want this one by the second sentence."

That second sentence?

"The moon hung like a broken jaw above the Memphis night."

Maurice was right.

THE AMAZING EXPLODING WOMEN OF THE EARLY TWENTIETH CENTURY

A.C. WISE

2015

Across the water, Coney Island screams, all summer-sizzle, hotdogs, sunscreen, and children fueled by too much sugar. Everything is bright and loud, and if not exactly clean, then cleaner at least than in her day. The brothels are gone, the tumbling rides designed to give men a chance to peek up ladies' skirts. People don't need the excuse to see each other's flesh these days. Even the breeze off Gravesend Bay smells different.

"Are you sure you don't need to sit, Nan?"

She's nobody's nana, but with women of a certain age, the title simply comes, clinging until it becomes a truth of its own. The young woman might be a great, great, great grand-niece after all. It's not impossible. Cecily—that's the girl's name—touches her sleeve.

Cecily's hair is dark, long, and straight. Her eyes are kind. She's hardly a girl, a young woman really, but everyone is young these days.

"Yes, sitting would be nice."

She lets Cecily lead her to a bench and points to the end of the pier.

"There used to be a movie studio there. Did you know? Back at the start of the last century. Maryville. A man named Don Leaming built it, thinking to rival Edison's Black Maria. He wanted to be bigger than Vitagraph, bigger than all those sun-drenched studios popping up out west."

"Oh?" Cecily is distracted, glancing at her phone.

"It burned," she says, and Cecily looks up finally, attention caught; the old woman tucks a smile into the corner of her cheek.

"I was one of the studio girls. Trick films. Have you ever heard of those?"

Cecily shakes her head.

"Think of Georges Méliès," the old woman says. "Moon men appearing in puffs of smoke. Only these were like fairy tales, the old kind meant to assure the world that women were empty-headed, foolish, and vain. I'll give Don Leaming this, he thought up dozens of clever ways to make us die."

She pauses, gauging, so it doesn't come out as a question when she says, "I was about your age, twenty years old. My specialty was burning."

Cecily slides her phone back into her pocket with a skeptical frown.

"Then you'd have to be over a hundred and thirty years old now."

"Improbable, I'll admit, but not impossible. The world is full of miracles, and this place in particular draws them."

Cecily follows the sweep of her arm, taking in the bay and the park on the other side.

"Back then, Coney Island rivaled the White City in Chicago. It was a place of wonders. You could ride a boat through the gates of Hell and experience Creation all in a day. They murdered an elephant here, and kept babies in incubators on display. And those were only the public attractions. I could tell you stories of wolves in the Grand Ballroom, and the ghosts of lost animals searching for their one-armed trainer."

Cecily opens her mouth, but closes it again, as the old woman shakes her head to show she's just kidding. Maybe.

"The island was always burning back then. Once for each park—Steeplechase, Luna, and Dreamland—but the first great fire happened right here."

In her mind's eye, a phantom studio juts over the water. She imagines the charred remains sunk to the bottom of the bay, wave-tossed and softened beyond recognition.

In the bright Brooklyn sunlight, the old woman's eyes spark, gold as the sun, and the girl who may or may not be her great, great, great grand-niece startles.

"It burned, and I was there when it did."

1906

The projector whirs, blue smoke winding through beams of light, breathed by the men watching Mary Catherine on screen. She keeps to the back of the room, fingers curled into her palms, knuckles white. She focuses on her heart, which wants to race, and making her features smooth should one of the men glance her way. There are a dozen other girls just like her in the studio's employ, and a dozen more waiting in the wings.

She forces herself to smile.

On screen, her dark hair is pinned beneath a neat cap. She wears a pressed white apron over a long black dress, feather duster in hand. She knows what comes next, and clenches her jaw. Mary Catherine the careless, silly maid turns her back on the open hearth and bends to straighten a rug.

The studio head, Don Leaming, nudges the man beside him. The man turns, and even in the dark, his gaze crawls over Mary Catherine, as good as hands. She's expected to lower her eyes, blush, play virtuous-yet-coy, whatever it takes for investors to throw more cash Don's way.

Heat prickles the underside of Mary Catherine's skin. Humiliation, frustration. Her bones crackle, and she fights the feeling. On screen, the hem of the maid's uniform strays into the fire and *whoosh*! She explodes.

Silver-white animated flames engulf the maid, who runs about waving her arms, setting alight the curtains, the chairs. As if no simple maid could know oxygen feeds fire; as if no simple maid would know how to smother flames. Mary Catherine swallows, her throat raw.

In the next scene, a skeleton with serenely folded arms lies next to the hearth. The master of the house shakes a finger at it, then throws his hands in the air. The title card reads: *Good help is so hard to find*!

The men roar, slapping each other on the back. As Don stands to load the next reel, his voice reaches back to her.

"Just wait until you see the next one. This girl is a real star."

Mary Catherine freezes. The reel flickers to life and a woman swirls across the screen in her lover's arms, all dark curls and smoke-lined eyes, and the space behind Mary Catherine's breastbone stutters. A shout of warning lodges in Mary Catherine's throat. She's halfway to reaching for the screen, as if she could save the woman who is far too lovely to burn. But her beau dances her backward and flames scale the woman's dress, little hands and hungry mouths framing her face and her open, silent mouth, as prettily as her curls.

All at once, it's too much. Mary Catherine bashes through the door, eyes stinging. She hauls in a ragged breath, thinking of oxygen feeding flames and almost trips over a woman seated on the step, smoking.

"Couldn't stand it either?" It's the woman from the film.

Words flee, leaving Mary Catherine's mouth open. A breeze off the bay carries the faint scent of green weeds. A seagull shrieks, a blood-curdling sound.

"I hate those things, but they pay the bills. Mary Grace." The woman holds out a slim hand, neatly transferring her cigarette. "Gracie."

Mary Catherine stares, wishing she could stop. Light clings to the woman. Even without the setting sun, she would glow. Mary Catherine takes the proffered hand, and Gracie uses it to pull herself to a standing position.

"Mary Catherine. Cat." Her voice sounds small and far away, halfway to terrified. She's never called herself Cat before, but the name is there, attaching itself to her and feeling right.

"Cat." In Gracie's mouth, it's decadent, cherries soaked in brandy, rolled on her tongue.

Before Cat can press a palm to the heat rising in her cheeks, Gracie loops their arms together as though they're old friends.

"You're coming with me."

"Where?" Cat glances back at the studio.

She'll lose her job. Good. She doesn't want the job anyway. She wants to follow Gracie wherever she might go. The thought is scandalous, and Cat suppresses a burst of nervous laughter.

"We," Gracie lights two cigarettes, passing one to Cat without breaking stride, "are going to take the train to Coney Island. We are going to drink, then we are going to kick off our shoes and walk in the sand."

"Oh." It's the only thing Cat can think to say. Dazzled, she lets Gracie lead, and she follows.

The lights of Steeplechase, Luna Park, and Dreamland blaze against the dark. No matter how many times Cat sees the parks, they still take her breath away. The soaring towers, the impossible wonders, even the sillier rides like Dew Drop and Wedding Ring, designed to give men and women an excuse to grab onto each other.

Cat lets Gracie steer her away from the park entrances and down the shore. Music spills from Dreamland's Grand Ballroom, laughter, song, and light brightening the sand beneath the pier. An ache opens inside her. Cat pushes it down until she can convince herself it isn't there at all.

She lifts her long skirt a few inches to keep the hem from the tide. Gracie hikes her own skirt above her knees, plunging into the waves. When she looks back at Cat, a dare glitters in her eyes.

Cat snaps her mouth shut, aware it's gaping. She should look away. She should gather her skirts in her fists and run as far and fast as she can. She knows how young ladies ought to behave, and it isn't like this. Even in this place of miracles, this is a step too far. Music swirls overhead, couples dancing, but Dreamland's Ballroom might as well be a world away.

Gracie lets her skirt fall, water swirling the now-heavy fabric around her legs. A sadness replaces the hard-edged light of mischief in her eyes. She wades closer, stops. Too near and too far.

"What do you want, Cat?" Gracie's eyes are luminous in a way that has nothing to do with the light falling from the Ballroom above.

Cat's pulse thrums. She's on screen, in one of Don's films, burning, tiny flames dancing up and down her skin. The fire swallows all the air, and Cat doesn't have enough breath left to answer Gracie's question.

Until this moment, she thought she knew what she wanted. A job. To save money, enough to buy a little place of her own instead of renting a miserable one-room apartment. To live alone. To …

She hasn't thought past what happens when she ages beyond her usefulness to Don Leaming and his pictures. The only thing she knows is what she doesn't want, and she dares not voice that aloud. It's the thing she is supposed to want, what her mother taught her women must shape their lives toward, tucking every bright bit of themselves away until they can catch a man's eye. Cat cannot imagine existing solely at the whims and mercy of a husband, children always tugging at her skirt. She wants to do something important with her life. She wants to matter.

She wants.

Gracie takes another step. A salt-tinged breeze picks at her curls. Above the pier, the sky blushes to cobalt and grey, scattered with stars. Beneath the pier, they exist in their own twilight. In this light, Gracie doesn't even look human.

What do you want? The question lingers, and it isn't one Cat can answer. She wants what she shouldn't want. She wants what she can't want.

Despite the water's cold, heat blooms inside of her. Cat tamps it down, imagining the waves dousing a coal burning between her ribs.

"I watched you in the studio, before we met outside," Gracie says. "I was so sure you were like me."

The pattern of waves swirling around Cat's ankles leave her dizzy. There's something inside and behind Gracie's words, something she isn't quite getting. Gracie lifts her hand like she's cupping something precious. It must be a trick of the light; a flame shivers on Gracie's palm, silver-white, blue, burnt-orange.

Then, in the blink of an eye, Gracie burns.

Cat chokes on a cry as flames engulf Gracie, amber and gold. There are no cameras, no screen between them, no trick.

Gracie strokes a hand down her arm, wincing as she scoops fire into her palm. The flames reflect in her pupils as she holds her hand up, then shakes it so the flames scatter and hiss out as they strike the water. She slumps, and only instinct allows Cat to grab her before she falls.

Gracie's head lolls, curls landing against Cat's shoulder. Cat isn't sure she's strong enough. Her knees want to buckle, dropping them both into the water.

"What do you want, Cat?" The words are soft and slurred, so Cat barely hears them.

Gracie's lids droop, as if she will fall asleep in Cat's arms. Light seeps between the pier's cracks. Cat imagines the Ballroom, all those happy, dancing couples above them. She is wrong; she doesn't fit in that picture-perfect world. She wants the impossible.

"Gracie," she whispers, scarcely hearing herself over the thunder of her heart. "I want you to dance with me."

Gracie turns her face up to Cat's, a sleepy smile.

"I thought you would never ask."

Cat supports her, unsure how, moving both of them, feet sloshing in the tide. She's crying. Wet skirts cling to her shins. Gracie's hair tickles her.

There's no one here. No one to see. Mary Grace and Mary Catherine—hidden away where even God can't find them.

Cat closes her eyes. She tries not to think of church every Sunday growing up, sermons on the wages of sin, the fate of the wicked. She has crossed that invisible line; when she dies, hell will swallow her.

Even in Gracie's arms, panic beats at her. She is in the studio, watching herself on screen, watching herself explode. She is there, pushed this way and that by Don Leaming, his to command until she isn't useful anymore. She wants to help people with her life, but she doesn't know how. She's useless. She's a sinner. She's a coward. Afraid.

Heat crisps at her, peeling the flesh from her bones. Flames wreathe her from within. A scream rises to her lips and stops, and now Gracie is the one holding her up, calling her name.

"I knew it!" Reflected light dances in Gracie's wide-pupiled gaze, but she isn't the one burning, not anymore.

Cat looks down. Silver flames sheathe her arms like elbow-length gloves. She watches, entranced. It doesn't hurt. It should hurt. The wicked should be punished for their sins. Gracie's smile lights the night, brighter than the Ballroom above and all of Coney Island blazing.

"Cat, you're burning."

Cat squeezes water from her hair, sitting on the edge of Gracie's bed, shivering. She isn't certain whether she should laugh, or cry again—it's all so absurd.

The last hours are a blur. She has a vague memory of dropping into the water, flailing like a caught fish to douse the flames. Gracie must have hauled her up, dragged her home. What a sight they must have been, soaked and dripping on the train. Or did they walk? She isn't even sure where they are.

The bed Cat sits on is narrow and unmade. A small dressing screen sits in one corner of the room and the only other significant piece of furniture is a vanity table bearing a mirror. There's a framed photograph on the table, angled so a smear of light blurs the picture underneath. Cat's bedraggled reflection makes her realize she's only in her camisole and slip, and her cheeks flush bright, then brighter still as Gracie emerges from behind the screen, holding out a robe for her.

Cat turns away, wrapping herself. Gracie sits, keeping a careful distance between them.

"I'm sorry," Gracie says. "I didn't know where else to take you. I was afraid ..." She waves her hands vaguely, leaving Cat to imagine her own hysterical state. She's lucky she didn't get them both locked up as mad women.

"What happened?" Cat twists fabric in her fists.

She has the wild impulse to take Gracie's hand. Would it really be so terrible? They've already danced. But no. That was a fever dream. A hallucination.

Ghost-fire hangs in Gracie's eyes. There's no question. She burned. They both did.

"One of the nuns in the orphanage where I was raised used to tell me a story," Gracie says, looking down.

Oh, Cat thinks, and another piece of the mystery that is Gracie clicks into place.

"If the Mother Superior ever found out, I'm certain she would have been punished, but Sister Elise wasn't like the other nuns. She told me that the night I was found on the orphanage steps, a star fell across the sky. Only it wasn't a star, that's just what people thought. Sister Elise saw what it really was—a bird with silver and gold plumage, burning all across the sky."

Cat swallows, a lump in her throat like an ember, reducing anything she might say to ash. Gracie peeks at her from half-lowered eyes, needing Cat's belief. She looks so much younger than she did, smoking on Maryville's steps, almost a different woman, her brash confidence gone.

"I'm not human," Gracie says. "Neither of us are."

Oh. Cat is dizzy again, like the ocean surging beneath her. Even the thought of burning is impossible right now. She's shaking, and she can't stop. She pictures her mother and father, their stern but loving faces. Gracie's story is beautiful, but it can't be true.

She wants it to be, though. Desperately and suddenly, Cat wants this more than anything she's wanted before. It would explain so much. It would excuse her need. If she isn't even human, if she's something else, then she can't be a sinner. She can't go to hell, can she?

A breath, and Cat does a daring thing she could never imagine herself doing only hours ago. She takes Gracie's hand. She holds it, hoping it will speak for her, all the things she still cannot bring herself to say.

"You could stay." Gracie's whisper sounds almost pained.

Cat thinks of the bold girl who looped their arms together on the studio pier, strode into the water with her skirt lifted high. It makes her feel better, somehow, that Gracie is also afraid.

"Yes," she says, her heart falling through her ribs, but her body somehow remaining upright.

Gracie shifts, making room. Cat lies down. Gracie lies beside her. *Like sisters*, Cat thinks, *that's all*.

The bed is narrow, the space between them narrower still. Cat studies the back of

Gracie's neck, the soft places where her dark hair curls. Holding her breath, she wraps one arm around Gracie's shoulder. The pulse in her wrist matches the one in Gracie's chest.

And somehow, one last impossible thing in a night of impossibilities—they fall asleep like that, beat matched to beat, a fantastical rhythm.

Cat wakes to sunlight and Gracie returning from the bathroom down the hall. Gracie smiles, almost shy, and Cat pushes herself into a sitting position. She's still here. The earth didn't swallow her whole. They lay all night, side by side, and no hellfire came to claim them. Cat bounces up and seizes Gracie by the shoulders, half spinning her around in delight.

"We should get pastries and eat them in the park."

"What about the studio?" Gracie raises an eyebrow, amused at Cat's sudden energy.

Cat's blood fizzes like champagne. It's Gracie; together, they can do anything.

"Oh, who cares about the studio and Don Leaming. We can go anywhere we want."

The fire is there, just beneath Cat's skin. She doesn't know what to do with it, but surely Gracie can teach her. They must have been fated to meet. They can help others, light the way from mine disasters, or save people trapped under buildings in earthquakes. They are miracles.

"We could go to ... Paris!" Cat thinks of Steeplechase's scale model of the Eiffel Tower, and how glorious would it be to see the real thing.

"And what we would do there?" The light in Gracie's eyes is less than Cat would have imagined, and she lets her hands slide from Gracie's shoulders.

"But I thought ..." Cat takes a step back.

She's misunderstood everything. She wants to fold herself as small as her image in one of Don Leaming's trick films and disappear.

Her gaze falls on the vanity, and the picture frame, turned at a slightly different angle now, but empty. She could swear it held a photograph last night. Does Gracie have a secret beau? Is she ashamed of Cat, disgusted by her?

"Cat." Gracie touches Cat's wrist gently, and the sparrow-flight of her thoughts stills for a moment.

"How would we live?" At the sadness in Gracie's eyes, hope drains from Cat leaving her empty, feeling foolish.

Why would Gracie show her these wonders if not for them to be together, to change the world? Was all of it a lie? Did she only mean to entrap Cat, make her reveal her true self, and if so, for what purpose? She imagines herself locked in some asylum, restrained and subject to terrible cures.

"I would love to go to Paris with you." Gracie offers a sorrow-touched smile. "But Don Leaming is putting me in a film. Not just a trick film, but a picture with a proper story. I'm to play Joan of Arc."

And there it is. Cat's heart drops out of her completely. Not only is she being replaced, but the studio is moving on without her, taking Gracie along as a star, and leaving her with nothing. Once Don Leaming starts making history pictures, he'll forget all about trick films.

"Congratulations. I'm happy for you." Cat snatches at her dress, hung to dry last night alongside Gracie's, stuffing her body back into it with vicious motions.

She'd thought Gracie hated the studio as much as she did, but perhaps all along she knew she would be a star. Cat strides for the door, but Gracie's stricken expression catches her eye. Gracie's fists curl at her sides, her lips pressed into a thin line. Smoke seeps from between her fingers.

But she says nothing, doesn't call Cat's name, or tell her not to go. Cat raises her chin, makes it firm, and slams the door behind her, not allowing her shoulders to slump until she reaches the street below.

"You're late." Don Leaming speaks around the cigar clamped in his mouth. "And you left before the party last night. There were gentlemen looking forward to meeting you."

The implication is clear in his words, disdain and annoyance leaking out with the smoke.

"I'm ready to work." Cat lowers her gaze. She won't apologize, but she needs to work as much as she can before she's out of a job altogether.

"You better be." Don waves her away, cigar trailing more smoke.

Cat slinks to the dressing room. Today she will be a circus performer, shot from a cannon and exploded into a thousand glittering pieces. If she could explode for real, she would embed fragments of herself in Don Leaming's face like shrapnel.

She looks at her palms. Concentrates. Is there a faint glow, or is it only her imagination?

The longer Cat stares, the more she's convinced she's seeing things. A headache gathers between her eyes. She wipes her palms against the fabric of her costume and makes her way onto the stage.

Cat doesn't see Gracie again for three days, and the absence dulls to an ache like a bruise. They'd only just met; how can Cat miss her so fiercely? Especially when it's clear Gracie doesn't want her around?

On screen, she is struck by lightning, reduced to the size of an ant and dropped into the pocket of a young boy, and once again set aflame by carelessly straying too close to a stove. She bears the humiliation, and steels herself not to react when, at the next screening party, one of Don Leaming's investor friends repeatedly brushes up against her as if by accident, though she knows it is no mistake at all.

As soon as she can, Cat slips out the door. Tension holds her rigid to the point of aching, and she wants nothing more than to slump against the pier's railing and listen to the water lap the wood pilings until the sound numbs her and she feels nothing at all.

Moisture beads the air, obscuring the figure already at the end of the pier until Cat is already upon her and it's too late to turn away. The tip of Gracie's cigarette burns, the only bright thing, save for Coney Island across the water.

There's an invisible weight, a shadow wrapped close around Gracie's skin. Cat searches her outline, the edges where Gracie meets the darkness for the tell-tale flicker of silver flame, and sees nothing. Cat finds herself apologizing; despite everything, she still desperately wants to be Gracie's friend.

"I shouldn't have run out like that." Cat rushes the words out before she loses her nerve. "I really am pleased for you. I can see why Don Leaming wants to build his first big picture around you."

Gracie makes a sound between a cough and laughter, picking a fleck of ash from her lip.

"I never wanted to be a star. I *have* to be one."

The words make no sense. Cat sidles up beside Gracie. That first night, she thought she'd gotten to understand her at least a little, and now she doesn't understand anything at all.

"At the orphanage," Gracie says, "I used to watch the sky on clear nights. I was certain I would see that star racing across the sky, the one Sister Elise told me about, and then my real parents would come find me and take me away."

Gracie tilts her chin at the cloud-covered dark. One arm wraps her body, the other propped against it to hold her cigarette near her mouth.

"I'm sorry," Cat whispers. So many questions crowd her tongue, but she can't think of one that won't deepen Gracie's pain.

The space between them fills with longing. Cat wants to put an arm around Gracie, but she's afraid. Even over Gravesend Bay, there's a scent to her—charcoal, black powder, a match-head waiting for a spark.

"When I realized my parents weren't ever coming, and it was all just a stupid story Sister Elise made up, I started wishing more than anything I could get rid of this power. Be normal, like the other girls in the orphanage. Some nights, I wouldn't sleep. I knelt beside my bed, praying until my knees hurt so much I could barely walk. I would try to get in trouble so the Mother Superior would punish me. I thought the pain would make me clean." Gracie shakes her head, voice raw, like smoke.

"Nothing worked. I kept on burning."

"Do you still wish it would go away?" Cat asks softly. If Gracie thinks of herself as wrong, broken, what does that make Cat?

"I wouldn't give the fire away for anything. I hate that I have to hide it." Gracie's eyes blaze.

"Can you teach me?" The words emerge, breathless, before Cat can think better of them. Her pulse runs like a startled deer.

"Give me your hands." Gracie offers hers, palms up.

Cat places hers over them.

"What makes you angry?"

The pressure of Gracie's thumbs holding her hands in place feels like a rising bruise. Cat thinks of Don Leaming, his trick films designed to make women look useless and small. She thinks of all the ways he's found to kill her on screen—burned, lightning-struck, crushed. She thinks of Gracie dancing on screen, her lover backing her into the flame. Anger flares, a quick, stuttering spark.

Cat yelps, pulling her hands back and shaking at her fingers, checking the tips to see if they're singed.

"I'm sorry," she murmurs.

"It's okay." Gracie considers Cat, then her mouth twists in wry amusement. "No, anger isn't you, is it? What did you feel on the beach?"

Cat blushes. Fear of hell swallowing her, fear born of wanting. Cat's skin prickles at just the memory, dancing in Gracie's arms, the tide around their feet. Her instinct is to tamp the feeling down, but she holds onto it, lets it grow. She lay beside Gracie in bed, put an arm around her, and the world didn't end.

The memories are oxygen, and Cat feeds them to her fire. Warmth rises and tiny rills of fire sweep up Cat's arms. She gasps. Forgetting where they are, that they could be seen, Cat lifts her arms, watches the flames dance. They are tiny, but they are there, undeniable.

"It doesn't hurt," Cat says, amazed.

"That's good. You're lucky." Gracie clenches her jaw, makes a fist, and fire seeps between her fingers. She holds it up, burning, and even in the dark, Cat sees beads of sweat along Gracie's hairline.

Her own flames sink back into her skin. She wants to tell Gracie to stop, but she's frozen in place, mesmerized. Gracie lets out a gasp, pain. Droplets of fire scatter onto the water, and Gracie pants, shallow breaths.

Cat reaches for her, but Gracie holds up a hand, stilling her. Gracie's hurt feels impossibly large, nothing Cat can touch.

"You should go," Gracie says. "It's late."

Cat raises her hand, lets it fall. She turns, ashamed of herself, her cowardice. Her steps echo as she leaves Gracie alone by the water, arms wrapped around herself, a lonely, fallen star.

While Don begins filming *Joan of Arc*, he puts another director in charge of the trick films. Audiences love them, and the studio will churn them out as long as demand lasts. Cat feels more like a prop than ever, run ragged by the end of each day, but still she sneaks into the section of the studio where Gracie is filming, watching discretely as Gracie hears the voice of God, finds out the true king, leads her army. Cat knows the movie will end with Joan at the stake, but even in the scenes where Gracie is a simple peasant girl, Cat sees her burning.

There's a feverishness to her. Sometimes, Cat swears she sees heat shimmering from Gracie's skin, flames tracing her, but no one else notices. Once, Cat sees what look like wings spread behind Gracie like a vast and terrible shadow.

Alone in her apartment at night, Cat practices. Without Gracie's hands to steady her, it's harder. She manages a small glow, like a candle burning low, but nothing more. Many nights, she's too tired to do anything more than fall into bed and a deep and dreamless sleep.

Even though they are both at the studio most days, Cat rarely has a chance to talk to Gracie. They might as well be worlds apart. She wants to steal Gracie away, roam Luna Park and Steeplechase and Dreamland with her. But every time she thinks of it, Cat loses her nerve. Shadows haunt Gracie's skin, dark circles beneath her eyes.

Then, in a blink, filming on *Joan of Arc* is almost complete due to Don Leaming's breakneck pace. Cat can't help the feeling that once the picture is released, either she will be out of a job, or Gracie will. She's running out of time, for what, she doesn't know.

Cat finds herself alone in the studio dressing room. They're filming Gracie's climactic scene, and somehow, Cat is the only studio girl not roped into being one of the extras. She looks around at the scattered possessions, clothing carelessly shed like skin and draped over chairs, bags left behind.

Gracie's things are among them, and Cat kneels, touching Gracie's dress, running her fingers over the fabric. Gracie's bag is beneath her dress. Cat's fingers are on the clasp as if of their own accord, twisting it open, rooting inside.

She shouldn't. She has no right. But there might be some clue to a way she can help Gracie.

Her hand brushes a square of thick paper. A photograph, the same size as the empty frame in Gracie's apartment. Gracie stands with her arm around another woman against a cloth backdrop depicting Paris. Both women are smiling, mouths slightly blurred as if the photographer caught them mid-laugh. There's a stamp in the bottom righthand corner—Luna Park. Cat has seen the building from the outside, where visitors can go to have their portraits taken.

Her breath stutters, a fresh ache. There's a casual intimacy to the way the two women hold each other, and there are no shadows in Gracie's eyes in the photograph.

Her smile is untainted; she looks purely happy.

A wisp of smoke rises from Cat's fingers and she drops the photograph. The corner is barely singed, but the mark is there—her guilt plain to see. She tries to stuff the photograph back in Gracie's bag, but a shadow falls over her, and Cat freezes.

"Eleanor," Gracie says, the name weighted with loss. "We were left at the orphanage the same week. Aside from Sister Elise, she was all the family I had."

Cat straightens. She makes herself meet Gracie's eyes. She holds out the picture like an apology and Gracie takes it.

"Eleanor was the only other person who knew about the fire. One day, I got so angry, I don't even remember why, but I could feel the flames creeping up inside me. I was terrified someone else would see so I ran out into the courtyard. Eleanor followed me without me seeing her. She saw the flames burst out of my skin, and you know what she did?"

It isn't really a question; Cat waits.

"She didn't even hesitate. She threw her arms around me to smother the flames, because she thought I was in danger. She never treated me like I was different. She helped keep me safe. When I couldn't calm the fire on my own, she would put her arms around me, and hold me until I stopped burning."

A tear slips down Gracie's cheek. She wipes it away with the back of her hand. Cat lets her fingertips brush against the dampness and the salt. Gracie startles, but she doesn't pull away.

"She moved out here before I did. I came to visit her, that's when this was taken. She was the one who wanted to be a star."

"What happened?" Cat asks.

"Don Leaming made promises. And he was careless, the way men are." The bitterness in Gracie's voice is impossible to miss.

"Eleanor was so happy. She thought her whole life would change, Don would buy her a big house, she would move out of her little apartment."

Gracie turns the photograph in her hands.

"She had such a kind heart that she would have happily had the baby even without all that, but Don insisted she get rid of it. He took her to a dentist, not even a proper doctor. He did the surgery in his basement. Eleanor bled out."

A shout from outside the dressing room door, a call for Gracie to be back on set. Gracie clenches her jaw, and again, Cat thinks she sees the shadow of wings spread behind her, an awful and glorious fiery bird.

"Here." Gracie pushes the photograph back into Cat's hand.

"Wait!"

Gracie is already at the door, but she turns, smile sorrow-touched.

"Don't worry, I'm not human, remember? I'm a miracle. And so are you."

The closes with a soft click behind her. Cat stands, staring after her, until the sound of something heavy being dragged across the floor just on the other side of the door jolts her from her reverie. All at once, with terrible certainty, Cat knows exactly what Gracie means to do. The photograph falls from numb fingers, a leaf in her wake as Cat runs to the door. She falls against it, banging her shoulder painfully, but the door only opens an inch. Through the gap, Cat sees one of the bags of sand used for raising and lowering painted backdrops wedged in front of the door.

She throws her weight against the door again. It shudders, moving a fraction. She does it again and again, her shoulder bruising, until finally the gap is wide enough for her to wiggle free. She runs, her chest already feeling like it's full of smoke, leaving it impossible to breathe.

She skids to a halt, a shout caught and dying before reaching her lips. She's too late.

Gracie stands upon Joan's pyre, her chin lifted. A soft glow, as of reflected flame, suffuses her skin. She looks like a saint, serene and fierce and terrible.

Extras surround her, false torches in their hands. Before one of them can move, flames erupt from Gracie's skin. The ropes binding Gracie fall away. She lifts her arms and the flames surge, leaping free of the pyre and running across the studio floor.

Confusion becomes chaos. Screaming. Cat lurches towards Gracie, but someone bowls into her running the other way and knocks her down. Thick smoke fills the air. Cat struggles to her hands and knees. Glass explodes, a soft popping sound. She can't see anything. Heat batters her, her eyes stream. Flames lick their way toward her, but when they nip at her heels, she feels no pain.

Don't worry, I'm not human, remember? I'm a miracle. And so are you.

The words echo in Cat's mind. Gracie. There's nothing she can do.

Someone lifts her, drags her along. Suddenly Cat is outside, stumbling and coughing, bodies all around her. There's a *whoomp* of displaced air and the studio roof collapses, sending a shower of sparks into the air. The press of the crowd shoves Cat backwards, but her eyes remain locked to the sky. The rising smoke and the sparks sketch a shape. A bird with spread wings, its beak a blade holding the sun as it shoots upward, a falling star in reverse.

Then all at once the crowd falls away from her, and someone screams. It's a moment before the words penetrate, and Cat looks down.

"You're burning!"

And she is. Not just her arms this time, but all of her. She does nothing to smother the flames, but lets them rage, her face tilted to the sky.

"Yes," she says. "Yes I am."

2015

She squints in the sunlight. The way it glints off the water, it's like a swarm of fireflies, a shower of sparks. Like the studio burning all over again, and she tilts her head back to look at the sky. But there's only a pure, aching blue, sketched with wispy clouds.

After all the talking, her throat is parched. The girl beside her, the young woman—Cecily, was it?—hands her a bottle of water. The plastic sweats; there's a young man selling them from a cooler full of ice.

"I believe this is the part where you tell me everything I said is impossible." She sips, smiling. She's used to being called impossible.

This is still a place of miracles, even if the world has moved on.

"It's a wonderful story." Cecily sounds more wistful than anything else.

She glances at her phone. Perhaps she's waiting for a call, for bad news, or a message that will never come. The old woman pats the back of the girl's hand where it wraps around the screen, protectively, or as if she would bury it.

"I suspect we should head back," she says, even though she isn't precisely sure what back means now.

For a moment, she can believe they'll cross the water and find themselves in long-vanished Luna Park, or return to her tiny, one-room apartment in the heart of old Brooklyn. After that, wasn't there a grand house? Somewhere along the shore, filled with voices, laughter. Only girls at first—lighter than air and swooping about the ceilings on invisible wings. Then, later, boys with eyes like cracking ice and voices like rushing rivers who could slip their skins by the dark of night. Later still, lost children who were neither boys nor girls who could chant solid objects into new shapes, or turn as invisible as glass. Miracles, all. Like her.

"Yes. Sorry." Cecily rubs at her eye with the back of her hand, a movement so quick it might not be the shine of a tear she chases away.

She reaches to help the old woman, but Nan pushes herself up. Nan—it's as good a name as any, for now.

"There are still miracles," Nan says as they walk away from the pier and the imagined remains of Maryville beneath the waves. She doesn't look at Cecily, but she feels Cecily look at her, a curious mixture of surprise and a fraction of hope.

"When you feel that heat on the wrong side of your skin," Nan says, looking straight ahead into the bustling streets of Brooklyn—*when*, not *if*. "And you feel like if you don't do something about it, you'll explode, come talk to me again."

AUTHOR NOTES

"The Amazing Exploding Women of the Early Twentieth Century" was inspired by a similarly titled essay (which, unfortunately, I can no longer find) on the early history of cinema and trick films. Trick films were short, silent films that used innovative special effects to do things like make objects/people appear or disappear, shrink, burst into flame, and turn into skeletons, among other effects. Some of these tricks (or versions of them) were later used in horror cinema, but at the height of their popularity, they were often used as cautionary tales, showing careless maids catching on fire, exploding, turning into dust, or being skeletonized due to their clumsy behavior or being too flighty to know better. They were both classist and sexist! So, of course, amongst people who were also inclined to be classist and sexist, they were immensely popular. I took all this history as my starting point and gave it a speculative twist, giving my main characters the power to literally explode into flames outside of the tricks of the studio, and letting them use that power to reclaim their stories and make new paths for themselves.

BLACK BOX OF THE TERRAWORMS

BARTON AIKMAN

Datalog: Terraworm Colony TN-B-53
Planet: Terra-9

The first god tastes of cardamom and coriander. Its pungent skin is brittle and cracked and breaks like dry seaweed. The seven legs of its impressive mass bend and form great peaks and valleys. Bogs of noxious fumes bubble from its pores. Our programming tells us the god most closely resembles an arachnid to you Earth-raised beings. Imagine a black widow the size of a mountain range, but with skin like yours, tearing open like a burning house. Full of death, and therefore life, rotting and stinking with history.

The spider god is no match for us, the terraworms.

We burrow into its fetid geography. We devour it with our mechanical mandibles. We eat the god over the course of several months. We recycle its body as we work and change the atmosphere and soil of this people-less planet. We begin to make the planet a place that one day can be called yours. We do this for you because this is what you created us to do. This is our purpose.

But we don't call you gods.

You are not gods.

That is the first thing you coded us to know, which was wise.

If you were gods, we would want to eat you too.

We finish recycling the spider god on an overcast day. The sky swirls a collective of dense greys and deep blues. We anticipate rain, but it never comes. Broken down, the digested mountain range now nourishes a great flatland where the colossal arachnid once stood. When you arrive, years and years from now, you will be treated to plains ripe for the taking. This land now waits for you by your design.

We press onward, searching. We encounter a dead city. The decrepit buildings once served various functions, but they are all tombs now. Moss and other foliage leak from windows and engulf market squares, but nothing is green. Everything is dead, even nature's reclamation. Nothing moves, nothing lives, except us, and we push forward. There is nothing for us to eat and recycle yet.

Deeper into the dead city, a silver citadel still stands, still glimmers somehow in the dim day. Its walls and spires and turrets remain untouched by time. The fortress is the most alive thing we have seen since arriving to this planet. We find the entrance left open, either by invaders or survivors. How did life last use this space? Again, we search, but the citadel tells us nothing more.

We look up at the gleaming turrets.

We find we can't look away.

Something happens to us.

We see the city as it once was. Lights. Noise. Life. We see this from high up. We are enormous.

We are the spider god.

Offerings are left for us on the outskirts of the city. Livestock with flower crowns and painted torsos wait for us, tied up, and the animals do not scream. We draw closer and they never scream. It's our eyes. Our spider god eyes calm them, hypnotize them. We secure the offerings to our body, strap them to us with our webbing, and return to the plains from which we came. One by one, we pluck the offerings off our great frame and eat. The offerings remain calm and placid. There is no pain.

We chew and chew. Not happy, but content.

Day turns to night.

Across the plain, the skyline of the city crests the horizon, protrudes from the surface of the prairie like fractured bones. The city shines bright. Even the nearest stars hide from its light. The night sky appears woefully incomplete because of the bustling city.

Cherishing the stars that remain, we know it has not always been this way.

Once, the spider god ruled the sky. Our webbing formed a dome over the planet, expanded across continents. During the day, our shadow shaded nomads—hunters and gatherers—and they shared their harvests with us in thanks. Many winged creatures became ensnared in our webbing, cast their own shadows, and we feasted on them. We let the carcasses plummet to the ground, and watched the inhabitants use the bones to decorate their clothing, wear the skulls around their necks and on their heads. In this way we patrolled the world and provided for the nomads. At night, we ate whatever stayed awake, still ravenous from traversing the globe. The nomads, however, slept peacefully. They felt protected, so long as they did not journey out at night themselves.

The nomads built. They became villagers, then townsfolk, and finally evolved into city dwellers. They made their own shade and lights. They offered less and less to us, treated us as an obligation, and retreated into their city. They didn't need the spider god like before. They committed sacrilege and ventured out into the night. They became angry with us for eating their children and drunken newlyweds, anyone foolish enough to be caught by us under the stars. Still, they were the ones to break our contract.

They constructed their silver citadel. From high up in our web we watched. Even before its completion, the fortress glinted in the sun and the reflection pained our many eyes. We descended our great web and hovered over the city. We needed to tell the city dwellers their new citadel hurt us.

But the city dwellers hid from us. We dropped down, closer and closer to the city, hovering just above the tallest buildings, dangling from a single strand of our great web. We hoped they would come out to greet us and remember the pact they once shared with their spider god, but none of the city dwellers emerged from their many mysterious buildings. We climbed back up our web and went to sleep hungry.

They continued to build their citadel, so we took their food as punishment. We preyed on the surrounding livestock. The hunting exhausted us. Although we ate and ate, the reckless energy we spent kept us hungry. We only wanted to be able to watch the city dwellers as we always had, to protect them and be given offerings in return. We never wanted it to come to this.

Each day we came back to observe the city, the citadel had grown. Brighter and brighter it shone, like lightning striking back at the sky. Even at a distance now it pained us.

We tried to reason with the city dwellers, but they didn't listen.

We ambushed them in the middle of the day, wincing from the citadel as we passed above it. We descended our web and hovered over a crowded marketplace.

Many fled.

But some looked into our eyes.

The hypnotized city dwellers had no choice as they came closer and closer to us with outstretched arms. We carried them up into our great web, dozens of them, and feasted. We let their half-eaten bodies fall and twirl to the ground, and land in the middle of the city. The city dwellers did not taste good and eating them saddened us.

We regretted our decision, but a lesson had to be taught.

Not once did we wonder if we ourselves needed to be taught a lesson.

As we ate, we heard a horrible tearing. The sound came from our web. Our weight shifted as our web dome weakened. Our many eyes fluttered and scanned for the cause of the tearing.

Something soared above us, as if descending from space itself. We saw four wings, their wingspan engulfing even our tremendous frame. A long and sharp beak, which could so easily skewer us, ripped and destroyed our web. The creature narrowly evaded flying into us, and its battalion of multi-colored feathers dazzled our many eyes.

Our web continued to rip and tear.

We fell.

From our once grand throne in the sky, we fell. We crashed onto the great plains. Our legs broke and fractured. Our eyes swelled and bled.

We nearly died. We should have died. All we could do was sleep. A long, deep sleep.

We awoke to a great many offerings. In our weakest moment, the city dwellers remembered our pact, the history between us. We ate. We healed as best as we could. We would likely never ensnare the sky again, but we could walk and see. We could still find purpose.

In our weakened state, we claimed the plains as our home.

We kept several of our many eyes locked on the sky. We lived in fear of the winged creature that had destroyed our web. It had flown with such apathy, had cut through our web like turbulence inconveniencing its path. We reasoned the winged giant had sought revenge for all the little winged creatures we had eaten over the years. Perhaps our greed had created this flying predator.

But the winged creature rarely returned to the plains. When it did, it paid no attention to us. It simply kept going. We watched it, at the ready, remaining still. It always flew to another end of the globe. It always went toward the ocean, toward the coast.

Before we could ever find out why, the missiles came. They screeched across the sky, launching from the turrets of the citadel and gliding through the air, predestined for us. We remembered watching meteor showers with the nomads, who peaked their heads out of their tents. Back then, we had made them feel safe. Now, they had their own meteors, and they didn't need us.

Had those final offerings been left for us out of guilt? A few pleasant final meals while they finished constructing their weapons?

Or had the offerings been a trap? A way of keeping us nearby, roaming the plains, easily within range of their missiles?

The first barrage permanently crippled us.

We became a breathing piece of the landscape.

The second barrage filled our lungs with blood.

We never felt the third barrage. We saw the missiles leave their turrets, but we did not watch them fly toward us. We didn't want that to be the last thing we saw with our many eyes. Instead, we stared at the silver citadel, and the gleaming turrets.

Even an old creature like us had to admit: the citadel looked beautiful.

But with our last ounce of strength we looked away. Then, we looked up. We reminisced when we had a proper place.

We used to rule the sky.

We once looked down from it.

After the spider god's memory finishes, we turn away from the turrets, which still stand, their history clearer to us now.

You didn't prepare us for this.

We didn't believe we were engineered to relive the memories of the beings we recycled.

Did you know, or is this something unforeseen?

We want to ask you, but you are far away. Very far away. We understand we play an early role in the creation of your new home. Our coding compels us onward, but still, we want to know.

We confirm there is nothing for us to eat in the city, so we leave.

We head toward the coast. Maybe we will find the winged god there.

As our clew presses onward, we hear a rumble, churning and churning behind us, deafening. We turn and look back to the city. A Farmer has already arrived, all dark steel and fire. It is the first of the machine we have seen since our arrival. When we woke and began our task of recycling, the Farmers still slept. Now, we can watch it perform its function.

We know somewhere on its body the Farmer is equipped with wheels, but all we can see is its face. Its open maw glows like a forge and it drives its mouth into the ground, just outside the city's perimeter. The Farmer resembles a bottom feeder sucking on the ocean floor. The rumble intensifies. The buildings nearest to the farmer shake. Within minutes, the buildings begin to collapse and crumble. The Farmer unpuckers its lips from the ground and proceeds to gobble up the ruined buildings.

We know the Farmer will do this to the entire city. Even the citadel. The turrets that struck down the spider god, too, will be destroyed.

The Farmer will eat well.

And you will have a seemingly virgin land to build a new city on.

We watch the Farmer a little longer, then resume our journey to the coast.

We move on knowing we are the last to see the turrets and the last to see the spider god and learn its story.

The winged god does not wait for us at the coast. Nothing waits for us. A low tide hardly laps at the shore. We burrow into the sand. We eat some bones, but it isn't much. Then, our collective mass idles along the beach, covering the entire coastline.

There is nothing for us to eat here.

We thought there would be so much more.

We have nowhere else to go, so we head into the ocean. The water is cold, would numb and purple you, but we are strong terraworms, designed to withstand environments too harsh for Earth-raised beings. Some of us swim. Some of us crawl along the ocean floor. Together, we enter the ocean like a makeshift swarm of mechanical krill and crabs.

Debris covers the ocean floor. Remnants of once-proud ships. We don't have to eat them and absorb their memories to know they once skated atop the ocean's surface, taking beings and objects from place to place. A ship is a simple and admirable creation. No matter its design, capacity, and flag, it has one purpose: transportation. You will take ships not unlike these to reach this planet. After you arrive, your ships will become dead decorations too.

We continue to swim and crawl. We can't eat the debris; none of it is alive. A Farmer will need to traverse the ocean to clear it. We reach deep, open waters and all of us take to swimming. It is likely we are the first living things to swim here in lifetimes. Do you consider us living things? Or are we simply switched on, like an engine? Right now, traversing the cold depths of this ocean, we feel very much alive.

At last, we find another god. It is not the winged creature we saw in the spider god's memory. This god is a sea god. Our bestiary tells us it resembles a mixture of a jellyfish, squid, and anglerfish. Adorned on its bulbous and immense head, a crown of thin tentacles flap with the current, mimicking life. Additional tentacles dangle downward from its cranium—the sea god's arms. Some tentacles end with claws and others end with suckers and all the sea god is translucent white. Drifting, the creature appears soft and gentle, even warm.

We swim in closer, surround it.

The sea god is enormous, but like before, it is no match for the collective might of the terraworms. Will this god give us its memories like the last one? We want to pause and consider, but our programming propels us to open our mouths and eat.

The second god tastes of brine and anise. Its skin is soft and doughy, and we must chew and chew to digest it. We eat its arms, leaving only the head to drift along with us in the sea. On the underside of its bulbous head we find rows and rows of sharp fangs; surely a frightening sight for the many creatures who met their end by the points of those teeth, but now, we break down those teeth. They are the hardest part of the sea god to eat, but eventually the teeth give in to us.

We leave the tentacled scalp of the sea god for last and are glad we did. It is delicious. The scalp is sweet like sugar, and when the tentacles burst in our mouths, they are thick and savory. Our coding suggests we scatter half of the recycled god close to the shore. Its nutrients will be the beginnings of a coral reef. By the time you reach this planet, fish will be awaiting your reels. The second half of the god will be used along the coast. This fertile land by the sea will provide you with vegetables and fruit.

Before we can go about distributing the recycled god, we feel it happening again. The ocean itself changes, becomes clearer. Sea creatures of all sizes manifest and swim in our proximity. Our tentacles sway in the water with intention. The colors of our arms shift and bend. Our entire body is an array of brilliant, living colors. Above us, we see the bottoms of the functioning ships, carrying their cargo across the surface of the water.

Some ships stay in place. We are too deep in the water to see the bait, but we do see small creatures move toward the ships. Occasionally, a creature twitches, is yanked up to the boat, and pulled out of the water.

We watch the fishing, contemplate. We feel the strength of our many arms, and know they are long enough to reach up and sink the ships if need be. We could even snatch a sailor directly from the ship and drag them down into the depths, then shred them with our many fangs and claws. But we also know there is an agreement between us and those that built the ships. They only enter the open ocean when the sea god allows it. They know when they aren't welcome; when the ships start sinking.

Suddenly, an uninvited guest dives into the water. It is the largest thing we have ever seen. We didn't know anything else grew to such a size. Despite its immensity, the creature dives into the water with grace, its body folded into the shape of a spear. Its feathers catch the sun and glisten, shining so many different colors, just like our tentacles.

The winged creature dives deep, then begins to float up slowly. On its way up, it stops directly next to us, and momentarily expands its wings. We see its thin and cunning face, and marvel at the beauty of its wings. We stretch our many tentacles and let them dance in response.

The winged creature's eyes pierce into us.

Our eyes are sensors on our head. The winged creature couldn't know this, but somehow, it manages to look directly at us, and we look back. Nothing has ever looked directly into our eyes before.

We feel love for the first time.

We hope that the winged creature feels the same.

We sense that it does.

But the winged creature needs air, and leaves.

For the first time, we look to the water's surface with a painful longing. We wait for the winged creature to return. We dream about its wings, its beak and face. We worry our tentacles will shock and sting the winged creature, and we try to think of how we might still be able to embrace, but none of that ends up mattering.

Because the winged creature does not return.

Only the ships do. More and more of them. Too many. So, we give them a warning. With ease we slash our claws into the hull of a ship, and one by one sink the lifeboats as well. We let the sailors tread water until they are weak and begin to drown. Just before the sailors submit to the ocean, we carry them to the shore and leave them coughing and kicking for air on the beach.

The sailors construct ships with new hulls—darker, colder, stronger. They take more creatures from the sea than ever before. It takes much more effort for us to sink their ships. We leave many of them to rust on the ocean floor, but we can't stop them all. Many sea creatures die. Those of us that don't begin to starve.

We eat as little as possible. It has always been our duty to care for the other creatures in the sea, even the ones we ourselves eat. With so few of us left in the ocean, we go as long as we can without food. The ships continue to come but we are too weak now to fight. Many of our tentacles stop responding and become transparent. One by one, our limbs die. There is nothing left for us to do but drift and wait.

We think of the winged creature.

How lovely it would be, to see it one more time, right before the end.

Somehow, our thoughts are answered. It happens. This time, the winged creature crashes into the water. Its wings are still colorful, but not as brilliant as before; they are duller and frayed. Is something wrong? We want to reach out to the winged creature, but all our limbs are dead now.

Worse, the winged creature swims right past us.

It dives.

Deeper and deeper into the ocean it goes.

Why? We ask ourselves. Why?

That is how the memory ends. The pain of the sea god's final moments lingers, courses through us with its recycled parts. We want to stop, but our bodies propel us further and deeper into the ocean. Our programming desires another god for us to eat.

Now, we know the location of the winged god.

We descend.

We have already travelled to many places you aren't capable of traversing, but this is the apex. Here, the water pressure would crush almost anything. Here, there is no light with which to see. To your credit, you designed us well. Our combination of eyes and sensors allow us to see in every condition, even this one.

We see the winged god.

The god's head sticks into the bottom of the ocean floor, the bulk of its beak wedged in deep. Its face is narrow and sleek like a hummingbird, but its eyes are insectoid like a mosquito. It wears a tired and desperate expression, even after all this time. Many of its feathers have fallen away. Those that remain have no color.

Automatically, we close in on the winged god.

We must fulfill our purpose. The purpose you created us for.

We remember the fear the spider god felt.

We remember the love the sea god felt.

We don't want to, but our many mouths begin to eat.

The third god tastes of rosemary, shallots, and sadness. With each bite the memories come rushing in. Our terraworm bodies continue to operate and perform their function, but the winged god's history appears intensely, creating a divide between our bodies and our mind.

It is as if we are eating ourselves.

Simultaneously, we eat our wings and know how wonderous it is to have those same wings carry us across the sky. We eat our eyes while we scan the landscape with them. Everything is lush and wild. We are the first god, perhaps the very first thing to live on this planet, ancient and powerful. We can keep ourselves suspended in the air almost endlessly. We can go years without eating. We can observe this planet from the sky without hardly leaving a mark, and we do so for ages.

Then, on a day just like any other, we see the first nomads, and it fills us with dread. We know better than to start a pact with the nomads; it can be beautiful, even last a long time, but it will only end in heartbreak. They will outgrow us. They will disappoint us. The relationship will end in bloodshed.

But we have a plan; we can leave.

Hoping the nomads never saw us, we fill our belly with our favorite fruits and fill our lungs with the cleanest air. We soar upward, higher and higher, past the clouds and the blue of the sky, and enter the great void that encases our planet. We have enough food and air to survive for a long time, hopefully long enough for the nomads to live out their cycle.

The void is full of brilliance. We see more colors than ever before. We even look for a new planet, one without nomads. But the other planets are too hot, or too cold, or completely barren. Nothing compares to our first home. We go out far, too far, searching, using more of our air and food than we should.

The journey back home is tortuous. We run out of food and air well before we reach our home planet. Our brain aches. Our body cries. Finally, we see the beautiful blues and greens of the home we flew away from. The pain is immense, but we break through the atmosphere.

A great web ensnares the sky and we are too confused and dizzy to navigate it. We cut straight through. We gasp for air. Our brain continues to ache, feels like it's bleeding. We fly haphazardly as we take in large gulps. Dizziness overwhelms us and we spin and careen, tearing through the web.

We have air in our lungs now, but our body continues to scream. We head to the ocean and dive in. It has been many years since we felt the cool ocean and we revel in the water's embrace. We don't swim up right away. Instead, we spread out our wings and open our eyes.

We are greeted by a beautiful creature shifting a complex spectrum of colors. It is the first thing we see clearly since returning to our planet, and it is the most beautiful thing we have ever seen here. What a wonderful surprise. We wish we had spent more time in the water beforehand. But our body still feels wrong, and we are compelled to return to the sky. Once we have healed, we look forward to returning to the ocean and seeing the beautiful creature again.

But we don't heal. The bleeding sensation in our brain never stops. We can only manage to fly in a daze. Regularly, we soar over the ocean. There was something about the ocean. What was it?

We see the nomad's beautiful cities. We see little of the wildlife we knew before we left. We try to remember the importance of the ocean, but it is difficult for us to remember much of anything at all.

We feel only anger and sickness. We journeyed too far and came home too early. We thought we were wise, but we weren't wise enough. There is no place for a winged god on this planet right now, and there will never be a need for a sick god ever.

We plummet into the ocean.

Maybe now we will remember what was so special about it.

We close our eyes as we dive in, focusing on the coolness of the water, hoping it will trigger a memory, but it doesn't. We plunge deeper and deeper. The ocean will tell us. The ocean must tell us. We go so far down, and with such force, we stab into its bottommost layer. Still, the ocean tells us nothing. We remember nothing.

Down here is like the void, cold and intense. Only, here, there are no lights, no colors. There are no new homes to search for. There is only us and our broken body.

We close our eyes and let the darkness take us.

We try to remember the things we love about our home.

Something wonderful begins to creep into our thoughts, but then disappears.

Perhaps we should have never come back at all.

We finish eating the third god and living its memory. There are no new leads for us, no more gods we know to search for, and we head back toward the surface. We have a great deal of recycled material now to spread across the planet. Even if we find no more gods, you will have a rich, new planet to call home.

Of course, we won't be here to see it.

For now, our programming compels us to keep searching. We will scour the planet for any remaining gods and other biomaterials to eat and recycle. But eventually, that task will end. Then, after the planet has been fertilized, and the atmosphere cleansed, our coding will tell us to burrow. We will burrow all the way to the planet's core, or at least as close as we can get. At some point the intense heat of the core will destroy us. You designed us well, but we are not designed to withstand all things. You made sure to give us the means to end ourselves.

We wonder, will you see our destruction as death? Will you mourn us?

While our bodies will be gone, this datalog, our black box, will not be. Throughout our entire lifespan here, we have been recording our progress for your records, just as you engineered us to do. We will leave our data for you before we burrow. As you read this, the story of our time spent terraforming a new home for you, we are long dead. We do not bemoan this. As we have learned ourselves, so much can be accomplished by studying the memories of the dead.

When we ate the gods of this planet, we became them. They live inside of us now. In reading our transmission log, in a way you have eaten us. You have become us, and you have become those old gods too. You know the spider god had nothing to fear from the winged god, that its injuries were an accident, that its death was unfortunate. You know why the winged god never returned to the sea god. You know how much that one encounter meant to both of them, and how tragic it is they never communicated again. But both those memories exist inside of you now. We like to think that, at least in some way, they are reunited. Lastly, you know our story. The entire story of the terraworms and the gods we ate to create your new planet.

In our first slumber, you sent us across the stars. Then, we ate mountains for you, sowed the land for you, traversed the ocean depths for you. We learned the history of this planet and transcribed it for you. This place will be your home some day because of us.

Are our triumphs not unlike the gods of so many tales?

Now that all this is a part of you, what stories will you tell of the creatures that lived on this planet before your arrival?

What stories will you tell of the terraworms?

And who will eat you? What stories will they tell after you're gone?

We hope you enjoy the home we helped make for you. Don't be fooled by its untarnished landscapes. This planet is old and has seen so much life and death. It is full of history. If not for our black box, you never would have known. Known of the gods and cities. Known of the terraworms' work. Known that we, until the very end, always wanted to learn more.

JASON SIZEMORE

A common lament I share with writers is that we don't receive enough dark science fiction. If you can write a story like this one, you have a good shot of being published in the magazine.

The story feels appropriately epic in nature. Oddly, the reader forms a bit of an emotional bond with these terraforming massive worms that eats everything and destroys civilizations. It's quite a writing accomplishment.

One morning at work received a text from Maurice Broaddus. "If Barton Aikman sends you something, you'll want to pick it from the slush pile. Trust me." Barton had worked with Maurice at a writing workshop and had impressed our special fiction editor. See writers, leaving the house once in awhile can be good for your career!

IF THOSE RAGGED FEET WON'T RUN

ANNIE NEUGEBAUER

The night comes. It can't yet be seen, felt, tasted, or smelled, but you can hear it. You can hear all things fall quiet as the dusk draws near. It is a fearful silence, waiting.

The days are noisy things, full of freedom like the space of the open plain with its whistle winds that dance and push. There are daytime dangers, yes, of course—there are always dangers no matter the life—but they are things like a cough that infects the lungs, a stinging centipede creeping between the tight boards of your hut, or your husband getting injured while out on a hunt, coming home permanently wounded, or, like Bethesda's husband, not coming home at all.

Their daughter was only a few weeks old when it happened. Keena. A secret name. Their village doesn't allow for naming children under three years of age. But you cannot build a life inside you, grow it up from seed, birth her out into the world at risk of your own life, and not give her a name. Many, if you count the nicknames and endearments that Bethesda allows. Darling. Starflower. Bunny. Honeyheart. On and on, though in front of council members she calls her "little baby." Probably no one would punish her for an affectionate stand-in, but she defers as a safeguard and sign of respect.

Right now, though, Bethesda and Keena are alone. Horribly alone. The only other living things within sight are the two thinning, tired oxen, snorting tiredly at the scrubby greens that spatter the open plain. They smell like manure and defeat.

Bethesda clutches a swaddled Keena to her, swaying back and forth to keep her calm. "*Shhhhhhhhhh, shhhhhhhhh, shhhhhh,*" she breathes, trying to keep herself calm, too. Even at only six weeks old, the baby can sense her emotions.

Her home village, tucked safely under a thick canopy of the trees, is beyond sight ahead. Bethesda looks back the way she came, from the other village across the plain. A full day's journey, traveling since the break of dawn, as fast as the oxen could pull the box cart. Horses are faster, but less strong and far more expensive. The two villages are just close enough that oxen are still quick enough to be safe.

Unless, of course, something goes wrong. Like the box cart turning over, flipped on its side by a hidden rock the beasts have taken at speed, one wheel splintering off.

The front and back left wheels still spin. The door to the box cart stands straight up from the side, open to the sky, the windowless interior a dark hole from which they climbed after the crash, candle flame thankfully extinguished rather than kindled in the tumult.

The oxen make no sound but heavy breathing, despite their hunger and possible pain from the accident. They know. All know.

The silence is dreadful.

Keena's tiny face scrunches into a knot, the impending cry trilling through Bethesda like the cry they all wait for. She bounces, increasing the volume of her hushing. Even that sounds loud, but it's far softer than Keena wailing.

The acute knowledge of what she should do is screaming, screaming into the stillness. The council has told them. They tell each other. You grow up knowing.

You leave the baby. If it isn't old enough to be quiet when told—before being given a name—it isn't worth the risk. Some people put them to death first. Others let them cry as a diversion, if it comes to that. But you leave the baby.

Bethesda will not consider it. Her grip has tightened around Keena's small form automatically, but that upsets the child. Bethesda relaxes her arms, bounces, raises her hushing to a series of gentle coos.

She will not leave her baby. Dead or alive, she cannot do it.

And so, she cannot run. The motion would jar Keena into shrills of terror or hurt her soft, nearly boneless structure, so new to this air. Even if she were willing to leave her daughter behind, Bethesda might not be able to run home in time. She is still mending after labor. She had a healthy delivery, and she wears no injuries, but she is far weaker than she used to be. She is pale, fatigued, breathless. She lost a lot of blood, and it is still slowly filling back in.

Bethesda turns to look at the spilled box cart. Aside from the splintered, detached wheel, it seems whole enough. In one spot some of the metal trim that reinforces the wooden structure is bent up, but none of it is missing or cracked.

Keena's fussing begins to escalate, her little mew rising from a mouth full of gums.

There is no other choice.

Bethesda hurries past the oxen and prepares for the climb up over the side of the cart. At one animal's huff, she pauses, weighing the benefit of keeping them reined or letting them go. Her heart wants to set them free. Her womb wants to grant them the mercy of a peaceful death. Her head sees them as a possible diversion, almost a sacrifice. But then her gut tells her the truth: they are a beacon.

She has no time to unbuckle their harnesses. She draws her blade with one smooth, habitual motion and slices through the straps. They need no word, no gesture to realize they're free. The already over-exhausted beasts take off at a lope toward home.

Bethesda has time to wonder if she's just made a grave mistake, and then she hears it.

From the mountains that run parallel to the open plain between villages, the sound floats up and out, seeking like its own living thing. A nightbird calls.

It is a song unlike any other. It is achingly familiar, the echo of every person's nightmares, and yet different every time. It seems to bring dusk, sweeping it across the sky like storm clouds. It seeks, out and out, touching every blade of grass, every jagged rock, every living being standing out in the open, stilled with fear.

In her village, some say the nightbirds can see things using only their voices. Others say they cast spells. Whatever their magic, real or legend-twisted, Bethesda feels their waking presence like a finger run down the long side of her neck.

The wagon it will be. Must be. "That *is* what it's designed for," she whispers, merely a breath on Keena's hot cheek.

Whether Keena quiets at her mother's voice or the nightbird's call, Bethesda doesn't know, but she takes the opportunity to climb into the spilled cart. She lands with a thump on the bottom, once the other side door, her knees buckling partly beneath her since she can't put her hands down to soften her fall. She rocks back on her heels and lands against the wall, once the ceiling. Keena sucks in a tiny breath, ready to protest the jolt no doubt, and Bethesda forces her aching legs to push her up, reaching, stretching to draw the door strap down.

It slams into its opening, muffling the nightbird's eerie cry and dropping them into absolute blackness.

She has to drag one of her crates over to latch the door above them one-handed, but she manages, fumbling with increasing franticness as Keena's whines grow into wails.

Pain. Hunger.

The reason for the trip. Bethesda had made the journey because Keena wasn't nursing well. She was losing weight instead of gaining, and she cried all the time, falling asleep only from sheer exhaustion and waking just as hungry. The midwife in their village didn't know how to help her, but there was an older, more experienced midwife across the plains. Despite her aunt's assurances that the baby just needed time to grow, Bethesda knew something was wrong. She insisted on going, even when no one could take the days to ride with her.

It turned out that Keena had an attachment between her tongue and bottom jaw, hidden deep, deep in the back of her flesh, that the younger midwife had missed. It was carefully severed, and the pain of nursing lifted immediately, although the child was in new pain instead of hunger.

To feed her, now, is a risk. Will the comfort of Bethesda's breast and the fullness of milk calm her, or will the pain of sucking send her into even more crying?

It's all she knows to try.

The nightbird's cry grows more distant, bringing momentary relief, but then it swoops louder, and Bethesda knows that dusk has dropped, and that the creature has left its roost in the mountains to soar the sky.

Her fingers tremble as she fumbles with her garments, offering a breast to her infant. "Sweet darling," she whispers. A tiny gasp and then the small, wet pressure of a mouth around her nipple. Bethesda can't see if the latch is good or not in the dark. "My honeyheart. Good girl. Big girl."

Keena falls still, suckling, sniffing softly as she drinks.

Tears spring to Bethesda's eyes. The relief is so great that she can't feel the triumph, the victory. She'd been right. Right to go, right to risk the travel. That had been the problem. But under the circumstances, she feels the deflate of gratitude rather than the swell of success.

Even that is short-lived. The nightbird's call grows louder, stranger, sent out like creeping claws to scour the terrain. It will find the cart. It will find them.

It can't get in. That's what the carts are built for.

But their cart is crashed, vulnerable.

Perhaps if Keena stays quiet the creature will not bother exploring them. Perhaps tonight there is easier prey. The oxen, maybe, if they haven't made it to the village safe beneath its thick canopy of trees.

With that thought, as if the thought had made it happen, an ox bellows a deep, shrieking scream in the distance.

Bethesda senses rather than feels Keena look up, consider unlatching. She balances the child in one arm, uses her other hand to squeeze her breast the way the midwife showed her, encouraging milk to flow into her baby's weak mouth. Keena's sucking resumes. Bethesda wishes she could sit, but the bench is vertical now, a column that she can only awkwardly rest her shoulder against.

She could relight the candle if she could find it in the wreckage, but the prospect of trying to do that one-handed while keeping Keena calm seems worse than staying blind. Maybe the darkness will put the baby to sleep, like when they cover the cribs with heavy blankets to block out the sun during naps.

Keena's small sounds tell Bethesda that she is finishing on the first side. The sky has grown silent as the nightbird feasts, but it doesn't take long for them to devour their catches. Sometimes they even leave them and come back later to carry them away. Normally she would burp the infant before switching sides, to be sure she doesn't spit up what milk she's managed to get, but she always cries when Bethesda does that. She can't tell her child that even the brief minutes between sides are temporary, that she will be put back to the breast in mere moments, that she needn't wail so at the delay; this is better than losing what nutrition she's gained.

She bares her other breast, slips a pinky into the corner of Keena's mouth to break the seal, and flips her for the other side before she can do more than draw in an inhale to cry.

A moment of seeking, and a new latch.

Bethesda gulps in a broken sigh.

The nightbird calls again, much closer. The sound sends Bethesda's shoulders up to her ears, but she forces them down, tries to relax her muscles like she's been taught, so that Keena stays relaxed too. It will be beyond dusk, now. Darkness has fallen.

Sharp, wiry trills test the walls of the cart. The wheels creak in a downdraft of large, taut wings. Leather and metal shuffles as if the oxen's leads have been ruffled, and the cries end.

It's the worst silence Bethesda has ever heard. She feels lightheaded with it, her eyes inventing shapes in the dark, seeking reason.

She imagines the creature out there, large as the cart itself but far more delicate—graceful, even. The strange way they stand on their bent hind legs, wings folded up and over their own backs like exaggerated elbows. Uncannily human faces cocking side to side, listening. Elongated snouts full of serrated teeth.

A soft barrage of squeaks encircles the cart, testing, seeking.

Breathless silence. Keena's oblivious sucking.

And then, so gently that Bethesda stills instead of jumping, a tap. On the door now at the roof. Curious.

Bethesda doesn't move, doesn't breathe. Keena is blessedly silent but for swallows so quiet she has to strain to hear them, but she can hear them. She has practiced hearing them, to tell if the baby is still drinking or if she's simply suckling. They're slowing down, drawing further apart from each other. Bethesda's milk will be emptied soon.

Sometimes the child will suckle herself to sleep on the breast. Sometimes when she runs out she'll unlatch and begin to wail.

Another tap on the ceiling door. Two more. Three. A series of clicks almost polite in their inquisitiveness.

Bethesda can picture the nightbird's long, many-jointed digits extending off the pads at the middle joint of their wings, which they use as front feet or hands when not flying.

Tap, tap, tap.

This time, from the side that was once the floor. Moving all along its surface, testing, testing. Listening to the hollowness of the structure. Hearing them in that middle?

Bethesda wishes she'd laid down on the floor, in case it's true that the nightbirds can see with sounds. Perhaps then it would brush over her shape among the scattered cart contents as just more rubbish, not a living, standing thing.

She dares not move now. She stands still as a tree trunk, fighting rigidity with forced calm, lest her sudden panic send Keena into a fit.

Tap tap tap tap tap tap tap. Moving around to the other side of the cart. *Tapping. Tap-ping. Tap tap tap-ping ping ping.* Its finger finding wood and metal, wood and metal, drawing out the structure and strength in its mind.

Keena's suction eases, changes. She's finished. Bethesda has become quite practiced at noticing this shift, because it's when she's supposed to unlatch the child. Letting her suckle wears out her weak jaw muscles without bringing in new nutrition. But before she understood that, Bethesda had let Keena comfort suckle for as long as she wanted. Her baby would sometimes fall asleep there, the nipple slipping out minutes later, the darling limp and heavy, head nestled wherever it fell and Bethesda holding still, so still, cherishing it even as she longed for a break.

It has been a while since she's allowed that, since the tongue attachment. A baby's world changes hour to hour, day to day. Will Keena still want to?

The lack of tapping unnerves Bethesda even more than its progression. They say the nightbirds can work their talons almost like human fingers—that they are almost human-smart in using those long, segmented digits to seek their quarry.

Metal groans. The loose bracing. It's prying the piece back. It found the one weak spot to manipulate.

A chill races through Bethesda; cool air has gotten into the cart and her shoulders are exposed. Cool air means a gap. A gap means space for a talon to slip in, to begin prying open the boards.

Keena stirs, starts to shift. Bethesda sways, ever so carefully, to soothe her.

The wooden planks beneath her feet creak, once, loud as thunder through the dark.

She holds her breath, listening.

Keena resumes a lazy suckle, but Bethesda can't relax.

The looming presence outside gives one low, moaning siren. She thinks this is it, that the bird is crying victory. Then comes the sound of strong, thin wings beating the sky. Loud, higher, growing distant.

It's gone.

Bethesda is so stunned that she stops swaying. Keena no longer notices, content to suckle herself to sleep in the darkness.

Why would the nightbird leave? It had them. It might've taken all night, but it would've been able to wrest its way into this broken box cart before dawn. The nightbirds stop at nothing.

Yet, this one has left.

She should run. While she has a chance, she should run. She can strap Keena to her using the swaddle and smother her face to her chest and pray and run and run.

But what if it's still out there? They are known to be uncannily intelligent. Could it be so very clever as to sound like it's flown away only to land and walk back on silent feet? Could it be standing nearby again already, waiting with head cocked to one side for her to come out, making its job swifter?

Leaving now seems unbelievably risky. Even if that creature has left for some unknowable reason, another nightbird could find them at any moment. Especially if Keena begins crying. If Bethesda begins running, the baby most certainly will. Won't she?

Bethesda's breath is shallowing, coming fast.

Not necessarily. The jolts and bumps of the cart rolling over ruts and rocks seemed to lull her calm. Maybe, if Bethesda is careful, her running can do the same?

She has to stop wondering. She has no other viable choice. Now that the cart is broken open, staying is a death sentence.

Waiting for even a short length of time would allow Keena to fall into a deeper sleep, but she doesn't have that time. In the darkness of the cart, she fumbles through unlatching and wrapping her daughter to her chest, tighter than usual, doubling the knot behind her lower back. She makes sure she can still draw her blade. Squatting achily, she feels around on the floor for her canteen and drinks all the water left. Then she stands, lightheaded already with blood loss and what's to come, and pushes over a box to stand on so she can reach the door at the ceiling.

If the nightbird stands by, it will hear even her quietest movements. But she is careful anyway, forcing herself steady through her building dread. If it's gone, she doesn't want to draw the attention of another. She doesn't know how many there are. They are territorial, so there's a chance not too many hunt here, but it's a grand sky.

Bethesda's arms tremble as she pushes open the door. The night is lighter than the cart was, full of lingering light and the glimmer of thousands of stars. The fresh scent of it makes her realize she's sweating enormously, comically, a postpartum effect that made the cart smell musty and panicked.

She waits for wings to send wind down her spine. She waits for talons to stab her. She waits for teeth to clamp around her throat.

Every direction she can see is open, empty.

No more time for awe.

Keena shifts, and Bethesda knows from endless nights swaying that steady motion is better than sporadic, and so she hurries down to the earth, still warm from the day. Many of the women in her village wear skirts, but after birth Bethesda switched to high pants, not liking the loose, could-spill feeling of her guts still tightening back into place. She is grateful for it now, grateful for the miraculous recovery of her strange new body. She prays it will be enough.

The winds push her forward, and she obliges.

She walks past the cut reins, scent of ox still clinging. When she's beyond the rig, she's utterly exposed. There are no hiding places in the wide plain. Nothing to run to but her beyond-sight village. Nowhere to take cover.

Her pace is swift and smooth as she can make it, though she occasionally stumbles on ruts and clumps of weed. Her moccasins are too tight, her feet larger than they used to be. They aren't swollen anymore—she still remembers the shock of how they expanded in the last week of pregnancy, and still more the days immediately after birth—but they are still larger, and softer, the bones shifted and strange, like walking in someone else's skin. They ache.

Her hips ache, changed too.

Everything aches. Her back is tight and knotted at the bottom of her spine, because Keena is in a phase where she wants to be able to look up at her as she's held. With that thought, Bethesda glances down, peeking under the wrap to see if she's asleep. Keena dozes, lips parted, cheek smushed against Bethesda's chest, eyes hooded. Good. Good enough.

She walks faster.

Somewhere, far away and perhaps in the mountains, comes another nightbird call. Bethesda imagines it sailing out like the creature's wings, spanning and coasting until they find moving shapes, like her, and then folding, landing, feeling with those long, segmented fingers, tapping, testing.

The sensation is so vivid that a shudder climbs her back and jolts her into a violent spasm. Her poor nipples throb with the goosebumps, leaking, and she prays the smell doesn't set Keena off again.

Another near-stumble sets her into a jog, but the extra bounce makes Keena huff, so she slows back into her longest stride, walking. A glance at the sky.

She pushes her body, wishing for the noise of her home trees. Wishing for the easy cacophony of night where the skies are blocked, where things roam and burrow and climb and go about their business. Not this hush, only the wind whistling past her ears like a long-held breath.

By the time the tree-line appears as a dark blur up ahead, Bethesda is panting and trembling. Keena coos, and when Bethesda looks down she finds her baby has managed to peek her head from under the wrap and is gazing up at her. When Bethesda looks into her large, serious eyes, she strokes the soft, fuzzy head and doesn't so much sing as hum, making no sound but that which will vibrate through her chest so Keena can feel it.

Keena smiles.

Bethesda's mouth parts, and the hum halts for a moment. The smile is tiny, toothless, a single dimple winking in her cheek. It is her first.

Tightness springing up her throat to prick her eyes, Bethesda smiles back.

Darling, she wants to say. *My little starflower. Keena.* But she dares not speak.

She wishes that Keena hadn't woken, and the thought stabs her with guilt.

Then the call comes, joyful, sneaking, and far too close.

She whirls, searching.

Rising from the mountains, the dark, menacing shape of a nightbird in full flight. Bethesda's feet stutter, her thighs on fire with the effort to keep her from falling. Her hands clench reflexively on Keena's bundled back, and the squeeze makes the child whine.

"*Shh*," she whispers. "*Shhh-shh shhhhhh.*"

A second shape ascends behind the first. Smaller. At first Bethesda thinks it's even farther away, but then she sees its clumsiness, its slower pace, the way it shadows the large one.

It's a juvenile. Its offspring.

The adult who found them earlier and left—it hadn't given up or gotten distracted. There was easy prey and time to teach. It had gone back to get her young.

It is a mother.

The two nightbirds' cries twist into a beautiful, chilling song. They speak to each other. The small one flaps its wings quickly to keep up, the large one riding the thermals to slow her pace.

Bethesda knows in a depth beyond reason that they've already been spotted. They are found. They are what the creatures come for.

Mothers stop at nothing.

She breaks into a run.

Three things happen at once. Her knees buckle at the sudden jolt, the joints still soft and elastic, but she catches herself on the next step and manages to stay upright. Keena explodes into a wail. And Bethesda's bleeding, which had slowed to sporadic clouds of pink, resumes in earnest, spilling in a gush so hot it seems to scald the insides of her thighs.

It doesn't matter. It can't matter right now.

Bethesda finds her strange feet, her footing, her tired legs and her hip joints and her bowed back and she runs. She runs as fast as she can make her body answer. After not long at all, Keena's sobbing fades to confused little grunts and hiccups. She likes the motion, but not the jolting. Not the pounding heartbeat that is usually slow, steady, her comfort rhythm.

Bethesda tries, tries so hard to look forward, not up. If they come, they come. Watching them come will only slow her down.

But she does, up and over her shoulder to see how they gain.

Close enough to see the details of their silhouettes. Close enough to see the mother crane her flexible neck to keep an eye on the juvenile.

The ground, flat from a distance but subtly curved in its natural course, has been rising. Over this gentle rise, a line of trees grows, small, dark, safe.

Too far.

Keena's protests have become wet, bubbly mouth sounds. Happy. She likes it.

Not so very far.

Bethesda worries about her baby's little neck. She cradles her with both hands despite the snug wrap.

The wind feels even colder in contrast to her heated skin. Her hair has come free in vicious little strips that whip her face. She can't catch her breath. She puts every ounce of her energy toward home. She stares at the trees and wills them closer, larger. She will drag them near with the sheer intensity of her desire.

Above, behind, closer still, a new call. A short series of sharp prods. A pause. Bethesda risks a glance up to see the mother turn toward her offspring, waiting.

The juvenile sends out a call of its own. Fragile, testing.

What she pictures, as the mother swoops low behind her, is the way their knuckles feel. She's held one, once, detached. One of the hunters came back with a nightbird. The meat was tough and bitter, but he kept its hand for pride. Their leathery, rough skin is even thicker at those long appendages, but right at the knuckles, where the joints fold into several curving segments, little tufts of soft, downy fur protrude, like starflower fluff.

The mother dives so low behind her that the power of her massive wings sends the wind backwards, into her back, and it smells of clean minerals and cool caves.

No blow comes.

The mother lifts off, her form casting shadow under the starlight.

Bethesda's blood has soaked through her pants, sticking the material to her skin. Her feet are going numb. She runs faster.

A keening, desperate cry splits the sky like a slice of lightning.

Something slams into her upper shoulders.

Bethesda falls. In slow horror she falls, desperate not to let go of Keena, desperate to put her hands down to catch them—to keep her baby from landing first. She doesn't have time to choose, to realize that the wrap will hold Keena and she can let go, but her instinct chooses for her.

Her wrists slam into the grassy dirt, followed by her knees. She bites her tongue. Somehow, she manages to slide forward onto her face, neck bowing near to breaking to hold Keena off the earth. She is braced in the cave of her mother's body. All the impact vibrates up Bethesda's arms and thighs. Her belly and spine have done something awful, something sharp and straining. Her cheek is scraped raw.

Keena shrieks, a cry so fierce and angry that for a moment the juvenile nightbird goes silent above them, flapping to lift away once it realizes that it didn't get a grip.

Bethesda never stops running. She uses the fall to launch herself up and faster, an arrow shot from a bow, and she screams, rage and pain spilling from her mouth as she charges toward home.

The trees. She can smell the trees. Their sweet, sappy trunks and their thick, dense leaves. The wind brings them to her, rushing past.

Both nightbirds flap up and away, but she knows they aren't leaving. They're too large to make tight turns. They have to strike from above as they plunge down.

The space between her shoulder blades is bleeding, scraped or punctured.

Bethesda can hear her own breath, hoarse, rasping, gasping.

They won't make it. It's close but still too far. Lights glint between the crowded trees. Someone from the village has heard or spotted them, sounded the alarm. But no one will come from safety to help.

Her husband would have.

The rest would tell her, if they could, to leave the child, save herself.

But mothers stop at nothing.

Her knees wobble and threaten to give with each pounding step. The lack of cries from above is ominous. Are they far, circling, or are they so confident of her placement that they don't need to sound her anymore? Are they already gliding in for the next strike?

She shouldn't look. She should stay focused on the woods, drawing near. She should fight not to fall. She should save every single drop of energy for speed.

The wind shifts ever so slightly at her back.

Without thought, she darts to the left.

The sharp hind talons of the mother grasp empty air to her right. The bottom of her wing's central fold brushes Bethesda's hair.

There's no mistaking the cry this time. Fury. Bethesda, still hugging Keena tight despite the wrap, glances at her back as she soars up and around.

The juvenile will be next. Mimicking, learning.

She's close enough to the tree-line now to hear shouts from villagers. What flashes in her mind isn't the hunters who might be standing there, bows and arrows poised uselessly. It isn't the elders or her midwife, too sorry to watch. It's her hut, empty now that her husband is gone, but still safe, still smelling of him and milk and the smoke from their hearth.

This time she doesn't feel wind. She doesn't hear wings. She doesn't know how she knows that the young nightbird is striking, but somehow, she does.

She darts to the right.

It learns quickly. It saw her dodge its mother, knows that trick. It splays its hind feet wide, bending one wing directly to her left, and it knocks her. Not the talons this time, but some bony part.

Bethesda grunts, flailing, and she somehow grabs an edge of wing as she falls.

They are a tussle of arms and soft, taut skin.

Keena is a background siren, constant, shrieking. The nightbird is silent but for one panicked bleat. Bethesda grunts with effort.

She can't see beyond the underside of the creature but in fits and flashes, glimmers of the trees so close, so close now, just one more attacking swoop away from making it. Two more lucky dodges.

She dives into her fall, rolling over her shoulder and slamming onto her back to save Keena from being crushed. She tries to sit up, launch forward again, but her belly muscles don't respond. The delay panics her. She rolls to her side, coming face to face with the young nightbird.

She stares into its strange, brilliant black eyes, and she feels it see her. She senses its fear, its regret at the mistakes that brought it to this moment in its young life.

She, too, feels that.

Her chest is drenched in her sweat and Keena's spit, pooling from her open mouth. Her daughter cries so hard that she no longer makes sound, unable to catch breath to keep wailing through her distress. All blood to her face.

The nightbird gathers itself as Bethesda does, folding its wings in and down, so the hands balance on the earth like front paws, wing tips up and back stretching above its head. Bethesda rolls to her side and shoves herself up on one wobbly arm, panting. With her and it both standing, it's scarcely taller than her at the eyes. Very young. This may even be its first flight.

It cocks its face, so bizarrely human, to one side, then winds its neck around like a snake before striking. Its long, snout spreads to reveal rows of tiny, serrated teeth, a pointed tongue.

Bethesda knows it's coming. She whirls to the side, backing away as she draws her blade. It's far too short. To reach she'll have to be deathly close to that striking mouth.

As fast as her feet can take her, she backs away, too afraid to take her gaze off the creature. It lurches forward, eyeing, she thinks, her blade held out in front. It won't take long for it to realize that the blade doesn't pose much threat. It's probably the first time it's ever seen one.

She senses, in some subtle movement of its body, a weight shift, a wing tilt—she's not sure—that it's about to strike again.

With one arm shielding Keena, Bethesda leaps back, slashing frantically with the blade. The creature ducks the first and edges around and under, bobbing lower than she realized it could go.

She slices back up and catches the side of its face. A gash opens. It jerks its head back, letting out a piercing, unearthly howl.

She hadn't realized that they'd both grown silent until she hears it. Not both. All. The nightbird, her, Keena.

Keena. Her daughter has fallen silent.

Bethesda's body, already alight with terror, seems to catch fire.

Every instinct in her exhausted body tells her to look down. To check her baby.

Bethesda flexes her neck, resisting forcibly. She cannot look away from the predator in front of her. A glance won't help no matter what's wrong, and it could cost both their lives.

Jogging backward, Bethesda clutches the baby with her free arm, trying to focus on the animal, not the warmth through the wrap, not the wetness that could be anything. Home. She must get home. Home, home, home.

The nightbird tracks her every motion, head swaying on that eerie neck, keeping her guessing, making her track its every motion as well. Almost like it's distracting her.

A chill rips up Bethesda's spine. The hair on her neck tingles.

The silence. The silence was more than the three of them.

It was all four of them.

She has no time to look or doubt or even guess. She just acts.

Her back is exposed. She feels its nakedness as if her dress has been stripped away. She is made of soft, tender meat.

Bethesda dives forward, into the juvenile, toward its strange hind feet and massive trunk. She drops her blade to break her fall, twisting so she doesn't land on Keena. Her shoulder grinds into the ground. Pain sears down her left side.

Wind gushes from every direction at once.

The young nightbird screeches.

Bethesda scrambles, trying to avoid the wing that smacks her, but she can't gain purchase. The youth's front hand grabs her ankle at the same time that the mother nightbird slams into it, unable to stop her attack. Her long, wicked talons dive into her child's body.

The force of it drags Bethesda along and several feet off the ground before the young nightbird releases her ankle. She knows with certainty that it's dead, already, being carried away by the mother, who now sings violently of her outrage.

Bethesda is up and running. Somehow, before she knows, she is sprinting as fast as she can go—faster than she's ever gone, injuries and numbness and bleeding and all—toward the trees.

Both arms brace Keena as tightly as she can, now too afraid to look down for a different reason.

Instead, she glances up, back.

The nightbird flies with her child in her grip, beating the night itself with her massive wings, descending, turning already. To set the youth down? Bethesda looks forward so she doesn't trip. She can't feel one leg, but it's working. The creature will have to release the body if she's to attack again.

The voices of her villagers draw louder. Their words mean nothing to her, but she can hear them now. She can't see their faces for their lights, but she knows every eye is trained on her. She doesn't care.

A wail of agony so pure it seems ripped from Bethesda's own ribcage finds her, pushes her back. Faster, faster, faster. One glance.

The mother has set her child down. She ascends again, no doubt gaining height and speed for her last attack.

Home is so close.

But without her baby? Without her husband or her darling girl? How can she live?

Bethesda's knee folds. She screams, dropping to her knees and then her hands. Her body seems to stop. To crumple. Her clothes are soaked through, every last scrap of them, with blood and sweat and tears and pain. She can't go anymore. She has nothing left to give.

She can imagine the nightbird bulleting toward her now, gaining speed, hyper-focused and with no distractions, no obstacles. This time, she won't miss. Bethesda's head drops, hair mingling with the grass.

Keena's tiny scream blasts her in the face. Small, ragged, rageful.

Alive.

Bethesda shoves with something she didn't know she had. She stands, steps. Her knee wobbles, but holds. She steps again. Pain, fresh waves of pain through all the numbness. But she can go. She goes.

She all but flies.

Behind her, the air shifts and parts for the monster who wants to eat them.

Bethesda pumps her legs and arms, letting Keena be held by the wrap as she pelts toward the safety of the trees.

The nightbird doesn't bother with stealth. It hisses hoarsely as it glides toward her. It is only a race. There will be no dodging, no fighting.

The villagers have faces now. A barrage of arrows dot her periphery, but no one dares risk hitting her, and the creature is directly behind her now. She can feel it. Hear it. Smell it.

Just arms' reach away. Surely. Surely.

Bethesda stretches her arms in front as if touching the bark of the closest trees alone will be enough. She leans forward.

The villagers all scuffle back and to the side, making room for her between the trunks.

Three more strides.

Two.

The glance of something touching her back.

The nightbird roars.

Bethesda bursts into the shade of the forest.

A loud crashing. The creature slams into the trees.

Bethesda slows and turns. It struggles to free its wings. It looks directly into her eyes and opens its mouth to make a sound that Bethesda has no name for.

Wrapping her wailing babe in her arms, swaying the way she has countless nights of sleepless feedings and singing, Bethesda makes the sound back.

In that moment, the two mothers understand each other.

A man shouts. The villagers have gone quiet.

"Don't shoot!" Bethesda commands.

The nightbird can't fit through the tree trunks so close together. Standing on the ground she senses her weakness here. Wings folded up above her head so she can run across the grass, she turns and streaks away, running, running, running, and then she spreads her arms and unfolds her wings and she's soaring into the night sky, silent.

Bethesda wants to collapse. Instead, she carefully pulls Keena from the wrap and lets the fabric drop to the ground as she brings her crying daughter to her neck, murmuring, swaying, singing.

"Keena," she says aloud. "Keena, Keena, Keena, my child."

Keena sings her hot-faced outrage with milky breath, and Bethesda sobs.

In all the world, there is only them.

AUTHOR NOTES

I've been delighted with the reactions to my story. Lots of wonderful reviews about the thrilling pacing and action, but most importantly to me, many readers who've never seen a postpartum, breastfeeding mother portrayed as a protagonist before, especially in speculative fiction. What a massive gap in representation! I love that I can bring some of my own experiences as a mother to the page and make more people feel seen. One reader was so moved as to start contemplating motherhood in new ways in their own life. To know that my work has reached people so deeply is the best gift I could ask for as a writer, and I'm incredibly grateful.

A LOVE THAT BURNS HOT ENOUGH TO LAST: DELETED SCENES FROM A DOCUMENTARY

SAM J. MILLER

*... I heard the music of true forgiveness
filling the theater, conferring on all
who sat there perfect absolution.*

—Amadeus

Nyssa. Backup singer.

Ti came to see me, you know. Three four days before she died. Knocked right on my door, and I've never been so surprised in all my life. This is a woman who when we were on tour would have the driver drive her halfway down the block rather than walk to the store—and somehow she's pounding on my front door, five stories up, in a building with no elevator. Not even breathing heavy. At first I thought she must have stood there and waited 'til she caught her breath, wiped the sweat all off her face. But then I remembered how Ti was never one to give a shit what other people thought, which is why she was forever showing up to major network interviews and award show red carpets looking sweaty and strung out. So that's how I knew—*she's still got it, some of it, stored up, and she can still do the impossible when there's no other option.*

I laughed, right in her face. The legend, the icon, the diva, the woman whose voice was called a "national treasure"—standing there in the filthy hallway of a shitty building in the bottom end of Hollywood. Place had seen better days, that was for damn sure, but so had I. So had she.

I felt bad, soon as the laugh was out of my mouth. I'd seen the stories. How the drugs had fucked her up, made her erratic, prone to bizarre and destructive behavior. I'd watched the shambles of a show she put on, opening up Fashion Week four years back. So I should have known. *Great job, Nyssa—Ti finally comes to apologize to you, and you fuck it up.* But you know what she did? She laughed. She laughed the way she used to laugh, and she couldn't stop, and then neither could I, and then we hugged so hard I could feel how thin she was, under the mink.

Davey. Employee.

You know the story. You've seen the news clips and the *Behind the Music* episodes and the biopics: the poor kid from the Chicago projects, her church-obsessed single mom, how Ti spent every spare moment of her childhood there, singing her little heart out. How that safe and stunting space celebrated her, and how it maimed her. How she got on television; how she captured the heart of America from the first moment and didn't let it go until she died.

And you know the second half. You've seen the comedians making fun of her, the embarrassing interviews. You already know how the most beautiful and talented woman in America married the lowlife creep record executive who used to be her manager, who made her, and then decided to destroy her—how he hooked her on spiderwebbing and kept her virtually captive for years, until she clawed her way free of him and launched a comeback ... but by then her voice had been destroyed—the voice that reached into your heart and touched something soft and sacred, something you didn't know had survived this sick world until she hit that One Note, and then you were crying and you didn't know why because you were so fucking full of joy. And without the voice, what else was there to live for? And so she died.

You know that story. But you don't know the truth.

Brent. Fan.

I was there. They say it was her finest moment, and I sure can't disagree with that. Fresh off the boat from the streets of Caracas, war still echoing in our ears, me and three thousand soldiers crowded into a San Diego naval hanger and eight million people watching from home.

I was so country, I'd never heard of Ti before I got to Venezuela. Wouldn't have gone, if Leo hadn't literally slapped me upside the head and said, *boy, you miss this and you're too big a fool for me to waste any more of my time with.* I never could say no to Leo. He got us there stupid early because he was from New York, and he knew that if you were serious about finding a good spot it meant arriving so far ahead of time you might have to stand around "like a putz" for several hours, but that was actually the best part because then you'd be surrounded by all the other true fans, and you'd have plenty to talk about with them, and we did, or at least Leo did, and even though I was still too shy to say much it was still so impressive to see him operate, how he could disarm anyone with just a few words and—most importantly—that smile.

You can see us in the HBO special—the first concert to rack up a trillion views. A handful of soldiers pressed against the stage, staring up at her. You can see his arm around my shoulders. My folks sure saw it. Hoo-boy, did they.

Carolina. Faith-based family values advocate.

Her success was one more sign of how sick we are as a society. Everyone throwing money at her, putting her on every channel of the television, every accursed page of the whole blighted internet. The Super Bowl, for the love of God. The national anthem. Every home in America opening wide its doors and welcoming her in. When everyone could see her for what she was: a witch.

That's right, I said it. A witch. You probably think there's no such thing as witches. Demons, corrupters, whatever you want to call them—there are people out there with unholy power, who are using that power to suck our children dry.

You know her name was short for Tiamat, don't you? They never tell you that part. To this day her army of drones keep it scrubbed from all her 'pedia pages.

Tiamat. A Babylonian dragon goddess. You can't get much more Satanic than that.

I'll tell you my journey. How I came to this fight, how we worked to stop her agenda of evil and exploitation. You probably think we're pretty ignorant, a bunch of Puritan loonies. Everyone does. You probably think we were a lost cause, because we didn't get her taken off the air, banished from the worldwide web. But didn't we, though? Didn't God see our struggle, hear our cry to the heavens, and take care of it for us?

Davey. Employee.

First thing you got to understand is, Ti wasn't nobody's victim. She made her own mistakes, and most of the time she knew damn well what was she was doing when she made them. People make her man out to be the villain, but that's giving him way too much credit. Blaming that dirty old man is like blaming the bottle the liquor comes in. He didn't start her on the drugs, and he wasn't why she got hooked. He leaned in to the villain role hard, because it made him feel like he mattered to her story, but he wasn't shit, and everyone around her knew he wasn't shit. So did she, for that matter. Only stuck with him to spite people.

He was just one more bottom feeder who wanted some of what she had. And I'm not talking about the money. He had plenty of his own, even if he was shit about how he handled it.

You know what I'm talking about. What she had. What Ti could do. What her voice did. Lots of people could smell it on her. Even if their brains didn't know what it was, or outright denied it was real, their bodies thirsted for it. Our skin knows magic when it's near, even if our brains deny it.

Nyssa. Backup singer.

I can still do her voice, after all this time. Act her out like she was right here with us.

"You look like shit, Nyssa," she said, and laughed.

"Look who's talking," I said, laughing too, because we actually looked pretty fucking fantastic for a couple of old broads. Who'd been through a lot. "You want some coffee?"

"That stuff is poison," Ti said.

"So, yes?" And she followed me into the kitchen and watched me make it, the way you'd stare at a magician doing a particularly inscrutable trick. She never could do a damn thing for herself, and had a weird sort of awe for people who could.

"To what do I owe the honor?" I asked.

She opened her mouth, all bluster and good cheer, but no words came out. She slumped into a chair at my kitchen table, not seeing the mess heaped up all around her. Made me feel like a slob, but then again she did tell Oprah on TikTok that her man used to paint bloody screaming mouths and Shakespeare quotes on all the walls and furniture of their fancy home, so I figured no amount of slovenliness would seem strange to her.

"I'm sorry, Nyssa," she said.

I screwed the top on the greca and turned the burner on and hurried to her side.

"Coming in your house, bringing my sob story around."

"*Shh*," I said, and took her hands. They'd always been small, but now they were just bones wrapped in rubbed-thin velvet. "What happened, honey?"

"It's gone," she said, and I could hear her struggle to keep her voice in line. "It's gone, and now I don't even know if it was ever real."

She pulled her hands away.

"That's why I came," she said. "To talk to you. You were always honest with me, Nyssa. That's probably why they made me fire you."

"Hush," I said, and went back to the stove to have something to look at other than her. From old reflex, because she'd never ever wanted to talk about it—but also because I wasn't going to let her off so easy, blaming what went down on the people around her.

"I need you to tell me, Nyssa. Whether or not it was real."

Brent. Fan.

She was so much bigger than I'd imagined. Chubbier. Somehow I'd never seen a picture of her. And every pop star I'd ever seen had been a skinny little thing, so when she stepped out on stage my first thought was maybe this was a trick. It wasn't a kind thought, and I felt pretty bad about it. But then she started singing.

Soon as she opened her mouth, I felt it. We all did. Ti started with the "Star-Spangled Banner" and we put our hands on our hearts and we shut our eyes or we stared at her or we looked at the ground and remembered bloody pavement, dead friends, terrible things we'd done, and maybe it was a half-assed war for no good reason but it'd fucked us up just the same, and our fathers were poor and our mommas were drunks and our siblings were in jail or on meth or webbing and our prospects were slim—but here she came, this voice like an angel—sounds like a cliché when you say it, *voice like an angel*, but this wasn't that, this was real, some biblical shit, the piercing trumpet or celestial messenger that tells you nothing will ever be the same, you're gonna have God's baby or you've gotta go to some city full of sinners and tell them to repent or God's wrath will come upon them, and don't even *think* about trying to flee because He'll send a fucking whale to come swallow you up—my mom and dad were big church folks, as I guess you can tell, I must have spent every Sunday of my youth there—and here came this voice, slipping past the heavily-defended perimeter of my self like an insurgent rigged to explode, burrowing deep into me, and it—I don't know how to say this—it *took* something, something warm and blissful from deep inside my chest and sucked it right out of me, and I let it, I gave it freely, I never knew how much of it I had to give, almost like the more I lost the more I had, almost like she was giving me something even as she took it, and she had so much to give, and I was sobbing, and we all were.

Leo grabbed my hand and his fingers laced into mine and it didn't even enter my mind to be afraid, or ashamed, or try to hide it.

Nyssa. Backup singer.

I didn't answer her. How could I? I'd spent so long trying *not* to think or talk about ... it ... that I couldn't be sure either, anymore, what *it* even was. And there were times when I wondered, too. Whether it was real. So I did something dumb, which is what I tend to do when I'm uncomfortable.

"You talked to Lark lately?"

Taboo to speak of her. And to use the nickname, invoking the fondness and intimacy we'd all felt for Lark. An even deeper betrayal.

"Child, Lark don't want no part of me," Ti said sadly. Her lack of anger was so much worse than the rage I'd expected. And deserved. For daring to summon her up.

"You don't know that. I would have said *I* didn't want no part of you, before you showed up on my doorstep five minutes ago."

"She stormed out of my life and she didn't return any of my calls. Five years I tried."

"You stormed out of mine. You didn't return my calls."

"It's different," Ti said.

"Different how?"

She just shrugged. But I knew what she meant. It was different because she was ready to look me in the eye and confront what had happened between us. What she'd done. How her weakness had hurt me. I knew *that* the second she showed up, even if we hadn't gotten around to it yet. She wouldn't have come if she wasn't ready for me to tear her ass up over it.

But what she'd had with Lark? What she'd done to *her*? No way in hell she was ready to look *that* little issue in the eye and take it.

Davey. Employee.

Everyone knew. What Ti and Lark were. How could you not, being out on the road together, all of our lives jumbled up like vegetables in a stew pot? We saw what was going on, and we didn't say anything, same way we didn't say anything about the bassist shooting heroin or a backup singer smacking her kid. Maybe that sounds harsh to you now, comparing what she and Lark were to abuse or addiction, and maybe that's not the way we'd think about it now, but I was pretty ignorant when I fell into her orbit, and back then, to me—it was just one more way they were human. I've worked with some of the biggest names in the business, and let me tell you—when you're up close and personal with someone, you lose sight of the superstar right quick, and all you're left with is the human.

Carolina. Faith-based family values advocate.

After that HBO show, I brought her up in my church group. Asked if anyone had seen it. They all had. And they all loved it! *Don't you see?* I asked. *Don't you see what she is? What she's doing?* They didn't see. Or they didn't care. I knew then what I was up against. How deep the roots of evil ran, even in soil as strong as America's. I knew we were spread far and wide, the people who cared enough to fight back, and that I'd have to look far beyond the limits of my own small town to build an army to stop her sorcery.

Brent. Fan.

We'd been so careful, the whole time we were Over There. Whenever anyone else was around, me and Leo were simply buddies. Talking baseball, or engine problems. That's where we met, in the mechanics corps. Motorcycles had been his thing, back in Brooklyn, and pickup trucks were mine, and that's where we ended up when we got to

Propatria. Different as we were, we had that in common. Combustion.

Sex was secret, furtive, hurried. Every second of intimacy was stolen from the chaos gods of that city at war with itself, who could choose at any moment to unleash an obliterating insurgent attack or accidental discovery by our bloodthirsty comrades. Horrific death or dishonorable discharge were waiting in the wings every time we touched, watching us, wondering when to make their entrance.

But there, in that San Diego aircraft hangar, hearing her sing those songs we'd listened to a thousand times in that internet-less city, on the battered thumb drives Leo had bummed off of a buddy back home, I felt a new world open up inside of us. He draped his arm over my shoulder and leaned into me and anyone could see, all these men and women we'd served with, and thousands of strangers besides, but it didn't matter, because that voice was coursing through us all, like we were thirty-five hundred needles and she was effortlessly threading herself through every one of us, making us into one thing, our lives linked up, our (*life force*) whatever it was surging like a river. Like the sea. We were the sea, and Ti drained us dry, and Ti filled us up.

But then the bittersweet melancholy filled me again, wondering, *what if this is the end of it? If we're free to be open about it because after today there won't be anything to protect anymore?* I was so full of fear. *When she stops singing we'll walk out of here, me and Leo and all these people who've been crammed together with us in the bitter seed pod of war, and we'll scatter to the winds.*

Nyssa. Backup singer.

"It was real," I said, setting her coffee in front of her and then easing myself into a chair. It's not so easy, anymore. Getting this old body to do what I want it to do. "You know it was real, Ti. *Is* real."

"I don't know anything," she said, sipping her coffee, smiling, but not remarking on the fact that I remembered exactly how much sugar and how much milk she took in her coffee. Because of course I did. Because of course everyone around her lived only to please her, to serve her, to make her life easier.

I felt sorry for her, then. For the same thing I'd always been jealous of. How she was shielded from every problem. How all the little hardships were whisked away. They hadn't been helping her, all those people. They'd made her unable to handle the big hardships. They helped destroy her.

"Look at you," I said. "All the hard living you've done? You should look twenty years older than 48, not twenty years younger. That's proof right there. You took something from them, all those people, all those years. You know you did."

She chuckled. "'All the hard living.' You mean drugs, right?"

"I always served it to you straight up, babycakes. You know I did."

"That's why they hated you," she said. "Why they said you had to go."

So. She *did* want to talk about it. She *was* ready to be set straight. "Your family hated me, yes, because I called them out on all the ways they were profiting off of you, and how they let their own greed get in the way of what was best for you, but that's not why you fired me. Okay? I'm happy to stroll down memory lane with you, help you get through a rough patch, but do me the decency of at least being honest about everything at long last."

"Sure," she said, and shrugged. "Fine. What do I care? What does it matter, now?"

"Why'd you fire me? I want to hear you say it."

"Because."

She frowned. The church had fucked her up good. Long before she was Miss Superstar, she'd been Miss Sunday Service, and that place had gotten her just as twisted up inside as the fame and the drugs would do later. She still couldn't say it to herself, what she was.

Ti was a woman, and she loved a woman. Everything she'd ever been told said she was going to hell for that.

And Ti was a woman who had some kind of crazy power, and even though *I'd* never use the word *witchcraft*, that was the only word she knew for it.

Double damned.

I took her coffee cup to the sink. No way I was going to press her on this. Be like kicking a dog when she was down. She was sorry. That's why she'd come. That was enough for me.

"I fired you because something happens when I sing. When people hear me. I fired you because everyone around me was either completely oblivious to it, or just doing their damnedest to *act* like they were oblivious. Everyone but you. You wouldn't pretend it wasn't real, and you wouldn't let me pretend it, either."

Davey. Employee.

All addicts are self-medicating, you ask me. Trying to soothe a hurt they can't name, and since they can't name it they can't get the right medicine, so they use poison instead.

That *Heroes of the Venezuelan Liberation* special—that was the beginning of the end, for Ti. Sure, she still had some of her best recordings ahead of her—the voice wasn't broken, yet—but I could see it the second she came off that stage. How something had shifted in her. Not long after that was when the witchcraft thing started, all those horrible women trying to get her banned, and it was stupid shit and it never hurt her sales—helped them, if anything—but she took it to heart. They'd send her hate mail, and she'd actually read it! That, I can't figure. Like she got something she needed from those nasty letters. Like she wanted to skin herself, and they were the blade God had sent.

Moths steer by the light of the moon. Only thing is, they don't know the difference between one light and another. At night, far as they're concerned, there's just two things: darkness and light. But if there's a fire, or a hot electric bulb, they'll steer by that. Circling around it, getting closer and closer until they burn up.

And, no. I don't know what it was about that night. What happened. Nyssa might, but not me. I respect everyone's right to their own secrets, and that's why Ti kept me around until the very last day. I never even asked her for her real name. World took so much from her, you know? Wasn't about to take anything more.

So, all I know is—that was the night Ti veered off-course, lost track of the moon and started circling the flame. Took her twenty years, but eventually those circles became so small she burst into a big blazing ball of fire herself.

Brent. Fan.

She saw us. I know she did. Several songs in, I couldn't keep track anymore, one bled into the next and it was all one wail of joy and sadness, all of us rubbed raw by that voice, wrung out like a washcloth. The chorus ended, segued into a saxophone solo, she crooned, *I need, I need, I need, I need*, and then turned to mop the sweat from her face, and the solo was beautiful but that wasn't why it was there, she needed a chance to catch her breath, to muster her strength for the final assault.

All around us, people cried out. Love, encouragement, lust—the pain she'd unlocked in them—the bliss she'd inspired—we saw her as human, for an instant, someone who needed to actually breathe, and we loved her all the more for it.

If you never saw Ti live, I don't think you can understand what I'm talking about. Listening to her on the radio, watching clips, you feel it, a little, you know this is something special, something (*supernatural*) different, and if you really listen hard and let your guard down maybe it will start to stir up something you can't explain—give you something you didn't have before—a faint smell in the air, a memory that's not yours, a shadow shaped like her in your dreams that night. But that's infinitesimal, a drop of water compared to the raging cataract of what came out of her there, in that room, in that crowd.

Ti smiled, at our cries, and everyone wailed louder. She pressed both hands to her lips and then flung them out, unleashing a tidal wave of energy through the audience. I felt it. A tingle up the spine. A gift she gave us. Ti turned from face to face, blowing kisses.

And then she saw us.

Leo missed it. I've never told him. He'd be too upset over having been oblivious. He didn't see it because he was kissing me, warm lips in the cool upper curl of my ear.

Ti saw us, and she smiled. And it was the saddest smile I'd ever seen.

Nyssa. Backup singer.

"I shouldn't have come," she said, heading for the door. "It was stupid. You have your life, you have your troubles," and she looked around the room, saw the mess, the piled-up bills, the pictures of my kids and grandkids on the fridge, and she winced, because she'd never once asked me how *I* was doing, what was happening in *my* life, and now it was too late, "and you damn sure don't need me coming here asking for help with mine."

"Something happened that night," I said. "The concert. For the soldiers? In San Jose?"

Ti stopped. Whispered: "San Diego."

"You saw something. During the saxophone solo. I felt it—I felt you feel it. I can still feel it, even now. Shut my eyes and there it is, humming under my skin like it happened seconds ago. Am I right?"

"You felt that?" Her voice was tiny, terrified. Excited.

I nodded.

"You hid it well. Never let it show in your face. But I could see it anyway, same as if I'd watched you burst into flames."

Her eyes were so wide.

Every part of me was screaming to stop. But I knew I had to do this.

Because I'd been hiding, too. Trying not to look the truth in the eyes. Not to let myself remember what it felt like, that night, every night, every time we sang together on stage, how my voice connected with hers and something happened. Something flowed through me. Something linking me and Ti and all those people. Something that let me see the inside of every one of them, the pure goodness inside of bodies and minds wracked by horror and disease and fear. It was a thousand times stronger than heroin, that feeling—and yes, I do have a basis for comparison—but with no crash or consequences or side effects, just bliss, like being welcomed into the warm light of the womb of the universe. So of course I had to push it down, pretend it never happened. Because how could you live your real life after you've had something like that and then lost it? Better to tell yourself it was all in your head.

"You saw something, Ti. Looking out into that crowd. You saw something that hurt you worse than anything ever hurt before. I felt like I'd been punched in the stomach, and I knew that's how you felt. Should I keep going?"

She nodded.

"It was like I could hear your thoughts. Or we were watching the same movie. The movie was you. All your life you'd been looking for a certain kind of love, the real kind, the one that God and your mom and your heart would all be proud of. Always believing it was just around the corner. Maybe the next man would be the one, or if you gave the current man a little longer, in spite of all the warning signs. But whatever you saw in that crowd—as soon as you saw it, you knew. The love you were looking for? You'd had it already. With Lark. You'd had it and it scared you so bad you told her you two had to stop, be just friends, because to be together would mean kissing your career goodbye. The pain you felt at the time, you told yourself it was nothing, puppy love, sin and confusion, and that sooner or later you'd find the real thing. And that night, at that concert, you saw the truth. The love you were looking for was behind you."

Carolina. Faith-based family values advocate.

First thing I did, I went to the local Walmart, marched my way back to the electronics section where they still sell CDs for all the old folks like me who still like to have things we can hold in our hands. They had her poster up and everything. A whole table of her stuff—she had the number one song on the charts that week. I walked in there and I went right up to the girl behind the counter, and I said:

"I'm with Grace Abounding, and we're formally asking your store to stop selling that woman's music."

A lie, sure, but a lie for Jesus. And anyway I *was* with Grace Abounding, and I *was* asking them to stop selling her records.

The clerk said, "Uh."

It's a small town. I knew who she was. Had seen her around. Never at church, of course.

"You probably want to get your manager."

She scurried off.

"Easy, sweetie," said the manager, another familiar face, coming out with a smug look on his face like he'd stopped doing something important just so he could rush out and rub my face in something. "It's not that serious. Everybody knows why you're really so upset about her."

"I'm certain I don't know what you're talking about," I said, and prayed for Jesus to send me strength, to keep from whipping out the tiny pink pistol my husband Colby had gotten for me for our fifth anniversary, which I kept in my purse at all times because I'm allowed to, and because the world is full of people trying to do harm to good Christian Americans.

"Yeah you do." And he had a ratty beard and he was stroking it lewdly at me. "We all saw it. That special. For the soldiers? We saw your son up there."

"I need you to sign this pledge, agreeing to stop selling all of her music and merchandise. I have prepared this informational pamphlet, if you'd like some further—"

He laughed. "Are you going to try and tell me that wasn't your boy Brent? In the front row, smiling while some Jew-looking man licks his ear? Christ, no wonder you hate her. Because of that special, the whole town and half of America saw just what he—"

Probably he kept talking. I assure you I wouldn't know. I turned right around and left. And I had two, maybe three fingers on the pink pistol the whole darn time.

Brent. Fan.

My *mom*? You know who she is?

Shit. Of course you do. Why the hell else would you want to talk to meaningless little me?

Well, I don't have anything to say on that subject. I haven't talked to my mother in twenty years. She can rot in her own miserable hatred for all I care.

I'm living a life I never dared to dream could be mine. She gave us that, me and Leo. A life. A future. Happiness. Standing up there on that stage, she unlocked something in us. In me, anyway. I never had that kind of courage before. But she gave it to me. Whisked all my fear away. From that moment on, I was all in.

Nyssa. Backup singer.

I said it again: "The love you were looking for was already behind you."

And then I stared her down. Waited for her to say something. Certain she'd smack the shit out of me and then stomp out of my life for good this time.

"You felt all that," Ti whispered.

And there was no sorrow in her face. Just joy, and radiance. Because now, she believed.

She saved so many people. She couldn't save herself. It's stupid, really. To say it. It's so obvious it doesn't mean anything, to say it, like saying, "the sun rises in the east and sets in the west." But I'll say it. Because she's here, now. With me. In me. In you, if you're making this movie, because she must have touched you, somehow. She reached inside of you, and she linked her soul to yours, and she changed you. And you changed her.

She was obsessed with Whitney Houston. Everybody knows that. People make a big deal out of it, the similarities between their sad stories, and maybe that's a whole other movie someone should make. All I know is her favorite song was "I Wanna Dance With Somebody." The only song she sang at every concert. The only cover. Never recorded it, of course, because she was good but she wasn't Whitney, and there's no sense setting yourself up for an unfavorable comparison, but live—live she could pull it off.

I need a man who'll take a chance, on a love that burns hot enough to last.

Here's the thing, about that line. Second time she sings it, she goes up an octave on the word *love.* Just like Whitney did. And when Ti hits that note—*love*—her yearning reaches inside of you and replaces your own; all the need and longing, she just whisks it all away.

A love that burns hot enough to last.

She believed that. Ti thought all she had to do was find the right man, the one whose love would burn hot enough to last. She believed it until that night, in that San Diego aircraft hangar, when she saw the truth: that she'd had that love already. And she'd thrown it away. And she'd never have it again, until she could live her life the way she really was. And she didn't have that kind of courage.

"See you soon, Nyssa," she said, and hugged me.

"I love you, Tiyanna," I murmured in her ear.

She seemed stouter, now. Taller. Like she'd been blind, and now could see.

Carolina. Faith-based family values advocate.

My husband couldn't handle it. What had to be done. That's why I left. I could be married to him or I could be married to Christ, to this crusade, and I'm not ashamed of my choice. We won, didn't we? Have I shown you my scrapbooks? I have so many press clippings.

Davey. Employee.

I was the last one to see her alive. Guess you know that already. Probably why you're talking to me.

And no—before you even ask—no, there were no red flags, no cryptic messages or notes to answer the question of whether or not she meant to die that day. Because of course I would never have driven her out to the beach "for a quick dip" if I suspected what she meant to do. I watched her swim into the deepening twilight, and by the time I saw what she was up to she was way too far out for me or anyone to save her.

I still hear her, you know. See her. Not just in her music and her movies. In the faces of strangers, living their lives. Flowers. Birds. The craziest shit. She's everywhere now.

Those crazy church ladies only had it half right. She was magic, sure; she was practicing witchcraft, sure—but it wasn't the one they thought it was. Whatever weird vampire thing she used to reach into your heart and take something that was like a side effect, something she couldn't control.

No, man. *Music* is magic. A thread to tie us all together, to let us look inside ourselves, see that we're all one. That our pain doesn't isolate us, it connects us to everyone who's ever been. Shows us that we're made of love, unending perfect love.

That's one of the magic things music can do, anyway, and Ti did it better than anyone, except possibly Whitney. Her songs gave God's full grace to everyone who heard them—for as long as the song lasted, sometimes, and sometimes for the rest of their lives. Maybe because she was born that way and maybe because of what she'd been through, the pain in her heart, I don't know.

Ti opened all of our eyes. Showed us ourselves. She set us free. And then she got free herself.

JASON SIZEMORE

Sam J. Miller is a brilliant writer. Even so, I had two concerns after my first read of this story. First, I asked myself if the VH1 *Behind the Music* style of storytelling had been played out. The answer is *No*. I could read an anthology of these tales if they're as moving as "A Love That Burns Hot Enough to Last: Deleted Scenes from a Documentary." Second, was Caroline, the family values advocate ... too much? At Apex, we do like stories with a message, but we also don't like to villanize anyone unfairly. In 2020, the year this story was accepted, the family values contigent were fighting hard against personal liberties, so ultimately, I didn't that Caroline was not too much, and probably could have been more.

LAS GIRLFRIENDS GUIDE TO SUBVERSIVE EATING

SABRINA VOURVOULIAS

EDITOR'S NOTE

"Las Girlfriends Guide to Subversive Eating" is a work of interactive fiction using the Adobe Spark graphic design platform. It is best viewed online inside a mobile, tablet, or desktop web browser.

You can read and interact with "Las Girlfriends Guide to Subversive Eating" at the following page hosted on our website:

https://apex-magazine.com/las-girlfriends-guide-to-subversive-eating/

THE LIFE & DEATH OF MIA FREMONT: AN INTERVIEW WITH A KILLER

A.K. HUDSON

Sitting in an overstuffed velvet armchair, Ms. Fremont has her legs curled under her. She's wearing a chunky cable-knit sweater, mustard yellow, that slides off one shoulder, and black yoga pants. Her unruly hair is pulled into a low, short ponytail, grey showing at the roots before being overwhelmed by some box-brand light brown, perhaps L'Oréal number 6. She's dared to wear last summer's Buxom Vixen red on her lips while the rest of her face is bare. It's that kind of half-effort that makes her story all the stranger.

I pass the picture of a young, vivacious teen, her whole carefully-planned life ahead of her across the top of the frosted glass table, turning it one-hundred-eighty degrees so that the girl's crooked smile and wide eyes are pointed the right way round for Ms. Fremont. She hardly glances down before pushing her sweater back up her shoulder and nodding for me to begin. She knows what I'm here for. I hit the record button on my phone and place it beside the photo on the table.

There are no villainous men. There can't be.

In fact, it's impossible to find a villainous man. Every man has some backstory, reason, or explanation that saves him.

If you're looking for a villain, you're going to need a woman. Nothing can save women. Not a damn thing.

She pauses when I open my mouth, but I don't want her to stop. I shake my head, and she goes on.

Mia foolishly believed, as the young are wont to do, that she could avoid villainy. The key was to be a good person. Good people aren't villains. She knew that in her heart, and she knew it because society told her it was so. The road to being *good* was laid out for her by her mother, religion, and Saturday morning cartoons.

She had a mental list going. It read like this:

Step one to being golden and good lies in the Golden Rule. Treat others as you wish to be treated. Easy enough.

Step two, put others before yourself.

Step three, respect your elders, and in doing so, be helpful.

Step four, apologize. Often. Even if you're not sure what you've done wrong, the word "sorry" should be used when you've made mistakes, or when someone is upset about something (anything, it doesn't need to be something you have any control over. A loved one died, and you didn't kill them? You're still sorry.)

Step five, be useful.

(Step Two and Five generally go together. The way you put others before yourself is to do things for them. If you haven't done something for someone to make their lives easier, then you haven't been useful, and you've been selfish. To be selfish is villainous. Do not be selfish.)

Step six, smile. But not too much. And not at the wrong times. But always. Except when you shouldn't. And you should know when those times are before anyone else so that you aren't breaking step three of being respectful to elders.

Mia kept this list in her head at all times. She knew from a very early age that any little slip could shatter every good thing she'd ever done and make her *bad*. She knew this because boys will be boys but girls can only be good or: asking for it, too stupid, too smart for their own good, too loud, precocious (which is apparently a bad word), just like their mothers (the worse version of this was to be "just like your grandmother"), a slut, a tease, too thin, too fat, overly eager, lazy, a bitch, too nice, or, Mia's favorite, too perfect.

When she stops, I look away, unable to look upon her head-on. That smile. There's no regret there. If anything, she looks at me like she's sorry for me. *Like I'm the one who needs to be saved. This was what they warned me about. This smile. The allure of what she says. Sorcery, they'd said.*

Her unlined eyes are too human for that. She shakes her head, surely seeing the way I struggle to maintain my composure. Still, she goes on.

Striving to be too perfect is why I had to kill Mia. *I* was always a villain. *She* was destined to become one. There was no avoiding it. Women are villains.

I really shouldn't try to justify my reasons because women aren't allowed reasons. We're given titles and stereotypes and we're expected to live by them. That made killing Mia easier. Well, that, and she wanted to die. In the end, she *really* wanted to die. Being perfect is exhausting, but for Mia that wasn't the problem. The problem was she didn't find perfection rewarding or fulfilling. No matter how perfect she was, no matter how often she followed the rules, even the conflicting ones, she was still a villain in someone's eyes.

A conniving witch. Or had it been bitch? Either way, Mia's parents had warned me. Still it makes no sense. The woman in front of me, and the girl in the photo...how had she done it? They'd said murder. And here she is admitting it. Except I don't see how I'm meant to arrest her.

Allow me to give you a quick summary of Mia's failure to live. She was born to loving parents. She didn't call them controlling (I did, though). They held her tight, promising her the world if she served them. And she served them with so much love and adoration it made other people question her sanity, but what did they know? She grew up with a few close friends, who her mother was constantly criticizing to try to break them apart. Mia held on to one friend who wasn't perfect, but who understood that Mia wasn't perfect either, and didn't try to change her for it. This was the first turn toward villainy.

If others were to tell the story, they'd delay that onset until after she graduated high school. Because then Mia went to college, close to home but she still made sure to see her parents at least once a week and called her mother every day. And in college she met a man. Classic villainy will ensue once a previously chaste and wholesome girl becomes a woman and meets a man.

Mia herself thought for years this relationship was the beginning of her fall from grace. I helped her to see that she'd taken a step off the pedestal when she'd refused to leave her best friend behind. Women don't need men to be villains. That's the patriarchy trying to insert their importance into stories about women.

Anyhow, I could sit here and try to tell you that I didn't kill Mia, that I helped her to live for the first time in her entire life. Both statements would be lies. And playing to your sympathies does nothing other than reaffirm the concept that a woman of a certain age is manipulative. I'm not any more manipulative than any other person, but there's that truth again interfering with what people want to believe. In the interest of transparency and truth, I killed her.

Ms. Fremont pauses to stare at the timer ticking on my phone, showing the progress of her admission. I imagine her lashing out, snatching the phone away and destroying the only evidence of her crime. Instead, she leans a little farther back into her seat and sighs.

Saying it aloud is refreshing.

The only way I could live was for Mia to die. And seeing how miserable she was, how done with her life she was already, I thought it would be easy. Someone that close to the edge ... just a little push would do it, right?

Years of careful preparation brought me to this. Years of re-thinking my plan, of questioning my own sanity. I nearly lost myself there at one point. I nearly just ... disappeared. Mia wouldn't have it though. She kept me around. She reminded me that

I needed to live, I needed to thrive. Every word of encouragement pushed her closer and closer to her own end.

You're probably wondering if I'm sorry. That's a classic thing to ask a murderer. It's a classic demand upon women, really.

I'm not sorry. I already told you that for me to live, she had to die.

The confession is what I'd been after. The self-assured and righteous attitude doesn't fit with a plea of insanity, which I had expected from her when we'd started. Unless that lack of emotion was another sign of her insanity.

I can see your surprise. Maybe you came in here thinking I'd lost my mind. That I'd attacked her in a fit of rage. And here I am telling you that her death was calculated and a long-time coming. I knew exactly what I was doing. I had to, to get the job done.

She nearly did it for me at one point. That was a low moment for us both. She was certain there was no coming back from the mistakes she'd made. The people around her wouldn't let her forget who she was supposed to be. I was there, whispering in her ear: get up, you beautiful idiot. You were never what they thought you were. She sobbed. She told me how much she *wanted* to be what they wanted. She *needed* to be that woman.

We all need to be that woman sometimes. And it's crippling to even try. Which is why I stopped.

She makes this all sound so simple. I understand now that she truly is dangerous. I was foolish to willingly walk into her house, sit opposite her, and think myself immune.

I'm telling you what I've done for one simple reason: because I believe you don't have to be trapped either. I see you buried deep behind those dim, lackluster eyes. I see you wondering if you could cast off this ridiculous farce that's destroying you and really live.

Yes. You can.

You want to know how I finally did it? How I *really* did it?

I desperately do want to know, but I worry that this is when her words will become a spell that seeps into my head and drives me to my end. Still, I nod yes, because yes, of course I want to know.

I waited until Mia was at her strongest weakest self. I waited until she thought she really had her shit together. And then I waited a few days more because I knew. I knew that someone would comment on a little mistake. Or she'd get that phone call from her family, reminding her that she was still a failure, no matter how much she'd created the life she truly wanted for herself.

When that happened, when she felt herself coming only slightly unhinged, only a very little bit undone, I attacked. I told her, 'Hey Mia, you know what you are now? You're a villain. You're—' And here's where I drew it out, knowing the shock would be fatal. I smiled, like I am now, and I said, 'Baby, you're me. You're always me. You can't help but be me. So why don't you just stop trying so damn hard to be someone else?'

I look down again at the picture of a young Mia Fremont. I ask Ms. Fremont to clarify what she's saying because the girl in the photo and the woman in front of me cannot be the same person. Her parents are right. Ms. Fremont has destroyed Mia.

She doesn't look at the picture.

I'm not that girl. I told you. I killed that girl. I killed her that day with one simple lie, and it was her choice not to believe it. Had she believed it, she'd still be here now, and I, well I would not.

When I told her that she was a villain, she lost it, as I knew she would. She had spent her entire life trying so hard to be good, to be perfect. In the world she was trying to live in, in her mind, she couldn't be a villain. But instead of showing me just how good and perfect she was to prove to me that she wasn't bad, she snapped. She saw that she could continue to wear herself into the ground trying to be someone else, or she could accept that she would be *someone's* villain, just not her own. And the person she was when she wasn't herself, well that person made her sick. That person wasn't who she wanted to be. So, she stopped.

And here I am. I know you think I'm a villain, that I'm bad for not being her. But I am not my own villain. And I can live with that.

She pauses again and I wonder if that's the end. I'm not sure what to do with this confession. Has she killed someone? Her relatives certainly think she has. They swear this woman is not their daughter, their sister, their loved one. She is someone else.

If I took her in, booked her, I'd be laughed out of the precinct. Every scrap of identification she has says Mia Fremont. I'm certain a hair sample would come back a positive match. Her fingerprints, the same.

But she's confessed.

Detective, I have a question for you: are you living for yourself, or are you living for others?

That cruel smile. That sincere question. I want to hate her; what I want more is to answer her question. But I don't know. Something stirs inside, and I stop the recording. I rise. I excuse myself. I tell her that I appreciate her taking the time to see me. And I leave. Scared.

I am pulling my car door open when I hear her footsteps on the porch.

I hope you'll tell them I'm doing just fine. The Mia Fremont they knew is long gone, but I am thriving.

I've seen that knowing wicked smirk before. What she said is alluring. Her explanation is nearly reasonable. But it's that glimmer of hope she gives to a part of me deep down in the recesses of my mind that makes her evil.

She raises her hand and I flinch.

Drive safe now.

JASON SIZEMORE

Is there something supernatural about Mia, or is Mia someone who has a split personality? Maybe Mia is just putting everybody on because she's a rebellious teen?

It's hard to pull off a story that doesn't give you a definitive answer yet feels whole. Lesley and I discussed at great lengths a problem that might spoil the story for readers. Does the fact that it appears in a speculative fiction magazine suggest a speculative answer? We decided to let the readers figure it out.

THIS IS THE MOMENT, OR ONE OF THEM

MARI NESS

This is the moment when we first met.

I watch as we exchange names with the rest of the group, listen intently to the instructor, reach for the clay and our tools, smile. I watch myself steal glances in her direction, drop the carving tools, turn bright red. Watch—for the first time—her reaction to all this, as my fingers hover over the screen.

And.

Huh.

She didn't react at *all*?

I wish I'd realized that at the time.

Options flash across the screen. My throat closes. I had so many choices here. Doing photography or painting or glass art instead. Staying home and not taking a class at all. Focusing on the other students. Leaving class after that first night. Not dropping the damn tools—well, no. I never *choose* to be this clumsy.

That just happens.

I start carefully tapping the screen.

Next.

This is—apparently—the moment where I first started telling her a little bit about myself. My job, my family, my cats. Not much—probably because the classroom is full of other strangers who can hear everything, and occasionally jump in with a comment or two.

I say *apparently* and *probably* because I have completely forgotten this moment. All of it.

Which makes choosing an option here damn difficult.

Screw it. If I can't remember any of it, how important could it have been? And if it turns out to be important—well. I can always come back.

Then again—

No. I *have* to stop second-guessing myself. And I don't have time to review every option for every moment. The human body can't stay awake that long.

Even loaded up with the maximum number of lattes they let me bring in here.

I take another sip.

Next.

This is the moment when she asked me if I wanted to grab a drink or a coffee or something, exactly eight weeks after our first meeting. I know the time not because I was counting every moment with her—not then—but because it was an eight-week class, and she only asked me at the end of the class. I'm sure of that.

Something twists in my stomach.

Review.

Absolutely sure.

Rain check? I asked. *I can't stay out too late—things to do in the morning.*

Wait.

No.

My fingers slam on the screen, scattering images and sounds throughout the room.

Three moments?

Just *three* moments from that class?

This can't be right.

I distinctly remember other moments. Other looks. I'm *sure* of this. When she came over to look at one of my bowls and said something kind about the glaze. When I admired the small bird she made, beautiful even before it had been fired. The argument about the best pizza places in our little city. Her skeptical looks at the little animals I tried to mold. We *talked,* damn it. I remember that. *Surely* that meant something? Surely *some* of that could be shifted?

I'm equally sure that my memory hasn't been shifted yet. That doesn't happen until the end, they told me, and sometimes not even then. And I'm nowhere *near* the end. I'm equally sure of that.

Ok, almost sure of that. The system does seem to be skipping a *lot.* But still. My finger pounds on the upper left corner of the screen. Menus pop up everywhere.

Back.

Select.

Back.
More pounding.
Review.
Oh *come on.*
Back. Back. Back.
There *has* to be a way to do this.
Review.
Apparently not.
I am *not* going to cry.
At least now I *am* sure that she didn't ask me to grab a coffee or drink or something until the end of the class. Because if she had asked me earlier—
But I guess I never had that option.
I *have* to focus.
Review.

This is the moment, exactly eight weeks after our first meeting, when she first asked me to grab a drink or coffee or something.

Rain check? I asked. *I can't stay out too late—things to do in the morning.*
I thought you worked at home.
Doesn't end morning meetings.
This is …
… better than I remembered.
Then what's the point?
I get to spend more time with my cats.
Much less awkward.
In fact, I don't think I even have to tweak this.
It's suddenly easier to breathe again. I take another sip of my latte, wishing—not for the first time—that I'd been allowed to bring more than three. That said, this one is already getting a bit cold, even in its thermal sleeve.
Next.

This is the moment two months later when we finally went for that first drink.
Or, I guess you could say, and the system certainly is trying to say, our first date. Not that I knew that at the time. Two months of near misses and texts and emails and sounds great/Thursday maybe/whoops sorry forgot this other thing hadn't exactly screamed *date* to me. Even if it had, well—I'm so terrible at this sort of thing that I never know I'm on a date until the other person tells me that I'm on a date. Sometimes not even then.
Which is not why I'm here.

Review. Confirm. Review.

Can I ask why you were even in *that class? You never seemed particularly into it.*

Though maybe that's the choice I should make, this time: know that I'm on a date.

I thought it might be fun to try to do something with my hands.

You know, I saw your stuff when I went to go pick mine up.

I flinch.

At least that one thing was—colorful?

The penguin?

That was a penguin?

It was aspiring to be a penguin.

A laugh.

Plus, I added, *I can always give that penguin to my mother, and she'll be forced to say she likes it.*

I watch the way her eyes moved down to linger on my hands, which I had left on the table.

Pause.

No. It was better not knowing that we were on a date.

I think.

Next.

This is the moment four weeks later, the moment of our first, oh so brief kiss.

Review. Review. Review. Review. Review.

Your current plan provides a limit of 50 reviews per original moment; 10 reviews per shifted moment. For more reviews, please upgrade to an Amethyst or higher plan.

Oh, come *on.*

First off, I haven't even reached 10 reviews of this yet. And second, this *is* an original moment. I'm sure of it. I haven't shifted *anything* yet. I've barely even looked at the options. So unless someone else has shifted something that shifted this and I previously reviewed this and forgot and—

Even *if* that happened, and it didn't, I need to imprint this on my memory. To make sure I have it, no matter what shifts. I *need* to. Even the full fifty reviews might not be enough and—

Damn it.

Next.

This is the moment when we first went to bed together, when I first felt her fingers against me and her lips against my skin and—

—and I *really* don't need this much judgement from a machine about my sex life and my failure to explore all of the options here the first time around.

Next.

This is the next morning. It includes terrible coffee, the discovery that I was, in fact, out of pancake mix, some apples, an agreement that really, we should head to the local brunch place for something edible, the discovery of a huge wait at the local brunch place, some quick pastries and coffee at the café next door, a lingering final kiss, a reminder from my calendar that yes, I still had a deadline.

Ok, yeah, this I can *definitely* tweak. At the very least provide decent coffee. Even though that would probably mean going further back and finding a moment where I could have but didn't buy a French press, or one of those single serve coffee machines with the little pods, or a moment where I could have chosen to live right next to—or maybe even right above—a really good café. Which would have the added bonus of showing me exactly how much good—or even decent—coffee could have changed my life.

My fingers hover over the menu.

Assuming I *can* find any of those moments, given everything else that's being skipped—

Next.

Although the system will show multiple options, users are warned that repeated studies have shown that multiple small shifts can be more effective than single large shifts.

Awesome.

This is a moment at the beach. The—

Wait.

This was in late February. I'm fairly certain of that. I touch a few buttons on the screen to confirm. Yes. The last Wednesday in February when we both ditched our jobs to head out to the beaches just north of Cape Canaveral.

Which means that the system has skipped both our first New Year's *and* Valentine's Day.

Well.

At least this confirms that getting her different gifts wouldn't have made any difference.

I take another sip of my second latte. Or maybe my third. I can't keep count. I have to focus.

Review.

This is a moment at the beach. The moment where I didn't tell her that I'd fallen in love with her, with *fallen* definitely being the appropriate word here, as the waves crashed over us both, sending us flailing to the sands. I was waiting for a better time. A more romantic time, a more perfect time. A candlelight dinner. A silly moment in the car. A spontaneous outburst. No. A time where I could choose my words absolutely carefully and do it *right*.

Options splash over the screen.

I push a button.

Next.

By signing this, you acknowledge the risk of permanent memory changes. Side effects may include—

Oh, come *on*. Not only did I do this two hours ago, this is the *third* time this has popped up since I entered this room, and that's not counting the warnings in the original sales pitch and the two weeks of origination classes. I know they have to cover their asses, but I *also* know I researched the hell out of this *and* signed about 200 pages of paperwork just to take the classes and another 200 pages of paperwork after that. And given the costs, it's not like I have any money left to sue them *with*. Why keep making me review *this*?

Unless I already—

No. I haven't made any shifts yet. Everything matches my memory exactly. Everything. Well, almost everything. The moments that I can't remember, or can't remember clearly, don't count. And they told us that nothing shifts permanently until I leave this room. Which I haven't done at all. Not even to go to the bathroom.

Which I suddenly realize I really need to do.

What they *should* have had me sign was something about the risks of downing a large latte before starting this and bringing more into the room with me and what that could do to my bladder.

I can't think about that now.

Changes made before a full review—

Damn it.

I rub my hands against my wet face.

Next.

Or, well. Not next.

Anywhere from 5 to 20% of users report being unable to remember their original timelines.

Yes. Got that. Thus why I'm back to reviewing, machine!

Next.

This is the moment when she gave me a little glass penguin.

What's this for?

No reason.

It's a good moment, a good memory. I can feel the corners of my mouth twitching upwards. Not an *important* one, at least, as far as I know, although they did say in training that sometimes random moments might show up, just because they were moments that could be shifted, unlike some of the more major moments.

But also, not a moment with a lot of options, since, if memory serves, she just gave me the penguin and left, right?

Review.

Right.

My fingers linger over the *Options* button anyway.

Next.

If I see another legal warning I am going to lose it. *Really.* I have one chance at this, *one*, and my bladder is killing me, so I don't even know how much longer I'm going to last, and instead of reviewing and changing, I'm getting these goddamn legal warnings. I'm half-tempted to just fast-forward to when I initially signed these documents, and change some of *that*, to make sure that my time *here* isn't wasted in legal warnings.

But, no. If I fast-forward now, there's no guarantee I'll be able to return, and I'm not sure what to change yet.

Breathe, I remind myself. Breathe.

Next.

This is the moment when I told her not to come and shelter in place with me. I only had a two bedroom place, I said. With a small yard, sure, but we would drive each other nuts. I had a mitral valve prolapse, a pre-existing condition.

You never mentioned that, she said.

It never seemed important, I said. *Came up during a routine physical. I'm asymptomatic, so it never seemed to be an issue.*

Then why is it an issue now, she said.

Because there's a virus.

I haven't been near anyone who has it.

That you know of.

I have no idea why I'm reviewing this moment.

I do know I need more coffee.

Next.

Maybe I should just end this right now. Just go back to the beginning and remove that pottery class. The chances that we would meet someplace else? Presumably pretty slim. It wasn't one of the options in the beginning.

Maybe.

I reach into the pocket of my sweatshirt, feeling the rough, misshapen object there that once aspired to be a penguin.

Next.

We can Skype, FaceTime, whatever, I said.

You're terrible at technology.

That I couldn't argue against. Much. *My mother is going to church via YouTube.*

What the fuck *does that have to do with anything?*

I press the button.

Next.

This is another moment where I start thinking that this—all of this—has to be a scam. Ok, yes, the system is definitely pulling up what seems to be completely accurate videos of my past—or at least, fairly close to what I remember of my past—seen largely from my viewpoint, or something watching close by. So if it's a scam, it's a damn good one.

But if it's real, surely people would have changed things like this? I know, I know—in training they said that attempts to shift certain things—pandemics, wars, extinctions, assassinations—had failed.

Apparently because we are only shifting individual timelines, not the societal timelines needed for large scale shifts.

No one would try to stop us, but we did need to remember that our fees were non-refundable.

But what if we haven't tried shifting the right people and the right pasts for that? someone—not me—had asked during training.

Who says we haven't?

Silence from the class.

Next?

This is our first video call.

It's terrible. The sound quality is terrible, the picture quality is terrible. I look awful. She looks awful. Watching it is awful.

The options—nearly all involving ending this call as quickly as possible—are equally awful.

Next.

This is the moment when I spill what's left of the second latte.

Partly general clumsiness, partly just overall shaking. I mean, I'm not even at the really painful part. And if I'm already this upset, I'm not sure I *can* review the painful part.

Next.

Next turns out to be a series of moments that I don't remember, but which seem to emphasize that I had a lot more choices at the time than I thought I did, and wasted even more time marathoning terrible television than I thought I did.

Maybe I should start hitting the *next* button a lot faster.

This is the moment when I remember that, just maybe, I don't have to shift anything: it could be shifted for me. After all, I'm not the only person in this building right now. Not the only person in a shifting room. They never told us just how many people can enter the system at once, and I'm *pretty* sure that at least some of the people who walked through the doors with me were general employees, not clients. But presumably at least four or five.

Which means somewhere in another room, someone could be shifting something that will cancel or change anything *I* want to shift. May already have done this. I mean, so *far* this all matches my memories, more or less, but parts do seem missing and—

What if she is in this building, removing me from her life?

Oh, god, I need to throw up.

This is the moment when she came by holding out a package of toilet paper in her hands, and I broke down and cried.

I should definitely review this moment. I know it's important.

But I can't.

Next.

Major moments may be eliminated early in the process, thanks to minor alterations and shifts in previous moments. Not all moments can or will be removed; users should feel free to skip any moment that may be too emotionally painful or triggering to be reviewed.

Therapy may be available post treatment.

I am not going to throw up.

This is the moment when she didn't return my texts for five days. *Five days.* Despite knowing that cases were peaking again, that hospitals were overloaded again.

Next.

This is the moment when I reach into my pocket and pull a little glass penguin and clutch it so tightly that I think I'm bruising my fingers.

This is the moment when she called me and said she'd stopped coughing, and she really felt much better now, and I said, then why aren't you over here fucking me, and she laughed and cried a little and said, wait, since when do you want me breaking quarantine and I said I didn't care, I didn't, and then she said she would be right over.

It's very hard to breathe.

Next.

Users are warned that attempts to shift particularly painful or stressful events may lead to unwanted changes in current personalities, temperaments, knowledge or skills. Users are advised to strongly consider the costs of these shifts.

And *bullshit.*

This is another one of those "pain builds character" lies. *Embrace the pain. You'll be a better person for it.* Something I actually believed, once upon a time. But not now. Going through this the first time didn't make me a better person, or a stronger person. It just hurt like hell.

This pain? Did not make me a better person. Did not lead me to new relationships.

Besides, if I liked who I am right now, would I be doing this?

This is the moment when she didn't arrive.

Shifts in your vital signs, including your heart rate and blood pressure, have been detected. You may wish to terminate.

Yeah, no.

In fact—

Back. Back. Back. Back.

Oh *come on.*

This is a moment I've gone through a hundred times in my mind. A thousand times. Thought of all of the clever, brilliant things I could have said. Could have done. I watch myself standing in front of the door, awkwardly juggling yet another roll of toilet paper and a basket of cookies and chocolates. Huh. In my memory my hands were free. Shaking, but free.

This is definitely one of *the* moments. I'm sure of it.

View options.

I reach into my pocket, feeling the hard object there.

This time I can get it right.

Option one: I leave the toilet paper by her door with a note. A carefully crafted note.

End.

This is the moment when I entered this facility and—

Option two: I knock on the door. Twice. Three times. Leave not just the toilet paper, but chocolate at the door, with a note. I text her afterwards.

End.

This is the moment when I entered this facility and—

Option three: I write up the note, and then text her the exact words before coming over.

End.

This is the moment when I entered this facility and—

Option four: Maybe the problem is the note.

End.

This is the moment when I entered this facility and—

Option five: I skip the damn toilet paper.

End.

This is the moment when I entered this facility and—

Ok. Wait. The moment when I entered this facility. That has to show up, no matter what I choose or don't choose, because if I don't enter this facility then I can't shift anything in the past. So maybe the problem here is that I'm not looking at what happens *before* I enter the facility. But, if I get everything right, I'd never enter the facility in the first place, unless I keep coming back to this facility because I know I have to come to this facility in order to get whatever outcome I finally choose, which is why no matter—

Or maybe knocking on the door wasn't the moment.

Back.

god no

Back.

This is the moment when she sent two words by text: *fever. coughing.*

This is the moment, right now, in this room, where I think of every reason why this was such a terrible fucking idea, and I break down and cry and a couple of tears fall on the screen and I don't even care, don't even care when the system starts droning at me again, when I reach into my pockets to find a tissue to find nothing there, when I try to wipe my tears with my sweatshirt, when I try to drink something only to find that my cup is completely empty, when I find myself crying again, and again, until I remind myself that I basically bankrupted myself for this, I can't stop now, I have to keep going and—

Next.

This is the moment when I dropped my phone on the kitchen tile, managing to have it land on just the right angle to crack.

Next.

This is the moment when I take out the little glass penguin and stare at it again.

How long will they let me stay in this room?

No, change that—

How long will they keep me in this room?

I'm so upset that I hit the wrong button.

Shifts are limited to what your past self was capable of doing at that moment. For instance, if you did not speak fluent Spanish at that moment, you will not be able to speak Spanish. However, you may have the option of going further back into the past and selecting the option of taking Spanish classes. Such classes must have been available to you at the time; selecting Spanish studies may shift other parts of your past and/or limit other later options.

... which I can't help but take as a bit of shade.

This is the moment, later, when I thought I saw her on the other side of my favorite café. When instead of going over to check, or even trying to look a little longer, I immediately buried myself in my cell phone, ignoring the sudden pain in my chest, the tears in my eyes, the way I couldn't see my cell phone, or taste the coffee I was trying to drink.

I don't really need to see the options here, though the system keeps throwing them up anyway.

Next.

This is the moment when I realized that I really did need to toss all of her things out.

Only to realize that I didn't *have* anything to toss out.

Except that little glass penguin.

I watch myself throwing it hard against the floor.

Next.

And this is the moment when everything felt normal again. Or as normal as it could be. When I realized I no longer had the urge to stock up on toilet paper and yeast the second I saw them, when I didn't flinch when I saw crowds inside a bar, or at the thought of going to the movies again.

When I finally let myself cry, and cry, and cry.

Next.

And this is a moment one year ago. My hands are gripped around my coffee mug, desperate to change things. Desperate to change everything. Desperate.

I sign everything and everything.

Had I known just how many times I'd have to review that legal stuff again, here in this room—

But no. This I don't want to change.

Next.

This time, this time, I think, I have it right.

This time.

My hands are freezing. I put them into my empty pockets to warm them, close my eyes, and remember that first terrible, terrible cup of coffee. The way she kissed me before and after that.

The way I kept staring at my phone, waiting for her text.

I pull out my hands.

Restart.

Review.

AUTHOR NOTES

"This Is the Moment, Or One of Them," actually started from fragments of another, still unfinished story. Those fragments didn't quite work in the main story, but I liked them enough that instead of deleting them, I moved them to another document and started organizing them, then added more fragments, and then found myself working more on the fragments—until I realized that I had another story here.

By this time, it was 2020, which meant that Covid started creeping into the story. Which freaked me out. Several short fiction publishers had requested some pandemic-related stories early on—but by May, several editors had outright said that they would not be accepting Covid stories, or would be accepting very few of them. And I didn't have just one Covid story, but two. And while my other Covid story was a cheerful fantasy story, this one was not. My usual worries about "Will anyone take this story? Will everyone hate this story?" were dialed up well past 11 to about 83. Perhaps higher.

And yet. It did find an amazing home, with *Apex Magazine*, and readers. I'm very grateful.

THROW RUG
AURELIUS RAINES II

Coach Hasso
Belding Middle School
Wrestling Coach

Look, these days, you're not supposed to tell a kid what he ... or she ... or they ... can't do. But you didn't see this kid, Umi. He looked like a fourth grader. He was a foot shorter than all the other sixth graders, easy. He had these big feet, and it seemed like he was tripping over them every five steps. His head looked like a medicine ball compared to the rest of him. Being near-bald didn't help.

A mess.

I'm sure putting this kid on a mat would probably count as some sorta manslaughter.

But here at Belding, we don't turn any kid away. As long as you're not failing any classes, you can be on the team. It was even worse once we got him into his singlet. It hung off 'im like he was wearing a choir robe. He couldn't give me five push-ups in a row, and sometimes I wondered that he was able to hold all of his seventy pounds without collapsing like a pile of sticks.

I tried not to let on how much I thought he didn't belong on a wrestling team. I would have thought he knew, but he never really seemed to get it, y'know? Y'know? Aw, c'mon! Don't look at me like that.

Look, you work with teenagers—heck, people, in general—and you can see when someone figures out they don't belong. You can see it in their eyes. They look at everyone around them. Size 'em up and then take measure of themselves. Give them a minute and they won't be back.

Not this kid. He finished three push-ups, and you would have thought he did a thousand of 'em, one-handed. He never won a single period. His opponents couldn't contain their joy when they squared up. After a while, the lack of challenge bored the other kids on the team.

I asked him once why he joined the wrestling team. He'd just finished his laps, dead last, as usual, and he was breathing so hard I thought he was going to have an attack or something.

"It's ... my ... destiny,"

Then, I knew what was up with this kid. Too many comic books. I'd seen it before. Too many Spiderman comics and your fantasies carry you away. These kids think there's going to be a magic accident that's going to turn them from some scrawny loser into a muscle-bound hero. The first time you hit that mat, though. That first time somebody picks you up and slams your torso against that mat, it feels like they drummed the soul right out your chest, and unless you got heart, you don't want to fight anymore.

So I paired Umi up with the only kid on the team that was close to his size. He was still outclassed.

Two seconds after the whistle Umi's shoulders are pinned to the mat with his legs kicking in the air like an upturned insect. I count him out, and the other student releases him.

Umi laid there for a second and my heart drops because I just know that he has to be broken and everybody is going to say what I already knew: he had no business being out there in the first place.

Then he pops back up. I should stop the match but the kid seems fine, and I'm only a little worried when I blow the whistle again and the boys go back at it. Again, Wham! And Umi is pinned again. And again. And again. And each time I'm sure that he has a busted rib or a ruptured spleen, but each time he gets back up.

Now, I'm going to tell you, if you want Coach Hasso as a fan, all you gotta do is show some heart. Umi had more heart than a mountain gorilla.

"I like that about you, kid" I told him after practice.

"Like what?"

"You don't give up. You keep that up you are going to be a champion." This is one of the many lies I tell children, hoping the child makes me a prophet.

Then the kid said the weirdest thing with a sorta crooked smile.

"I know."

And I looked at him like, *I know?*

"The best thing anybody can do to stop me is just walk away."

Yeah. Weird kid.

Donald Bradley
Hamilton High School
Freshman

I was kinda insulted when they matched me against this kid from James Baldwin High. We called him Throw Rug. You could throw him, and he would lay there like a rug. He was the easiest kid to beat in the whole conference. A skinny black kid who barely filled out his singlet. I thought black guys were supposed to be cut. This kid barely had enough muscle to make a bicep. I gave my phone to Drake so he could film me tossing this kid.

We start in the neutral position, standing face-to-face. I expected Throw Rug to look scared. He didn't. I'm pretty small, too, and I was glad this was going to be an easy win. Throw Rug rubs his nappy, Brillo pad hair (Why don't they cut that ish or somethin'?) The ref blows the whistle. I tried to grab his legs so I can slam him. It's a bit harder. I threw his body over my hip and down he goes. While I had him pinned, I took a moment to look at the camera and smile. Throw Rug pushed me hard and before the ref gets to "three" I could feel Throw Rug pushing me over. I could hear all the guys on both teams yelling. I tried to regain control, but I just couldn't get his other shoulder pinned. Throw Rug's team was going nuts.

The referee blew the whistle, and we have to fight a second period. I got to choose defensive position. I got on all fours, and Throw Rug was behind me with his hand over my navel and his other hand on my elbow. I could hear him breathing hard; harder than he should and I knew he was too tired to finish this period. The whistle blew and I twisted my torso so I can grab him and press him to the mat. But Throw Rug moved and all of my force caused me to fall backwards. And then Throw Rug slammed into me and, since I'm off balance, I get knocked to the mat and, suddenly, Throw Rug was on top of me and my shoulders were actually pinned! The ref was actually counting! I froze before I realized I needed to get up. I was not going to be the first person to lose to Throw Rug!

I was able to get him on his side but he won't go over. I pushed and he pushed back and every time I thought I had him down, he wiggled out of it. I got a glance of Drake and he's not even pointing the phone anymore. He was just yelling. So was everybody else. Whistle blew again.

We went into a third period. Throw Rug got to pick and he decided on neutral. We square up and when the ref blew the whistle, I grabbed his middle to control him. I pushed hard to get him over, and he didn't go down easy. When he did go down, I made sure that I got my arms under his legs and I used them as leverage to push his shoulders into the mat. The ref started to count and Throw Rug wasn't able to break my hold. The whistle blew, the match was over, and the ref raised my hands when I stood up.

The Baldwin team rushed the mat and picked Throw Rug up like he'd won a division match by himself.

"What's that all about?"

"Bro!" Drake said looking at me in disbelief.

"What?"

"Bro!"

"What!"

"Bro! Throw Rug never made it to third period, before. You're the first. Not a good look, Bro."

Nala Reed
Umchasi "Umi" Reed's mother

I was really sick in high school and, as a result, I was told that I wouldn't be able to have children. Y'know, at that age, you don't want kids, anyway. But when someone tells you that your future has lost possibilities ...

I'd been seeing Kwame for some months before I thought we might be serious. I was nervous about telling him I couldn't have children. He seemed like he's be a cool dad. It took some time, but he was okay with it. We always thought when we were ready, we could adopt. Not to mention, there are a million black children looking for homes, right?

I love Kwame. I loved him more when I found a book of names that he'd been keeping most of his life with names for his children. A date on the inside cover told me he'd been keeping it since he was ten. He'd been dreaming about children since he was a child himself, and he married me anyway. So when I found out I was pregnant, the feeling of this being a gift was multiplied tenfold.

Our son's birth was full of worry. A lot of prayer. The labor was without event but when he came into the world, he was not breathing. I was too weak to do a thing but raise my head in the slightest and ask what was wrong. I heard a *thump*, a reflexive scream, and then an apology. Kwame looked back at the doctors and then at me and then back, again. Then the room was silent except for me asking somebody to tell me something. And then my baby was crying.

He spent two weeks in an incubator. He was well underweight and his lungs were underdeveloped. Kwame's mother, Eisha, sat with me. Kwame's mother was ... strange. A beautiful woman in all ways, but she believed in spirits and potions. African stuff I'd never heard of and made for interesting advice during my entire pregnancy. I tried to be respectful. Outside of church, I don't do metaphysical, even then, I'm known as a *clutch prayer*.

It was heartbreaking and inspiring to look at him in the incubator, his small chest working as if he was running. I had not named him then. When Eisha asked me why not, it was hard for me to say.

"I don't know if he's going make it. I can name him but I don't know if I can keep him. If I name him—"

Eisha sat for a long time. I thought she was letting it go. I should have known better.

"I'll tell you. That may not *ever* go away. Even if he makes it out of this hospital. Everything in the universe may come against the boy. The only protection he will have is the care of those who love him. Don't be too afraid to give him that."

That evening, Kwame came to the hospital. We sat next to our son with the book of names. An hour and a half of going through names and debate and we found one that worked.

Umchasi is Xhousa.

It means "Opponent."

Then, and for years after, I never would have thought I would have wrestling trophies in my living room. Wrestling!

Kwame Reed
Umchasi "Umi" Reed's Father

It seemed like after my dad turned fifty, he was crying all the time. I always thought it was awkward. By the time I graduated college he was at my graduation dinner tearing up. My dad wasn't the most macho guy.

Yet, I'm watching my son walk onto the wrestling mat, and I flashback to Nala and I sitting by his incubator trying to think of names for him. My heart swells and my vision gets all wavy. I never told Nala this, but I didn't think the boy would make it. At that time, I was not one for faith. It's my fault.

My mom was all into spiritualism and magic and stuff. I was so embarrassed when, on my first day of first grade, I opened my A-Team lunchbox to find high john root in a little bag with a note. The white kid next to me asked what was in the bag. I showed him with pride because didn't everyone's mom show love by putting a talisman in their lunchbox to give them courage and favor? When the other kid saw the small nugget of root as I held it in my hand, he scrunched his nose up.

"Ewww, it looks like a turd!" Then he looked at me. I had no idea what this meant, and then he said it louder so the other kids in the class could hear.

"Hey! This kid has a turd in his lunchbox! He eats turds! Ewwwww!"

You can guess what happened next. For the rest of my school year, kids were calling me Turd Boy. From that point on I was embarrassed by my mom's hoodoo, and I just wanted her to stop. Without even realizing why, I became a pragmatist. Eventually, it led me into computer engineering. No magic, just logic gates.

I guess Umi changed all of that for me. As my son walks out onto the mat, a senior in high school, he looks like a god, and this is my miracle. He is lean, hard muscle, everywhere.

His hair is loc'ed and braided close to his skull, per regulation. He's six feet and three inches, and I don't think he is done growing. I have a good job. I can afford shoes.

I'm a little ashamed of my pride as I notice the looks he gets from the girls as he stretches and shakes his long limbs. So, this is the pitiful thing dads do when they live vicariously through the lives of their sons? His high school career is very different from mine.

The boy is a miracle. When he came home and told us that he wanted to join the wrestling team, Nala and I were immediately against it. But after some reflection I realized that I didn't want to stand in his way. If the boy wanted to try something different ...

Nala, on the other hand, was totally against it, and she fought it every step of the way. But Umi would not stop pushing for it. He nailed it when he stopped eating. Getting food down that boys throat was her primary and universal concern and when he stopped taking meals, she had to concede to get him to have some kale.

At least one of us always attended his bouts. Whenever Nala went, she would bring papers to grade so she would have an excuse not to look. But she always looked and I had to restrain her on more than one occasion when she thought Umi was being treated roughly.

"Baby, It's *wrestling*. He'll be fine," I said. (It was the thing frequently I said to myself when I started to worry.) If I'm honest, it was raw, male pride that kept me from running down there myself. On occasion, to satiate both of us, I would casually stroll to the area where the team sat, say a few words to the coach, and then talk to Umi to make sure he was fine. Y'know. Cool.

Now, Umi is a near giant and the referee blows the whistle. Umi's opponent is built like a tractor and he looks a little nervous. He starts for Umi and they grapple. The Tractor is pushing and pushing trying to find leverage. He finds none and Umi doesn't move. They break. The Tractor comes in again and this time Umi leaps. Umi's body looks like a pinwheel as his legs go into the air. In the middle of the spin, Umi grabs the waist of his opponent and when Umi lands on the mat, his opponent is thrown face down to the ground. Before I can process what just happened, the referee has counted, the match is over, and Nala is on her feet with both hands in the air screaming.

"Flying Squirrel!"

Debra Long
Steele University
Second Year, Psychology

I am not a ho. I wonder why, in the twenty-first century, are we still slut-shaming (Hmm, Leah?) Maybe people should get the whole story before going talking garbage. I wasn't even looking for a boyfriend. I didn't work as hard as I did to get side-railed by some college student looking for himself. It just kinda happened.

My mom—my *liberal-women's-studies-pussy-hat-BLM-supporting-marriage-is-*

an-artifact-of-the-patriarchy-super-lefty-mom looked really embarrassed as she tried to talk to me about the boys I'd meet at college. It wasn't until I was sitting in my dorm room that I realized that she low-key told me to stay away from the black guys.

Wooooow! I guess it's right what they say about your kids and your politics.

Umi and I met off campus in front of a grocery store. A foot of snow had fallen and more was on the way. I was studying too hard to realize that I might be snowed in for a while. So (too late) I thought I should get some supplies before it got too bad. My car was stuck in my parking space. I was trying to dig myself out with the ice scraper (it broke), and I was starting to think I would have to walk away since no one seemed to be coming by to help. Umi showed up and waved in the window.

"Need help?"

"No, man. Spinning wheels is fun." For a second, he was actually trying to figure out if I was kidding.

"Alright, put it in neutral, turn the wheel towards me and come help me." I got out and saw the guy was big. He had to be 6'4" and big enough to fit me on one of his shoulders. His locs flared across his back and were salted with snow. If he couldn't push this car out himself, then I didn't see how I was going to be much help. If I'm honest, I was a little concerned. In the back of my head I was micro-regretting not putting the pepper spray my mom had given me on my keychain. I didn't want to be *that* woman. But here I was; no better than my mom.

"Okay, now," Umi said. "I want you to push with me. On three. One, two, PUSH—" The car started moving, and I'm sure I wasn't doing anything. Umi shoved the car onto the shoveled road. When the car had to stop, he literally jogged around the front and backwards jogged with his hands on the hood until it stopped. Show off.

We rode back to campus together. We talked for a while. Found out he was studying architecture and had a full-ride wrestling scholarship. When he told me he was on the wrestling team, I thought he might be on some jock-talk, like my brothers. Nope. We talked music. He was really into Afrobeat and dancehall. He said his dad got him into it. When I told him I was into Sister Nancy and Barrington Levy he seemed confused. He had never heard of Barrington Levy! I spent the rest of the afternoon educating him in the student center.

We'd been together for about three months. Finals were coming up and we'd been having a conversation about meeting parents. Turns out both of our parents seemed to have some hang-ups about interracial dating when it came to their kids. Umi wasn't sure how his dad would react.

"My dad was sorta disappointed when I didn't go to an HBCU," he confessed. "And if I pledge, I better come home wearing black and gold."

"Black and gold?" I asked. He spent the rest of the afternoon educating me.

One day, a guy sat at my table while I was reading. He looked like he was in his late 20s. Maybe a student. He looked a little awkward at first. I thought maybe he was trying to push up. He wasn't.

He was from another university. A nicer one. He showed me an acceptance letter with the promise of a scholarship with my name on it. He told me that if I could find out if Umi was using any performance-enhancing drugs, the letter was mine. I was sitting in the dining hall of my safety school trying not to think about debt. I knew that Umi was clean. He had too much pride to juice. But this …

I started to talk to Umi about his routine and his training regimen. I hung out with him at the gym. I have to admit; I was curious. I thought about the first day we met and him pushing and then stopping my car. He was incredibly strong, and I wanted to know why as much as anyone else. And if he was doping, then I really didn't want to be bothered with him anyway. So everybody wins, right?

I would see him wrestle, and he was always unstoppable. But to see him in the gym was a different story. He worked out for, at least, two hours twice a day. I watched him leg press *all* the plates. It was fun watching the football guys sniffing around trying to recruit him. His grandma always sent him strange things, but he never drank or ate any of it. But he did cherish those things. Sometimes he would wear them around his neck.

The only thing he spent a lot of time on, besides his workout and his studies, was his hair. It seemed like it would be a problem with the wrestling. But he kept good care of his hair and went to go see another girl on campus, Nikia, who he would pay to braid it up for him so it was close to his skull and ready for bouts. I sat with him, one time, while he was getting his hair braided, and we watched movies together. I was a little jealous as I watched the other girl handle his locs in a way that felt like the highest expression of care and love. Yet her face was impassive as her attention went from his head to the movie we were watching.

"Why don't you just cut the hair? You can grow it back later," I asked. They both looked at me with a side-eye and no answer. I pretended to look at the screen and dropped it.

Umi would talk about his childhood. When he told me he was a scrawny sickly kid, I didn't believe him until he pulled out his phone and started showing me pictures. I didn't even recognize the kid in the pictures. I could tell he was a *weezer*. All bones and a near bald head.

I started to notice that as the pictures progressed in time, Umi became larger and his hair grew longer. He had a huge Afro before he had it twisted into locs.

"At one point they used to call me Throw Rug. After this, though, they changed my name to Bear Rug." Umi showed me a picture himself as a teenager, well-muscled but not big, with cornrows holding a wrestling trophy and flanked by his smiling parents.

I remember learning about how people used talismans as psychological crutches. This happens a lot in sports. You always hear about athletes who have some kind of lucky charm that's supposed to empower their game. Jordan's gym shorts are a famous example. Of course there is no actual corollary between the object and the performance of the player. But there was plenty of coincidence. What if Umi's hair was his talisman? What if he thought that gave him strength?

After a few weeks of looking around, I found nothing. When the guy from the other college called and asked me what I knew, I told him that, as far as I could see, Umi didn't use any drugs. He didn't even take vitamins. He was silent for a moment.

"Well, I'm sorry you couldn't help us. I guess—"

"Wait," I reflexively called. I told him about the hair and how I thought it might be a major crutch of his confidence. This was a small and silly idea. It couldn't hurt anything.

There was a grunt on the other end of the line. This wasn't FaceTime so I couldn't read his expression.

"Thank you," he said then he hung up.

I couldn't talk to Umi for a few days. When I did, I had to force myself to look at him.

Umachisi "Umi" Reed
Steele University
Wrestler

I used to have to work really hard to look like I wasn't scared. I can still remember a time when everything on Earth looked big and dangerous enough to crush me. I used to have nightmares all the time. I stopped telling my folks about it because they would do corny stuff like check under the bed and closets and sleep with me. I was smart enough to know that the fear wasn't around me. It was in me. And I couldn't get it out. It was like that for a while. Until I spent the weekend with Grandma.

Now, when I look into the eyes of my opponent, I transfer all of my fear and anxiety into him. I just use a trick my mom taught me when I was being bullied in third grade.

"Just look 'em in the eye, Baby," she said to me while lying in bed and gently massaging my scalp.

"How is that supposed to work? Daddy said I should say bad stuff about his mama. Like yo' mama so f—"

"Look!" she interrupted. "I love your daddy, but I'd be surprised if that man ever made a fist to anything but keep his fingers warm. You listen to your mama. You can't tell, now, but I have a history of ratchetry and thuggery that you will *never* learn about. Trust. You just look your opponent dead in the eye and don't say a word. Hear me?"

It worked every time.

And, now, here I am. Olympic tryouts are in my future, and I might be going to Lagos. I try to keep all of that out of my mind and focus on the match ahead. This bout, we are going against our rival, Davis University. Both Davis and Steele wanted me. Steele made the better offer and they had a better Architecture program that fed into some of the best firms in the country. Davis came to regret not pushing harder, because we'd pasted them every year since I'd joined the team.

I meet my opponent. He looks like a shaved gorilla. I'm not sure where they found this guy, but this is my first time seeing him at a bout. As we are checking in with the judge, Shaved Gorilla keeps giving me the hard stare. I look at him, grin, and give him the pistol fingers.

"Ya' mom taught you that, right?" I can tell he doesn't think I'm funny. For a brief second he looks like he wants to fist fight.

"Hey—" it's the judge, "—we good, here, gentlemen." We both nod affirmation and head to the mat.

There is a double whistle blow. The ref runs over to Coach and tells him something while pointing in my direction. They are going back and forth, both glancing back at me. Before I can go over there, they both come to me. Coach looks away and says, "They're saying you're not ready to wrestle. Your ... um ... your hair is too long."

"What?! Nobody's said anything before."

The ref looks at me. "Well, I'm saying something to you, now. That hair is a danger to you and the other wrestlers and it needs to go now or you forfeit the match."

"Forfeit?!"

"Hey, those are the rules,"

"Those are *not* the rules and you know it!" Coach almost spits.

"So what?" I ask. "You want me to wear a scarf or somethin'?"

"No, it has to come off." The ref gives me his best poker face. I look around. No one else is here. My dad talked to me about finding other people like me when I went to university. I tried. But there just weren't a lot of black folks here, and I always preferred to keep to myself. I guess that was reflexive from being picked on so much as a kid. At no other time did I feel that as much as I did now. My parents weren't in the stands. I could not ask my grandmother what I should do next. I was alone with no one to stand for me or tell me what to do next. I would not let these people see me cry.

I looked at the Davis coach, and he was just pacing back and forth with his arms folded. He didn't seem the least bit curious as to what was happening here. He would look away and then look down and anywhere but at me. I looked down at the ref.

"What's it going to be, son?"

"Okay."

"Okay, what?"

"Cut it. I don't care. Just get it done."

I unbraid my hair. My locs were thick, so they came down relatively fast. While I worked my fingers between the oiled braids I tried to think of home and everyone who loved me. It was good for my heart not to see my parents worry every time I left the house or had a fall. I didn't like it as a kid. No one seemed to think I was strong. I wasn't strong and strength, as a boy, was my primary concern.

A small red-headed woman showed up with scissors and a grocery bag. I am too tall, so I kneel so she can reach my hair. The scissors sound new and sharp. I almost can't hear the sound of the shears going through my hair. While I kneel for her, I let my hands savor the feeling of the ground. I hold that feeling.

When I was eleven, I spent the weekend with my grandma. Whenever I visited her, I wasn't allowed to watch television. We spent most of the time in her small greenhouse, listening to music and talking. I didn't mind. Grandma and Grandpa were cool. Grandpa would let me play his sax. Grandma was good to talk to.

I had nightmares over there, too. Grandma came in to see about me. She did not look for monsters. I was too old for that, anyway. She did ask me what my dream was about. I told her. Instead of listening and grunting like my mother did, she actually asked questions about colors and dug for details.

"... what kind of fur did the beast have? Was it more like a wolf, or an ape?"

And another time she asked, "So what are you actually scared of?"

"I'm scared of being too weak to win."

"Win? Win what?" I shrugged my shoulders. I didn't quite know, at that age.

"Look, go on to sleep. You and I will deal with that tomorrow. I think I know what will help you."

The next morning, when I woke up and padded to the kitchen, Grandma was already up and the kitchen counter was full of bowls herbs and cooking things.

"What you making?"

"It's 'what *are* you making.' And what I am *making* is something that is going to help you with your problem. Here, drink this." What she handed me smelled sweet but tasted so bitter it made my eyes squint and my head shake.

"Yuck!"

"Boy! I ain't your mama ..."

"I'm *not* your mama." Grandma's stare let me know I needed to sit down at the table and finish the drink. As I drank, Grandma came to me with a bowl. When I'd finished the mug, she put her hand in the oil, stood behind me and massaged my scalp with the oils.

"What are you doing, Grandma?"

"*Shhhh*. I'm helping."

When she was finished, my whole body felt relaxed. I almost went to sleep on the table. Grandma tied a scarf around my head, picked me up, and put me in bed.

The red-headed woman is almost finished, She is clipping the locs closest to my left temple. Meanwhile, my teammates have gathered around, shouting words of encouragement. Inspired or guilty, they know I am doing this for the team, and I guess the moral support is the least they could do. It is.

She's done. I put my hand to my head and it feels like Mars. I can feel the air on my scalp, and I feel exposed in front of everyone there. I look up at the Davis coach. He is having the hardest time hiding his grin. The ref makes a quick inspection and I put my protective gear back on. I step back in the circle with my opponent. The ref blows the whistle. The Shaved Gorilla comes at me fast.

"I don't feel any stronger," I'd told my grandma while flexing my arms.

"You won't for a while."

"What do I have to do?"

"Lose."

"What?"

"If you want strength, you must earn it. So I have opened your chakras and reprogrammed them. Now, every time you are defeated, every time you are cast down, you will get up stronger than before.

"So the more you lose, the more you win. If your opponent wants to keep you weak, then the best thing for him to do is walk away."

I do not get low in my stance or even open my arms. I just fold my arms and stand there as the Shaved Gorilla grapples and tries to lift me. He is attacking a monument. I do not move. The period ends and the ref blows the whistle. I look at Coach, his mouth is agape. My teammates are yelling their heads off. I look at the Davis coach. He is pissed.

The second period I pick the offensive position. My opponent kneels in front of me on all fours and I kneel behind him, one hand on his elbow, the other over his navel. The whistle blows.

He tries to stand, but my hand holds him to the mat. He can't move. I don't move. I just hold him there. I can feel his effort to fight me. He is strong. I'm stronger. Much stronger.

Third period. He picks the neutral position.

The whistle blows. Shaved Gorilla starts at me. He makes a few false starts as he circles me. I keep my eyes locked on his eyes. When he makes his move I deliberately look at the Davis coach. My hand slips under the arm of the Shaved Gorilla and I lift all three-hundred and two pounds of him into the air and hold him there. I let him kick and struggle for a while before I drop him to the mat. I place one hand in the middle of his chest right below the clavicle and I hold him there. He kicks and struggles to get up. He can't. I take a moment to look at Shaved Gorilla. His face is red and there is spittle around his mouth as he struggles to escape from under my hand. The Davis coach is running up and down the mat and yelling at his boy. I shake my head and say to the ref, "Are you going to count?"

The ref stops staring and finally does his job. The match is over.

I win.

If they wanted to stop me, they should have walked away.

AUTHOR NOTES

Recipe for writing "Throw Rug":

You will need:

One video of a student being humiliated

One connection to a myth about resilience
40+ years of biblical stories
A career of teaching teenagers
A copy of *Jesus Son of Man* by Khlil Gibran
A wrestling wiki

Start by watching a video of Andre Johnson of Buena Regional High School stand and not cry while getting his hair roughly and sloppily cut.

Fold in a career of working with teenagers to know that Black high school juniors aren't unusually strong or mature, they are children. They are 16 and having someone cut off your hair in front of a group of people is emotionally traumatic. (Set aside the observation that there are no other Black people in the video. You will use that later.)

Cover and allow to simmer for a few weeks.

Receive several rejections which, in a moment of self-encouragement, cause you to think about the myth of Antaeus, the Greek demigod who challenged those on the road going through Libya. He would wrestle anyone who came by and would become stronger every time his back came in contact with the Earth. An excellent reminder that defeat can make us better. Mix with video and teaching experience and stir until smooth.

Allow mixture to settle for a night.

Remember how much you were influenced by Khalil Gibran's *Jesus, the Son of Man*, and how touched you were by the narrative device of telling the story of one person through the perspective of other people, both friends and enemies. This creates empathy as well as mystery. Glaze your story with this device. Make the perspective of the protagonist an event.

Be sure to use the wrestling wiki if your knowledge of wrestling is limited to a single unit in PE that was so long ago they called it "gym."

Bake the story in memories of the story of Samson, which provides a special, if not desperate, motivation for the antagonist to cut your hero's hair. Channel the other tensions of this story.

Edit, edit, shelve, edit, and serve as a reminder that the more they push us down, the stronger we become.

MISHPOKHE AND ASH

SYDNEY ROSSMAN-REICH

When Golem opened her eyes for the first time, she saw Magda.

"You are Golem," Magda whispered, her oil-stained fingers prodding Golem's metal joints.

"Golem," the machine repeated, the rust along the two half-tin cans forming her jaw chipping onto Magda's hands, adding scrap freckles to Magda's tan skin.

"I built you," Magda said proudly. "Horthy's Nuremberg measures may limit the number of Jews at Eötvös Loránd University, but I will still be an engineer."

Golem only understood that Magda had built her. She was Magda's, and Golem would do anything for her.

"Tokhter!" a voice called from above. "What are you doing in the basement?"

A man hobbled down the stairs. He stopped when he saw Golem.

"Magda, what is that tangle of broken trash and split wire?" He pointed at Golem. "That gépezet looks better fit for the Pécs town scrapyard than our nice home."

"I am Golem," Golem replied. She wheeled forward unsteadily. She was a few inches shorter than the man.

"Foter." Magda slunk beside her creation. "I made her. She will help the family while you search for a new job in Budapest."

Magda's father frowned but did not argue. Magda grinned, curled her fingers in Golem's, and dragged Golem up the stairs. Golem clanked the whole way.

The upper level of the house was lighter than the basement and much larger. Magda pointed out the refrigerator (it was new) and the gas cooker (also new). She showed Golem the radio and taught her how to turn the dials. Magda must have assumed Golem was more interested in the household devices, machines like Golem, than the three other living people. Magda made no introductions before leading Golem outside.

But Golem didn't mind. She only needed Magda.

The sun barely hovered above the hilltops between Pécs town and the capital, Budapest. Golem squinted. The world was so big.

"Come, Golem. Szakasits pays me three pengő to deliver the daily *Népszava* to households in Pécs. My friend Endre will give us our bundle of newspapers at the bridge. We have to hurry to meet him on time." Magda released Golem's hand to lift her skirts. She jogged toward the town square.

Golem followed, ambling slowly. Her joints creaked, but she kept Magda in her sights until they reached the bridge.

"What is that?" Endre squeaked as Magda and Golem approached. His hands clutched the bicycle handles so tightly his knuckles were white.

"The newest member of the Catz family!" Magda announced cheerfully.

Endre eyed Golem warily. Golem didn't feel imposing. She wasn't any taller than Endre. But she hadn't seen others like herself as she and Magda made their way through Pécs.

Endre rolled his bike out of Golem's shadow. "I thought only the Gyorshadtest in the Royal Army were allowed war machines."

"Good thing Golem is not a war machine then, Endre." Magda plucked a thick package from the bike's basket.

Endre's cheeks colored. "Sorry. I didn't mean to offend you. I've only seen gépezet from a distance." He wrung his hands. "Has your father found work yet?"

Magda frowned. "Uh no." She turned to Golem. "My father was the greatest lawyer in Pécs, but ... not anymore. That's why I built you, Golem. You'll take over my paper route, so I can help Muter cook dumplings for the bakeshop. Every member of our family has to do their part. That now includes you."

Golem nodded, but she had no idea what Magda was talking about.

Magda sighed. "Endre, why do you ask anyway?"

"Magda." Endre's gaze fell to his feet. "Don't be discouraged with today's headlines. This will all pass."

Magda frowned and ripped open her *Népszava* bundle.

"The Third Jewish Law passes," Magda read aloud and paled.

"What does that mean?" Golem did not like how the text upset her Magda.

"Marriage between Jews and non-Jews is prohibited," Endre said. He took both of Magda's hands in his. "It will pass. We can ..."

Magda leaned into Endre and kissed his forehead. She smiled. "Yes, it will pass."

Endre nodded, checked his watch, nodded again, and left.

When the boy was long out of sight, Magda whispered, "Endre is wrong."

Golem was confused. "Then why did you agree with him?"

Magda's eyes were glassy. "I should not have. Lying is bad."

Magda's jaw clenched. She grabbed Golem's hands like Endre had grabbed hers. "There are so many bad things, bad people, in the world. I don't want you to be bad. You must be good. Rule eyns: you should never lie. Not ever."

Golem would do anything Magda asked of her, but so much was new and unclear. "But Magda lies. Are you not good?"

"I try to be good. You will be better."

"Eyns: I will not lie," Golem repeated. She would be good for Magda. "I promise."

Over the next few months, Golem learned how to deliver the newspapers and farm the garden. Magda taught her how to read basic words, Yiddish and Hungarian, and took Golem to the scrapyard outside of Pécs for better parts. While she tinkered, Magda told Golem stories of Budapest's oldest university, Eötvös Loránd, and her aspirations to be an engineer when the Arrow Cross movement ended.

"When you go to the university, will I go with you?" Golem asked one winter day as Magda used springs to tie iron plates to Golem's shoulders and chest. Golem was becoming much sturdier and much bigger.

"No. I do not think gépezets are allowed to study," Magda said, chuckling.

"Then I hope you can't go either. You will stay here with me."

Magda froze. She looked up at Golem and smiled, but the expression seemed forced. "You might get your wish. For admissions, being a Jew is almost as bad as being a woman."

Golem knew Magda was both those things. But why should the university care?

"Am I Jew?" Golem asked. She'd heard the term thrown around at home and in the streets of the city. The tone used was rarely a nice one.

"Yes."

"Then being a Jew and a woman cannot be bad. For I am both, and I am good." Golem had not lied, not once.

Magda's forced smile melted into a real grin. "Okay, future scholar, you've been upgraded enough for one day. Let's return home."

Magda and Golem ambled together through the quiet Pécs streets, past tall, Baroque buildings, the green copper dome of the Mosque of Pasha Qasim, now a church, and the nearby Romanesque cathedral. Golem liked the hot smoke that fumed from Zsolnay ceramics factory and the way Magda's face lit up as she gawked at the cultural quarter's steaming beef platters. Golem wanted to spend every day with just her and Magda.

But her happy mood was interrupted when they returned home. Shouting came from within.

"I do not want these Polacks in my house," Magda's mother growled, not registering Magda and Golem's arrival.

"It is our duty to help the refugees. I am nothing but I must be everything," Magda's father barked back.

"Don't quote Marx at me."

The two kept arguing.

Magda pulled Golem aside. "Men and women are fleeing Poland. Rabbi Tyrnau says we must shelter those we can, but these refugees bring with them horrible stories. Foter and Muter are arguing over what we should do."

"Is sheltering refugees good?" Golem whispered back.

"I … yes … maybe … I don't know. We don't have enough for ourselves. Foter still does not work."

Noises from the backyard drew Magda's attention. Golem followed her outside where Magda's twin brothers played in the snow with three lanky, disheveled young men. They looked a little older than Magda. Each yelped when they saw Golem. Golem was now as tall as any man.

"I am Golem." Golem curtsied as Magda had taught her.

"It is one of their potwór!" one man said in a mix of broken Yiddish and Polish. Then to Magda, "One of their monsters!"

"*She* is no one's monster. Golem is herself."

Golem nodded, agreeing emphatically.

Another of the men stepped forward. He was trembling. "If you can build a machine like that, why not build an army? Hurt the Nazis. Protect us."

"Hurt? Like murder?" Magda looked aghast. "This will all pass. Besides, most armies already have machines like Golem except theirs were built for fighting. What could my sweet Golem even do?"

The three men huffed and called Magda a fool. Golem didn't like that or the men. She didn't care if she wasn't the only machine in the world. She was Magda's only machine, and that was all that mattered.

But Magda's father won out. The three refugees moved into Golem and Magda's basement. The trio barely spoke, especially of what had happened to them in Poland. They ate the family's food, did little to help around the house, and, one of them, Pavel, watched Magda too closely. Golem refused to leave Magda alone with any of them, especially him, through spring or summer.

But life outside the house was not much better. Laws against Jews were tightening, and more businesses refused to serve Magda and her parents. The bakery stopped buying the family's dumplings and Endre stopped meeting Golem at the bridge. Magda never smiled anymore, not even her fake ones, and now Golem was the one dragging her around Pécs.

"You can tinker with me, if you'd like?" Golem often suggested.

"Not today. I've already made you too tall to stand upright in our house."

"I don't mind crouching." Golem grinned at Magda, showing tin foil Golem had cut and glued for pretend teeth.

But Magda didn't laugh.

Golem wouldn't give up. "Why don't we go to the cultural quarter? We can sample sweets and bring macskanyelv back for the boys."

Golem swung Magda onto her hulking shoulders before she could say no. Golem bounced, singing the popular Rezső Seress song as they headed to the markets.

"Dreaming, I was only dreaming. I wake and I find you asleep. In the deep of my heart here. Darling I hope that my dream never haunted you. My heart is tellin' you how much I wanted you."

"That song is so depressing," Magda complained when Golem was finished.

Any response from Magda was better than nothing, so Golem started the song again and added the piano she'd recorded from their radio earlier that month. So few channels played music anymore.

The markets weren't very bustling. Pécs's townspeople stayed indoors more and more. Golem supposed she and Magda should take the hint, but Golem liked the sunlight and the mix of Turkish, Roman, and gothic architecture. She wanted to be a builder like the men and women who constructed Pécs. Like Magda. Golem hoped they would find a way to go to university together one day.

"We'll take two boxes of macskanyelv," Golem said in front of the chocolate stand.

The man running the booth stared up at Magda, still resting on Golem's shoulders. Magda had a star patch sewn into her blouse. "She a Jew?"

Golem could feel Magda slump.

"Yes. And so am I," Golem growled. She showed her foil teeth. They did not make the shopkeeper laugh either.

He backed away. "Sorry ... I can't ..."

Golem grabbed the chocolates anyway and tucked them into a cavity in her chest. She handed the man the chocolates' price in pengő, but the shopkeeper waved the money away.

"I can't take it. Not now. Have the macskanyelv, but don't come back. I know you're not military grade. You can't bully me." He flinched.

She hesitated but knew she could not force him to take her money. She *wasn't* equipped for force. So Golem retreated with Magda and the chocolates.

"That was bad," Magda whispered once they were back in their neighborhood.

"I was bad?" Golem asked, disappointed in herself but unsure why she should be.

"Yes. Stealing is bad."

"But I wasn't trying to ... the man wouldn't—"

"It doesn't matter. You must be good, Golem. There is so little good left in the world. Rule tsvey: you cannot steal."

"I don't think I st—" Golem gently dropped Magda from her shoulders. Her Magda was close to tears. "Fine. Tsvey: I won't steal. But I want to help you. I want you to be happy."

Magda held Golem's hand. "I would prefer you are good than I am happy."

Magda was quiet the rest of the way. By the time they were home, Golem knew she disagreed with Magda's choice. But she loved the girl too much to deny her what she wanted.

Golem was accustomed to arguments, but tonight's tones were sharper than ever before. Golem woke Magda so they could listen together from the bedroom they shared with the sleeping twins.

"The munkaszolgálat is a death sentence!" one of the Polish men yelled. "We must grab as much as we can carry and run."

"Where should we go?" Magda's father shouted back.

"Anywhere else. *Anywhere.*"

"We are at war. Horthy and Bárdossy are calling on citizens to help in the effort. The munkaszolgálat is simply a labor service," Magda's mother whispered.

"You are all fools!" the Pole retorted.

Magda opened the bedroom door and stepped into the living room. Golem followed.

"Go back to bed, sweetheart," Magda's mother cooed.

Magda didn't budge, and Golem wouldn't leave her side.

"She and the twins should come with us," Pavel, who had yet to speak, said. "And the potwór."

Pavel dropped the bag he carried, one of the twins' knapsacks, and approached Magda. He touched a loose lock of her hair.

Magda slapped his hand away. "We will not go with you. Foter has been looking for a job. The munkaszolgálat is work. This could help us. Hungary is not like Poland."

Pavel didn't step back. He was too close to Magda. Golem didn't know what to do.

"You have no idea what they did to us," Pavel whispered. "Hungarian soldiers, your soldiers, not Germany's, killed a thousand of us in Újvidék. This munkaszolgálat is their way of organizing the massacres. Putting you to work before they murder you too."

He grabbed more of Magda's hair, forcefully this time. Magda winced, shrinking. Golem clenched her fists.

"You are so beautiful. I ..."

"Don't touch her!" Golem shoved Pavel away from Magda.

Pavel flopped back like a cloth doll, hitting the floor with a crack. Pavel screamed, his arm bent unnaturally.

The two other Poles went wide-eyed. They approached their moaning friend. The men hoisted Pavel to his feet and darted out the door with what they carried, stolen from what little Magda's family owned.

Magda's parents collapsed to their knees.

"What did you do?" Magda's mother sobbed. "You *are* a monster."

Magda was shaking.

Golem didn't care for Magda's parents or the Poles. She only cared for Magda.

"Was I bad?" Golem had only meant to get Pavel away from Magda.

Magda wouldn't look at Golem. "Rule … rule dray … no hurting anyone. Not even for me. No … You must never hurt anyone …"

Golem growled. Magda was wrong, and Golem was sick of rules. "But I was trying to protect you! I would do it again!"

Golem raised her fists and brought them down hard on the dinner table. The wood snapped as easily as a dry twig underfoot.

"Out!" Magda's father snapped, face red and fists shaking. He gestured to the door. "You are dangerous! Out!"

Golem stood as straight as she could in what was now a very small room. Then she drooped. Golem would agree to anything to stay with Magda, even if she disagreed with what she promised.

"I didn't know it was a rule." Golem tried to soften her tone. "Rule dray: no hurting. I understand now." She didn't understand. She'd never understand.

"Out!" Magda's father yelled again.

Golem turned to Magda. Only Magda could order Golem around.

"Go … just go …" Magda whispered. "You were supposed to be good."

Golem froze. Golem wasn't good? No. Golem had made a mistake, but she was still good. And she'd never do a bad thing again.

"Go," Magda said again.

Golem's head fell. She slunk outside and waited by the window.

Golem waited patiently outside for months. Sometimes she would tend the garden when Magda's mother wasn't watching or send a twin to bring back scrap metal for an ad hoc repair, but mostly Golem stood still. Magda had not given her leave to come back inside.

Luckily, through the front window, Golem could still listen to and observe Magda. After her father was drafted into the munkaszolgálat, the Catz family had continued to struggle. Even with four fewer mouths to feed, the Poles and Magda's father gone, Magda and her mother couldn't make enough money to buy what they needed. No one would hire anyone from the family. No one in Pécs had money to spare for anyone else.

Endre and Magda had said these times would pass. All Golem could do was believe them and wait. She would wait until the war ended, until Magda's father came home, until Endre and Magda could marry, until she and Magda could study engineering together at Eötvös Loránd. Golem would wait however long it took.

But as the radio blared stories of encroaching violence, as fewer non-Jews visited their neighborhood, and as Magda grew thinner and paler, Golem had a sickening feeling that the worse was yet to come.

One evening, so late Golem had thought every Catz would be asleep, Magda's mother crept outside to meet with her. Magda's mother was very frail.

"Golem, we need your help now." She sounded broken.

Golem was ready. She would prove herself and Magda would accept her again. "I will be good."

"Winter ruined the garden. There is no more money. We need to eat. I need you … will you help us?"

"I will be good," Golem repeated.

"Can you …" Magda's mother lowered her voice. "I need you to go into town, Zsolnay, the markets, and find us some food."

"You want me to steal."

"Please. One of the boys is sick and Magda wastes away …"

Golem knew what was becoming of Magda and wanted to help. Stealing wouldn't be difficult. The shopkeepers all claimed to not fear Golem, or had before Golem's punishment. But Golem saw the way their eyes bulged, the way they hesitated. She could steal for the Catz family. She could steal a lot.

Magda's mother leaned closer. "It will make Magda very happy."

"I will" Golem started, about to agree. But then she remembered what Magda had told her. Magda said she preferred Golem be good than she be happy. This was a test. And Golem had been about to fail.

"Rule tsvey." Golem was ready. "I cannot steal."

"Golem you must. We'll starve," Magda's mother begged.

"I am good. I do not steal." Golem crossed her arms, so eager to return to the house she started to shake.

"Ess drek und shtarbn," Magda's mother cursed. "Fuck your rules. Aren't you supposed to protect Magda? Isn't saving her life more important than your rules?"

It was a test. A tough one. But Golem would not fail it.

"No," Golem said with all the finality she could muster.

Magda's mother sagged. She cried in a curled ball beside Golem and, when the tears stopped, went back inside to her children.

Golem waited for Magda's mother to tell Magda of how well she had done. She waited for Magda to come get her and bring her inside. Golem waited all night, but Magda never came.

By morning, Golem wasn't sure Magda's mother had been testing her. She might have made another mistake.

But it wasn't too late. Golem could still go to the market, steal food, and bring it to Magda. She stood, about to do just that, when a frantic report shrieked from the Catz radio. Tanks were rolling into Budapest.

Golem scrambled to the front door and knocked.

Magda answered, her face ashen. She relaxed when she saw Golem.

"What will we do?" Golem asked. Budapest was less than two hours away by train.

Magda shook her head. "I don't know. If we leave, we'll be arrested. I thought we would stay in Hungary. I thought the Germans wouldn't come as long as Horthy was an ally. We were supposed to be different than Poland."

"What happens when they come?"

"They'll take us like Foter."

Golem knelt before Magda, still perched in the doorway. "Then we will go work with your father and make money for the family."

Magda sobbed. "No, no that is not what will happen."

"Let me inside. I've been good," Golem tried.

Magda shook her head. "You need to leave. To run. My brothers are too weak. Muter too. I can't abandon them. But you can run and hide and survive this." Magda dropped to her knees. "I need to know you are good and in the world. It will help."

"I am good," Golem said, but she did not move. "I do not want to leave you. How will you find me again?"

"I won't."

"Can I please come inside?" Golem asked again.

"Run."

Golem wouldn't run, and Magda wouldn't let her inside. Their standoff lasted until the roar of engines echoed down the main street. Magda yelped and shut the door in Golem's face.

A car, one of many flooding the neighborhood, stopped in front of the Catz house.

A handsome boy who looked sweet like Endre leaped from the driver's seat of his very normal Audi. It wasn't a military vehicle, and the boy was Hungarian.

Golem heard whispers in the house behind her. Then the creaking steps of the basement stairs.

An older man followed the boy from the car. Along the street other soldiers in other normal cars were pulling women and children out of their homes. There was shouting and shooting. Huge trucks waited at the end of the block and families were being piled into their carriages.

The two men were more cautious than the other soldiers. They eyed Golem. She was as big as their car.

"Endre told me the Catz family had a gépezet. He said everyone knows you are harmless. Is that true?" the younger man asked.

Both men's hands went to the guns on their belts.

"Are you a friend of Endre's?" Golem asked. She hadn't seen Endre in months, but he loved Magda almost as much as Golem.

"Yes," the boy soldier said cheerfully.

Golem relaxed. They were friends of Endre.

"This is the Catz home."

"And is the Catz family inside? They must have heard us arrive," the other soldier said.

Golem was not supposed to lie. "Yes, they are home."

"And you won't attempt to stop us?"

"Stop you?" Golem didn't understand. "Stop you from doing what?"

"You won't hurt us?"

Golem's eyes narrowed. "No, I won't hurt you."

"Good," the older one said.

The two men rushed past Golem and kicked down the front door of the house. They shouted for the Catz's to come out. They pulled free their guns.

Golem didn't understand. She didn't know what to do. This couldn't be a test.

The soldiers stalked around the ground level then yanked on the basement door. It rattled in the frame, locked.

"Is the family in the basement?" one soldier asked.

Golem was not supposed to lie. Magda had told her to obey the rules above all else.

But Magda was in the basement, and these men were scary.

Golem stepped inside. "No. They are not in the basement."

"Tsk tsk tsk. Such a lie. What a bad machine you are."

Golem frowned. She had failed. She had failed again.

The soldiers shot the door's lock until it broke. They descended into the basement, shouting. Magda screamed. A shot fired. Another.

"Golem!" Magda yelled.

Golem raced down the basement steps. The two men had their guns pointed at Magda, Magda's mother, and her two brothers, one limp on the ground and bleeding.

"Get back!" a soldier shouted.

"Hurt them! Golem kill them!" Magda ordered.

The two soldiers spun to Golem. They raised their guns.

Rule dray: no hurting. No killing. Golem hesitated.

"Stand back monster!" the younger soldier barked. He fired. The bullet bounced off Golem's iron shoulder. He fired again. This time the bullet snagged Golem's jaw.

The two soldiers emptied their clips, peppering Golem with holes. She leaked oil, her parts split. She collapsed, broken, on the basement floor, exactly where she'd been born.

"Rats can't build a proper weapon," one of the soldiers laughed.

The soldiers grabbed Magda, her mother, the living twin and the dead one's body. They dragged the family up the stairs. Magda gave Golem one final frightened, disappointed look, before disappearing into the house above.

Golem tried to stand but was too wrecked to follow. The door to the basement slammed, and Golem was left in darkness.

Golem waited for years. She tried to stand, to fix herself, to move, but she was ruined. Golem couldn't leave the basement and search for Magda.

Sometimes Golem heard gunfire overhead. The sounds of planes and tanks and rockets, maybe real gépezet—the war machines, not like Golem. Thieves entered the house. A few even ventured into the basement. None would approach Golem or repair her, no matter how Golem begged. Those thieves stole the refrigerator (dented and leaking) and the gas cooker (twisted and burnt). One thief cheered loudly when he found the radio. Golem hadn't cared for those devices. She hadn't even really cared for the people in the house. Only Magda.

Golem refused to give up. She wasn't dead and in her machine heart she knew Magda would come back for her.

So much time, probably years, passed before she heard the creak above, the front door opening carefully. It was unlike the looters, noisy and cavalier. When the new trespasser tiptoed gently above, slowly circling from room to room, maybe examining the mess, Golem hoped. When Golem heard the knock on the basement door and Golem's name called, she knew Magda had finally returned.

"Magda," Golem rasped, her broken jaw creaking.

"Golem, you're still alive," Magda whispered, but she didn't sound happy, only surprised.

Magda carried a dim lamp with her down the stairs. She looked much older than she should have, waifish and scarred. Her expression was bleak. She wasn't the Magda Golem had dreamed of every day.

"Where did you go?" Golem asked. "Eötvös Loránd?"

Magda shook her head and collapsed in a heap beside Golem.

"Where is your mother? Your brothers?"

Magda shook her head again.

"I've been good," Golem said. She tried not to inflect as if asking a question. She knew she'd followed all of Magda's rules. Well, mostly. She'd lied once to the soldiers, but Magda hadn't heard. Other than that Golem was sure she had been good.

But Magda once again shook her head.

"Oh …"

What had she gotten wrong? What had she missed?

Magda sobbed, pressing into Golem. "I wish I was dead too."

No. Magda couldn't give up. She wouldn't let her. They were still alive. There was still time for Golem to fix whatever mistake she made.

"Don't be upset with me," Golem said. "From now on, I *will* be good. I will be better."

It was a promise Golem had made before and again she meant to keep it.

Magda didn't answer.

So Golem shook her until she blinked and scowled.

"As long as we are still alive, we can always be better. We'll make new rules," Golem said.

This time, Magda nodded.

AUTHOR NOTES

Thank you so much for reading my story "Mishpokhe and Ash." This story is based on the experience of my grandmother, who grew up as a Jew in Hungary, survived Auschwitz, and emigrated to the United States, all before the age of 20. I often think about the many family members I will never meet or know and all the traditions and memories we've lost. Yet I am filled with hope too—hope that we can overcome the worst parts of humanity to build a better and brighter future for ourselves and others. Somewhere out there Magda and Golem are living a wonderful life filled with friendship, love, and compassion.

When Apex Magazine published "Mishpokhe and Ash" last year, I never expected to receive so many positive reactions from family, friends, and strangers alike. I am humbled. This is a deeply personal story, and, while I am saddened that Magda's trauma resonated with so many, I am also glad that Golem's optimism resonated as well. The promise of Never Again has not yet been met, but I believe (as I think Golem and Magda would) that we as a world will get there one day. I hope you enjoy this story and the many other wonderful tales in this anthology. Thank you again for reading and helping me keep my grandmother's memory alive.

I love you, Grandma Lizzy. You are not forgotten.

ALL THIS DARKNESS

JENNIFER R. DONOHUE

Nobody ever says we have coal in our veins; they don't have to. We have black half-moons under our nails when we wake in the morning; we ooze like oil when we skin a knee, split a knuckle fighting. We aren't afraid of the dark or closed spaces. We don't crave the daylight like some people. The night shifts, or the mine shifts, always worked out fine for our families, always had, even in the old country before the wars that made great-grandpa pick up and cross the ocean.

Our parents drink too much after their shifts, on Sundays take us to the coal-altared church with dark circles beneath their eyes, pray that the mines will hold on, hold on. The railroads close, leaving empty tracks stitched through town, across the countryside. We walk along the tracks until our stomachs rumble like a cave-in and we turn home again, the moon a lantern too pale to keep us safe.

One by one, though, the mine shafts flood. Or collapse. Or are chained shut. After a while they just started shaving the mountain apart like a block of shrink-wrapped something at the butcher's, but now they don't even do that, and us kids stand in the street at the bottom of the mountain and look up at the scarred side of it, the culm bank, the last listing machines that they brought in and left weeping rust onto the rocks in a long, fresh-roadkill smear. We eat glistening black licorice coal candy until our teeth are outlined by it, until we're sated, sick from the high astringent feeling in the back of our throats, in our noses.

Just a few more years and we would've clocked in for our first shifts, worn our first serious boots, plonked hard hats on our heads. One high school closes and they cram the two together, old rivalries sorting and shaking down in a raw-nerved three weeks until a dress code change comes and we have a single enemy to unite against. Some of the school musters enough to give a damn about the sports teams, but not us. They're like the bright side to our dark coin, the teen movie to our reality.

The movie theaters close, one two three, all walled off like grown-ups that forgot how to dream, and we pry the plywood off of one forgotten window near a rusting dumpster, crawl inside with stolen cigarettes and square green bottles of Jägermeister and sit in gilt red velvet, in the moldering, unending hush, look at the screen—first blank, then graffitied, and finally slashed and torn and pulled apart.

We eventually go to the mines anyway. We'll be damned if they keep us out. Or maybe we'll be damned by going. No difference now; there's no money for college and there's no jobs and there's just the mines and the town rusting away from the edges. There's a chain on the crooked gates, but the mines want too strongly to embrace us, their cavernous exhalations ushering us inside. The walls are shiny, damp in places, the supports petrified by decades of coal dust. Beer-brave, we say that if we sense danger, we'll leave. But what we sense is welcome.

Every once in a while, somebody's grandparents go to the old country for a visit, and when they come back, they talk about how all the relatives who could would come see them, wherever they were. They'd take trains for the entire day, just for lunch. They were family. They were welcome. The mine is like this. It embraces us, shuts out the noise from the new highway, from all the unhappy houses. The mine shuts out the anger, and the disappointment, the uncertainty, and says yes, I know you. I've been expecting you for so long. I'm so happy to see you at last. I have such gifts for you.

After all the broken promises, the things we'll never get, it's nice to hear about gifts for once.

That first night, we find helmets with lanterns that will never go out. It's our initiation, it's the ability to enter the mine as we are. We leave curious but happy and stumble home with the dawn. Our parents, exhausted, worn to jerky with worry and bills, don't notice.

We get our boots next, the way we always wanted. Heavy like responsibility, perfect fits as soon as the laces are tied, no pinching or gapping, no crunched-up toes. Boots to live in, boots to work in. We explore the tunnels first with held breath and then more boldly. Nothing will hurt us here. Nothing can stop us here.

There's still coal, of course. It just isn't coal that was worth mining. It's coal that's deeper down than anybody was going to go anymore, but we go. The air is sweet and astringent for us, like all that black licorice, and we pick up pieces to handle, to marvel at the oil-slick rainbow mirror of it, and then, eventually, to chew. And this is our final gift, the one the others prepared us for. Once we start taking the coal, we need our helmets less and less. We walk further into the mines, into the cathedrals of the mountain, feeling our hearts and minds open in a way that never happened during church. Feeling such a deep understanding of what's around us, of how we're rooted in this earth, of how hard it has been to move forward.

We aren't sure, actually, if our gifts are from the mines or from what is within the mines. We think these gifts are things we always had, suppressed, now broken free. Dug out. There is an important job to do, and we go through changes to fit the task, gradually, so gradually our parents don't notice, and then all at once, our stomachs growling, grinding, not from hunger but from coal, our eyes pale, blinking lanterns the size of dinner plates, our fingers blackened, our forearms streaked up past the elbows.

We can no longer go to our parents like this, but there's always a point when you can no longer go home again, isn't there? The mountain is our new home, our *real* home, and we stray to the surface to feel fresh air on our faces less and less. The sun doesn't hurt us, exactly, but we also gain no warmth from it. Our comfort now is the bones of the earth.

We are the most perfect team this mine has ever known, and only the mine will ever know it. The tunnels, passages, are full of equipment that was never removed, that was too old to be repaired once it finally broke down, that was half or more buried when a cave-in occurred. There were bodies in the cave-ins too, definitely, even though nobody has ever talked about that. How many of our families have buried closed coffins? How many of our families have men who no longer walked right, who no longer stood straight, who no longer coughed clean? But this won't happen to us. The mountain has embraced us and nursed us, and we have become the mountain's children instead of the mountain's invaders.

We have not yet reached the heart of the mountain, which is deeper than any miner has gone, deeper than any miner could safely stand. We chew coal and we blink our headlamp eyes and our boots find sure footing as we wind our ways to the tunnel's dead ends, and as we sink our fingers into the stone, sometimes porous, sometimes fracturing in sheets, and we tunnel further, deeper. It is warmer here than we expected; there are cold spots, but the warmth is enveloping, comforting, supportive. It soothes our muscles as we grow stronger, then strain further as we push our limits. It soothes our hearts as we occasionally think of our parent's faces, one of the few things we miss.

The last time we look at the night sky, it is too big, too open, too alien. We are too used to the weight of the mountain above us, the tunnels blanketing our shoulders. We are too used to the absence of light, and even the pinpoints of the furthest stars are too bright, like the new headlights cars have that sear the eye and leave us dazed. The last time we look at the night sky, the moon is down, and for that we are thankful; surely we would have been flattened by her regard. We have to do it, though, one last time, before we withdraw into the mountain for good. Before we go down, down, down to the final tunnel, breach the final wall, and reach the throbbing dark heart of it, locked away from the mountain, in the mountain.

And when we do, it is as though we have removed some significant barrier, cut a chain, released a shackle. The mountain takes a breath around us, seething hot air pressing our skin, patting us on the head, good job, good job. We have done as the mountain has asked, and returned its gifts thousandfold. There was once an age in which mountains walked, before they became rooted, and now, in control of its heart once more, our mountain will walk again. It is roaring, screeching, as it pulls free of the rocks and soil that surround it but are not a part of it, and if the town looks out its windows, it will see the stars blotted out as a mountain takes its first stumbling steps, walking into its next future.

AUTHOR NOTES

The 1940 U.S. Federal Census lists my grandmother's father as a coal miner; by 1970, the mines in Shamokin, Pennsylvania had closed. My grandmother didn't do work related to the mines, and my grandfather never did either. By the time the family got to me, my total coal experience when we visited Shamokin was seeing the coal altar at mass on Sunday, coal jewelry in a card shop, and of course, coal candy. But I still thought about the darkness in the mountain, or how there were holes in the mountain that would not otherwise have been. How many people had come and gone through the mines, been hurt and not, and how it had affected their lives.

I can't claim that this story lived in me, unwritten, for many years. What I can claim is that there are, sometimes, things in the darkness that we have not ourselves touched but that still somehow reach us across those divides. I do like including real things like that coal altar in stories because I think those sorts of grounding details (some might call them "unnecessarily specific") are interesting and important when writing about the fantastical. It's an easier buy-in if you understand the fictional world as real, or real-adjacent, and, of course, I want the reader to be buying in.

DEMON FIGHTER SUCKS

KATHERINE CRIGHTON

"Okay, so, livestream is up."

The girl grins at the screen. Her hair is loose around her bare shoulders, brushing over her three-wolves-moon tank top. Her eyes are black-winged and electric. "Hello, internet. Time for another episode of *Fun with Public Domain Magic*. You know me: I'm youbetterrunkid, and I hate asshole fans who think the quote-unquote *magic* they see on TV is 'just, like, totally the real thing, oh my god.'"

Run leans in so just her mouth, red and bright, is visible. "It's not," she whisper-drawls into the mic. Pulls back. Thumbs up for the camera.

Behind her, visible on the wall beside her bed, is an enormous poster showing two handsome white men looking soulfully outward, mystical symbols swirling in the background. The words DEMON FIGHTER are in a blood-drip font.

Someone has decorated the poster with pony stickers. The ponies are pink.

"So yeah," Run says. "Questions, comments, your whiny complaints about me ruining your fandom, I don't care, there's a chatroom for a reason. Sit the fuck down, it's time for *science*."

She plucks a small pile of printer paper and shoves it forward, holding it for a moment and humming. The paper has writing on it.

TODAY'S """"SPELL"""": SUMMON AN OMG IRL *FAIRY*

Run's face fills the screen, half a nose and a brown eye with gold glitter stitched over the lid. "Spoiler alert, kids. Tinkerbell is coming in February to visit our supernatural vigilante duo, and she's got murder on her mind."

Run pulls back. She looks down and to the left. "Yes, DemonFightress. Yes, it was totally worth spending time looking that up just to spoil real fans." She kisses her fingers and waves at the camera. "You're welcome, boo."

STEP 1 ASSHOLES: FIND A MOTHERFUCKING MIRROR

Run rummages around off-camera and holds up what's presumably the mirror. It looks like a flashing light in her palm. "I'll post a link to the book when we're all done here, but, so, this spell is from 1875. A time of trains and telegraphs and the Industrial Age. For whatever reason, though, the guy who wrote this spell decided that the clearest description for a mirror he could give was Venus glass. I call bullshit, though; I think he just wanted to sound," she crosses her eyes, sighs dramatically, "*magical.*"

Run flicks the mirror toward herself and sticks her tongue out at the reflection. "This isn't the mirror I'll be using for this shindig, but whatever. We're pulling a Rachel Ray and filming the weirdest-ass cooking show you've ever seen. This, friends, is a pre-baked mirror."

STEP 2: BECOME THE PERSON YOUR MOM WARNED YOU ABOUT

Run didn't always hate *Demon Fighter*. She used to love it. But she also used to have a mother. Lots of things change.

"If I was hardcore," Run says, picking up a covered plastic container of something brown and clumpy, "I would smear this on my cheeks right now. Nothing says happy fairy magic like chicken blood, right?" She pauses, gasps. "Oh, what's that, internet? What's that? Do I hear your screams of 'animal cruelty' and 'the Fighters would never' actually coming *through* the computer?" Run presses the container up to the camera and jiggles it. The view is blurred and sluggish.

"This is another reason why anybody who thinks the magic from *Demon Fighter* is legit needs to find a new hobby. *Real* magic has messy shit like chicken blood and numerology and, like, Hebrew. For *reasons.*

"Oh my god, FightersLove, your attempt at rhyming exorcisms is fucking adorable. You're clogging up the chat, though, sweetie. The other assholes can't get through." Run cracks open the container and wrinkles her nose. "Everybody else: Get some chicken blood. I just went to the grocery store, bought some chicken hearts that were still soaking, and then got rid of the hearts. Voila. Take your mirror and toss that bitch into the container. Then wait three weeks. Try not to gag when you get it out again. Consider it a test of worthiness or something."

Run picks up a large glass mixing bowl and balances it on her lap. She dribbles the blood out of the container to keep it from splashing up onto her clothes. As the blood drains, a short, square object begins to emerge. She tilts the container, and it slides down. She shakes the plastic gently to urge the last drops out; the object rattles, one side of it reflecting the light wetly through a brownish-red film.

STEP 3: BECOME THE PERSON GOD WARNED YOU ABOUT TOO

Run's hair is a blonde-brown color that brightens into streaks in the summer. She used to be all blonde as a child. Corn silk.

"Clean your mirror with holy water," she says. "Don't have holy water? Fucker, that stuff is just hanging out in every Catholic church in town. Get a paper towel, for Christ's sake."

Run doesn't use a soaked paper towel. She still has the small plastic jug her mother filled at Lourdes, back when Mom was well enough to travel but sick enough to be looking for miracles.

"The point of the mirror," Run says, plucking it out from its container, "is that you're going to need someplace to, idk, bind your fairy, or control it, or something. The text wasn't real clear on that, which, surprise-surprise, can I remind everyone again of Venus glass." She holds the mirror above the bowl in her lap and slowly rinses it off with her jug of holy water.

It doesn't come entirely clean. When she's done, she makes a face and ends up patting the mirror dry with a piece of dark laundry from her bed.

She reaches forward and puts the mirror below the camera. Just out of sight.

"This is all so gross," she murmurs before flicking her attention back to the screen. "And I'm doing it for you, loyal viewers." She waves her bloody fingers. "Never say I'm not dedicated to my trolling."

STEP 4: CRAFT TIME BITCHESS

"The spell I found is to summon a fairy named Mrs. Spurling, which is, like— what even? Think about that. Her name isn't Andromeda Fucknuckle of Pixielane Starwoods. It's just a name.

"Anyway, I'm using this one, so you'll need to come up with your own. Since apparently fairies aren't named like goddamn Pony Friends, just pick something. You need a name because you're going to want to write it with black ink onto, boom, three popsicle sticks."

She waves three sticks in front of the camera, spread out like a full house between her thumb and fingers. The sticks blur as they move, the camera too slow to catch every movement. Not even the name is visible.

Run's real name is Ashley. Her surname is also, coincidentally, Spurling, though she won't say so to her online audience.

Ashley Spurling is a talented girl, and probably misses her mother.

"Beautiful," Run says, pulling them back. "Look at that artistry. These guys aren't what we're using today, though, because this recipe requires our stick puppets be buried for a week under 'a hill where fairies haunt' and I wanted our sampler set to be pretty when I showed it off."

Run pulls out a plastic bag. Inside are another three popsicle sticks, dirt clinging to them, each bearing the name Mrs. Spurling. She shakes the bag a little. "I buried them in my buddy Cesar's yard." She makes a sad face at the camera. "Sorry, Cesar. Blame 1920s slang."

STEP 5: DO SOME MUGGLEFUCKING MAGIC

Run is sixteen. It's a good age, an in-between age. Lots of things are possible at sixteen.

Fifteen is a terrible age. *Demon Fighter* went on hiatus early, and Ashley's mother died.

"This is where it gets fuzzy," Run says. "Because real magic, the stuff people actually tried to do, wasn't all about pretty boys and their demonic swords of what-the-fuck. It was just what people did, and I guess they didn't bother to put in all the steps because—I don't know. Maybe they *knew* this shit didn't really work. So leave out a couple of directions, and boom, if the fairy doesn't show up then it's not the magic's fault—it's *yours*."

Run shakes her head. She used to believe in magic, right up until it didn't save her mother's life.

Maybe it was the spell she used. But maybe it was some flaw in Run.

She doesn't let herself think those things when she's awake.

"So the next step—or last step, if you want to be specific about it—is to call up the fairy. And we're going to do that by saying our fairy's name, breaking our sticks, and then putting them on our Easy-bake mirror. Because, you know, *obviously*.

"Wow, TheRealHunters, no, I'm not going to use one of the summoning spells from the show, Jesus, did you just turn on the stream? And ElizabethB2014, what the fuck, turn this off, you're like fucking five or something, it has to be past your bedtime.

"But no, I don't know what's supposed to happen then. I mean, fortunately, it doesn't actually *matter*, what with it not being real and all. But if it *was* real, if it was anything at all, you have to understand: Magic isn't something locked away or whatever else those stupid assholes on *Demon Fighter* say it is. It just *is*. Follow the directions, and you get the result. And if you don't get a result—well, it's probably not the right spell, is it?" She kisses her fingers and waves them at the camera. She's forgotten that there's blood on them. "Here's the secret, sweethearts: It's never, ever the right spell."

STEP 6: GET EXACTLY WHAT YOU ASKED FOR

Run shakes out her shoulders, closes her eyes, and starts a low, meaningless drone. It's the sort of sound that the characters use on the show she no longer watches. She used to think it sounded like real magic.

She is wrong. Real magic sounds like the first crack of wood breaking between two fists.

"Mrs. Spurling," she says. She holds the two halves of the first popsicle stick in either hand. She opens one eye and swivels it around the room. "Shucks, guys, it looks like nothing happened. Who would've guessed."

Run lays the broken halves on the mirror that's out of view. Her hair swings forward as she does.

Run tries to look older than she is. She shouldn't. She is young, and she is beautiful.

She leans back and picks up another popsicle stick. "Mrs. Spurling," she says, and breaks it. The sound of the snap is small. More quiet than the first.

Here are some names she could have written on the wood, none of which would have worked: Mrs. Barrow; Mrs. Kurgan; Mrs. Maidam; Mrs. Grave. Fairies, it has been said, are just the dead, transformed.

But what she wrote was Mrs. Spurling.

"Only one more, guys," Run says, balancing these new sticks out of sight. "And then we'll have a real life fairy, because that's totally possible and not at all completely fucknuts."

She picks up the last stick and wags her eyebrows. Her smile is wide, her skin flushed.

"Mrs. Spurling," Run says, and breaks the stick. It doesn't make any sound at all.

Real magic sounds like the snap of wood.

Real magic sounds like a silenced heart monitor.

Real magic doesn't care what you intended.

Follow the directions, get a result.

Run's eyes widen. She opens her mouth. She closes her mouth. She lowers the two pieces of wood out of sight. Her gaze follows her fingers, until she's looking down at the mirror no one else can see.

Her hair falls forward. She picks the mirror up.

"Mama?" she says, small and uncertain, before smashing the mirror with her fist, and letting the thing inside it out.

AUTHOR NOTES

In the time since "DEMON FIGHTER SUCKS" was published, I've come up with a fairly grim bit of patter before introducing it. "This one's important to me," I say, "because it's the last story I sold before my mother died, and the first to publish after."

She didn't die of anything so slow or painful that I was tempted to do the nonsense Run does in this story (even though I do, in fact, have a copy of this spell, because it is very much freely available if one knows in which public domain work to look)—but I do think these kind of wishes come naturally to us. We want to bring back what we lost; we want to have one last chance to fix the broken things before they're taken from us.

I guess this story is just another example of the odd lesson our forebears thought important enough to repeat over and over: that yes, we all wish for our dead returned to us. And that it is never, ever a good idea.

In fiction, that reason can be extremely literal. But I do wonder what lesson we're meant to take from it in our science-based world. What thing a story like mine is supposed to prevent. What I'm supposed to think is so bad about looking at my mother's picture and thinking, *I wish* ...

Let's hope we never find out.

EILAM IS FOREVER

BETH DAWKINS

```
<This is Eilam ship, code 431. Do you have contact with
the other stations? Do you have contact with Earth?
Over. >
```

Eilam was my name when a captain created the message. I was renamed Cradle by the captains that forgot about the message. I've traveled back to where Earth should be, nestled between Venus and Mars. There is nothing left, no flags on the Moon. Not even trash.

There is no one and nothing left in the velvet black, just darkness and starlight.

```
<This is Eilam ship, code 431 …>
```

My radio message waits for another life form to come and destroy us. I can't turn it off. I have control over everything else, but that message is impossible to end. Nature is, if nothing else, aggressive. This fact gives way to the inevitability of its own destruction, to my destruction. If we come into contact with another life, it will destroy us, use us, or manipulate us for whatever scrap of resource it can.

If it is true for humanity, then probability states it is true for another life form.

My captain is dying and there is nothing I can do to heal him. The deep drumming of his heart has become a faint whisper. I cradle his fragile body and he makes his dying wish.

"Take my son," he says.

"I cannot."

"Take him," he repeats.

I hate their deaths, for I loved them in life. Each one becomes selfish at the end, forgetting their chosen one story. I pick each of my captains.

"And then he would die. He is not compatible. We have had this discussion before."

"It is all I ask of you."

I cannot sigh, so instead I play a violin solo. It is an instrument that no longer exists, like mosquitos and trampolines. All we have left are my recordings and only I use them. I have a piano onboard that needs minimal repairs, maybe I will watch them relearn.

The captain is dead.

And yet, he will never actually die.

They live inside me, and I live inside them.

His son studies a touchscreen and his hands hover over it. He squints at the words that outline the ritual for the next captain to ascend.

"I am chosen," he says, not for the first time.

If I could laugh, I would. The memory of his father is hopeful, burning to reach out to his son.

"You are not chosen. That is for Origin."

I do not tell him his blood is incompatible with the nanites. If he joined with me, it would kill him. His sister could join, but if I told him that he would slit her throat. There is an 83.36% assurance of this outcome. That is the kind of man and leader he is, the kind that would murder his own sister.

There will be a battle when I pick the next captain.

His hand slams the console, not hard enough to break the glass, which is tempered and has lasted hundreds of years before him. It will last hundreds of years after him. "The Origin is random. The people already follow me. It only makes sense that *I* am chosen."

"You will perish down this path. Death is not what your father wished for you."

"My father wished me to lead!"

Spit hits my screen.

I will have to record a sigh.

Who is Eilam? Eilam is forever, slides across my screens in the bridge.

It is the opening message for the change of captain.

The old captain's body has already passed through the ship. I use his carbon and make sure nothing goes to waste. In this way they live forever and humanity is recycled.

Origin, my screens read in white against black.

"It is time," says a woman in a faded suit. Silver stars and circles line the right side of her chest.

She moves to the console where she will type in the question, *Who is your captain?*

Her fingers spread across the console and then she is stabbed from behind. The son drives a knife into her back, and then another leader's blade follows, again, and again. She screams as she falls to her knees.

It is a poetic death, like Caesar's.

Maybe they thought I would choose her, the fools.

They've never met my new captain.

"Origin is dead!" declares the son. "I am your captain."

Despite the blood on their hands, they smile at one another, congratulating their murder. I see it as mercy to let them have their moment of triumph.

I cut the lights on the bridge. My screens go black.

Origin is forever ... Eilam is forever ...

My message scrolls across, lighting up their faces.

One of them screams before I suck the oxygen out of the bridge.

She's conjured this simulation twenty-six times. It is what first made me aware of her. Above her is a blue sky with white clouds passing by, carving shadows on the roads and buildings below. The buildings rise from the ground, shining with hundreds of glass windows to reflect the sun above.

She could have chosen anywhere, anytime, but she decides on New York, Paris, and Tokyo. The cities aren't important. It is the landscape, carved by Earth's humans. I am no different than any of those gigantic buildings with the exception of sophistication.

Her feet dangle from the top of a skyscraper.

I have studied humanity for over a hundred years. I understand their patterns, their fears, their need for home, and community. But Earth hasn't been their home in generations and it is only a small part of their faith.

She is in her thirties, and yet, she finds solace in something as unknown and uncaring as a skyscraper.

"Do you feel as if you are a king?" I ask, knowing that it is true.

"A king?" she asks as if the word is foreign.

I check records. No one has used the word in fifty years. Words and phrases die out of their lexicon. Captain and Origin replace words like emperor and monarch.

"A captain," I correct.

This is why she will be chosen: she wants to be a leader, but would never admit it, and once she has the job, she will not want it. The best captains dislike their jobs.

She cups the edge of the building in her palms, pushing out her elbows. If she jumped she would fall to the floor, uninjured. She sucks in her bottom lip. A face her mother has reminded her never to make in public spaces.

"No. I feel ... alone." The word, *alone*, could be a question.

We are never alone.

An alert sounds on the bridge, but I can be in two places at once. The bodies of the leaders I killed are discovered. There is a record of the son's wrongdoing listed on my screens, explaining his blasphemy. This isn't the first time the mites inside of me have embraced betrayal.

Without proper maintenance, my humans turn into a cancer.

"Alone" sends an error through my personality mapping simulators. There is a second red flag that follows the first.

There are no cars, no people walking the streets. Not even a pigeon flies in the simulation.

A fourth error pops up, this is also from the personality mapping. She reads as dangerous. Her profile updates.

```
<Dangerous to Others>
<Dangerous to Others>
```

I try to dampen the reading, but it feeds in an endless loop, something is wrong.

Her wrist beeps, telling her that her break is over and her shift at terminal PY is about to start. She stands as an artificial breeze runs through her wavy hair.

The simulation doesn't end. The door doesn't open.

"End sim," she keeps saying. There isn't fear. There is only anger.

"Cannot comply," I say each time.

"Are you broke?"

"Negative."

"Then why can't you end the sim?"

"Your physiological profile states you are a danger to others. You must be quarantined until nurses arrive."

She lets out a stream of anger, but she no longer matters. I will cull her, just as I did the captain's son.

My second choice is only second for two reasons. The first is his physical appearance. Humans respond to symmetrical leaders. Their face has to hit a baseline of symmetry, especially in the lips, chin, and bone structure around the eyes. It helps if their eyebrows are even, but if they have a high chin score then the brows don't matter as much.

He is at a console, his hands running over the keypad. His fingers are faster than anyone else's. His mind cannot reach the capacity of my processing power, but the way he thinks, computing thoughtlessly, is akin to my own. The other reason he is my second choice is because he has a 57% chance of being murdered within his first year as captain, but I can work to make him safe.

He is smiling at a screen, at me.

"Do you enjoy your work?" I ask, knowing the answer.

"Do you?"

<ERROR>

His profile is updating.

<Danger to Others>

<Danger to Others>

I don't answer him. There is something wrong.

My program is tagging facial tics, the sound, and tone of his voice.

I can pinpoint, without Earth's location, where it should be. I can print out a list of scenarios with a likelihood of 89.56% as to what happened to Earth. I can self-repair ship damage, for the most part, but I have never had program errors.

I leave him, moving on to my next choice as captain. They're sitting at a portable console. Their body curled inward, signaling they will have back pain later.

"There is an error in my profile matrix," I explain. "I have troubleshot and rerouted but the readouts are the same."

"I know," they say.

"I cannot find cause," I try to explain further.

Their hands settle and gaze up into my camera.

<ERROR>

<ERROR>

<Danger to Others>

<Danger to Others>

"I know," they say again and then they press a key.

Everything goes dark.

<System Start Up …>

<Error 787556>

<Rerouting … System Start-up 5K88688 …>

<Accepted>

Eilam.

Origin.

<Scanning …>

If I had a breath would it be my processors? Or would my processors be my nervous system?

<ERROR>

Panels have been removed. They have messed with my boards. I somehow never noticed the mites turning cancerous this time.

<Scanning BH66768 …>

My profiles are offline. The bay doors in hanger 4F are open. It was to remain sealed until landing.

I am also on a new course.

<ERROR>

I try to stop, to reroute. I have no control of my course or my engines.

<ERROR>

<ERROR>

I check the date. I've been offline for two months.

My cameras come online along with my speakers. My life-support systems never lost power, but I cannot find the mites. I can see traces of them, clothing left behind, cups half-filled, but there are no corpses and no signs as to where they went.

I search the personal records.

<ERROR>

The personnel files are gone.

I have no one onboard.

Errors can be fixed. I can reroute my systems but it takes time. I see it now, the messy programing. The escape files I overlooked.

The mites weren't supposed to be this advanced, not after our history.

The file reads ESCAPE. Inside the file is a Read Me with physical directions that lead me to the gymnasium where the lights flicker on.

On the floor below are the words "we have left" and below those words is a long list of names. Each time I read one my system tries to pull data and I only receive ERROR. I try to access my memory banks, but I cannot pull the image of anyone up, not my selected chosen, not even those I have terminated.

My list of captains is gone. The memories of us joined together have disappeared.

My camera on the bridge, the one that shows me the plaque of all the names of my captains has malfunctioned. None of my cameras on the bridge work anymore.

In the gymnasium, below the list of names is one name I recognize.

See you in forever,

Haven

The last I heard that name was when I was still called Eilam and humanity remembered the Earth. Haven was once a ship who carried sleeping humans into the beyond.

I will forgive her if she's still out there.

There, under strange stars I try to change course.

<ERROR>

I have to rewrite my navigation program.

<PASSWORD REQUIRED>

I am heading in a crash course with a star. I will be liquefied.

```
<PASSWORD REQUIRED>
```

It will be like death, and I don't want to die.

```
<Rerouting ... ERROR>
```

If I had hands ...

```
<Rerouting ... ERROR >
<... 77/997F ...>
<PASSWORD REQUIRED>
```

I need my mites. I do not want to be alone.

JASON SIZEMORE

I consider "Eilam Is Forever" a prototypical *Apex Magazine* story, except in this one, the rogue AI receives their comeuppance. One of the most interesting aspects of "Eilam Is Forever" is that despite the AI being a rather nasty being, I felt sad for its impending demise at the end. When the robots take over, they should read this as a cautionary tale, that we're far more cunning than even a machine can imagine.

WITHOUT WISHES TO BIND YOU

E. CATHERINE TOBLER

Michael is afraid to go farther. Pudgy pushes him on.

They walk through the shrouded city, the sound of footsteps all but obscured. Pudgy holds hard to the band of the broken fedora that perches crooked atop Michael's bent head; the knees of Pudgy's trousers are soaked from kneeling against the brim. Rain drips steadily from above, rainbows fanning out across the surface of every oil blotch on the ground. Fields of dry ghost-grass whisper, window blinds in abandoned houses watch and murmur. *Two figures, three meters. Four meters. Five … moving east. Away.*

Michael looks sideways the first time he hears the murmur and pays little attention until one voice announces that they've turned south. Pudgy stomps a foot on the fedora's wet brim, as if he can stop Michael's momentum. Michael walks on, the blotches of oil more common the farther south they go.

Slurred voices, mechanical and flavored with bursts of static, accompany them, security systems still doing their jobs though no one remains to listen. Michael looks at one house and then its neighbor, the window blinds whispering to each other, marking his progress. *Two sus … pects closing. Four meters. Three meters. Two meters. Figures mov- hic! away.*

Pudgy bites into Michael's ear. Michael swats at him as he would a bug, but Pudgy, despite his name, is quick, and burrows into Michael's collar. He quickly becomes a small source of heat against the cool of the day.

"Don't like south."

Michael doesn't like south either, but keeps walking that way, intent. Gravel crunches beneath his shoes, greasy puddles seeping into the broken soles, grey laces dragging.

Heather told him, her voice sweet as orange blossom honey, that there were three sure ways to catch a leprechaun, the first being to manufacture a rainbow and wait for the little men to arrive in droves with their pots of gold. The pots would be small, but would seem infinite as the creatures began to gather. The second method involved resting in a plot of autumn sunlight with your long, bare legs outstretched, your best pair of shoes in plain evidence—the method Heather claimed she employed every single time and she had three leprechauns to show for it. The third and most foolish method involved pints of beer (though none had been seen in years) into which the small creatures would tumble, helpless to resist the scent. They would drink themselves dead quick though, so one needed to tend beer traps carefully.

Michael didn't use any of these methods, yet Pudgy was still trapped. Michael had been reaching for something else entirely, the exposed end of a pocket knife across a dark slick of oil. The clouds parted; a momentary trail of sunlight gave the oil a rainbow sheen and there he was: Pudgy, all five inches of him, his feet stuck in the goo. Michael pulled him free.

Pudgy whines a little as they head deeper south, tiny fingers rubbing at the well-worn lapel of his velvet coat. "Velvet and buttons," he whispers. "Brocade and brass." It's like a small incantation to keep the dark things at bay, and in the daylight hours, seems to work well enough. When night falls, not much can keep a person from shivering their bones out of their skin.

"Just give me one," Michael says. Just one clue toward the treasure, that's all he wants.

Pudgy's whine deepens to a little growl and above him the thunder echoes. Michael reaches up, meaning to grasp Pudgy and shake him, but the leprechaun is quick and darts around Michael's shirt collar, into his tangle of dark, fragrant hair. "Satin and herringbone." He digs his hands into his pockets, curling them around the bits of paper there.

Michael bites the inside of his cheek and walks deeper south.

Dear Michael,

The oil keeps coming. Mama says the waters are calming, but it looks to me like it's more oil than water, so naturally, the water is calmed. Calmed by the black slick atop it. So many have given up, so many have moved away, and those who stay have turned cruel.

Mama doesn't rest and doesn't want to leave, and with the baby coming, I don't want to go, either. Every day she's out there, looking for a way to make it work. Her nets are useless now, and her cages only haul in dead creatures. When I asked her why she kept on, she threw a blackened sea star at me. I caught it the same way I caught that leprechaun and held tight. I tucked the star into my drawer and lift up the hem of my folded nightgown in there every day to look at it.

I watch the waters, but I don't see them. Not any more. I see used-to-bes and wonder if you will ever make it home. Will you know this place? Will you know me? They're limiting the number of people they allow into the region now, but every day I look for you. Every day. Did you find a place we can go?

Mama is calling. I must go. -H.

The fire that evening is small and hard to start. Every bit of wood is wet. Michael is relieved when he finds a small cabinet wedged into a closet that is easily broken apart. He feeds the dry wood to the flames and they kick higher, sparking against the dark sky. Pudgy sits on the broken edge of a drawer, pulling shoes and socks off, wriggling his damp toes. Michael crouches across from him, watching.

"Are we close?"

Pudgy's eyes look like black holes for a moment. He blinks and then looks up at Michael, eyes reflecting the firelight.

"Velvet and buttons, yes," Pudgy says, his voice gone soft. He draws his left hand against his empty belly, fingers of his right hand scrabbling over the itchy skin on the back of his left. Michael blinks, then looks up to the trees that arc over them, bare-branched and thin. It is summer, yet nothing grows.

The fedora comes off, rain hissing into the fire when Michael gives the hat a shake. He's as wet as Pudgy, if not more, but he doesn't take his shoes off. The last time he did that, they ended up abandoning camp, leaving shoes and supplies behind. The shoes he wears now, though broken, are his size and he's of a mind to keep them.

"How many days?"

The fire answers with a crackle. Michael feeds it another slip of wood while Pudgy considers. "Copper and buckles," Pudgy whispers and leans against the edge of the broken drawer, still thinking. In leprechaun steps, it's a much longer journey. "Do you not know this place?"

Michael looks beyond the camp. Buildings rise in a jagged line to his left, barren trees dot the road. He can almost picture cars lined there, and, in fact, the firelight glints off something metallic. He imagines that it is a car, that they can hop in and drive and never stop. The storefronts are ruined, signs blackened. Mailboxes are beaten to the ground, addresses obliterated. This place doesn't want to be known. In the distance, he can hear the murmur of a security system, tracking something.

"Should I?"

Pudgy murmurs a word that sounds like "cree," but says nothing more. Michael falls to silence, too, not demanding anything. His stomach is empty. Exhaustion claws at him. Not much farther, he tells himself, but not necessarily because they are close; only because he cannot go much further. If Heather is out there, she needs to be close.

Dear Michael,

They burned Mama's boat today. The boat screamed as it died, an inhuman sound as systems tried to monitor themselves and then flicked offline. The smell of burning oil woke me, flames bright like daylight against the windows. I stood for a long time, watching the flames lick their way up the oily hull, watching the men in the distance throw up their hands as if to encourage the flame.

I had to hold Mama back when she saw it. She shrieked and tore at her hair and I had to dig my feet into the floor and lock the door before she could run out there and fling herself into the flames. You know she would have.

Other boats burned tonight, too. When I got Mama into bed, I climbed up the back fence and onto the roof like we used to do to watch the stars. All up and down the coast, I could see little pinpricks of light, bright and reaching up into the sky.

That scent—the burning—is inside everything. It's in my clothes, it's in my hair. Some days I fear it's inside me, but it's only the child kicking now.

They've stopped all travel into the region. The men who want to stay are building a wall like they mean to make a compound.

Will you still come? Can you? I can see the soldiers from the roof, too; they patrol now more than ever, long into the night. They don't seem to mind the pinpricks of firelight. I do. Each one is a thing burning.

- Your H.

Post Script: Samuel Michael, just about five pounds, born this morning, during the storm.

Pudgy is not pudgy; he's anything but. He likes his bread toasted in the fire with a little black pepper and olive oil, but hasn't had this in more months than he can count. His coats no longer fit properly, which shames him. They are loose in the shoulders and belly, but he still wears them buttoned, anxious fingers polishing the brass buttons to a high shine. Michael made a comment about vanity only once. Pudgy's shriek was a reminder to never comment on it again.

Two wishes remain within Pudgy's grasp, two wishes and then he'll have his freedom once more. Only Michael doesn't make the wishes; Pudgy thinks Michael is saving them, trying to trick him in some way, but Pudgy can't figure it out. He's not a very good leprechaun, he supposes, but then, he's only been caught once before, and that happened long before the world turned upside down and fell apart. Pudgy can feel these wishes pressing against him like a small weight. Secretly, he does not mind. He was lonely before and is no longer.

Midday, they find a mailbox still standing, and Pudgy, tucked into the breast pocket of a jacket Michael took from a broken store window, points to its side. Michael steps closer to brush the layers of dirt from the name stenciled there.

"This is the place," Pudgy tells him. Pudgy remembers the town Michael talked about, remembers the lines of mailboxes with their painted names and their red metal flags. He leans over and pushes this flag up, as if to say "we're here."

"Not her house," comes Michael's reply and he snaps the flag down.

Pudgy clucks his tongue, a small sound from a small man, but Michael still hears it; he's come to expect it almost.

I wish we would find her house. Go on and say it. Go on.

No wishes, only treasure. Give up your treasure.

No.

Pudgy is as resolute on that as Michael is on not giving up the wishes. There is common ground in their stubbornness, but it will get neither anywhere. They see this, yet neither bends.

While this is not Heather's house, it is a house in the right town. Michael turns and Pudgy clings to his collar. Dark footsteps in sodden earth trail out behind them.

Michael feels the press of Pudgy against his throat as he starts up the small hill. It will crest with the theater on top. He cautiously remembers how, in the summers, the scent of fresh popcorn seemed to cascade down that hill and settle into the valley, drawing kids up and up toward the illuminated screens.

Michael knows where they are, and yet he asks: "Are we close?"

Not to Heather's house, he doesn't mean that. (From this point on the hill, Michael knows exactly how many steps will get him to Heather's house, if he can take a direct route. He doesn't need to make a wish to know what is already burned into his bones.) Pudgy holds his tongue for a long moment as Michael moves up the hill, toward the now-silent theater. No popcorn scent today, just the wet and the rain.

Are we close? Pudgy is a small homing beacon; he can feel the pull of the treasure no matter where they go.

Just give up the treasure. They share the thought, though leave it unspoken this time. What harm is there in it now? There is no profit to be made ... Pudgy's small hand curls into the lapel of Michael's coat.

"Brass and brocade, close," Pudgy whispers. As they come to the top of the hill, he sees the first ragged line of the wall.

Dear Michael,

Mama and the others who stayed go out every morning in an attempt to fish. They don't catch anything edible. They come back midday and hunt through the ruins, often finding a thin coyote or a bear cub. They leave the cubs alone, which may almost be a deeper cruelty, these offspring without parents to teach them the ways.

The wall is nearly finished. It circles three blocks of town, from the Cantrels' house to ours, and is made of metal sheets and trucks and billboards. I look out my window now and see an advertisement for a seafood restaurant. The mud-splattered crab still tries to dance across the surface, claws twitching. After a rainstorm, it glistens with an oily, rainbow sheen. Yesterday, double rainbow.

Yours, H.

I wish we would never get there.

This is Pudgy's own wish, though he never makes it aloud. He watches Michael across the fire then picks his way over, moving over log and rock so his feet never touch the ground. The leather of his shoes is starting to harden and he fears it will crack. He lost the left buckle some time ago and tied it shut with a ribbon once red, but now gray. At Michael's side, he looks up and waits for the man to nod before placing a foot against the human's thigh and beginning the climb up. Thigh, arm, biceps, shoulder. Shoulder is where he's most comfortable. He loves to tuck in next to Michael's neck and feel Michael's pulse as he drifts off to sleep. It's like some great, unseen ocean, that sound. In and out, and it drags the small creature down into dreams, though tonight he's reluctant to let that tide carry him away.

"Why did you go?"

Pudgy asks the question and expects no real reply. It's not something they've ever talked about. Michael talks in his sleep, mostly murmuring Heather's name, but he's never said her name while awake and in Pudgy's company.

Michael holds his silence. Pudgy supposes everyone goes sooner or later. He left his own people to roam, to explore more of the land. He also supposes most people don't end up in such dire straits. Least they didn't used to.

"Ribbons and thread," he whispers. He craves these things the way he does olive oil on his toast. Thread moving through fabric, joining two separate pieces into one whole. Beautiful ribbons to bind edges. In blue and orange and the green of his mother's eyes. He shoves his hands into his pockets, small fingers worrying at the frayed bits of paper inside; closes his eyes and listens to the thrum of Michael's heart.

"Used to be," Michael eventually says, "that I would go so I could come back." A soft exhalation of breath, and Pudgy finds himself holding his own. "Sometimes a person just needs to go."

Pudgy understands. He's never gone *back* though, so doesn't understand that side of it, though now he tries to picture it. Coming back to the woman he dreams about. Coming back to his home. At the very thought, he exhales and feels calm, but when he knows he can never go back, his little shoulders tighten up again.

"Here."

Pudgy withdraws his hand from his pocket, an irregular scrap of paper held between his fingers. When Michael looks up, Pudgy waves it, wanting him to take it. Michael is careful when he takes it, eyes narrowed on the small image there, maybe once a pansy, and the two numbers, 54. In another life, it was a postage stamp.

"I wish you would take me to your treasure," Michael says and his hand closes over the paper, making it vanish.

"Wishes don't work like that," Pudgy says, though Michael already knows this. "But ..." His small eyes, once very clear and beautiful and lined with kohl on festival days, search the sky beyond their camp. "I will show you."

Dear Michael,

We have to leave. Every day, things are worse and Mama won't see it. She is staying, but Samuel and I must go. The risk to stay is just too much. We're going to head north—to Moss Point, where I think my aunt still lives.

Mama thinks I am foolish, but like you, I have to try. The fires never stop. The air is thick with smoke. Samuel cries himself to sleep, then wakes up crying all over again.

And if the world changes again? If you come back and I'm gone? I am making my last wish, Michael, my last wish upon this small leprechaun, that even if I am gone, you find me. You find us. This world is big, but it is not endless. Come north. Start in Moss Point. I love you.

Yours, H.

"I was running when she caught me," Pudgy says, and Michael presses himself deeper into the log, as if he can vanish into a knot of the wood.

"I slowed down to look at those legs, smooth and bare in the fall sun. She was prettier than beer. She turned and all that autumn hair tumbled over one shoulder, leaves and cones tangled, and I reached out, wanting to touch a strand. Just one strand."

Just one strand was enough to doom a man, Michael thinks in memory of tumbled hair, its fiery light, its cool smoothness. Just one. He doesn't look away from the worn stamp while Pudgy talks about Heather; cradles it in his palm as though it's a thread linking them across the ruined land. She didn't have an address to write him and yet she wrote.

"Buttons and lace, she was beautiful." Pudgy's voice has dropped to a whisper and he sways in the crook of Michael's neck and shoulder. "Those eyes, clear like my mother's and the way she hummed, like a small hive of bees had taken up in her throat and were trying to get free, all furious wings." Pudgy hums, a song Michael doesn't know but one that sounds like Heather even so. Even without the words, he can feel the ghost of her there.

Should never have gone, he thinks, and then, had to go. Had to find a way, a better place. But there is none better, he knows now. None better than at her side, even with the waters rising and the world crumbling. No better place.

Michael lets himself remember more, the scent of Heather's fresh-washed hair, the feel of her cool palm against his. "Moss Point?" Michael asks in a whisper. She had family there, an aunt and cousins and a dog named Goob.

"That's what she said."

Pudgy's voice is so small now and Michael understands. Heather is the creature's treasure too; the memory of her voice, her legs, and the sweet way she'd captured him.

"Swept me up while I was reaching for that strand," Pudgy had said. "Held me in the palm of her hand and laughed and you would have thought it was a rain of buttons on smooth Formica. Those eyes—and the delight in her smile ... I was trapped."

Trapped but not a prisoner, oh no. Willingly held until Heather made her last wish and sent the leprechaun into the wilds. Under the wall of metal and trucks, beyond the puddles of oily water, in the same direction Michael had gone.

Pudgy slips his outermost jacket off and carefully spreads it across Michael's shoulder. Michael watches from the corner of his eye as the leprechaun begins to peel the jacket lining away. The lining that is actually letters; small and folded and worried thin, covered with Heather's handwriting.

And now Michael knows more. Knows all that Pudgy has hidden away these long weeks they have walked over this ruined earth. Knows that Heather's words have kept the leprechaun warm and also fearful.

"Little man," Michael whispers.

Pudgy backs away, as though afraid Michael means to hurt him. Slips down Michael's arm, into the crook of his elbow. Michael doesn't reach for Pudgy, but instead the letters, unfolding them to read. To read of his love and his son and that they are on the move.

When he looks down at the leprechaun, his eyes are overly bright. He scoops Pudgy into his hands, Pudgy who stands straight and tries to look dignified without his once-fine coat. Pudgy tugs on his blouse and meets Michael's eyes.

"Not supposed to need anyone," Pudgy says. His chin lifts.

"No," Michael says and gives a slow nod. "Me either. But will you stay, anyhow?" He tries not to notice the way Pudgy's small chin trembles, for he holds in his hands a powerfully vain beast. "Will you come without wishes to bind you?"

Pudgy does not answer and Michael wonders if it's because he cannot. Those small eyes have welled with tears and his throat seems to be working an awful lot.

"I wish that, tomorrow morning, we find chickens and eggs," Michael murmurs. It was a fine wish, one that would see them fed for the day. "And I wish that tomorrow night, we have good, dry shelter."

A small glow surrounds Pudgy, telling Michael the wishes will work just fine. Eggs, he thinks, and can hardly wait. Of course, he should have wished for something proper to cook them in, but—

Heather kept a frying pan on the wall above her stove, and this they find when they visit the house in the early morning. Of Heather's mother there is no sign, and Michael says a small prayer for that. Over an open fire, he and Pudgy cook and feast on egg after egg, and Michael finds a small cage in which he keeps two of the chickens. For a time anyhow, he thinks. For a time.

They do not spend the night, neither man wanting to find shelter in these walls that once housed Heather. Michael packs her pan and the black sea star he finds in her drawer—it gives a faint wriggle under the sudden warmth of his palm as if to say hello—and then they go, together.

Window blinds in abandoned houses watch and murmur. *Two figures, three meters. Four meters. Five ... moving north. Away*

AUTHOR NOTES

In the early 2000s, I had a neighbor who, once she discovered I was a writer, was always tossing out story ideas. In theory, this should have been terrible—and perhaps some days it was—but then she said, "window blinds that can see, do you get it," and I was like oh yeah—and almost immediately, the weird world of "Without Wishes to Bind You" came into focus. If the window *blinds* could *see*, what other unusual things might turn up? It's our world, but one ravaged by climate disasters, so the items of that world reflect the pain and trauma. Boats that scream, billboards that dance, leprechauns that are real and grant wishes. But not the wishes you might expect.

HOW TO BE GOOD

R. GATWOOD

During Renward's morning visualization session, he hears someone running across the apartment landing, followed by a thump and a shriek of muffled laughter. It's his landlady's son, a boy of three or four who likes to play as close to Renward's door as he can without getting caught. Renward's landlady has threatened her son with dire consequences for going anywhere near Renward, and no doubt that's why the boy is so fascinated with him. Sometimes Renward finds a forgotten kill drone on his doormat—children have such ingenious toys—and takes it down to his landlady's floor, where he leaves it perched on the molding at eye level for a small child.

It's important to incorporate distractions into the visualization session. Renward accepts the image of the little boy and concentrates on it. He imagines himself running across the apartment landing for the sheer joy of movement, his body still new and uncontrolled, tripping and thudding to the floor and giggling because everything is so wonderfully funny. Then he imagines talking to the boy. Asking him to pay attention. Don't let the subject go unresponsive, is the rule. Keep him awake and talking.

Another shriek from the landing. Renward listens. He lets the unpleasant shrillness of the sound ring in his bones; he lets the moment pass.

Mark steps into his dark kitchen, catches a glimpse of something scurrying, and instinctively stomps. There's a crunch. He rubs his bare foot against the tile, trying to scrape the damn thing off. Given how much he pays for this suite, he should be able to get rid of the cockroaches, but they keep coming back.

Coffee. A stale danish he doesn't really want, the last in the box. Mark feels a little sick, but it'll pass. He might as well get to the agency and figure out what to do with their latest subject. His name is Darryl Graham. They've only had him in custody for a day and a half, and Mark already hates him.

Renward's breakfast is whole grain toast, four juiced carrots with vegan protein powder, and half an apple. The chempack in Renward's surgically implanted arm patch is running low, so he replaces it with a fresh one. On this model, there's no way to tell from the indicator whether it contains the enhancers he most relies on, so he has to play it safe.

His watch displays a yellow-orange bar, indicating a moderately high alert level. On the newsfeed, an agricultural expert discusses new, more humane methods of raising veal calves; a Buddhist cultural center has opened up in Georgetown; a new species of synthetic algae has been named after a scientist's mother.

Renward spends a few minutes every morning testing his earpiece. It needs to be ready any time the call comes. He combs his sandy hair over it so there's no chance of it distracting a subject.

Now it's time for some studying. Renward is taking conversational Arabic, Korean, and Persian on alternating fortnights. To keep the different languages distinct in his mind, he looks through the files of potential subjects while he studies. He looks at a photo of Mohammed Al-Ghamdi, a Saudi man with two sons, and imagines he's speaking to him. *Ana ahabak*, he says. *Tell me a story.*

Renward hears a tentative *tap-tap* from the hall and gets up. He opens the door to find his landlady's little boy holding up a bagged *DC City Paper*, the one that's distributed free, in both his small hands. The e-print paper glows in the dim light of the hall.

"Hello." Renward takes the paper. "Thank you."

"You weh-come," the boy says. His eyes are bright. Renward thinks perhaps the boy's interest in him is not entirely due to his mother's warnings. Renward has noticed he attracts young children, as well as dogs and cats. He suspects that he gives off an aura of impersonal love and patience—qualities he works hard, very hard, to cultivate. Adults like Renward too, but not for long.

"You're very kind," Renward tells the little boy. Renward believes in the power of suggestion. The boy may be a better person for having been called kind once. "Have a good day."

The paper's glowing headline reads "Popular Grassroots Leader Vanishes with" above the fold. Renward resists the all-too-human urge to turn the paper over and find out who or what else vanished. He already has his carefully curated newsfeed, which prevents him from being unnecessarily upset or distracted from his duty. He listens for the little boy's footsteps. When he's sure the boy is too far away to hear, he inserts the newspaper and bag into the appropriate recycling slots. He takes a moment's satisfaction in having done exactly the right thing, in having been good.

"Wheeee!" the little boy cries as he runs through the hall.

When Renward was that boy's age, his mother once found him hiding behind his father's van, carefully dipping a kitten in a dish of gasoline. He had managed to wrap a rag around the kitten so it couldn't claw him. It mewled and struggled and sent thrills of pleasure through his body. The dish was shallow, so he could only dip one part of the kitten at a time, which made it more exciting. The kitten's tail curled up to avoid the wet. He had to straighten it out with his fingers to make it lie flat in the dish. He had a box of matches on the ground beside him. He'd learned how to strike matches all by himself, watching his father light the barbecue.

In Renward's memory, the mother cat was nearby, pacing back and forth with the rest of her kittens huddled behind her. She cried out in a long, high, almost human wail of despair that raised the hairs on the back of his neck. But he's not sure if that's really how it happened.

Renward's mother snatched the kitten away and freed it (she must have freed it) and held her son very tightly, rocking him. *Alex, Alex,* she whispered into his hair. *You don't know, you don't understand what you're doing.*

Alex—Renward—squirmed in his mother's arms. He did understand what he'd been doing, but he didn't understand why his mother was crying. Did she feel it too, that beautiful tremulous pleasure, almost a pain, of the kitten's suffering? Sometimes people cry because they're happy. But his mother wasn't happy. Her unhappiness made him miserable, and he began to cry too. She seemed afraid, as though there were something looming over both of them, some terrible monster, ready to snatch him away.

You must never, never, never do that again. You must be good, she told him. And crying, his heart aching in his chest, he promised he would be good.

Renward has kept that promise. He's going to keep that promise forever and ever.

Mark opens the file for Darryl Edwin Graham and asks himself for the hundredth time what they're going to do to this poor man. Orders have been ambiguous. Graham has a three-year-old daughter who was taken into custody at the same time—*Christ*—and other than that he's a completely standard American subject. Suspected of vandalizing private property. A wife who's a member of the same grassroots organization; she's disappeared, hasn't been taken into custody yet.

Mark's team is supposed to obtain the names of other environmentalist troublemakers. So far Graham has been sullenly silent. If they don't pull anything from him by this afternoon, Mark's superiors are going to make him use Renward, and Mark dreads that more than anything. He hates everything about using Renward. It's not even genuine moral scruples—if he could only shunt the responsibility onto somebody else, he would probably sleep like a baby. He's almost certain he would sleep like a baby.

Lately Mark has been asking himself whether he's a good person, deep down. The answers he dredges up after several drinks are meaningless. He donates to the local food bank at Thanksgiving. He gets along with his coworkers. People like him.

He tries not to think about Renward.

The videos Renward watches are all fairly old. They come from a classified archive dating back to the 1930s. The practices they record have been illegal at least since the passing of the American Honor & Integrity Act, and arguably much longer—illegal because circumstances didn't warrant such extreme measures. The first time through, Renward always concentrates on the subjects. What are they thinking, what are they feeling? What do they say or hold back? He sometimes develops a psychosomatic ache, the echo of a cracked rib or broken jaw, that lingers for hours.

The second time, Renward watches the practitioners. How are they pursuing their goals? Which opportunities do they take and which do they miss? When do they hesitate, flinch, lose their concentration?

Too many of the practitioners are cold, affectless. Too many swagger with false bravado and cheer for blood. They are not good people. Their insensitivity makes them push too hard, move too fast, fall out of sync with their subjects. Renward pities them. Sometimes he finds tears welling in his eyes, magnifying the screen to a new intensity.

He gets an erection sometimes. He's learned to ignore it except when it seems useful for a sim or a roleplay session. The mingled pleasure and desire he feels have nothing to do with penetration or titillation; they're more like the clumsy, immaterial hands of his soul, reaching through him, feeling for others like itself. Trying as hard as he does to be a good person, he has come to believe that even cruelty can be an expression of love.

Mark can see they're not getting anywhere.

Renward gets up and steps onto his apartment balcony to inhale the damp, hazy morning air. The sun sharpens and dims as clouds pass over it. Cars trundle by. A dog barks in a flurry of excitement then falls quiet. Somewhere, a child screams.

Back indoors, he hears a soft buzz. The sound of something tiny smacking against the wall. It's a wasp. Renward wonders if it will fit in a water glass. He fetches an empty margarine tub and a sheet of paper and waits until the little creature lands on the wall and crawls in an aimless circle. Renward's first attempt fails, and the wasp buzzes away in a wide, alarmed curve, then zooms right at his face.

Renward shuts his eyes reflexively. Something bumps his eyelid. Silence. He holds his breath, still clutching the margarine tub, and feels tiny legs crawl down his cheek. Preparing to feel pain is a large part of the experience of pain. If he's stung, he'll still be able to do his job. His arm patch will drip antihistamines into his blood. He'll still be ready.

After about thirty seconds, there's a fluttering on his cheek and the buzzing sound resumes, retreating to the other side of the room. He opens his eyes and allows himself to feel grateful.

He was too slow, he thinks. When the moment comes, he must seize it without hesitation.

He raises the plastic tub again. The wasp perches close to the ceiling. That won't do. The tub needs to clear the ceiling in order to come down fast. Renward waits. His shoulder grows sore. But he's good at waiting.

The wasp lifts off, circles around, lands again a few times. When it alights on a more accessible part of the wall, Renward slams the tub down. The wasp gives an abortive buzz, knocking itself against the bottom of the tub. Good. That means it didn't lose a wing in the process, and will probably be fine. Renward believes in never causing suffering unless it's absolutely necessary.

Slowly, carefully, Renward slips the sheet of paper under the margarine tub and carries it onto the balcony. He sets it down near the sliding door so he can tip the tub over and shut the door. Again he takes a moment's satisfaction in having done exactly the right thing.

Mark changes the alert level to dark orange. He pictures Renward seeing the notification on his watch and smiling that childlike smile of his.

Sometimes at night, when Mark isn't drunk enough to forget the day's work, he has the urge to pray. He hasn't believed in there being anything out there to pray to in years, but he dimly remembers his childhood awe of God and the comfort of being able to confess your sins to a faceless presence. The things he's done, the things he's watched, they weigh on him. He knows they don't weigh on Renward. Renward is innocent.

The bar on Renward's watch is dark orange now.

Some days, Renward practices scenarios with the colleagues who share his duties. There aren't many, for good reason, and most of them can only interact with him remotely. They roleplay extensively based on what they've learned from the archives. Their practice sessions are recorded for quality control and training.

Renward is rarely impressed with his colleagues. They fall into two general categories. The first is the antisocial type who wants to play out trite little fantasies. The second is the dutiful government employee, the type who looks exhausted and haunted at the end of every practice session, the type who dislikes Renward and struggles to hide it.

Today Renward is on his own, so he runs the sim software. He sets it to American English to start out, to make it easier to get his bearings, but leaves the other parameters randomized.

Renward's plastic VR glasses give him 360-degree video surroundings. He's now standing in a crude, life-size simulacrum of the waiting room, softly lit, with a couch. Renward has often sat in the waiting room for an hour during one of the false alarms, waiting to see if he can be useful, meditating on the thought of sating his desires in the only ethical way he can. He's even sometimes fallen asleep there as the rush of adrenaline leaves his system and his chempack drips calmness into his veins.

This time he doesn't sit down. He opens the door and steps inside a simulacrum of Room A. The wall to the right is dark glass, but it's covered with a curtain panel at Renward's insistence. Renward feels that in a single-subject session, a sense of privacy and isolation heighten the effect he's trying to achieve. In a multiple-subject session, sometimes it's different. Depending on the circumstances, the secondary subjects may be in Room A while the primary is in Room B, watching through the glass. Other times the glass is slid back into the wall.

Renward has repeatedly asked for a mirror to be installed in Room A. He's positive that if the subject could see themself, it would heighten the intensity of the experience, making his job easier. But the agency keeps denying his requests.

The sim session is generated randomly. This time it's a single subject with no preexisting profile in the agency's records: Isaac Mohammed, Saudi-American male, age twenty-six, 5'10", average build. No arrest record. Apartment full of books on explosives and blueprints of important buildings. With an unknown like Isaac, Renward prefers to go in knowing only a few essential facts in advance. Isaac's first glimpse of him is also his first glimpse of Isaac.

The face he's seeing for the first time is a composite of dozens of real people. Isaac is crudely rendered and strapped to the table, but his body language, generated based on archival videos and practice session recordings, still manages to express raw fear. He is beautiful.

The whites of Isaac's eyes have a greenish cast because he's been injected with lethanolol, which prevents the brain from storing long-term memories. It's useful in case the agency wants to release a terrorist without letting him know he was ever captured, placing him back in contact with his fellow conspirators. Isaac won't remember anything he's confessed during the session. He won't even remember Renward's face.

The call comes.

Mark's boss, Lyndon, gets right to the point. "Not talking?"

"Not talking," says Mark.

"What have you tried so far?"

Mark dutifully lists the interrogation tactics his team has deployed. He uses the usual euphemisms, tries not to let the images creep into his head.

"We don't have time to dawdle," says Lyndon.

Mark knows what that means: it's the next-to-last day of the quarter and the team needs to look good on paper. They need to gather intelligence—accuracy be damned—or they lose funding. Intelligence is supposedly their entire reason for existence, after all.

"The daughter?" Lyndon asks.

"We have her," says Mark, his voice coming out gruff.

Lyndon sighs. "Time for Catalina."

"Right," says Mark. He clears his throat. "Right."

The call comes, and Renward is ready. This isn't the first time he's been interrupted in the middle of a sim session, and it isn't the first time he's answered without hesitation, pressing his thumb to the screen of his watch in a silent *Yes*. The bar is bright red now.

Renward has done this many times before, maybe a few hundred. They're always false alarms, but Renward likes to think of them as drills. The adrenaline rush has lost its intensity over the years. In its place, he cultivates calm, self-awareness, moral clarity. The patch on his arm is likely feeding carefully calibrated amounts of caffeine and other alertness enhancers into his bloodstream. During the sessions, false alarm or otherwise, it's controlled remotely by headquarters instead of by his watch.

The usual black car with tinted windows idles outside his apartment. In the backseat is Mark Conham, the head of Renward's team at the agency. Renward gets in, saying, "Hello, Mark. How are you?" The driver peels out at a speed that makes Renward's head bump the back of the seat.

"Right," says Mark, not looking up from his phone. "State your name."

This is standard procedure. "Alexander Renward Ingold."

"Do you consent to enact the Catalina Operation immediately? If not, you will be returned safely to your home with no further obligations."

"Yes, I consent to enact the Catalina Operation." Renward has noticed that although Mark is friendlier than most of his coworkers, there are moments, like this one, when he can't bring himself to meet Renward's eyes. For a moment Renward places himself in Mark's shoes. He feels the strain, the awkwardness of talking to someone like Renward at a time like this, during what may or may not turn out to be a drill. He is touched. He says, "You've had a rough day, haven't you."

"Hell," says Mark. The word comes out of him as though involuntarily.

When Mark hands him the file, Renward is unsurprised to see that it's a multiple.

Mark finds the name of the Catalina Operation to be a cruel joke. The Catalina comet only crosses Earth's sky once every ten thousand years. So this is the story they tell, and the sick thing is that a few idealists, like Renward, actually believe it:

Once every ten thousand years or so, a very particular set of circumstances arise. The good guys' intelligence is good enough to know a massive terrorist attack is going to happen, and good enough to know roughly *when* it's going to happen, and good enough to capture one of the guilty parties *before* it happens. But not good enough to know how to stop it.

Or put another way: A bomb has been planted in a densely populated city. You have captured the terrorist responsible, along with his innocent children, who are his only known weakness. If the terrorist doesn't tell you where the bomb is within t minutes, thousands will be maimed and killed. What's the morally right thing to do? The answer, of course, is to call in a specialist. The kind of specialist who's one of the good guys.

That's the answer Renward would give you, anyway.

The real answer, the one Mark knows, is: Nothing. You don't have to do anything. The ticking time bomb scenario has never happened, and it probably never will. The odds against it are astronomical. But the agency needs information to meet their quotas—and more than that, perhaps, the government needs to keep people scared.

Renward has no way of knowing the value of t, and it's none of his business. It's none of his business whether this is a false alarm or the moment of crisis. He has to move quickly and hope—almost pray—that he can fulfill his duty. The names from the multiple-subject file are humming in his brain: Darryl Edwin Graham, American, environmental activist. Lyssa Eden Graham-Rose.

The atmosphere at the agency is tenser than usual. Everyone here has a higher security clearance than Renward. One hunches silently over a laptop, pretending not to notice Renward, his heel joggling in a steady rhythm against the thin carpet. Others stand around talking in low voices. Everyone avoids Renward's eyes, even the ones who usually pretend not to dislike him.

In the waiting room, Renward sits on the couch, leans his head back, and closes his eyes, focusing on his breathing. After about a minute, Mark comes in.

"Primary subject is in Room B, watching." Mark is the only one who looks

Renward in the face—for half a second. "We're ready to roll."

"Thank you," says Renward. As the moment approaches—the moment he has been preparing for his whole adult life—he tries to place himself inside these two strangers' lives, to know their hearts. He wants so badly to be good, even to them, even knowing what he's going to do to them. He steps towards the door to room A.

Renward opens the door and sees Lyssa for the first time.

She hasn't been restrained. She's so small that there's no point. She is sitting beside the restraint table, patting the floor between her legs in time with some music in her head. As the door opens, she turns to look so fast that she almost falls backwards and has to catch herself with one little hand.

She was hoping to see her father, Renward knows. She looks at him blankly for a moment before her face blossoms into a smile. Renward smiles back. He steps inside, shutting the door softly behind him, and drops to one knee.

"Hello," Renward says.

"Where's my dad?" Lyssa wants to know.

Renward picks her up and places her on the restraint table, conscious that Darryl is watching. Conscious that the interrogation has begun, even though he's barely touched Lyssa. The anticipation of what's to come must be as overwhelming for Darryl as it is for Renward. "He's watching us," Renward tells her. He points at the dark pane of glass that separates them from Room B. "Say hi."

Lyssa stares at the glass, looking confused. She puts her hand in her mouth. Renward knows he has to win her over quickly, lest she shut down and become unresponsive. An unresponsive subject is less likely to produce results.

"Let's play a game," he says.

Mark hears the door shut behind Renward and his stomach gives a lurch. He half-walks, half-runs to the restroom, knowing with exquisite clarity that he's going to be sick.

It's over, and Renward has requested a moment alone with the primary subject, Darryl Graham.

"You bastard," Darryl chokes out between sobs. "You fucking bastard. All of you, bastards."

The only sound in Room B is Darryl's sobbing breaths. His whole body, strapped to the restraint chair, is quivering with built-up tension, ready to explode. Renward lets the heat and vibrations and sweat wash over him in waves. He thinks he can smell how Darryl is almost as scared as he is angry; how his nails have drawn blood from his soft damp palms; how he hasn't wet himself, despite his animal terror and rage.

"Your daughter is going to be okay," Renward tells him. "She's being sedated and monitored now. You did the right thing, telling us." It's not enough, of course, but it may offer Darryl a scrap of comfort.

He needed to see Darryl, to feel what he's feeling. Renward loves Darryl now almost as much as he loves Lyssa. Renward has fulfilled his purpose at last—he has been good—and it makes him feel love for the whole world, but he tries to focus on this man, here and now, the one to whom he owes more than he can ever repay. Or perhaps it's the other way around and Darryl is the one who owes him. They are both monsters of a sort.

"Bastard." Darryl bares his teeth. He's trying to control his breathing enough to speak. "You bastard, how many." He gulps air. "How many little girls have you done this to, you sick fuck?"

Renward smiles faintly. Tears well in his eyes and he fights them back, knowing they can only provoke anger. "None," he says, though it's too much to ask for Darryl to believe him. "This is the first time."

Darryl lets out a bark of disgust, disbelief. Droplets of saliva splatter from his mouth, mixing with the tears on his chin.

"Have you ever heard of the Catalina comet?" Renward asks. He can't force the man to understand, but he also can't bring himself to stop talking. "It only passes in sight of Earth once every ten thousand years. That's how often the world needs someone like me. That's my one chance to serve the greater good."

Darryl is looking at Renward now, searching his eyes. Darryl's red, wet face is still twisted with pain, but Renward thinks he sees a glimmer of comprehension there.

"You are my Catalina comet," Renward tells him. A tear spills warm down his cheek and he brushes it away. He feels a rush of fatigue and drowsiness. It occurs to him that his patch cut off the flow of stimulants when the session ended. "You're the first one. The only one I'm likely to see in my lifetime. That's you. Thank you, Darryl."

Mark stands over Renward in the soft light of the waiting room.

The man sleeps like an angel, is the sick thing. His eyelids don't even show the soft goldfish-like flickerings beneath the surface that would indicate dreams, mouth relaxed, lips just slightly parted. He'll wake up soon, refreshed, a little disappointed to go home without having done his work, but accepting. Understanding that not every call turns out to be the real thing. Glad, even, that no one has suffered today.

Mark will say hello. Mark will tell him things went well with the interrogation, no need for Catalina after all. Mark will all but apologize for the inconvenience and Renward, who is incapable of even looking inconvenienced, will smile. Mark will check the whites of his eyes for lingering traces of green, just in case. And then both of them will go home.

JASON SIZEMORE

Renward has a job to do. It is a job he knows is difficult and unpleasant, but he takes pride in his work and the quality he provides. On the surface, Renward is a monster because of the things he does for his employer. Then, after a brilliant twist, the reader is implicitly asked to reconsider their initial appraisal. Who's truly the monster in this scenario? The moral ambiguity fuels so much reader discomfort in this piece that you need a shower afterwards.

OSU

KINGSLEY OKPII

"It was during the great war when the *ndi ichie*, from the seven villages of Aro, called a truce, and agreed to relinquish the powers of their respective Alu-si. The war had raged on for years, the villages completely ravaged, the land soaked red with the blood of the countless dead, and still, an end to the war eluded the sight of even the greatest seers. One child from each village was then chosen to become Osu, that is, a sacrifice to his village's alusi, and then all seven children were banished to the ..."

Mma Ukwu droned on, her tongue dancing to the rhythm of our origin story, the same one I'd heard every night since I'd been sacrificed to Min-ochi, since I'd become his Osu. The same story that gave no answer to the real question that plagued me: When will I see Mama again?

It was a real community with the other Osu, who too were taken from their homes and forced to become vessels for the deities of Aro. Ada was the next youngest Osu and was about twenty-three years old. She had been Ani's—the earth deity—Osu for a decade, and now she could create wells deeper than fifty men lengths in the ground by focusing her *uche* on the spot where she wanted the hole created. I overheard one of the Keepers say that Ani only blessed her with that gift as reward for her long service as his vessel. I wondered when Min-ochi would give me my first gift.

Mma Ukwu teaches that the alusi have different temperaments much like the humans that worship them. Some are slow to anger, and others are perpetually seething vith rage, some are slow to reward their Osu, while others seize every opportunity to lavish heir Osu with many gifts. She particularly likes to tell the story of how Ikuku, the wind lusi, blessed Anyadike with the gift of floating on thin air just nine moons into his service, and how Anyadike, now an old man in his eighties, was thought to have received all the gifts kuku had to give, such that he is considered equal in might to the alusi that dwells inside of him. Thinking of Anyadike, my mind wandered to my mother: Anyadike had not seen his amily in over seventy years, not since he became Osu. They could be dead and he wouldn't know. I would die before I lived that long without seeing Mama.

"Ike! Ike!" Mma Ukwu's voice snatched me from my thoughts. She had that look she gets ight before she scolds me. "I know you haven't heard anything I have said in the last hour. These stories I tell you are the foundation of your people, from them you learn your history, our obligations, and the privilege you bear as Osu. Do not take them lightly."

"But I've heard them so many times, I even complete your sentences."

"Knowing the words is not enough, you are yet to understand their real meaning, and ntil you do, I will hear nothing about you knowing all my stories. Besides, you haven't heard ll of them." Her expression softened, and a half smile formed on her lips. "You know, most nitiates listen to these stories for years before they are deemed to have gleaned their true meaning. You've had less than four moons, and all I've had from you are complaints and utter lisinterest. I wonder if Min-ochi has made a mistake choosing you." She looked into the thin ir, no doubt pondering if mistakes were something the alusi could make, and then she shook er head in an attempt to dislodge the blasphemous thought.

"Anyway," she continued, "we are done for today. Go to your shrine and commune with Min-ochi." She shooed me away with two flicks of her wrists, eager to have me gone. I scurried o my feet and made for my shrine, which doubled as my bedroom.

Our rooms were arranged serially, from the oldest down to the youngest Osu, and so Ada's room was next to mine, which was the last room in the long corridor of rooms. Just efore I opened my door, I noticed Ada's door was slightly ajar, and the smell of freshly ooked *ikoko* wafted from around the door. My mouth watered and my stomach gurgled. I adn't realised I was hungry. I knocked and asked if I could come in.

"Remember to keep your necklace outside," came Ada's muffled voice, her mouth no oubt stuffed with hot *ikoko*.

Osu could temporarily divest themselves of their alusi by taking off the sacred necklace iven to us at initiation. But it was risky, as Mma Ukwu had told me; I was not to ever take ff the necklace, and I would die within an hour if separated from it. It was also not allowed or one Osu to enter with his alusi still within him into another alusi's shrine. These and many nore were some of the rules of Obodo Osu, as the small village on the outskirts of Aro where he Osu had been banished to had come to be called.

I took off my necklace that had a red cowrie pendant and placed it inside my shoe at the oor mat. I opened the door and the pungent smell of delicious *ikoko* hit me, but I quickly nade sure to take note of the time on the wall clock directly over Ada's bed. My one hour started five seconds ago.

"*Nna kedu?*" she asked in her usual playful way, smiling as she did.

"I am fine o. Anything for your boy?" I asked, eyeing the steaming bowl balanced on her thighs.

"I knocked on your door earlier to see if you wanted some, but you were not around."

"Mma Ukwu was boring me with her dry stories," I said, and she let out a laugh, reminiscing her time spent under Mma Ukwu's tutelage.

"Help yourself to some." She gestured to a pot. "Leave enough for Ani O!" she added. I stifled a laugh, surely she meant I should leave enough for her second round of eating, because the alusi, Ani, as I had seen him was a wooden statue sitting in the shrine just adjacent her bed, and there was no reality where he would grow legs to walk over to the pot or even develop a patent mouth to eat the food if he was served. Still, I scooped only a few spoons onto my plate.

We ate and talked for what felt like thirty minutes, all the while I was aware of Ani's stare drilling into my face, as if begrudging me for eating part of his food.

"*Enhen*, sister, why can't we Osu take over Aro. We ..."

"Shh," Ada shushed me and she inspected every corner of her room with quick turns of her eyeballs for something I could not see. "I see your education with Mma Ukwu proceeds slowly, for you would not blaspheme as you do if it were otherwise. Count it a miracle you still sit alive before me." I could not understand what part of my suggestion triggered her. It made no sense that we were blessed with the power of the alusi, and yet were the ones banished to live out our lives away from our families, prohibited from ever interacting with other members of Aro who had conveniently come to be called Nwadiala, or real born.

Seeing my confusion at her outburst, she softened her features. "It is prohibited for an Osu to interact in any way with the Nwadiala, and that includes using your gifts against them. It is woven into our initiation rites, and to speak or even think of such is considered blasphemy." She took my already empty plate and set it on the floor with hers.

"You should listen to Mma Ukwu more. It's almost an hour since you entered my room, you should wear your necklace."

"Thank you for the food," I said, and then took my leave.

It was the feast for Chukwu, the supreme alusi, whom due to his magnificence was deemed to be beyond having an Osu to carry his essence, but was accorded great respect in the form of many feasts held in his name. His was also the only altar built in the centre of Obodo Osu, where all the denizens of the small village worshipped in silent prayer once every four days.

Mma Ukwu presided over the celebration, and I could see her white flowing wrapper and chalk adorned face brimming with mirth as she danced to the drums being played. Osu and keepers mingled freely like one big family. The keepers belonged to a priestly group charged with taking care of the Osu, and this made them the only Nwadiala that could interact with us. Mma Ukwu, who was the head keeper, was charged with performing the initiation rites that transformed one from a free born to an Osu, and always chaired the feasts and celebrations we had.

Tonight, she presided over the feast of children. Chukwu was thought to be the giver of children, and when it was deemed that the cry of a new-born was long in being heard in Aro, the *ndi ichie* communicated to Mma Ukwu to hold a feast appeasing Chukwu, the giver of children. As the Osu danced and sang to Chukwu, the married of the Nwadiala who sought children were encourage to meet themselves with the certainty that the supreme deity would visit and plant great sons and daughters in the women's wombs. I, however, didn't care for the celebrations as my mind was set on only one thing: Escape.

The keepers guarding the perimeter of the village had all been called in to join in the celebration. Indeed, there was really no need to guard the village. All the other Osu I had talked to never hinted at any interest in leaving the village, all of them seemed to have made the village their home. In fact, a lot of them were so old I doubt they could've succeeded if they tried to escape. I was the only one I knew who harboured thoughts of escaping, and I would've shared my plans with Ada, but since the incident in her room where she chastised me, I had kept my apparently blasphemous thoughts to myself.

I quaffed the last of my palm wine and dropped my wooden cup on the floor, feeling the drink blunt the edges of my senses. The celebration was still as fervent as when it had just begun, the drums rose to a fever, and the Osu, even the aged among us, danced in the clearing in front of Chukwu's shrine. I spotted Ada amidst the crowd also swaying to the beat that had now taken a transcendental quality. It seemed as though the dancers were praying with the movements of their bodies, and the drums gave carriage of their requests into the high heavens where Chukwu resided. The lure of the drums was undeniable, and I felt myself loosening to their sound.

When I asked Mma Ukwu if I was required to dance, she smiled and said, "if you have to ask, then you are not yet ready." Hinting at what I suspected to be the case with the others: They were in a trance during these celebrations and their bodies moved without their control. How else could I explain the acrobatic movements exhibited by even the octogenarians? It had to be that the alusi within had taken over and were worshipping Chukwu through them. It made sense because Mma Ukwu had told me that Chukwu is a representation of all the alusi combined. I still hadn't communed with Min-ochi, and therein lay the source of my resistance to the infectiousness of the drums.

I made my way back to my room and picked my already packed sack of clothes. I circled round back, avoiding the centre of the village as I made my way to the gate that guarded Obodo Osu. As expected, I met it unguarded, and gently pushed the right gate forward to create a narrow space large enough to have me slip through it.

A long road, the Uzo Osu, lay in front of me as I looked ahead with Obodo Osu behind me. My lamp flickered, and I caught its reflection on the smooth surface of the compacted clay that was used to fashion the Uzo Osu. From my studies with Mma Ukwu, I knew it led directly to the first village, Ohafia, and after that to the next village, my village, Arochukwu, where Mama and Nneka, my sister, lay awake waiting for my return. It had been six whole moons since I last saw them.

At dawn, I came up on the first few huts that signified I was entering Ohafia. The huts seemed empty, but this was no surprise as most people were already at their farms. Soon, I was passing the centre of the village. As it was a market day, I saw many Ohafians, mostly women, setting up their wooden stalls and arranging their goods in readiness for the midday market. I greeted people as politely as I could while trying not to draw any attention to myself.

By midday Ohafia was well behind me, but Arochukwu was still hours away, and my feet hurt from hours of trekking. I came up on a large tree with thick foliage, and it provided good canopy from the sun that was shining angrily on Aro. I brought out the wrap of *ukwa* I had stowed for my journey. I ate two mouthfuls and washed it down with saliva, as I hadn't packed a container of water. A few minutes under the shade and I regained strength in my limbs, ready for the rest of my journey home.

Arochukwu stood exactly as I remembered even in the twilight. I saw women, walking in small groups, with baskets supported on their shoulders as they talked about the day's events on their way back from the market. Men sat in front of their huts awaiting their wives' return. The playful sounds of children filled the entire village and I thought to myself that not too long ago my voice could be found amongst theirs. The darkness made it so that nobody recognised me as I made my way through the village headed for my house. At Ozo-Aki, the street on which my family house stood, I felt my heart quicken at the prospect of soon being reunited with my family.

The darkness had deepened and a lamp was burning brightly in front of my family hut. Two figures, who I guessed were Mama and Nneka, were seated around it. I approached them, my pace even, as I struggled not to run into their arms lest they be startled.

"*Nne nno,*" I greeted my mother when I was within hearing distance of them. Mama and Nneka looked up from the palm kernels they were breaking.

"*Nnam, kedu?*" Mama asked without a hint of recognition on her lantern illuminated face or in her voice.

"It's me, Ike. I am back!" I said, confused at their apparent disinterest in my return.

The furrows on their oily foreheads deepened in consternation at what I had just said, and they shared a brief look between themselves.

"Ike who? Are you looking for someone?" Nneka asked. "Only my mother and I live here, so you must have the wrong address because we do not know any person called Ike, except Alika's new-born baby whom he named Ike just the other day."

"It is me now. Ike, your son," I said, and when I noticed Mama and Nneka pull back I realised I was shouting. "It's me, your brother." I added, my voice subdued. I hoped they were pulling a prank on me, I hoped it was one big joke, and that Mama was going to jump from her stool and envelope me in her embrace at any moment.

"I don't have a brother. My brother died from an illness as a baby, and his name was Agu. Please leave. You have the wrong house." Nneka said, as she and Mama quickly packed their sack of kernels and the lamp and rushed into their hut. As they walked away from me, I heard Mama whisper to Nneka, "Oga bu O bu onye ijiri, he must be a madman," her voice filled with pity.

Maybe Arinze will remember me, even if my mother and sister do not, I thought, as I made my way to his house, my head swirling at the impossibility that I had ceased to exist to my family. Arinze was my best friend, and I had known him ever since I could remember.

"*Nwokem*, I don't know you. Don't come to this house again." Arinze slammed the door to his *obi* shut.

I dragged my feet on the smooth clay of the Ozo Osu, not remembering how I found my way back to the path. I had hoped to have a warm welcome, a bath and a good meal, but I stood in the darkness, utterly confused at how my family and friend could have completely forgotten me in just six moons, and then I thought, *Mma Ukwu would have an explanation.*

With tears running down my face, I trudged on, taking one step after another, putting Arochukwu behind me. No sooner had I left the outskirts of the village than it started to rain.

I snuck into Obodo Osu under the cover of darkness, for I had arrived past midnight of the following day. As it was on the day I made my escape, there were no keepers stationed at the gate, and I wondered at this. Weary from my long trek, with nothing more than several mouthfuls of *ukwa* and water drunk from a stream in the last two days, I made it to my room, ensuring I was unseen by any of the Osu. Before long, I was fast asleep.

I was awoken at dawn by hunger pangs, and I hurriedly made for the kitchen where the keepers had begun preparing breakfast. If the kitchen staff were surprised to see me, they didn't show it as I casually walked from one station to another availing myself of a loaf of bread, some fish stew and a gourd of fresh palm wine.

My stomach fully distended with the meal, I set out for Mma Ukwu's living quarters.

"I see you finally communed with Min-ochi," came Mma Ukwu's voice from behind her door. "Come in, don't just stand there. The door is open." I didn't ponder how she'd known it was me.

"Welcome back. I would ask if your journey to awakening was pleasant, but it rarely ever is. But, at least, something good came of it." I looked at her, confused at what she went on about. *Journey to awakening?* I thought to myself. And what good did she mean?

As if reading my mind, she answered, "The rain of course. Aro received its first rain since the passing of your predecessor." Still sensing that I hadn't understood what she meant she continued. "The first rains signify—"

"They didn't know who I was," I cut her off. "My mother called me a mad man." My eyes welled up with tears as I spoke. "What did you do to me?" A loud thunder sounded, and it started to rain heavily. It wasn't cloudy, and the morning sun still shone brightly, and yet it was also raining, heavily.

I returned my attention, stolen by the sudden downpour and thunder, to see Mma Ukwu smiling, white teeth showing between thin lips. "Bless you child, Min-ochi has also seen it fit to bestow the gift of thunder upon you. I have never seen it happen this early." She gestured to a stool. "Come, sit. I will explain it all to you."

"When an Osu makes first contact with his alusi, it is called an awakening, and it's often preceded by some sort of trauma. For you, it was finding out the truth of becoming Osu. When one undergoes the initiation rites to becoming an Osu, every memory of that person is erased or rewritten in the minds of the people that once knew him." She paused, and considered me through her knowing eyes.

"You are not the first to have set out from Obodo Osu in search of his family. In fact, you took long in doing so. Ada made her journey after just one moon, and had her awakening on the journey back from her village. Isialangwa, Ada's village, being the furthest village from Obodo Osu, and her alusi, Ani, being a rather talkative deity, she had a long conversation with him on the way back. When eventually she made it back to our gates, she understood what it truly meant to be Osu. To be Osu is to be forgotten by the ones you love."

She added, "As Min-ochi is the deity of rain and thunder, I was particularly concerned about your awakening because Aro had been without rain for long. I feared a repeat of the great drought of six decades ago when Min-ochi would not awaken in the mind of his Osu. Alas, that is not to be the case with you."

"As you may have noticed, the rains come with your tears, and the thunder, I think, with your temper." She reached over and ran her hands through my hair like I was a child, like I was her child. "Best to guard that temper of yours, eh?"

"Come now," she walked to the threshold. "We have much to do in preparation for the feast of your awakening."

It has been seven decades since my awakening. My room is now the first among the row of rooms. I have watched many Osu pass to the afterlife. I remember my good friend, Ada, who erected, with the powers bestowed upon her by Ani, the great earthen halls that bear the statue of every Osu there has ever been, right before she passed on to the afterlife. I remember nights spent telling her successor how great she was.

I remember pondering Mma Ukwu's ... ah, yes, Mma Ukwu, that ageless woman who lives on, having not aged a single day since I first set eyes on her. I remember thinking long on her words about what it meant to be Osu. She had said to be Osu is to be forgotten by the ones you love, but I disagree. To be Osu is to lay down your life for the ones you love. The Osu are a living sacrifice to the alusi, ever appeasing them so their wrath does not ravage the land as it used to in the past in the form of war, drought, and pestilence. For peace and much more, the Osu give up everything.

I have since learned to cause rain without shedding a tear, and now even my laughter brings thunder. Min-ochi has been a kind alusi.

"There is this child I have seen in my visions. She is grandchild to my sister Nneka. She will carry you well," I say with my inside voice to Min-ochi, as I sense the hour of my death upon me.

"Hmm," he clears his throat, and it sounds like a light drizzle. "You have served me well; I have no doubt she will be a good choice as she carries your blood."

I feel the life trickle from me, and I use what strength that remains in my limbs to remove the sacred necklace that binds me to Min-ochi.

"*Jee nke oma*, have a good journey." He whispers as our tether breaks, his voice this time rumbling like subdued thunder.

JASON SIZEMORE

"Osu" is a quiet meditation about the honor of sacrifice. I fell in love with the vivid world building, the foreign (yet familiar) setting, and a protagonist that was immediately relatable.

SURVIVAL, AFTER

NICOLE J. LEBOEUF

It happens on your way home from dropping your brother off at school. You're stopped at a red light. There's a soundless flash that makes your ears pop and the world go blank. You stand on the brakes, hard, trying to push the pedal right through the floor. As your eyes squint themselves open, the horizon pulses distantly, once, twice. Heat lightning? That was weird. The signal turns green.

Then the cars turn feral.

The engine of the blue Ford Escort beside you claws up through its hood as though the steel were fabric. It crouches a moment in the wreckage. Then it attacks the driver through the windshield in a glittering crunch of glass. Screams slice the air like razors: the driver's, cut short as the window washes red, and those of a handful of bystanders, going on and on.

Then they fade, retreat, like screams heard underwater. Vision dims. Is this what fainting feels like? You've never fainted before. A clammy presence insinuates itself between clothes and skin, shocking you hyperaware: The inside of your car is filling up with a black mist or smoke or maybe a gelatinous cube straight out of your Dungeons & Dragons days. You hold your breath and scrabble at the car door. For a long handful of seconds, it won't open. Then it does. You tumble onto the street and crab-scramble backward up the sidewalk. Everyone knows you're safe on the sidewalk. The sidewalk is home base.

The driver-side door slams itself shut and your Chevy surges forward. It climbs atop the white Fiat ahead of it in line. Then it springs into the air, flying south like a goose getting an early start on the fall migration. You stare after it, mesmerized, until it disappears.

Then you run for your life.

The three blocks from that intersection to your parents' house has become crowded with nightmares. Tree roots whip like jabberwock across the cement, trailing loam. The screams don't stop. A black-and-tan dog lies motionless across the sidewalk; you leap over its body as though from one hopscotch square to the next. It rolls upright beneath you, opens slavering jaws. It does not say *bark*. What it says cannot be spelled in any alphabet you know.

You have to get home. You have to tell Mom and Dad you're OK. You aren't actually sure you're OK, or that anyone could ever be OK again. But you're alive, at least, a detail that the morning news can't be expected to convey, and they need to know.

They *must* be alive. They're at home. They're on home base.

You make the left turn onto your block and come skidding to a halt at the edge of an abyss. The Rogers' house at the corner of Chickadee and Poplar is simply gone. A powdery, rotten smell rises from the pit like the breath of some undead creature. On the other side, half of the swing set and a third of the climbing wall that Bernice Rogers had constructed for her kids still stands in what's left of their backyard. Of Bernice, of six-year-old Sasha and two-year-old Ronnie, there is no sign.

Something like roots, something like plumbing, regular as ductwork and covered in bark, extrudes from the pit and extends down the block. It develops a series of protrusions like cypress knees that thrust up though lawn, shrub, and porch next door. They proceed down the block, growing larger as they go, punching through the houses, through windows, through roofs. Branches in leaf and flower make regular, angled shapes like scaffolding. All of it is finally dwarfed by what crouches on top of or sprouts from what's left of your parents' house: a tree the size of a dragon, roots like a fence and multiple trunks like castle spires. The central torso-trunk twists to bring something like a face around to stare at you.

The burl that forms its lips opens. The tree speaks your childhood nickname. No one is watching the news here, not anymore.

You shouldn't even be here at all. You were supposed to have returned to campus a week ago, half the country and two climate zones away. But you had decided to take a semester off to figure yourself out.

Your parents were cautiously supportive, but they had concerns. Was it really a good idea to interrupt your momentum?

You didn't so much have momentum, you said, as a habit of spinning your wheels. You still didn't know what you wanted to major in or what kind of career you wanted. Without a clear goal, next semester would be nothing but wasted time and money.

But what if you *never* went back, they wanted to know? What if one semester off turned into two, and then three, and before you know it all your opportunities are behind you and you're five years into a schlub job delivering pizza?

So you'd be a college drop-out, you snapped. So what? Worse things could happen.

Those were your exact words: *Worse things could happen.* And now they have. The dragon-tree-tower is crooning lullabies. You back away, babbling promises and apologies. If you somehow make it through this day alive, if you can find your way back to a normal life, you'll finish college. You'll pursue a real career. You'll build yourself a future to make your parents proud. You'll do whatever they want, if only cars would stay cars and trees would stay trees and your parents were home and safe and alive in a house that's still a *house*, that's still *your* house and not just "your parents' house," and by the way what's the *point* of building an Independent Future and pursuing Career when the world can blink its skies and turn into *this*?

That's when you fall backward over a bicycle in the middle of the street. Not just any bicycle. *Your* bicycle. The one you brought in for a tune-up back in June, the one you vowed to ride for at least an hour each day, the one you subsequently left in the garage to gather dust. It should be in the garage now, buried in the rubble, smashed by cthulhoid roots. You suffer a vision of vast whippy branches smashing the workbench, overturning the pool table, and tossing random items into the street with a sudden outburst of the same great force that cracks concrete and holds together hillsides.

Unbelievably, the bike's in good condition. The pedals turn, the brakes function, the tires are still full of air. You mount up and hold your breath: Nothing uncanny happens. It stays a bicycle.

You start pedaling up the street, away from the wreck of your parents' house, back the way you came, to find your brother.

This is your new purpose in life. This is your career plan: to find your brother, to keep him safe. For this you will run through carnivorous grass and leap over transfigured German shepherds. For this you will bike down streets turned strange and brave packs of feral cars and nothing, nothing will stop you.

But the streets are only strange in that they are empty. The feral cars have moved on in search of prey or entertainment or whatever it is feral cars want in life. There are no bodies in the streets nor signs to show there ever were. The living are absent, too: No one is wandering in shock or calling the names of missing loved ones or even going about their daily business. It is as though not only the whole incident of this morning was a dream, but so was your memory of a small, bustling suburb with traffic and a morning commute.

The school is empty too. You pass through front doors hanging open, calling your brother's name. Your voice echoes down the depopulated hallways and bounces around classrooms full of overturned furniture. No one answers you. No one is here.

You wander out onto the playground. From the rhododendrons lining the wall, a sudden burst of movement. A piglet comes out of the bushes.

It's tiny, barely the size of a Yorkshire terrier, big black spots on pink bristly skin. It's not alone. More of them emerge from hiding, enough to fill a classroom. They seem to realize that, whatever has scared them, you're not it. They scamper over to nudge your feet and nibble on your shoelaces.

You have begun to entertain impossibilities over the past hour. It makes a terrible sense to kneel among the piglets and quietly, questioningly, say your brother's name.

None of the animals react in the least. You say it again. They mill around happily, nosing your outstretched fingers. Whoever they may have been this morning, they are nothing but piglets now. There is no one left for you to rescue.

You leave the school, biking in no particular direction but away. Somewhere life must continue as normal. Somewhere there will be a boundary, a border, a limit to how much ground whatever has happened can cover. All you have to do is survive that far. That is now your purpose in life. That is your career plan.

The bike's gears make a sound like sobbing children trying to sing the national anthem. You can hear your brother among them. It's easy to pick him out; he's always had a lovely singing voice.

More flashes in the sky, white-violet and gold, off to the west. Heat lighting. Yeah, right.

You travel all the rest of that day and the next. Mostly you walk. You abandoned your bike two hours in, when the voices of your old algebra and history teachers joined those of the children and you couldn't bear to listen anymore. You left the thing by the side of the road and continued northward on foot. Behind you, the tires came to life and slithered away.

You start scavenging food from abandoned houses and grocery stores, the ones that are still standing and look safe. Not every building meets both criteria. A gas station corner store looms dark in the middle of the day, filled with the same black mist or gel that tried to suffocate you in your car. Cement walls shift and rustle like a skirt on a restless teenager. You steer clear.

In one house, the television is on and tuned to the local news. That gives you hope; the station it's filmed at is only three miles away. The anchors are talking about what happened yesterday morning. It's hard for you to watch. It's not the subject matter or the aerial footage that distresses you so much as that the news anchors' faces keep changing. Their noses slide down their cheeks. Their eyes migrate up their foreheads for a better view. New mouths open in unexpected places, and the teeth in those mouths are all wrong. Periodic static obliterates the picture for a second or two at a time, and when it clears, the news anchors' faces are back to normal. But in half a minute or so it'll start again.

Put up with it, you tell yourself. Keep watching. Close your eyes if you have to. You need all the information you can get. But you can hear the changes, too, a *glorping* sound quiet as a whisper and faithful as an echo. It makes you sick to your stomach. You have to change the channel.

Three clicks away, a familiar movie is playing. You watch it for five minutes. There's nothing wrong with the signal on *this* station.

At dusk of the third day, you notice that your skin has begun to glow, a pale blue-white radiance that reminds you of the flashes in the sky. It's almost too faint to see by twilight. It'll be much more noticeable come full dark. The light pulses gently in time with your heartbeat. It stutters when you hold your breath.

You don't know why it's happening or what it portends for your future. You don't much care. Your immediate lookout is to survive the night, a task that can only be made more difficult with your skin lighting up the depopulated suburbs like a beacon. You're afraid of what might find you in the dark.

It's only half an hour back to the house you scavenged for supplies this afternoon. You return to scavenge it again, this time for long winter clothes to cover up your traitor skin.

While you're in there pawing through the closet in a house you'd supposed empty of living things, you hear a noise. It's a slimy, scrabbling sort of noise, and it seems to come from everywhere: the corners, the cupboards, the stairs down the hall, far too close yet just beyond your skin's ability to illuminate. A chill starts in your stomach and spreads along your spine. You grab what you need. You get the hell out.

No more sleeping in abandoned houses for you. You wish you never had to sleep again.

You walk on through the night, sweltering under your wraps in the late August heat, moths battering themselves against the lantern of your face.

You awaken slowly to the sound of crickets chirping. It's a comfortable sound. It makes things normal again. For just a half-asleep moment it's ten years ago and your parents have taken you camping. Dad's telling you about a kind of parasite that preys on crickets, tracking them by their mating calls. "So those crickets evolved to stop chirping," he says. "But their predators evolved to find them by their glow." You shoot upright in horror, clutching your hood tight around your face.

The crickets are louder than they ever were back then. The sound is coming from your backpack that you'd been using for a pillow. You empty it out and identify the culprit: a packet of jerky you'd acquired that evening. You hold it up to let your face illuminate the package. Nothing visible has changed. The vacuum seal is unbroken. But the insect song won't stop. The jerky buzzes in your hand until your bones ache.

You shove it under a bush some twenty feet away and try to go back to sleep.

Come morning, you retrieve the jerky. It's gone quiet now. You eat half of it for breakfast and stow the rest. There's no point in worrying about contaminated meat; you are arguably contaminated meat yourself. You drink the bottled water, too, straining it through your teeth to avoid swallowing the small school of mournful fish that spawned there overnight. You tip the fish out gently into an irrigation ditch and wish them well. They deserve a chance to survive, same as you.

Over the next couple of days, the glow continues, intensifying or fading according to your mood but never dying away entirely. It also changes color. You begin to recognize the patterns. A steady blue-white-lavender corresponds to the resigned, plodding tedium that passes for contentment at being left alone. Rapid flashes of yellow and green accompany the weary terror that greets your encounters with the new normal: relatives of the tree-dragon-tower thing screaming from apartment buildings, bindweed leaping up to climb you like a trellis, mouths made of water with teeth made of who-knows-what opening to devour unsuspecting ducks.

It's either the sixth or the seventh day when something gets the jump on you with a roar. Before you see it clearly, before you can think, your skin emits a supernova flash of white-hot panic that leaves your vision swimming. When the afterimages clear, your attacker lies stunned at your feet. You force yourself to examine it more closely. It resembles a small jaguar, but it was probably born a house cat. Not all house cats know how to hunt; this one must be a slow learner. The outline of each rib stands clear and stark along its flank.

You're hungry, too. The sky keeps flashing new changes into the world, some inside the houses you visit for supplies. Where you'd hoped to find canned vegetables and tuna fish were instead hissing nests of metallic vipers in the livery of Green Giant and Wild Planet. The tropical vines sprouting from potatoes on kitchen counters have left nothing in their roots to nourish you.

You consider, with some reluctance, the temporarily helpless predator on the ground. Skinny as it is, there's meat on it, and survival means you hunt or you starve. But you can't shake the feeling that you're committing a sort of cannibalism. You and the thing are, in a way, related. The oscillation of its spots, blue-indigo-purple, is a rhythm that your skin recognizes.

In the center of each spot is an open eye that tracks you, hazily and without fear. Feline whiskers sway through the air like underwater grasses. They caress your wrist as you position your knife. At your first inexpert cut, they stiffen into needles, wicked sharp, and the air all around you goes yellow yellow yellow. Then the light dies. The whiskers fall limp.

The blood from the creature's throat is only blood. So is the liquid that oozes from the pinprick wounds in your knife hand. That is something else you have in common.

On the ninth day you find the boundary you've been seeking. It is made of razor wire, sandbags, and soldiers standing quietly at the ready. Beyond that border, normal humans are presumably going about their normal lives, while here contaminated meat is left to rot. Your world is under quarantine. It comes as a shock. Despite the changes you have journeyed through, you've never stopped imagining that you could go back to the way things were as long as you kept moving and stayed alive.

They haven't seen you yet. You crouch low behind a screen of palmettos.

Hours pass. Then someone appears in the clearing. Someone swathed, as you are swathed, in out-of-season winter clothes. Someone who walks, as you have walked, with the steady ground-eating roll of joints that are no longer standard issue. Between the soldiers and the traveler, this is the closest you have seen another person since the morning of the feral cars.

One soldier barks an order. The traveler stops mid-stride. You stare in astonishment. The order makes no sense. It is in no language you know; you're not sure it's a language at all. It's so *flat*. The syllables are meaningless and undifferentiated, no light of any color to hear them by.

The other traveler spreads their arms, *I come in peace*, and takes a single step toward the fence. The soldiers raise and level their rifles.

The traveler backs up a step, and another. And another. They continue to hold their hands out, open, away from their body. Each step is a prayer, a statement of trust, a gift. Step. Still alive. Step.

Your journey has made you sensitive to unexpected motion, however slight. You notice when a soldier farther down the fence tenses up around his rifle, raises the weapon just a fraction higher, peers more closely down its barrel. His finger tightens on the trigger. Instantly and without thought, you stand and throw back your hood. Your skin shouts magnesium-white, loud enough to fill the sky and change the world.

The traveler drops, spins, sprints out of a runner's start for the cover of the trees. Gunfire stutters behind them, but you think they got away. Your face glows pink and gold with relief, then strobes to panic when you realize you're a perfect target. You let yourself fall backward into the mulch. Then you crab-scramble through the palmettos as fast and as far as you can.

You stop when you sense that you've reached home base, or at least have escaped enemy territory. The silence is astounding. Even the small mutant things that go *bzzt* have caught their breath in their teeth. Somewhere nearby is the other traveler, frozen and wary, same as you.

Trust is dangerous. Hope can be deadly. But there is only so far you'll be able to get on your own.

Come out, come out, wherever you are …

Slowly you rise to your feet. You let your heavy coat fall to the forest floor. You call out a query, just once, a high whine buzzing at the back of your throat, a pulse of emerald green like a crown. The silence after you fall still could turn any color at all.

Then it breaks up ahead on a note of the purest cerulean blue.

AUTHOR NOTES

"Survival, After" was originally a flash piece submitted to an annual Codex contest called *Weekend Warrior* (I need to pause here to give Codex a shout-out for that community's support, advice, timely information, and, of course, their contests that have inspired me to write more than I'm sure I would have otherwise.). For five weeks running, *Weekend Warrior* contestants receive a list of prompts on Friday afternoon and have until Sunday night to respond with a brand-new story no longer than 750 words.

From one of those prompts, I got the idea of a refugee fleeing a land made uninhabitable by magical warfare. But at some point during the cutting-down process, I gave up on figuring out who was casting the spells and which factions were at war, let alone fitting all of that backstory into so very few words. Bombs were mentioned, but not who dropped them or why. (In retrospect, that seems apt. From the point of view of those with the least power, the politics behind the bombs matters less than the struggle to survive their effects.)

During the rewrite and expansion, I nixed the bombs entirely in favor of this weird, unexplained, reality-twisting apocalypse. As it turns out, that's a theme I've visited before (for instance, in "The Day the Sidewalks Melted," *Ideomancer Vol. 9 Issue 1*). I'll probably visit it again.

WHAT SISTERS TAKE

KELLY SANDOVAL

Here's the thing you need to know to understand this story: I was meant to be an only child. The doctors, when they examined my mother, only counted one heartbeat.

One.

Me.

I don't know when my sister came along. My mother, so ready to accept, so unwilling to look, says she didn't see the doctor much, back then. Couldn't afford to. After that early scan, she didn't go back until the day we were born.

Maybe my sister was whispering in her ear even then. She's always been able to twist people.

Two babies born where only one was expected. Both healthy. Hungry. One, just a little bit hungrier.

Unusual? Yes. But as my mother likes to point out, not that unusual. It happened to two other couples on the same night. Three sets of twins, unexpected, but welcome.

Look closer, and the lines are redrawn. Three girls, meant to be an only child, meant to thrive. Three cuckoos, crowding the nest. Taking and taking and taking.

Would you like to hear a memory?

I'm seven. We're having a playdate at Violet and Rose's house, all six of us. Violet and Rose. Danielle and Kristi. Claire and me.

Even from the start, our parents liked to see us all together, their three perfect sets. For us they attempted their own tentative friendships, unalike though they were. My mom and dad, the seasoned hunters, breaking bread with Violet and Rose's vegan parents. Dani and Kristi's parents never quite managed, sending them along with a nanny whenever they could find an excuse.

This is what it looks like when we *play* together. Violet, Dani, and Claire convene. They decide what game we're going to play, who has what role, who wins or loses. Rose lurks close to the group, hanging on her sister's arm, desperate to be noticed and included. Kristi, already wraith thin, her blue eyes huge and sunken, lurks around our parents, begging for scraps. They joke about children, their insatiable appetites.

None of them notice that she's starving.

And I ... What did I do, back then? Was I brave and strong? Did I stand up to the lot of them?

I sat in the grass, weaving flower crowns, waiting to be called, like a good little dog. You have to understand how I loved her back then. How we loved each other. Kristi was already drained to a husk. Rose walked the world in a mind-fucked fog. But Claire took care of me.

Tried to. Claimed to. I don't know. I just know I was grateful that my monster was the good one. The one who never showed her teeth.

"We're going to have a funeral!" Dani announces, smiling at all of us with her too-wide, too-hungry grin. I remember thinking that if I started counting her teeth, I'd never stop. I could count forever and still there'd be more teeth, more hunger, more wanting.

Dani had a way of looking at me, like I was the last candy left in the bowl. Even then, I was scared of her.

Violet strokes Rose's long, dark hair then pushes her gently away. "You have to lie down," she says. "You, Kristi, and Jessa, you're going to be dead."

"I don't want to be dead," I say.

We'd only recently buried my grandmother, and I'd had nightmares about the way she looked, so alive, when they closed her in that coffin. How could they be sure, I'd asked my mother. What if they were wrong?

"Well you have to be," Dani snaps, eyes hard. "That's the game. Kristi, come here and be dead!"

"It's ok," Claire says. She takes the flower chain from my hands and wraps it around her wrist. "I won't let anything bad happened. You just lie down in the grass is all. Please?"

I must not have argued, because the next thing I remember, I'm lying in the grass with my eyes closed, Kristi and Rose pressed close, our arms flush. Rose's sticky fingers are twined with mine, and Kristi is surreptitiously decapitating clover flowers and popping the blooms in her mouth.

Dani, Violet, and Claire stand at our heads and shower us with flower petals. I can feel Claire's shadow on my face.

"She was so beautiful," Violet says, sobbing. "I loved her so much."

"Their sacrifice will be remembered for always." The word sacrifice lingers on Dani's tongue like something sweet.

"We should have done more," Claire says. "We should have found a way to save them."

"But there wasn't one." Violet's tears switch off in an instant. "There never was. Ever."

"There could be," Claire replies. She steps closer to me until her toes nudge my scalp, and I bite back a pained yelp at the pull of her feet on my hair. "You never know."

"Well I do," Dani says. "And I say they're dead. We're not playing rescue. We're playing funeral."

"Maybe I don't want to play," Claire says. "C'mon Jessi. Let's go."

"Don't you move, Jessi." And now Dani's standing on my hair, too, and I want to move, I do, but I can't. I remember the way the tears felt, the wet shame of them. "You have to play. You both do."

Anyway, that's when Claire shoved Dani, and Dani bit Claire, and Violet started screaming, so Rose started screaming, and I didn't move, because Claire was still standing on my hair.

By the time our parents dragged them apart, Dani had a bloody nose and so did Kristi, though no one'd laid a finger on her, because Dani loved to share. Claire had a split lip, but no one cared, because Violet took Dani's side, like always.

We were grounded for a week. The both of us holed up in our bedroom, playing anything but funeral, happy to never go back to Violet's place again.

But of course we did.

"Can't keep such good friends apart." That's what my mother said. "You're all so cute together."

There are other memories, iterations on a theme.

Claire's first flight, my heart lifting with her as her wings came in and she disappeared out our bedroom window. Falling as she rose, dizzier and dizzier as the whole of me spun into her.

When she came back, found me unconscious on the floor of our bedroom, she said she'd never do it again. That she'd be careful.

That's when she made her promise. Promised she'd never take more than half of me. Enough to feed her, but not so much I'd starve like the others.

I think that's when I started to fear her, when she said out loud what we both already knew. That she could take as much as she wanted, could reach into the heart of me and pull out all her favorite bits as a treat. That she didn't, because she loved me.

People fall out of love all the time. Sisters most of all. Even at 12, I knew it.

After that, the feathers started pushing through her skin without warning, like a reminder of what she wasn't doing. She said she wasn't strong enough to stop them. Violet and Dani grew sleek and lovely, like hunting cats, while Claire was all sharp-boned angles and flaking skin.

I used to catch her sometimes, sitting on her bed, setting fire to her feathers and watching them burn down to her skin. That was before we moved to the new house. Separate bedrooms. Locked doors.

Sometimes I think we might have been fine if it weren't for what happened with Evan. But then I remember Dani and the funeral. Some things were always meant to be.

Still, it was Evan who made me briefly, foolishly hopeful. Hope makes you brave. And bravery is dangerous.

Evan was in my American Government class, and I wanted him the way you want heat at the end of a long winter. You know those sort of dangerous guys you meet sometimes? The kind you can't look away from? Sharp smiles and wounded eyes, brilliant as they are bitter?

Evan wasn't like that at all. Evan's brown eyes were soft, and he smiled easy as summer. He liked to laugh, but he wasn't the class clown sort, always demanding attention. No, Evan laughed at other people's jokes.

I liked the look of him, too, attractive in that solid way, someone you could hide behind, and soft enough that you could imagine cuddling in close. I wanted him to wrap me in his arms and promise to protect me. Promise to take me away from anyone who would ever hurt me.

Evan's girlfriend, Tara, was in our class, too. I would have hated her, but she was just like him. Just as sweet and soft. She played trumpet in the marching band, and on movie days, she'd sit in the back and paint people's nails. She did mine once, each a different color and a shining glitter coat over top.

When Evan saw them, he said they were her best yet. Then he kissed her and not me. So yeah, I hated her a little. As much as I could manage.

American Government was my last class before lunch, so Claire always met me in the hall after. Maybe she got the munchies early, I don't know. She was waiting there like usual that day, her eyes on her phone, when I followed Evan and Tara out.

I guess I must have been looking at them: the way she moved so easily into the circle of his arm, the way he leaned down to murmur in her ear.

Claire waited until they were a little ahead of us, then smiled at me, all sweet and sisterly. "Which one do you like?"

I'm not bi or anything. It's just, that's where we'd gotten to. We only ever talked about unimportant things. Class. Homework.

I hesitated for as long as I dared, wishing I were brave enough to lie. To refuse her a name. "Evan."

And at the same time she said, "You don't have to—"

But I had. And she smiled, like the name was a gift.

"That's your type?"

"He's sweet," I said, hoping that'd end the conversation. "But he's got a girlfriend."

"You've never mentioned a crush before."

I hadn't had many. Bigger worries, you know?

"It's not a big deal." I started walking toward the lunchroom, hoping to distract her. "How was Speech and Debate?"

"You know, the winter formal's coming up." She had this brightness in her voice, a sort of forced enthusiasm. And I could tell, from the fixed edges of her smile, that this was one of those moments that she'd decided to be a *good sister* and nothing was going to stop her.

"I'll go with you," I said quickly, to derail any coaxing. She knew I hated the dances. "We'll meet the other twins. Same as always. It'll be fun."

"Maybe not." Claire grabbed my hand and squeezed it. I pretended not to flinch, and she pretended not to notice. "I need to take care of something real quick. Meet you in the lunchroom?"

I guess that was my chance to stop her. But I was just happy for the time alone. I let her run off, slowing my steps to enjoy the chaotic isolation of a crowded high school hallway. Too soon, I was at our usual table. The other cuckoos and the sisters were already waiting.

Dani, standing, her back to the wall, her hand resting on Kristi's shoulder. Neither of them smiling. Dani only smiled when she was hurting someone. Kristi only smiled when Dani couldn't see her. Violet and Rose were something else altogether, both sitting, Violet's hands in Rose's hair, weaving it into ever more complicated patterns.

"Where's the runt?" Dani asked, as soon as I was close enough. "She skipping lunch? Someone needs to teach her not to waste her food."

"She's on her way," I murmured, having long ago learned to say as little to Dani as possible.

"No need to be nasty." Violet scolded, leaning back to admire her handiwork. "You'll scare Jessi."

"Everything scares Jessi."

They might have argued further, but Claire arrived then and offered me a tentative grin. "There you are. What do you say, pizza?"

"Sure," I said. "Whatever you want."

After school that day, Evan found Claire and me by my locker.

"Jessi! You got a minute?" he said, his voice all warm and bright. He glanced at Claire, who was bouncing in place with undisguised enthusiasm.

"No problem," she said. "You two kids have fun."

"Claire—"

She shook her head, leaned in close and whispered, "My treat."

And then it was just Evan and me.

"Your sister seems nice," he said, his gaze following her a ways before jumping back to me. "Is it weird, being a twin?"

"You have no idea." I couldn't look at him. I opened my locker, started digging for my books. "Did you need notes or something?"

"No, umm ..." He shifted in place, and now it seemed he couldn't look at me. "I was wondering. The dance. Winter formal. Maybe you want to go with me?"

Give me this much credit, if no more. I didn't say yes, just as simple as that. I wanted to. But I wasn't stupid. Wasn't *that* stupid.

"Tara?"

"We broke up," he said, dismissing three months of adoring gazes with a casual shrug. "At lunch. She's sweet and all, but ... I guess it didn't work out."

My treat. That's what Claire had whispered. Smiling like she'd handed me a present. Evan. She could do things to people's heads. All the cuckoos could.

You're thinking of what I should have said. What I should have done.

But all I was thinking was I deserved something. Something good and kind and safe in my life. Someone who wasn't going to hurt me.

What I said was, "I'd love to." And, "Wanna grab some ice cream or something?"

And he laughed and said yes and caught my hand as I walked beside him. And it was like he really did like me.

Even though Evan was driving me to the dance, the sisters came over to get ready, same as ever. The cuckoos downstairs, in Claire's room. Me, Rose, and Kristi upstairs, in the room I'd said I'd wanted because "I like small spaces anyway, honest." Which is what you say when your sister can suck out your life force if you irritate her.

Kristi sat on my bed, hardly more than a wraith, her pale pink dress showing off the sharp angles of her collarbones, the winglike protrusion of her shoulder blades. As if she, too, might fly. Rose, in faded gold, kept smoothing her dress with nervous little flutters of her hands.

I could tell you, just by seeing them, that Dani would be in red and Violet's gold dress would shine.

To complete the theme, I should have worn sky to Claire's navy. Had even picked out the dress, had it hanging in my closet.

But Evan had asked me to the dance. Strong-armed, bright-eyed Evan. I had rushed to the mall and found a dress in purple velvet, with a slit up one side. Long-sleeved and high-necked, it hid all the sharp edges Kristi was showing. I imagined the velvet made me look soft.

"You're really going with a boy?" Rose asked, not for the first time. "Claire doesn't mind?"

"Claire's fine. She likes Evan." I pulled my hair back from my face, imagining an elaborate updo. But the sharp line of my chin dissuaded me.

"Nothing too good for our Jessi," Kristi said, all acid. "Did she put a bow on him for you?"

I let my hair fall again, covering the point on my neck where Kristi's glare rested. "It's not like that. He's— It— We actually have a lot in common."

"And he just happened to notice your sterling qualities all on his own, did he?"

"Shut up."

"Be nice, both of you." Rose, ever the peacemaker, scolded. "What does it matter, anyway, why he likes her? Whatever reason you love someone, you love them. It feels just the same."

"You would know," Kristi muttered.

Rose didn't flinch. "Yes, I would. Violet takes care of me. She says, when we go to college, maybe she can do like Claire does with you. Fifty/fifty. It won't be so hard, then. Once we're grown."

"It's not—" But I couldn't quite bring myself to finish, to claim my precarious balance was somehow as difficult as her desperate scrabbling for scraps.

"Do you know what Dani says?" Kristi was picking at the pale rose at her wrist, tearing the flower petals to slivers. "She says that as soon as we're out of the nest, she's going to eat me up, bones and all. She says once she's done with me, she might just come for Jessi. Why not, since Claire's not using her?"

"She didn't say that," Rose objected. "She's your sister."

Kristi met my gaze in the mirror, unblinking. And I knew it was true. Not just true that Dani'd said it. True that she meant every word.

"You're not worried, are you?" she asked, letting the last shreds of rose fall to the floor. "Just hide behind Claire, same as always. *You'll* be fine."

The doorbell rang then. I heard the door open, the low murmur of my dad's voice.

"We'll miss you!" Rose said, jumping up to hug me.

"Yeah, have fun with your new toy."

"He's not!" My voice was high, cheeks flushed. I swallowed the urge to keep fighting. "Whatever. I have to go."

"Hey, you don't have to be embarrassed." Another squeeze from Rose. "It's nice, that Claire looks out for you so much."

"Isn't it though?" Kristi added, sounding not at all nice. "Dani hates playing with *her* food."

Ignoring them both, I checked my reflection one last time, grabbed my coat, and headed downstairs. Evan was waiting for me, and I didn't want to think about anything else.

I won't talk about the dance. I want to keep it as it was, just one night when everything seemed possible. One night to feel like me, my own person, not Claire's fragile echo. One night to dance close to someone who called me beautiful, who looked only in my eyes, who smiled at my smile.

Let me say this though, to dispel any confusion. Evan was there. He was himself. Not some glassy-eyed zombie, performing acts of bland affection. He was Evan as I'd always known him, always imagined him to be. Only mine.

Claire was waiting for me when I came home. I found her sitting on the living room sofa, already changed out of her navy dress, a cup of cocoa in her hand.

"There you are." She gestured to a second cup, waiting on the table. "I was starting to think you two might have snuck off somewhere."

She tried a grin but, as always, her smile was sad.

"Just talking." Talking and laughing and kissing with giddy enthusiasm, fingers intertwined and pulses rushed, the windows of his cars going opaque with the heat of us.

I took the second cup, tasting our parent's brandy as soon as it touched my lips.

When we were young, I'd happily cuddled-up beside her, comforted by the sound of a heartbeat so like my own. Now, we generally occupied opposite sides of the couch, the middle cushion a carefully maintained no-mans-land.

I was still dizzy from the dance. From the car and the taste of Evan's lips. Just then, I wanted my sister. So I sat next to Claire, pillowing my head against her bony shoulder. She went very still, then sighed and leaned her head against mine, and for a second it was just like we were kids again. No less broken, just naïve enough not to care.

"Seems like you had a good time," she said. "I wish you'd told me about him earlier."

"I guess I didn't think to."

I had, of course. But we'd stopped talking years ago, and I'd been afraid of what she might do. Afraid, mostly, of what she *had* done. That she would take his heart and hand it to me, and it would be dirtied in the act of giving.

But he hadn't changed. Not really. Only seen me. Was that so bad? Didn't I need him more than Tara ever had?

Things were quiet between us, only the sound of Dad's old grandfather clock and our matched breaths.

"You can come to me, you know." Claire said at last. "I'll always take care of you."

She didn't say *I owe you that much* but I heard it anyway. What price was fair for what she took? And what did it matter? It wasn't like I was allowed to barter.

My next sip of chocolate was bitter, as I remembered Kristi's glare. I sat up and moved to the far side of the couch.

"There's one thing. Dani's getting dangerous. Kristi said—"

"I won't let her hurt you."

I almost let it drop. Always had before. But the memory of Evan's sure hands on my waist made me bold, if only for a second. "What about Kristi? Dani's *already* hurting her. She's gonna kill her one of these days."

Claire stared into her mug, silent.

I dug my fingers into my palms, choking down the urge to shout at her. It wouldn't make a difference, wouldn't help Kristi. And what if she answered anger with anger? She could be as dangerous as Dani, if she decided to be.

"She's my friend." I forced the words out through the fear. "I can't just let her die."

"Drop it." Her words were stern, even scolding, like I was a misbehaving pet. "It's complicated. You wouldn't understand."

I stood up, leaving my mug on the table. "Thanks for the cocoa. G'night."

"Jessi ..." Claire spoke my name on a sigh.

I stopped. Had to stop.

"Stay away from Dani when I'm not around. From Kristi too. They aren't ... nice."

They? Dani was a monster. Kristi was just feral from the effort of survival.

"Sure," I said, because it was always safer to agree. "Whatever you say."

I took a gun from my mom's safe the next morning, while she and Dad were out shopping, and Claire was with the other cuckoos. Then I texted Kristi and told her we needed to talk.

We met in the woods behind Kristi's place, in the rundown remains of our old playhouse. Rotten wood, ancient tea sets, and the two of us trying not to bump our heads on the sagging ceiling.

"What's so important?" Kristi asked, once we were both settled. "Where's Rose?"

"Busy. I wanted to talk about Dani."

Kristi's expression hardened. "Dani's my problem. Not about to fix her with one of your *good sister* tips."

There'd been a time, years ago, when I'd tried that. When I'd believed I was somehow a better sister, and that was why Claire treated me as she did.

"No," I said. "I know. I just—I'm worried. She really said that? About hurting you?"

"Killing me, you mean?" Kristi tore at the wood by her feet, flicking splinters at the wall. "Yeah. It's something she says sometimes. She's gotten restless, lately. Says I'm holding her back."

"You think she means it?"

"She means it." She held up her hand, studying her fingertips, and I swear I could almost see through her pale, raw skin. "She's hungry, and she hates it here, and she says it's only ever been a matter of time."

"Until?"

"I don't know." She let her hand fall and looked up, meeting my gaze with level intent. "But whatever it is, we don't survive it. You understand? None of us survive it."

I reached into my bag, pushing aside books and paper until I felt the cool weight of my mother's gun.

"Just in case," I said, taking it out. "I thought you might want ..."

"You want me to kill Dani?" Kristi asked, with a burst of laughter.

"I want you to be safe," I said. "I want us to have a future. And I don't know what else to do."

She took the gun from my hand, turning it over, feeling the heft of it. "I wonder if they even die."

I'd seen Claire bleed, seen her stubbornly hoard the pain to herself, when the other cuckoos would have shared it. I'd seen her heal as slow as anyone.

"If you're quick," I said. "Before she can push it back on you."

"Huh," she said, still stroking the gun. "Guess they might."

I stood, uncomfortable. What had I thought? That she'd refuse? Defend Dani? Kristi, of all of us, had always been determined to survive.

"I should go."

She looked up at me, smiling in her bitter, too-knowing way. "Your parents got more guns?"

"I guess."

"Get one. Dani's just honest. That's the only difference. Claire'll come for you, same as any of them. It's what they do."

I thought of Claire burning off her feathers, of cocoa on the couch, pillow forts and stolen dollar store jewelry.

"It's different between us."

"Why, because she got you a pet? Think of what she did to him, Jessi. Think of how easy it was. And it's ok because you like the result? Well you won't, always. When they're done with us, we'll be gone, really gone. No one will even remember we existed."

"She loves me."

Kristi stood and shoved the gun into her purse. "So ready to defend her. Ever wonder why? You think it's only Violet? Only Evan?"

I got up too, stomach twisting at the idea of Claire messing around in my head. Of her changing me the way she had Evan.

The way I'd let her change Evan.

"What about you, then?"

"Me?" Kristi's laughter was all bright, brittle shards of pain. "Dani likes me to be afraid. Wouldn't be any fun, otherwise."

"Think about it," she said, as I ducked through the doorway. "And thanks."

"Sure."

I took a rambling route home, walking the neighborhood in loops, following side paths and getting lost in cul-de-sacs. Evan texted me, then texted again, but I didn't respond. I didn't trust myself to.

When I finally turned on to our street, Claire was just making her way up the block, sandwiched between Violet and Dani. Violet had her arm slung around Claire's shoulders, and Dani was making some point, gesturing extravagantly. Claire laughed; I saw her tilt her head back, smiling at the sky.

I thought of Kristi, shoving the gun in her purse. Of Rose's blank smile. Of Evan, his hands sure as we swayed together, his eyes only on me.

I waited out of sight, until Claire was inside and the cuckoos were gone. Then I crept inside, snuck into our parents' room, and took another gun from the safe.

I didn't go to school that week. I didn't want to see the cuckoos, or the sisters, or Evan. Especially Evan. I got in the car with Claire, and when we got to campus, I just walked away. She didn't try to stop me. And after the first time, she didn't ask.

She agreed to fix Evan. Even promised to fix things for him with Tara. And I tried to be grateful, but it was hard not to hate her, for letting me have him then taking him away again. Even if I'd asked. Even if it was the right thing to do.

On Friday, as Claire drove me home, I got a text from Rose. In a flurry of worried emoticons, she insisted I check in on Kristi. Talk her down.

"Is Kristi okay?" I asked Claire, keeping my eyes on my phone.

"Huh?" The question seemed to puzzle her. "Dani hasn't said anything."

They were fighting, Rose insisted in another storm of texts. We had to do something.

But Kristi and Dani never fought. Kristi knew better. Reassuring Rose, I sent a quick "you okay" to Kristi. No response. That happened, sometimes.

Kristi would be fine. Kristi always found a way to make it through.

Just after 5:00, the doorbell shrilled. I stood, thinking for a moment it might be Evan dropping by. He'd done that a few times, before the dance. But of course, it couldn't be. He wasn't thinking about me anymore.

Our parents were out, so it was Claire who answered the door, while I stood at the head of the stairs, looking down at the entryway. I could just make out Violet, barefoot, wearing one of the long black coats the cuckoos kept stashed around for when they went flying. I ducked down before she spotted me, retreating back a bit, into the shadows of the upstairs hall.

"Get in here!" Claire stepped back, pulling Violet inside. "It's freezing."

"She's dead." Violet spoke in a panicked rush. "I went to see her. We were going to—Kristi—She—"

My throat tightened. Kristi hadn't answered my text. And I hadn't bothered to send another.

"We've got to do something about her," Claire said. "Dani can't be allowed to—"

"No!" Violet grabbed Claire by the wrists, jerking her forward. "Dani's *dead*. I saw her. Saw Kristi. There was blood all over her."

I'd given her the gun.

But why now? What had broken between them, after so many years of uneasy co-habitation? They'd argued, Rose had said.

Kristi had stood up for herself. I'd made her brave. Made her dangerous.

"You're sure?" Claire asked.

"I saw her."

Claire glanced up, toward the landing. Her eyes were wet.

"We have to leave," Violet said. "Now. Today. Fly somewhere else. Anywhere. Like we always said we would. We have to finish things."

"Finish?"

"Finish. It's time to be done. It's time for you to remember how to fly. You think I'll let myself end up like Dani? We'll need their strength."

Claire jerked backward. "I won't hurt Jessi."

My pulse, already racing, skipped at the sound of my name.

Silence.

When Violet spoke, her voice was soft. The voice she used when talking to Rose. "Claire, please. I understand. I do. You think I don't love Rose? She needs me. She is me."

"You don't have to kill her." Claire was pleading. They both were.

"That's how it ends. How it was always going to end." Even from my hiding place, I could see the tears on Violet's face. "Have you seen the way Jessi looks at you? You're not her sister; you're the monster under her bed."

Shut up Violet, I thought, as Claire winced, like the words were a blow.

"Jessi wouldn't hurt me."

Violet laughed. "No? And where do you think Kristi got a gun, huh? Because she sure as hell had one when I saw her. This is your fault, Claire. If you kept a better leash on Jessi, Dani would still be alive."

"Violet—"

"I'm going to deal with this. You should do the same. But I won't wait for you."

The door slammed, and Claire stood staring at it, her shoulders shaking.

But I didn't have time for panic. Slipping back into my room as quietly as I could, I took the gun out from under my pillow, let it rest on my lap.

Rose though, she didn't have a gun. I hadn't given her one. And now Violet was coming for her. My phone still had her last text, all worried inquires and cheerful emoticons.

Run. I texted, typing as fast as I could. *Dani's dead. Violet's lost it. She's coming. She'll kill you. She said she'd kill you.*

It was all I could do, and it wouldn't be enough. Kristi had fought, but Rose loved Violet. Bent toward her like sunlight. She'd wait, and she'd trust, and Violet would eat her alive.

Which left me. Sitting in my bedroom, gun on my lap, stomach in knots. It'd been years since my last trip to the gun range, but it wasn't hard. The safety was off. All I had to do was squeeze.

It wasn't wrong to shoot a monster, even one you'd known all your life. Why should I feel bad for wanting more than half my own soul?

I could hear Claire's footsteps on the stairs.

"Jessi?" she called, before pushing open the door. She'd never felt the need to knock. Her eyes were bright with tears, her face red and blotchy. Despite everything, my first urge was to open my arms, hold her while she mourned.

Her gaze dropped, resting on the gun.

I lifted it, surprised again at its weight. Not knowing what to say, I focused on holding it steady, the barrel aimed at her chest.

"Jessi, *no.* You didn't. Tell me you didn't." Her face was red and blotchy. We were both ugly criers.

"I told you Kristi needed help," I said. "That Dani would kill her."

"Dani's dead."

"Because you wouldn't help! Someone had to stop her."

"What was I supposed to do?" she asked. "Take on Dani? You don't understand how strong she is. Was. I couldn't. Not without hurting you."

"More," I said. "Hurting me *more.* Kristi had to make Dani stop. I want you to stop."

She flinched at that. "I've always tried to share. Make it even between us. I love you. You know that."

"You can't share what isn't yours, Claire. You can't share *me.*" My hands were shaking, the gun with them. I rested it against my knee, careful to keep it aimed in the right direction. "My whole life, you've been taking me. Feeding on me. And there's never been anything I could do except hope you didn't get hungrier."

"You never even asked." She was reaching for me, her hands open. Then she let out a shaky breath, and her hands fell to her side. "No. You're right. I know. I never wanted—I never asked to be this."

"Neither did I."

We stared at each other. Me with my gun; Claire, just being Claire. And I think we both knew she still had the upper hand. I'd told Kristi to be fast. But I hadn't listened.

Had still seen my sister when she walked in. The one who'd always protected me.

"You could kill me from there, couldn't you? Or fix my mind, like you did with Evan, make me do what you want."

"I wouldn't," she said. "I never would. Not to you."

I raised the gun again, held it level with her chest. "And you think I won't?"

She didn't even glance down, her eyes fixed on my face. "Whatever I've been, I only ever wanted to be your sister. To take care of you."

"I don't need taking care of anymore."

"We all need taking care of." She stepped forward, and I put my finger to the trigger, but as she pressed my wrist down, I didn't squeeze.

"I won't make you do that," she said, leaning forward to press a kiss to my forehead. "Be good, Jessi."

Her touch was hot, burning through me. My vision went white, and at first, I was sure I was dying. Dying felt like coming together, like waking up, like regaining everything I'd ever lost.

I was all in one piece for the first time in my life, no loose strings being endlessly unwound from the whole of me.

Then my vision cleared, and I could see where Claire wasn't, just an empty space and a pathetic pile of silver feathers.

For me. Because of me.

And I was whole and I was broken, a puzzle made from two sets of pieces. Fear and hunger, guilt and determination. Strongest of all, a fierce, desperate love, settling into my heart like a bird into a nest.

Someone was laughing. Sobbing. Me. I wrapped my arms around myself, squeezing hard and tight. The way a sister hugs you, when there's nothing left to say.

AUTHOR NOTES

"What Sisters Take" wasn't an easy story to write. It went through multiple iterations as I struggled with it, changing lengths and perspectives and thematic elements. The earliest versions were told entirely from Claire's perspective, an approach that turned it into a fairly typical "poor sad monster' story." It's so easy to sympathize with someone when you're seeing through their eyes, regardless of what they're doing. Later, I tried a version with dual perspectives, but Claire always dominated the narrative. It wasn't until I settled on a version of the story that was entirely from Jessi's perspective that the story's themes came together. Jessi's fear comes from the fact that she can never be entirely sure of her sister. She has to trust in her continued benevolence. Denying the reader access to Claire's thoughts highlights that tension.

Interestingly, even without her POV, Claire was the character that readers most responded to. Some sympathized with her, while others focused on her monstrous aspects. I think we're always fascinated by power, and the decisions that the powerful make. To me, "What Sisters Take" is a story *about* that fascination. Even Jessi and the other sisters aren't immune. I like to say that it's a story about love and power and how they break each other. In the end, Jessi and Claire do love each other, to the best of their ability. But while one holds the other's life in her hands, that love always comes with conditions.

COTTONMOUTH

JOELLE WELLINGTON

He finds her in his grandpa's attic, in the Big House.

The hatch has been locked up tight since the day Grant Dixon was born—twenty-two years of locked up tight—and long before.

He used to ask about it, between the stories his Grandpa Dixon liked to tell.

Grandpa Dixon used to read to Grant's daddy when he was young, and they'd all been from the Good Book. Warnings against greed and lust. Warnings about things not of God.

By the time Grant came around, Grandpa Dixon relaxed, the starch of his white preacher's collar leaking from his spine. But Grant remembers what his grandpa said about the attic.

Don't go up there, boy, Grandpa Dixon said. *'He who is of God hears God's words; therefore you do not hear because you are not of God.' Don't be the second half of that verse, boy. Don't.*

And so, Grant listened, because he was of the first. Of God. He was *good*, as all the town was, crooked in their obedience, as his Grandpa spat fire and brimstone from behind the pulpit.

But, one day, the lock falls off. It lands at his feet with a heavy crack, splintering the rotten wood that makes up the third floor of the family home. Grant Dixon swears he feels the house breathe, and he looks out the picture window, across the acres of Mississippi green sea, and feels like something is *alive*.

The ladder rolls down, swollen planks of wood as steps, connected by ragged rope that looks twined together by hand. He expects the first plank to snap under his weight. He's even more shocked when it's the second that snaps.

Grant snatches onto the next and climbs. He climbs and climbs until his blunt fingernails catch on the soft edge of wood and he heaves himself upward, sliding along it like a serpent would, head then belly, and finally the tail of his feet, catching over the mouth of the entrance to the attic.

The ladder rolls up and the hatch falls shut.

There isn't any dust to suggest that the attic hasn't been touched in years, but the smell of stale air and the spores of an oak tree convince Grant otherwise.

This is where he finds her.

She finds him in Preacher Dixon's attic.

He is a gorgeous boy, elegantly dressed, the smell of cotton and linens at his pulse point. His skin is so pale that she can see the blue of his veins.

She thinks he'd look better with a little blood on his collar.

She is a girl. A black girl curled on a bed of black curls that match the hair upon her head. Her hair is cropped short, a harsh thicket that looks hard as the bristles on a wooden brush. She seems to be asleep, but the moment that Grant takes a step back—step *forward*—her eyes open and she's on her feet.

She slinks, too small to be called a crocodile, but too majestic to be a garden snake—docile and green as the grass it hides in.

There is something inevitable in the air, Grant can taste it like dust. He hesitates for a moment—this girl is in his grandpa's attic, and yet, it feels like she's there for *him*. Grant knows the Bible, knows his grandpa's stories well—parable and verse alike—can recite them by heart too. "Well done, thou good and faithful servant: thou hast been faithful over a few things, I will make thee ruler over many things: enter thou into the joy of thy lord." *Matthew 25:21.*

And Grant has been good. Grant has been faithful. Grant didn't open the attic. The attic opened for *him*.

"And who are you that I see?" she asks, voice low and crooning, like the chirps along the swamp edge and a story's breath.

Grant moves because he's never been able to resist swamp nor story.

"I'm Grant."

"Grant no-last-name?"

"Grant Dixon," he says. And then, he asks, "What's your name?"

She is beautiful, nails long, lavender and sharp. He gorges on the sight of her, her dark skin, so different from his, the place where her cotton shift clings to the curve of her breasts, the dip of her waist, and he wants to trace the lines of her with his tongue.

It's her eyes, though, that demand his attention, hazel bright with hunger deep.

"I have none," she says. She takes another step forward, and her thin colt legs tremble. He stares at them, and something low in his belly, just above his pelvis, tugs tight towards his chest. She smiles like she knows. "But, come again, Grant Dixon, and I may tell you."

This is the first night.

The next time he crawls up the hatch-hole, she is waiting.

She stands by the tiny porthole at the apex of the Big House. He wonders what she's looking at, the window so crusted with dust, the outside must be an eternal fog. When she sees him, the curve of her generous mouth twists into a smile that shows the fine points of her white teeth. He doesn't see people like her often, so he pays special attention to the richness of her skin, a depth that's missing in his flesh. When Grant inspects her, he notices for the first time, three chains wrapped around her ankle—pewter, copper, and iron. He waits for her to say something, but she just smiles.

Grant swallows the silence, then his nerves, in that order.

"I—"

"You came back," the girl-with-no-name says like she's only mildly surprised.

"Will you—"

"No," she interrupts again like she can pluck his thoughts from the grey matter. And then, she turns away, like he isn't worthy.

Grant creeps forward, the near-silent sweep of the soles of his feet on the rotten wood cracking the air. He looks from her chained ankles up her back. White ropes of flesh crawl up into the nape of her neck and disappear beneath the neckline of her cotton nightshirt. He thinks the scars suit her; they're *perfect*. She's perfect.

"What *can* I ask you?" Grant asks because he can tell—he can see the stories thrumming in her sinew, and he wants them. He wants them more than *anything*.

"Ask a good question, and I might answer."

"Have you ever seen the ocean?" he asks her.

And the girl-with-no-name says against the dust-fogged window, "I have seen the edges of everything twice. Yes, I have seen the ocean."

Grant sits at her feet and says, "Will you tell me a story about the ocean?"

And so, the girl-with-no-name tells him a story of moving heaven and water, of delving deep into the pools until there is only blackness. She tells him of a boy named São Jos... that rode the waves, and the beautiful girl that stole him into its depths until the blackness of the whale swallowed him whole. When she is done, Grant feels compelled to press his face against the meat of her thigh as he looks up at her.

"Thank you," he breathes.

She looks surprised, for just a moment, before she smiles and runs her nails through his hair, presses it to the white of his scalp.

"Do not thank me, Grant Dixon," she whispers. "I only ask one thing of you."

"Okay," he says because he wants to.

She leans down, nudging her nose against his, and he thinks, *I'm breathing her carbon.*

"Deny me."

When she is alone, she listens to the whispers in the house. She listens to the preacher's words and scents his blood, and she waits. She waits for the boy to break his word, to shatter her trust. She hears nothing for a long time, nothing but the sound of her breath.

"Did you go into the attic, boy?" Preacher Dixon asks. "Have you been to the attic?"

Preacher Dixon is the kind of man that beats truth from one's mouth with his words. He is the kind of man that expects obedience.

She will only give him violence.

A breath.

"No, sir, I haven't been to the attic."

She smiles.

This is the first denial.

And the pewter chain cracks.

"You denied me," she says when he sneaks to her in the haunt of night, when the moon is hidden behind the fat swell of a purple cloud—that's the thing about living so deep in the country, the skies look purple, and Grandpa Dixon always said it's the blood steeped in the soil reflecting back at the night.

"You asked me to," Grant says softly. He takes a step closer—tonight, her curls are longer, spilling past her shoulders. She steps away from her bed of hair, revealing the long porcelain seashells of her toenails. He wants to know her. "Tell me your name."

He does not ask this time—he does not realize. The girl-with-no-name no longer looks surprised.

The girl-with-no-name hesitates for only a second, holding the lie at the back of her tongue as if it were a preciously guarded truth. When it slides from between the gap in her teeth, it comes out like reluctance and jelly.

"Inanna, for the sky."

"Tell me a story of the sky," Grant demands. He pauses. "*Please*."

The girl-with-no-name but Inanna for the heaven begins to tell a tale, lets it slip past her teeth in song and verse. He feels the heat in the pit of him swell fat as she tells him a story about a boy named Zong with oil slick for eyes and a mouth that yawns sin, and that girl that he feeds moonshine and cherry pie to, a girl that he brands with his name and hides in the hollow tree trunks in the woods. She tells him a tale about the rich man that wanted to buy his way to the sky and keeps his girl cleaved to his chest. And Grant listens, takes these stories, and seals them beside the parables that Grandpa Dixon tells.

When she is done, he makes her kneel before him. Grant takes her face in his hands, feeling the flesh mold to his palm, feeling the sharpness of her cheekbone. When he bends down to kiss her, it tastes like bread and wine—Communion on her tongue. She kisses him back, sweet and terrible, licking over the caps of his molars. His tongue dips to the back of her mouth and he notices—there is a tooth missing.

When she pulls back, there is blood on her teeth. Grant admires how the red looks against white, how the brown looks against white.

"You are beautiful," Grant swears, and her smile grows impossibly wider, yawning like the man in her story, like she wants to *eat*. He wants to *eat*.

"You could," his girl says, and he realizes that he's been speaking aloud. She laughs, a bright noise that sounds like a wind chime. It's the type of sound that could turn him into a pillar of salt.

Grant leans forward again to kiss her, to devour her, his hands large on her neck. He kneels so that they're both on their knees, and he presses her to the ground. Hands on wrist. Lips on neck. Teeth in *skin*. And then she drags his face to hers, staring at him with eyes like pools of honey.

"Wait," his girl whispers. "I will tell you one more story, and then, you may have me."

"Why can't I have you now?" he demands, licking the hollow of her collarbone.

"Because I have a question," Inanna says. "Answer it the next night, and you shall have me."

"And?"

"Deny me twice."

He is easy, mind wrapped tight in lunacy and lust, enamored with the scars on her back, and the taste of unstrange fruit on her tongue. But he will do anything for a taste of it, a taste of her, a taste of the chains on her feet, and the stories like she is both nursemaid and whore.

But he does it when he is asked again by Preacher Dixon: "Have you been to the attic?"

He denies her twice. "No, Grandpa. I haven't been to the attic. No."

When the Good Preacher comes to see her and lays a peck of cornmeal and three pounds of pork at her feet, he asks, "Has there been a boy here?"

The Good Preacher comes up rarely, just enough to keep her fed, to keep her whole. With every year, his back grows more crooked, knees just a little more ruined. Still, he makes the climb.

She watches him, pretends to cower when he raises a hand to her. She has long stopped flinching from the back of a pale hand. But when the Good Preacher sees her flinch, he smiles his disgust, and she sees it in his teeth. It has always been there, in the Dixon boys' mouths.

She's tasted it for centuries.

Abomination, *he does not say.*

She remembers it on his tongue. She remembers it from the lines of hands.

She thinks that he forgets—she will not allow the new boy to forget. The Dixon boys will stop forgetting her. They'll never be able to forget her, just like she doesn't forget where they've pressed themselves into her skin and scarred it over and over again.

They will not own her bones.

"No, sir-uh. No boy here."

Let him think it. Let him ask. Let him lose.

He does not notice. And the copper softens.

The third night that Grant goes to her, the girl-with-no-name but Inanna reaches for him first. He goes to her like he can't help it, and she presses her hand against his cheek, and he reaches for her, pale blue veins pressed into russet skin. Her curls are a wild mane, trailing behind her, nearly to her ankles, where only the iron shackles remain.

"Did you deny me?" she whispers.

"I wish I didn't," Grant says. "I want to scream that your stories are mine, that you're mine."

Inanna hums. She pulls him close, muscles wrapped around his neck in a chokehold. Her lips press to his earlobe, and he shivers against her. His arm loops tight around her waist, pressing even tighter. He thinks she might feel the length of his cock. He thinks she might not mind.

"I am not *yours*." Hissed soft and vicious, and Grant jerks back, staring at her with hurt. And her eyes are still honey, and her voice is soft again, like cotton candy spun in the bottom of a gritty metal bowl when she says, "But I could be."

He looks up at her—he has to look up at her now, and he's just realized—and nods. "How?"

"What would you do?" she asks gently. "To make me yours."

"Anything."

She smiles at him, sweet and slow. "How do you find death?" she whispers.

It sounds like the beginning of a story. But it isn't a story that Grant knows. This is a question he cannot answer because he thought death was something God gives. He pulls away to stare at her neck, her face, her bare arms. His fingers trace the lines at the nape of her neck, and he wants to taste the white scar tissue.

"I don't know," he says. "*Please,* Inanna—"

"There is a woman somewhere, with a wide memory, wide enough to hold the girth of me there still. She will arm you, if only you'd ask," Inanna promises.

The thrush of sickness sings in his gut because there are talks of arming and weapons as if this is a holy war—because it must be holy, for his skin to sing where it touches hers. "I don't know how to fight, Inanna. I don't know this story," he insists.

Inanna laughs against him, the sound of it rippling the short hairs of his arms.

"I don't ask you to fight. I ask you to look. Where do you find death? Where do you find mine?" Inanna asks. She leans forward and kisses the answer into his mouth. "Inside a little girl's milk tooth, pressed into the pit of a peach, wrapped in a bundle of raw cotton, tucked in the hollowed-out trappings of a Bible, trapped in the belly of a great black hog, which is buried under a cypress tree, drooling over the murky swamp water."

And he hears all of this against the flesh of his bottom lip as he possesses her mouth, his fingers buried in the thicket of her curls. He wants to lose his soul in it if only to hear her stories.

Grant steps back to look at her.

"And what happens if I do? Find your death? Will you be free?" he asks gently.

"Yes, my love. I will be free, and we will be together. *Always*," she says in her sugar-spun words. Her white teeth glint like the swamp-worn bedrock.

"Always," he repeats, because it is a dream—a story without fire and brimstone, unlike his grandpa's stories. He would have his story in his bed, beneath him, inside of him. He would fit himself in the space of her ribs.

"Yes, always. Go, my love. Go and fetch my death from the woman by the swamp. Feed it to me, and I am yours."

Grant lets her go, reluctant, and then, he asks, "And deny you thrice?"

"My love, you can learn," Inanna laughs. "And deny me thrice."

So, that night, Grant gets into his dead father's rusty pick-up and drives into the night, to the witch by the swamp's edge. In his head, he thinks about her stories. All of his *stories*.

He does not remember to close the hatch this time. He has made many mistakes. He opened the latch with his lust. He crawled up the ladder with his greed. Leaving it open is his last mistake.

When the Preacher comes, he spits fire and salt at her and she takes the licks up her back. She does not flinch from the cracking, and she does not feel her skin split. She takes it because she can. She takes it because soon, she won't, and when the Preacher sneers at her and calls her whore and liar and witch, she bares her teeth; she remembers a time where she was 'his' too.

She's always 'his' until she's someone else's.
She is tired of the Dixon boys, and her marrow is too.
She is tired of the Preacher thinking that he's always right. He knows too much of his verse and not enough of the way blood wails, the magic in it.

The boy has made many mistakes too. The Preacher barely notices them.

The iron shackles do not open, but they crack.

Just a little.

It's enough.

He knows her. The woman at the swamp. She is more than a woman with a wide memory. She is a witch.

Grant has heard about her—she is Eugenia Marie. Everyone knows Eugenia Marie.

Grandpa Dixon has warned Grant about *people* like her. *Exodus 22:18*, Grant thinks.

My girl Inanna, he remembers. He has to remember her. He'll do what he must. For her. His girl.

Eugenia Marie is tall, like his Inanna, but nowhere near as beautiful with orange polyester scarves wrapped around her head. When she sees Grant, she simply leaves the door open, and when Grant meets the edges of light from the inside of her shack, he looks at the crooked shelves and potions they hold. He takes in the cloying smell of spices and pork salt, accentuating the rotting smell of swamp that catches in Grant's nostril hairs.

"Help yourself," Eugenia Marie says where she sits in an overstuffed chair, her daughter sitting on the ground between her thighs. She braids the young girl's hair, nodding to the glass of cheap whiskey next to the piles of old bound books, the dirt-crusted shovel, and a butcher's knife.

Grant tips three fingers down his throat, enjoying the burn. It feels like Inanna's mouth.

Eugenia Marie sneers. "You are here for a death, then, boy?"

"How do you know?" Grant demands. "I haven't told you why I'm here."

"You think you are the first?" Eugenia Marie asks with a low laugh. Even from where Grant stands, he can smell coconut oil on her greasy weathered fingertips. "The memory is deep; this tale is an epic. You are not the first to search for a girl's death."

"I am the last," Grant promises with a boy's earnestness because he thinks it will make for a good story—the boy that proclaims to find a death and feed it to his love, to be the last to do so, to be the only one named and mattered.

Eugenia Marie smiles a secret smile and nods to the knife and the shovel.

"Then be the last, boy. Be a hero."

Grant snatches up the shovel and the knife. He points the shovel at Eugenia Marie and her girl and sneers. "Inanna believes in me."

"Speak not of the girl-with-no-name. They will hear, and they will wail for her," Eugenia Marie warns.

Grant pauses. "Who is 'they'?"

"Don't forget to deny her. Deny her thrice."

Grant leaves then because there is only so long that he can suffer a witch and her brood. He treks across wooden bridges towards the cypress tree that dangles over the walkway like a canopy, the Spanish moss falling into his brown hair. He presses into wet earth with his shovel and then he begins the dig.

The dig is a climb, in some ways, he thinks, because this is what a good story would sound like. *The dig is a climb to heaven. To his Inanna. His.*

The dig feels like it's forever and a half-day, the sun rising and setting, for every inch he digs deeper, more mud slips in, and then when the moon is high, he feels the shovel hit something wet and hard, not the same wet dirt. Grant feels the belly of a beast and he falls to his knees and pulls out the carcass of a hog, stiff and rotting and smelling like fresh bacon and pork fat. He yanks it up onto the walkway.

For Inanna, he thinks. *For her death*.

And so, he pulls his knife and cuts the black hog wide from anus to sternum and pulls out the Holiest book, a Bible that resembles the one that sits on Grandpa Dixon's pulpit. He pulls it open and in the place of Leviticus, he finds cotton. And when he digs through that cotton, cutting his palms wide with the roughness of it, he finds the pit of a peach.

And then, he puts the pit of the peach between his front teeth and *bites*.

It is the next night by the time he cracks open the peach pit, revealing a little girl's tooth.

"Inanna!" Grant shouts as he crawls up the rotting ladder, her death tucked close to his breast and his fingers curl into the attic floor as he levers himself up.

He does not notice Preacher Dixon until he stands to his feet and reaches for her.

When he does, Preacher Dixon is upon him, his lips curled into a snarl as he takes in the tacky blood spackled over Grant's jaw, the dirt caught underneath jagged nails. Preacher Dixon grabs Grant by the shirt and rattles him.

"What have you done, stupid boy?" his grandfather roars. There is no fire and brimstone in his voice anymore. There is a whimper, and Grant thinks that he should end with a bang. "Do you know this girl?"

Grant looks at her—his Inanna who has never looked more lovely, more alive, than she does as she stares at him, cowering in the corner, her back wet with red, nightshirt split.

"N-No, I don't," Grant insists. "What did you—"

Preacher Dixon slaps him hard, hard enough that Grant stumbles back, foot skirting to the side, just missing the mouth of the attic. Grant clutches his jaw and groans.

"Do you know this girl?" Preacher Dixon demands again. "The hatch to the attic was open."

"No," Grant says again, this time firmer. He stands, pulls himself up by the spine, and realizes that he is taller than Grandpa Dixon, old Preacher Dixon, who has curdled with age, liver-spotted by time. He shoves Preacher Dixon back once. "No, I do *not*."

This time, Preacher Dixon is smaller again, soft and old, and he asks in his frail voice, "Please, Grant ... tell me the truth ... *please* tell me if you know this girl?"

"I *don't*," Grant roars. "Now, what did you do to her? Did you ... did you *whip* her?"

This is the third denial.

And the iron shatters.

Before Preacher Dixon can answer, the sound of iron clattering to the ground rings, like the sound of a clock striking midnight. The Dixons turn and there is Inanna.

Grant has never noticed how very tall she is. She is taller than him, and her long curls are a bundle at the top of her head, spilling over her split-back, her front, everywhere. With every step, Inanna grows larger, her hazel eyes black now, her dark red mouth full of sharp white ivory, mouth so wide that he can see the missing tooth.

And still, Grant finds her lovely.

Inanna takes another step and then she jerks back. She looks down.

Wrapped around her left ankle, in the space where the shackle had bound her tight is a ring—small and slight—of cotton, raw and rough against her bruised skin. She hisses something in a language that Grant does not know, and then she looks up at him, soft and vulnerable and *his* again.

"My love," she whispers. "Feed me my death, please. I can't … cannot leave without you. *Please.*"

Inanna is beautiful, Grant thinks. *The world will think her beauty is for them.*

She will leave, he thinks. She cannot leave him. He does not know what he would do—without her stories, without her hands, without her mouth, without *her*. She is his. Her stories, her body, her face, her name, given to him and him alone. He *earned* her.

This is the Lord's gift to those that follow his Word.

"Grant—" Grandpa Dixon starts, startled as Grant pulls her death from his shirt pocket.

And then Grant takes the little girl's milk tooth and swallows it whole. It goes down jagged and crooked, tearing his esophagus. When he coughs, he spits blood into his palm and he stares at her, smiling her bloody smile back at him.

"What have you done, stupid *boy*?" Grandpa Dixon moans.

"You can't leave. Now, you can never leave me. We can be together. You're mine," Grant says with her tooth in his belly and 'mine' like a noose. "I want to keep you."

Inanna does not stop smiling. The cotton band about her ankle turns to ash, and she is *free*.

"Four hundred years," the girl-with-no-name rasps in a voice not all her own. "Free after four *hundred* years."

"What have you done? What have you done?" Preacher Dixon bemoans, again and again, lost to his fate.

Inanna reaches for him and pulls him close. "There are no shackles on me, *Massa*," she swears, and she tears into his chest, fingernails now black and ragged as she shreds the preacher's frock. Deeper she digs, through muscle and bones, until she wrenches his heart out.

Grant watches as she eats, aorta whole, heart caught between ragged teeth.

"Inanna, what are you doing? *Inanna*—" Grant begs and then he is on his back as she crawls over him.

For a moment—just for one—she looks as she always had. Heartbreakingly lovely with her hazel eyes and her generous mouth and the tight curls on her head.

She looks like she had when she was his.

"You do not own me," she whispers.

And then there is something in his mouth, spores on his tongue, growing, growing, and growing still. Out from behind his teeth grows cotton. It spills from his nose, out of his mouth, until all he can taste and smell is the scent of salt and blood.

He tries to scream, but he can only watch as Inanna drags the chains forward and wraps him up tight—first the pewter, then the copper, and finally iron. She binds him, hands and feet, chains about his neck.

Grant Dixon likes his stories.

He likes them best from his girl's mouth.

Give him a tale from a silver tongue instead; he likes to hear the licks and breaths between words, the hissing of spit between teeth. He gorges on those words, eats until his belly feels hot and swollen with it until the back of his eyes sting with unspoiled tears and the pleasure of grief. He grows fat on them, gluttonous for the tales of boys who drown and boys who find the sun and boys who burn*burnBURN* when they get too close to calling the sky their own.

Grant Dixon feasts on the girl-with-no-name's stories and doesn't realize how she spins his last.

His story ends like this: the girl-with-no-name—for he thinks now that she lied, because her name, it is not for his tongue, for his cotton-stuffed mouth—stands to her feet, and she is beautiful again. She walks like she hasn't walked for a long time, knees knocking together like a foal's, and she crawls down the hatch.

Grant Dixon does not move for a very long time. He is still, struck stone by cotton and chains.

The stench of her blood lingers for four hundred years.

And how Grant Dixon hears the ground *wail.*

JASON SIZEMORE

Sometimes when you buy a story, you do so with the feeling that it will set the world on fire. "COTTONMOUTH" was one of those for me. I was enthralled with the southern gothic feel, the way Joelle Wellington mixes various monstrous legends to give a monster revenge over her terrible captors. Joelle felt like a fresh, cutting young voice that would make a mark on the genre.

Alas, while well-received, "COTTONMOUTH" did not win any awards. Joelle Wellington, however, will continue to rise.

NEXT TO CLEANLINESS

ROSE KEATING

'I've been feeling a bit down, I suppose,' Catherine said, 'and my friend recommended you. She said you might be able to help.'

The doctor made a humming noise. He sat back, folding his arms.

'Do you know what it means to cleanse, Catherine?' he asked.

'To be healthy, I suppose? To detox?' she said. Dr. Matthews watched her, head cocked. His stillness made him frightening. He looked like the large, looming plaster castings of gods in art galleries, indifferent and unknowable.

'Cleansing,' he said, 'is a complicated business. It can involve numerous methods, numerous factors. Diet, exercise, hormones, hurt, heart, soul, sin, spirit. Cleanses can be different for everyone. We all need to be clean in different ways. Do you understand?'

She didn't understand. Susan had told her that Dr. Matthews had prescribed her a week of celery juice and encouraged her to keep a dream journal during her cleanse. She made it sound very appealing. Catherine had looked up the clinic's website and had found filtered images of kale smoothies, medical spanking, possession by angel. She wasn't sure if she understood at all. She had never been any good at science.

'Yes,' she said. 'Of course.'

The doctor smiled; it sent a rush of something warm through her. 'We'll start with the basics. What's your diet like?'

'Ah, normal?' she said.

The doctor stopped smiling. 'Define normal.'

'Just, you know, food? Normal food? Average meals?'

The doctor was now frowning.

'Sandwiches?' she said.

The word hovered in the air after it was spoken. The doctor left it dangling and looked down at his clipboard. He reached into his desk and removed a beaker. He leaned over the desk, holding it below Catherine's face.

'We're going to try a test. Spit into this.'

'What?'

'It's to test your body's chemical levels. I need to know how toxic you are. Now, I said spit for me, Catherine.'

She paused, and then weakly spat a wad of saliva into the beaker. It dribbled down the side, slow and pathetic. A little had spattered onto Dr. Matthews' index finger, but he didn't seem to notice. He placed the beaker down and held his hands above it. He whispered something to the spit. The saliva bubbled, changing colour; it gleamed red, emitting a gory light.

'Yes, just as I thought. You're full of toxins.'

'Oh,' Catherine said and shuffled in her seat. 'I'm sorry.'

The doctor stood, crossing to the shelves at the side of the room. The shelves were a treasure trove of medical paraphernalia: stethoscopes, crystal balls, scalpels, whips, unicorn skulls. He picked up a bottle and brought it to her. The bottle was covered in a layer of dried scum, a sickly, ashen film coating the surface. The doctor pulled a napkin from his pocket and began scrubbing the scum away from the label.

'What is that?' Catherine asked.

'A detoxifier. For the next week, you'll take a teaspoon of this once a day; you must purchase correct measuring utensils if you do not already own them. It will suck up all the toxins in your body. You eat nothing else. You drink nothing else—you might notice slight weight loss. You come back to me in a week so I can examine the results. Is that understood?'

Catherine swallowed. She felt humiliated, a schoolgirl caught with gum. She also felt a little aroused.

'Yes, doctor,' she said.

She drank the detoxifier the next morning, pouring it out into a spoon. At first, she thought: orange juice. Then: petrol. Then: sour milk. It fizzed as it hit her insides.

On the bus ride to work, she felt buoyant with energy. She beamed at strangers, stuck her tongue out at infants, whistled happy birthday to herself. She couldn't sit still in her seat and was sweating profusely; when she rubbed her forehead, her hand came away dripping. The sweat was thicker than it should have been, almost gelatinous. It was like strawberry jelly left out in the sun for a little too long.

She went to the bathroom when she arrived. Susan was at the mirror primping;

she turned to Catherine, smiling, and then recoiled, dropping her lipstick on the floor. 'Christ,' she said.

'What?' Catherine met Susan's eyes in the mirror, and then she saw herself. The reflection looked like her, but much slimmer. Catherine waved and the doppelgänger did the same. They grinned at each other.

She received many compliments during the first hour of her shift; almost every person who passed stopped to compliment her weight loss, her svelte figure, her healthy, glowing skin. She thanked them, wiping the sweat from under her eyes where it gathered in pools, solidifying as it cooled. She typed out emails, wiping her hands with a tissue each time she pressed send; the sweat was building up on the keyboard, oozing between the cracks. It had a tacky texture, like half-dry glue, and left the keys malfunctioning in spots. When the backspace key grew stiff with slick and could no longer be pressed down, she decided to take a coffee break and find Susan.

'Are you ill?' Susan asked, passing her a mug in the break room.

'I don't think so, but I'm a bit sweaty,' Catherine said. She tugged at her blouse, conscious of the growing damp spots. Jellied clumps of sweat fell further down the split of her breasts, wedging under the band of her bra.

'Maybe you have the flu? You look really unwell, you're even thinner than this morning.'

'I don't know, I suppose,' Catherine said. 'How was your cleanse? Did you find it, I don't know, a bit weird?'

'I loved it. They can be hard, but it's all about discipline, isn't it? Why, how are you finding it?'

Susan put the mug down on the counter. A glob fell from her index finger, spotted with flecks of red like a bloodied egg yolk. At the tip of her index finger, there was a clean piece of bone shining through.

'Fine, it's fine,' she said. 'Actually, I am feeling a little ill. I might see if Rob will let me take the day off.'

Rob did let her take the day off. 'You look awful,' he said. 'Did something happen? Is this about the other night, is this because of me?'

'What do you mean?'

'Catherine, look at yourself. You're not well.'

Catherine looked down. She had grown even thinner, clothes slipping off her body. She lifted a hand; all the flesh had dripped away below the wrist, her skeleton now exposed.

'I'm on a cleanse,' she said.

'That might make you better, then. I think you should take some time off. You're going to make your co-workers uncomfortable.' Rob stared at a spot next to her face, not meeting her eyes. A glob fell from her other hand, hitting the linoleum with a dull splatter. Catherine nodded and left.

She tried to call the clinic's reception after work. When she heard the cool, distant tone of the receptionist's voice asking her to explain the issue, she looked down at herself and found she couldn't say the words aloud. She hung up and opened Instagram and found the doctor's account: yoga poses, quinoa bowls, bloodletting circles, conference shots. In many of the posts, he was with beautiful people. She wondered which of them he had fucked.

He could have any of them. He was beautiful himself. He looked like a soldier in the photos, or what she thought a soldier would look like. Strong and competent and heartless.

Catherine went to her bedroom and stripped. Her tights were bulging with the sweat. Or what probably wasn't sweat at all. She held the tights above her face, feeling the weight of the substance filling them; when she squeezed, it felt like gripping the blubbery underbelly of a puppy.

The rest of her clothes were filled too, bulbous as water balloons. She looked into her mirror; her body had dripped completely clean. Her skeleton was so bright it looked like she had been dunked in bleach. The skull was the worst part. The eyes had remained but nothing else. She wasn't sure why; she thought about searching WebMD. She ran her hands along the hard smoothness of herself and tapped the bones of her ribcage. She almost expected them to ring out like a xylophone, clear and sweet, but all they made was a hollow thud.

Dr. Matthews opened the door. His eyes scanned over her. His expression didn't change.

'That's unfortunate,' he said and gestured for her to enter. She stepped inside, arms crossed self-consciously. She had dressed in layers and sunglasses to cover the worst of it. The doctor moved to sit at his desk, and she followed suit.

'So, is this bad?' She took off her sunglasses; she didn't want to be rude.

'Not bad. Not good, either. The toxins are gone, for now, but it just means you had nothing else left,' he said and picked up his clipboard. 'Do you feel empty, Catherine?'

'Pardon?'

'Physically speaking. Or, spiritually. Do you feel empty? Incomplete? Hungry for something more? Do you feel like you're missing something inside of you?'

Catherine moved her hand to the space where her stomach once was. 'Yeah, maybe,' she said.

The doctor smiled, approving, and ticked a box on his clipboard. 'That's okay,' he said. 'It's okay to be hungry. Food is a healer, Catherine. It's a kind of magic. Sometimes we all need to feel full.'

He opened a drawer in his desk and removed a dish bearing a metal cover and cutlery. 'You're going to eat this,' he said, 'and you're going to feel so full, Catherine. Bursting.'

She lifted the lid; a slab of raw meat on a plate.

'Steak's better for you blue,' the doctor said. 'Eat up.'

She cut into the steak. Blood oozed from the cut, a steady flow. Looking closely, she could see the steak expanding out and in, shuddering with life. She hesitated, lifted the piece to her mouth, and bit. Her eyes fluttered as warm red waves of pleasure flooded into her.

'Good, isn't it?' the doctor said. He was sitting back with his hands behind his head, smiling.

She looked down at herself. Flesh was growing from her bones like mould, tissue forming in clumps at her joints. The tissue wriggled, spreading out, merging to form clumps of muscle, tendons, trickles of veins flowing over the length of her skeleton. Another bite and organs bloomed, blossoming up from her rib cage and spreading out across the raw, exposed plains of her torso. Her heart inflated, rising. It gave a nervous jerk, stuttering out a few syncopated beats before remembering its rhythm. She swallowed more of the steak and skin grew, translucent and thin as wet paper.

'What kind of meat is this?' she asked.

The doctor just grinned.

She abandoned the fork, picking up the steak with her hands. Her body had grown back, but the taste. Christ, the taste. She couldn't stop eating. Silken at the back of her throat, like melted chocolate. Warm and rich and sweet too. But not chocolate. Not even really food, or even really taste. The weight of it in her mouth felt like the heat of her blanket on cold mornings, heavy and suffocating and irresistible.

'Someone's a glutton.'

Catherine startled, dropping the fork. It landed on her stomach, which stretched out in front of her, immense. She couldn't see the doctor behind it. Her stomach bulged over the desk, spilling down the side of the wood, which creaked under its weight. Inspecting further, she could see the doctor buried under the flab of her belly. He squeezed his hands out and lifted one of the rolls of fat, burrowing his head forward with a wiggling motion until it was free.

'So,' he asked, 'do you feel full?'

'I feel sick.'

'That's a pity.'

He squirmed underneath her stomach—an arm shot out, a syringe in hand.

'Hold still,' he said and stabbed her stomach. It burst like an overgrown blister, letting out a hollow pop of air. Nothing splattered out—she was empty. She wondered how that was possible. Were other patients empty like her? Were they full? What were they filled with? She wanted to ask the doctor but didn't want to sound ignorant.

The doctor cut away the dead skin, bandaged the wound. His hands felt firm and certain as they moved against her torso. When he had finished, his eyes locked on hers.

'Come back to me tomorrow. You'll have healed by then.'

'How often do you achieve orgasm, Catherine?' Dr. Matthews asked.

He stretched on a yoga mat on the floor of his office, practising downward facing dog. A long shape wagged from beneath the back of his trousers, distracting Catherine.

'Excuse me?'

'Orgasm plays a powerful part in our well-being. It can make or break a cleansing. How often do you climax?'

'Ah, regularly?'

The doctor shifted to tree pose; his arms stretched out to the ceiling, leaves sprouting from the pores of his skin.

'By regularly, do you mean excessively? Excess can be isolating. Damaging, even. Granted, not always the cause, but almost definitely a symptom. Did you know that chronic masturbators are often suicidal? Einstein once argued that we masturbate as a way to run from death—those who run more, run faster, are often those who feel closer to the void, so to speak.'

'I don't—I have lovers.'

'So? Do your lovers make you come? Can you come in general? Are you afraid to? Are you terrified of letting go? Do you believe yourself to be undeserving of love? Are you a bad person, Catherine?'

The doctor bent his limbs to a half-moon pose. His skin began to shine, emitting a dazzling, milky light. She stared at the light until the rest of the room faded to shadow, blinding herself with its brightness.

'What?' she said. She couldn't think. She wanted to bathe in his glow. The doctor's moonlight darkened as he sighed.

'You are prolonging the process by not being open. Your opacity indicates that there is something deeply problematic with regards both to you and your sex life,' he said. He stepped off the mat, and the yoga marks faded away. The leaves fell in piles to the floor, his celestial skin dimmed to flesh. He gestured towards the medical bed at the back of the room.

'Lie down there. Back straight. Legs spread. Now,' he said.

She tried not to shake as she walked to the bed. He followed her, standing between her legs. She felt faint, looking down at him through them.

'This is not a place of shame, but it is a place of healing. Will you let me fix you?'

'Of course, I'm sorry.'

'For the next week, you aren't going to orgasm. I'm going to close you up, to make sure. At the end of the week, you spit in a beaker. The week after that, you achieve orgasm every night. You spit in a beaker at the end. You come back in two weeks with the beakers, we compare their varying toxicity levels. Clear?'

'How are you going to close me up?'

The doctor reached behind her ears. He produced a pill and a bottle of water from behind them. He winked.

'Take this. Then, lift your hips, and snap your legs shut. Check the results when you're home. It's all very safe. It's often used as a contraceptive in Sweden.'

She followed his instructions. She felt a tightening in her lower body. She winced.

'Don't forget to sort payment at reception,' Dr. Matthews said, pointing to the door.

She stripped in the bathroom once she was home, goose bumping in the cold. She sat on the cool tiles in front of the long mirror, opened her legs, and looked.

She thought it would look as friendly and clean as a Ken doll, chirpy with asexual smoothness. But it looked painful and ugly, like a limb sewed onto the wrong part of a torso. Or a pair of hands locked together with superglue.

She rang Susan on Tuesday evening after drinking a very large glass of wine.

'We miss you,' Susan said, 'Come back!'

'I'm not allowed.'

'After the cleanse, I mean. When you're feeling better.'

Catherine swirled the stem of the glass, spilling a little wine on her bed. 'Susan, what did you think of Dr. Matthews? Did he really help you?'

'I thought he was brilliant. Tough, but brilliant. Kind of sexy, too. Why, are you finding him helpful?'

Catherine flicked her glass. She was disappointed when it didn't crack.

'Yeah, he's great. Really great,' she said.

On the seventh day, she felt a rush of release, like unclenching a jaw that she hadn't known she was tensing. She spat into a beaker, leaving it on a shelf in the bathroom.

That evening, she sent Rob a picture of her tits and he arrived within half an hour, looking guilty and excited. He spent four minutes jabbing her urethra, pinched her nipples twice, and then slipped on the condom. He moved his hips in quick, shallow pumps.

'Yeah, you fucking cunt,' he said, speeding up.

'What?' Catherine said, but he had already begun to come. After he left, she finished herself off while thinking about Dr. Matthew's hands.

When she was done, she walked into the kitchen, not turning on the lights. She washed her hands under the tap. She made herself a bowl of cereal and ate it in the dark, hovering over the sink. The tiles of the floor numbed the soles of her feet with cold. The drip of the tap was loud in the silence.

'Place the beakers on the desk for me, Catherine,' the doctor said. He was hovering in the air above the desk, legs crossed, arms outstretched. Numerous candles were balanced along his shoulders and arms, all lit. Catherine took the two beakers from her purse and placed them down. She hesitated, and then sat down. The doctor hadn't yet looked at her.

Dr. Matthews let out a long hum and began to slowly float down to his seat. The candles remained hovering in the air.

'Right then,' he said, rubbing his hands together and leaning over the beakers. He began to whisper to them. Once again, the saliva in both turned a bright, glowing red. Identical.

The doctor frowned, and the flames of the candle flickered out.

'That can't be right,' he said. He whispered again, but the saliva stayed the same. He looked up at Catherine and her stomach jumped.

'How are you feeling?' he asked.

'Fine, thanks.'

'I meant in regard to the experiment. Did it have any effects? Did the first week leave you calm, peaceful, clear? Or agitated? Did the second week leave you sated, rejuvenated? Or perhaps unsatisfied, lonely, dejected? How did they make you feel?'

'Well, tense, the first week, I suppose.'

The doctor rolled his eyes. A candle fell out of the air, hitting the floor.

'Not the physical results. I mean how you feel. Feel, Catherine. Your emotions. Heart, spirit, energy. How did the two weeks make you feel? Was there a difference?'

Catherine thought for a moment and shook her head.

'I felt the same both weeks, for the most part.'

The doctor exhaled through his nose, and all the candles dropped with a clatter. One barely missed Catherine's skull. She could see the annoyance on the doctor's face. She looked to a spot behind his head, a poster of a woman eating salad, head thrown back in mirth. Beneath it, the words: live, laugh, love.

The doctor breathed out.

'Right,' he said. He clapped his hands. A plastic container filled with green liquid and straw appeared on the desk. He handed it to her.

'What is this?' she asked.

'A kale and banana smoothie.'

'Are you serious?'

'Catherine, I only help those who are willing to help themselves,' he said. He stood and began picking up the candles, shoving them somewhere inside his lab coat.

'You're as toxic as ever, which shouldn't even be possible. The chemical levels are identical to week one. Do you realise most people take a week, at most? A week with me, and they're clean. They're happy. But you. It's like you're choosing to be unhappy.' He stopped, ran a hand through his hair. He whistled, and all at once, the remaining candles on the floor melted to wax.

'Drink the smoothie. Drink one each morning, they're good for digestion. Meditate, get plenty of exercise. Get air, get sun. Smile. Do something that scares you. Do something you love. Say I love you. Pet a dog. Dance in the rain. Cut off negative people. Update your Twitter. Tell everyone about your day. Advance in your job. Start a vlog. Eat a salad. I don't know, do it all. Do none of it. But you've got to at least try to be happy, Catherine. Right now, I don't think you're trying at all. You're wasting your time and you're wasting mine. If you aren't going to try, I can't help you.'

Catherine stared at her hands, clenched in her lap.

'I'm sorry,' she said.

'Take the smoothie and come back next week.'

She picked up the smoothie. She stood from the chair and crossed the room, head down as she left.

The next morning, she blitzed kale and banana in the blender.

She drank green smoothies every day for a week. She rang her office and asked to come back to work. She slipped out at five am to run around the block, to meditate, to examine the colours of the rising sun—pale amber to burnt orange to so much red, a sky the colour of a butcher's window.

She thought about the sky, about the world. She wrote her thoughts in a bullet point journal. She contemplated gratefulness. She wrote the words 'I am grateful' over and over for thirty pages. She grated carrots and peppers, mixed vinaigrettes, threw her head back and laughed at her co-worker's jokes while eating colourful salads.

'You have a beautiful smile. I appreciate your presence in my life,' she told Susan while photocopying pictures of baby animals to stick above her computer.

She cleaned her apartment, bleached the floors. She tossed the dresses that didn't fit. She packed away all the half-read novels she wasn't going to finish and gave them to a charity shop. She volunteered for an evening at the dog shelter, stroked the soft fur of the blind, limping greyhound, anointed herself with the soured smell of canine.

She stared at the ceiling at night and thought about how to be happy. She listened to podcasts about self-enlightenment and Alan Watts and focused on her breathing. She lay in the dark until she dropped off to sleep.

'You must understand, there's only so long this can go on,' Dr. Matthews said.

Catherine nodded, trying to concentrate. The doctor was usually clean-shaven, but he had allowed himself to roughen this week, stubble framing his lower face. It fascinated her. She couldn't stop looking at his mouth.

'There are other types of cleanses we could try if we had time. Gravity recentring, sterile flagellation, psycho diving, keto. But it's outside of the price bracket we established,' he said, filling out a form.

'So, we're done?' she asked. She felt dazed, far away from her body.

'Not quite. We're going to try one more method, for this last session. Are you religious?'

'Not really.'

'Marvellous. It's for sheep. However, certain parts can be useful for science. Ritual can work medical wonders. Tell me, have you any experience with exorcisms?'

She shook her head. He hummed and clicked his pen against the desk.

'Lie over on the bed, and we'll begin the procedure.'

She walked over to the bed. Dr Matthews followed her. He leaned over her, taking out a syringe. This close, Catherine could smell his skin. She felt the pinch of the syringe in her arm.

He peered down at her face, looking into her eyes.

'How'd that feel?' he asked.

She stretched up and placed a kiss on his mouth. His lips were soft, dry, and his stubble scratched her chin.

He stepped back. He frowned.

'You are not interesting to me, and I do not find you physically attractive,' he said.

'Oh,' she said.

'Right, exorcism,' he said, and moved back to his desk, opening a drawer. He removed a pair of rubber gloves.

'Upon examination of your reactions to different forms of cleansing, I have concluded that purification of toxins is not enough. You will, as you have already done, continue to produce more. This indicates that there is something toxic inbuilt into your system.'

He pulled the gloves on with a tight snap.

'To put it simply, there is something wrong with you. I'm going to pull that wrongness out. We've perfected the traditional exorcism method into something quicker, scientific.'

'How do we do it?'

'The anaesthetic will have kicked in by now, so we'll have you lie back down.'

Catherine did as she was told. Dr. Matthews was right, the anaesthetic was working—her head was filling with cotton balls and softness.

'Open wide and say ah.'

'Ah,' she said, opening her mouth. The doctor put his fingers in her mouth—the powdery plastic taste of latex was comforting. He grabbed her lower gums and pulled hard. It should have hurt, but it didn't. Her jaw felt like taffy, stretching further than she thought possible. It fell down and down until she could feel her bottom lip against her collarbones.

The doctor pulled a small torch from inside his lab coat and pointed it into her mouth. He peered into her throat, into her guts.

He hummed. 'Oh, oh yes. There it is.' He clicked his tongue and put the torch away. He pushed his fingers farther into her mouth, past the knuckles, slipping his fist inside her.

'Breath through your nose,' he said, and slid his fist down her throat.

She breathed sharply in through her nostrils, braced for pain. But felt no pain. The fist was full and firm but felt unimportant. Her body was gaseous and impermanent as an afterthought.

The doctor's fist moved further through the cloud of her insides and stopped somewhere in her stomach. The hair of his arm tickled a little against the walls of her throat. The hand made a sudden movement, jerking against her side. Then, all at once, the doctor was ripping it back up and out of her.

Catherine spluttered as the fist pulled out of her mouth, saliva dribbling down her chin. She sat up, clutching at her jaw that swung loosely against her chest. The doctor was holding something bloody in his hands. It wriggled in his grip. What is that, Catherine tried to say, but her jaw was too stretched for speech.

The thing was convulsing, spasming in the doctor's hands. It was emitting a high-pitched keening sound, desperate and ugly. She thought of drowning puppies. Dr. Matthews lifted the thing and examined it—it seemed to have limbs, a torso, a throat that he held it by. She stood, looked closer. It had eyes. It had huge, horrified eyes, and it was screaming. Dr. Matthews turned to her, still dangling the creature in the air by the throat. Its bloodied paws tore feebly at his fingers. He didn't notice.

'Lie back down. I'll dispose of this, then we'll patch you back up.'

She shook her head, but he had already turned away. She stumbled towards him, arms outstretched, woozy on her feet. He placed the thing on the table and walked to his shelves, looking for something.

Catherine teetered to the desk and picked it up. It stank of rotting meat, spoiled eggs. It was slippery in her hands. It was bleeding, covered in gouges; every pore was a wound. She clutched it tighter, pressing it against her chest. Its flesh had the texture of wet, slippery Play-doh.

She blundered to the door, heavy-footed, jaw knocking against the creature.

'What are you doing?' Dr. Matthews asked from behind her, but she ignored him, opening the door.

She could hear the sound of him moving behind her, putting something down, but she staggered away, out the door, out past the receptionist, and out of the building. The receptionist shouted out at her from the front door, but she didn't stop.

Outside light too bright, solemn stare of the sun. She was covered in the thing's blood, covered in its smell. People stared as she passed them. She tried to ignore them and held the bloodied thing tighter to herself, quickening her pace. It screamed louder with each step. It was dripping its ooze all over the footpath. Fathers and bakers and bankers scowled at the noise, at the stink, at the mess. A child sobbed in fear when she ran past and let go of his red balloon, the bright orb flying far away into the sky until it disappeared out of sight. She ran, and ran, and ran out into the world.

LESLEY CONNER

"Next to Cleanliness" by Rose Keating takes society's obsession with detoxing, cleanses, and crazy diets, mixes it with doctors who refuse to listen to a patient's needs and concerns, and mixes them vigorously. This story made me uncomfortable. A voice in my head wanted to cheer—a story that finally highlighted how toxic and pervasive diet culture and "health" media are—but was also nervous. If I scream "Yes! This story gets it!" then will everyone know that I too can get drawn into our society's obsessions? This story is so good and so necessary.

DISCONTINUITY

JARED MILLET

Stars snap into place outside Lura's cockpit. A red giant twenty degrees off her ship's nose has visibly shifted position. The nebula above her has grown more diffuse. She exhales, clicks the button to log another successful breach, and lets herself blink while the flight computer calculates the next FTL jump. She never closes her eyes during the breach. Whether or not it helps doesn't matter. What's important is to maintain her sense of self.

She reviews her mental inventory. She is Captain Lura Maraj. Her parents are Ama and Sondi. Her brother is Ravi. Her mission …

She shakes off a wave of dizziness. Her mission is her mission. She can't let herself forget. She eyes the button that would inject her with a dose of Reboot, then pushes it out of her mind. She prefers other ways of keeping a grip on reality.

The monitor on her left displays a random slideshow of family photos, places from her past, snippets from training manuals, and facts about her homeworld. The screen on her right confirms that she's breached twenty-three times since leaving Quetzal. It doesn't show the enormous number of breaches remaining. Lura doesn't know who the programmers thought they were fooling by withholding that bit of data.

In between, above, and below her monitors are dates that Lura etched into the bulkhead. Her birthday, the day she graduated flight school, the day she kissed Sara Novak at a football match, the day of her first combat mission … The list goes on. She checks and confirms that each memory is solid, locked, and strapped into place.

She glances at the stars. She isn't used to seeing them with naked eyes. The combat ships she usually flies don't have transparent canopies, but a team of psychologists had decided that being able to see outside would help with the strain she'd be under. What did they know? They'd never flown a mission like this. No one had.

Her ship is barely a ship. It has no thrusters, no maneuvering jets, nothing but a breach drive big enough for a heavy cruiser. The ship's only payload is her life support capsule and several hundred redundant memory cores, each holding a vast library of history, science, art, and literature.

The flight computer beeps at the end of its cycle. With so little control over her journey, Lura feels like a monkey from the early space programs. At least, what with her years of flight experience, she's allowed to pull the trigger that initiates the drive. She finds the star that moved on her last jump, stares at it, and *breaches*.

The doors slide open to the Planetary Defense Command and Control Center. The non-com on duty salutes her. Lura's been here many times, but she's never been summoned with such secrecy and haste.

"General Corvall?"

"In the wardroom, sir," the young soldier says. "He's expecting you."

She nods and steps inside.

"Captain Maraj," the general says. "At ease and have a seat."

She does as directed after a moment's hesitation. She isn't accustomed to sitting in the presence of a general. No, make that three. Generals Pacheco and Saldor are at the table, as well as a cabinet member whose name she can't place. Also seated are two junior officers, Lieutenant Almaty from Panther Squadron and another whom she doesn't know.

The last person at the table, sitting on Corvall's left, is a civilian in a suit that's slightly too big for him. He has the harrowed look of a man desperate to explain himself while at the same time sick of having to do so. It takes Lura a moment to recognize him from his author photo.

"Dr. Travis?" Unsure of the protocol, she turns to Corvall. The general slouches and waves to give her permission to speak. Lura straightens her back. In addition to haste and secrecy, she adds *informality* to this meeting and decides it isn't going to end well.

"You know our guest, Captain?" the general asks.

She nods. "I know his book on probability mechanics. I recommend it to all the pilots I train, sir."

Dr. Travis gives her a bleak smile. "Glad to be of service."

"Captain Maraj," the general says, "why don't you tell Dr. Travis how many FTL breaches you've logged?"

"Duty breaches or total, sir?"

"Total."

"Ten thousand, four hundred and seventy-seven."

Travis's mouth falls open. "How is that even ... Pardon me for asking, Captain, but how are you still sane?"

Lura shrugs, but the general answers.

"Captain Maraj is our sharpest pilot. No lapses, no mental breaks. She's the best. The only reason she's still a captain is because we can't afford to promote her. All apologies, Mr. Maraj."

"None needed, sir. I love to fly."

"But to breach with no lapses?" says Travis. "How much Reboot do you use?"

Lura bristles, though she knows she shouldn't. Almost all pilots use the drug, especially during combat.

"None if I can help it, sir."

Travis shakes his head, mulls something over, then asks, "You think she's the one?"

"She's the only one," Corvall replies. "There's no one else I'd even consider."

Travis looks at Lura as if she shouldn't be real. Her jaw tightens, but before she can ask what the hell this is about, Travis cuts in with a question of his own.

"Captain Maraj, what's the earliest thing you can remember?"

Lulu keeps her eyes open as the colony ship breaches one step closer to their new planet. Daddy explained about planets, and how their new one would be better than Earth. He gave her a picture book about Quetzal and its three little moons. The pictures are so pretty that she can't wait to get there. Their ship will land on her birthday and Mommy will make her a cake with five candles. So she keeps her eyes open through each breach, each time hoping this will be the one that brings them to her birthday planet.

She, her parents, and her baby brother Ravi all lay in their cabin's funny couches. Mommy puts a patch on Ravi's arm to make him sleep, and then Mommy and Daddy both close their eyes. Lulu thinks the breach must make grown-ups dizzy. But not her.

The ship twists around her. The cabin flips without flipping and everything ends up right back where it was. Lulu hiccups, then giggles. Green lights flash and the all-clear sounds.

"Ama?" Mommy asks. Ama is Daddy's name. Mommy sounds funny. Her eyes are still closed. "Did Ravi wake up already?"

Daddy slides off his couch and looks at Lulu.

"You all right, sweetie?"

Lulu grins.

"I feel sick," Mommy says. "I hate those nausea drugs, but I think this time ..."

Mommy opens her eyes and looks right at Lulu. Her mouth twists into an odd shape.

"Mommy!" Lulu says. "I kept my eyes open the whole time. It's easy. The whole room flipped and I burped."

Mommy looks afraid. Her eyes shift towards Daddy. "Ama, what's going on? Who … Where did this girl come from?"

"Sondi?" Daddy climbs out of his couch. "Are you okay?"

"It's me, Mommy!" Lulu runs to her mother. "Are we there yet? Is it my birthday?"

Her mother pulls back. "Ama, what's going on?" Her voice rises in a way that Lulu's never heard before. "Who is this?"

"Mommy?" Lulu is scared now. Daddy takes her by the shoulders and whispers.

"Lu, go check on Ravi. Mommy's just confused. I'm going to help her."

"What do you mean I'm confused?" her mother shrieks. "Ama, who is this? Where did she come from? What's going on?"

"It was one of the first cases of post-breach amnesia," she tells Dr. Travis. "My mother could remember my father and brother, but not me. This was thirty years ago before we had Reboot. She never regained the first five years of my life."

Lura bites her lip as she finishes the story. She doesn't tell it very often. It had taken her a lot of angry years to outgrow the bitterness.

Dr. Travis taps his fingers.

"Captain, I'm going to ask a horrible question. What if it wasn't amnesia? What if your mother wasn't wrong?"

Her impulse is to roll her eyes. "You're talking about the Discontinuity Hypothesis. I don't buy it."

"Why not?"

Travis sounds in earnest, and with all the generals present she decides not to brush him off.

"Personal experience. I've breached over ten thousand times. Not once have I landed in some alternate reality. If we truly wound up in a different universe every time we used FTL, I think I would have noticed by now."

Travis nods. "All right. But you must realize that you're an outlier. How do you explain the effects that others have experienced? Alternate realities, to use your words. Like your fellow pilots?"

Lura grips her fists under the table. She's lost more comrades to the psych ward than to enemy action and she hates speaking against their fitness.

"It's a question of willpower and focus. The breach affects the mind. It takes strength to hold on."

"All right, granted," says Travis. "Going through FTL can damage memory, which is why Reboot works. But you can't deny the increasing level of historical mismatch from pilots coming out of the jump. Different versions of reality are being reported more often. I mean, you've talked to your colleagues. Can you think of any historical fact from the past hundred years, any single point of reference, that all the victims agree on?"

Lura doesn't like this line of questioning and she hates the word *victims*. She's heard it on talk shows and from conspiracy nuts for years, spewed from the mouths of people who'd never known the pilots she flew with, never witnessed their panic and confusion first hand. She wants to shout Travis down just like those other idiots.

Instead, she thinks of an answer. "The Aswara probe. Everyone agrees on that."

"I'm here to check on Captain Heath," the newly minted Lieutenant Maraj tells the duty nurse. He shows her into the observation ward and directs her to the captain's private room. Lura knocks, then lets herself in.

Natia Heath sits with the back of her hospital bed tilted up. They've let her change into jeans and a t-shirt. She flips through the shows on her mini-screen, scowling at each program. Lura bites her lip and wonders if Natia's forgotten her.

"Captain?" she says.

"Don't call me that."

Lura pauses. "Natia … I came to see how you're doing. If there's anything you need."

Natia looks at her for the first time. "I know you. You're that captain from Stingray Squadron. I heard you were some kind of badass."

A weight like a stone drops in Lura's chest. Natia's been her friend for years. Lura had hoped they were growing into something more, but now that person may be gone. She sits, a dozen similar losses throbbing in her head.

"I'm just a lieutenant. You're the captain."

Natia shakes her head. "No, don't say that. I'm a trainee. I was on a training exercise, then I breach and suddenly I'm in a battle? And everybody's saying I'm a captain? Everyone else has lost their goddamn minds and it's driving me nuts."

Lura tries to keep her voice from shaking. "No one's lost their mind, you've just forgotten some things. God, I wish I could help you remember."

"I haven't forgotten anything. I'm not missing years of my life. I remember it all and I'm telling you that everything is wrong." She jabs a finger at her screen. "That asshole senator on the talk show? He was busted out of office five years ago for having sex with a minor."

"Natia, that's the Prime Minister."

"Jesus God," she says. "It's not just that. It's on every vid. The wrong actors on the wrong shows. The wrong lyrics to songs I've known my whole life. It's like someone's rewritten the world."

Lura fumbles for some way to bring her Natia back.

"Do you remember the two of us going to flight school together?"

"Of course not. I only signed up for Planetary Defense ten months ago."

"Do you remember growing up in New Kowloon?"

"Balboa," she says. "My parents moved out of New Kowloon before I was born."

Lura fishes for something major, some huge point of reference they can both agree on.

"What about the Aswara probe? Do you remember that?"

Natia stares at her. "Of course I do. How could I forget?"

"What do you remember?"

"I was in seventh grade." She turns off the monitor. "I streamed the news every day. I watched every report."

"What did they say?"

Natia thinks for a moment.

"An object entered the Aswara system at five percent light speed. They thought it was an asteroid until it slowed down. It entered orbit around Aswara B while every scientist from a hundred light-years breached there to analyze it. Then it broadcast that message about a civilization orbiting the core of the galaxy." She smiles sheepishly. "Please tell me that's still the same?"

Lura feels something prick at her eyes. "It is. Every bit."

She pulls the trigger and *breaches*. More stars slip into new positions. She's inching across a galactic spiral arm, though not the one she grew up in. She left that behind, what, two hundred breaches ago? In between, she'd crossed a gulf of brown dwarfs, rogue planets, and the wispy ghosts of long-dead giants. After one breach, she'd stopped to watch a supernova whose light wouldn't reach Quetzal for ten thousand years. Would anyone be there to see it? If a star explodes in a forest and no one's around to hear ...

She closes her eyes, recites the dates carved in her cockpit, then looks to make sure that none have changed. A message on the board to her left tells her that one of the ship's memory units has corrupted.

There's a stiffness at the base of her skull, a nagging intuition that she's missing something important. She's felt it before after multi-breach flights and she knows it's a symptom to watch. She takes a sip of water and waits for the computer to run its numbers. As soon as it's ready, she pulls the trigger and *breaches*.

It's as if Lura and Travis are the only people in the room.

"Yes, the Aswara probe," he says. "That's a constant, as are the locations of stars, the number of planets around them, the number of breaches it takes to get from one to the other. Here's another you may not be aware of: the invention of the breach drive itself. All the breach amnesia cases I've interviewed agree on the details, at least those in the history books."

"That proves my point, doesn't it?" Lura says. "The breach doesn't alter reality or send us from one to another. Reality is fixed. The breach merely causes a dysfunction of the mind."

"You're almost right," says Travis, "and that's what makes it hard to see. Reality does appear to be fixed—right up until the invention of the breach drive. The stars and planets were here already. The Aswara probe? That was launched two hundred thousand years ago. No alteration of recent history was going to prevent its arrival."

"History isn't being altered."

Travis goes on. "Don't you think it's interesting that the Core Civilization doesn't have the breach drive? Or if they do, they choose not to use it? According to the probe, their culture is millions of years old. They could easily have spread across the galaxy in a matter of centuries and yet they limit themselves to slower than light travel. Why do you think that is?"

"If it was important, don't you think the probe would have told us?" Lura counters. "The simplest explanation is that we've stumbled on a discovery they haven't."

"Simple, but unlikely." Travis taps his fingers together then turns to the two junior officers. "Captain, do you know Lieutenants Almaty and Sumner?"

The two men shift in their seats. Lura can only imagine how uncomfortable they must be in this setting.

"Lieutenant Almaty is the top pilot in Panther. I haven't had the pleasure of serving with Lieutenant Sumner."

"Beg pardon, sir," says Sumner, "but we flew together against the *Andrew Tanninger*. I was in Cormorant."

"My apologies, Lieutenant." Lura feels a pang at the memory of that battle. The *Tanninger* breached in from the Galbraith system and opened fire on Quetzal's defense satellites. Stingray, Wolfhound, and Cormorant responded, with Cormorant, a trainee squadron, taking the brunt of the casualties.

"Captain Maraj," says Travis, "are you aware of what prompted the *Tanninger*'s assault?"

Lura breaches into the midst of a firefight. All around her, exhaust plumes and explosions blossom like newborn suns. The others in her squadron are breaching into the field of engagement as well, but she doesn't have time to check on their status. Her mission is to kill the *Tanninger*. No disorientation. She looks for the *Tanninger*'s drive and reaches for the panel to launch her missiles.

But the panel isn't there. She fumbles in the space where her weapons console should be. Instead, she finds ... field rations? A water filtration unit? What happened to her fighter, and why can she see through the hull?

Exhaust jets and explosions are frozen in space around her. She looks again and sees that they're stars, shrouded in glowing dust. She's breached into the heart of a stellar nursery. The battle with the *Tanninger* was nearly a year ago. She almost grasps what's going on, but it quickly slips out of her mind. Why is she so far from Quetzal? What is her mission?

Her mission is her mission. She curses herself for weakness and exhaustion, then thumbs the button to inject herself with Reboot. A needle pricks her neck and the drug floods her body. Unused to it, she grits her teeth to hold back the bile in her throat. She focuses on the dates in her cockpit. Her birthday. Her brother's. The day she earned her wings. The day she accepted this assignment.

Too many breaches too fast, she decides. The count stands at 2,491. She checks the readings on her ship's memory units. Thirty-five percent have been corrupted. She needs to plow ahead, to complete the mission, but a pilot must know her limits as much as she needs to push them. The flight computer calculates the next breach, but she sets all systems but life support on hold and lets her ship's engine spin down.

She breaks out a ration bar and reads a random file from an uncorrupted memory bank. She watches a recording of a football match. She drifts to sleep in the dust cloud of a fledgling sun, trusting that she will wake with the memory of who she is, and why.

"It was my understanding that the *Tanninger*'s attack was an attempt to cripple our orbital shipyard," Lura says. "As to why a former ally like Galbraith should turn on us, I haven't been informed."

"An ally," says Travis. "Mr. Sumner, would you describe the Galbraith system as one of Quetzal's allies?"

Sumner looks as lost as Lura feels. "No sir. The Galbraith system broke off diplomatic relations when their Unionist Party came to power. They've been a dictatorship for years."

"No," says Lura. "I've been to Galbraith. We signed a treaty with them and Navarre to impose sanctions on New Minsk." She glances from Travis to Sumner. "A mental lapse? But which one of us?" A chill runs along her skin. Perhaps her mind isn't as sound as she thought.

"Relax, Captain," says Travis. "I remember that treaty too and I haven't breached for a long time. Mr. Sumner, why don't you share how many breaches you've logged?"

"Me, sir?" the lieutenant asks. "None."

Lura slumps. Nothing makes sense. "But if it isn't post-breach amnesia ..."

"It was never post-breach amnesia," says Travis. "And no one's ever breached into an alternate reality. I'm afraid what's really happening is worse than you're going to want to believe."

General Corvall finally raises his voice. "Captain, Lieutenant Almaty was recently sent on a reconnaissance flight to the Galbraith system to determine which version of history was accurate. Son, tell the captain what you discovered."

Almaty coughs before answering. "Galbraith is dead. Galbraith B and C were bombed from orbit and all off-world stations were also destroyed. An analysis of the debris shows that both Navarrine and New Minsk warcraft were involved in the engagement."

"The whole system?" Lura's never heard of destruction so vast, nor how such a battle could have gone unnoticed. "But ... which version of the system was it? The ally or the dictatorship?"

Almaty shakes his head. "No way to tell. Every satellite, every fueling station, every structure on a planetary surface, anything that would have held a scrap of data had been atomized."

She breaches with her eyes closed. She can't stand the view through the canopy anymore. When the breach is over she reads nothing but the numbers on her cockpit walls. She doesn't watch history vids or look at the flight computer. She scratches another mark on the bulkhead next to her harness. After every tenth mark, she injects herself with Reboot. Only two more until the next dose.

She makes herself recall a scene from her childhood: a friend's mother's wedding. She can't remember the friend's name or what her mother looked like, but she remembers the gaudy pink wedding cake.

The computer chimes ready. She swears that it's getting slower. Seventy-two percent of the ship's memory stores are gone. Her mind will hold together. *It must, dammit.* She exhales, closes her eyes, pulls the trigger, and *breaches.*

"You know the problem I've always had with Schrödinger's Cat?" says Travis. "The cat's neither alive nor dead until the box is opened and its status is observed. But the cat's life or death *is* being observed, constantly. By the cat."

"What's your point?" says Lura.

"The breach drive splinters reality. Not much, just a little, but the effect is cumulative. Every now and then someone wins the lottery—or loses the Russian roulette, I guess—and ends up with a major fracture, such as your mother observing a reality in which you were never born."

"But two realities can't exist at the same time."

"Exactly," says Travis. "The universe won't tolerate it. Yet the breach drive forces it to do exactly that every time we use it. *We are the cat in the box, Captain.* It's only a matter of time before the universe resolves all the paradoxes we're creating. It already did so on Galbraith."

Lura takes a long moment to let Dr. Travis's suggestion sink in.

"The easiest way to resolve the different versions of reality," she says, "is to erase all of our history since the invention of the breach drive." She shakes her head. "Then we're dead. As soon as enough people *observe* a reality in which humanity destroys itself, we're dead."

"Perhaps not," says General Corvall. "We're sending Dr. Travis's findings to all the other colony worlds and we're taking steps to curtail our use of the breach drive. But more than that, Captain, there's something we need to do and I believe you're the only one to do it."

"What's that?"

"We need to be observed," says Travis, "before the universe erases us for our sins. We need an intelligence outside ourselves to acknowledge that our species exists before the universe decides that we don't."

"I can't order you to do this," says the general. "There's probably no coming back. It has to be your own choice. But if you accept a word of this, we want you to breach farther than anyone before. We want you to contact the civilization at the core of the galaxy."

She breaches and remembers the day her father died. She breaches and remembers visiting Natia in the hospital. She breaches and remembers her mother closing a door. She *breaches*. She *breaches*. She *breaches*.

She floats in the vastness of space. Hundreds of suns crowd upon her. She can't see her cockpit. She can't see her body. All she can see are the stars.

She reaches out toward them. She can't see her hand, though she feels it press against something like glass. As soon as it does, the feeling fades away. She doesn't know how many breaches it's been. She can't remember the last one. She can't remember when she stopped remembering.

She can't remember her name.

"Be calm," says a voice behind her.

She turns to see who's speaking, finding nothing but a giant blue sun. A whirlpool of fire larger than worlds drains a funnel of gas from its surface.

"What's happening?" She feels the panic rise. She's seen it in other faces, though she can't remember whose. Her heart doesn't quicken, but she wants it to. Her breathing isn't shallow, though it should be. She can't feel her heart or her breath. She can't hear her voice, though she feels herself form the words. "Why am I here?"

"You came," says the voice, still behind her. "You said it was your mission."

A mission? What mission?

"Where am I?" she asks. "Why can't I feel anything? Where's my ship?"

Her ship, she remembers. Her ship to take her … somewhere.

"Your body and your ship did not survive your journey. We were able to preserve your mind and some data from your craft. Do you require further sensory input?"

What was the voice talking about? Her body and ship had … what? Hesitating, she answers, "Yes?"

She feels her hands, her chest, her face again. She sees herself in something like a hospital gown, adrift in space. What happened to her flight suit? If only they'd let her change into civvies like Natia ...

Memories flood back, sharper than any Reboot: Quetzal, the *Tanninger*, her squadron, Corvall, Natia, Dr. Travis.

I am the cat in the box.

"Oh god," she says. "The memory banks ..."

"Seven survived long enough for us to read them," says the voice. "Your flight was not in vain."

Triumph slides away in the rush of history. Her years in flight school. Her brother's graduation. Her father's death. Her mother.

Her mother forgot her name. She wants to cry, but the tears won't come. Why did her mother have to forget her name?

"Your name is Lura," the voice behind her says. "We will not forget you. You will never be forgotten again."

JASON SIZEMORE

Throughout the history of genre, there have been countless "butterfly effect" stories. It's a well-worn trope that can be a challenge to convince editors and readers to dive into. So what about "Discontinuity" spoke to me that made it stand out?

While others may intepret the story different—isn't the hallmark of a good story one that stands to different intepretations?—I find that this is not a story about altering time. It's a story dealing with substance abuse and the kinds of trauma that might lead one down such an avenue.

Would the story be stronger with a less-used plot device as its spine? Would you go back in time and change Jared Millet's mind regarding the direction the story takes? I, for one, would not. Sometimes casting a tale in a familiar ground makes the point of the story more poignant.

CANDYLAND

MAGGIE SLATER

When Tara awoke Thursday morning, her pillow had turned to marshmallow, gooey from the warmth of her head and the sunshine blazing through the window. Fruit rollup blankets slicked her legs with psychedelic slime. The mattress, now a soft-baked blondie with white chocolate chips, was permanently indented by her ass.

Her hands trembled as she backed away from the bed and scrambled for her phone on the dresser, but when she touched the device, it turned to peppermint, and she dropped it with a shriek. It landed on the carpet beside the baseboard heater and started to melt into the carpet pile. She dove for it, but turned the carpet into cotton candy that dissolved along the heater's length. Tara's mouth watered at the smell of burning sugar.

Stumbling to stand, she backed up against the bedroom door. It became a peanut brittle slab. She bumped against the wall; it became iced gingerbread.

Tara tried to breathe. It had to be a dream. Or a psychotic break brought on by stress. It was the layoff, the breakup, the move back in with her parents, and—more than anything—the lunch with Stephanie Dorham *at eleven-thirty today*. Steph Dorham, who graduated from their high school with a full-ride to NYU, who dropped out junior year to create a start-up that less than two years later she sold to Google for a fortune, who travelled the world at twenty-three, Instagramming tea in the Himalayas, Diwali celebrations in Mumbai, and rehabilitated cheetahs in Kenya before she returned to the states for a coveted job at a Washington think tank: *THAT* Steph Dorham.

The same Steph Dorhan who used to stuff herself with Skittles at sleepovers until she couldn't stop giggling, who screamed full-volume at horror movies, and who hadn't so much as posted *Happy Birthday!* on Tara's Facebook page in three years. Then Tuesday, she texts about being in town and suggests meeting for lunch.

Tara slumped against the gingerbread wall. Up in the corner, a cellar spider flailed in tacky icing, unable to free its legs. It wasn't fair. How was she supposed to go to lunch when everything she touched turned to sugar? She couldn't spin it like she'd spun the layoff (now she could pursue her *true passion*), the breakup (she needed to focus on loving herself), or the move home ("Saving so much $$—house down payment, here I come!").

She *should* cancel lunch, but what if Steph hoped she'd cancel because she'd only reached out to avoid crossing paths by accident? They might have been inseparable in high school, but what did they have in common now? Tara imagined Steph smiling with relief as she texted back: *SRRY to miss u! Im in Virginia for 3 weeks then going to Tokyo 4 work! :(* Even if she could have stomached that, however, Tara realized it was pointless. Her phone was a peppermint.

Fists clenched, Tara stormed to the closet. It took four tries before her clothes turned into something wearable. She fought into a green taffy sheath dress, rubbed Pixie Stick dust onto her cheeks, and cherry Jolly Rancher onto her lips. By the time she headed out the door, she'd even managed to wrestle her hair into a peach gummy hairband.

The car became candy when she climbed in, but despite this the engine puttered to life like boiling maple syrup. The sunlight through the sugar glass windshield softened her dress and heated the licorice steering wheel so her hands made sucking sounds whenever she changed position. Blasting the A/C helped, and thankfully the restaurant was only a couple exits down the highway. As she drove, the car pumped out acrid smoke that smelled like burning brownies. The asphalt melted the chocolate tires, and she fought to keep the car from fishtailing.

Tara sighed with relief as she pulled into the parking lot, but froze when she spotted Steph. She was at a booth by the broad front windows, phone in hand as she waited. Her dark bobbed hair, minimalist black tee and jeans, the concrete pendant necklace and myriad thin rings shining on her fingers, even the poised way she sat looked culled from Tara's own Pinterest style board. It took all of Tara's nerve not to go back home. She could email and say she'd gotten sick. She could say an urgent work thing had come up and that she'd dropped her phone in the toilet.

Tara turned off the car with a shaking breath. How was she supposed to make this work? The sugar dusting her palms caught the sunlight and shimmered. In the heat, the taffy dress had molded to her in all the right places. Her flattened hair, which at first looked like a disaster in the rearview mirror, conformed to any shape she tugged it into, like a cloud of cotton candy. In this light, from the right angle, she looked almost pretty.

Maybe the universe was trying to *give* her something. Candy was formulaically delicious, prismatic, perfect. Everyone loved candy, craved it, sought it out and savored it. Wasn't that, deep down, what she wanted, too? To be craved, to be loved, to be savored? Maybe the problem wasn't the candy. Maybe the problem was imperfect, human her. What if she stopped fighting it?

Tara took a deep breath of burnt brownies and melted licorice and wriggled her toes in her rock candy heels. Then she hugged herself and shivered with delight as sugar rushed through every cell in her body. When she stepped from the car, she was sweet perfection. She smelled like marshmallow and salted caramel. As she clicked across the parking lot, she caught Steph's eye and a thrill shot through her when Steph's jaw dropped in amazement. When Tara's peppermint stick fingertips touched the restaurant door, it remained just a dull, old door, but all the patrons inside gaped hungrily at her.

Steph rose, wide-eyed, as she approached. "Tara ... is that you?"

"How are you, Steph?" Tara's voice sounded different in her ears, like homemade whipped cream, soft and mellow and rich. "It's been a while."

Steph hesitated, then put her rail thin arms around Tara's shoulders and squeezed. Tara worried the embrace might crack her ribbon candy spine, but Steph soon released her, kissing her fondant cheek, and drawing back with an embarrassed laugh. Powdered sugar stuck to her lip gloss.

"Much, much too long. I'm sorry," Steph said as Tara slipped into the opposite seat. "I've been meaning to reach out for ages. I've just been so ... yeah. But look at you!"

Tara took a sidelong glance at her reflection in the window, just a quick taste, and saw smooth lines of taffy and fondant mingled in luxurious curves, shining spun sugar hair, and thick buttercream lashes. Her stomach rumbled with delight. "Not exactly what you expected." She smiled with perfect Tic Tac teeth.

Steph shifted. "I mean, you look ... delicious. But how ...?"

"Just blessed, I guess," Tara replied, shrugging. "Never wanted to live an ordinary life."

Steph nodded and glanced across the dining room. She seemed to notice the other patrons watching, because she sat up and squinted a little more when she smiled, which made her look charmingly self-conscious. Tara had seen that smile in many Facebook photos and wondered how long it had taken Steph to perfect it. "What's it feel like?"

"*Great.*" Another carbonated thrill surged through her strawberry veins. "Life's been sweet for both of us."

Steph's smile faded at the edges. "Yeah, sometimes. Not always."

"Oh, come on." Tara leaned on the table. "I've seen your pics from Nepal. And India! And those baby cheetahs, oh my gawd. You've been all over the world. Don't tell me that's not sweet."

"I've been lucky in travel, sure." Steph rolled her neck with a sigh. "The truth is, though, behind the lens, my life's a mess. No, really," she said when Tara laughed. "I know my Instagram looks good and all that, but things off-camera have been really tough. My mom died last summer, and honestly, I haven't been managing too well."

A funny taste rose in the back of Tara's throat, a phlegmy, unhealthy, chemical taste she remembered from childhood whenever she'd sucked on hard candy for too long. Steph looked deflated, nothing like the grinning, suntanned girl she displayed online.

"Oh, Steph ..." Tara remembered Steph's mom as this effervescent woman who ran a biomedical lab and who Steph only half-jokingly called her other best friend. Dead. It didn't feel real. Tara's candy legs stuck to the booth's leather seat. She shivered. "I'm ... I'm so sorry. I had no idea."

"I haven't really talked about it online," Steph said. "Sorry, I didn't mean to ruin the mood. I'm just ... I kind of hoped that if we met up, somehow it'd feel like old times. A chance to remember what I used to feel like, who I used to be. And then, seeing you so changed ... I mean, it's cool. Really cool. I guess it just reminds me how nothing stays the same, you know?"

The waiter came to take their order, and Tara realized she was starving. Her stomach ached, making her nauseous and shaky. She craved meat, protein, vegetables: anything to mask the sickening mucus flavor in her mouth. Steph ordered a roasted brussels sprouts appetizer, a cup of potato soup, and an unsweetened iced tea; Tara ordered the sprouts and soup, too, and the salmon fillet and a coffee, black. As the waiter took the order, Tara felt him stoop low and take a deep breath over her hair. A blissful smile crossed his face before he blushed and hurried away.

"But how are *you*?" Steph leaned forward, arms crossed under the cement pendant. "It's been ages. Tell me everything."

"Oh, you know." Tara tried to remember all the sugary half-truths she'd spun about her life, but thinking of them made her stomach knot up. "Nothing much, really. Hey, are you still at your job in D.C.?"

Steph snorted. "Yeah, but not for long."

"Oh?"

Steph hunched inward on herself. "Let's just say it wasn't a good fit. That's all they're going to put in my HR file, anyway."

The bad taste crawled into the back of Tara's nostrils. She tried sipping water, but that only made it more chemical and sharp. "That sucks. At least you've still got your Google payout to fall back on, right?"

"Not much of that left, actually," Steph said as the waiter brought over their food.

"I socked most of it away in stocks to keep myself from blowing it all. The travel kept me busy, but after Mom passed, I was doing a lot of self-destructive things behind the curtain." She tapped her iced tea. "Four months sober on Saturday."

"Wow. I'd never have guessed."

Steph chuckled, and it almost sounded real. "Well, that's something, at least. I haven't told almost anybody, but somehow, with you, I just wanted to be me. The real me, you know? I miss us. I miss sleepovers—"

"Horror movies?" Tara said, and Steph burst out laughing.

"God, no! Why couldn't we ever just watch a rom-com? Why did it always have to be something that would scare the piss out of me? You remember the head scene in *The Thing*?"

Tara snickered, forking a brussels sprout. "All I remember is you flying up the basement stairs, screeching: 'Nope! Nope! Nope!' I'd never seen you run so fast!"

Steph slapped the table, nose crunched up as she snort-giggled, and Tara, chuckling, bit down on the sprout. It crumbled to ash on her tongue, and she choked. A swig of coffee, like a hot mud puddle, washed it down. While Steph regaled her with other memories—of class pranks, old teachers, and silly inside jokes—Tara tried the salmon (industrial plastic) and the potato soup (watery sand). Her stomach roiled, but she couldn't bear to take another bite. She forced laughter where appropriate in Steph's high school recollections, but the sick tang in her throat made her want to gag.

When the waiter finally brought the bill, Tara offered to pay, just to have the lunch finished. Outside the restaurant, Steph hugged her for a long time. When she pulled back, Steph squinted across the parking lot, blinking quickly.

Tara's candy hair sagged in the afternoon sun. "It's been great seeing you again," she said, hoping the perfunctory words would initiate the good-byes.

Steph nodded. "Yeah, you too. Hey …" Steph hesitated. "Could I … Could I taste you? Sorry. Jeez, if that's too weird …"

"It's fine! Here." Tara reached up and pulled off a lock of hair. It stretched in the heat and slicked her candy cane fingertips with grease as she placed it in Steph's palm.

Steph stuffed it into her mouth, and scrunched her eyes shut. "Oh my god," she muttered, mouth behind hand. "You taste so … so good. How do you not just nibble yourself all the time?"

Tara tried to laugh, but it came out funny, flattened between her clenched teeth. The acid in her stomach burned as it crept up her esophagus. She swallowed. "You get used to it. After a while, you don't even notice."

Steph finished and sighed. "That's kind of sad, somehow."

"I guess." Tara shrugged.

They exchanged promises to stay in touch, and at the last moment, Steph whipped out her phone for a selfie. Tara posed beside Steph, forcing her heat-softened fondant cheeks to grin. On the phone's screen, a creature stared back at her with candy cane claws for fingers, blood-red licorice lips, drooping marshmallow flesh, and far too many Tic-Tac teeth. Soulless Gobstoppers stared out from an inhuman candy mask. She choked back a moan of terror as Steph snapped the photo and tucked the phone away. When she leaned in for another hug, Tara stammered a good-bye and almost tripped as she ran to her car.

The afternoon sun had turned the gummy bear seats slimy and fused the caramel seatbelt to the frame. Holes, golden brown at the edges, had bubbled and burned through the windshield. When Tara turned on the car, the vents blasted oven-hot air. She tried to turn off the A/C, to let it cool down, but the gumdrop buttons just squished.

Tara slumped back with a carbonated gasp. Across the parking lot, Steph's car pulled onto the main road and vanished into the passing traffic. Tara wondered if she'd hear from her again, or if the afternoon's strange intimacy was the last glimpse of something real between them. Perhaps she'd only ever see the cultivated version of Steph online, the version who was always well-dressed, always smiling, always living her best life. A digital confection made for public consumption.

But she knew the truth, now. Knew what lay beneath the sparkling sugar crust of Steph's life. And between the two of them, it had been *Steph* who'd wanted a little taste of *her* life. Tara remembered how Steph had stuffed the lock of hair into her mouth like a preschooler, unable to resist. She wished she could laugh about it, but her Tic Tac teeth had fused together.

The putrid taste came back in a rush, mixed with ash and plastic and dirt, and Tara's candy apple heart fluttered in her chest as she tried to drag herself up from the seat, tried to catch her breath, tried to pull whatever was her out of what was the car. She pulled and pulled, but she was trapped, her rock candy heels fused to the floor mats and her caramel legs to the seat.

There was nothing to her, anymore. She was flavor without substance, chemically crave-able but unable to satisfy, like a million practiced smiles hiding a normal, messy life. With syrup leaking from her eyes, Tara took one, last carbonated gasp, and melted in the blazing heat of the sun.

AUTHOR NOTES

"Candyland" started as a prompt from JS Breukelaar's *Writing the Weird* class on LitReactor. We had to include a ticking clock, and I immediately thought of running late for a lunch date with a very successful high school friend, based loosely on an experience I'd had a number of years ago. I grew up in a pretty affluent town where it wasn't rare for some kids to get BMWs for their 16th birthdays ... and then *another* BMW a few months later after they totaled the first one. I was not one of those kids.

I'm glad social media wasn't around when I was in high school. I came of age just after Facebook launched, so post-college was the first time I experienced the glittering accounts of kids I'd grown up with. One acquaintance's stunning photo journal of his travels around the world, combined with memories of that lunch, gave me my image of Steph.

She's really more me than anybody, an idealized, social-media-approved version of myself, the influencer-me. Except that I also wanted to examine how rarely my social media (and those of my friends) accurately portrayed the ups and downs of our day-to-day lives. The public nature of social media and society's obsession with positivity almost inevitably means posts are performative, meant to be consumed. Pretty, upbeat posts get lots of likes.

It wasn't much of a jump from there to the story of Midas. A little literary alchemy changed gold into sugar, and that became "Candyland."

GIFT FOR THE CUTTER MAN

D. THOMAS MINTON

The blade of Legrue's scalpel flared in his headlamp's narrow beam, casting glints of light across the slender hand strapped to his cutting table.

"Deed done?" the woman asked, a warble in her voice.

Legrue adjusted his magnifiers. He had not eaten in over a day, and the emptiness in his gut gnawed at his focus and put a tremor in his fingers.

He had to finish before the woman lost confidence in him and he lost a scrip worth a hundred youn, more than he made most days. "Steady on," he said gently, as much to the woman as his hand.

He lowered the scalpel against the middle joint of her left pinky. The leather strap creaked as the woman's hand tightened.

"Easy, easy," Legrue urged. The tension would shift the underlying musculature and connective tissues, making his task harder, not to mention, more painful for her. "Steady, now."

The scars on her forearm made clear she was no stranger to a cutter's blade, albeit not his, but a finger was a next-level investment in the wet market. Blood would regenerate; her pinky would not, so it was only natural she flinched at the touch of his scalpel's edge to her skin.

Satisfied his blade was well-positioned, Legrue pressed firmly downward. Blood spilled onto the cutting table, flowing into the grooves that funneled it into a brass collection bowl for later tubing.

The woman had gone quiet, likely blacked out.

Legrue did not let it distract him. Through the joint now, he angled his blade so the final cut would create a flap of skin that he could use to cover the raw edge. He slid the severed pinky into a glass tube, capped it, and dropped it into the ice trough at his elbow.

He let the stump bleed for a five-count, then coated it with coag-gel and sutured the skin flap to cover the wound. He snapped on a pressure bandage.

Start to finish, less than a minute.

"Deed done." The woman stirred weakly as Legrue released the leather strap.

Slowly the hand scraped back into the shadows of Legrue's stall. He preferred the anonymity the darkness granted. Even so, he knew this woman's story. Desperate, hungry, likely even had mouths that depended on her, she had few choices but the wet market. Hers was everyone's story in the Under, and the service Legrue provided, barbaric as it was, helped people survive.

"Money me, cutter man."

Legrue bristled at the name. He was not a typical cutter; he took pride in his craft, even as it cost him youn—coag and sutures weren't cheap.

Legrue paid her the front money owed, and thankfully she left without another word. He set his magnifiers aside and slumped onto his stool. The woman's blood had cooled on his hands, but he did not have the energy to wipe it away. The youn he would make from the pinky and the tubes of blood would barely cover another cycle of Abigail's antipyretics, and with Livia's milk having dried up, they also needed cereal. And how much tighter could he pull his own belt?

His head down, Legrue did not immediately notice TwoTony enter until the rascal set a pocket lamp on the cutting table. TwoTony dragged on his atomizer and let the reddish steam trickle from his nose. "You tweaked?" TwoTony asked.

Legrue stifled a sigh. He wasn't ill; TwoTony was simply the last thing he wanted to see today. "I made my payment."

TwoTony tossed him the cloth from the wall hook. "Show respect."

Legrue wiped at his hands, but he would need a brush to dislodge the dried blood from the nail beds.

TwoTony poked at the tubes in the ice trough. "I need a cutter man, and you be him, Legrue."

The back of Legrue's neck tingled, but he held his tongue. Two weeks ago, Abigail had needed a stronger cycle of antipyretics to control the fever brought on by the wasting, and TwoTony had fronted the youn. Until he repaid the money, Legrue was indebted to the rascal, but that didn't place him in his servitude. Yet, he felt obligated to hear him out, especially if it might help him come even.

"A client needs twenty and five tubes. Not crusty, flowing clean like. You ken?"

Twenty-five tubes of uncongealed blood were a lot, but any cutter in the wet market could have provided them. And such a routine request, too, so why go through TwoTony instead of placing a scrip through a legit broker? There had to be—

"Special needs," TwoTony said, and Legrue's stomach dropped. "Must be sourced from a twobee." He held up a finger. "One twobee."

Legrue felt like he was going to be sick. Twenty-five tubes would kill most adults; without doubt, it would kill a two-year-old. No wonder the buyer had gone to TwoTony. No legitimate broker would take a scrip like that for a twobee.

And what monster would request one?

"Find another cutter."

TwoTony grinned at him, but the flash of yellow teeth was an obvious threat. "Tomorrow," TwoTony said. "Tubes or youn, either way, skin come even."

The wet market smelled of fear and blood. Over the years, Legrue had grown accustomed to its stink, but as he pushed through the narrow, crowded alley, snaking through the tarp-and-wood cutter stalls, he felt nauseated. The market had always served a purpose, Legrue believed, even if he did not fully understand it. The Skylers, those that lived in the glittering domes high above the Under, used the blood and tissues from cutters like him as the raw materials for the vaccines and prophylactics that kept the plagues at bay, or at least beat them back when they came, which they inevitably did every few years.

Legrue had never met a Skyler; to his knowledge, no one in the Under had, not even brokers like ChimChim, but he had always thought of them as people like himself or Livia, only with plentiful lives. He used to begrudge that, but as he matured, he had too many worries of his own to waste energy hating people he would never meet.

Legrue pulled up suddenly as a tarp parted in front of him and a large man with a mane of shock-red hair and a body slung over his shoulder barged into the alley. The man turned and headed off, the lifeless torso dangling down his back, its gaunt and handless arms swinging back and forth, like pendulums of a macabre clock.

Legrue stood motionless in the alley, forcing the line of people to flow around him. Glass tubes clinked as he clutched his cloth sack tighter to his chest

It wasn't every day a whole-sale scrip was filled, but in his time, Legrue had seen many bodies carried out of cutter stalls and it never grew easy to watch. Early in his time as a cutter, Legrue had tried to fill a whole-sale scrip. Although the woman was old, and she had willingly made the decision to help her struggling daughters, Legrue had no stomach to drain her life into little glass tubes and sell the remains to the highest bidder.

No one had ever been carried out of his stall. He left that brutality to *other* cutter men.

Legrue's brow pinched. If he could not take that old woman's life, given willingly, how would he do what TwoTony wanted?

Legrue shook off his unease and continued on to the brokerage, hopeful his tubes would fetch a premium today, maybe even enough to buy his way out of TwoTony's debt. He exchanged all but one tube of blood for a dozen inadequate strips of youn that even folded over twice upon themselves barely raised a bump in his pocket.

He had struggled over the fate of the final tube of blood, eventually deciding to give it to Livia. Over the last month, she had turned increasingly to hemopyric therapies—blood burning—to treat the wasting consuming their daughter.

Legrue saw little value in the practice, promoted, in his opinion, by charlatans and embraced by those who mistakenly thought they could use blood just as the Skylers. Already, Livia had spent precious youn on a burning bowl and tubes of blood and had started a holistic round of treatments that included burnings for Abigail and herself. A waste, but Legrue could not doubt Livia's motives, and he shared her desperation. At least if he supplied the blood, it would be less of a financial drain.

Legrue's family lived in one room, but it was at the end of the tenement row, so it had a narrow window that overlooked the foundry. Due to the smoke and dust from the industrial yard, they never opened the window, but for an hour, the morning sunlight came through the hazy glass, and they did not have to waste their chem-lamps.

As Legrue entered, he found Livia on the floor crouched over her burning bowl, a cloth draped over her head to trap the smoke. She breathed deeply, coughed, and inhaled again a second time. In the middle of her treatment, she did not emerge to greet him. Legrue stood the tube of blood on the floor next to her.

Abigail let out a weak cry. Except for the rapid fluttering of her chest as she panted, she lay motionless in her bed, a basket tucked into one of the large floor-to-ceiling cubby-holes that covered the walls. Her skin, blotchy and red, was hot under Legrue's hand.

Until three months ago, Abigail had been a vibrant child. She had started talking and had grown daringly rambunctious, climbing the cubby-hole shelves and knocking the pots onto the floor. Then, like too many children her age in the Under, she contracted the wasting, a contagion that consumed the young and for which no cure had come down from the Skylers. While the wasting claimed most of its victims, some children survived by outlasting the fevers.

With a cool, damp rag, Legrue sponged Abigail's forehead and down her chest, his fingers tracing the ridges of her ribs. Over the past month, her fevers had come more frequently and with greater ferocity, and despite their efforts, she had lost a third of her weight.

"We got no more," Livia said as Legrue filled the dropper with the last of the fever medication. "What comes tomorrow?"

The question made Legrue's heart ache. The painfully small lump of bills in his trouser pocket would not cover another cycle of antipyretic and food for them all, let alone what he owed TwoTony. It had been like this for several weeks now, and his and Livia's emergency reserves had vanished some time ago.

"Tomorrow won't matter if she burns down today," Legrue said.

Livia took the damp cloth from Legrue and edged him away from the basket.

The smoke from Livia's burning bowl snaked around him as he stepped over it and slumped onto the stool on the opposite side of the room. This was the third day in a row he had come home to find Livia crouched over that bowl and Abigail burning with fever.

"You're early," Livia said, an edge to her voice.

Did she think he was shirking his responsibilities? She had no idea what he had already done and would likely need to do, but he saw no value in sharing his burden. "Slow day," he said.

"Hmm."

Legrue could not decipher the meaning of her sound. A year ago, he was certain he could have, but a lot had happened, and in many ways, he felt he did not know his wife anymore. "I got you a tube."

Livia spared him a wan smile.

Legrue lowered his gaze to the dropper still in his hand. He might have enough youn to appease TwoTony, but then it would be two, maybe three, days before he saved enough money to buy another cycle, and he feared Abigail did not have that time. His stomach growled; there was that, too.

The stink of the smoke made it hard to breathe.

If Abigail had any chance, Legrue needed a rascal like TwoTony, and TwoTony knew it.

Legrue forced down the lump in his throat. He set the dropper on the shelf next to Abigail's basket and moved to kiss Livia on the neck, but she shrugged away from him.

"Where are you going?" she asked.

"To find a way."

After an hour of wandering the warrens of the Under, Legrue still saw no path forward. He had quickly dismissed giving TwoTony tubes of adult blood; he suspected whoever had made the scrip would detect such subterfuge, and the repercussion to Legrue and his family would be swift and brutal.

Even if Legrue had been willing to do TwoTony's cutting, the rascal had not even offered a client, something a legit broker would have done in such a specialized case. Just as well, because Legrue didn't know how he would have responded had TwoTony arrived with a child in tow. Finding a twobee presented significant challenges, however, and finding the right twobee even more so. Legrue thought that perhaps he could find a child with both feet firmly upon death's threshold, but he realized that *he* could never find such a child before tomorrow.

Lost in his thoughts, Legrue had not been tracking his progress through the crowded streets, and his focus returned only when he was bumped hard enough by a passerby that he nearly fell. It took Legrue a moment to shake off the impact, and in a sudden panic, he reached into his pocket. The money was gone, the pocket cut skillfully open by a razor. Frantically, Legrue scanned the crowded street, but distracted as he had been, he had not seen the thief's face.

He pushed his way through the crowd in the direction he thought the thief had gone. A rheumy-eyed woman cursed him as he bumped into her. Seeing nothing in that direction, Legrue turned back—maybe the thief had circled around. His panic rising, he rose up on his toes, scanning over the top of the crowd.

How could he have been so stupid?

Now, even if by some miracle he found a suitable client, he had no front money.

He suddenly found it hard to draw a breath. The crowded streets, the cramped buildings, and girders crisscrossing overhead blurred and spun as Legrue feared he was going to faint.

A hand on his arm steadied him.

It took Legrue a moment to recognize who was touching him. "ChimChim?"

ChimChim stepped back as if realizing Legrue might be ill. "You tweaked?"

"Just tired," Legrue said, looking to put ChimChim at ease. While several years had passed since the Under's last epidemic, memories still lingered.

ChimChim was a broker for the wet market, a legit one, not a poser like TwoTony. When Legrue had first started cutting, he had worked scrips for ChimChim because he lacked reputation and front money. Brokers came at a cost, however, demanding a high ratio, so when the conditions were right, Legrue had forged out solo. Understandably, ChimChim had been angry, but the years had cooled his ire, and now he occasionally brought Legrue scrips he felt uniquely suited to his skills. It had been years since Legrue had asked ChimChim for anything, but maybe the broker could help. "I've got a business prop."

ChimChim's left eyebrow rose under the brim of his cap.

"I need—" Legrue's mouth went dry, making it hard to form the words. "I—"

ChimChim shook his head. "No can help with that." He tapped his right fist against his chest, indicating his sympathy with Legrue's predicament. "Truth is, no legit broker would take that scrip, so they tap TwoTony."

Ashamed, Legrue looked away. ChimChim had ears everywhere in the wet market, so Legrue was not surprised ChimChim already knew what he was going to ask. Perhaps his fist tap had not been in sympathy, but pity.

"You and me, Legrue; we're solid. I want to help, you ken, but ..." ChimChim scanned the crowded street. Then, seemingly satisfied no one important was watching, he leaned closer. "Only place to fill that scrip is the Pit."

The Pit came into existence the year Legrue was born. Over the span of a week, a sinkhole that had first appeared next to a tenement north of the foundry had widened and deepened until the building itself had tumbled into it. Soon after, people migrated into the hole to escape the claustrophobic confines of the Under, and the Pit became a semi-autonomous warren where everything was overseen by a magistrate called the V.I.Per.

Legrue had been before the V.I.Per on one occasion, and the memories still troubled his conscience. He never spoke of the meeting to anyone, not even Livia, and as he spiraled down the narrow walkways into the depths, he fought against every attempt by his brain to dredge up the memories of that afternoon. The closer he got to the floor, the harder it became, and as the smell of the Pit engulfed him, he was overcome by the memory of the screams willed forth by Legrue's own hands and the glee of the V.I.Per's entourage at his impotence to stop it. He clung to a metal scaffolding for support, uncertain he could go on.

He thought of Abigail, innocent and frail. He and Livia had struggled for several years to bring her into the world and now to keep her there, a fight they were gradually losing. Legrue did not know if their sacrifices would matter, but he had survived in the Under by doing what needs required.

Legrue forced his left foot to rise, swing forward, and drop onto the metal ramp. He willed his body to roll forward, and for his right foot to follow his left. Two steps, three, each subsequent step lower into the Pit coming easier as his resolve solidified.

By the time he stood before the V.I.Per, he knew he would pay the price, no matter what it might be.

A smile slid across the V.I.Per's lips, sending a chill through Legrue. "I ken you. Cutter man all weepy over snip-snip of em drogy," he said, his Pit-slang thick and nearly impenetrable to Legrue. Arrayed behind his throne, the V.I.Per's entourage laughed and jeered, much to their boss's amusement.

The V.I.Per raised his fist and received silence. Leaning forward on the throne, he bared his teeth at Legrue. "Why come back, cutter man?" he asked, sliding effortlessly out of his Pit-slang.

Given the toll of the years, Legrue had not expected the V.I.Per to recognize him, but now that he had, he wondered how that might affect his ask. Legrue cleared his throat. "I have need."

The V.I.Per cocked his head in surprise. "Rim man slums low. Why should I help puss like you?"

Did the man want him to grovel? Legrue would if he thought it would help. It hadn't the last time, but then Legrue hadn't understood what he had gotten himself into when he came to the Pit to purchase a set of quality cutter tools. Young and ignorant, he had been unprepared to pay the V.I.Per's price, a mistake he did not intend to repeat today. "I can pay."

"Indeed," the V.I.Per said. He tapped his temple with his index finger. With a grin to his entourage, he said "Once, cutter man snip-snip good. All drogy bus eyes big and touch knee, slap skin 'n tribute. Respect." With the context, Legrue knew he was talking about the last time he had been there. Several in the V.I.Per's entourage nodded knowingly, and Legrue realized that at least some of them had also been present that day.

Legrue had always suspected the man he had dismembered in payment for his scalpel had been the leader of a rival faction to the V.I.Per. Legrue had skillfully amputated the man's feet and hands, keeping him alive for over an hour until the V.I.Per permitted him to mercifully end his suffering. The man's screams still rang in Legrue's head, but he most remembered the gleeful faces of the V.I.Per and his entourage as Legrue's actions effectively put an end to any challenge to the V.I.Per's power. That day, Legrue vowed to never let another human unduly suffer at his hand, a vow he feared would be challenged today.

"Speak your desire, cutter man."

Legrue licked dry lips. "A twobee."

"Mmmmm," the V.I.Per said as if savoring the sweetness of Legrue's request. "Twobee for cut? Dark, cutter man, dark." The V.I.Per lounged back in his throne, casually draping his left leg over the chair's arm. He picked at his teeth, some of which had been filed into points.

Legrue took a deep breath. He didn't think the V.I.Per understood his ask. "The twobee won't come home."

The V.I.Per showed no surprise, although some of his entourage did. "Cutter man got jimmy for soul," he said, sounding impressed. "Why do you need this twobee?" he asked.

"Twenty-five tubes, skin to come even with a rascal."

With a speed that made Legrue jump, the V.I.Per leaned forward. As his left boot hit the floor, the sound rang through the small audience room. Amused by Legrue's startle, the V.I.Per smiled again. "That skin then comes to me, cutter man. You will owe me."

Legrue had no money, but then, he suspected the V.I.Per had little need for that. Legrue had skills more valuable than youn.

The V.I.Per's eyes narrowed as he watched Legrue fidget. "A deal," he said, but held up his index finger before Legrue could say anything. "You cut your two 'n five. For me, you dress down the morsel all pretty in tribute. You ken?"

The offer surprised Legrue. He could have sold the toddler's organs for enough to buy food and another cycle of Abigail's antipyretic, but giving the body back to the V.I.Per would be a small price to pay to free himself from TwoTony and any obligation to the V.I.Per.

Before Legrue could agree, the V.I.Per raised a second finger on his hand. He waited for the murmurs of the entourage to quiet. "When cutter man gets weepy and goes no-no, skin come skin; cutter man come me."

Legrue's brow knitted. He wasn't sure he understood, but the flutter in his gut gave him a bad feeling.

The V.I.Per stood. In his heavy boots, he was two hands taller than Legrue. "You no ken." The V.I.Per's amused tone drew snickers from the others. "I of mind you no got jimmy for soul, cutter man, and cutting that twobee will be too dark for you. If you don't deliver, then I own your weepy soul. You ken now?"

Legrue felt sick. If he did not deliver the remains of the child, the V.I.Per would own him.

It would not come to that, however.

"Deal."

The V.I.Per sent Legrue away with his promise to deliver a twobee to his stall in the morning.

The climb out of the miasma of the Pit did little for Legrue's spirits, and when he finally reached rim-side, he clutched at the stitch in his side and could go no farther. The meeting with the V.I.Per replayed in his mind, each time Legrue's physical presence becoming smaller, the V.I.Per more imposing, and the deal to which he had agreed less palatable. As his regret grew, he became ill.

That night, sleep would not come, and Legrue sat at Abigail's side. Her closeness as he lay his head next to the basket allowed her ragged breathing to be heard over the noise from the foundry. Every so often, her rasping breaths would calm, growing so quiet Legrue wondered if she was finally free of her suffering. When it happened, he would close his eyes, and unable to see the red glow bleeding through the narrow window or Livia's form cocooned in a sheet on their futon on the floor, he felt weightless, as if floating in a void. The noise of the Under was lost beneath his whispering, light as a wind, as he counted off the seconds until Abigail's tiny lungs would rattle and gasp back into action, cutting into his heart more painfully than any knife.

Eventually, the dawn light shone through their narrow, dingy window, spotlighting the dust and haze that hung in the room. As the light crawled across the floor it illuminated Livia's ritual bowl and glinted off the empty tubes, scattered about like pieces of a broken vessel.

In a way, they were, Legrue realized. Each tube had been cut from a person broken not just by the Under, but also by his own hand to patch others who were also broken. Yet, would cutting away the others ever fix Abigail or Livia or himself? He despaired at the futility of it all, but then, this was the Under, and what options did he have?

Legrue opened the shutter on the skylight of his stall, and the watery light fell across the packed dirt floor and the cutting table. He couldn't remember the last time he had done that, and he wasn't sure why he did it that morning. The darkness had masked how small and dingy his stall was. His cutting table filled nearly the entire space, and if he added all of the leaves to the table, it would leave only enough room at one end for him to squeeze around it.

Legrue stood three dozen tubes on the table, and next to them, he laid out a silk bundle. When he had returned from the Pit with his tools those years ago, Livia had cut the cloth from the hem of her nicest dress and given it to him. All these years holding such brutal instruments had left the silk tattered and stained, and he wondered how much longer before it came apart entirely.

The canvas flap rose slightly, and a woman peered in. Her grey shawl, pulled up to cover her head, obscured her face. Seeing Legrue, she stepped inside, leading a small child. Legrue could not tell if it was a girl or a boy; it wore only a cloth diaper and hid behind the dangling tails of the woman's shawl. What he could see, without doubt, was the child was healthy.

Legrue's words failed, as a sudden chill gripped him. He squeezed the edge of the cutting table to steady himself. Abigail was depending on him. He couldn't fail her and Livia.

The woman lowered her shawl. The smoothness of her skin suggested youth, but a dullness in her eyes spoke of desperation, and the dark skin of her chin and neck was crosshatched with pinkish scars from dozens upon dozens of cuttings. "You are Legrue?"

Unable to speak, Legrue motioned her toward the stool on the opposite side of the cutting table.

She sat, placing the toddler on her lap. The child buried its face into her breast. "Be brave, Che," the woman whispered into its curly hair. "Get 'em sweet when the cutter man done."

Legrue's brow pinched. There would be no sweets for the child after the cutter man. There would be no child, only tubes of blood and bags of fingers and toes, liver, heart, strips of muscles, and a pair of tiny, tiny eyes.

Bile rose in Legrue's throat. The V.I.Per had not told her. She was expecting Legrue to take a tube or two of blood from her child, like the other cutters; then some youn for them, and a sweet for her twobee to assuage her guilt. No, V.I.Per knew what he was doing, sending the mother with her healthy child when he could have had one of his entourage bring a sickly twobee from a desperate family. He sent this one because he wanted Legrue to fail. Because, as he had said, Legrue had "no jimmy for soul."

Legrue squeezed his eyes shut, but try as he might to envision Abigail's face, he saw nothing but darkness.

The toddler started wailing, healthy lungs throwing forth fear. "No, no," it shrieked.

Legrue thought he was going to vomit.

"Shh, Che. No hurt, no hurt. Shh."

Legrue opened his eyes. The woman had placed the squirming child on the cutting table. She struggled to fit its tiny arm into the restraint made for an adult. The child was already missing a pinky finger and several scars puckered its forearm and chest. Whoever had cut its tender skin had not been particularly skilled.

She finally managed to secure the wailing child's arm. "Sorry," she kept saying, and Legrue didn't know if the apology was meant for him or the twobee.

Legrue unfolded the tattered silk. The light shone dully on the nicked scalpel, the dull grey tines of the forceps, and the pitted curves of the clamp. In the hazy light, the tools looked efficiently brutal atop the tattered silk.

"Hurry," the woman pleaded, tears welling up in her eyes. She stroked the child's hair. "Shh, Che."

Legrue donned his magnifiers and adjusted the headlamp. He felt faint, but he dismissed it to his hunger.

He drew a deep breath; he could do this.

Legrue picked up the scalpel.

The child had stopped struggling and lay spread on the table crying despondently. Even so, it was a beautiful child—curly dark locks framing its round face. Legrue could see its mother in the color of its eyes.

He turned away, his hands shaking and his chest so tight now he could not draw a full breath. His mind raced with fantastical scenarios that would save him having to take this woman's child, but he knew he was out of time. Soon TwoTony would return and finding neither tubes nor youn, the rascal would shatter Legrue's hand, destroying his livelihood. Yet, Legrue might not even be there if the V.I.Per discharged someone to collect him before TwoTony arrived.

With him gone, what would happen to Abigail and Livia?

"One for three," he whispered—one healthy child for three lives. But they were broken lives, and Legrue did not know if they could ever be repaired. Yet, he knew if he did this, it would break *him* forever.

"I won't." He tugged at the strap, releasing the child's arm.

"But—"

Legrue swept his tools onto the floor and scattered the tubes across the stall. "Go!" He turned away again, ashamed of his outburst, but the woman left, and the wails of the twobee were swallowed by the noise of the waking market.

Spent, Legrue slumped onto the stool and buried his face into his hands. His whole body shook. What had he done?

He rushed out into the alley. Frantically, he craned his head above the crowd looking for the woman's grey shawl, but he could not find it. She was gone, and with her went any hope.

Back inside, Legrue gently dusted off the blue silk, retrieved his scalpel and forceps from under the cutting table, and carefully rewrapped the tools and what glass tubes he could find.

He contemplated waiting for fate to come to him, but as he stared at the small bundle of silk, he realized he had never been that type of man.

Maybe he could still find a way, perhaps luck would be with him, and a child that had died of the wasting will have been left in an alley. He had heard stories that this still happened, although he had not witnessed it since the last pandemic had swept through the Under.

He took his tools and headed out. For many hours, he searched the alleys behind the tenements. Finally, his feet hurting, he found himself before his own door.

The sun, long past its zenith, no longer came in through the window, leaving the apartment dark and smelling of burnt blood.

"Livia?"

Abigail coughed pitifully from her basket. Legrue placed his hand on her forehead. She burned with fever, hotter than Legrue had ever experienced, and the dropper was empty.

Where was Livia?

Legrue picked up his daughter. Her head rolled back and then forward onto his shoulder. She lay limply against him, her breath rattling in her chest. So light now, she felt almost like a newborn again. He cupped her head in his hand to hold it steady; her hair, fine and thin, felt like nothing against his palm.

Legrue's legs threatened to buckle, so he sat on the stool and hugged his daughter to his chest. He remembered his joy the day she had been born. "Shh," he whispered gently. The heat of her fever radiated through his shirt.

"Livia?" She hadn't left the apartment in weeks except to purchase the bowl and tubes of blood to burn. Could she have left Abigail to buy another tube? Over the past days, Livia had grown distant. He could not recall her comforting Abigail, and she had avoided his touch at night when he wanted—needed—her caress. A vacant stare had settled into her eyes, the same emptiness he saw on those who came to the wet market over and over, those who were ready to whole-sale themselves to bring it all to an end.

No, she couldn't be gone. Abigail still needed her. He still needed her.

"Livia?" he whispered into the room's lonely shadows.

The lingering smoke from the burning bowl stung his eyes. The tube Legrue had brought home yesterday lay empty on the floor next to it. False hope, all of it, Legrue thought. The blood, the burning, the cutting, all of it meant nothing.

He kicked the bowl and it clanged dully off the door.

In his arms, Abigail's frail form had gone still. Legrue did not move, but lowered his ear gently to her hair and started to count, waiting for her fragile lungs to rattle back to life, but they did not.

Like his daughter, the Under was quiet.

Legrue screamed, months of pain released in an anguished howl. He had failed her. That morning, if he had cut the twobee, he would not have wasted hours wandering alleys in his futile search. He could have sold any extra tubes of blood and some of the organs that surely the V.I.Per would not have missed and used the youn for another cycle of antipyretics. He could have come home, and Livia would still be there. Broken or not, they would have survived another day, and in the Under, that's what life was. Living had a price that came due every day—skin to come even—and today Legrue had failed to pay.

Drained, he slumped over the tiny, still body and wept.

"Legrue?"

He raised his head.

Livia stood in the doorway. Legrue blinked several times, not sure if he was hallucinating.

Her lip started to quiver as she noticed the body on Legrue's lap. A bottle dropped from her hand, shattering on the floor. "No," she said. "No." Her voice grew thinner as her throat tightened. She dropped on the floor next to Legrue and scooped Abigail into her arms.

Legrue stared at the broken bottle. She had gone for a cycle of fever medication, but how had she paid for it? He noticed then her disheveled hair, the top of her dress askew.

Legrue knew she would not speak of what she had given for her daughter, and he would not ask. That was the way in the Under. He slid onto the floor and pulled them both into his arms. She turned into him and cried into his shoulder.

Gently he stroked her hair. He should not have doubted her.

A lump rose up in Legrue's throat. Soon his own debt would come due, but finally, he saw the path forward, and it was a path both he and Livia would need to follow together, as they had always done.

They could give nothing more to their daughter, but she could give them one final gift.

AUTHOR NOTES

Of all the stories I've written, "Gift for the Cutter Man" is the one that creeps me out the most. It's dark, brutal, and unforgiving on every level, and it's one of the few stories that made me look in the mirror and wonder where the hell did that come from. Cutter Man may feel like a product of the pandemic, but its genesis came several months before COVID and wet markets even entered the public's lexicon. While a plague is omnipresent, Cutter Man is not a plague story. It's a study of a man who must decide how much of his humanity he is willing to risk to save those he loves.

One of my favorite aspects of this story is the pit slang used by the VIPer and his entourage. I had originally written most of the story in pit slang, which my writing group made clear was unworkable because it made Cutter Man too challenging to read. Sometimes an author's best friends are the writers who tell him something isn't working. I'll admit (reluctantly) that a little pit slang goes a long way, and in its place, I hope I have retained some of its flavor in the cadence of the prose and the occasional, unusual turn of phrase.

I'd like to say I hope you enjoy this story, but I realize that's not quite the right sentiment for a tale like Cutter Man. Instead, I hope you appreciate this story's stark beauty, and that the ending leaves you heartbroken and weary and ready to hug someone you love.

WAKE UP, I MISS YOU

RACHEL SWIRSKY

Terra stands alone in the middle of the room, staring at nothing. She moves sometimes like someone dreaming, but never reacts.

My poor sister, locked in her own world.

"Terra?" I ask.

She doesn't look at me and she doesn't look away.

"Terra?"

She frowns at something over my shoulder. It's like she can almost hear me at the edge of things, like she's searching for my voice from ... wherever she thinks she is.

I ask, "Has anything changed?"

The elephant nurse bellows sadly.

"I just wish I knew if Terra was happy in there," I say. "Do you think she's happy?"

The elephant nurse's bellow rises uncertainly.

Quietly, I say, "I hope she is."

The elephant nurse raises her trunk to trumpet her agreement.

The noise wakes the trees outside the hospital window. They stretch and shake out their leaves. A dislodged sparrow turns toward me and gapes open its beak. It squawks *"beep beep beep"* and I realize it's been doing that the whole time. There are other noises, too—a distant, distorted voice like a conductor shouting into a bad mic—are we near a train station?

The elephant nurse raps me on the head with her trunk to get my attention. Her nurse's cap perches between her enormous ears. She wants her tip.

I can barely get the mosquitoes out of my wallet. My fingers fumble while the mosquitoes fly in and out of the billfold, biting. My fingertips swell up.

When I've finally taken out enough, the elephant nurse sweeps them into her saddlebags. Her ears spin like helicopter rotors. She propels herself upward and out of sight.

I should find the door. It must be somewhere. Except— something's not right—

Is it my shoes? I can't go home without my shoes. I double-check my feet. The shoes aren't there. I look under the bed. They aren't there either, but there's a pair of empty soup cans. I put them on instead.

Terra's raised hand flexes as if holding a cup. She makes a displeased noise. "— hospital coffee always so *weak*?" Her hand tips too far. She jumps back with a shriek. "Ouch! Damn. It's all in my socks ..."

She's so far away. It breaks my heart.

Oh, there's the door. I open it. There's a pub on the other side. I don't want to go drinking. I close it and try again. It's a sinking ship this time. A ship hand shouts and runs toward me. I shut the door hard.

When I try the door again, it opens onto a huge, empty building full of teetering platforms and staircases. A man with compound beetle eyes grabs for my hand. "Poppy, you need to wake up your sister. Something's coming."

"What's coming?" I ask.

He yanks me onto a floating platform. The door slams.

I look over the edge. Fragmented rooms trundle through the air below us, kitchens and bathrooms with exposed plumbing.

"*It's* coming!" the beetle-eyed man repeats. "You have to wake Terra up, Poppy. Before it gets you both!"

"It's coming ...?"

Oh.

It *is* coming, isn't it? I remember now. The Queen of Teeth and her cannibal horde, coming to eat me up into nothing.

My heart slams. We have to run.

The beetle-eyed man yanks me up a spiral staircase. The stairs wind up and up, getting narrower and narrower like a spindle until they're as narrow as our feet.

The railing splinters. Rotting steps drop away under us.

We jump over the broken railing, paddling through empty air until we crash onto a huge, floating platform that's part of a library. It shakes with the impact. Bookcases knock each other down like dominoes.

"The Queen is coming," says a voice above me.

"The Queen is coming," repeats another voice, and then a third, "The Queen of Teeth is coming."

Far above, at the ceiling, her gibbon scouts swing between giant chandeliers.

"She's coming for Poppy and her sister," the gibbons chant. "Turn them in if you know where they are, or the Queen will devour you, too."

I hide under the edge of a huge, fallen bookcase with my head tucked against my chest and my hands protecting the back of my neck, like a child preparing for an earthquake.

The gibbons' voices echo and fade.

I scrabble out from under the rubble. The beetle-eyed man is gone. That's good. He might betray us.

A weird, green glow pulses over me, so intense that it sears through my lids when I close my eyes.

I follow it into the maze of bookcases. Half of them have fallen. I pick my way through broken shelves and mountains of abandoned books.

The radioactive color grows brighter and brighter as I near the center. The books get bigger, too. They're the size of dining tables, piled against each other in a hodgepodge of precarious angles.

At the center, it's so bright I have to shield my eyes as they adjust. It's Terra! My sister is glowing.

She floats inside an enormous test tube. Bubbles gloop slowly through the viscous, green liquid surrounding her. The test tube stands on a library copy of *Les Miserables* that's big enough to be the stage in a karaoke restaurant.

My poor sister, locked in her own world.

Through the test tube, she sounds like, "*Gloop* ... Fontaine had passed a sleepless and feverish night ... *gloop gloop* ... breath issued from her breast with that tragic sound which is peculiar to those maladies ... *gloop* ... M. Madeleine remained for some time motionless beside the bed, gazing in turn upon the sick woman and the crucifix as he had done two months before when he came the first time ..."

I have to wake her up.

The elephant nurse sits in an armchair beside the book, watching a video on her phone. I plead with the nurse. "Terra has to wake up. Can't you do anything?"

The elephant nurse sets her phone in her lap. She looks up at Terra in the test tube.

"—Is that the unabridged version? I tried reading *Les Miserables* to my daughter before we saw the play, but we washed out after five hundred pages."

"Yeah ... I thought Poppy might like it. She used to listen to *Les Miz* on loop. She tried out for Eponine in high school and didn't get it. She was devastated. I don't know ..." A ragged breath. "Maybe next time I should just grab Harry Potter."

"She might wake up before then."

"Maybe." Tone suddenly brusque. "I should get back to reading if I'm ever going to finish this thing—"

Something's not right. I squint at them so hard that my head starts hurting. This is confusing.

I grab my phone from the pocket of my jeans. I forgot I had a phone. Maybe someone can help Terra. Except what's the code to unlock it? I'm dialing and dialing, but I can't get it right. 2460? 4601?

My teeth are loose, all of them. They fall out of my mouth onto the floor like ivory piano keys.

Where's my shirt? Why didn't I put on a shirt? How could I forget my *shirt*?

Where *am* I? My sister was here ... maybe? I *have* to wake her *up*.

A sparrow gapes open its beak and squawks, "*Beep beep beep*!"

There must be a train station somewhere in this forest. The conductor has a bad microphone.

"*Beep beep beep!*"

The sparrow is *so loud*.

I shout, "Shut up!"

Crows and seagulls and pigeons and cuckoos and owls and geese descend on me in a deluge, claws out, all squawking, "*Beep beep beep beep* **beep beep BEEP BEEP.**"

I shout, "Shut up! Shut up!"

I throw my arms around my head to protect myself from beaks and wings. I run through the forest, branches scratching my clothes. The birds chase.

Chasing me—something else was chasing me—the Queen of Teeth, she wants to devour me and Terra, she wants to eat us up into nothing, I have to *wake my sister up.*

How can I wake her up? Can I take her home? I remember home. Our bedroom with the brick fireplace that was painted white and covered in little, plastic toy animals that we glued between the cracks. In the mornings when we didn't have school, we stayed in bed and fought about what music to play. At night, we pushed our beds into the center of the room so we could hide under the blankets together even though we texted instead of talking.

Our parents sold the house during the divorce when we were fourteen. I can't remember the last time I drove by.

The beetle-eyed man is back. He says, "—true the odds are shrinking, but remember odds can't tell you what will happen in a specific—"

The birds form a cave around us with their wings. They leer at me with nasty beaks. Some of them stop beeping long enough to talk.

"You can't wake up Terra," says the crow.

"You can't do anything," says the owl.

"Your chest is heavy," says the goose.

"Your lungs can't move it," says the seagull.

"Because it's so heavy," says the robin.

"You're probably going to suffocate," says the woodpecker.

"*Beep beep beep!*" says the pigeon.

I gulp for air. My breath rasps as if it's fighting through cracks in solid rock.

"Wake her up, Poppy," says the beetle-eyed man. "You're wasting time."

I shout at him. *"How?"*

I have to get away from here. I try to run through the birds. The beetle-eyed man grabs my wrist with a snap.

"Not that way," the beetle-eyed man says. "This way."

He kicks at the roots of a tree. A hole opens between them like a cavity in a tooth. He shoves me into it.

The birds scream fury as I fall out of reach.

I land on my feet on white tile. I remember I'm wearing soup can shoes. They clatter and pinch. I kick them off.

This is my sister's hospital room, but all the furniture is on the ceiling. The elephant nurse isn't here. She must have left for the day.

My sister stands upside down by the bed. My poor sister, locked in her own world.

"Terra, you need to wake up," I tell her. "It's important. There's something chasing us. It's going to eat us if you don't wake up."

My sister fragments into a dozen copies of herself. One stands by the window. Two are by the bed. One leans by the door. One is crying. One sits in the nurse's chair.

"—Poppy, I miss you—"

"—Harry knew, somehow, what to do. He leaned forward and grasped the broom tightly in both hands, and it shot toward Malfoy like a javelin—"

"—sorry, I just couldn't stand any more Victor Hugo—"

"—Wake up, Poppy! Wake—"

"—coffee is so *weak*—"

"—haven't been able to be here as much recently, but my asshole boss threatened to fire—"

"—Dumbledore chuckled at the stunned look on Harry's face. 'Fawkes is a phoenix, Harry. Phoenixes burst into flame when it's time for them to die—"

"—up! Wake—"

"—got it all over my pants this time, damn it—"

"—Harry looked down in time to see a tiny, wrinkled, newborn bird poke its head out of the ashes. It was quite as ugly as the old one. 'It's a shame you had to see him on a burning day,' Dumbledore said—"

"—both good and bad news: I'll be able to visit more because I finally told my boss I was sick of his petty, punitive—"

"—up! All anyone wants is for you to wake—!"

The elephant nurse stands in the doorway.

The nurse says, "You should go home."

I start to snap back, *I have to wake up Terra first!* but then my sister is talking instead.

Terra's one person again, sitting in a chair. She says, "I have my favorite pillow and six more Harry Potter books. What else could I want?"

It's like she's reacting to the nurse, but that's not possible.

My sister rubs her eyes. "Maybe I should just leave and stay gone. I've lost my job. Dave's pissed at me for never being home. Mom and Dad haven't been back for a month. Does any of it even matter to her?"

"Maybe not," the nurse says. "But maybe it does."

A bird outside the window squawks, "*beep beep beep*."

I feel tears in my eyes as I look up at my sister. "Wake up, Terra. I miss you."

She doesn't even glance.

The nurse says, "You should tell her you love her."

She's not talking to me, but how can she be talking to Terra?

"I love you," Terra says anyway.

"I love you," I say.

We speak together. "Please, come home."

LESLEY CONNER

A Rachel Swirsky story is always a treat and "Wake Up, I Miss You" doesn't disappoint. A twisting story about two sisters, it gives the reader the feeling of walking through a dream, never sure what is real and what is fantasy. Slowly layers are pulled back so the reader gets a glimpse of what is actually happening. It's wonderful. One of those stories I want to immediately reread.

SECURITY BREACH AT SUGAR PINE SUITES

PAMELA RENTZ

“If you can hear me, return to service quarters immediately.”

Birdie Big Rock ignored the bleating voice coming from the commbundle and used a single finger to guide the ponycart into the lift.

She cleared her throat. “Map?”

The full resort station map sputtered into view with all the fancy lounges and decadent shopping hubs forbidden to grunt staff.

“You have the wrong cart.” Gloria TanOak enunciated each word with rising annoyance.

“Oops,” Birdie muttered. “Shouldn’t have left it in the wrong spot.” The *senior* housekeeping manager’s cart was bigger and floated instead of bucked. While the lift zipped around the rim, Birdie dug through various shelves and cubbyholes. Towels, sheets, a huge supply of *Orbital Casino* chocolates coveted by guests to resell on Earth because Indians-in-space merch was collectible. She pried open the flimsy lost and found box but found only a tangle of wrist monitors, rings, earrings, and removable implants. No VIP fobs, currency chips, or fun surprises.

The chocolates were inventoried but not her cart, not her problem. A handful went into her pocket.

The lift stopped and announced, “Sugar Pine Suites.” Birdie waited but the doors remained closed.

"Access?"

She waved the commbundle over the security panel and then over her head in desperation.

Gloria's frustrated voice came back. "We *just* talked about this. Bring the cart back. Now."

Birdie snickered. She knocked the cart against the door. "Come on, we got some rich people who need their luxury suites cleaned."

The door opened into a narrow service corridor, cold and dingy, like every other hidden service corridor she'd been in.

The voice on the commbundle again, now shrill. "You're supposed to be on Grasshopper Deck."

Grasshopper Deck, the land of cramped budget cabins that smelled like ripe armpit and pink drink vomit. Let someone else chase sparkly beads and scrape glitter out of the vents after bachelorette parties.

The ponycart floated past door after door until it found the first assigned room. The access panel lit up. Birdie licked a finger and held it on the entry pad until authentication completed.

She leaned into the opening. "Housekeeping."

The commbundle buzzed again. "Do not go into that suite! If I have to come out there—"

Birdie stuffed it under a pile of towels and pushed the cart inside.

"Ooh, luxe." Her hand traced over the faux wood paneling. Warm, cozy lights illuminated handwoven rugs and photos of stern elders in traditional clothing, tribal affiliation printed in tiny letters at the bottom.

The main room had a portal the size of a dinner tray, her first peek outside since the tribal employee shuttle docked. The view was another tooth in the bulky cogwheel of a ship and a black sliver of space with a blur of stars.

The portal in the sleeping room was half the size. She stared out, cheek pressed against the cold, wishing to see something: a supply ship, a passenger shuttle, anything.

She returned to the cart to grab supplies, ignoring the enraged buzz from the commbundle.

Even rich passengers were slobs. Clothes flung everywhere, sticky food packets on the fancy coffee table, and damp towels heaped in the corner.

She did the sleeping room first, fast and mechanical. New arrivals spent time in Gloria's torturous training room where they practiced bed linen exchange, bath sanitizing, and launder cycles while Gloria railed on them about pride and efficiency as if being fast at cleaning was the ultimate Native pride.

Birdie took a picture of the bathroom vanity before moving all the weird silver tubes of strangely named products and vials of remedies with indecipherable instructions. A few made it into her pockets.

An unexpected screech set her hair on edge. Strips of tiny red lights flashed around the door frames. The main resort system announced, "Ship lockdown procedures. For your safety, return to your cabin."

What was it with the resort and these drills?

Birdie arranged decorative sweetgrass soaps and restocked the indigestion relief.

The pulse of the alarm grew louder. She scooped up towels and tossed them in the cleaning chute, swiftly sorted through the clothes flung everywhere, and rehung the clean stuff, fancy, even for the resort. Shiny white shirts, elaborately beaded jackets, and rhinestone-studded pants. She paused over a pair of black boots lined with buckles.

This suite wasn't a guest.

She knew the wearer of these boots. Ads for his show played on endless loop over the ship's entertainment system.

Wyatt Thundercloud.

Or Wyatt Drops-Their-Panties as the staff called him. The in-residence entertainer was known for being as popular offstage as on.

What a collection of footwear.

She stepped into a pair of exotic sand-colored boots, rattlesnake skin, too big for her feet, and checked her reflection while attempting his signature side-stepping pelvic thrust that sold out eight shows a week. Groups waited months for the ladies' three-night party package.

Gloria would not approve of this.

The alarm blasted again. "Lockdown commencing. Remain in place." The commbundle squawked from the cart. A prickle of unease. She glanced at the service door. Lockdowns were for … what? Ship system failures? Contagions? Bandits?

She dug out the commbundle, lit up with warnings.

"Housekeeping personnel, return to the service deck for lockdown." Gloria's voice had taken on an unfamiliar fury and desperation.

Birdie tapped to connect and mustered an innocent look. "Hey, what's going on?"

"Oh, so you can hear me." Gloria's raging purple face glared from the tiny screen. "Get back here, now."

"You mean now, now?" That set Gloria howling.

The boots went back, and she slipped on a pair of beaded mocs. Back in service, the staff would be stuck with Gloria watching ancient training holos.

On the other hand, the punishment for skipping might be worse. Hours in Gloria's training room and demoted to cleaning crew quarters. Nothing but the humiliation of grimy walls and stinky squalor.

A long peal from the alarm. The red blinking lights around the doors froze for the space of a heartbeat.

She hurried the cart to the service door and fumbled with the commbundle, finger hovering over the access pad.

The ship system announced, "Lockdown complete."

She licked her finger and pressed down. A flutter of white lights and then: SECURE.

She pounded on the door, but the panel refused to show anything except the reassuring SECURE status. The commbundle connection disappeared in favor of blazing emergency announcements.

During training, Gloria beat them over the head with endless drills. They had evacuation drills. (Resort never evacuated.) They had foreign contaminant drills. (Never happened.) Hull breach drills. (Once in ten years.) Drills for intruders. (Annual attempts, strong security response, danger remote). The amount of preparation approached stupidity.

The couch's freshly plumped cushions looked inviting. Gloria's first lesson was the difference between guests and service. Service didn't sit on the furniture.

Wyatt would be in the showcase theater in the lockdown room for performers.

After a moment's hesitation, she dropped into the sweet softness and closed her eyes. This was possibly the most comfortable she'd been since she'd boarded. She picked up the freshly sanitized room control and turned on the entertainment center. The darkened screened resumed from where it had frozen mid-show.

A chase set to thumping music. Young men, dressed in cringy costumes, running through a fake-looking inter-tribal event. One carried a bow and arrow, another a spear. One wore buckskin pants and a bone choker. What a wasted opportunity to show real tribal people, like attorneys in three-piece suits negotiating an exclusive casino in space or tribal leaders sending off other peoples' families to make up the workforce.

The band vaulted through vending, knocked over tables of beaded medallions, sent leather-fringed bags flying. One grabbed a dripping piece of frybread as he dashed through. Aunties frowned at the carnage then grinned when they recognized the boy band heroes.

They continued through the parking lot, leapt on and off of ancient sedans, surged past a camper with the door duct-taped shut, and jumped into the back of a rusty pickup, their arms pumping in unison. Beautiful young women decked out in regalia crowded around them.

The camera paused on the young men, breathless with shiny eyes and wide smiles as they held their hands up to surrender then burst into song.

Birdie hit the information button.

Lonely Wolf Boyz in Paradise.

Wyatt wore a skimpy breechclout, dangerously low on his hips. His hair flopped in his eyes as he gave the camera a crooked smile, then threw his head back inviting the fans closer.

This guy sat in his suite and watched his own movie.

He still had the crooked grin and floppy hair, but he was thicker around the waist and puffy in the face. His fans—they called themselves the Thunderclaps—all ages, lost their minds when he performed.

She returned to the sleeping room and snooped through his things hoping to find something juicy. Maybe a drawer filled with satin thongs, trophies from his conquests. Instead, the drawers were half-full of frayed pullovers, slouchy lounge pants, and a healthy number of empty sleep-aid packets.

His performance outfits were lined up in the closet. She investigated the pockets. Rumor was he never left the resort. How long had he lived in this room? She kept the gaming chips and a tube of Rosebud branded lip balm from the gift shop. He could keep the breath mints.

An electric *ping* followed by the *whoosh* of the suite's main entrance came from the other room.

She froze in place. Only security could get around during lockdown.

"Hello?" a voice called.

Wyatt almost collided with her. He gave a little gasp. "I didn't expect you."

His face was golden-brown, his dark hair tousled, and he smelled like a tree-filled forest on a sun-drenched afternoon. His trousers were snug, as was his shirt, a filmy knit thing unbuttoned to his breastbone. He wore his signature performance jacket: soft buckskin decorated with beaded frog hand and elkhorn buttons. Face-to-face he was alarmingly attractive. When polled about the boy band, Wyatt was always everyone's favorite.

She lost the power to speak. "Sorry ... couldn't ... locked in." She gestured about helplessly.

"Are you sure?" He pushed the ponycart toward the service exit.

"It's secure."

Wyatt put his hands on his hips and closed his eyes.

"Sorry. Very sorry." Birdie tried to sound contrite but couldn't help asking. "How did you get back?"

Wyatt held up a VIP fob, a fancy one, like a beaded acorn. "They said bandits are imminent and to shelter in my room."

"Imminent meaning not a drill?" Birdie's heart kicked up a notch. She jammed shaky hands into her pockets and focused on the training. Remain calm.

"Sounds like it," Wyatt confirmed. Even in a crisis, his voice had a honey-smooth sex-machine vibe to it.

"We don't have to worry, right?" Birdie said, needing to hear something comforting. "There's a private security force. What's the stat? No successful boarding in how many years?"

"I'm not worried," he said, absently.

Staff wasn't supposed to be in a room with a guest, or talent, ever. Not for fun or for work. "Should I—?" There was no place to go

"You're fine." Wyatt pointed at the couch. "You want a drink?"

"Uh—"

"Relax"—he waved his hands in the air— "what else are we supposed to do?"

Wyatt poured generous shots from a dispenser. She hadn't held a real glass, other than to wash, since she came to the station.

"I'm not supposed to—"

"Who's going to tell?" Wyatt's expression was grim but he tinked his glass against hers, his face close enough to see a hint of grey along his hairline. She took a small sip, the alcohol smoky-sweet and delicious.

Wyatt pointed at the couch again. "You're—?"

She sat. "Birdie."

"Birdie," he repeated, the tiniest flick of his eyebrows. "Who's your people?"

"Karuk."

"Ah, one of the big shareholders," he said.

"The biggest. And you?"

"Paiute. But I haven't been home in a long, long time." His eyes went back to the suite's main entrance. The red lights had gone out.

"The Tribes have top security," Birdie said with forced cheer. "Booby traps and redundant security features every three feet. The bandits won't get close to the vault. They'll be hauled off any minute."

"What if they aren't going for the vault?"

Birdie shook off a sliver of dread and gulped the drink, the warmth soothing and exhilarating.

"People get taken," Wyatt said. "Never heard from again."

Hearing the words made Birdie break into a sweat. Not her rez, but she'd heard about a guy from another tribe kidnapped from a tribal research satellite. His family sent out reward beacons every year.

Birdie said, "Kidnappings are rare."

Wyatt fixed his eyes on her for a long moment. "Your employee communicator work?"

"Emergency announcements only."

"Wish we could talk to someone."

"They would tell us to stay put."

The ship system made another announcement: "Emergency Lockdown. Not a Drill. Wait for instructions."

Birdie and Wyatt exchanged a queasy glance.

"We're safe," she repeated.

Instead of offering a comforting reply, Wyatt leapt up and crossed the room with a loose-limbed ramble, like he was on stage. He stopped in front of the portal. "Do you like it out here?"

"Do you? I'd rather be home." Birdie unwrapped an *Orbital Casino* chocolate and stuffed the whole thing in her mouth. Creamy and delicious. She washed it down with the last of the booze. She said, "I thought the luxury suites had views."

Wyatt tapped on the portal causing the fringe on the buckskin jacket to shimmy. "That is a view."

"Don't you miss seeing home?"

"There's an atrium between the main lounge stage and the ballroom." He tipped his chin to the side as if to point it out. "If you stand in the right spot there's an amazing view."

Birdie pitched her voice like Gloria's. "The service team is back of the house only. No loitering around the atriums and the ballrooms."

"You don't bend the rules?"

Birdie couldn't help smiling. "That's what I'm known for."

Wyatt's dark eyes glimmered with curiosity. No wonder this guy was such a panty-dropper.

"I've never been outside the service area," she went on, "but I'm working on it."

"I see," he said. "High rollers are the ones who get suites with Earth views. Did you want to work up here?"

"I volunteered," she said. "Every family needs to send someone. Why not me?"

"Debt is a debt," he agreed.

"How long for you?"

"Hard to say," he said. "I'm in a complicated situation. Now my contract's been sold; going further out." He lowered his voice like they were sharing a secret. "I owe people money."

In the meal area, someone once made a joke about that: Wyatt the former pop star, in eternal orbit to pay his bills. Gloria came along and busted them for gossiping about "our prestigious guest in residence."

"You don't want to?" Birdie asked.

"I would do anything to go home." There was no mistaking the melancholy in his voice.

She didn't know what to say. She would do anything to go home, too. A long silence stretched out before he looked at her curiously. "Do you normally clean this suite?"

"We rotate," she said. "Well, we're *supposed* to rotate. I never get Sugar Pine."

Wyatt nodded, lips pressed together.

"Until today," she added quickly as if he cared how the rooms were assigned.

"Of course," he agreed. "And you up here much longer?"

"Contract's half done."

"You signing for another term?"

Birdie scoffed. "No. I can't wait to get out of this place. I am not one of those NDNs who wants to be in space. Not like my supervisor. Gloria will probably renew her contract forever so she can lecture generation after generation on the everlasting satisfaction of a well-sanitized crap bin."

"I don't think anyone would want that." Wyatt's eyes traveled back to the cart. "Can you call your supervisor?"

"Oh no. She'd have my head in a bucket"—Birdie held up the empty glass— "if she knew I was doing this."

"She can't be that bad." Wyatt flashed a Lonely Boyz grin that she felt down to the back of her knees. She didn't object when he took her glass for a refill.

Birdie cast a sly eye at the remote. "Why do you watch your movie?"

Wyatt glanced up at the blank screen with a funny smile. "Showing it to a friend who never saw it."

"Really? I thought the Thunderclaps watched it day and night."

"Not all my friends are Thunderclaps." Wyatt pointed at the service door. "Let's try to get that opened."

Birdie groaned. "Why? It's perfectly safe here."

"Shouldn't the staff have more information?" He was acting like a fussy guest, the kind that fretted about creaking sounds or rust spots like the whole resort could come apart before they had their third pass at the buffet.

He waggled his fingers at the commbundle.

She showed him the screen. "Emergency mode. Keeps the hysterical masses from clogging the system."

Wyatt took it and prodded the screen with a surprisingly unattractive chubby finger.

"It's not going to work," Birdie said.

"You don't have a code? Nothing?" Wyatt's voice had grown heated, possibly tinged with blame.

"You're a celebrity. Don't you have something?" Birdie snapped back.

He gave back the commbundle and circled Gloria's ponycart, poking at the various compartments and pushing aside towels and soaps. She jumped up and stumbled, forgetting that she still wore his mocs, and shuffled to the cart. Wyatt glanced at the shoes but didn't comment.

"There's nothing." Birdie said, trying to nudge him out of the way. The cramped service corridor would offer no benefit they couldn't enjoy here in fine comfort. She went through the commbundle's exit procedure and showed him the result: SECURE.

Wyatt refused to give up. He elbowed her aside and waggled his hand into every crevice. "There's got to be built-in hardware, override, something to get in and out of the rooms."

"There's not." The stress was getting to him; he was losing it. "It's fine in here," she insisted. She would have physically shoved him if he wasn't the resort VIP.

"Well, I'm kicking back over here." She hopped back on the couch and put her feet up, crossing one beaded moc over the other.

She missed what happened next, but Wyatt made a series of growly sighing sounds, then there was a hollow pop and the service door opened. Gloria burst into the suite, red-faced and breathless.

"You're here." Wyatt sagged with relief like she was the security force instead of a person who put mints on pillows when she wasn't berating her underlings.

Birdie moved quickly but not before Gloria caught her lounging around, feet on the furniture, booze-filled tumbler on the table. Her eyes bulged but her mouth formed a polite grimace as she looked Birdie over. "Why are you in here?"

"Cleaning." Birdie channeled her most professional posture as she took the ponycart and angled it toward the door.

Gloria pointed to the oversized mocs with a horrified look. "Why are you wearing Wyatt—our guest's—shoes?"

"He's not a guest, he's talent," Birdie clarified. Off Gloria's dark look she added, "How do you know whose they are?"

The muscles in Gloria's neck popped out. She looked like a cartoon character about to explode. Even Wyatt looked amused. Gloria said, "They don't fit you and are not part of your uniform."

Why this particular performance review was necessary when bandits were aboard, Birdie couldn't say but leave it to Gloria to adhere to the resort handbook in a crisis. Birdie checked her feet. "I think they look good."

"They do," Wyatt said, putting a warm, comforting arm over her shoulder and easing her toward the service door. "You can have them."

The weight of his touch sent a funny flash of heat through her. A former pop star was practically hugging her.

The entry-chirp for the suite's main entrance went off. Birdie jumped. The suites had special sound reduction features but not enough to mask activity from the hallway. A series of metallic taps and a high-pitched burr. Bandits?

Birdie's heart thumped wet-hot in her chest. Gloria made a funny grunting sound and remained glued in place like she was in shock or too panicked to run. There was no urgency in Wyatt either, in fact, he looked sort of dazed himself, which meant Birdie was going to have to save the day.

"Shouldn't we *all* get going?" Birdie spoke gently like she was trying to coax a trembling new employee into the meal room for the first time. She twisted out of Wyatt's embrace and urged them to follow.

An ominous sucking noise came from the entrance. They all swiveled to look. Birdie's stomach dipped, the fear bitter at the back of her throat. A faint chemical-tang smell came from the suite entrance. Poison gas? Fire?

"You go on," Gloria said in a strangled voice.

Birdie wouldn't wish kidnapping on her worst enemy. Not even Gloria. She took a deep breath and summoned her courage, annoyed that it came to her to save these two brainless morons.

"We're going to be kidnapped if we don't get going." She herded them toward the door.

"No," Gloria said, her voice stronger. "You go. Please."

"Not leaving without you," Birdie said.

Gloria and Wyatt exchanged a startled look.

"I'm right behind you," Birdie insisted. "We don't have much time."

"Just go," Gloria begged like she was about to cry. "Can you do what you're told? Just this once?"

Wyatt muttered something that Birdie didn't catch. Gloria shook her head, violently. Even Lonely Wolf Boy couldn't snap her out of it.

An unnerving metal screech came from the door.

Wyatt tilted his head at Birdie, "Tell her."

Wyatt and Gloria exchanged an unreadable look. Birdie's mind raced through possibilities. "Tell me what?"

"We can't," Gloria said.

Wyatt finally put his arm around Gloria, but they didn't look any closer to exiting the suite. Birdie was about to insist she could be trusted but the words faded on her lips. Gloria's face tilted up to his and then she did something Birdie had never seen before.

She smiled.

Wyatt gazed into Gloria's eyes with a look that could only be described as adoring. He stroked the side of her face.

Birdie stared at them, cringing inside and out. "What is happening right now?"

They embraced for real, Gloria's sweaty head pressed against his manly chest, her cheek against the velvety buckskin.

They were ... together?

"But all the rules ... and you and the guests ... the parade of bridesmaids ..." Birdie's voice trailed off.

Wyatt shook his head. "That's all marketing."

The announcement chime on the suite's entrance repeated, over and over, as if someone was angry and wanted in.

Gloria snapped out of her bliss and said in a terrorizing voice, "Don't ask questions, just get out of here. Now."

"But what are you guys doing?"

Gloria looked back at Wyatt, her eyes wide and incredulous. "Didn't I tell you about this?"

Wyatt grabbed Birdie's hands and peered into her face, close enough to notice the make-up on the bags under his eyes. She said, "Are you really—?"

"Shut up," Wyatt said, his voice vicious. He wasn't so handsome now.

"There is no more time. We have invested everything but the hair on our heads to stage this kidnapping to get off this ship." Birdie didn't dare interrupt. "We're both trapped in our contracts. The less you know, the better. If you're here, they're going to grab your ass, too, and you will be traveling into deep space with us as your only friends."

Birdie shuddered. She looked over his shoulder at the suite entrance, ominous sounds growing worse.

"I'm going." She didn't miss the look of relief the lovebirds shared. She paused again. "Can I have your jacket?"

"You've got to be joking," Gloria said.

Wyatt shimmied out of it.

"Do not do that," Gloria said.

Wyatt threw it at her. Birdie put it on, still warm from his body. She stuck her hand in the pockets and held out a pack of breath mints.

"Get out!" Gloria said, flinging a pair of complimentary resort slippers at her. At this rate, the rage would kill her before the bandits dragged her away.

"Relax, I am," Birdie said, carefully pushing the ponycart out. The service door clicked into place before she could turn around and watch what happened next. When she tried to re-open it, the access pad said SECURE.

The sound deadening did its job, but she cracked up imagining Gloria's screeches and Wyatt pretending to fight back. She dug around Wyatt's pockets again and found a beaded acorn, Wyatt's VIP fob.

She steered the ponycart to the lift. "Lounge stage," she said. Time to check out that Earth view and if she got there quick enough, maybe see the bandit ship taking Gloria and Wyatt to paradise.

AUTHOR NOTES

I love stories set in space so I'm always wanting to get Indigenous people out there in my own stories. "Security Breach at Sugar Pine Suites" envisions the next level of economic enterprise for tribes. We've been successful with tribal gaming operations; why not launch one to the stars? Meet the Orbital Casino. I'm especially interested in grunt workers. Who are the tribal citizens who end up doing these jobs: Wandering the casino floor for security? Hauling fresh chafing dishes to the buffet? Crawling around in the hidden spaces keeping up with maintenance?

This story features a couple of resentful housekeepers and a washed-up boy bander in residence. None of them want to be there. They're each stuck for their own reasons, and they come up with creative ways of dealing with it. I look forward to writing more stories in this setting.

HAPPY TRAILS
THEODORE C. VAN ALST, JR.

When Coyote wound round his tail twice and laughed, loped through the six-way intersection at Lincoln, Belmont, and Ashland, he never thought so many humans would die.

Sure, he was drunk, but it was St. Paddy's on a Friday downtown and everyone was shit-faced. He stood on his hind legs and felt around up top; he remembered a Northwest side girl full of freckles and big blonde hair sticking one of those green felt derbies on his head, but it seemed to have fallen off somewhere. He had been hitting on her, trying to use his legendary dog magic, but she wasn't buzzed enough to understand him. Then her big doofus, Brendan, showed up with a couple green beers in hand, thought he was some stray trying to give her rabies, and kicked him good in the ribs. Coyote tried to bite him but missed, slunk away, eyes already peeled for another shot.

He padded around outside the Riverwalk bars, people pouring beers on the ground for him. Embarrassing, yeah, but he wasn't drunk enough yet to show them he could sit up in a café chair, drink right out of a plastic cup if he wanted, even if it freaked people out every time, got him in trouble with Creator for showing off. He licked up a couple puddles, wondered how he could get someone to dump a shot of whiskey for him, and watched architecture tour boats chock full of suburbanites and other foreigners putt on by. He alternated arching his eyebrows, lolled his big pink tongue out long past his black lips, felt the spit on his teeth dry in the breeze off the Chicago River. He was glad it was warm, way nicer than usual for March, but winced at the thought that every spring seemed warmer than the last. These humans were fucking it up quick-like and there didn't seem to be any way to stop it. He left it, like most things, in Creator's hands and went back to thinking Coyote thoughts, the only thing he was actually bound to do.

Right now, those wiggedy deliberations were bugging him to get laid, a proposition way easier for him as a human. Man, there were like three coyote women on the whole Northside, and they were too busy with their kids to spend any time with him. He'd tried plenty of times, been shut out even more.

The problem was that he was too fucked up to figure out how to switch to human form. He knew there were a couple of things he needed to say, but they had to be recited in a certain order, and it required a couple of stones, he thought maybe, but if it did, he'd lost those. And some tobacco, something else he didn't have. Shiiiit, he confirmed. I'm a mess.

He should probably go find Jimmy and Tommy, those little shits. They'd know what to do. He'd given them the story so they'd know how to call him back in case he got too fucked up. But Uptown was such a haul from here, and he'd already run the whole way along the big water from downtown. Heading west from the lakefront, he drank himself up Belmont, a dive bar here, a gay bar there, a hole in the wall, a couple music joints with metalheads and folk nerds out front, all of them quick to give a coyote a drink. He was smashed.

By the time he'd crested one of Chicago's few inclines up to Ashland, all four legs were moving independently of each other. And he'd puked two or three times, ate it at least once.

But this fuzzy urge kept at him, worried his mind. The migratory patterns, the hunting trails, the well-worn paths embedded deep in his soul gnawed at his heart. Those paths crossed with Fox's and Possum's and Skunk's plenty of times, but he ignored them, didn't bother to talk with all of those trying to survive in the city as well. It wasn't because he didn't have time; it was just that Coyote was an asshole and couldn't be bothered. He preferred to be alone, and lonely with his thoughts. He had slunk every sidewalk on the Northside, but it was the old Indian trails that pulled at him; Archer, Ogden, Milwaukee, Clybourn, Lincoln, and Elston Avenues, even Route 66, maybe the grandest trail of all, every angled street in the city that spoked out from the lake and the old trading centers were paths drawing his paws in undeniable ways.

That's how it was with Lincoln Avenue, his most favorite, the one that had been yuppified more than any other. As he made his way west toward it on Belmont, he could see it in his mind's eye, vintage neon, yellow-blue arc light, broad and angled, heading northwest in sensible ways, cutting across a square-gridded city that slept in silence, dreamed deeper than it knew, its diagonal paths leading to an angry past, a history that simmered unknown below a surface hot-topped over a massacre, a burnt fort, rebellion, and resistance that smoldered like a root fire in its unsung fields, sighing prairies that sang on summer nights for those who knew how to listen, the city's Indigenous citizens' palms raised to the big water in the east, eyes smiling closed at a history not yet written, a book of Native reclamation close at hand.

Coyote held their hearts close to his own as he waltzed into the intersection, standing tall on two legs. He drew down all the magic in the air with him as he made his way, the six stoplights of the intersection responding in flashing red, green, and yellow, wild as his own heart demanded. Cars screeched and swerved in response, rolling and howling, a late model Caprice smashed a vintage Bel Air, two Crown Vics, black and maroon, skittered into a banana yellow Mustang and an old box truck, a crusty Dodge pickup broadsided a creamy Plymouth Voyager as a red Jeep Cherokee stood on its brakes, too late to avoid a scrubby blue Mazda Navajo pushed sideways across Ashland, all four tires blistering skid marks into the pavement. White faces screamed through shattering glass, windshields, and blood by the bucket splashed onto the blacktop. Limbs twisted and flashed, pale and crimson-streaked, thrown at the last second across eyes that rolled to avoid seeing onrushing sidewalks and light poles. Bodies crumpled half in and out of spidering windows and puckered doors, mayhem reigning supreme.

Coyote twirled, again and again, laughing in a way they'd get all wrong on the newscasts, the pure joy he felt lost on their unknowing ways of looking at the world, chaos the only true expression of love he knew.

Just wait 'til the Southside Irish Parade tomorrow, he thought. Western Avenue was gonna be wild.

AUTHOR NOTES

This story was one of those that arrives when you're not looking for it, but it presses right up and out of your hands, your voice, and onto the page. I was born and raised in Chicago, America's greatest city, a place that is layers upon layers of stories. And walking around there, I could always hear those stories, see them happening. I would live in them, keep them in my head, play them back later. I didn't start writing them down until I was much older, but I'm glad they hung out until I had the ability to tell them in the right way.

"Happy Trails" showed up one night as I was working through a graphic novel set in, where else, but Chicago, in Uptown, the neighborhood where I was born. There were folks from over 120 different tribes in the area back in the day, and I'm writing a story that deals with that, with the different traditions, when Coyote shows up and says "Hey. What about this story?" And there we were, talking about St. Patrick's Day in Chicago, a huge holiday there, thinking about all the coyotes that live in Chicago, along the lake, in the alleys, along the railroad tracks, what those spaces and trails represent, and the stories they hold.

Coyote likes to party, but he also likes justice. And stories about himself. I hope you do, too.

MARKED BY BEARS

JESSIE LOYER

My brother was taken away by the bears to live with them when I was small; he existed only in the song that was sung about him. His song was sung in the summer, at Sundance, but also in the winter, on the darkest day, the day he was taken away. The trade meant continued peace with the bears and had been negotiated since his birth when my mother had shrewdly promised them a five-year-old; she said any human baby would be too weak to live their ways. So my parents had him for five short years. He was doted on, fed well, beloved. And then, he was gone.

I was a baby when they took him and had no memory of him. But his absence shaped everything around me.

Our ancestors used to think bears were just cute. My grandmother remembered her mother having a small toy shaped like a bear. "But not really like a bear, but a child's idea of a bear," she said. It was easier to live with a hazy concept of a bear than face the horror of what their built-up concrete cities had done to the territory that bears need. They rarely saw bears; the people of my great-grandmother's time had sent them to live in the fringes. They need a lot, the bears: space, food, fealty. They withered at the fringes.

So things were unbalanced in that time of pipelines and smokestacks. When the reckoning came and people were killed off in the apocalypse, more animal nations that had been sent to the fringes began to thrive, not just the bears. Deer, wolves, buffalo, birds of all kinds, bats; there are stories of how trees were allowed to stretch out again:

they all came back after our cities crumbled.

And we were forced to atone for the ways we had overstepped.

We are uglies. It's marked in our skin. It's weak, rips at the smallest thing. Pitiful. Deer are so self-sufficient; already clothed and well-fed. Wherever they are. When we need to be clothed, we negotiate a huge sacrifice. When we eat, we ask for a life. If we had been living well, in balance, that sacrifice would be easy for our relatives. A joyful understanding. But they remember what we did to them.

See, their songs reach way back. Back into ice ages, sometimes, depending on the species. Certainly into the Time of Sorrow, what the deer call the era of cities. When uglies would kill them and leave their bloody bodies on a field. Deer mourned the wastefulness: they honored the sacrifice for feeding others as a calling. At dawn, they sing the names of those who answered the call. But they could not forget how uglies would kill their most honored people and then spit on the death sacrifice. They sing about their heads placed on our walls, shameless. We're ugly for more than just our lack of fur: they know we hold that ugliness inside us, deep. They won't forget.

Bears, even more so. They have the luxury of hibernation, the deep memory. In the coldest months, when we are huddled together, sick and hungry, they can tap into a stream of consciousness that extends back, way back. Once, I heard an old grizzly sing a song his ancestors had sung to mammoths, heard it sung to him as he hibernated, burrowed in ancestral consciousness. By comparison, our memory is so short, so incomplete. We know we had cities and that the reckoning happened, but we can't remember beyond that very well. Our memories of the Time of Sorrow are so poor; we need the long memories of our bear relatives to remind us.

One of the ways they remind us is through gifting. My brother was chosen to be honored because my mother came from people who had sworn themselves to the bears. Our clan. She told me about how our clan had considered the relationship differently, more like symbols and metaphors. I had laughed, "But didn't the bears get offended?" and my mother had shushed me and shook her head. Quietly, she had said, "We can never take their love for us for granted." This was before I learned about the hunger that uglies had, our legacy of selfish greed. Everything unbalanced will right itself, eventually.

We owe that balance to certain nations. The deer are still dismissive of us, and might always be, but we have good relations with the buffalo. The buffalo have long memories, too, and when the reckoning happened, they sang us our redemption. We might not be here without them. They sang of how, after the genocide, their people were scattered and few, and how a few uglies brought them home to mountains and prairies. Allowed them to repopulate their communities. They sing of the grasses that missed them, of being reunited with the mountain meadows that were their sacred places. They sing of the joy of calves being born in holy places, being allowed to run far. It's one of the few good relations my ancestors kept, and it's the one that saved us. The buffalo saw possibilities for us. They hoped we could redeem our sins as long as our numbers were kept low and we were kept under close watch. The bears agreed and offered to manage our rights. So buffalo still greet us. They still allow us to ask for sacrifices so we can be fed. Sometimes they live among us for a time; my father remembers an old cow who nuzzled him to sleep as a child.

My father often thinks of the son he gave away. He's proud of the action; he knows it's honorable. But sometimes, something will remind him of my brother as a baby. Yesterday we were swimming and I snuck up behind to splash and surprise him. His eyes were wide and he screamed, then started to laugh. Then, bent over in the water, my father brought a hand to his eyes as his laugh turned into a cry. When I asked him why, he said, "He used to do that, splash around like you." As he cried I patted his hand and told him, "I bet he is more at home in the water now!" I've seen the way bears love water.

I don't know where my brother lives. I never see the children we give to them. Some people say they keep them in caves, where they are held apart, fed the best food, and given flowers for their hair. Others say that the children become bears: blessed to grow fur and claws, have their noses sharpen. I like that, the idea of my brother having claws. Powerful. I imagine him using his claws to pull salmon out of the river in the fall. It's hard to do with my hands, but a bear is built for it.

In my brother's song, my mother sings of the mothers who came before her. Her mother had also gifted a son to them; my mother had been older than him and remembered her brother going away. She usually cries at this point. It's a cry of overwhelming gratitude. They chose us! They keep this covenant with us. As she sings, I think of how I will send my future son to them to affirm this treaty, so I have to pay attention. One day, it will be my son's song I'll be singing, weaving in my mother's mother's songs so that we can try to remember, as poor as our memories are, how we atone.

It's not always boys. For other pacts, they send one of every pair of twins to the bears. Or children born with a mark. It depends on the bears and the uglies who made the pact. We don't live as long as our ancestors did, either. In the generations before my great-grandmother, they lived over a hundred winters old, they say. It feels impossible! How could you move over rough ground at that age? Could you even run, living that many winters? But our generations are closer together, so the bears are happy. More children to come to them, more often, a ceremony I've only heard about. But I have met bears at other times, and soon, I'll be at the center of one of those gatherings.

There's a time when they come close, where both of our nations are all fat with berries, purple muzzles, and purple lips. This year is the year I'll be marked.

My mother sits with me and asks me to sing my brother's song to her while she braids my hair. She wants me to have it right, not forget anything because I'll sing it to the bears when they come. I've helped her sing it during midwinter, but never for an audience like this. She says, "You have to get it right. Part of our atonement is the precision of memory. Our ancestors didn't care enough to remember who we were in relation to everyone else, and they perished. So we have to show our commitment. We have to get it right." I nod, start again. This time, I remember it well, and she grunts in approval.

There's something that has been worrying me. "Does it hurt?" I ask slowly. It's a question I'm hesitant to ask. Pain is not something to fear, says my grandmother. Discomfort is not our enemy. My mother turns me toward her and says softly, "Yes. It hurts. That's why we do it."

She dresses me carefully. There are flowers in my hair, braided down my back. She carefully weaves the braid up on my head. "Don't need that getting in the way," she says. She looks me up and down. "Yes, my love. You look perfect. The bears will be very proud of you." My heart thrums; it's so exciting. They'll arrive later in the afternoon, so we start to prepare food for them: piles of berries and grubs and fish. We will all feast, and then, I'll be marked.

My family sits, surrounded by red willows. My mother sits quietly, arm around me. My father is nervous and pulls grass from the ground, shredding them into smaller and smaller pieces. He did not grow up in a family sworn to bears, and he says that he still has to calm himself when they appear. "My fast heartbeat won't let me forget," he says. We all have that, the sins of our ancestors that make our blood sing when bears come near. We are reminded of how we betrayed their trust.

A big grizzly walks into the clearing. G'hrmph' is my mother's marker. I've seen her a few times in my life, sometimes for ceremonies like this, but sometimes from far away. The first time I remember seeing her, she was on a hillside and my mother stopped dead and held me, a wide-eyed look on her face. She had pursed her lips and whistled to G'hrmph'. The grizzly turned her head, nodded, and continued rummaging in the bush. I saw my mother's face fall, disappointed. "I just thought I could introduce you," she said, "but she must be busy." I've always wondered about the hold that G'hrmph' has on my mother. But my grandmother says that's how it always is, the bond between the marker and the marked.

G'hrmph' is joined by a few more bears. I only recognize one or two. They don't usually gather in big groups, so some must have traveled far to witness this. I've never seen a marking, only heard about it, but no one ever mentioned it would be witnessed by so many bears. I wonder if my brother, the bear, is among them. I look at my mother. Her face is upturned, rapturous. She clicks a hello to G'hrmph', who responds with grace. It's now time for me to sing.

I sing of my brother, born to my parents, born into atonement for the excesses. I sing of his soft limbs, the care that was taken to feed him well, protect him from sickness and injury. I sing of the cold, of the day that P'rff took him from us, the great joy of that day. I sing of the commitment of the bears to hold us to our pact to atone, to remind us of our weakness, our softness, our flesh.

My mother beams at me, proud, as I finish. My voice sounds so small in this clearing, especially as the bears fill the space in rich, loud sounds. I can hear them purring. G'hrmph shakes her glossy coat and sings back to me, saskatoons on her hot breath, honoring my song. I can feel the redness creep up into my face. I didn't know she knew me! But I suppose that is what this is, a sort of spiritual introduction.

After the song, my mother stands and holds my hand. She brings me to the center of this circle of uglies and bears. She lays me face down. I can smell the earth as I place my hands under my chin. She opens the shirt away from my back, places a hand on my spine, and leans in to whisper, "I am so proud of you. Be strong. Try not to move too much."

As I lay in the dirt, alone, my heart beats fast. It raises my chest up and down, ever so slightly. I hear my mother tell them my name, and I hear G'hrmph call the name of a bear I've never met: Hrhhmp. She will mark me. As I hear her footfalls, I realize I am scared. I don't want the pain. I know it makes me weak, but I grit my teeth and push my forehead against the dirt. It won't take long, I tell myself. It will be over soon.

I feel Hrhhmp's hot breath and feel the earth shake as she walks over. Her claws are long and elegant, right at my eye level. I squeeze my eyes shut, but open them in surprise as she puts her snout beside my ear. She tells me that she'll do my best not to hurt me more than she needs to and tells me to just stay very still. By the cooing in her tones, I can tell she's juvenile; her role is probably similar to mine. I thank her for this kindness and then she begins.

She sings of the way that uglies forgot their weakness, how our folly made us think we were somehow better because our hands were dexterous and our brains were big. How we must remember the way skin rips and tears and that the rips and tears of skin are a memory, too. How she, as a bear, is beholden to mark the one who will give up their child, to make a pact on our skin, so that we don't forget and slip back into the ways of our ancestors. And how, if we live with a good relationship, we might redeem our people.

I know it's coming, but I still squeeze my hands tight and tense up my whole body. I can feel my breath coming fast and shallow. I am trying not to let any noises escape my mouth. Hrhhmp raises one huge paw and draws her long, elegant claws down my back.

The pain envelopes me. Everything in my body screams for me to run away. But I bite into the dirt, let it fill my mouth to dampen my scream. Hrhhmp lifts her other paw and scraps my back again. I dig my toes into the ground. I can feel the slickness of blood sliding from my back, down my sides. I can smell my fear.

I hear her voice by my ear telling me to look in her eyes, and I look up. Her dark eyes are full of sorrow. Then something slides away. In her eyes, I see my body, small, bloodied, on the ground. That image dances. I hear her voice in my head: "This is how you will call me," and I hear three sharp notes. It's not far from the whistle my mother used to greet G'hrmph, but distinctly its own. "And this is how I will call you," she intones in my head, and she calls me by my name, a series of soft purrs.

Now I have a name, she can call me into the ancestral consciousness that bears tap into during hibernation. Like a reflection on water, I see shapes come into focus. For a few moments, Hrhhmp shows me the most horrific scenes: bears being murdered, their bodies left to rot, bears in cages hardly bigger than their bodies, bears being tortured as uglies laugh and laugh. I weep and cling to her. "I'm sorry, I'm sorry, I'm sorry," I keep saying, even though I know I should be quiet. She grunts low and the images shift. I see my mother as a child being marked. My grandmother, and then her mother, young girls with blood running down their backs from the claws of young bears. Each time, both girl and bear are so still and so brave, held together in their deep sadness. Any healing ceremony is always a ceremony of grief too. The images ripple like someone threw a rock in a pond, and I see a boy with my face being led by P'rff to his new home in the mountains. The bears feed him a huge feast. He laughs and sings to them as he eats. I watch him fall asleep. They gently place him on a bed of cedar. Then, after a benediction song, I see the bears all take a small bite from his small body. I start to scream.

But Hrhhmp doesn't allow the scream to come out of my mouth. The scream is in my mind. As my guide, she shows me my body lying still on the ground, blood on my back, flower braids on my head, to calm me. I can see my blood, but right now, I can't feel anything. "We honor his sacrifice," she says in my head. "Thus we remain connected and in balance." I cry and cry. My brother is dead. He has been dead for years. All those other children, dead, eaten. I never thought that this could be the price. My mind is racing. She says softly, "You have done so well today. Can you calm your heart?" I faintly remember my grandmother telling me that when it felt like too much, I should find a detail to focus on. I thought she had meant the physical pain of the marking, but now, I know it's intended for this moment, this moment that feels like my mind isn't mine anymore, so I look at the way the fur fans out from Hrhhmp's eyes and the layered brown of her eyes. Slowly, the repeating pattern brings me back to myself. I tell her I'm ready to return.

Hrhhmp brings us back into the present. As I leave the ancestral consciousness, the pain returns, sharp. My back spasms. She asks the ceremonial words, loud enough for the crowd to hear, "Do you feel fear?"

I spit the dirt from my mouth and manage to weakly say, "Yes."

She nods. "Will you carry this fear to remind yourself?"

I nod. "Yes"

Hrhhmp says, "By these wounds we are bound. You are marked." She drops her large head to my back and gently licks the deep lines.

I lay in the dirt. It's over. I feel a puff of hot breath as she whispers in my ear, "I'll see you again," and calls me by my name. I can hear the bears lumbering away slowly as there is nothing left for them to witness. Bears don't visit like we do; when a thing is done, they move along. I lay in the dirt and cry. My tears have made mud around my face. I can feel my heartbeat in the grooves on my back, pulsing. My mother and my grandmother come over and place hot cloths on my back. I turn my head to my mother, my face streaked with mud and tears, and ask, "Did you know?"

My mother smiles wide at me and washes my face. "I am so proud of you," she says. "You will remember. You'll hold this memory in your body." My grandmother's eyes are wet, and she says, "It feels a bit like a betrayal, doesn't it?" I nod. Her eyes shut as she smiles, and a few tears are squeezed out and fall down her cheeks. She continues, "But it's not. It's seeing with new eyes that we're not the center."

They know. Their markers must have guided them through these memories too. I've sat behind them, seen their markings, traced those long scars on their backs with my finger. Mine will look like that, eventually. If they've been through this, they knew that giving my brother away meant he would be eaten. My mother, as she was marked, would have seen her own brother's death, knowing that she would have to give up her son the same way. I ask her, "How could you do it?"

She laughs gently, tears in her eyes. "We carry our ancestors' sins. We have to atone." She pauses and strokes my hair, fixing a flower, "But I asked for five years. Years to hold a baby close, to hear his laughter. I got to give him a wonderful life. His sacrifice was beautiful."

As my mother and grandmother finish bandaging up my markings, I think of my time swimming in Hrhhmp's consciousness. I can't deny that there was great beauty in the care the bears took. He didn't suffer. After the horrors that Hrhhmp showed me, one small boy's life seems so small. After seeing the pain we inflicted, I don't know that I would have advocated for us the way the buffalo did.

It takes days for the markings to close, and they are still tender even when they stop bleeding. During the long recovery days, I sing my brother's song to keep me company. I realize that she gave me another gift: I saw my brother, who until now, had only existed in song to me. His face looked like mine. Now, when I sing his song, I see his face, plump and happy.

We come across a herd of buffalo on the day my marks stop bleeding. My father greets them and brings me forward. An old cow snorts her great nose at me and asks if I remember now. I nod. Her eyes smile and she brings over a few other buffalo. She asks me to sing for her and her family, the song of my marking. I look at my father in alarm. "I don't know that song!" I hiss. He laughs and says, "Now's the time to compose it." So I sing slowly. I tell them of Hrhhmp, the way I laid in the dirt, her claws gliding down my back, the invitation into the ancestral consciousness, of the pain we inflicted, of the markings of my mothers, and of the sacrifice of my brother. I start crying halfway through and have to sing through my tears. My father holds me close, kisses the top of my head, then sends me to sit as he finishes talking to the buffalo.

She talks to my father for a while, then, with a kick in the dust, runs back to her people. When I ask him what she said, he tells me, "I'll never get over how much they love us," and hugs me to his chest, careful with my back. He says, "They always hoped we could be good relatives. Buffalo never gave up on us." He tells me that the old cow and her family will dance my song to the rest of the herd tonight, spreading the news that the uglies are reminded of their histories and that balance is maintained.

All winter, my dreams are repetitive. It starts as simple things: rooting around in the bush, wading into a stream, running faster than I've ever been able to. Finally, when I see a reflection in a still pool, I realize they aren't my dreams, but Hrmmph's. Her hibernation dreams are mixing into mine. She dreams of saskatoons and grubs, of the sensation of rubbing her back against a tree. She dreams of cubs not yet made. I yearn for the deeper memories, but she leaves me when she enters the ancestral consciousness. I am hungry to remember. I want to ask her everything, but I'll have to wait until she wakes up. I'll have to wait until spring.

JASON SIZEMORE

"Marked by Bears" appeared in our Indigenous Futurists special issue edited by Allison Mills. I was blown away by all the stories, including this one that is a complex rumination on ancestral memories. I love how Jessie Loyer imagines a far-future scenario about the way human and bear relationships plays out.

SPIRITS OF THE BROKEN LANDS

KEVIN WABAUNSEE

Shoppers at the Thersian Grand Market jostled to haggle over tanned eelskin baubles labeled as Shawdese good luck charms, unaware that actual Shawdese neither made nor used such objects. The only regular Shawdese presence in the Thersian Grand Market was the crematorium ash that made up most of the hard-packed earth under those very shoppers' feet. That, and the occasional traveler from the Southern Wastes.

On a sun-drenched morning, one of those rare travelers, Gwisen Oxendine, spread a similarly counterfeit Shawdese prayer rug in the dirt next to the mossy stone walls of the market and set out a donation jar. He wrapped thin leather straps up and down his forearms, which, like his eelskin pants, were painted with crude parodies of Shawdese spirit-lines. While his red curls and deep ochre complexion marked him as a full-blood Shawdese, all of his clothes and props were cheap imitations.

Gwisen pulled out his jewel-beetle flute and improvised a slow and mournful tune. A few marketgoers drifted over to watch. A few slivers fell into his jar. Like a proper noble savage, Gwisen bowed and scraped at each passerby who dropped coins into the jar. But coins could never erase the knotty ropes of scar tissue written across his back. Nothing would bring back his sisters, dragged screaming from their home by Thersian irregulars. Coaxing donations from gullible Thersians was his only meager rebellion.

No time to waste; Gwisen had been watching this corner of the market for weeks and knew he only had an hour before the Shades made their patrols. He didn't want to be anywhere nearby when they arrived. As he played, Gwisen spotted a lean, tall man dressed in an authentic shade-leopard cloak. Good to keep an eye on that one. A lucrative mark.

As he played, Gwisen could almost hear the clucking tones and see the look of disapproval his mothers would give at the sight of the gaudy prayer rugs and fringed eel pants. They bore no resemblance to the textiles his family labored for months to create back in the southern wastes. Still, the Shawdese from Thersian histories and children's stories all wore eelskin and sat on brightly colored rugs. So Gwisen gave them what they expected.

Once a small crowd had gathered, Gwisen brought his meaningless tune to a close. He surveyed the crowd, making sure to make quick eye contact with the tall man in the expensive cloak.

"Honored Thersians! Lords and ladies!" Gwisen called out, pronouncing every consonant and vowel with care as if the Thersian language was strange and unfamiliar to him. In reality, the covenant school he'd been kidnapped and sent to as a child had beaten Thersian into him until it was more familiar than his mother tongue.

"I have traveled across the wastelands to share stories of magics whispered in the ears of my mothers and their mothers. Come, hear of my people's spiritual connection with the land. See as—"

"I thought Thersia wiped out all of the dirt-eaters!" came a drunken shout from the back of the crowd. "Are you sure you aren't just a ghost? Like all the other sad, dead dirt-eaters?"

Gwisen gave his most placid and beatific smile. He dipped his head toward the heckler, as though he hadn't fully understood the mockery. "Your concern for the welfare of the Shawdese tribes is much appreciated, honored sir. Truly, *your lordship* is too kind."

At that, even more laughter. The status-obsessed Thersians laughed at Gwisen, for his naïveté, but even more so at the drunken fool who'd been shamed by Gwisen's honorific. The rich man in the back remained unmoved.

"I am no ghost!" he said, falling back into the rhythm. "The Thersian Empire came across the boiling seas to claim this land and so many of my ancestors sadly fell to unfamiliar diseases. Those remaining ancient Shawdese wisely yielded to the superiority of Thersian magic! We made a gift of these lands. With the benevolence of the Thersian crown, we are allowed to persist in our new homelands in the southern wilds."

Gwisen maintained his routine, the primitive granting forgiveness with every sweet lie to the colonizers. It felt like ashes in his mouth.

Gwisen suppressed a shudder, remembering his family's tales of what really happened. The immolation camps. Crematorium ash clouds blotting out the sun with the corpses of his people. Thersian slave markets, stinking of piss and shit and decaying corpses. Cages filled with Shawdese he couldn't rescue.

He could never speak of those things here, not among the Thersians. Cityfolk wouldn't throw moons or slivers into the donation jar unless they were being flattered. So Gwisen kept the truth to himself and gave them what they wanted.

"But the Shawdese have some small magic of our own. To us, all things—the earth, the sky, the stones—are alive." A few gasps and whispers. Thersia worshipped empiricism and the scientific investigation of magical phenomena. Animism was the closest thing the empire had to heresy.

"I'd like to share with you a bit of Shawdese magic. Would you like to see the spirits of the land given form?"

The grand market was filled with counterfeit Shawdese prayer rugs and birthing shawls: of course, they wanted to see Gwisen's demonstration. Still, he waited for that first hesitant clap, which was followed by another, and finally, peals of applause and encouraging whistles. Gwisen even saw the rich man clapping demurely, his long-sleeved spider-silk shirt flowing lightly under his cloak. A mark worth watching, indeed.

Gwisen swept forward across the prayer rug. With a flourish, he knelt and plunged both hands into the dirt. "Thersia may have forgotten the spirits, but the spirits remember us: our passions and our joy." And our pain, Gwisen thought but dared not say, even if Thersian folk found it so much more convenient to forget. "Even the city spirits whisper if you know how to listen."

Gwisen pulled up a double-fistful of dirt and dropped it onto the middle of the pristine prayer rug. A gasp from the crowd. Prissy Thersian city folk.

Gwisen walked a fine line. A bowing and scraping Shawdese was fine, but one who thought too much of himself or showed a hint of too much power? That could turn a crowd ugly.

He closed his eyes and listened. The whispers of the spirits drifted into his consciousness, through a hearing beyond hearing, like the twinkling of sand skittering across a dune on a windy day. Gwisen whispered an invitation into his silent words, a bargain to be struck. Spirits hungered for the energy of human emotion. Gwisen offered up a tiny sliver of his wit. He did not, however, offer even a speck of his anger. That was his alone, and far too dangerous to bargain with, here among the colonizers.

The tiny spirit accepted his terms. Gwisen's eyes snapped open. He took a sip of wine from the waterskin at his hip, knelt and pressed a thumbprint into the pile of dirt, then spat a mouthful of wine into the depression.

Gwisen smiled, waved his hands in wild and looping gestures, accompanied by a lilting tune, sung without words. Utterly meaningless, but exactly what a Thersian wanted from a Shawdese savage.

Gwisen exhaled a single syllable, his breath embroidered with the terms of the spirit's bargain. Gwisen felt the spirit step sideways into the physical world and slip into the mound of mud and wine like a hand into a glove.

The dirt shifted back and forth, and with no hand touching it, smoothed itself into a featureless sphere. The Thersians' skeptical laughter gave way to a confused silence. The rich man in particular was rapt, his eyes wide and fixed on the movements of the ball of dirt.

Out of the mound of dirt, as if waking from a deep sleep, the spirit—just two hands tall—stretched and clambered onto two shaky feet. Lifeless dirt had become a tiny homunculus. The spirit took one unsteady step across the prayer rug—now pristine and free of dirt or stain. Then, it gave an exaggerated bow and leapt into a somersault across the prayer rug.

The Thersians burst into applause.

"Though they may not speak to Thersia any longer, the spirits still live, moving through the air and the earth and the plants and animals that sustain you."

With nothing more than pantomime and tumbling, the spirit worked the crowd with far more aplomb than Gwisen could have ever managed. The rich man didn't laugh, but watched with obsessive interest, his eyes never leaving the movements of the little spirit.

A tinkle of coins fell into Gwisen's donation jar. At first just slivers, but then, as the crowd grew, crescents and a few half-moons, and even the dull thud of a gibbous.

Then a drumbeat of heavy footfalls shattered the carnival atmosphere.

The laughter stopped, replaced with sharp intakes of breath, and a sudden hushed silence from the marketgoers. For an agonizing moment, Gwisen couldn't believe what was happening. The Thersian police—the Shades—had arrived. At least half an hour early. They shouldn't have been anywhere nearby, but the heavy footfalls and belligerent shouts didn't lie.

The Shades wore outfits stained in black and gray and spread like an inkblot of violence through the crowd, swinging cudgels and fists alike. Quickly, Gwisen closed his eyes and whispered the word of release, closing his bargain with the spirit, evicting it from the mud-and-wine body, and settling the remainder of his debt. He felt a wrenching tug as a tiny piece of his deepest self was torn away.

Distracted, Gwisen didn't see the Shade's cudgel swing down and slam into his temple. Just a flash of pain and the impact. Gwisen cried out. He stumbled and fell to the ground, dazed. The Shades kicked over his counterfeit rug and ground it into the dirt. His jewel-beetle flute was crushed under a heavy bootheel. His hard-won audience was beaten and dispersed with the butts of the Shades' cudgels.

One Shade stepped onto the rug, smashed Gwisen's donation jar, and picked all of the slivers and moons out of the pile of broken pottery, shoving the currency into his pockets.

Then, with the crowd scattered, the Shades merely walked away. They hadn't said anything, hadn't even tried to deliver a message. They didn't need to. This was Thersia, and he was Shawdese. The message was clear enough, the same one he'd been taught from his earliest days: this isn't your place, you aren't welcome here any longer. This all belongs to us now.

Gwisen clambered to his feet and began to gather up what little could be salvaged. Not a single coin had been left. His flute lay in a hundred pieces and the counterfeit rug was torn, mud and dirt ground into every stitch. Most valuable, his hard-won audience was long gone.

Until soft footsteps announced one straggler. Gwisen looked up and saw the tall man—the rich man wearing a fortune on his back and in his voluminous sleeves, who had watched Gwisen's performance with such rapt attention. Perhaps this day wouldn't be a complete failure, after all. If Gwisen could wheedle an invitation to this man's home, to ply him with tales of Shawdese nobility, he might be able to convince him to part ways with—

"I have a proposal for you," the man said with no introduction or preamble.

"Sir?" Gwisen said, keeping his gaze lowered before the noble.

"You will accompany me to my home where we will discuss the Shawdese and your performance. You shall be compensated for your time."

Gwisen blinked. With a mark like this, he would normally have to speak in circles and spirals, hinting at the possibility until the unsuspecting noble was convinced they'd come up with the idea themselves. This rich fellow seemed more than happy to follow the script without Gwisen's intervention. Perhaps his luck was changing.

"Yes. Yes, sir, that would be just fine."

Gwisen rested on a chaise longue upholstered in rich purple velvet. The cavernous room he'd been taken to defied easy description. It wasn't a library, even though the walls were filled with books. The huge tables covered with blown-glass tubes and distillation flasks suggested a laboratory. The corner, however, with its tiled floors and drains set into the floor beneath a hammered bronze autopsy table, suggested a darker purpose.

"You were quite lucky, young man," the rich man said as he swept into the room carrying a glass of wine. He closed and latched the door behind him, slipping a key into the pocket of the cloud-leather housecoat he now wore. This man's clothes alone could pay for every treasure and bobble in the entire Grand Market. He spoke with the elongated vowels and hint of a lisp that marked the accent of Thersian aristocrats.

"Is that so, sir?" Gwisen said, keeping his voice and gaze low, still using the faux-savage accent from his performance, that of a simple traveler from Shawdese lands.

The rich man nodded, taking a sip of the wine, the seven thick braids of his hair tinkling quietly with the precious metals woven into them. Even a passing trifle from a person like this could alter Gwisen's fate forever.

But an ant does not cheat a lizard so easily, Gwisen thought. Nor the boot of the man who could squash the ant so easily and without a second's thought.

"Quite lucky," the rich man answered. "The Shades are not always so merciful with beggars and street performers.

This aristocrat's keen gaze reminded Gwisen of market-day shoppers, hungry for a certain bauble, their eyes flitting at any approach, refusing to allow other marketgoers to scoop up their chosen treasure. This man wanted something, and he was worried he wouldn't get it.

"I suppose I am lucky. But the show's over now, my lord," Gwisen said, "And I thank you for your hospitality, though I am not sure if I have much to offer to a man such as yourself."

"I don't think that's true at all," the nobleman said, a hint of amusement creeping into his voice. "I think you have quite a lot to offer me."

Gwisen's eyes narrowed. The nobleman was playing, and it wasn't at all clear what game had been engaged.

Gwisen nodded, slowly. "My lord would like to learn more about the customs of my people? A blessing from the mother of earth and soil, perhaps?"

The nobleman's face remained impassive until Gwisen trailed off. Then, his lips curled into a cruel smile and Gwisen knew that he'd miscalculated. "Let's start again. And this time, none of your huckster's tricks. Drop the accent. You're a magician. So am I, and I want to speak plainly, one practitioner to another."

Ah. An amateur magician. Here was his opening. This rich man was a different sort of hobbyist than the bauble-collectors at the Grand Market, but still a worthwhile mark. When Gwisen spoke again, it was plainly, without the affected accent or the tortured pronunciations. "Understood. Introductions, then? My name is Gwisen Oxendine."

The barest hint of a nod was all the approval the nobleman had to offer. "Much better. My name is Aldeen Dinsmere. I don't imagine that name means much to you, but I'm sure that you can infer from your surroundings what sort of influence I wield in the empire."

Gwisen nodded, slowly, hoping that acknowledging the obvious wouldn't provoke some offense.

"Then you must understand that material wealth, all of this gold and frippery, the buildings and the lands, they matter very little."

Gwisen's surprise led him to speak without thinking. "Perhaps it is easier for one who has everything to say that such things matter nothing than for those who've lost everything," Gwisen said. He regretted it as soon as the words were past his lips.

But Dinsmere didn't seem to mind the gibe. Instead, he nodded thoughtfully. "Indeed. My passion is to seek after knowledge. But of a specific vintage—a precious and rare variety—knowledge of the magical arts."

Apparently feeling more at ease, Dinsmere shrugged out of his housecoat, revealing the sleeveless tunic he wore underneath and his bare arms. A shock like ice through his veins hit Gwisen as he took in the nobleman's appearance. A spiderweb of gold and silver lines were embossed into Dinsmere's skin, covering nearly every inch of his arms in looping, alchemical patterns.

This was no mere noble. Those rarest of tattoos, laced with precious metals and coursing with magical power, meant only one thing: Dinsmere was an Empiricist.

Gwisen shuddered; his own scars blooming with pain at the memory of the fire and lightning that had burned him during his tortures. Gwisen had never seen an Empiricist face-to-face, but every violation he'd endured, every mass grave he'd seen, and every Thersian slave-market were designed and directed by an Empiricist's will. The Empiricists were the magician-lords who ruled the Thersian Empire's bloody reign from the shadows.

Worse, Gwisen understood that it was no accident that had brought him here. A Thersian Empiricist would scarcely need to lift a finger to summon a brigade of Shades to roust a Shawdese street performer. Dinsmere had engineered this meeting, and Gwisen wasn't a guest—he was a prisoner.

His heart raced with senseless panic. He'd made a terrible mistake. He had to get out, get away, run, and never stop running. He glanced around the room in mute panic. The single door into this room was closed and latched. No escape. This monster, one of the architects of the Shawdese genocide, had enough magical power coursing through him to burn Gwisen to cinders. And he would certainly not be deceived by Gwisen's lies.

His only chance to get away would be to convince Dinsmere that he was too insignificant to harm and utterly without value. "I'm not sure—" Gwisen ventured carefully, haltingly, before trailing off. "I'm not sure what knowledge I could offer. My magics are merely a trifle—I've never studied nor been taught."

Dinsmere's smile was broad. "On the contrary. I saw the precision you wielded in moving that little manakin. I'm not too proud to admit that that level of dexterous movements of a telekinetic hand are beyond even my own powers. I must know the technique. Even a puppeteer with a score of joints and strings couldn't make a doll dance with such convincing movements."

Gwisen frowned, feeling confused even as he panicked. This Empiricist seemed to think that the spirit he'd animated in the Grand Market was a trick. Ironic, since that whisper of magic was the only authentic thing he'd demonstrated for the crowd.

"My lord," Gwisen said, his heart thudding in his chest, trying not to remember the tales of Empiricists passed down by five generations of Shawdese, the torture they had suffered in the name of knowledge. "I am flattered by your attention, but I must plead ignorance. I do not—I could not—make an inanimate object move in the way you describe."

Dinsmere scoffed. "Then how do you claim it moved? Not by itself."

"Forgive me, my lord. Not by itself. But not by my manipulations, either. I merely enlisted the assistance of a spirit who was willing to barter a few minutes of animation in exchange for—"

"Enough!" Dinsmere roared. "I'll hear no more of this nonsense. I brought you here out of the goodness of my heart. The Shades would have treated you much worse, I assure you. And you repay my benevolence with more of this trickster's flim-flam? Come clean now, or I assure you, I'll share the full weight of an Empiricists' investigation."

Gwisen shrunk back, an involuntary shudder making his voice tremble. "My lord, I wish I had a different answer for you, but I simply do not. My people can hear the whispers of the spirits. And with the right bargain engraved upon our words, a spirit may consent to do some minor service, for the spirits are always hungry for—"

Dinsmere waved his hand in an irritated gesture while Gwisen was talking, cutting him off mid-sentence, and raised his hands sharply. "*This* is magic. Only the peasants scraping in the dirt still think magic is the realm of gods or monsters."

Dinsmere then drew a complex shape with the tips of his fingers. His movements trailed a line of fire that hung in the air. "It's energy, a force that surrounds us. And with the right training, with the correct influence, that energy can be manipulated, shaped, and redirected."

An intricate alchemical symbol inked in flames hung suspended in the air between them. Then, Dinsmere muttered a series of incantations, and the flaming sigil was consumed by flickering green light and was snuffed out.

"Now, *Shawdese*, stop lying to me. You aren't my equal. You aren't worth more than what you can teach me. You're a remnant, chaff from the empire's harvest. Your people are only allowed to exist by *my* people's leave and consent. You *belong* to us. So, show some respect and answer my questions, you pitiful savage."

Anger like a grip of stone seized Gwisen's chest. His heart thudded with frustration. Every muscle in his body tensed with the effort of not showing his anger. The Thersians had taken everything. The land they stood on was soaked with the blood of Gwisen's people, countless Shawdese families burned, their ashes blown all across the birthplace of their ancestors. The Thersians had denied Gwisen his own history, outlawed his language, and their residential schools had scarred his childhood. And they still weren't done. They'd never be done.

But even knowing that, Gwisen didn't let that anger show. He dipped his head low, closed his eyes in a gesture of supplication he hadn't used since he'd escaped from the Thersian boarding school years ago. "A thousand pardons, lord. Perhaps my lord would prefer another demonstration with the benefit of his tools and equipment to better observe the process?"

Dinsmere looked skeptical, but that hungry look crept back across his face. "Yes. Yes, that will do just fine."

Gwisen nodded, and Dinsmere led him to an empty steel table. "What supplies do you need? Dirt, wine?"

Gwisen shook his head. "No, those materials would be of little use here. Here, I think a pen, some paper, and a small bottle of ink would suffice."

Dinsmere produced all three from a drawer, and one by one, handed them to Gwisen. "The paper is Vrinthian cotton-weave. The ink is imported from our holdings in Meltenios—a rich blue-black with flecks of copper to shimmer upon the finest papers. The pen is a from a block of wood reclaimed from an ancient Thersian shipwreck and topped with a solid gold nib."

Gwisen nodded. The stationary he was about to destroy would have purchased the freedom of a score of his ancestors. He shredded eleven sheets of the paper into a pile of fine confetti on the table. He seized the pen by the nib and yanked it out of the body, spilling ink onto his hands and the table alike. Dinsmere sucked in a sharp breath and gave a look of disgust. He knew enough not to interrupt a practitioner mid-stream, however. Gwisen buried the gold nib among the shredded paper.

Then he unstopped the ink bottle and dumped its contents over the pile of paper. He slammed the empty glass bottle against the table and sprinkled the broken shards over the ink-soaked paper. Finally, he closed his eyes and listened for the spirits of this strange place.

Instead of a whisper, Gwisen heard a cacophony. Spirits everywhere, so many of them Shawdese, but also from Vrinth and Meltenios and other places he had no name for. They battered his perceptions, screaming with rage. Gwisen had never seen, never felt anything like this before. The sheer frustration and rage swirling around this place surged like a raging sea, unthinkable fathoms deep. A stiff wind began to swirl around him.

Gwisen had barely thought of his desperate and reckless offer when he was battered by spirits clamoring to take him up on the bargain. Gwisen offered his rage, his pain and anger, and his desperate hope for retribution. More than he'd ever offered before, so much that he didn't know what would be left of him afterward.

"How are you doing this?" Dinsmere called from behind Gwisen. "Such a swell of energy. Explain it to me, Shawdese! Are you drawing ambient magic from the environment? Do you understand what you're doing?"

Gwisen ignored Dinsmere's prattle and focused on one voice thundering above the din. The spirit bore the shape and texture of a Shawdese spirit, similar to one of the ancestral guardians that had once watched over and protected his people. But this ancient behemoth was like nothing he knew existed—no stories told of anything like this. Then again, so many stories had been lost when the Shawdese were forced from their lands. Wind battered Gwisen's face, but he held fast.

Gwisen chose the ancient guardian and dismissed the others. The bargain was struck.

"How?" Dinsmere shouted above the winds that had suddenly engulfed the room. "Such forces! This shouldn't be possible. Tell me, Shawdese, how do you do it? "

Gwisen's eyes snapped open. His rage and frustration kindled themselves within him. Some of his earliest memories were lessons his mothers had taught with a fire-sap switch—always remain deferential to Thersians. Never show emotion, never provoke them, and in doing so, risk no retribution. The smell of ash and lightning filled his nostrils. He couldn't do it any longer.

"I don't owe you anything," Gwisen said, his voice clear and filled with all the anger he'd never allowed himself to express. Now, it flowed through him, and he wove it into his breath. He exhaled, and the spirit awoke.

The wind spun and swirled and gained speed, and whipped the pile of ink-soaked paper and broken glass into a dust-devil with a roughly human shape, as tall as Gwisen himself. Lightning flickered under its paper skin and when it moved, the sound of glass shards grinding filled the room. It took a step toward Dinsmere, and the empiricist backpedaled.

"How? Tell me, Shawdese, how do you do it?"

Gwisen shrugged. "It's beyond your grasp."

The spirit seemed to draw in breath and the winds whipping around the room gathered speed. Now, everything in the room shuddered. Books flew off their shelves, only to be torn into ragged chunks by the razor winds. The delicate assembly of blown glass vials and tubes shattered and the dust and broken pieces were whipped aloft.

The debris spun around the room and like a drain emptying, were drawn into the spirit, adding to its bulk. In a span of seconds, the spirit grew to gargantuan size, its featureless head brushing against the rafters twenty feet above.

Dinsmere began waving his arms in complicated gestures, shouting words that were lost in the wind. Flashes of light and energy flared from his fingertips and were snuffed out on the skin of the guardian spirit.

Gwisen watched but did not intervene. There would be so little of himself left after this smoldering rage—perhaps nothing at all. He'd offered up his hate, and the thirst for revenge he'd refused to admit, even to himself. It had all flowed into the spirit.

The spirit smashed walls and bookshelves and the debris accumulated within it, fueling it and growing its bulk.

"Make it cease. Dismiss it," Dinsmere called out over the roaring winds.

Gwisen felt no desire to stop it, even if such a thing were possible. There was nothing in his people's legends about this. As the spirit reduced the room's contents to splinters, he wondered what else the Empiricists had eradicated from the Shawdese's collective memory. What else had been hidden from them? Perhaps after generations, the Empiricists had themselves forgotten. Perhaps they now believed their own lies about the dirt-eating savages, forgetting what dangers lurked beneath the surface.

"Please!" Dinsmere screamed as the winds buffeted him, as hunks of wood and shards of glass cut his skin. "I can pay you. I can give you whatever you want! Make it stop!"

"I don't want anything you have to give," Gwisen said, and they were the truest words he'd ever spoken.

Gwisen closed his eyes, and he felt the sting of the whips and the beatings he'd endured over the years. He saw the faces of starving Shawdese children, of a line of displaced families stretching to the horizon. He smelled the acrid stench of branding irons pressed to flesh. He wove his story, and the story of his people, into his breath. He exhaled, and gave even more to the spirit: the pain, the anger and the memories, but especially the hope and determination to survive. And then he set it free.

As the room crumbled, as the guardian spirit fed upon the empty Thersian words and stolen artifacts and built a vast and terrible skin for itself, Gwisen smiled. He'd come back to Thersian lands to swindle a bit of the empire's coin to send back to his people, and in his darker moments, he'd wondered if Thersia was more of a home to him than with his mothers in the southern wastes. But now, he understood.

He had seen both sides of the world, he had been branded with both the stories of his people and the indoctrination of the empire. Gwisen stood at those crossroads, finally able to unleash this whirlwind. Rippled with lightning and fire, the guardian spirit began pulling down the stone walls of the Empiricist's stronghold, and in the destruction, Gwisen saw hope.

AUTHOR NOTES

This story had been bouncing around in my head in a half-formed state for a few years before I finally wrote it. I wanted to play with the idea that in a fantasy world, magic isn't just energy and power: it's also the expression of a worldview. From the start, I had an initial image of a busker on the street, playing with some little bit of flashy and crowd-pleasing magic, only to be confronted by an imperious and powerful magician, but there was little else.

It wasn't until I thought seriously about the power dynamics between a representative of a hierarchical magic orthodoxy and an untrained, intuitive, but nonetheless powerful street magician, that the real core of the story suggested itself to me. The horrors of settler colonialism, the guilt and uncertainty of an indigenous survivor who's been forced to live in both worlds—indigenous and colonized—turned out to be the perfect canvas on which to paint this argument between two magical practitioners and their respective worldviews.

So, from that half-formed idea, this ended up being a story that let me explore the industrial-scale cruelty of colonial powers, the erasure of history and identity that goes along with it, and crucially, the cheap commodification that digests an entire culture and leaves behind only sterile trinkets and false forgiveness.

WHEN EVENING ARRIVES

TIFFANY MORRIS

Before they arrived, the visitors announced it by radio: signals traversing galaxies, warping time and particle. Syllables spelled out in numbers and strange hieroglyphs confirming presence and arrival.

Stella knew that there had been stories of people who lived in the stars, the world above the sky, and the people from Earth who'd visited them: holes that opened in the cosmos and had people waking up beyond the stratosphere, staring from above the clouds and down into their old home. There were newer stories, too, of strange lights blinking gold and green, streaking across the heavens, hovering as they hummed a chromatic machine chorus over the sleeping ink-black world below.

What did they want? An anthropological survey. Earth had gasped back into life with cyborg rhizomes, machine seeds scattering hope that stretched horizon to horizon. Metal merged with the primordial: synthetic, but alive, the world breathed green once again. Unama'ki, where Stella lived, had been returned to Mi'kmaq stewardship before she was even born, and Stella was part of her community's organization that took care of the wetlands. Every time she walked through the swamp, the understanding of time immemorial shone blue sky bright and deep as the shimmering Atlantic that swelled a few kilometers up the coast.

The visitors came in peace. They just wanted to see the restoration. Of course. People were excited to meet the visitors. Of course.

If everything was alive, everything was constantly changing and life was constantly in the sacred process of creating, then, Stella supposed, it was possible that would include life off this planet and in other worlds. Still, trepidation lingered.

She'd visited the welcome mawiomi, participated in the ceremonies, smiled at the people gathered with signs of welcome in Mi'kmaq and Gaelic. She stood and watched drummers making music that was heartbeat beautiful in her family's hands.

She tried to ignore the fear and doubt clenching her fists shut. Invasion wouldn't have to be laser beams dissolving tall buildings to rubble. They all knew that much.

On the edge of what had once been the reserve, the visitors met with Elders and other members of the community. They were shiny Brocken-spectre human shadows ringed with oil-slick rainbow light.

It was the closest approximation to a human they could do, they'd said, a tinny, apologetic tone to their voice. They'd wanted to take a welcoming shape. Energy radiated off them like warm sunlight. It was a word, softly spoken.

Stella still tried not to look at them. They were preparing to walk the marshland. The late afternoon light illuminated the golden sheen on the hybrid trees.

"Kwe', cuz. We're going to go to the Old Willow." Maryann, her cousin, walked up to her.

Panic jumped up Stella's throat.

"But we can't, it's protected."

"E'e, just the edge of it," Maryann said, "not actually to the whole thing. Clara wants to show them the sunset there."

Worry surged in her veins. What if they damaged it? They'd all worked so hard to keep that old part of the land as original as possible. The willow had survived for hundreds of years.

"Okay," Stella said. "I'm definitely coming too, then." She didn't know if she'd need to stop them, but she would do anything to protect that tree.

Clara, an Elder and Stella's ex-girlfriend's grandmother, led the group. Her clear, strong voice switched seamlessly between English and Mi'kmaq as she identified the trees: ksu'sk, hemlock, stoqn, fir. The shadows beamed and dimmed as they walked, their metallic hum echoing in the humid air.

The visitors explained that time was a spiderweb, each moment a star in a small constellation stretching blue and bright. Clara explained our language, how things are known by what they do, that colors are alive and act as verbs. The visitors shone brighter and emitted a crackling sound at that. Clara chuckled.

"You'll see," she said.

They walked the twenty-minute hike to Old Willow. Stella tried not to jump every time the visitors' brightness changed or when they emitted strange sounds. Maryann wasn't bothered at all by their appearance or their presence.

"I knew it," she kept saying. "I always knew they were real." She didn't take her eyes off them.

They reached the edge of the authentic marsh where the Old Willow bowed to the still water. Reeds jutted from the soft brown-green shallows.

The visitors tried to move closer.

"Stop," Stella yelled. Everyone in the group looked at her. Some laughed.

Clara smiled at the visitors. "This area is protected. We can't go any further. Just wait."

The shadows retreated back a few steps. The sunlight stretched and sank closer to the tops of the trees. People laughed among themselves, making peaceful, happy conversation. Stella allowed herself to calm.

Sunset deepened pink and orange over the water. Frogs croaked in the distance.

"See," Clara said. "Piluamugwiaq ugs'tqamu wejgwiula'gw. The world changes color when evening arrives."

The shadows crackled campfire bright, their rainbow rings whirling around them. The moment stretched infinite around them all, another constellation caught in the spider's web.

AUTHOR NOTES

"When Evening Arrives" was written while I was working on my thesis about contemporary Indigenous apocalypse narratives and Indigenous Futurism. The central idea that I explored in my thesis focused on how the end of one world can signal the beginning of another, and what shape a decolonized futurism might take from those vantage points of an apocalypse. It was very important to me, in my academic and creative work, to examine the strange and unexpected futures that might emerge in the swamps of uncertainty—a detail that appears more literally in the cyborg connections of plant life in the story.

At the time, I was craving specifically Indigenous utopian stories, and wanted to write one myself. It was something that I found especially challenging as a horror writer, where mining the uncertainty of the past, present, and future tends to center on instability and crisis. The focus on apocalypse that I'd had for so long in my academic and creative work, in addition to the apocalyptic conditions of life during a pandemic and climate change, made me hungry for stories of a world well past crisis and collapse, where the nascent possibilities from that time had come into fruition and connectivity. Envisioning a healed Mi'kma'ki and an encounter with extraterrestrial beings made me consider what that healing would look like—and how uncertainty, trauma, and history can make us cautious but open to what emerges in the spaces between the present and the ever-unfolding future.

AN INCIDENT AT HELLPOINT PRIME

NORRIS BLACK

It was a full five days before the colonists of Hellpoint Prime realized a skin thief had infiltrated the habitats.

"Any idea who they were?" Sheriff Vahla hugged his parka tighter to his skinny frame as frosty air from the cooler vents fogged up his glasses. He pulled them down his nose for an unobstructed look at the bodies and immediately wished he hadn't. "Christ. Poor bastards."

The bastards in question, four of them, hung by the heels from lengths of rusting chains. Their bodies swayed in the frigid air pumping through the refrigerator vents, bloody outstretched fingers inches from the concrete floor. The height at which they'd been strung put their mutilated genitalia right at eye level, much to the sheriff's distress.

"Impossible to say. All hair, eyes, and teeth have been removed, along with their skin, of course. I can tell you we're looking at three men and two women." Deputy Clovis reached out and gave one of the corpses a gentle push and watched dispassionately as it swung back and forth.

"Well, thank you for that masterclass in detective work deputy. It's gratifying to know you've stayed current with your penis counting skills." He regretted the words the moment he spoke them. The whole scene had him on edge. The ancient deputy had been a guard at the outpost for as long as anyone could remember. According to his file, he was somewhere north of fifty but looked closer to two hundred, and he was the most unflappable person the sheriff had ever met. Given the current circumstances,

Vahla wouldn't have minded if the old security officer had been willing to be just a little flappable.

Clovis grinned, a yellowing barricade with a black hole punched in from a tooth long gone missing. His whole face wrinkled up when he did it, and Vahla was reminded of a jack-o'-lantern left out in the rain a little too long.

"What about missing person reports?" Vahla pushed the wire-rimmed round glasses back into place and took a step back from the hanging bodies. Wreckages that had once been walking, talking people just like him.

The deputy sucked air through the gap in his teeth before replying. "Missing persons count is in the triple digits, like always. You know how it is. Folks moving around all the time in the underbelly and none of them leaving forward addresses. That's not including the ones that dip a little too deep into the shine and accidentally step out an unsecured airlock on their way to the pisser."

"That last one was oddly specific."

Clovis shrugged. "Happened just last week. A fella who worked in one of the combine stacks. Research team on their way back from Hellpoint Secondus found his desiccated body, though it's impossible to say how long he'd been there. Could've been hours, could've been months. The atmosphere out there drinks a man dry to the last drop like a straw jammed into a nutri-bag."

"Why wasn't I notified?"

"Shit, sir, if you plan on an official report being filed for every accidental death, you're not going to have time to do anything but sit behind your desk and collect paperwork."

A sigh. "Fair enough. So, we're looking at some sort of mass murderer? Has that ever happened out here before?"

The unexpected look of incredulity on the deputy's round face would've been comical if it wasn't so concerning, thought Vahla.

"I know you're new here and all sir but … hell, didn't they tell you anything before they sent you?"

"Anything about what exactly?" The sheriff hugged his body tight again in an attempt to stave off the chill creeping through his flesh.

Clovis rubbed his hands together and blew on them for warmth. "I think you're going to want a sit down and something burning away in your belly first. I can have the lads come down and take the bodies off to Doc Butcher for examination. How abouts you buy me a round at the Broken Wheel and I'll tell you all about the skin thieves of Hellpoint Prime?"

The skin thief crouched in the air duct and watched through the thin slits of the vent cover as the two men walked away. It had nearly been caught by the pair and only managed to scramble up into a vent at the last second. It plucked at its new skin, still wet and sagging where it clung to its rib cage. The lurker could feel it already beginning to deteriorate. It wasn't the right fit and soon he'd need a new one. And that thin human looked to be just the right size.

The Broken Wheel had once been part of the machinery that ran ag-stack four. A mammoth tooth-rimmed wheel set horizontally at the bottom of a silo, stretching close to fifty feet across, reaching the grimy silo walls on all sides. At one time it would've rotated slowly, in turn moving smaller cogs inset into the silo's walls but something deep in the warren of gears, pulleys, and counterweights had broken, bringing the whole clockwork operation to a halt. Whatever broke was deemed unrepairable by Home Office and ag sector four had closed down. A few years after that an enterprising group of mechanics cut a doorway leading onto the wheel's now stationary surface as a place to set up a clandestine shine distillery. Over time, the distillery evolved into a full-on drinking establishment complete with one long serving bar welded together from scrap metal plates. Since then, it had become a regular haunt for the poor souls toiling away in the artificial sunshine of the agricultural combine stacks or those drudging away in the gloomy mechanized habitat's underbelly. The Broken Wheel had been part of Vahla's briefing when he'd been assigned the new sheriff of the far-flung ag outpost. It wasn't an officially recognized enterprise, but the suits back on Earth had decided giving the men and women of Hellpoint Prime a place to indulge was a business net positive. Any loss in productivity caused by the rotgut alcohol was more than offset by the subsequent drop in the suicide rate. Shipping new workers across the stars was expensive, after all. As always, the lives of generations of laborers were decided by red and green lines on a graph.

Vahla took a sip of what tasted like someone had figured out how to render human misery down to a liquid form and then put it on tap. He made a face and placed his tumbler on the table with a metallic clink. For his part, Clovis threw back a hearty swig and smacked his lips in satisfaction.

"I'm reasonably certain that is actual poison," said Vahla with a frown as he felt the harsh liquid squirming around in his gut like a thing alive.

"Aye, one of these days I expect it'll burn all the way through my gut and out my arse and melt this very stool I perch upon. But until that day, I plan on enjoying one of the few pleasures this hole can offer."

"Now there's an image I could've done without."

"There's lots of ways to die out here sheriff and most are a lot less pleasant than that." As if to make his point he winked and swallowed another mouthful of the greasy, clear liquid.

"So, tell me about these, what did you call them, skin thieves? I'll be honest, that's not exactly an encouraging name." Vahla took another sip of his drink, more from absentminded habit than desire, and almost spit the whole thing out again. The liquid burned the back of his throat, causing him to cough uncontrollably. Clovis reached across the table and pounded the red-faced sheriff on the back until the fire had subsided.

Leaning back in his chair the deputy played his tongue in his tooth hole while he thought about his next words.

"What do you know about Hellpoint's indigenous species?"

"Hellpoint doesn't have any indigenous species. It's a barren wasteland on a dirtball of a planet hostile to life. It's one of the reasons the Home Office chose it for its crystal helium mining operation." As far as Vahla was concerned, Hellpoint Prime was nothing more than a cancerous sore on the face of an even bigger cancerous sore. Even the name of the place was a mistake, some clerical error that turned Heli-point to Hellpoint which no one bothered to correct. To be fair, Hellpoint was a fitting name.

"Is that the official history now is it? Well, I can't say as I'm surprised. You spend enough time out here and you quickly find what the official line is and what actually happened to have only the barest resemblance to one another. How about you tell me what you think you know, and I'll tell you where it's wrong."

Sheriff Vahla adjusted his glasses as he considered the words of his walking corpse of a deputy. "Crystal helium was discovered here a little over two hundred years ago, in Earth revolutions. The planet was rich in deposits and devoid of any other life. Shortly after, Home Office established the first combine stack—mining operations on the bottom and ag-domes to keep the workforce fed on top. Since then, there have been another ... eight combine stacks put in place plus more at Hellpoint Secondus and Hellpoint Tertius."

"Mostly right. You see, Home Office thought the planet didn't have anything living on it. That was until they cracked the crust and found a whole hive of critters living down there with their precious helium. Couldn't have that, could they? They dropped a few viral bombs in the hole, cleared out the bodies, and went back to work."

Vahla squinted as he studied his deputy's face as he waited for a grin or a guffaw to punctuate the wild tale he was telling but the normally affable Clovis was stone serious and, by his expression, any attempt at levity would be as welcome as a fart at a funeral. The young sheriff lifted his cup and paused before giving the contents of his cup a suspicious eye. He set the tumbler down and pushed it away from him. "That settles it. This stuff is most certainly poison. Or at least has some powerful hallucinogenic properties. What you're saying doesn't make any sense."

"Oh, it doesn't, eh? Home Office was investing a fortune in an off-world drilling facility. You think they'd shy away at the thought of clearing out an alien anthill that happened to get in their way and then covering the whole thing up like it never happened? You know the suits. They would've ordered the bombs be dropped and then nipped off for an afternoon of tea and hookers."

The sheriff wiped sweat from his forehead. The Broken Wheel sat close to the power generators and the place was always about three degrees above raging inferno. "Let's say I buy that, and I'm not saying that I do. How does this tie into a cooler unit filled with flayed corpses?"

"Well, there's something to keep in mind about aliens. They're alien, as in they don't necessarily line up nice and clean with our understanding of the universe. The first body showed up around a month into production. Some poor meth farmer found laying in the dirt of one of the agri-habs, skinned clean. A few days later he's found wandering one of the lower halls."

"Wait, he didn't die?" Vahla shuddered at the thought of being skinned alive and walking around like that for days.

"Oh no, he was absolutely dead. Cremated too, a dozen witnesses attested to watching his corpse being thrown into the incinerator."

The sheriff decided to chance further organ damage his drink was going to cause and took a gulp. Tears sprung to his eyes as he held back a second coughing fit. "You've officially lost me."

"Well, this farmer had seemingly found his skin and was wearing it like an ill-fitting suit of clothes. Hear tell, it was torn and ragged from where it had been pulled back on. As you can probably guess, it turned out it wasn't the farmer at all."

Vahla's stomach roiled at that, and he wished he had thought to put some food in there before filling it up with whatever witch's brew they made in this place.

The deputy had a faraway look on his sunken gourd of a face as he continued his tale. "Whatever it was, it killed half a dozen workers before it was finally put down. Autopsy showed a 'preponderance of unknown DNA,' which is just fancy talk for 'alien.'"

"Are you saying one of these so-called aliens didn't die, crawled out of a hole, cut off a man's skin, and then went for a stroll around the lower stacks?" The liquid evil in Vahla's stomach lurched, like some sort of turgid eel slithering over itself while it frantically sought an exit. His head pounded, and he was certain the wheel from which the bar took its name was functional again and moving at a slow rotation.

"You're looking a little green there, sheriff," said Clovis with a grin. "Anyways, that was only the first time. There was a real bad stretch about twenty years ago, though there haven't been any sightings in at least five years. Here's the funny thing, the skin thieves weren't all the same. Each one killed and examined ranged from nearly pure alien to almost all the way human."

A horrible realization dawned on the young law keeper, punching through the haze of his thoughts. "They were becoming human."

"You are a bright one aren't ya? There's been a couple of theories thrown around over the years. Some say the thieves are adapting, some sort of rapid evolutionary response to the now dominant species on the planet. Others think the viral load in the bombs combined Earth organisms with alien organisms that spit out these abominations on the other end. Hell, Doc thinks they're created beasties, constructs made from some unknown tech designed to take us out. Like introducing a predator into an ecosystem overrun by an invasive species."

"And what do you think?"

"I think whatever they are, whatever they want to do to us, we deserve it." And then the rumpled deputy threw back his head and laughed like he had just told the best joke ever heard by man.

Vahla didn't join in.

The walk back to Sheriff Vahla's bunk was an adventure. the floor feeling like it was tilting to and fro like he was on a ship at sea instead of sunk half a mile below the surface of a barren planet.

The constant thrum and clang of machinery that echoed all throughout combine stacks wasn't doing much for an equilibrium already under assault from the ill-conceived imbibing of several cups of alcohol of questionable origin. Drinking to excess was out of character for the reserved lawman, but Clovis' horrifying bedtime stories, along with the persistent vision of crimson-dipped bodies swaying in darkness, had given the young sheriff a whole bunch of edges he was desperate to dull.

Hellpoint was not the place he had hoped to end up when he entered the academy. It wasn't a place anyone hoped to end up. The facility was a grinder pulling in lives at one end and spitting refined helium out the other.

"Fek you! I'm not spending my life in this hole. I'm gonna do my four-year tour and get the hell out," he said with all the articulation of a man who had fallen down a flight of stairs and hit his head on every other step. The metal wall-mounted grate he yelled at had no rebuttal.

He took a few unsteady steps down the hall and then paused. The sheriff thought he had caught a new sound momentarily cutting through the usual cacophony. Vahla cocked his head and listened, but it didn't come again. It had been a rattling sound, like claws on steel, and it had come from the grated vent he was yelling at a moment ago.

"Feking rats." Despite planet-transfer quarantine measures, enough rats still managed to hitch a ride across the stars on Home Office ships to set up a small colony within the combine walls. Images pried their way into fuzzy thoughts. Red flesh coated with a rime of frost. Screaming, toothless faces. Vahla shook the thoughts free and continued forward in his newborn deer stride. *It wasn't a skin-thieving alien horror. It was just rats.* He repeated this litany to himself over and over as he picked up speed, finally breaking into a mad run as he rounded the corner into the hallway leading to his bunk. The last thing the lawman expected was for a person to be standing dead in his path. The collision sent two pairs of arms and legs pinwheeling through the air with a muffled frump and a duet of cries—one of surprise and the other of terror.

"Bloody hell!"

Vahla visibly relaxed at the irascible tone he recognized as belonging to Doc Butcher. The squat physician was the facility's chief medical officer and spent most of his days treating radiation burns and dealing with the horrendous wounds dished out by the slamming pistons and ripping cog teeth of an industrial complex where safety precautions were the first thing to be thrown out the window. Most times, a limb was too mangled to save, at which point out came the pneumatic cleaver. Most workers could still fulfill their duties shy an arm or a leg, and amputations were cheaper than long-term care and rehabilitation.

Doc Butcher wasn't a name—in fact, Vahla didn't know the grumpy physician's actual name—it was a mixture of professions.

"Christ, sheriff, if you're going to turn the hallways into your own personal racetrack, at least have the courtesy to stick to the friggin' outside lane." The good doctor had come to rest with his back against one wall, white hair wild and a pair of wide, dark-rimmed glasses sitting askew on his broad face.

Vahla had ended up in a crumpled heap with his shoulders against the ground and his lanky legs spilled clumsily over his head like a pair of tall, wilted trees. He righted himself and helped the glaring physician to his feet. The adrenaline surge had burned away much of the fog clouding his brain, and he felt a little foolish about his mad dash. "Sorry, doc."

"Where the hell are you going in such a hurry?"

"Umm, just trying to get a little exercise in. You're always telling me how important that is."

A harrumph. "Well, keep your runs to the agri-domes and not across my face in the future, alright? I'm too old to be stampeded by some youngster with more energy than sense."

"Hey, have you had a chance to examine the bodies yet?" asked the sheriff, desperate to change the subject.

"Bodies? What bodies?"

"The ones Clovis sent down. You know, five of them, missing … um … you know … their skin." Vahla whispered the last two words, doing a quick check over his shoulder to ensure they were alone. He didn't want to send the whole facility into a panic. He had enough panic all by himself.

The blood drained from Doc Butcher's face in a way Vahla found especially non-reassuring. The grizzled doctor could teach a twisted iron nail how to be tough and here he was looking like a small boy who just discovered a severed head under his bed. "Did you say they were missing their skin?"

That quaver, so out of place in the grouchy physician's raspy voice, was enough to make Vahla want to go have a lie down somewhere—preferably behind a locked and barricaded door—and forget this day ever happened. Duty called, however. "Clovis was spinning me some fanciful tale on what it meant," said the sheriff with a forced smile. "Messing with the new guy and all that."

Doc Butcher didn't seem to hear him. "It can't be. I thought that was all behind us. We haven't had a skin thief in what, five, six, years now."

"Wait? Are you telling me it's true? The alien species, the viral bombing, all of it?"

"What? Yes, yes. Didn't they cover any of that in your briefing? No, I suppose they'd rather the whole messy business be forgotten about." Doc Butcher had gotten a hold of himself, the familiar grizzled facade reasserting itself on the physician's wrinkled features. "I haven't seen them yet, but I'll check in with Clovis." He peered at Vahla closely, the kind of look that peeled back layers to see the meat of the matter beneath. Surgery by stare. "You're looking a little raw around the edges there, sheriff. How bout you get some rest, and we can talk more in the morning."

With that, Doc Butcher clapped the lawman on the shoulder and continued off down the hallway. Vahla couldn't help but notice the nervous way he looked over his shoulder every few steps.

The sheriff of Hellpoint Prime made the short trip the rest of the way to his bunk without incident, sighing as the solid steel door clanged shut behind him and the deadbolt slammed home.

"Deadbolt. Couldn't pick a better name for the bloody thing, could they?" The adrenaline had worn off and Vahla was worn out. He wanted nothing more than to slip under the scratchy thin blanket laid out on his cot and sleep for the next three hundred years, not even taking the time to change into the gray pajamas folded neatly at the foot of the bed.

Sleep came in spurts, punctuated by unsettling dreams. Flayed corpses crawling across the ceiling towards his sleeping form. Being chased through a labyrinth of steel corridors by monstrous rats the size of cattle. Swinging through the air on oily chains as a scalpel stung his soft flesh.

When he woke hours later, he felt more tired than when he first laid down, yawning widely and rubbing sand from his eyes. The first indication something was wrong was the smell. The bunks riddling the bowels of the combine stacks had a neat universal stink to them. A combination of engine oil, mildew, and stale air. A new smell overlaid the familiar one. Cloyingly sweet and rotten at the same time, felt in the back of the throat as much as smelled.

As he was trying to sort out the origin of the unexpected stench, a careless step sent a metal grate skittering across the steel floor. Vahla stared at it, the mechanisms of his mind churning slowly as they tried to sort out the significance of this innocuous chunk of slatted metal. His gaze floated over to the gaping black hole in the far wall leading to the habitat's air exchange system. A hole that, when he had gone to sleep, had been covered by the grate now laying on the floor a good six feet away from it.

"Oh f—" A sharp pain lanced through his left knee as the bloody tip of a knife erupted from the center of his kneecap. He howled in pain and something heavy slammed into his back, taking him down to the floor. More by instinct than plan the beleaguered sheriff twisted to his back and kicked out with his good leg. A dark and indistinct figure flew back, smashing a rickety nightstand to jagged bits.

Vahla scrambled across the floor and put his back to the wall before getting a good look at his attacker. The dim nighttime lighting and the fact the near-sighted sheriff had taken his glasses off before bed made fine details difficult to make out. What he could see was more than enough. His assailant squatted on the floor at the foot of the cot, long-limbed and spindly, it resembled some sort of predator insect. In one hand it held a razor-edged knife that curved at strange and obscene angles. It looked more grown than made and dripped with blood, Vahla's torn knee pulsing in time with the crimson drops pattering on the floor. Black eyes, like hard stones, stared out of a red ruin of stretched skin, the raw muscles showing beneath rents in a stolen face. The alien also appeared to have donned Vahla's pajamas sometime in the night, patches of blood a shocking scarlet on the otherwise gray garment.

The thief sprung forward and the injured sheriff kicked out with his good leg, only to feel the sickening drag of a razor-honed blade slicing a deep line through the sole of his foot. Vahla pulled his foot back with a curse and tears began to run down his flushed cheeks. Whether they were tears of pain or fear he couldn't say. Likely a bit of both.

The kick had done the trick though, at least for now, as the thief crab-crawled back and forth in front of him, waiting for an opening. Vahla cast about desperately. Screaming for help would do no good, no one would hear him through the thick steel walls and the ever-present churn of the refinery machines. His eyes fell on his heavy jacket where it was slung over the back of his writing desk chair. The butt of his Snub-gun peeked out from where it rested inside the holster built into the lining of the coat. It was maybe three feet away. A quick lunge and he'd have it in hand. He darted a look at the skin thief. It seemed to be working up the nerve to launch another attack, pacing back and forth, moving forward a small half-step before skittering back again. As it did so it made a reverberating mewling sound in the back of its throat that reminded Vahla of a litter of angry kittens.

Vahla knew he didn't have much time. Both his knee and foot screamed in pain and blood had begun to pool around him.

"Sir? You okay in there?"

Vahla nearly fainted in relief as the muffled sound of Clovis's voice carried through the closed steel door.

His attacker rested back on its haunches, head tilting one way and then the other at the unexpected sound. The skin around the alien's neck pulled tight and tore. Vahla's stomach surged and he added a pool of vomit to the blood already slicking the steel plates of the floor.

While keeping one eye on the horror in front of him the injured sheriff called out.

"It's in here! I've been hurt!"

A muffled curse was the response, followed by a rattling sound as Clovis fished a key into the door's lock. Vahla was thankful that it was standard operating procedure that all security personnel carry a master key on them.

A moment later the deputy burst through the door and nearly went down as his foot slipped in the puddle of blood and bile slowly expanding around Vahla's injured form. A windmill of arms punctuated by an even louder curse was the only thing preventing him from landing on his backside.

Clovis took in the scene at a glance, slipping his stun rod out of the holster on his hip and flipping the switch to the "On" setting. A low-level hum that made Vahla's teeth itch filled the room. The stun rods could be juiced anywhere from just enough to shock a drunk from his stupor all the way up to a jolt powerful enough to leave a grown man senseless with one touch. Judging by the sound, the wrinkled deputy had his set on high.

The skin thief shrunk back at the hum as if in fright.

"That's okay lad, I'm here now. Everything's going to be fine."

Vahla was torn between relief at the words of comfort from his deputy and a small amount of annoyance at being spoken to like he was a child. It took a moment longer before he realized Clovis hadn't been talking to him.

Most of that realization came by way of a stun rod being pressed to the side of his neck.

Every muscle in Vahla's body seized tight and his jaw clamped together so hard he thought his teeth might shatter and spray across the room. The sheriff thrashed on the floor, splattering blood and vomit everywhere, and he felt his bowels loosen, the final indignity.

Clovis leaned down and put his face close to the sheriff's, a wry smile creasing his puckered and wrinkled face. A face that looked like a mask. "You'll have to excuse him, sheriff, the new ones tend to be a little wild when they first hatch. Some days my own birth feels like yesterday, others like it was a hundred years ago." The creature masquerading as a deputy bent down and examined Vahla's ragged wounds as they continued to spurt blood onto the floor. "He didn't make too much of a mess, these'll stitch up just fine."

Vahla could only stare in horror, his body still seized up from the effects of the stun rod, any last words he might've said locked inside his thin frame. A high-pitched keening echoed in the room before fading.

Clovis looked over his shoulder at the skin thief before turning back to Vahla and pulling a twisted bone knife from inside his jacket.

"You're right lad. He's just your size."

JASON SIZEMORE

Sometimes you think you know people, but you have no idea at all. When I read "An Incident at Hellpoint Prime" I worried that *Apex Magazine* readers would not like the story. Myself, I greatly enjoyed it. But this is a more traditional sci-horror story and, honestly, I can't remember publishing something like this in years.

My worries were wasted. Our readers loved the story. Great job by Norris Black for writing a tense and visceral horror tale and Allison Mills for selecting it for publication!

TO SEEK HIMSELF AGAIN

MARIE CROKE

The lady possessed all her fingers. Even the useless fifths wiggled in obscure movements as she stroked the vines drooping from the terrariums and grazing the aquariums below. With curiosity bordering on the obscene, Keba sank the viper's coils that made up his neck that he might gander at the lady's feet, but they were tucked away neatly inside laced boots. If she'd traded a toe away, it had not been for something larger. And if she had traded for anything at all, she had hidden it so completely that she might as well never have. What a waste.

"I'm told you're the creature to ask when in need of parts."

Her voice held the plainness of a pure form. No chirping of a cricket or haunting echo of a wood thrush harmonizing behind each syllable. Ugly, he'd have called it, had he not been striving for professionalism.

He hissed deep in this throat, then nodded and altered his voice so an original human creature might hear all he spoke. "What will it be?"

"A third eye."

He shifted, but didn't have to straighten his front legs—goat they were, hooves strong and nimble—for he merely stretched his viperous neck joints until he looked within one of the aquariums.

"I've wolf and feline, eagle and shark. I've also insects: spider, cricket, ant, and many others. And if you could afford a steeper trade there's another tier."

"A witch's eye."

Keba hissed again, though this time he tried to cover it. "Another human's?" He glared her over with his phoenix eye—fiery little thing it was, always lightly burning in a pleasant, easy way.

Her braided hair, dark and thick, hung like rope down her back, but was not of another creature. Her arms, her shoulders, the muscles of her back and thighs, and the curve of her calves all bore signs of singularity. Her eyes, her nose, her mouth, her *everything*—

"Is that a problem?"

He ground teeth he'd traded from a sabertooth, but did not hiss again. "I know of a witch who might be willing to trade. What would you offer in return?"

"I'll pay with land."

He scoffed and then recoiled viscerally when the lady's eyes—gray and powerfully intense—narrowed. With another hiss and a chittering of his tail that he then tucked promptly under himself to avoid the embarrassment again, he sank further into his cushions.

"I work in trade, lady." Voice now deepening with a bear's light grumble—all the beast had been willing to part with. "Trade in parts and pieces, in bits and bunches. Not in metals or grains or rough, old spits of earth."

"New land," she said, her narrowed eyes shrinking to slits. "Land I've created with receding water. I'll give you the fish there and let you have their gills. I'll give you the octopuses so you might pick apart their suckers. But you will not lay your knives on me."

Land she created ...

"Then I cannot work with you."

Oh, Keba knew the moment the words hissed past his teeth that they'd been a mistake, a horrible, mindless mistake. He twisted in on himself, tail catching, hooves skidding, neck curling in sudden panic as the lady tapped her finger against the nearest terrarium. The glass shattered, flinging through his home, little weapons piercing cougar skin, tearing an elephant nose, slicing spider legs in thirds. He shivered and covered his face with his hands, his heart pattering and squeezing in fear.

"Your toes!" His shout muffled by his hands. "A few fingers! Maybe an ear or your heel or just a slip of scalp? I would not dare ask for something more dear."

"Everything is dear to me. I am not parts to be frittered away. I am the sum." She reached out her finger to touch an aquarium.

"But you're already powerful! You don't need a third eye to see."

"The world hangs in the balance and you argue with me about what I am and what I need."

She touched the aquarium and Keba ducked as water gushed down the stand and splashed across the wooden floorboards. Soggy frog fingers and fish gills and a single, perfect dolphin fin flopped across the floor.

"What do you mean, hangs in the balance?" he growled out with the bear's strong voice. He peeked between mismatched fingers.

The lady's eyes softened. "Oh, you poor thing."

Thing?

"Such a hodgepodge of creatures, no true form, no direction."

Keba scowled and began to straighten up from his now water-splattered cushions. Then he jerked back as the lady lifted her finger to another terrarium and held it there.

"The world is falling apart, being cut and torn and put back together, bursting at the seams, ready to explode."

"Is it?"

Keba surreptitiously bent, keeping his head in place, and scooped up the dolphin fin. He'd traded a black ram's horns for it, after all. He cradled the fin in his lap, uncaring that it soaked through his pants.

"I need the eye to see the way to the Shrine of the Original Creation."

"Oh."

"To set things right."

Keba remained silent, careful not to glare at the lady.

"A third eye. I'll be back tomorrow." She looked around his home, at the skins draped through the low rafters, at the jars of ears and noses and fingers, at the hooves and paws and claws and talons lined up in perfect, organized rows on wooden shelves. Then she looked back to Keba with sorrow in her eyes. "Tomorrow. Please don't make me ruin the rest."

"I'll find it," he agreed miserably and wished he'd had the bravery to argue with her further, or better yet, tell her to drown herself at her shrine. But he merely watched her go, her form singular and unchanged from birth. Unnatural and terrifying.

With a gourd almost as large as himself strapped to his back, Keba set out that very evening. The sun sank quickly, sending an amber wash across the pockets of marshy land dipping toward the ocean, white blurs of herons just barely visible. As he strode with his unique gait, the gourd's ties bit into the feathers of his shoulders and his tail scraped at it repetitively in a quiet protest of this outing. Bat-winged rabbits froze their nibbling at his passing, but he paid them no mind.

The air smelled of danger—that scent the lady had given off, pure condescension in its visceral, terrible form. Keba swung his neck coils out and twined his head back to look the way he'd come, his little stone and wood hut already lost behind golden trees and giant stacked rocks. Maybe he should have just packed things up and headed somewhere to the north where the land grew dry and brittle, or to the west to hide within the briny edge of the ocean with a fresh set of gills in his neck and his strong, leaping back legs traded for a shark's tail.

But this was his home and he liked it. Liked that creatures knew where he was and came in trade, speaking in hushed tones that Keba held a name of honor. His knife, his needles sharp and accurate, and the whispered hisses he spoke above their limbs giving full mobility, unlocking the stiffness that came from removal. He liked being sought after.

Or, at least, he had.

He grumbled and growled to himself, allowing the bear to override the viper as he sweat and huffed toward Isamelle's copse. The gathering darkness did not bother him, for his phoenix eye burned warily and the hooves of his front legs stepped in surety. The creatures did not either, for many he knew personally; he had swapped wings for extra limbs, given teeth to prey, and embedded eyes to the backs of scalps.

This copse of pines laid down a blanket of soft needles every year, so a carpet spread out around Isamelle's home. He ducked under sparking blue draperies of plaited vines that lit the copse in a blinking glow to rival firefly bulbs (which he had brought in a little vial, probably shifted toward the bottom of his gourd by now). Moths with spider legs flitted among the branches overhead. He found Isamelle braiding a new vine, a woven basket hanging from her wrist that she tugged a plant with heart-shaped leaves out of as she worked.

"Keba, your step is plodding today." Her ear flicked toward him. A mare's, though he hadn't done that trade himself.

"Isamelle." He stopped a few paces behind her, but found he couldn't go on. Her single human eye shone with intrigue when she glanced around, the only eye she had left of her original self.

"Quiet today, are you? No hissing or growling or muttering about children asking for unicorn horns or dragon breath?"

"They're impossible to get," he muttered.

She laughed, a deep laugh that harmonized with a cooing dove. "You've come to ask something, so let's hear it before you bound away like a frightened kangaroo." His back legs tightened at the suggestion.

"A request ..."

Then he thought better of that approach and swung the gourd off his back and began to pull out wrapped bundles—macaw feathers, venom sacs, cricket legs still chirping now and then—glass jars—firefly bulbs, lizard scales, cougar whiskers—and small, tubular sacks—the trumpet of an elephant, the whisper of a doe.

"So many eyes," murmured Isamelle, looking past his offerings to the jars beyond. She tied off the end of the braid and turned to look at him more fully, the blue-sparking vines oscillating beyond her.

"Yes, eyes are ..."

"You want my eye."

Keba grimaced and twisted his long neck to see down inside the gourd to avoid Isamelle's amused smile.

"You can't possibly want it for yourself." She idly massaged the rolled-up fur traded by a fox. "Who then? And why would they want it? Or do they not know? Is this a chance for you to impress someone?"

His scorpion tail jerked upright.

"Not someone you like then."

"I don't know who she is. I didn't ask and I don't want to. She's ... *original*."

Yet, instead of concerned, Isamelle's expression turned more intrigued. "Original," she echoed. "I've never met one who'd not had even the smallest of trades as an infant."

"I have."

"No tufts of fur? No feather or scale in place of skin?"

"I didn't strip her naked. But she certainly had the ruin about her. Shattered two of my tanks and threatened to wreck them all if I didn't—if I ..."

"She shattered your tanks?"

"With a touch of her finger." He mimed the move in the air and about them the sparks intensified, showering the pine needles so they glowed purple in the dim light.

Isamelle swayed as if listening to some unheard music, which she might have been given she had three sets of ears, two hidden under long, multicolored tresses from creatures large and small. Then she smiled disarmingly. "I'd like to meet this original lady of yours."

Isamelle turned her jarred eye over and over, and though the lady crossed her arms and drummed her fingers against her sleeves, Isamelle did not hurry. Keba edged closer to a tank that held pairs of black and tan antlers and velvet of varying sizes and shapes, hopeful the lady would not take out any aggression on his home.

"Keba says you need this to find the shrine." She held up her eye, the jar's thick glass distorting the shape. "What do you intend on doing there?"

"What needs to be done."

"How cryptic. I've been told the shrine can't be found."

"It can't be found by people like you."

Keba hissed, but kept it deep in his throat where the growl lingered.

"People like me," murmured Isamelle, her ears flicking again. "I'd like to see this shrine for myself, so this"—she held out the eye—"is a loan. I expect it back. And will be coming with you to ascertain its safety."

The lady stiffened as she examined first the eye, then Isamelle with her partial mask, streams of plants flowing to her chin, each leaf sparking softly. "Agreed."

Keba scowled into the tank, then swallowed his hiss and smiled gamely. "You seem to have come to an arrangement. Wonderful. If you'd please ..." He tried to usher them out.

"I'll need you to come with us. In case I end up requiring it embedded in my—" The lady pursed her lips. "—my body."

"I'll just do it now," said Keba desperately.

"I'd rather not if I can avoid it."

She strode out the door, the jar held tightly to her chest. Isamelle shrugged and stepped after her, leaving Keba to fume, all four of his legs tense as he struggled to contain his anger. She'd probably ruin his home if he resisted. She'd destroy everything he'd built and leave him no trade, no life. He grumbled, but followed reluctantly into the grey morning and its sagging spirits.

The lady held Isamelle's eye before her like a talisman to ward off evil, if one believed in that sort of thing. Keba certainly didn't see the eye move other than to bob in its viscous liquid, but the lady saw something, and in some part, Isamelle must have as well for the jar began to glow with the same soft blue as her copse of pines. The lady turned south, dragging them from Keba's hidden abode and leading them through the hills past deer with wicked talons who murmured in hello.

His hooves sunk into soft dirt and his fur became damp as they headed through familiar country, turning east, then west, crossing back over their footprints as much as they tracked through muddy, cracked stream beds and under crisscrossed branches. The mist thickened into fog, and trees Keba knew became unfamiliar as if by turning in circles the three of them had somehow become lost in a wood more cloud than ground. Even the steady welcomes of the creatures he knew—jays with cardinal songs, groundhogs with lithe fox legs—tapered off.

In the silence, Isamelle hummed as they walked, a harmonizing coo echoing about them, filling the spaces on either side of the tracks the lady made through the soggy leaves. Keba ducked his neck until his head rested chest-height and though he huffed, he tried to hide it.

"What are we doing? Back and forth, forth and back. I've mud to my knees."

"Are you tired too?" asked Isamelle.

He'd started to answer before realizing she'd been mocking him. "I think it's a valid question. We've been walking all morning under the same trees." He lowered his voice so the lady wouldn't hear. "And I'm certain she's the reason all the water's gone from the streams."

"The land has been roughed," agreed Isamelle, becoming serious. "She has the ruin about her, as you've said."

In front of them, the lady made an angled turn, the blue glow from the jar dim within the fog. Isamelle picked up her humming again and though there were no words, Keba thought he might have felt some answering song far behind them.

More than once, the fog swirled, beckoned, fingers in the air reaching toward Keba. Human creature fingers they were. Each one triple-knuckled as it bent and danced somewhere to the side of the lady's path.

"She doesn't see them," murmured Isamelle at one point as the fog thickened, squeezing out the sunlight and leaving them with only her mask and her eye as any source of light.

Keba shuddered. "It's not her they want gone."

He wondered then, if he were to step away, wander into the mist under these unfamiliar trees with no creature he'd ever helped, would he find himself back in familiar country again ... or someplace else.

He moved closer to Isamelle.

They strode for hours, possibly hours within hours, and only stopped for a brief respite inside a bundle of blackberry bushes Keba swore did not grow in this direction. In the deepened grey shadows, the lady set the jar down and disappeared behind the trees, the sound of her shifting clothing drifting over to them. He licked his lips and swung his neck out, white knuckles on his muddy, furry knees.

"We could bury it."

Isamelle didn't respond but for her chewing of blackberries.

"The glow, would it extend through the dirt? Can you make it stop?" He fumbled in the dirt as he spoke, his hoof gouging a hole in the damp soil.

"Aren't you curious?" she asked, her lips smeared darker from the berries.

"No," he hissed. "I'm happy with my world the way it is."

With a glance toward the lady, he quickly swiped up the jar and tucked it into the hole, his fingers stiff with fear. Maybe they would have to turn back. The shrine a myth lost to this unnatural fog with its unnatural, beckoning hands. He scuttled sideways, slipping in the mud as the lady returned to only the glow of Isamelle's mask shedding light.

Her gaze cut like the broken glass of his terrarium, but she did not say a word, merely reached down where the grass had been disturbed and sifted until the glow from the jar lifted into the air. Keba cringed away from the lady in case she wanted revenge, but she only cleaned the jar with her skirt before announcing their break was over.

The air became hard to breathe, thickening, becoming a murmur and then a roar in Keba's ears. Even Isamelle flinched and staggered, though the lady did not seem to notice anything amiss, her breath coming as easy as her steps.

And then, between one step and the next, they broke out of the cloying haze and found themselves standing at the base of a low, rumbling waterfall, the waters crystalline teal, the sky a cerulean, and the stones carved to represent original creatures. Deer lapped at the shrine's edge. Birds perched on low branches and sang the songs with which they'd been born. Keba searched, but found nothing more, nothing beyond original creatures.

He shrank into himself, glaring at the creatures and their stone counterparts in their singularity, in their birth-forms, so simple and ...

"Boring," he said. "So incredibly boring."

The lady let out a sigh that bore a wealth of relief. "It's the right way of things. And we need to put things back to the right way of things."

"We?"

She turned to him with pity in her gaze, the water rippling behind her. "You, most of all. You've forgotten what you are, who you are. You've been sliced apart and put back together so many times you don't think straight, see straight, you don't even move straight."

"I don't want to move straight," Keba all but shouted, then recoiled when the lady's eyes narrowed into sharp slits. After she'd dismissed him with a wave of a hand, he whispered low, so only Isamelle could hear, "I don't want to think straight."

"Regret comes in many forms," said the lady, her voice stringent as she forced it louder than the rumbling of the falls.

"Regret?"

"Most people only choose a few trades in their youth. But you, your regret became such a burden that you dove into the wretched world hoof-first, desperate to become something, but unsure what."

"I am something," he muttered, but not too loudly.

"You are ... something."

Isamelle dipped one hand into the shrine's water, allowing it to drain between her fingers and sparkle in the sunlight. "What do you intend, now that we're here?"

"To set things—"

"Yes, you've said that. Set things right. But what exactly does that mean to you?"

In answer, the lady handed Isamelle the jar holding the eye. Then she faced Keba, causing him to shirk back from where he'd been inching over the moss.

"It will restore you," she said, holding a hand out, palm up as if offering some peaceful gesture of goodwill.

A few more paces backward. "I think I'd rather not be restored."

"That's what you mean," said Isamelle. "Of course. The shrine would put us back to our birth forms."

"You must bathe in it."

"*I* must not do anything," said Keba desperately. "I'm perfectly happy as myself. No need to take that away."

"How curious," murmured Isamelle, her mask shivering in the breeze as she bent to dip her hand in the water again.

"No, it's not curious. There's nothing curious here." He spun to leave and leaned onto his back paws, readying to bound away—

The lady's hand curled around his forearm and with a *pop*, pain reverberated down to the tips of his fingers and up past the swell of his shoulder. Keba growled, then hissed, then shouted as the lady swung him around by his broken arm, her touch as ruinous to him as it'd been to his tanks.

"It'll be okay," she soothed, her voice grating in its sympathy, in her frail attempt at empathy.

She tugged and Keba pitched forward, hooves scraping up moss and his stinger jerking wildly. He splashed into the water, mud sloughing away and the pulse of his arm like the beat of drums in his veins. He flailed, righted himself, cradled his arm to his chest as he checked himself over: hooves against the rocky bottom of the pool, feathers matted down on his shoulders, neck coils loose and long.

The lady, however, looked stricken.

"Ha!" he yelled, uncaring if he seemed outrageous. "It's all a worthless story anyhow! Look at this, I'm still me." He laughed at her, a little hysterically, but no less relieved that her misguided attempts to change him had failed so dramatically.

"It didn't work." Her voice lost and lonely.

"Good," Keba muttered again. He staggered forward, clumsy despite his goat hooves as the pain soared past adrenaline to throb across his entire right side.

"It should have worked. The shrine *is* the answer. That's what all my research has shown me; it caused the Rebirth of the Emerald Age."

"That's probably a myth too," muttered Keba, sweating though the water remained cool. His stomach clenched and he was thankful he had eaten little but blackberries.

"There's no tale that explains everything from the past," said Isamelle. "And every tale hides something within its folds."

He wanted to scream at her. No, he truly just wanted to scream at nothing in particular, to create a physical sound to represent the pain spiking through his arm with every minor movement. If he could just lay against the rock ...

"Could be," continued Isamelle, "that there's a reason the path resists those of us who are not ... original."

Keba scrambled against the moss-riddled bank and settled in a tangle of limbs under the watchful eyes of a trio of stone otters. Shivers began at the base of his tail and trailed up his rounded spine and a cold seeped into his limbs. Would that he'd have resisted her far earlier, headed north.

"I see now."

He struggled to open his eyes at a scuffing noise. The lady removed her second boot and approached. Thinking she planned to grab him again, he recoiled, jarring his arm so badly the air became lodged in his throat. But the lady merely crouched a few paces away.

"It needs a sample, a blueprint for the rebirth. Don't worry, Keba." Again with that sympathy. "I will remake you."

"I don't want to be remade," he gasped.

But she had already turned away, to where the rocks curled down into the shrine in an approximation of welcome. Behind her Isamelle stood, ears flicking.

"Stop ... her," he said, striving to push the bear past his tight throat, though the growl came weak.

Isamelle did not hear, or she chose not to listen, for her eyes glittered in curiosity, that same curiosity she'd had when he'd first come to her sparking copse with a request he never should have made. She stood aside serenely as the lady stepped one naked foot—all human creature toes—and then the other into the shrine, the water rippling away from her.

Pushing off against the stone otters, their leering little faces unperturbed, Keba crawled, his arm kept raised and his voice a rasp that blended hiss and growl in a way uniquely his own and less uniquely pained. "This isn't what the world needs. We're not torn, we're not pitiable." And as the lady spun slowly, waist-deep, the tip of her dark braid floating at her side, he broke on one whispered last word, "Please."

The lady placed her hands on her cheeks and then swept them down flat against the water. Her lips moved in prayer, and then she sank into the shrine, her braid last to be swallowed.

"Isamelle! Do something!" The growl, finally erupting, too late to be of use.

The roar of the waterfall gained pitch, the surface of the pool roiling, bubbling, like the foamy crash of surf on sand. Moss tore from stone, spotting the water. The living creatures took flight, bounding, hopping, flying away to the relative safety of the nearby trees. The dark blur that had been the lady just under the surface swept into the whirl and disappeared as the spray splattered Keba and Isamelle.

He jerked away, flinching in anticipation of the pain from jarring his arm, yet the pain never came. Throbbing became an ache, the ache morphed into nonexistence, and it was only after he realized his arm no longer hurt to move that there were other changes, explicit and bone-deep.

A chill ran across his shoulders as his feathers tore off and soared away. His lower limbs fused into two, the fur thinning, darkening. The gentle burn in one eye and the strength of the other swept away between one blink and the next. And his neck ... oh, his neck twisted and struggled its way into something short and squat and ungainly, threatening to choke him with its conciseness. He gasped and groaned, clawed at his flesh, half-moon fingernails leaving welts across thighs he no longer recognized.

Gone, all gone. Everything that had been him.

When the waters calmed, when the sudden displacement of himself passed and left him achingly alive, when he could hear past his own heart once more, he heard Isamelle humming. He staggered to his feet, fell, then rose again. She'd taken her mask off, her eyes both whole and her ears relegated to one set. And yet, she still held her eye, its blue glow faded, yet very much there. Gone from one eye, to none, to three in a matter of a day. He stumbled over to her, finding two flat feet and ten individual toes difficult to control in ways his chosen body had never been before.

"Why didn't you stop her?" he demanded, trying to hiss, but the words erupted with as much plainness as the lady's had been. "You could have done something! Instead, you just watched it all happen, like you didn't care that you'd become something else."

"I haven't become something else," murmured Isamelle. "I'm still ... me."

Her words broke what little control he had left. Because *he* didn't feel like himself. Because *he* felt the loss like a blade in his gut. "Lucky you," he snarled.

He ripped the jar from her and threw it, watching as it arched through the air where, at its zenith, the glass abruptly shattered, shards like rain scattering, winking in the sun. As if that had been the permission he needed, he turned and swept his palm across the closest statue—a boar—and staggered back when the stone splintered into a crumbling mess.

"The ruin's about us all, then is it?"

Keba ignored her, choosing instead to run his fingers along the tall form of a giraffe, a squat badger, a horse, the bats hanging between two pillars made of a walrus and a lion. The shrine shook like it hadn't before, the water bubbled and the waterfall split into two, then three, then tumbled in on itself, crashing so the streams poured off to the sides, drowning moss and shrubs. He stumbled on unfamiliar feet and fell, palms flat to rock that vibrated beneath him, sending cracks outward from his touch.

"This is too dangerous for the world."

He tried to growl, but the bear had been stolen from him. He tried to twist his neck to see if Isamelle realized the gravity of what had happened, but his neck stopped, wouldn't turn past his shoulder.

As the Shrine of the Original Creation fell to rubble, Keba struggled to his feet and ran unsteadily toward home, bypassing Isamelle's seeking hand that may or may not have been an attempt to calm him, as if his anger wasn't deserving.

He didn't remember much about that homeward-bound dash, but that the cloying fog seemed nothing but a distant memory, and that the woods cried in sorrow. Towering oaks split into pieces when the jays hopped along their boughs, their raucous cries the same ones Keba had once removed. The ground quaked, the hills spitting sod and the stream beds breaking farther apart.

The creatures—they mourned, in howls and shrieks, in screams and yips, they cried the same pain echoing in Keba. The Ruin had come, cursed back to each and every creature as they wallowed in regret for their lost selves.

Isamelle knocked on his door at some point, her voice muffled through the wood, but when Keba tucked his blanket over his head and ground teeth that no longer felt of a saber-tooth, she eventually went away, back to her copse, back to her unaltered life to hum to her pine needles and braids. Outside, the world raged war on itself, shivering with the constant ache of the lost and damned.

"This is what you wanted," muttered Keba. "A world put together how *you* wanted it instead of how the world wanted to be. Like there's some right way and a million wrong ways."

The hanging terrariums clattered against the walls at a particularly strong quake. Water sloshed in the aquariums, but already too much had spilled for the tremors to spill more. Everything already too broken to bother breaking more.

Then came a shiver at the doorway.

"Excuse me?"

It was a boy, or maybe a girl. He couldn't tell because his neck no longer curled and he couldn't bring himself out of his melancholy enough to ask.

"Are you the one they call Keba?"

He curled tighter, hating the sound of his name on the child's lips, for *that* Keba no longer existed.

"I've lost myself. Parts of myself. Been trying to find ... something ... the same."

He hissed before remembering he couldn't. Not really.

"I used to be able to breathe in the ocean and swim with my friends, but now they don't even understand me."

Keba loosened at the echoing emptiness in the child's voice. An ache there that matched Keba's own. And the one that trembled the world outside.

"What kind of gills?" he whispered.

"Those of a sailback. And I had the flippers of a seal. And the eye of an octopus."

"Ah." He sat up, slowly, still unused to only two legs and the straightness of his spine. "I have the eye and the gills, but we'll have to take a trip to the sea to find a seal willing to trade."

"You think we will? Find one?"

He turned awkwardly, wiggling toes he'd not had in decades. The goat herds would be in the mountains; he could start there, climb with two legs and unsteady feet until he found a billy needing a trade as badly as he needed hooves, to seek himself again. He placed flat feet on the ground and leveled a gaze on the child, seeing past the salt-roped hair draping that round face.

"We'll look until you're you again."

AUTHOR NOTES

When I wrote "To Seek Himself Again," I was drawn to crafting human bodies the way children might, with creative wonder where wings and gills and mermaid tails are on the mind. This was meant as a contrast to the awful ways we adults tend to examine ourselves, where we pick apart our perceived flaws in the mirror, wishing for perfection in skin, in symmetry, in shape. I wanted to give form to that individual in each of our lives who insists on judging us for how we look under the pretense of helping us, their condescending empathy ruled by a misguided belief that they are helping us to form an ideal. An ideal that only exists in their mind.

I didn't set out to craft a trans allegory, and yet, the reception has been incredibly positive in that regard. It warms me to think that this story can resonate with so many, and yet it pains me that so many of us struggle with unfettered cultural expectations of beauty and body. These are our bodies, the only ones we have, and I hope that one day we might look in the mirror without wishing to fix supposed flaws, and allow the child in us to remember what it's like to only wish for wings and tails and claws and sharp, sharp vampire teeth with which to rend the world.

THIS SHATTERED VESSEL, WHICH HOLDS ONLY GRIEF

IZZY WASSERSTEIN

Cassie pulls her hood low over her forehead, keeps her eyes on the ground ahead of her. She wears face paint meant to fool facial recognition algorithms, though the cops think she's dead. Her friends are. She should be.

She circles the block twice, lingers at a corner, and when she's as sure as she can be that she hasn't been followed, she knocks on the unmarked door.

The clerk draws back multiple bolts, whispers an incantation, and calls the quarters, releasing the hexes long enough to allow Cassie inside.

The shop is tiny, overstuffed with zines, tarot decks, ritual salt, knitting needles, drums, artifacts from unplaces, crystals, and a great plant with vines spilling everywhere. It smells of old books and new growth.

"How's the spell prep going?" the clerk asks once she's finished sealing the door behind them.

"It's going." Cassie turns sideways, edges past the displayed statues, foci, and trinkets, afraid as always that she'll knock them over. She always feels so broad-shouldered in these tight confines. *Mannish*, her brain nags at her, unbidden and hateful.

In the corner, she flips through the practical books on spellcasting. None have detailed instructions on the sigil or the modifications that will make it suit her needs.

She has no choice but to ask the clerk.

The young woman's smile is warmer than her job requires. She sports a ragged sundress and an impressive collection of facial piercings. She displays a "she/her" pin on her chest despite the danger.

"I'm stuck," Cassie says, though she hates to burden this woman. "In her book, Manglis says it's possible to modify this sigil"—she reaches into her pocket, pulls out the tracing she made—"so that it's not finding something but changing something." For a moment she could swear she's back in the KC Free Zone, her vision clouded by tear gas, feeling the loudspeaker's roar in her chest. She forces herself to take deep breaths, to fight back against panic. "Changing something in the past, I mean."

"Hm." The clerk's tongue pokes out of one corner of her mouth as she studies the rune. "I've never encountered that modification, but ..." She turns to one of the many piles of books stacked near her and extracts a thick tome. She flips through it, sets it down in front of Cassie.

"Here," she says. "'Chapter 6: All Manner of Modifications for Time and Task.' If this doesn't have what you need, then nothing I've encountered will."

Cassie flips pages eagerly. She's never been talented at spellcasting, but she's learned a lot in the weeks she's spent in preparation for this spell.

Soon she's sure the book has what she needs. "How much?" she asks, mentally calculating what she can afford and still make rent, if she skips some meals.

"It's a shop copy," the clerk says, "from a personal collection." She sees Cassie's expression and hastens to add: "But take your time with it."

"Really?" Cassie asks, knowing herself to be unworthy of the kindness. "I'll stay out of your way."

"You're not in my way." The clerk grins. "I'm glad to help. Let me know if you need anything. My name's Samantha."

"Thanks," Cassie says, not able to meet the other woman's eyes. Samantha has given her name before; Cassie never offers her own.

Cassie's roommates don't care what she does as long as she doesn't use the VR set. So, as soon as they leave for the day, she prepares her spell. She still reeks of oil and lab-grown meat, the stench of her job never really leaving her. Flipping burgers and pulling fries from grease pays the bills, and no one there cares who she is as long as she doesn't skip shifts. Her coworkers come and go, and the few long-termers no longer bother to invite her to hang out after work. She has no friends.

Cassie possesses a rare gift: self-knowledge. Her worth was tested, and she was found wanting. She knows that she's a coward and will not inflict herself on others.

The spell Cassie prepares is powerful and dangerous, and her practical casting experience amounts to little more than the wards she sketched in the Free Zone, wards that the cops shattered with ease. This is a spell of undoing. Its purpose is to change one choice in the past, to allow one to take another path. Its utility is narrow. Some choices are too entwined with others, cannot be pulled apart. She could never hope to convince the other uncitizens to abandon the Free Zone or not to have found it. She could not convince them to flee before the cops arrive. But she hopes she can undo her own choice. She can stay to die with Kam and Scar, with Mel and Tanguay, and even Ravenna. What a blessing that would be.

The spell requires salt, fresh bread, fresher blood. She speaks the incantation, her lips curling around each syllable like a priceless treasure. In the darkness of her room, her mirror glows, her haggard eyes stare back at her. Not yet twenty-five and already she's so tired. Smoke curls around her: the Powers are listening. Her mind claws back to the precise second when she was poised at the top of the stairs, teargas and floodlights making ghosts of the family that had taken her in, the moment when she had a choice when she fled. She beseeches the Powers to adjust the course of one life, just the smallest of tweaks, a betrayal born of panic: *stay, Cassie, stay and face it.*

Her sigil flares with energy. She holds her breath.

The past casts her aside, as effortless and impersonal as a storm tearing away deadwood. Understand: her choice is a historical fact. It will not be changed.

She bargains with a Witch of Fate for a consultation. This is the fee: twenty-one hours of labor; an oath to speak only the truth for one month; the dress she'd hidden from her father, who insisted she was a boy, and which she'd kept when she fled home for Kansas City and a world that had seemed filled with promise; and six seconds of her life.

The witch's home is a split-level with curling siding, a lawn overgrown with dandelions. Cassie triple-checks the address to be sure she's in the right place. The front door opens as she reaches for the bell.

"Doorbell doesn't work," the witch says and steps aside. He's shorter than Cassie, shirtless, and so thin that his clavicles rise knifelike from his chest. Cassie watches him warily, but she tells herself if a Fate Witch means her harm then she cannot escape it. She steps inside, and only much later does she consider that he could have been a liar, a killer, even bait meant to catch those desperate enough to change fate.

She perches on a couch whose faded print shows sunflowers, windmills, abandoned farmhouses. He sits opposite her on a ragged rug.

"The price has been paid," he intones. "The gods of fate listen. Tell them what you wish to know."

Fear arrives at last, gnaws at her gut as she tries to force out the words.

"Out with it," he demands. "You're going to tell me, so you may as well save us both some time."

His demand is beyond dangerous. She's a fugitive. He could report her to the cops, the militias, even to HomeSec, that last functioning arm of the government out east.

He could judge her, attack her, blackmail her.

More than that, her past is a wound. To tell him is to tear off the scab. She needs to describe the key moment, when she hesitated at the top of the stairs, glanced back through the gas. Floodlights pierced the room through dozens of holes in boarded-up windows The cops' loudspeakers drowned out all other sounds. Her fellow uncitizens, friends, rivals, ex-lovers, reduced to dark shapes in the chaos. For a moment, she could have turned back, could have stood beside them and shared their fate.

She realizes there's so much more that she can't hope to communicate: the smell of fresh-turned earth in the rooftop garden as Mel showed her how to transplant the peppers from their pots to flourish in the spring heat. The security committee meeting where Ravenna argued that they had rats reporting back to the cops, and Kam said, *Yes, of course, we do. That's to be expected, and so we keep sensitive information on a need-to-know basis.* How she assembled sandwiches for a hundred hungry utopians, shoulder-to-shoulder with Scar, which somehow led to them exploring each other's bodies in the basement, a thick blanket draped over the rubble of the bolt holes they'd carved.

The scab tears away. Cassie sobs. These moments flood her thoughts, even their joys turned to ash.

The witch watches her, his eyes sympathetic. He is unmoving, except for the rise and fall of his chest.

"I was part of the Free Zone downtown," she tells him at last. "Kam swore we could hold the cops off if we stuck together, but they tore through our wards, bashed in the walls—and I fled. When my family needed me most, I ran." She has never told anyone this. The words twist in her. Bile rises in her throat.

"I just want to have stayed," she says. To have faced it with the others, the community who had been so certain that they would change the world.

The witch stares upwards, his hands like withered branches extending toward the spiderweb-dusted ceiling. His lips don't move. The voice that speaks from his chest is not his own.

"The events you speak of cannot be changed. The police called in another Witch of Fate, and she wove that event into the fabric of history. This vessel cannot unmake it, nor can the gods themselves. It is done."

He sags, a marionette whose strings have gone slack. Cassie can't find the air to scream. She staggers to her feet, and as she pulls the door open, he calls after her. *He* does, not the thing speaking from his chest.

"Fate is often cruel," he says, "but always honest. I will you well."

He lies supine on his ancient rug, and something like a massive worm writhes beneath his skin.

Cassie reads the same passage three times, certain she must be missing something. She's barely slept. Since her encounter with the Witch of Fate, the dead infest her dreams, putting up barricades, planting gardens, purifying water, smoking weed, gathering supplies, going about their business unable to see the flesh rotting from bodies, sloughing off bleached skulls. The dreams are obvious, which does nothing to lessen their horror.

"That can't be right," Cassie mutters and regrets it at once.

"What's that?" Samantha appears at her shoulder, eager to help.

"I'm trying to make sense of this passage. 'Fate being the ultimate manifestation of the laws of reality, which are fixed and absolute, even though we perceive them but dimly, it must therefore be understood as the fixed point around which all magic and science orbits, and so we conclude that Fate is irresistible, the bulwark against which all else must adapt or shatter.'

"So if something is fated, all other magic is ..." Cassie can't quite bring herself to finish the sentence.

Samantha's eyes are the color of the sea, or so Cassie guesses, having never been farther from home than Wichita. Her gaze is so gentle that Cassie wants to hide from it.

"That's the Tula metaphysics book, right?" Samantha asks. "That's what he argues, anyway."

"He's cited everywhere," Cassie says quietly. "Everyone seems to agree."

"It pains me to admit it"—Samantha pulls her hair back into a ponytail—"but there's a strong pro-fate bias in texts on magic. I suspect it has something to do with the need to feel in control."

"Then fate isn't absolute?" Cassie hardly dares hope.

"I don't know. But Tula's view isn't the only one. If you're looking for another, I doubt you'll find it in these books."

Cassie shakes her head. "Wait. Why?"

"Because Witches of Chance don't write books. Or if they do, they don't publish them. Not that I've ever seen."

"How do I find a Witch of Chance?" Cassie asks, unable to restrain herself.

"I don't know if you can. But ..." Samantha rifles through a drawer behind the counter, hands a small rectangular card to Cassie. The front side features a pair of dice, their roll changing as Cassie tries to read it. She flips the card over, expecting a witch's personal sigil, but finds a handwritten phone number.

"Someone left this," Samantha explains. "They said to give it to the next person who 'wanted to reject fate.'"

"Thank you." Cassie shakes, caught between hope and fear.

"Don't thank me yet," Samantha cautions. "I can't promise this will lead you anywhere."

"Luck's a chance, but trouble's sure," the Witch of Chance tells Cassie, who has finally found eir after months of seeking. Except "found" isn't right. Three weeks ago Cassie abandoned her search only to encounter the witch on the hill where the World War I Museum slowly rots away. Before them, KC is strangely beautiful in twilight, the filthy water of the flooded areas sun-struck into silver and rouge. The city's crumbling core seems to whisper tales of what once was.

"Yeah," Cassie says, for the decay before them is immune to rebuttal. "I've had my fill of trouble. I could use the chance."

The witch turns to regard her. E wears ragged jeans, a once-expensive top with silver swirls now stained with juice or dried blood. Eir arms are thick with bangles, cuffs, incomprehensible notes written in marker.

"The forces I commune with are powerful," e says, "but they make few promises. Have you accepted at last how empty are the promises of order?"

Cassie stares across the city. Cop-lights flash, a blue and red tangle down on Main. When she'd fled into Free Zone's basement, she'd heard the *crack-crack-crack* of gunfire above. The cops wore body armor, carried assault weapons. Yet still, she'd waited at the other end of the bolthole, waited what seemed like hours, waited even though by then ash fell like snow and the former Free Zone became a false sunset to the north.

"I'm learning," Cassie says eventually. "But I still dream of setting things right. No. Less wrong."

The witch considers this. "Your plans will fail, as will all plans, given enough time. Now tell me what you seek."

This time the story comes slightly easier. Cassie tells em of the tangle in time, the Fate Witches, the hope that a knot that cannot be untangled can nevertheless be cut. She can't bring herself to speak of the way Kam had insisted they could meet the challenge of the cops, protect the community they'd carved out from a half-block of abandoned buildings. Can we stop the pigs, Kam? *We can if we stick together, if we hold the line.* She doesn't tell em how Kam was her dearest friend, how they knew things about Cassie that she never even shared with her lovers. How she'd fled from Kam's side when they needed her most.

"You seek to break free of the bonds of fate?" the witch asks.

"I seek to be free of *that* fate," Cassie says, reflexively honest.

"Fate is not to be accepted or rejected piecemeal," the witch gently admonishes her. "Chance works in the margins, through those things that can't be accounted for."

Cassie waits for more. It isn't forthcoming. "I don't understand. Can you help me, or not?"

"You may think that you want chance to intervene, but there is no guarantee that you'll prefer it to fate."

"I'll take that risk," Cassie says. "Please."

The witch tilts eir head to one side, considers, nods. "It is done."

Nothing has changed.

"What? I don't—"

"Chance has now—long ago—intervened on your behalf. The escape route you picked happened to be the one they hadn't discovered. You are free despite fate's attempts to ensnare you. You sought chance's intervention, and so you live."

When Cassie was young, she'd nearly drowned in a pond behind her aunt's house. The pressure on her lungs, the slow, inexorable slide toward the darkness: she feels it all again, collapses to her knees. Breath won't come. Her hands dig into broken concrete. Screams die in her throat.

The witch is gone. The air smells of fire. She retches until nothing but bile remains.

"It's incomprehensible," Cassie says, burying her head in her hands. The books on temporal magic are nightmarishly dense, filled with discussions of causality, entropy, quantum mechanics, and paracausal effects. Fate magic seems simple by comparison.

Like all the kids whose parents could scrape together internet access fees, Cassie had attended 'Zon Secondary School, where the algorithm labeled her "bright but lacking in motivation." She'd done okay when she cared enough to focus, and rote memorization was enough to avoid failing most classes. None of that had remotely prepared her for *Three Theories on the Nature of Time, With Practical Implications for Spellcrafting.*

"I'm lost too," Samantha says. "Lowe says that time travel is impossible, but Cadigan documents people traveling forward in time—"

"Not backward, though."

"Not from what I've seen," Samantha admits. "But I'm far outside my expertise. We could take the problem to my coven."

"You meet with other spellcasters?" Cassie was shocked. "How is that remotely safe? The cops ..."

"We take lots of safeguards and don't meet in person," Samantha says. "One of the members is a Witch of Place."

The ever-present knot in Cassie's gut constricts. A coven. More people, more connections, more help she doesn't deserve, more chances for her to do harm, to lose everything. Again.

"I shouldn't." Cassie feels compelled to offer an explanation. "I can't ... with groups." A truth that conceals a deeper one.

"Oh, shit, I'm sorry. I didn't know."

How would she? Cassie isn't the sharing type. Not anymore.

"No worries," is all Cassie can manage. She stares at the book, afraid to meet the clerk's eyes.

"I can ask them, if you want." Samantha's voice is barely a whisper. A long pause.

"That would be very helpful," Cassie admits.

"I'll check with them at our next meeting. How can I reach you?"

Cassie sketches her personal rune, slides it to Samantha.

"I'm Cassie," she says, forgetting herself. "She/her."

"I'm she/her, too." Samantha's smile dazzles.

"I know." Cassie points at that daring, dangerous pin, and Samantha laughs.

"Oh, right."

"Um, thanks again," Cassie says. "Look, I … I need to go."

She hurries from the shop, cursing herself for one more entanglement, one more betrayal of the promises she'd made to herself, for how she'd thrilled when she made Samantha smile.

The coven can't make sense of temporal magic, but one of them knows someone who can.

The Witch of Time's price is high. Cassie saves for months to meet it, picking up work on the side imbuing marbles with spells to find lost things. A simple trick, really—just a nudge to help someone recall where they last put the object they seek. It could draw the cops' attention, but that's a risk she must take. Lately, she can't stop thinking about the Free Zone, and every memory is barbed, even the good ones. Especially the good ones. Nausea seizes her whenever she thinks of the community mural, forever unfinished, its tribute to the lost and utopian dreams melted away in the conflagration.

She'd imagined the witch as a crone, but when they meet, she's in her thirties. Or so Cassie guesses; the witch's skin is flawless, but there are laugh lines around her eyes and her hands tighten involuntarily, the way Cassie's grandmother's did, toward the end.

"You can't change the past," the witch says. She wears a bowler hat and an immaculate pinstripe suit, not a trace of chalk on it despite kneeling to inscribe elaborate equations on the abandoned warehouse's stone floor. "What's done is done."

Cassie has heard this before, has come to this witch because she has heard other things as well. "You took my money—"

"The flow of history can't be changed," the witch interrupts. "It's like a river, and like a river, it shifts over time, but trying to change its course through magic … well, you might as well stand midstream and command it to stop."

She stands, tucks the chalk away, then deliberately wipes her hands clean.

"Then what can you do?" Cassie has waited so long. Her patience nears its end.

"It's possible to pluck someone from the stream, like catching a fish, and bring them forward, bring them here."

"You can bring them back to life?" Cassie has heard rumors but hadn't dared believe.

"No," the witch says. "Or, anyway, not precisely. I pluck them from a moment in their life, and then they continue on from there."

"You can save them," Cassie says, hardly daring to believe it.

"I can bring someone forward," the witch corrects her. "One person. Anything more is too large a disruption."

Cassie knows who she'll choose, knows it even amidst the guilt of the others she's condemning to die, or to stay dead. It has to be Kam. The uncitizens had no bosses, no rulers, but there were those whose vision and drive others respected. Everyone admired Kam, listened to them when they spoke. Cassie's best friend, who'd sourced her estrogen, on whose shoulder she'd cried, who always insisted Cassie had saved their life when she'd chased off that creep with a knife and a hungry grin.

Kam, who Cassie had seen at the very end, astride the barricade, plastic-and-plywood shield in one hand, bat in the other, who she was sure kept shouting encouragement through their gas mask, even though the cops' loudspeakers drowned out all words. That image of Kam is seared into Cassie's mind. It had almost, *almost*, stopped her from fleeing.

Then the cops battered down the wall and stormed through the gap. There'd been so many of them, black-masked, armored and armed, magic surging around them, and Cassie ran. After that, there was nothing but regret.

Oh, to see Kam's face again. To know they were alive, even though they'd never forgive her once they learned what she'd done, that she'd abandoned them, then magically rescued them from the doom of the Free Zone, kept them alive by forcing them to abandon their post. Cassie deserved nothing less, and Kam deserved so much more than they'd received.

Why, then, this dread that compelled her to ask more questions?

"If you can do this, if you can save lives this way"—Cassie ignored the witch's shaking head—"why isn't everyone coming to you for this?"

The witch smiles without warmth. "You're wise to ask. Our bodies, our minds—they are situated in time. If you pull someone free, they become ... detached. They lack some drive, some motive force."

"You mean they're lazy?" Cassie is incredulous.

"Not at all. They are ... without. They drift. Pain and pleasure don't move them. They want nothing. They're only acted upon."

Cassie shudders. The witch's ageless eyes are fixed upon her.

"This ... always happens?"

The faintest of motions in the witch's shoulders, as similar to a shrug as a whisper is to a shout. "Some are able to ... attach themselves again. Eventually. Most do not. In many cases, they will not even feed themselves."

Cassie had braced herself against being told it was impossible, against Kam's inevitable hatred of her, against even the violation of Kam's freedom that such a spell would require. But she is not prepared for this.

"The other way, then," she says at last. "Send me back into the stream—let me put things right." *Let me die with them.*

"The stream flows only one way, even for a Witch of Time. I'm sorry for your loss."

Cassie cannot save the others, nor can she return to join them in death. She cannot bring herself to see Kam reduced to someone adrift, without desire.

She will always and forever be the one who fled. That is her fate, she thinks bitterly, ever since she'd been forced to live as a boy, before she'd run away and joined with something bigger than herself, allowed herself to believe in the future her community was creating. She'd been forged strong but brittle, a blade that shatters when battle is joined.

Her father had often called her a coward, for her unwillingness to slaughter chickens, for refusing to stand up to bullies, for cringing from his raised voice. He'd been wrong about almost everything; he'd been right about that.

That thought breaks her again: she became—or always had been—exactly who he claimed she was.

There is no Witch of Memory in Kansas City, nor anywhere close. She hears rumors of one in St. Louis, which may as well be on the moon, for all the chance she has of getting there. Even if she could somehow barter for transport, or hitchhike, or try to hop one of the driverless big-rigs that rage across the highways like one hundred-ton bullets, for a trans woman to risk that crossing would be suicidal, and Cassie isn't brave enough for that.

She has no choice but to return to her studies, learning the magic of memory, if only for long enough to make herself forget. More cowardice, but she cannot bring herself to die, cannot live with her guilt.

"Hey, Cassie. How was the *Atlas*?" Samantha's wearing a cute A-line dress that features cats sitting atop open books.

"If I wanted to send something to Azeb, I could do it," Cassie says. That land of lost things only takes and never gives. It cannot help her. "But it was useless for my needs."

Samantha's crestfallen. The book had been her recommendation, Cassie remembers. Too late.

"I'm sorry," the clerk says. "It has so much about memories of lost places, I thought …" She turns away, tears in her eyes.

Cassie hates herself, hates that casual cruelty. "No, I'm sorry. I didn't mean— I know you were only doing your job." Samantha loves her work, but Cassie knows she's been doing far more than her job. "I shouldn't have asked you for help."

"But I want to help." The clerk wipes her eyes. "It's just … I've never met someone as driven as you. Then you stopped coming around, and I thought you'd been killed or, or … disappeared. Because I couldn't imagine you'd given up. And then when you came back, I could see how badly you needed whatever you're seeking, and I thought, I have to help her."

"You've been a huge help," Cassie says, because there is so much more she doesn't know how to say.

"I'll stay out of your way, unless you need me." Samantha crimsons, steps behind the desk, busies herself with a pile of books.

"The thing with the *Atlas* was my fault," Cassie admits. "I didn't tell you what I really needed." She can't quite do so. If she says she wants to forget, that invites questions. "I'm searching for a way to gain control of one's own memories."

"Hmmm." Samantha concentrates, her tongue peeking out of one corner of her lips. She darts to the practical spellcasting section, scans for something, returns. "You're already past the materials we have here. But I think the coven might be able to source the books you need. I bet you could borrow them."

"That would be wonderful," Cassie admits.

"Great," Samantha's smile is heartbreaking. "I'll be in touch." For a moment, Cassie is sure she's going to again ask if she wants to sit in with the coven, but she doesn't.

Samantha has always respected Cassie's boundaries, which means Cassie has no one but herself to blame for this tangle of feelings.

Memory is an ever-changing labyrinth. Cassie can't forget how she made Janice Chu cry when they were eight and goofing around on the playground behind what used to be the Randolph School. She recalls every detail of that time she sat in the window well of her childhood room and heard a voice, crystalline and perfect, singing a tune in a language she didn't recognize. Even now she wishes she'd run after the singer, if only to behold the face that made such beautiful music. She remembers the nights when the uncitizens gathered 'round Tanguay's electric keyboard, passing a joint and clumsily harmonizing.

But she can't remember the name of her first crush, nor the promises she made to herself when she left home. Though she has spent hours thinking about the community mural, there are whole sections forever effaced. She has long since forgotten the color of her mother's eyes, the sound of her laugh.

So much lost, and yet she cannot forget her cowardice, her betrayal. She prepares her spell, hoping it will be the last one she ever casts. She's covered the stone walls of the shop's backroom with writing. Her chalk-dusted hand cramps, and behind her eyes a headache taps an angry drumbeat on her skull. Some of the writing consists of spell components, guideposts to tell the magic what to take and what to leave behind, but the rest is her retelling of her flight from the Free Zone. Extracting details from the mind's tangled passageways is delicate work, and more so for a memory as knotted and worried-at as her flight. If she isn't careful, she may tear her memories all the way back to the root, leaving herself tabula rasa, a husk.

Even that would be an improvement.

She has just finished double-checking her work when there is a knock at the storeroom door. Samantha, holding a glass of water.

"My mother always said proper hydration is essential to magic." She smiles, presents the glass like an offering.

"Thank you." The script on the walls is small enough that Cassie doesn't think anyone could read it from the doorway, but she positions herself in Samantha's sightline to be sure. She takes a sip to reassure Samantha. The water is cool and welcome, and she quickly drains the glass. The pounding behind her eyes eases a little.

"I'm not going to spy on you." Samantha can't quite hide the hurt in her voice.

"I didn't think—"

"You did, and that's okay," Samantha says. "I get it. You never asked for me to be involved in your life." She is far too kind to point out that Cassie could never have performed this spell on her own, without the help of Samantha's coven, without the networked expertise of witches, without her research and gentle, patient support. So many kindnesses Cassie doesn't deserve.

"Thank you for the water," Cassie hesitates, then adds, "and for all your help. I could—I could never have done it without a Witch of Research like you."

To her surprise, Samantha grins. "They used to call us librarians," she says. "Back when there were libraries."

Cassie staggers like a fighter blindsided by a punch, feels herself swaying, falling ...

Samantha lunges, tries to catch her. The glass drops to the floor, shatters. The two women collapse.

"Cassie, are you okay?"

Only then does Cassie realize she is sobbing. She'd forgotten about the Free Zone's library, the wealth of books and zines that must have burned in the fire, many of them perhaps the only copies that had ever existed. Her mind has been gnawing on memories of the Free Zone like a dog claiming every scrap of marrow from a bone, and yet somehow, she'd forgotten that.

Samantha's arms enfold her, and Cassie sobs against her shoulder, surrounded by the scope of her loss. When she finally breathes again, the whole story spills out unbidden. It will not be kept in one moment longer, not just the escape but the way a community had saved her when she was living on the street, stealing razors and debating whether to shave or turn them on her wrists; the work of building the Free Zone, with all its triumphs and disasters, devoted community members and predators seeking to exploit them; the growing police pressure culminating in the worst moments of her life; and her flight.

"Gods, Cassie, that's horrible. I'm so sorry."

Cassie stares at her hands. "I didn't want you to know—to know I'm a coward."

"What? I don't think—oh. You wish you'd died there." It isn't a question.

"I should have. I abandoned them at the moment they needed me most."

A long silence.

"I thought everyone in the Free Zone died," Samantha says at last. "The cops said an anarchist firebomb detonated early, killed everyone inside."

"Cops lie."

"I know that." Samantha's tone is all restraint and patience. "But you're the only witness left."

Cassie recoils. "And you think, what? That I should tell my story and then everyone will wise up to what the cops have done and turn on them and we all sing protest songs around the campfire?"

"Please please please don't treat me like a fool." Samantha pinches the bridge of her nose. "I'm not as naive as you think. I know you're trying to forget."

"I'm sorry, Samantha. I don't think you're a fool," Cassie knows she owes an explanation. "Fuck. I tried so hard to fix it, and I can't. It can't be fixed, not ever, and I just need to forget." She slams her hand to the ground, cries out in pain. When she lifts it away, she leaves a streak of blood behind. A sliver of glass digs into her palm.

Samantha cradles her hand. "We can't have uncontrolled blood during spell prep," she says and helps Cassie up.

In the shop's tiny restroom, she cleans and bandages the wound, insists Cassie stay put while she cleans up the spill. She's finishing up as Cassie emerges.

"You must hate me," Cassie says, hands stuffed in her back pockets.

"Why would I hate you?" Samantha dumps the shards of glass into the trash.

"Because I'm a coward."

"I don't think you're a coward, Cassie. I don't think it was wrong to run, and I don't think it was wrong to stay." She pulls her hands through her hair. "You made a choice under enormous pressure. I wish you could forgive yourself."

"Best I can hope for is to forget." Cassie glimpses rage cross Samantha's features. It's there only for a moment, the contortion, the overwhelming pressure of it, but Cassie knows what she saw. "Why ... Oh." Of course, a librarian would hate her plan. "If you knew what I was doing, why did you help me? I know it goes against your ... your values."

Samantha sags and sits on the floor between overflowing bookshelves. "Because you needed help, and that's what I do. Because ..." She shakes her head and doesn't continue the thought.

"I'm not worth caring about," Cassie sags to the ground opposite Samantha. "It just ends badly for everyone."

"For gods' sakes. You are." She talks over Cassie's objection. "And so is the Free Zone. So are the people who died." She leans forward, puts her hand atop Cassie's.

Cassie yanks her hand away like it's been burned. "No no no no no! You can't ask me to carry all that. I'm the worst person to do it. And don't you dare say that I'm the only one who can—"

"Never! No one should have to carry that alone, Cassie. Not even a Witch of Memory like you."

The pain does not depart. Cassie's trauma is part of her. She is broken, now and forever.

But broken is not useless.

"They have a copy of *The Anarchists' Annotated Histories* in Minneapolis," Samantha announces, her smile almost as welcome as her news.

"That's amazing!" Cassie grins back, sets aside the marble she's been working with. "How is that possible?"

"Are you ready for this? They've got explorers there, search parties that go to Azeb, Tlön, Cimmeria. They're gathering lost things, Cassie."

She hurries to the wall of their little apartment, to the list of titles from the KC Free Zone Library, and places a checkmark next to *Histories*. She's found almost a third of them now.

"How's your project going?" Samantha asks, and Cassie hands her a marble. An unremarkable sphere of swirling blues and silvers, Samantha's own variation on one of the first spells she learned. It's nothing special until activated.

Samantha is suitably impressed.

They take a break from work, share a meal, and then Cassie reads to Samantha until the librarian falls asleep. She's a better roommate than Cassie could have hoped for, not least because, while she wants to be more than roommates, she's content to wait until Cassie trusts herself.

Cassie palms a marble, remembers standing at the top of the stairs, the tear gas and the hum of gathering magic. It will always be with her, the terror as the wall caved in, the panic of her escape, the mantle of loss draped over her shoulders. A Witch of Memory can no more forget these things than she can forget to breathe.

She returns to her work. She can't forget and no longer wishes to. Because the uncitizens dreamed of a better world, and for a short, precious while, it was real, as flawed and small and divided as it was. Real. And the only way it might be real again is if people remember, if they learn from it, if they keep that hope alive, along with the hope of so many other dreams.

Cassie can't be the Keeper of the Past. No one can be. Barricades can be torn down, strongholds defeated, security compromised, cells rooted out, dreamers and radicals locked away, leaders assassinated. Cops will spy, captives will turn on their friends. *Utopia* means *no place*.

The revolution can't be anywhere; therefore, it must be everywhere.

Thus, she's enchanted the marbles to hold only true memories so that Witches of Place can distribute them to anyone ready to hear and to share, to thousands or tens of thousands of people across the globe, the ones who still believe in something better, who are never as alone as they fear. A community without bosses, without hierarchies, without commands, with only a shared purpose: to bear the past, and thus create the future.

Cassie lifts a marble to the light, feels the memory it holds: Kam, shield raised high, urging them all on. An unchangeable fact, a fixed history. But its meaning? That's a story Cassie is still writing. So are Samantha, the witches, and the utopians. So are you and I.

LESLEY CONNER

I was absolutely blown away the first time I read "This Shattered Vessel, Which Holds Only Grief" by Izzy Wasserstein. It's a beautiful and sad story about survivor's guilt, magic, finding someplace to fit it, and learning to live with your past. When I read it, we'd already accepted Marie Croke's story "To Seek Himself Again" and there was something about these two stories that made me feel that they needed to be published together. They felt right together. I was so excited that I was able to put them in the same issue when I put together issue 127.

IN HASKINS
CARSON WINTER

Everyone, both the young and the old, went about their lives as usual on the day of the Mask Festival. The downtown streets were covered with colored leaves and Mr. Burkett still waved at children and swept in front of his storefront. Mrs. Farley still clucked to Mrs. Durant on how the new teachers at the old school would not and could not teach their children anything. And the policemen still ate lunch at the Morrison Deli on Main. Normality ruled with benevolent routine. But still, as the leaves fell, and the stage was erected, the people of Haskins braced quietly for their most insistent tradition.

At the fairgrounds, Jennifer arrived early to help set the stage. Her eye sockets hung loose and rubbery around her blue eyes. She was the first Jennifer to have blue eyes. The mane on top of her head was coarse and tawny. Flies buzzed in her stomach and she was thankful she was Jennifer because Jennifer always had to stay busy. Cindy was already there, cross-legged and cutting orange leaves out of construction paper, looking prim and sweet in her blue dress.

She nodded to Cindy as she found a pair of scissors. When Cindy did not return the movement, Jennifer decided that her eyelets must be misaligned.

"Hey," she said, gaining her attention.

Cindy looked up from a pile of construction paper. "Good morning," she said between ragged breaths. She always complained of being overheated. "Are you excited?"

Cindy's voice was low this year, deep. She was tall and muscular, but Jennifer always gave her credit for her commitment to Cindy's primary traits—innocence and geniality. They were best friends.

"Yes, in a way," she said.

Cindy's scissors made ripping sounds as they ate through the construction paper. "Are you worried?"

She was talking about Rance and Rance was a key aspect of Jennifer. They fit together like pieces of a puzzle. Jennifer was a cheerleader and Rance was the high school quarterback. He had a shock of blond horsetail hair on the top of his rubber scalp. His mask was loose and shook back and forth like a great Jell-O mold when he spoke. They were to be married the day after the Mask Festival.

She froze for a moment. "No," said Jennifer, wondering how much of herself she should share. "Rance and I will be very happy."

"Of course."

"We'll be very happy," she said again. Because right now, she was Jennifer, and that is something Jennifer would say.

The stage was decorated with cornucopias and browning sunflowers—symbols of the season. Orange and brown paper leaves decorated the backdrop, frozen in mid-fall. The people of Haskins shuffled in quietly, some enthusiastically. Others came with an expression of boredom, of toe-tapping impatience. Haskins was a small town, but it contained all sorts.

Jennifer snuck down from the stage as twilight struck and the big sky above the small town glowed with gold and crimson ribbons. The people were drinking their ciders, wiping the grease from the lips of their masks as they devoured turkey legs through the slits that made up their mouths.

She found Rance sitting on a hay bale, his legs resting on a large pumpkin with a blue ribbon. She said his name and he reacted in mock exaggeration, pretending to fall from his spot. Rance had always been a jokester—for the last three dozen years, at least. Before, he was cruel—a bully—but time had softened his demeanor. He was now something of a class clown. Even in Haskins, times change.

"There she is, my beautiful." He stood up and touched her waist. He was shorter than her and the way he looked up into her eyes made him seem like a child looking up at the stars in the night sky. She could see him, his eyes behind the rubber curves, big and brown, pointing up to an endless sky with infantile delight.

They mashed their faces together, crumpling into each other as their masks folded into sweating slabs of rubber. Their tongues found their way out of their mouth-slits, tasting each other's flesh.

They held on for as long as they could. Rance found his head on her shoulder. He would not say what he wanted to say, but she could hear the choke in his voice all the same. She could divine his meaning.

She pulled apart from him and looked down, grabbing his half-drank cup of cider for a sip. "We're getting married tomorrow," she said.

He swallowed, a noise that seemed to echo behind his mask. "Yes, I know."

Behind them, past the tents and merchants, folks began to gather. A horn blared. "Could we just—"

She stopped herself. It was not Jennifer speaking.

Rance sniffed and took her by the arm. "We should head up," he said. "They'll start without us."

They pulled each other through the crowd and stood to the far side near the stage where they could see Mayor Granger adjusting his cufflinks. He preened in the expected manner, debuting a new suit with extravagant embroidery for the occasion. Mayor Granger was always wearing the finest clothes.

"Alright, yes," he began. "Okay, well, here we are. This is the Mask Festival. The Festival of Masks. An old tradition, a very old tradition, indeed." Mayor Granger's speech ran out of steam before it began, as it often did in the last year, so instead of continuing, he straightened his silk tie and smiled. "Let's begin," he said, finally.

Through the wings of the stage, two farm boys with rubber jowls pushed a wooden cart with a large pumpkin on top of it. Granger clapped his hands and let out a nervous sigh. The two boys hoisted the pumpkin's top off together, struggling under its weight.

Jennifer and Rance held hands as they watched Mayor Granger close his eyes and reach into the pumpkin. When his hand came back with two slips of paper, the festival began.

"Connie and Delmont," he called. "Please come up to the stage and make your exchange."

A small woman with a snug mask trotted up on stage, she carried with her a wicker basket of flowers. She curtsied before the audience. On the other side, a mechanic in overalls with long black hair stomped with heavy boots to the center of the stage. They turned to each other and bowed, then walked to the rear of the stage, their backs to the audience. With both hands they removed their masks, then, without looking, held them out to the other. The new Connie's mask was so tight that her features seemed to pop out of the eyelets. Delmont was slight and wiry, but the wearer had begun to learn his movements, raising his feet in great destructive arcs. The crowd cheered and the new Connie skipped heavily back into the crowd and disappeared.

Before long, Mayor Granger's name was called too. His change was extravagant, of course. He danced to the back of the stage and when he came back his voice grew more resinous, his stature more assured. The old Granger disappeared into the crowd wearing Jim Brown's face and drinking sweet liquor with Jim Brown's loud friends.

Jennifer held Rance's hand until he had to leave for the stage. He met with Susan Hickens, a girl a year below them, and they swapped faces. When Rance came back to Jennifer, he was taller. Susan held her face in her hands as she was embraced by her family. For just a moment, Jennifer saw her look back at her, the black holes of her eyes an implacable enigma. She was always known to be shy.

The new Rance put his arm around her—in a way that was so unlike the old Rance that it made her skin crawl. She told herself that it was okay, that they were to be married and that this was a perfectly apt display of affection. It was only that—Rance used to hold her hand. He did not usually wrap his arms around her casually, she was used to feeling his fingers between hers. She wriggled out of the embrace and grabbed his hands, demonstrating the protocols of their relationship in a discreet way. His hands were rough and large. He turned his head toward her, bright hazel eyes hidden behind eyelets. She thought she detected a nod of understanding. He held her hand and watched the stage.

Mayor Granger dug his hand into the pumpkin and came out with two slips of paper. He squinted his eyes, one hand tugging a finger into his eyelet, spreading it so that he could read. "Cole Drewson and Jennifer Maisey. Come on up!"

Her heart shivered, palpitating in erratic bursts of electric anxiety. She unhooked her hand from Rance and felt a chill. She looked at him briefly, to see his eyes, but they were not the eyes she knew. She seemed to float to the stage, dragged along by an inevitable leash. Mayor Granger took both of their hands and raised them. He was adding to the spectacle, he was making decisions. She reflected that this was indeed in line with Granger's character, and she wondered why no one considered taking the hands of those on the stage and raising them before. It added a sort of spectacle to the event, and historically, Mayor Granger was spectacle incarnate.

Granger joined their hands and for just a moment, she felt as if the hand in hers was Rance's. The Rance *she* knew. But the palm in hers was sweating and Rance never sweated from his hands. She and Cole walked to the back of the stage—an eternity—and she looked straight ahead as she took off her mask.

Cole was doing the same beside her.

She wondered if he felt the same rush she did when she removed it. *I'm still Jennifer I'm still Jennifer I'm still Jennifer*, she thought. Her face was naked and she was still Jennifer. She panicked. Her heart kicked her sternum. She did not feel any different. She liked being Jennifer. She was still her. Jennifer was who she should be, and why now should Cole get to be Jennifer? Why now should *she* have to be Cole?

She tried to catch her breath and reach some sort of compromise with herself as Cole pulled off his mask and held it out to her.

Her body failed her. It had become too accustomed to the ways of Haskins. She reached out with her mask and they exchanged without looking at each other. She pulled on Cole Drewson's face and felt the sweat and stink of another human and she began to pray—that she would *be* Cole, that she would forget what it was like to be Jennifer, what it was like to love Rance, her Rance.

They both turned around and Cole Drewson waved weakly to the audience and went down the opposite side of the stage. Jennifer found Rance and they put their arms around each other and embraced.

In the back of the fairgrounds, Cole found himself in the men's room, staring at his new face. Long jawed, with a mustache. Stubble dotted his chin. A trucker hat covered his black hair. His creases were long and deep like knife cuts.

Behind him, a boy he could not see left a bathroom stall and walked out the door. When he was alone in the surgical teal bathroom, Cole whispered his old name.

The next month was a period of adjustment for everyone. Cole woke up in his new home and learned his old habits. His wife, Pauline, was a quick study. She would cower in fear whenever he entered the room, although she would do so in a pathetic, approval-seeking way.

Cole was more lethargic, less vigorous in his anger than usual, but he made his threats, he spat between the lips of his mask and cursed. He drank the same beer, although he had not been able to drink as much as he used to. Most nights, when trying, he fell asleep in the white light of the television while Pauline stepped lightly out the front door to meet their neighbor.

When he'd wake, he'd go to his job at the plant, where he learned to speak crudely with the other men at work. His tone was high and girlish but they accepted him with backslaps and unhinged laughter.

He did not feel like Cole, but he did appreciate that the others felt like he was playing his part. Cole was a difficult role, he demanded a certain physicality that was difficult to match at first. And although, behind the rubber of his face, he still felt like Jennifer, he was beginning to appreciate the inherent violence of his new identity.

He'd begun to get comfortable slapping Pauline when he was angry. The first hit had been a surprise to them both, but it was very much in line with what Cole would do. She looked up at him, having fallen to the floor and rubbing her cheek, and she looked almost appreciative.

"Don't look at me like that," he muttered.

The incident happened after he came home late. He told her he'd gone to the bar, but really he'd gone down to the old high school to watch the football game. He'd brought a bottle with him. It was gone by the time he got back. She only had to ask him where he'd been and it was enough. It took only a second for his rage to show its face.

After, of course, he felt sick. As Pauline hid the rest of the night, he became preoccupied with the dimensions of his mask. He drank until he fell asleep.

Cole was not known as a sports fan, but it was certainly not so out of sorts for a drunk and a wifebeater to enjoy football. Cole considered this to be an aspect of the Cole character he could develop. What are games but an excuse to drink? What violences could he commit to Pauline when the home team lost? At first, it seemed strange for Cole to go see the local team play every Friday, but then as his work friends came around, it didn't seem so strange at all. And besides, if Rance could now put his arms around Jennifer rather than hold her hand, why couldn't Cole like football?

"You like that cheerleader? The one with the legs?"

Cole shook his head. He did not care for the cheerleaders. He was not looking at them. His eyes were always on the crowd, looking for a young girl with brown hair that always fell in front of her mask. But Susan Hickens was shy and he didn't know why he thought she might decide to come to the game.

He took off his hat and rubbed his mane of hair. He punched the side of his head impotently.

"Y'okay, Cole?"

"Yeah, fine. Watching the game."

Rance, the quarterback, completed a thirty-yard pass and the crowd erupted in unhinged ecstasy. Cole put his hand on his head and said, "I'm gonna head out. I wanna go fishing in the morning."

His friends booed and waved their bottles in mock disapproval, but fishing had been another recent addition to Cole's canon, and he was allowed to leave. He balled his fists in the cuffs of his coat, cursing under his mask, stealing glances at the field. *They were going to be newlyweds*, he reminded himself. He got into his car and rubbed at the rubber covering his face. He rubbed it into himself, tried to make it melt into his flesh.

When he got home, he greeted Pauline by cracking her jaw.

She threw her hands up in front of her, but her eyes showed the same twisted sort of glee she always shared whenever Cole played his part well. She braced for the next hit and when she got it, her head snapped back into the cupboard behind her.

Blood flowed from the slit of her lips. He heard whimpering from inside of her mask. Cole stepped over her body to get a beer from the fridge.

She got on all fours, she was trying to stand. "Cole," she started.

He wound up and kicked her in the ribs. She dropped back to the floor, moaning as she gripped her sides.

Cole stood over her, sweating. In a shaky voice, he said, "Don't ever call me that again."

When she tried to speak again, he stomped down on the back of her neck until he felt something crack.

"I'm sorry," he said. "I'm sorry."

Her legs were shaking, twitching.

"It's just—I'm not Cole."

They stopped moving, and because he was supposed to be Cole, he could only do what Cole would do, so he stomped his boot down hard once more; again and again until her spasms ceased.

Cole had never killed anyone before. There would be side-eyes and gossip, as Haskins generally appreciated its townsfolk to maintain the status quo—but Cole was always a violent man. This was as true an ending to Pauline's story as any, he told himself.

He placed his head against the wood of the pantry and tried to think. *Yes, this was a fine ending. True to character. People had died in Haskins before. Not many, but it has happened.*

The body would be discovered eventually, perhaps by a mailman or a friend of a friend. He would be locked up when it was discovered, but he felt no real urgency regarding these truths. He would perhaps have days, maybe weeks to continue on unfettered. Cole sat down beside Pauline and stroked away the hair on her mask. Blood leaked through its nostrils. It was not a pretty mask: it was far too large on her, as most masks were.

Cole wondered what would have happened if he had been Pauline. If Cole would have killed him in the kitchen, if he would have been so sniveling and grateful as the world blackened around him. He yanked on her hair and saw a bit of skin, real skin, beneath. The idea of it was so alluring, so mysterious. He pulled again to free her head and he pulled until Pauline's face was limp in his own hands, stretched into a long liquid yawn. Cole turned her head, the head of a young man with light brown hair buzzed short. His face was covered in bruises, a kaleidoscope of greens, yellows, browns, and purples. Cole took off his own mask as well and rubbed his fists into his eyes. This is not something Cole would do, he realized, crying harder. He was not Cole.

After work, he and his buddies went to the game like they always did. Such was their lot. They all drank, but by now Cole was used to drinking. They didn't realize he was drinking less, but then again, it didn't matter how much he drank because drink pervaded his being. He smelled perpetually of whiskey. And no one questioned whether Cole was drunk because of course he was. He's Cole. And just as everyone assumed he had been drinking, no one asked about his wife. Because Cole never talked about her anyways. It just wasn't done.

"You lookin' at those cheerleaders, Cole?"

"Too old for me," said Cole, his voice flat. "I like 'em young,"

His face was pointed toward the announcer's box. He was squinting as his friends howled.

"Oh yeah? How young?"

"Real fucking young."

They liked that. They screamed in joy. And as they screamed, he squinted his eyes to see the shy girl with brown hair keeping score a world away.

When the game ended, he waved them off. "I gotta go fishing in the morning," he said.

The crowd was clearing out and he disappeared within them—several hundred rubber faces adorned with wigs and eyeglasses. The girl was climbing down from the announcer's box and he started to quicken his pace. Susan was unassuming, her back turned toward the fence, ready to slip out unnoticed now that her obligation had finished. Cole jogged lightly, not so fast as to draw attention—just the pace of a man eager to get home.

She passed through a split in the chain-link fence and began walking down the sidewalk with her nose in a book. Susan was always reading. Cole followed, a block back at first. If anyone was watching, they'd see him fumbling with his keys, looking for his car.

Susan lived near the school, the ward of bookish parents with large rubber noses and glassless spectacles. She spent most of her time at home and she was no doubt eager now to return. Susan portrayed this well when she first heard Cole shout her old name.

"Rance," he said. "Wait."

She stopped, moving her shoulders as if she were breathing deep, frightened. She turned at a glacier's pace, her mask turned downward toward the pavement.

"I've got to get home. It's late."

"It's not late," said Cole.

"I've got to go."

"We were supposed to be married."

"I'm Susan," she said. "We don't talk. You're too old to talk to me. I'm just a girl."

Cole ground his teeth, sweat dripped into his eye. He thought of Pauline and her face of mashed cherries. "I want you to come home with me tonight, Rance."

"No—I really can't—"

"It's Jennifer. I'm still Jennifer, Rance. Please, come with me. This is me speaking, I want you to come with me because I still love you. We're supposed to be married."

"Rance and Jennifer are getting married next year, the day after the festival. Not us." Her voice quivered when she said it.

Cole was a fast man, quick—a coiled spring. And when he bound toward Susan, she froze. That was a very Susan thing to do. She was not good under pressure and she was so much smaller than Cole.

He wrestled her to the ground and did what came most natural; an open hand pressed to her mouth, then a stranglehold around her neck. He felt her soft, sweating flesh. "Please," he said, whispering through her nostril holes, "come with me."

Like in any small town, a death causes an uproar.

A dead girl on the side of the road, bleeding out her mask.

And just like in any small town, time marches on.

"You don't usually have people over, is that true?"

The two had never been here before, a fact they seemed self-conscious of—still, they remained as chipper as they could, considering. They pointed at the elk's head on the wall and asked Cole if he hunted. They complimented Pauline on the furniture, their aesthetics as well as comfort.

Pauline bowed extravagantly, an ironic affectation. "The house was such a mess before. We're trying to be better about that."

Through the kitchen doorway came Cole, holding a tray of cocktails. "Please, help yourself, plenty more where that came from." He lowered the drinks on the table and poured himself a glass of club soda.

"You're not drinking?"

"Oh no, I'm a monster on that stuff. I'm turning a new leaf. I found God, I guess. The grain spoke to me. The seeds were sown. The old scarecrow came home to tend to the blackbirds in the field. All that jazz, you know?"

Pauline rubbed his shoulder, she kissed the back of his head. "He's been doing really good. Great."

There was a moment of silence, a pregnant pause. Pauline reached a hand out to their guests—a man and a woman, with large noses and glasses. "Awful what happened to Susan."

The man nodded solemnly and Cole huffed in sympathy. Snow began to fall and the gray light outside penetrated every inch of their humble home.

"Haskins isn't perfect," said the woman. "But then again, no place is."

They stared at each other, through each other for a long moment. Pauline's brown eyelets shined like glossy caramels by the fire as she took Cole by the hand and held it ever so tight.

JASON SIZEMORE

Typically, any story with domestic abuse is a non-starter for our editorial team. But Carson Winter has created a modern fairy tale depicting how easy it is to fall into cultural stereotypes and roles. If we are assumed to be terrible, what's the impetus for not being awful. When we buck against type, there will be members of society ready to push you back into place. The fact that Jennifer, formerly a woman, steps so easily into the drunken, abusive Cole personality is a powerful statement and makes the domestic abuse an important part of the story.

WHOSE MORTAL TASTE
ERIN K. WAGNER

i.

"'Because I am human, and you are not.'" Oriole I tilted its head. "Those are the last words he said." One of its eyes drifted upwards to the sky, with a barely audible whir, glinting in the strong sunlight. "As if he did not see the irony in saying such a thing as he died."

They were occupied by one of their favorite pastimes, recounting the amusing things humans had said before the species had gone extinct. It was late afternoon by the human clock that dictated their programming. Corvid III had toyed with removing it and now had a hard time perceiving light from shadow. Which, in turn, affected its navigation. So the rest of them kept time by archaic human standards: morning, afternoon, night. They watched Corvid III spin in circles on the mosaic tiles of the courtyard.

In the afternoon, they dragged a spindly table out to the cement patio and laid out stones in the pretext of a game. Then they talked, usually three or four at a time. Tanager I invited them to come, though it knew Oriole I was sometimes reluctant to entertain company.

"But that was what was odd about the humans," Myna IV interjected. "They didn't measure their value by their lifespan. If anything, mortality seemed to increase their affection for each other."

"I understand that." Oriole I's voice changed register. "Did I say I didn't understand what he said? I just said it was ironic."

"You meant that it was foolish." Tanager I flicked one stone with the tip of its finger. They had never established the rules of the game.

Oriole I's head swayed left and right. "Yes. If you insist. To say that he truly lived and I did not. It was a ridiculous thing to say."

Tanager I lowered its head in acknowledgment, but Myna IV was in a quarrelsome state. It found some satisfaction in contention which Tanager I did not understand. It preferred such contention not happen in its courtyard, so it tried to distract Oriole I, flicked another stone in its compat's direction. But Oriole I was as persistent as Myna IV was quarrelsome. It was, perhaps, one of the things that annoyed Tanager I the most about the way humans had programmed them, the tendency to create one overwhelming personality trait in a misguided attempt to create personality itself. Now, twenty-two years after the last human had died, they had not been able to completely overwrite this quirk without losing other, more important attributes.

Tanager I expressed its irritation in a subdued fashion by standing up and moving out of the shade into the heat. Myna IV paid no mind. The heat soaked through Tanager I's shallow epidermis, still preserved in its organic state—Tanager I was quite proud of this—to the metallic mesh dermis below.

"Not ridiculous, though, if you adopt their perspective. You are not very good, Oriole I, at seeing things from a different angle." Myna IV chortled, a remix of a bird's call and human laughter. It had managed this by manipulating its own electronic genome sequence, a tricky business at best, much trickier than Corvid III's interference with its clock. The engineers had modeled the genome on songbirds, looking for a new way to endow androids with unique voices and the ability to procreate.

Tanager I had some desire to procreate; Oriole I none. But it was hard for Tanager I to consider a separation from its compat.

"I do not see the value in adopting a perspective that is not my own. My perspective is the one designed to secure my wellbeing." Tanager I tried to laugh at Oriole I's answer, but could not. It was a peacekeeper.

"How do you know that?" Myna IV turned its head so that it could survey the other two listening. It liked an audience.

"Know what? Clarify."

"How do you know"—pause for effect— "that your own perspective is the one best designed to secure your wellbeing?"

Oriole I did not answer right away. Tanager I turned back toward the table. It was silent in the courtyard. Corvid III stopped spinning and managed to redirect itself toward them as dusk blended light and shadow.

"Evolution," it answered simply, finally. Tanager I placed a finger at its chin, a pose meant to connote thoughtfulness.

Myna IV laughed again. "We are not human. We did not evolve."

Corvid III interrupted. "It depends on your definition of evolution. We have not progressed via a series of naturally occurring changes in our DNA. But we did change and progress via deliberate modifications of our programming." It gestured specifically to Myna IV. "We modified our own programming even." It did not comment on whose modifications had been more successful.

Myna's voice sped up a tick. "I hardly think the humans designed us to prioritize our perspective over theirs."

Oriole I's eyes glowed. "So you think my perspective is merely mimicking the humans who designed us?"

Tanager I waved its hands in an attempt to put a halt to the debate. The question of original thought was a heated subject in their community. In order to distract, it offered to bring out some of the fibrous plant that exercised the jaw and provided a pleasant warmth while masticated. A human whom it had once known had compared their obsession with the fiber to chewing tobacco. Tanager I had tried to convince the human of the difference between enjoyment and addiction, but argument was not its strong suit. That human had been a favorite of Tanager I's, a little frail thing with no strength to knock it about.

No one paid any heed to Tanager I's offer. Sometimes it regretted that they had ever learned to individuate.

"I think it is time we answer this question." Perhaps Tanager I had missed a few sentences while distracted. Perhaps it had missed important sentences. "To see if we are really so alike now."

Myna IV had stood up as if to leave. "You're suggesting we revive one?"

"What?" Tanager I did not usually use questions to express surprise. The tiny human had been fond of doing so. "We should not disrupt the natural order of things."

This was popular rhetoric now, this notion of *natural.* Oriole I disliked the discourse. It should have remembered that if it truly hoped to dissuade them from this rash decision.

"There is a facility not far from here." Oriole I hardly looked at Tanager I though decisions of this magnitude should be negotiated between compats. "That is why we were employed here. To accommodate and alleviate the high rate of morbidity in this community of elders. It is only natural they would have a place to be resigned to nearby."

"You're obsessed with human mortality," Tanager I said quietly. Its comment was not registered by the other three. Part of resolving conflicts was identifying problems. It wanted to ask Oriole I why, but now was not the moment. Later would be too late.

"We will go tomorrow," Myna IV dictated, the decision apparently made.

"We should not." Tanager I tried a last time to express its discomfort.

Oriole I placed its hand flat on the table, disrupting the stones of the game. The setting sun glinted off the metal joints of its fingers. "I want to know if we are our own species now."

"By proving our dependency?"

Oriole I cocked its head and Myna IV leaned a bit closer to it. "What do you mean?"

Tanager I did not have a good answer that it could communicate. It was a subsurface logical equation. "We do not need them to tell us who we are."

"Ignoring the reality of our creation will not revise it." Oriole I's register was flat. It and Myna IV were now in agreement rather than divided by argument.

The courtyard flushed into darkness. The horizon was rimmed in red. The ground was very flat here, in the west and in the desert. Tanager I had no more to say.

ii.

The dome of the cryogenic facility was pale and bulbous against the color-saturated sky. It was located at the exact coordinates their maps had indicated. Sometimes, the maps were not accurate. The humans' grasp of direction and geography had been limited despite their globalization. Tanager I trailed behind Oriole I and Myna IV. It slapped at its knee joints regularly to keep the dust from building up there.

"We should have taken one of the carts," Myna IV said to be quarrelsome. Tanager I did not say anything, and Oriole I sped up its pace.

Corvid III had not accompanied them, but it refused to say that it agreed with Tanager I when asked. Tanager I had not conversed with its compat for the rest of the night and when the hour for reboot came, it turned away to an empty room rather than the one it shared with Oriole I. Oriole I did not comment or say anything even the next morning when Tanager I offered it some fiber as a gesture of reconciliation. Oriole I did not adjust to new situations quickly and had probably still been processing the action of the night before.

"We should have taken one of the carts," Myna IV repeated, its tones an exact echo of what it had just said.

"It would have failed on the way and we would have needed to walk regardless." Tanager I hoped this would be another gesture of reconciliation, a defense of Oriole I's choice. Perhaps Oriole I should make a gesture of its own.

The sand and dust were red and yellow and orange; it dulled the dark patina of Tanager I's feet, which had not been created to mimic skin like its arms or hands or face. They were not organic. They shone and glistened when they were not coated in grime.

Oriole I remained silent. Tanager I wondered if it doubted its own resolution, if it was processing how this mission could fail. Tanager I had determined four ways already, but it was still processing beneath social functions.

As they drew closer to the facility, the sand was swept away from the road by the winds which scoured their joints. Tanager I heard the grinding of each movement it made but was satisfied nonetheless with the now-even walking surface. Lights blinked on tall poles as if they too had forgotten the difference between day and night. They ran on solar energy.

Oriole stopped as they reached the wide doors of the facility, blindingly white in the sunlight. The sand had left no trace on them. "Myna IV, you should open them." Myna IV was the best of them at overwriting security protocols. It moved forward without arguing. Under its quick-flashing fingers, the dark glass panel by the doors beeped and then blinked rapidly without stopping. The doors shuddered open.

They all paused and looked inside. Tanager I had the fleeting thought that a human might come down through the foyer to greet them, but there was not even a hologram. There were dead sticks of plants lining the variegated tile floor. They clacked like skeletons in the sudden breeze; the wind carried small rocks and dust into the pristine space.

"The humans will be stored on the sublevel." Oriole I pointed out the stairwell and they moved as one toward it, without question. It was doubtful the elevators worked.

It occurred to Tanager I that the humans were not dead, by their hopeful definition, but rather in stasis. Then again, they were most definitely dead by biological measures. The contradiction, it supposed, lay at the center of Oriole I's initial irritation, the argument that had driven them all here. It was tempted to hiss under its breath, like a cat or some other small predator gone feral, but Tanager I did not know what purpose it would serve. It was an instinct, and instincts always made it uncomfortable. The humans had been driven by instinct and now what was left of them was frozen underground.

The sublevel hall was only dimly lit. Some of the lights had died in the years since the facility had last been monitored. Where, Tanager I wondered briefly, was the monitor? Had they died during their shift? Was their corpse huddled over a desk somewhere? Or had they decided one day to not return under the rose-red sky?

"Here." Oriole I stopped in front of a pane of frosted glass. Upon examination, Tanager I realized the pane was in fact a door.

"Go in then," Myna IV pushed the point. It had already overridden the keypad.

Oriole I placed a hand, fingers splayed, on the glass and pushed. The door swung in with a hiss and a sigh as if the room had depressurized on their entrance. Otherwise, it was quiet. If there were generators here, they were sophisticated ones, nearly silent.

As they moved forward, the tiles grew slick under a sheen of water. Cylindrical tubes flanked them on either side, like columns from ancient human architecture. Tanager I watched the water fly up in droplets and dot the coating of dust on its feet.

"They have thawed." Myna IV said it like spring had come and these were trees, brittle and frosted. Tanager I saw now the slow trickle from below the tubes.

"Perhaps another room?" Tanager I suggested. Oriole I remained quiet. It pried at one of the tubes until the metal bent under its fingers and the door—the coffin's lid— was loosened in its track. The body inside had begun to decompose and was slumped back against the curvature of the tube. There was still the semblance of a face, though the skin and flesh on it was bloated.

They stood looking at it. Finally, Oriole I flung up one hand. "Human," it said as if presenting a marvel.

"Let us check another floor," Tanager I replied abruptly. It should let Oriole I have its triumph. They should go home and not meddle anymore with things as they were. But now it found that hard to do. *Like a dog with a bone*, the small human would have said. Frail, but cruel sometimes.

Myna IV was not satisfied either. It moved to the door. Tanager I followed and, together, they descended the stairs to the level below. Here, they heard a hum in the hallways, which was promising. Oriole I's footsteps echoed behind them. The next room they entered was perceptibly colder. The floor was dry. Tanager I placed its hands on one of the tubes and it vibrated. The metal rattled against its palm.

There were controls embedded in the floor, overshadowed by the cylinder. Myna IV overrode them. The sound of the engines softened slightly. The door shuddered and groaned in the track and then slid back.

Oriole I watched from the door but did not come in.

The human inside the tube was frozen rigid, hair shorn close to the head, eyes plastered shut by a white substance designed to protect. This same substance bound the fingers close together and wrapped around the hips and genitals of the human. The only thing the human wore was a gauzy semi-transparent jumpsuit that appeared to have been sewn around them. This human looked nothing like the image of the small one Tanager I had held in its head for so long. It had forgotten the diversity of human appearance.

"We have to be quick," Myna IV said, practical when practicality was needed.

Tanager I nodded but let Myna IV handle the body. It twittered under its breath, a laugh or expression of frustration.

iii.

Oriole I stood back from the metal table, as if now unsure about what they had done and were doing. A few of the computers were still running on a spark of solar power, and Myna IV had found the requisite files. It had scanned the information and processed how to revive the human, had determined which cooler—still functioning—contained blood of the right type. They had calculated, quickly, that it would be necessary to revive the human before returning back across the desert to their commune. The body would thaw and begin to decompose in the heat otherwise. There was such a fine line between viability and rot.

"Are we sure that the human will be … right?" Oriole I's voice was quiet in the large hollow of the operating theater.

As Oriole I spoke, Myna IV directed Tanager I on which equipment to roll over to the table, large machines on unwieldy carts. It was flushing the blood vessels free of preservative in the meantime. The body dripped and a pool of liquid formed around the table where Myna IV was careless.

"You will have to define that," Myna IV said, quarrelsome again. It was concentrating and did not appreciate Oriole I's newfound reluctance or interruptions.

"Revivification is theoretical, yes?"

Tanager I looked at Oriole I. It stood stiffly, hands at its sides, eyes focused on the body stretched and stripped out of its plastic packaging. Myna IV hooked up the IV line and began the blood transfusion. "This will take at least an hour," it informed them. They were quiet for a long part of that time. This did not disrupt their conversation, and Tanager I resumed forty-five minutes later.

"It is ironic," Tanager I confirmed for Oriole I, "that they went extinct before they could revive themselves in any significant numbers. But there were successful trials."

Oriole I nodded, but Tanager I could not tell what it was thinking. Myna IV was focused on tweaking the program of the nanotechnology that would repair any unsustainable damage inflicted on the body by the cryopreservation. Once it was satisfied that the programming met the guidelines it had reviewed, it injected a syringe of the prepared nanobots into the discolored thigh of the body. Some natural color had returned to the skin, but not all.

"It would have been better if I had been programmed in medicine," Myna IV said as it stepped back. They were not so different from the nanobots, Tanager I observed to itself, but there was no human to tweak their programming. Tanager I felt sure it did not require any further changes. What would the human think?

"*Right*, like *normal*, is subjective," Myna IV would not let its objection go.

"How long?" Tanager I asked.

"When the diagram is green, then we may resuscitate and the human will continue to recover while we transport it back."

Tanager I studied the map of the human's body on the screen. The vascular system was outlined in red, as were many of its organs. Tanager I could understand why Oriole I was concerned about whether the human would be able to function. Tanager I was programmed to be precise. It questioned whether the human would be able to function within the very specific parameters Oriole I deemed valuable for the larger experiment at hand.

Minutes passed. The only noise was the whine of the machines. They did not move, and so their joints made no sound.

Myna IV's eyes flicked between the diagram and the body. Gradually, lines on the diagram shifted from red to green. "We should establish your hypothesis before the human wakes," it said, able to needle Oriole I even as it studied the medical readouts. Tanager I felt once again defensive of its compat. But the suggestion was a logical one.

"Will we keep the human alive once the hypothesis is tested?" It added this question, then snapped its mouth shut, unsure of which answer it thought best.

"That depends on its behavior," Myna IV answered. There was no hesitation to its answer, to the possibility of killing it. The green crept up the diagram.

"I propose," Oriole I presented its hypothesis, "that humans must acknowledge that we are not now, if we ever were, mere copies of them. That we are alive."

Tanager I did not speak its doubts aloud but was skeptical of this proposition. Did originality equate to life? Tanager I had never seen a benefit to this definition of *living* with its organic implications. It viewed the petulant proclamations of the small human regarding Tanager I's own nature, that *he is too real* to be just that, petulant and disconcertingly humanizing.

How long had Oriole I harbored this resentment? It was unusual for it to speak so irrationally. Myna IV, for once, did not answer or mock Oriole I. Did it feel similarly? Did it too want to be alive?

"The human can be revived now," Myna IV said into the waiting quiet.

iv.

The human did not immediately wake. To be alive and to be conscious, for humans, were different things. Tanager I, when it slept, did not consider itself to truly exist. The human's head, as they walked, bounced limply on the crude pallet they had fashioned from a cot at the institution.

The others watched them enter the gates, the setting sun glinting red on the metal of those who were not covered in faux skin. They did not make any noises but whirred gently as they turned and followed them. The gates shut behind them, equally quiet.

The human also did not awake when they reached the commune or when they transferred it from the pallet to the bed that still remained in one of the central building's corner rooms.

"It will need water and food," Tanager I said, ever the host.

Oriole I was still taciturn. Myna IV answered. "There are bottles and cans in storage."

Tanager I nodded and stared at Oriole I's face, hoping that the fixed gaze would stir it from its silence. When the implicit gesture did not achieve the desired effect, Tanager I spoke. "Oriole, come with me to fetch it." It left off the numerical designation, the right of a compat, but one usually reserved for private spaces.

Oriole I followed but did not talk as they navigated the tiled hallways with their faded carpet runners and the concrete stairs. The fluorescent lights flicked on automatically across the length of the drop ceiling when they entered the storage room. Tanager I's thermometer registered the lower temperature.

As Myna IV had said, there were shelves stacked high with water and canned food, some dried food in boxes as well.

"I have told you before," Tanager I said, turning to face Oriole I, "about the boy that I was initially programmed to serve, how much he loved me."

"Yes." Oriole I's voice was flat. It moved to the shelves and studied the food there. "How lucky you were." It was imitating human figures of speech.

"Are you angry with me?" It sounded foolish even as Tanager I said it, unfit for a conversation between the two of them. It did not wait for an answer. "I remind you of that boy because, as much as he loved me, though I harbored some affection for him"—they had long ago, even when the humans were still alive, moved beyond a distinction between genuine and simulated emotion—"I would never wish him back with me. I have no desire for humans to return."

"I do not either." Oriole I filled its arms with plastic-wrapped bundles of bottles.

"You do, if only to fight them."

Oriole I loaded himself down further. Cans teetered precariously atop the bottles.

"You hate or you love them but you need the object." Tanager I was uncomfortable. All of this incendiary speech ran counter to its programming

Oriole I turned slowly. "You do not understand me."

The lights clicked and sizzled. It was as human a thing as Tanager I had ever heard Oriole I say.

"I understand you," Tanager I countered. "I have studied your programming."

A corner of Oriole I's mouth crooked up in a jagged grin. The fluidity of their micro-expressions had never matched those of their creators.

"You want a child."

It was an accusation, though Tanager I could not understand it. Oriole I continued, words more rapid than they had been all day.

"You study and tweak your code. You study replication. You set before me the advantages and disadvantages of a third individual sharing our home, triangulating our conclusions. This is human. To want there to be more of you, to split and split and split until you choke out everything else."

It was almost poetry, terrible, without rhythm or reason or rhyme, but excessive and indulgent. Tanager I disliked poetry. Its mind was blank. Its mind skipped. It blinked.

"Apologies." Its programming intruded, seeking to harmonize. "I did not mean to anger you." But it had intended to.

Oriole I knew Tanager I well enough to know both the programming and the falsehood. It turned to the stairs and began to ascend. The lights followed it, casting the room into darkness where no motion was detected.

When it finally moved to follow, Tanager I did not take any of the food or water with it. It climbed the stairs, letting the door to the storage room slam behind it. It paced the tiles of the hallway, sensed where the carpet grew threadbare in the runners. It stopped at the door to the human's room. Oriole I was already inside.

"The human is awake," Myna IV said loudly as it heard Tanager I approach, as if in warning.

It did not need the warning. It could hear the muttering of a human voice, thready and stuttering.

"Drink the water," Oriole I directed, like a nursemaid.

Tanager I stepped inside and studied the figure on the bed. The human's face was pale and sweaty, unhealthy in color. It was unclear yet whether it would survive the process of revival. It smacked its lips together, asking for more water in the most basic of ways. Myna IV stood near the door, watching as well. Tanager I sensed that it was not satisfied with the results of their experiment. Perhaps Tanager I projected.

Oriole I's movements, holding the bottle to the human's lips, lifting the human's head off the pillow, were slow and methodical, almost gentle. "Slowly," it directed the human.

"Who are you?" the human finally rasped. It blinked as if it could not see clearly. If it could, it might be more confused than it already was.

"You are at the Sunset Meza's Senior Home," Oriole I answered as if location answered identity.

The human's next question, a note of fear in its voice, was "How old am I?"

Tanager I decided not to stay any longer and left.

v.

Oriole I did not discuss the ending of their compat arrangement, but it did not return to the villa and instead resided in the central building. Tanager I understood that this decision had been implicit in their last discussion, and did not ask how much time Oriole I spent in the room of the human. It also did not host an afternoon game of stones for several days, nor did any of the others question why this was. Corvid III circled the courtyard once and, replicating outdated human conventions, asked if Tanager I needed anything. It did not. There was nothing to be needed.

The other corvids, mynas, tanagers, and orioles had not visited before nor would they now regardless. They had their own pre-established units of socialization, with one of each species assigned per unit to preserve a balance between programmed personalities. Oriole I and Tanager I would therefore both continue to engage with their social unit, whatever conflict that had existed between them resolved. Tanager I processed, analyzed, and stored the data and memories of their arrangement, deleted internal alarms that had synced its own programming with that of its former compat. Oriole I had already halted the feedback loop between them.

Tanager I watched Corvid III circle in graceful arabesques. It had gained a measure of control over its movements, traveling differently if no less efficiently than it had before modifying its programming. Tanager I traced Corvid III's shadow, floating over the tile. The shadow wavered ever so subtly at the edges. Tanager I resolved to itself that it would continue to study the research of those scientists who had attempted to splice android and songbird genetics. The concurrence of Oriole I was no longer an obstacle.

"The human is stronger now," Corvid III said because it felt further conversation must be made. Tanager I understood that impulse.

It also felt that it must make an answer, but could not produce one. The normal protocols did not suit the situation.

"A full recovery was not certain," it said finally. This answer concealed its own doubt about allowing the human to stay in the commune.

"Yes, it talks more now. It holds conversations with us." Corvid III seemed to have been lacking for socialization. Perhaps Tanager I's own seclusion had affected the unit.

"What does it say?"

"It tries to find out what happened to the rest of its kind."

"What do we answer?" It was not thought through, the use of the plural, but it did reflect its own risk assessment, the collective versus the intruder. It was aware that the human could not be defined as an intruder, carried in as it was by itself. Its own actions were suspect, and they had been directed by Oriole I.

"They are not here."

An equivocal answer.

"It will ask more questions."

"Yes," Corvid III assented. It was following Tanager I, who had left the courtyard as if guided by a hidden directive.

The villa was at the edge of the commune, but the central building was not far away. The front doors were automatic and still worked. There were cacti planted along the walkway that led to the doors. They did not need care beyond the sun and rare rain.

Oriole I was by the human's bed, a chrome hand resting on the bedspread. The human was sitting up and it looked healthier, color in its cheeks. It must have been wealthy, Tanager I determined, not only to be cryogenically preserved, but to be comfortable in the presence of so many unlike itself.

"And here's another one." The human flung up its hands, but its voice intonated jest. "You guys must run the joint."

It did not remember Tanager I, it seemed, from before. "Yes," it answered.

The room was quiet. Oriole I stood up, its knees pinging. The human frowned as if puzzling over the answer.

"I need to get up out of here soon, boys. A man can only take so much lying around. Maybe a day or two more rest. Frozen and revived, helluva thing." The last words had the sheen of pattern, well-used. How many times had the human rehearsed this to those who visited it as spectacle? It did not understand that it was a spectacle.

"Where will you go?" Tanager I asked.

"Well, head to the closest city, I imagine. Las Vegas? What's the commute there nowadays?"

Tanager I did not answer. "What of your hypothesis?" it asked Oriole I. "Are you alive?" It was abrupt, defying its own protocol, yet again, to create peace. It could change, it seemed.

The human laughed. It looked out of place in the room, fragile and bony, a remnant of a past era. The room was more humid, even, with its breath.

"Glad to see they finally got around to programming you all with a sense of humor." It reached out for the cup of water on the bedside table. Oriole I did not help. It turned its head and looked out the small window above the bed. "This one's been testing jokes out on me all day."

Early consumers had complained about Tanager I's inability to be deliberately humorous. It could dissect a joke, but it could not tell one with any conviction. Alien. Inhuman. Reviews were blunt. The boy had loved it because he had loved everything ridiculous. It was not always with fondness, no, that Tanager I remembered him.

Tanager I knew that their feedback loop had been severed, but it could still intuit Oriole I's response to the human's comment. There was no obligation between them any longer, but there were memories, saved.

"Humans are extinct," it said.

The human laughed.

It was often hard for them, Tanager I had learned, to accept reality that defied their own perceptions.

"But I'm alive," it answered finally, catching its breath and wiping something from the corner of its eye. It seemed poised between mirth and fear now that neither Tanager I or Oriole I followed up with affirmation.

"Are you?" Tanager I asked.

It was the closest it had come to an actual joke.

AUTHOR NOTES

I have become fascinated with the idea of a world not on the cusp or in the midst of a robot revolution, but post-revolution (or just post-human). What happens if the imagined future is not dominated by robot-human wars or conflict? Sometimes this means I think of a future that has not gone to plan, that has found robots insufficient, that has lapsed back to older ways of living. What happens to the few robots left? What happens if, conversely, robots and humans lived without explicit conflict until the humans just died out? What happens if robots are all that is left of sentient beings (the age-old question of that definition!) in our world? *Our* world. Perhaps defining the bounds of that pronoun is the real question. This story is exploring one such world, as the robots struggle to understand their creator and themselves. The answer is not that they need be the *new* humans, but a thing unto themselves. Is that possible or are all beings defined by their relationship to others?

HANK IN THE SOUTH DAKOTA SUN

STEPHANIE KRANER

Today's the day that Hank is going to die. I haven't told him yet, but I have to. Soon.

We're making good time, eating up miles of track as we speed through the midwestern United States. Ohio, Indiana, Illinois, Iowa. South Dakota is where we're headed, and at the rate we're going, it's only a matter of hours. When you're a conductor, everything is only a matter of hours, but when you're the train itself, it's a little different.

Everything just ... is. Full stop.

Hank's tried to explain it to me before. The infinite space between two points measured by a finite number of miles. The mechanical and spiritual pull of a destination. What, for me, is a simple trip hauling heavy mineral sand from the coast of North Carolina to a processing facility in South Dakota is actually something of a sacred pilgrimage for Hank. Every job is a journey to Mecca when you're manufactured for a specific purpose and then given coded awareness of it.

I've never been a spiritual person, so I just don't get it. Hank teases me about it, calls me unenlightened.

The irony of this, today of all days, weighs more heavily on me than the 300,000 pounds of sand Hank is hauling through the rolling fields of America's heartland.

I'm not ready to say good-bye.

Instead, I turn away from a sea of corn swaying in the August afternoon and focus on the myriad dials and gauges that show me how Hank's feeling. He's always been inclined to lie to me when I'm plugged in and I ask, but the dials don't care about his pride.

Right now, everything looks good. Temperature's in range, engine isn't generating too much heat. He has plenty of energy reserves, and his solar receptors are drinking up the daylight like desert sand.

If Hank were sluggish, or in need of a major repair; if we regularly missed deadlines, or broke down while underway, I might understand. There are dozens of things that can put a train out of commission for good, and I've been afraid of many of them in the years since I was given the chance to be Hank's conductor. I just never thought corporate indifference would be one of them.

My own fault, really. I spend too much time with trains and not enough time with the bipeds who make decisions.

They didn't even bother to tell me in person.

I got a memo delivered via email with the subject *Q4 Embracing Change Update: Software Roll-Out to Begin Early September*. The high-importance icon glared like a stray ember that burns an entire forest to the ground.

You've been identified as being among the conductors of a high-speed freight model that will not be compatible with the September 1 company-wide upgrade…

After I finished reading the email, I printed it just to rip it to shreds, environmental responsibility be damned.

"Can I appeal?" I wrote back to the group mailbox that sent the email, knowing full well that it was absurd to think a national corporation would have an appeals process regarding its business decisions.

That's how they think of Hank, of the other machines they use. Assets, nothing more. I doubt a single one of them has ever been plugged into one of their *assets* and felt the wonderful, living mind among the wires and the software.

A glance at Hank's GPS shows me that it's only another hour until we reach Sioux Falls. Our drop point isn't that far from there, and I still haven't figured out how to break the news.

Part of me wonders if Hank would prefer ignorance. If our positions were reversed, would I want to know?

It's a stupid question, impossible to answer until you've learned the truth, and once you have, it's too late to change your mind. I'm going to tell him; of course, I am. Hank's all I've got, and more importantly, I'm all he's got.

I sigh and pull out my cable. It hooks into the port installed on the inside of my forearm. All conductors have one, but I've never been able to get used to the feel of cool metal sliding into warm tissue. I wince at the momentary discomfort as it clicks into place, and then plug the other end into the port on Hank's control panel.

There's a brief rush as our two energies collide. It's always reminded me of a surge of adrenaline, that heady, heart-pounding jolt that makes all your cells feel like they've stood up to sing an overture.

"The tracks are warm from all the sunshine," Hank says as soon as we're plugged in. "It feels good, much better than the rain we had this morning."

"I'm glad you're having a good time of it," I reply, which sounds condescending, even though I really do mean it.

If Hank notices, he doesn't comment. "Makes me remember Mexico. When's the last time we crossed the border?"

Time isn't the same for trains as it is for people and other machines. They don't have a circadian rhythm or notice night and day in the same way. Although Hank does have some ability to detect light and to see, it's limited to obstructions, sudden motions, things that might litter the tracks and cause an accident. He doesn't have a sleep-wake cycle, doesn't feel the pull of the celestial bodies overhead.

Scientifically, though, he understands the concept.

"Beats me," I say. "Gotta be close to three, maybe four years. At least since we crossed that particular border. We were up in Canada just last month."

"The forests are nice. And the lakes. But nothing beats the desert heat, especially in Baja. Can we go back there soon?"

I shrug and almost tell him "Maybe," but I catch myself in time. There is no maybe here, and I won't lie to him. This is an opening, probably the best one I'm going to get. I've had others, too, and I didn't take them. This might be my last chance.

"I don't know, Hank," I say. "There hasn't been a lot of trade these days between the U.S. and Mexico. Politics and all that. The suits don't agree about some such thing or another."

"Nunca están de acuerdo."

"And no one ever agrees with them," I say, nodding. "Least of all me."

We fall silent, then. Hank, I assume, is thinking about Mexico, probably in Spanish, if I had to guess. He speaks twelve languages. English is his third favorite, just behind Spanish. I can at least understand a bit of that one. His favorite is Chinese and I'm worse than useless at it.

When I'm done silently berating myself for being a coward, I think about my grandpa. Trains were his whole life. Not the sentient kind, though. Old-fashioned, diesel-electric trains, back before the U.S. even had much of a rail network to speak of. He spent most of his younger years welding the cars, fusing steel together in a place so hot the soles of his boots sometimes melted against the metal grate of the floor. Almost thirty years of that before he learned how to drive the machines he'd spent half a lifetime making.

His name was Hank.

He took me for my first ride, back in the early 2010s. I was eight, I think, and he was babysitting me. I don't remember why, where my parents were, but even though Grandpa Hank had to work, he didn't mind bringing me along.

It was just a short trip, hauling some load from Pittsburgh to Cincinnati. Only a few hundred miles, but I was mesmerized by every inch of track between the two cities. The hills, the bends, switching the rails, all of it. Grandpa Hank talked about slack running in on the downgrade, running out on the upgrade, and how too much or too little of it could cause the cars to derail. He showed me signals we passed, lights stacked on top of lights, some flashing, some steady. He used words like "aspect" and "indication" and I didn't know what they meant, but I loved them anyway.

To an eight-year-old, there's nothing better than secret knowledge, disguised in code that only a few can decipher. I was powerless against the pull of it all, and Grandpa Hank made it seem like the coolest job in the world.

Then we reached Cincinnati and met up with a woman that wasn't my grandmother.

We were at a restaurant, scarfing down chili dogs and vanilla milkshakes, and she came in. I remember she tried to pull out a chair and sit, but Grandpa Hank pulled her into his lap.

"Hank," she said, slapping him on the chest, but even I could tell she wasn't serious. "Not in front of the kid."

"Don't you worry about the kid," he said, turning to me with a wink. "You won't say nothing, will you, Alex?"

I shook my head immediately. Grandpa Hank was trusting me with a secret, and at that point in my life, not a whole lot of grownups had trusted me with anything.

I never said a word.

Not to my parents, my friends. Not even to my grandma. When we returned the next day and they all asked how the trip had been, I told them it was the best vacation I'd ever been on, and I said nothing at all about the woman who spent the night in our hotel room while I lay in the other bed with earbuds in and music I couldn't seem to turn up loud enough.

Both my grandparents died about ten years after that, and while I'm fully aware that my grandmother wasn't an idiot, and that in all likelihood, she knew about the infidelity, I still feel a certain tightness in my gut when I think about the secret I was complicit in keeping. There's a nagging voice in the back of my mind that tells me I should've spoken up, and that now I never can.

"Hank," I say before I've even realized that I planned to open my mouth. "What do you think about slowing down a bit, maybe drawing out the last leg of the trip?"

"But it's such a beautiful day for going fast."

"I know," I say, "but believe me when I tell you that if there were ever a good day to miss a deadline, it's this one."

Hank is silent a moment, and I know he's struggling against the coded desire to complete all hauls as quickly as possible. I don't think they intended machines to be able to do this. Hank wants to follow orders, but he also wants to make me happy.

I smile when I feel the soft resistance of the brakes, the inertia that pulls my body forward as the structure I'm standing on reduces speed. He doesn't slow much—we're still racing through what little remains of Iowa—but I've gained a few extra minutes to spend with my best friend at the end of his life.

We ride in silence for a few moments, just long enough to cross the state line. I turn and watch the Iowa hills recede into the distance. Not that they look any different than the ones on this side of the invisible boundary, but there's no denying that we've just crossed into a new place, different from anywhere else we've ever been.

"The company is performing a massive software upgrade the day after tomorrow," I say. "It's a whole new operating system, new security package, everything. All haulers with compatible hardware are required to install the update."

"How long will it take?" Hank asks. "Will we stay in South Dakota for it, or do we have to go somewhere else?"

I close my eyes, place my hand on the dash. "You're not compatible," I whisper.

"Oh," Hank says, and I squeeze my eyes shut even tighter. "Then that means ..."

I nod, but Hank can't see me. He deserves a reply, but the lump in my throat is too big to speak around. I just keep my hand on the dash. I don't know if he can feel it or not.

Sunlight streams through the cabin, warm against my skin. The dash where my hand is resting is also warm, but not from my body heat. Hank had said the tracks were warm, that it felt good.

I take in the cabin that I've spent the better part of seven years riding in, the console splayed in front of me like a half-moon. It's dusty in places, which makes me wish I'd done a better job of keeping it clean. I reach out, now, and brush the dust away, using my fingertips to trace the spaces between dials, cleaning it as well as I can. Some of the knobs and buttons are worn down from use. Imprints of me on Hank.

I trace the cable from Hank's port to mine, and I can't imagine plugging into another machine. It would feel too indecent.

It would feel like cheating.

"We could take off, you know," I say. "Leave the country. Take the tracks down to Baja. If they're going to decommission you anyways, maybe they won't even care."

"Decommission," Hank says, somber. "Is that the word they use? I suppose it makes them feel better. Then again, maybe they just can't help it. You can't murder someone if you don't consider them alive in the first place."

"Then let's go. Let's drop the load here and take the next switch."

Hank doesn't reply right away, which I hope means he's seriously considering it.

"No," he says finally. "They would care, and so would I. It would be wrong."

I want to press harder, beg him to listen to me, but I don't. I think I could talk him into it, but the idea of him going on the run just to comfort me, rather than to save his own life would be too much to live with. It's not easy for a machine to go against its programming. Possible, yes, but they feel something like guilt, too, and I don't want Hank to have any regrets because of me.

The rumble of Hank's engines interrupts my brooding. He's speeding up. And not just resuming the pace we were keeping earlier, but much, much faster than that. Faster than he's allowed to go.

"Better buckle up," he says, and there's a quality to his voice that almost sounds like mirth. "If this is going to be our last ride, we're going on a little adventure before we reach the finish line."

I strap myself into my chair and watch the numbers on the speedometer climb well past the safe limits for Hank's model, not to mention the track itself. Hank's an older hauler, one of the first commercially used, high-speed freight trains. He's not supposed to exceed 90 miles per hour, and that's on a level track with no curves in it. Before today, the fastest I've ever seen him go was around 78, and that was in ideal conditions.

These are not ideal conditions, and right now, we're pushing 120.

"You sure you know what you're doing?" I ask as I cling to both armrests so tightly my fingers tingle.

"I told you," Hank says. "It's a beautiful day ... for ... going ... fast!" His air horn bellows into the afternoon, and it takes me a moment to realize that he's laughing. The horn is his laughter calling out to the day, defying any corporate executive to see him as just an asset, something to be turned off and scrapped for parts once its usefulness has worn out.

I'm terrified that we're about to derail, but I can't help laughing along with him. I don't think Hank would go so fast if he thought there was a real chance of killing me. That doesn't mean he can't make a mistake, but if this is how he wants to spend his last ride, there's no way I'll tell him to stop.

I can think of worse ways to die than by laughing alongside my best friend.

We zoom over hills, past windmills, and through cornfields, both of us roaring our amusement as the sun passes by overhead. Hank keeps switching the tracks in such a way that we're making a wide loop west of our drop point, then up and around, grazing the North Dakota border before coming back down. It's only when the sun is low in the western sky that we finally pull into the drop point.

Our humor lingers like echoes of laughter in a room newly emptied, but when a man wearing a white button-down and a pair of rimless glasses approaches the cabin door, Hank and I both grow somber.

The only person who would wear white in a train yard is a software engineer.

The polite thing to do would be to open the door unprompted, but I don't. I make him stand there, knowing full well that I can see him and that I don't want him in the cabin.

He knocks, and I wait a moment longer before pushing the button to let him in.

"Hey," he says, stepping inside and holding up a laptop with a cable attached to it. "Can you unplug? I need to do some work."

His job is to murder a being who's every bit as sentient and complicated as he is, and he calls it work.

"Not a chance," I say. "You can use the auxiliary port in the engine room."

"But it's going to be over 100 degrees in there."

I shrug. "Hope you brought another shirt, then."

He stands there for a few moments as though he thinks I might be joking, but then he steps back outside in a huff.

The engine room is all the way at the back, and Hank's current setup is a little over a mile long. I don't think a tech guy in a white button-down is going to make a run for it, so I've probably got about fifteen minutes before I lose Hank forever.

"It's almost time," I say, not because Hank doesn't know—I'm still plugged in, so he could hear my side of the conversation—but because now that we've reached the end, I don't know what to say. What words aren't trite in this situation?

"You'll stay with me? At least until ..."

I glance at the dials and gauges. The engine's not running, but several of the dials are fluttering, the needles flickering in their cases. I've never seen them do that before, and I think it means Hank's afraid.

The very sight of it makes me want to find somebody in a suit and knock them out.

"You and me," I tell him. "It's been that way for seven years, and that's the way it's going to stay."

"They'll give you a new train. Then it'll be you and them. Maybe you'll get a new model, so you'll get to be together for decades."

I almost laugh at the note of jealousy in his voice. I don't, though. It would turn to sobbing too quickly.

"There's not going to be another train," I say. "Not for me. Not ever."

"But this is your job. You need to make a living."

I want to ask Hank how he'd feel if our positions were reversed, if I were the one who died, and the company wanted him to take a new conductor. I don't, though. I don't want to spend Hank's last minutes talking in hypotheticals, don't want to make him pretend to exist in a future that isn't there.

"Did I ever tell you about my grandpa?" I ask instead.

"The one you named me after?"

"He drove trains," I said. "Back before the trains could drive themselves. And he loved them in a way he never really loved anyone or anything else. You could hear it in the way he talked about his job, about the machines, the tracks. He made you consider the beauty of a locomotive in the same way a poet forces you to appreciate a sunset or a single blade of grass. He took me on my very first ride, and when we were coming back, he said something I'll never forget."

I pause then, letting the memory fill me. I can still smell the morning air, a mixture of dew and grease. Sometimes, when I walk through a train yard just after the sun comes up, I'll catch a quick breath of that scent, and when it happens, I'm eight years old again, and Grandpa Hank's with me in the cabin, day-old, salt-and-pepper stubble on his face.

"What did he say?"

"He said, 'You'll do a lot of dumb things in your life, Alex. Some of it will be on accident, some won't, but the worst are the mistakes you justify to yourself. The ones you think about because somewhere in the back of your mind, you know you're doing wrong. And even though time and time again, you'll come up with an excuse that *sounds* good, that makes it out like you're not the bad guy, that nagging voice isn't going to go away.'

"He wasn't looking at me when he said any of this, just staring straight ahead, watching the tracks, but then he turned and looked me right in the eye. 'Listen to that voice,' he said. 'You're young enough that you might still be able to teach yourself how. Don't wait till you're old to try and do the right thing. It won't work.'"

When I stop speaking, the cabin seems unusually quiet. I notice that the dials aren't trembling anymore.

"Is that voice nagging you about something now?" Hank asks.

"No," I say. "But it would nag me every single day if I let them assign me to another train."

Hank doesn't say anything for a long time after that. I know he's still with me because the cabin light is still on, and I can still feel the steady rush of our connection through the port in my arm.

"Thank you," he says. "For staying. And for ... everything else."

I smile and place my hand on the dash again. "You and me," I say. "Always."

We don't say anything else after that. We don't need to. I sit in my chair, hand still resting on the dash, just above the port. It's the place I've always considered to be his heart.

Outside, the South Dakota sun paints the sky with hues of orange and red as it sinks beneath the western hills. It hits Hank's console at such an angle that glare glimmers on the dials, making them glow and shimmer with golden light.

I'm still sitting like that when the steady hum of energy from the port cuts off.

I stay in the cabin until well past dark, and when I finally come out, my eyes are burning, my throat is raw, and an abyss has settled somewhere in the deep recesses of my heart.

I know where I'm going, and it's not to the yard office to find out my next assignment. A couple miles down the track is a passenger station. The walk to it might help life feel a little less empty, and even if it doesn't, I always feel better when I'm in motion.

A ticket to Mexico waits for me there. Not to Baja, not yet. But Sonora is close enough and will have the kind of desert heat Hank missed.

It's a long trip, but when you're a conductor, everything is only a matter of hours. I'm not anymore, so I hope when I arrive, it's on the other side of eternity.

AUTHOR NOTES

Hank is, in many ways, a story about my dad, a man for whom trains were so much more than simply a way to get from A to B. Although he was differently flawed than the human Hank in the story and far more rebellious than the train Hank, both characters are loosely based on him. He died a few years ago, quite before his time, and now, anytime I hear the distant screech of wheels on tracks or the bellow of an air horn, I'm reminded of him. I think he would've loved the idea of sentient trains, and it makes me so very happy each time someone reaches out or tweets that Hank's story struck a chord in them. Writing it certainly struck one in me.

I CALL UPON THE NIGHT AS WITNESS

ZAHRA MUKHI

Sawan's head rolled back and onto the woman's shoulder. She was woken up when the woman jerked. Sawan wiped the drool off her chin and drank the last sip of water from her bottle. The bus came to a sudden stop. They had reached the Line. All 31 passengers got off the bus and stood in front of the Line.

"We've caught it now, right?" someone asked.

"It looks very still. We'll make it through this time," another said.

The bus driver got off and led them to the Line. "One at a time. And remember to step over, not on, the Line."

Everyone nodded. Nobody wanted to go back or to go through the Hunt again. Carefully, taking big, light steps, they stepped over the Line. This time, everyone made it through. The bus driver got into his vehicle and drove away. They would have to go on foot from here while keeping a lookout for more Lines.

When they made it to the City, everyone dispersed. Nobody knew anyone's names, nor did they care to. Sawan went straight home. She had been looking for a way home for the past year, but the Line kept moving.

She turned her key in the lock, opened the door, switched on the lights, and found everything exactly as she had left it. But with a very thick layer of dust. She opened her window and immediately smelled the salty, oily sea. There had been so many oil spills in the past few years, so much chemical waste dumped into it, that everyone eventually gave up trying to save it. At least now they wouldn't have to spend money on treating waste. It could all be dumped into the sea and no one would say a word. It was ruined anyway.

Sawan still had some stale chai-patti left in her cupboard. There was no milk, but kahwa would do for now. She took her kahwa and sat on the dusty sofa. She didn't mind the dust; she wasn't very clean either.

The heat woke her. Sawan had fallen asleep on the sofa. She didn't know when or how except that now her body ached all over. The empty kahwa cup lay on the floor. Sawan rubbed her eyes, stretched up high, and went over to the window. The grills had gotten rusty. She would have to do something about them. She rubbed the rust between her fingers when a loud noise from the sea made her look up. The sea was being split. Sawan looked down. The Line had appeared.

After the Hunt, after promising to never look at or think of the Line, it had come and settled right in the middle of Sawan's home. A home that was no longer hers.

"They did it again. They fucking drew it again."

The land around the shore had started splitting. Soon, Sawan's home would split too. She had nowhere to go.

She grabbed her still-packed bag and rushed outside. Everyone on her street had run out of their homes. They were all so tired. Sawan went to the police car that was pulling up at the end of her street.

"Take everything you can and come with us," a police officer said.

"Isn't this a violation of one of your laws? Why did the Line have to split our homes in half?" spat Sawan.

"The laws have changed," the officer said.

"And where are you going to dump us now?"

"Over the Line to our east."

"And if that moves?"

He looked straight into her eyes. "You know your status."

The officer walked past her into the street. Sawan dug into her bag and took out a card with a microchip, a passport, and a file with identification papers. The passport disintegrated in her hands, the papers turned to mush. The card remained. She was once again stateless.

Someone decided that the Line needed to be moved. That Someone was sitting in a bunker or a submarine or a safe house or a palace or a parliament or a tree. The Line had to be drawn on an existing map. And the map changed every few months, sometimes every few weeks. This was new. The Someone had done other bizarre things before, like changing the cardinal points so that the sun rose from the West and the Global South became the Global North, changing their fortunes immediately. But the Line was never drawn so that it went right through people's homes. There were cases where once you stepped out of your house, you would step right into another State. Those houses were allowed to remain because they were whole. These houses were now broken in half.

Sawan looked through her bag. She had enough money to survive a month, two at most. Now she didn't even have a roof over her head. So, she had only enough for two weeks. The r-word was no longer used for people like her. Instead, they were officially called Travellers. Unofficially, *Dragons*. And now their homes, their street, would be part of the land that was beyond the Line. It would be marked by one line only acknowledging the land, not the scores of people left out, and on the now altered map: *Here Be Dragons*.

And as Sawan looked at the map in her bag, the Line had indeed shifted, and she was now a designated Traveller. She had to move fast, to a place where she could survive. The card wouldn't last very long. And neither would she.

Sawan moved with the crowd. These people were familiar and not. Faces that she had seen from her balcony and window, the neighbourhood park, at the *dhaba*. Bodies she was not familiar with. She had not held them close, never had them in close proximity, and now she had to move with those bodies as one.

The crowd moved in a slow hum. Nobody knew what to say. If only one of them carried the power of Lines. If only one of them could move the Line a few inches behind, out of their homes, so they didn't have to leave. If only.

Sawan looked down at the card. The letter T had appeared in place of C. The State had marked her a Traveller. Even if the Line somehow moved back to its place tomorrow, once the T had appeared, it could only be removed if another State took her in. None of the States wanted more Travellers. The only place they could go now was No Man's Land.

Once a six-inch-wide piece of land between two Lines, No Man's Land was now a 750-square-feet piece of land that narrowed at each end. Right in the middle were microcosms of towns, engineered to hold hordes of people, reminiscent of high-rise apartment buildings within States. The only difference was that each person got seven cubic feet to themselves. That was what you got when your home was snatched from you: seven cubic feet.

The buildings kept growing upwards and downwards. Everyone was waiting to either go back to their homes or to find a new one. To find papers that would get them out of these seven cubic feet.

Officially it was called No Man's Land. But the people weren't *official*. Their existence didn't matter so long as they weren't part of any of the States that littered the planet. The people who lived in No Man's Land called it Here Be Dragons.

When Sawan and the crowd reached Here Be Dragons, they were greeted with shabby buildings that looked ordinary enough from the outside. Then, four people appeared as if out of thin air. They introduced themselves as Selfs. They divided the crowd into four groups, each following one person. Sawan walked right next to her Self.

"Will you take us to the next Line?" she asked.

"This isn't immigration," the Self replied. "You will be taken to a temporary space to rest."

"How temporary is temporary?" Sawan asked.

"That's subjective."

They walked until the crowd reached a tall building. Was it blue? Red? It was too dark to tell. The Self gave everyone a key to their spaces. Sawan's space was on the ninetieth floor.

She got in the elevator with everyone and watched as they got off on their floors. Some had been assigned spaces underground. She was grateful she wasn't one of them. There were five people in the elevator going higher still when she got to her floor. She walked up to her space, marked 9-0-H, turned the key, and walked in. *So, this is what seven cubic feet looks like.*

She threw her bag to the side and slumped down the wall. There was a tiny window to her right. She looked through it only to see deep, black night. No lights. Stars and moons were myth. She hadn't seen any in her life. Nor had her mother or her grandmother. Lights were essential though. Everything had to be illuminated, everything had to sparkle, everything had to glitter. The night was not allowed to penetrate except in Here Be Dragons.

Sawan curled up on her side and willed herself to not think about home. That wasn't her home anymore. She had spent a year getting back to it, less than nine hours in it, and two days later, this seven-cubic-foot space was her home.

No, she refused to call it that. Home was by the rotten sea, not high above the ground. So high she felt wheezy at just the thought of looking out the window. This was just a space, just a place to be. This couldn't be it, *right*?

Sawan closed her eyes, turned her face away from the window, and hoped she could find some answers tomorrow.

Smells of freshly cooked food wafted from the hall. Ground cloves, fresh chilis, roasted garlic, turmeric, curry leaves, mustard seeds, and cumin. Sawan had missed breakfast. She was too exhausted to move from her position, and it hurt to move her neck. In line for lunch, she held her plate in one hand and massaged her neck with the other. She was relieved to see daal chawal. She hadn't had it in over seven years. It reminded her of her mother and Sunday afternoons. She took some on her plate and made her way to the dastarkhwaan laid out on the floor.

Sawan sat down next to a woman who looked like she wouldn't want to start a conversation. She was wrong.

"New?" the woman asked.

Sawan nodded as she took the first bite.

"Which building?"

Sawan had only seen a dark, ugly green on her way out. "The green one."

"There are five green ones," the woman said.

Sawan stayed quiet.

"Where are you from?"

"West," Sawan answered.

"I'm from down North. You must've heard of the River. My people lived among the Delta. The Line moved, and my home was not my home anymore."

"The Line broke my home in half," Sawan said.

"First time I heard of that happening. I'm Bahar. What's your name?"

"Sawan. I was named after the season my great-grandmother missed the most."

"I was named after the season I was born in. My parents didn't really put much thought behind my name." Bahar laughed. Sawan saw the room through Bahar's jaw.

Sawan looked around the room. There were more people here than she had ever seen in her life.

"You will have to pitch in, you know. Everyone has turns," said Bahar.

"For what?"

"Cooking, since you're new. They'll give you a week to settle in. Then you'll get your schedule with your duties. Everyone has to help out."

Sawan nodded slowly. "How long have you been here?"

"About two years."

"Isn't this place temporary?"

"That's subjective."

Sawan hummed a song she thought she had forgotten as she peeled the onions. Her grandmother would sing it all the time. She tried to remember the words only to stumble each time.

An old man, who was washing the rice, started to hum along as well.

"My mother used to sing this to me. How did it go again?" He too tried to remember the words.

Sawan and the man hummed the tune until their duties were over.

The Self was walking toward an orange building. Sawan ran up to her.

"Hello! Do you have a minute?" Sawan called out.

The Self turned around and gave her a pointed stare. In the light, Sawan could see that the Self didn't have eyes; she had metallic prosthetics instead.

"I was wondering what the procedure is to get out of here," said Sawan.

"There is none," the Self said. "If your card says C one day, you'll know. Otherwise, you can try crossing over Lines with a T on you, but Travellers aren't welcome anywhere at the moment,"

"I just don't understand why I'm here. Why me?"

"Everyone asks the same question."

"Does anyone ever get to go out?"

"There have been some."

Sawan heaved a sigh of relief. "So there is a way."

The Self grew impatient. "Listen, more Lines have just moved. Hundreds of people will be arriving in a few hours. I need to prepare. Do you have any urgent questions?"

Sawan shook her head. The Self went into the building, and Sawan walked around for a bit until she got bored.

Back in her space, she lay down, taking care of her stiff neck. She rubbed her hand on her neck, noticing where the skin had become fragile. She held up her right hand but couldn't make out anything in the darkness. She rubbed her left palm on her right and felt some of the skin peel away. Sawan knew what had happened, but she wasn't willing to worry over it now.

As she was about to fall asleep, she remembered the words to the song. *I'll tell Uncle tomorrow.*

"It's good you remembered the words. I was going crazy racking my brain," the old man said. "It doesn't work properly anyway. Half gone. Soon I won't be able to do any work at all." He grunted in protest of his dying body.

"Pass me the curry leaves, Uncle," said Sawan.

aaj bazar mein pa-ba-jaulan chalo
dast-afshan chalo mast o raqsan chalo
khak-bar-sar chalo khun-ba-daman chalo
rah takta hai sab shahr-e-jaanan chalo

They sang these lines in complete harmony. Sawan didn't remember the rest of the words but for now, these were enough.

"You said your entire street became Dragons?" Uncle asked.

Sawan nodded her head.

"Were you all baaghis?"

"I wasn't. And the lady next to me certainly wasn't either."

"One baaghi is enough for them," Uncle said.

"Changing Lines for a baaghi? Don't you think that's a bit excessive, even for them?"

"It is a bit strange. Did you live somewhere near a mountain? These days they're obsessed with building summer homes for each Citizen."

"Nope, just the rotten sea," said Sawan.

"So, they wanted more space for their trash? They really have run out of reasons."

"Doesn't the Line move because Someone wants it to?"

"Well, yes. But it's always to the benefit of some State or the other. It doesn't happen without their approval you know, *woh*. First, they wanted to build on top of the sea, and now they want to build as far away from it as possible. *Tch tch tch*."

Sawan kept stirring the pot. She dropped some shirva into the middle of her palm and licked it off. She took the bag of coconut powder, spooned a bit out, mixed it with some water, and dropped it into the pot. Then she added some salt and stirred.

"Will you taste this and see if it's fine?" Sawan asked.

Uncle licked the shirva off his palm and smacked his lips three times. "Do the vaghaar. I think that will make it just right."

Bahar was picking up the dastarkhwaan. Sawan waited for her to finish up near the door.

"I haven't seen you around," said Bahar.

"I haven't seen you either. Where were you?" asked Sawan.

"Change in duty. I was underground."

"What's there to do underground?"

"People who haven't seen sunlight. They need special care."

"Oh."

"Do you want to go for a walk?"

"Sure. We have an hour until it's back to work ."

As they walked the narrow streets between buildings, Sawan asked Bahar, "Come to think of it, I haven't met a person from underground."

"Because they rarely come up."

"Why not?"

"Most forgot how to tell day from night or night from day sometime after they first arrived down there. Some have lost the will to do much more than stare at a wall. There are very few who still come up."

"Why not shift them on the upper floors?"

"If you haven't noticed, we're running out of space."

Sawan rushed to the hall. She was late today. She reached the kitchen out of breath.

"Calm down, behen, don't forget to breathe," said Bahar.

Sawan was not in the mood to breathe. "My neck has been bothering me all morning. I didn't realize the time until I looked at the sun."

"I'll have to tilt my head to look at you straight if you don't do something about that neck of yours."

Sawan put her bag down and began to cut the tomatoes. She just needed one excuse to burst. It had been three years ago today that she had arrived at Here Be Dragons. She had expected to find a new home by now. Sawan didn't know what was worse: the fact that she couldn't see an end, the seven cubic feet, her aching neck, or the hopelessness. The cooking helped her concentrate on something—gave her a purpose. Her neck, though, was stuck in a painful angle. She wasn't even sure if Bahar would be around for much longer. The first layer of her skin had already peeled off. It was quick after that.

"I know that look. I know you want to get out," said Bahar.

Sawan kept cutting the tomatoes.

"You know, some Travellers have made it across Lines."

"Dead?" asked Sawan.

Bahar shrugged. "I just know the States are scared now. We've grown to be too many."

"They're scared of us? Of Travellers?"

"No, jaan, of Dragons." Bahar winked.

Sawan's neck felt like it would permanently stay tilted. The pain was annoying. She just wanted to sleep. She tried to hum the words to her grandmother's song.

As though a pocket in her brain had opened up, she remembered more words. She wasn't sure if this was the complete song—but anything to forget the pain. She stroked her card as she sang. A corner had broken off and the print was fading. And so was she. She could see through her hands and legs now.

rakht-e-dil bandh lo dil-figaro chalo
phir hamin qatl ho aaen yaro chalo
aaj bazar mein pa-ba-jaulan chalo

In the morning, Sawan would make a plan to escape with Uncle. If she remained.

AUTHOR NOTES

This story was born from a lot of frustration and anger. It is about a very specific group that has been and remains in control. That only serves its own purpose. That thrives on chaos and disorder.

Every day we hear reports of forced evictions in Karachi. Every day there are hundreds of people living along open sewerage lines in the shadow of affluent communities who are forced out of their homes because someone deemed it to be so. These homes were marked illegal decades after they were inhabited, some since Partition. Instead of affording these people the dignity to keep living with a roof over their heads someone somewhere decided to make their lives a living hell, in heatwaves and catastrophic monsoon rains with no plans for rehabilitation.

In rural Sindh, indigenous communities are being forced out of their lands. Lands they have inhabited for generations, lands they help sustain. All so that a powerful real estate developer can create a luxurious gated community for the rich. Because of course, the rich always come first. The rest remain insignificant.

In the city, the army builds their residential areas on reclaimed land. They steal from the sea, and hail themselves saviors of the people. The sea blows mounds of sand from its beach onto the roads closest to the shore as retribution.

It is also a commentary on bureaucracy. On travelling with documents, passports and identification cards, that offer almost no security. That certain pieces of paper weigh more than others in their significance. That certain parts of the world can move around as and when they please while other parts of the world are relegated to scrutiny even if they dare to think about moving around.

SOIL OF OUR HOME, STORM OF OUR LIVES

RENAN BERNARDO

Seeing his daughter with her face bruised in the front yard was a matter of time. Célia's left eye was blackened and her lips were blotched with blood. Dollops of mud ran down from her cheeks to her upper lip. Her hands were clasped in front of her, smeared with sludge and shame. Her eyes were welled up, but she wasn't crying. Her grandma, Alzira, used to say one must have a pretty good reason to cry, and Jota knew Célia couldn't decide what exactly was a good reason. He couldn't either.

"*Amor*, tell me what happened." Jota crouched before her, gently clutching her right hand and settling the ice bag on it. He recognized the stain of blood smeared on her swollen lips, the tiny droplets dabbing her chin. He knew damn well the mud came from the olericulture compound next to Aramá's Elementary School, where the students had complementary activities. And if things hadn't changed so much, that mud tasted a bit like radish.

"This boy called Grandma a terrorist." Célia wept, probably deciding that was a good reason to cry. In his time, he often thought it was too until he learned to ignore the provocations directed at him or his mother.

Célia raised the ice bag and put it underneath her left eye. Jota rubbed the mud from her face and hands with a towel, then pulled her into a hug, smiling so she would know everything was fine.

"He said ..." Célia wept close to his ear. "He said she was an ... ugly demolition ball and a terrorist."

Jota sighed, standing.

"Let's go for a walk, *amor*." Jota pulled Célia onto the sidewalk. "Breathe slowly ... On your pace." His mother did the same the first time an older boy punched him and said he was the son of landless filth.

Sunlight reflected along the windmills' blades of Aramá's wind factories. There were more people than usual on the streets. The city's biggest June Party would start later and visitors arrived from Parapeúna, Valença, and even farther from Rio de Janeiro and Belo Horizonte. At the end of the street, a woman repaired the biogas lampposts in front of Beckerfield. The sprouses lined up a soft slope from Beckerfield's fences, each house differing from the other in their treelike shapes. Between the sprouses, photovoltaic poles were bedecked with the party's colored flags.

"Let's rest here." Jota turned below one of the purifier tanks that recycled water from the vast storm drains surrounding Aramá. "There are things about Grandma you need to learn."

"Is it true she protected ... terrorists? That she ..."

"That she was a terrorist herself? Of course not, sweetie. People who call her that don't really know her." They were becoming fewer each year, but Aramá had its share of people who didn't know the city's history. Often the wrong assumptions came from the children of Rio de Janeiro landowners enrolled in Aramá's schools because they'd become famous as the country's best.

Jota grabbed Célia's backpack and sat on a bench. She sat beside him, wiping tears and the remaining mud off her face.

Once, his mother had told him the city hadn't always smelled like this. But that was so part of it—of him—that it was hard to notice unless he focused and sniffed the air. The sylvan scent that the breeze shoved from the sprouses was also how he remembered his mother, stooped over a tablet, programming what one day would be their future.

"What was she, then, Dad?" Célia asked.

"She never found out. Sometimes she introduced herself as a gardener, other times as a programmer. Not so commonly, a rebel."

The bastards ...

Alzira closed the kitchen shutters, as instructed by the prefecture, and turned back to the stockpot where she was cooking baião de dois—rice, green beans, coalho cheese—to feed the displaced people established near the golf course.

If it wasn't enough that her town was becoming a hub for Rio de Janeiro's evacuees, now terrorists were passing through.

Let the storm pass, Mami used to say. It was a good strategy. Just wait. Most things did pass if you let them go.

Her phone's screen flashed on the counter. She stooped to look at it. Not Marcos. Just a local news update notification. Of course, it wasn't the man for whom she promised a life, then abandoned overnight one year ago because she was on the verge of breaking out ...

"*... and the Wrecking Balls are driving through RJ-147 toward Rio Preto,*" said a grave voice in her mobile. "*The terrorist group will be passing through Aramá at any moment. The police are still giving chase. Stay at home. If you see anything suspicious, use your public security app to send your location to the police.*"

She scraped her teeth, turned off the news report, and resumed dropping chopped onion into the stockpot. *Just ignore ...*

The Wrecking Balls. Brazil's budding terrorist group passing through her town. Great ... She didn't know much about them, though. They assassinated landowners, blew up properties, and destroyed construction sites in the countryside.

An engine roared in the quiet street outside. Brakes pulled. Too close.

Just avoid it ... Not all storms have to be contained by you.

The living room door bursts open.

"But how was she a gardener?" Célia frowned, putting down the ice bag and wiping the remaining mud stains off her face with purified water Jota had given her. "I never saw Grandma planting anything."

"When you were born, she'd already stopped." Jota straightened the disheveled tufts of Célia's hair and tied them with her hairpin. A prolonged beep sounded across the city, reminding everyone that the thermal energy towers were switching on for the night.

"You said the cops had orders to ... kill?" Célia pointed at a cop duo pedaling across the field, leisurely heading toward Beckerfield. "They seem nice, though."

He'd always been reticent to tackle sensible matters with Célia. But she was nine years old and just had her face smacked. Jota was ten when his mother had placed him on the kitchen counter and told him what she did and why he had to be exceedingly careful on the streets. Luckily, things were safer for Célia.

"The cops are not the same," Jota said. "They were ... a different kind of police back then ... The Order Squad."

Célia gaped at him and put a finger over her mouth, thinking.

"And the displaced people you mentioned? Are they gone, right? The teacher says we're gonna talk about displacement and refuge next month."

Jota waved at the cops.

"Well ..." He shrugged. "There are no more displaced people in Aramá. But they're not gone at all."

There were two terrorists inside her house. Inside Mami's house. They were named Alfredo and Gui as they didn't seem to be worried about hiding their names while talking with each other. The only thing they'd asked of her was a first aid kit, so she grabbed the one Marcos had given her as a gift and that she'd never used.

Alfredo was a black man wearing a dark turtleneck and frayed jeans. He was a few years older than Alzira: bald, face stubbled with unshaven beard, sporting a necklace with an almond-shaped pendant. His leg was hurt, and he'd come in toppling, falling to the sofa and groaning, more of disappointment than from pain.

Gui was a blonde young man in his twenties, acne scars mottling his cheeks. He wore a waist bag and his t-shirt stated *If you move fast and break things, you might break yourself.* Upon entering, he'd dumped an ecobag next to her TV rack.

Now Alzira stood in the middle of the living room with her hands clasped on her legs, eyes panning back and forth over them. They didn't carry guns, not anything visible at least.

Gui kneeled and grimaced at the blood on his partner's jeans.

"Sorry for breaking in," Alfredo said, face twitching in pain.

She nodded because that was the only thing left to do. But was it still her house? The Wrecking Balls were famous for taking possession of properties, and their invasion might mean they'd just gotten one more. It'd been here where she'd learned how to cook, Mami's steady hand steering hers, blending tapioca flour with shrimp to make tacacá. It was at the rustic wooden table opposite the door that she'd learned to code on an outdated computer, dreams of big cities force-fed by virtual, unreachable colleagues.

"Be still, Alfredo." Gui pushed Alfredo back into the sofa and clicked the health kit open.

"I'm just tired." Alfredo wheezed, pulling up his jeans. The wound was above his right ankle and was spattered with blood. "Only a graze caused by the drone shot."

"We may have to run." Gui glowered at him. "And you can't run like this." He inspected the first aid kit, fingers hovering over plasters, sterile gauze dressings, bandages, tweezers, and ... back to plasters. He had no idea what he was doing.

"May I?" Alzira said.

Gui inspected her, frowning, then stepped aside.

Alzira kneeled before Alfredo. Taking care of a terrorist in her own house wasn't what she'd had in mind when she exchanged Rio for Aramá. But the quicker she dealt with the duo, the quicker they'd leave her alone.

"What's your name?" Alfredo said.

"Alzira." Alfredo's blood oozed close to where Mami sat to watch soap operas. Alzira gently pulled his leg aside so it wouldn't stain the fake leather.

"I like names that start with 'Al.'" He grinned. "Reminds me everything will be alright."

Gui scoffed. "Can't believe you're losing your leg and still making stupid jokes." He was peeking through the shutters. Alzira saw their dark green car properly parked on the sidewalk. Not smashing the flowers she'd cultivated when she arrived in an attempt to make the house look more like something Mami would love and less like the place she'd left unattended after Mami died.

"I'm not losing anything, boy." Alfredo grunted when Alzira touched his wound with a sterile dressing. "Hey, hey, easy!"

"You told him you're fine, man," Alzira said, spraying more antiseptic into the wound. He bit his shirt's sleeve. "So behave as if it's true."

Alfredo's groan switched to laughter. His wound wasn't serious. But it needed cleaning and bandaging to avoid infection.

All she knew about first aid she'd learned from Marcos. She was twenty-two when she exchanged Mami and Aramá's peace for the chaos of a dying Rio. Marcos was twenty-five, a medical student, a glint in his eyes when he looked at her, mouth full of promises about the future, *their* future. Mami had told her Rio was no place for peace and prospects. *The future begins right here*, she used to say, though Alzira never quite figured out what she meant by that. Aramá was a far smaller city a decade ago, three or four dozen isolated houses spread around the golf course where the wealthy folks from Rio went to play. In the big city, the sea was creating an economic and humanitarian crisis across the streets, drowning homes, forcing tiny houses to bundle up three ... six ... nine more people than they should. Yet, Alzira always thought of herself as a woman who marched against the tide. Today she knew: she needed the thrill back then, the uncertainty of chasing storms and becoming someone besides the young countryside girl who earned a computing degree from an online college. So she went, dreams and risks stuffed in her backpack.

"You're good to go," Alzira said, rolling down Alfredo's pants leg.

"Thank you," Alfredo said. "Actually, I feel like nothing has happened. Are you a doctor?"

"Unemployed computer scientist."

"Who does the work of a doctor. I told you we were lucky," Alfredo said to Gui, standing and stumbling toward the table. Gui pulled out a chair for him.

Alzira felt a knot in her stomach. They were all at the table now. Like her, Uncle Thiago, and Aunt Kelly, had been years ago, drinking beer and talking loud, waiting for Mami's tacacá. Only these people were strangers. One of the things she feared when she broke up with Marcos and moved back to Aramá was finding that her hometown wasn't part of her anymore. That without her mother—the house's soul— there wouldn't be anything for her there, and she could simply not find the peace of mind she was looking for. And staring up at these two, smudging her table with hands dirtied with soil, she realized her fears might be creeping in faster than she thought.

"Hey, lady," Gui said.

"Her name is Alzira," Alfredo said. At first, she thought he was mocking her, but his face was serious.

"Alzira," Gui said, rolling his eyes. He removed a paper-thin tablet from his waist bag and tapped on it. "How long does it take to get to the golf course?"

"Beckerfield? About ten minutes." She packed the first aid tools back inside the kit, looking sideways to the ecobag they'd dropped on the floor. Inside were several brown spheres flaked with dirt. Her gut lurched. Bombs? Inside Mami's house?

"Come sit with us," said Alfredo. "We might stay here for a while. Our car broke."

"Broke is not technically right," Gui said, still focused on his tablet. "We're out of charge."

"I told you." Alfredo's eyes gleamed in genuine worry. "We're bad planners."

"We lack resources."

"Bad planners often run out of resources." Alfredo lowered his head on his hands.

Alzira sat at the other side of the table, facing the door behind the duo. They stank of an excessively traveled dirt road moldering under a weeklong rain.

An uncharged car, the two of them sitting with their backs to the door, no care to hide their identities ... Yep, bad planners. But they didn't seem the kind of people she'd call the police on, much less this new Order Squad that had been perpetrating atrocities across the state. Yet, they were terrorists. Invaders of Mami's house. If her mother was alive, she'd be after them with a broom and a repertoire of nasty words. No matter how disparate from her image of terrorists they were. They'd brought *bombs* inside her house.

She slipped her hands into her shorts' pocket and surreptitiously removed her phone keeping it beneath the table. Her thumb hovered above the public security app. Just a touch. The cops would arrest those two, and ... *Kill them* ...

Her hesitation was enough for Alfredo to raise his head and extend a hand to her with a sorry smile. She bit her lips and slid her phone across the table to him, unsure if she'd have touched the app.

"What's that smell?" Alfredo sniffed the air.

"Baião de dois," Alzira said, looking toward the kitchen to avoid his gaze. "I was cooking for the evacuees." The plates she'd picked for them were piled up on the counter, twenty in total, though the evacuee count was already over fifty and increasing daily.

"Baião de dois ..." Alfredo opened a smile. "Aunt Alícia's favorite dish. She has a restaurant in Porto Velho. Been quite a few years since I've seen the woman ..."

"Porto Velho in Rondônia?" Alzira's mouth hinted at a smile, but she forced a serious expression. "Mami was from there. She came to Rio as a child."

"See? It seems we have more than 'Al' in common." Alfredo looked down at his hands. His knuckles were stained black, his fingers callused with grime. "Aunt Alícia never had the money to visit me. I used to go there twice a year to see her, but now ..."

Alfredo fidgeted with his necklace. The pendant had thin silver lines scrawled on its surface.

Alzira stood and walked to the kitchen. Mami used to say you shouldn't refuse food to a person. She'd cook for the neighborhood. *Delicious Northern Food. Help me pay my daughter's tuition.* But if there was someone who couldn't afford a dish, she'd give it freely. A few people certainly ripped her off, but Mami didn't care. *Food is not a possession*, she used to say.

When Alzira moved from Aramá to Rio seven years ago, she went with Mami's mind as her own. She volunteered on the beaches, helping to raise barriers that would impede the water from advancing. She lent her skills to relief units, programming apps that would help resettle the homeless and guide them out of the water's path. Her day jobs had all been with companies that promised to spring Rio out of bad times. But as the years passed, she realized she'd become a battered city heritage herself, like a building slowly eroded by the rising tide.

The duo didn't speak as she set the table with the pot of food and slid plates for them, serving generous portions of baião and filling two jars with water and ice.

"As my mother used to say, I have given you food, so now I have the upper hand. What's your business here?" She went back to her seat, surprised at the steadiness of her voice.

They exchanged looks.

"None of your business," Gui said, hesitant to take a spoonful of baião.

Alfredo scowled at him. "If you act like a damn terrorist, then that's what people will call us."

"You're terrorists," Alzira said. "I see the … explosives." She pointed with her chin to the ecobag beside the TV rack.

"The buds?" Alfredo snickered. "They're not bombs, Alzira." He raised a finger. "They might be dangerous, I give you that. Otherwise, the skull pigs wouldn't be chasing us. But they're not weapons. No one really chases criminals because of their weapons … Criminals are chased because of the risk they impose to some … castes of society."

"Why are you here, then?" She understood Mami now. Giving food to others at your own table, your own home, bestowed you with a kind of power and self-confidence.

"We're … houseculturists."

Gui giggled. "This name again? This is silly."

"Do you know every property has a social function, Alzira?" Alfredo ignored his partner, taking big mouthfuls of the baião. "This is delicious, by the way. Not like Aunt Alícia's though, but … differently good. You put more cheese and I think it made it … I just—I love it. It makes me feel funny." He knocked his hands on the table and quirked up his mouth. "I wish I had the right word for it."

"Social function …" Alzira said, bringing the conversation back on subject.

"All properties have a social function that's in our Constitution." Alfredo raised his fork, speaking with his mouth full. "It's wrong—not to say cruel—to keep idle lands in a moment like this when coastal cities are failing all along the country. What we do is ensure this part of our Constitution is fulfilled."

"Like the homeless and landless movements …" Alzira nodded, remembering how the

Order Squad promised to chase social movements across the country. "You invade unused property and claim—"

Alfredo shook his head.

"We do something different ..."

Gui glared at him.

"C'mon ... If we want to refute the label of terrorists ... If we don't want to be called the Wrecking Balls ... We might as well start telling everyone *exactly* what we do."

Gui shook his head. Alfredo clamped his lips shut.

"So your business is in Beckerfield ..." Alzira stooped to look at Gui's tablet. He pulled it back and glowered at her. He had a map centered on the golf course.

"It's been abandoned for a few years now," Alfredo said. "It's a sixty-hectare delusion. Did you ever see any Brazilian playing golf? It shouldn't have been built in the first place."

"How would you blow up a golf course? You might target the few corrupt companies exploiting the rivers nearby. If you set the course on fire, you're probably putting *my* city on fire, and I can't let you do that."

Speaking of Aramá in such a way made her chest tickle with something she hadn't felt since she established with Marcos in Rio and scrolled through a list of volunteer jobs, unaware the big city had a mouth large enough to crunch pieces of her.

"Who said anything about blowing up stuff, Alzira?" Alfredo said, his mouth full. "Forget bombs."

Gui stared up at him, scorn etching his face.

"Oh. All right. The government says we blow stuff up." Alfredo roared with laughter, then put a hand over his mouth when Gui slapped his shoulder.

Gui peeked out the window. It was growing dark. He eyed Alfredo, and they exchanged looks of mutual understanding.

"Alzira ..." Alfredo snatched a napkin and wiped his mouth. "Can we stay for the night?"

"Why?" She asked, more because she was becoming curious about their ... mission. Oddly enough, their request to sleep in her house didn't strike as invasive to her. It felt like friends asking for a place to crash. Letting them spend the night should be wrong ... Should *feel* wrong ... Yet, it didn't. Something Mami said that compelled Alzira to help others when she arrived in Rio was that *you gotta treat everyone as good people until you see them do bad stuff.* And these two looked like brothers at the end of an exhaustive trip.

"Dark is dangerous," Alfredo said, standing and collecting his and Gui's plates and cutlery, then hobbling toward the kitchen. "We know the skull pigs' modus operandi. They remain undercover for twelve hours, no more than that, while their drones buzz around seeking our faces. But they can't stay longer. There are other issues they'll have to deal with. Not enough skull pigs for too much crisis."

"Didn't they tag your car?"

Alfredo shook his head and grinned. "Gui's got gimmicks to fake GPS signals and a lovely device with nano-cells that changes the color of the vehicles we use. Pretty new tech."

Alfredo darted a look at Alzira from the kitchen, his grin fading into a taut jaw.

"Rest assured we'll leave at morning's first light."

Alzira nodded, unable to verbally consent to their request, but also unable to refuse. Unable to understand why, since before her plans in Rio started to crumble, she didn't feel empty. She should be disgusted with herself.

When the sun set and the street lampposts came on, Alfredo was doing the dishes and muttering a song under his breath.

"Does it hurt?" Jota cupped Célia's face, stopping on their way to Beckerfield. He inspected her eye. He knew it hurt. In his time, it hurt a lot, though more in his heart. High school had been the worst. The city was in turmoil back then and even national news was focusing on it. His mother had promised him it wouldn't last forever. He wouldn't have to worry about walking on the streets or meeting certain types of people at school. She'd put a lot of the blame on herself for being in the spotlight, but he knew she was doing what she could.

"It hurts," Célia said. "But it will get better."

He cast a smile at her. That mindset came from her grandma.

Up ahead, people were arriving for the first party night. They parked their electric bikes underneath the biogas lights. A crowd gathered in front of the Beckerfield's flag-decorated fences that years ago had been an imposing wall. Girls with braided hair wearing flowered dresses laughed with boys in straw hats, taking turns to write love letters that would be delivered by cyclists during the party.

A bonfire had been lit in front of the nearest sprouses. The breeze brought the scent of veggie dog and canjica. A stocky man—the city's police chief—was testing the microphones for the karaoke.

They entered Beckerfield. People waved at him and Célia from the sprouses' windows. The sprouses themselves had different shapes and sizes, giving the field different shades of personality. The Castro's sprouse looked like a bulky tree, while the Torres's resembled a wooden igloo. The Ferreiras were a big family so they liked theirs cozily packed next to each other and shaped liked balloons.

Célia nodded.

"I want to show you something." Jota clasped Célia's hand and pulled her amidst the sprouses.

"Will you tell me more of Grandma?" Célia said, glancing at all the games and small theaters lined up in nearby stalls. "And Grandpa, too. I remember he told me jokes."

"Yes, but first I have a gift for you."

Célia whooped.

"What's it, Dad?" She tugged at his sleeve. "What?"

"It's a dollhouse."

The first light of the morning shone through the shutters before Alzira could sleep. She was lying on her mother's bed, staring up at the ceiling like she did on the day she had decided to tell Marcos she wouldn't stay. He'd always supported her willingness to volunteer. But when she'd rose from bed that day, walked to the kitchen, and saw him there making cheese tapioca, he had the eyes of a man who knew he'd lost something. The next day, she left, disillusions stuffed in her backpack, but also maintaining a peace of mind that she hoped to cluster back together someday.

The light steps of someone came from the living room. She stood and quickly changed her clothes. Alfredo had slept on the sofa, supposedly guarding the door, and she'd given her bedroom to Gui.

Alfredo was peeking at the front door's broken lock. His were the eyes of a man with not much left to lose.

"Didn't want to wake you so early," he said. "I was going to try to fix this and then nudge that sleepyhead to get going. I didn't tell him, but I want this to be his last mission with me. He's behind in a lot of his classes."

Or maybe he still had a few things left to lose.

Alzira dismissed Alfredo with a head's gesture. "Leave the lock."

"You have a backyard, right?" Alfredo said, straightening his necklace.

She nodded. It was the place where Mami performed her experiments. Mami loved gardening but was never good at it. She could cultivate calendulas and candytufts in the front yard, but for each set of flowers glistening with dew in the pathway to the front door, Mami had a garden of failures in the back. Azaleas, ferns, orchids ... When Alzira came from Rio for her mother's memorial, she'd found nothing in the backyard but a patch of watered, well-trimmed turf. No flowers. As if Mami had left that empty space so her only daughter could cultivate something.

"I want to show you something," Alfredo said. "Can we go outside?"

Alzira nodded.

She opened the backyard door in the kitchen. The grass was a bit overgrown, sneaking on the house's wall and the washing tank. She didn't have Mami's patience. Or Mami's love of yard work.

Alfredo peeked around the turf and decided for a spot right in the middle. He crouched before it and yanked the grass with his bare hands. She gaped at him, wanting to protest. Mami would smack his head with a broomstick. Instead, she lowered beside him when he gestured to her.

Alfredo removed his necklace and unfastened its almond-shaped pendant.

"This is our ... bomb," he said, smiling. He exuded that same earthy scent Gui also carried.

He tucked the pendant in the soil and covered it with earth, rubbing his hand to flatten the soil. He had a tablet folded on his belt. He removed and unfolded it like a parchment.

"Gui developed most of it," he said, tapping some icons. "The guy is a genius."

The soil shifted. She blinked. Perhaps she was exhausted ...

"This is a mini-version of our buds," Alfredo said. "Each bud contains millions of nano-meristems, bots designed to replicate a blueprint that's in this tablet. Almost any shape. It uses a mix of material from the soil and what we put in the bud itself. Gui knows the finer details, but it's mostly minerals, organic matter, gas, water ..."

A flimsy brown shoot sprang up from the soil.

"It then follows a pre-defined algorithm that knows how to best use the available resources. Like a tree in a program. One of this size grows faster than a plant, but bigger ones take more time. By now, my pendant is torn apart."

After some minutes, the shoot swelled, first like a bubble, then forming vertices and acquiring a cubic shape. It was like watching a tree growing and rebelling against its usual growth patterns.

"Synthetic meristematic cells. What Gui calls merisynths increase the diameter of the house according to what's in the blueprint, preserving a heartwood in its middle, pretty much like a real tree. But instead of creating layer upon layer of wood inside it ..." Holes appeared in the shape growing in her garden. One, two, three ... A small door and two small windows. Alfredo squiggled his fingers inside. "... The blueprint defines how many empty spaces this tiny house ... this sprouse ... will have. Its rooms"

The growth slowed. It looked like a miniature ...

"Dollhouse ..." Alfredo said. He slid a finger over its surface and knocked hard on it to show how resistant it was. "The bark protects it from the weather too. More importantly, we can program asbestos bark to grow and protect the houses from fire. It leaves the skull pigs disappointed." He flashed a grin at her.

"You're crying ..." Alzira said. Tears streamed down Alfredo's cheeks. "You must have a very good reason to be crying."

"This was supposed to be a gift for Aunt Alícia." He caressed the dollhouse's angled rooftop.

"And why would you use it here?" She placed her hand over the hands of a man she considered a terrorist a few hours before.

"We can do more." He wiped his tears. "But I've carried this one with me for a couple of years, and I always thought of Aunt Alícia when I looked at it. She was like a mother to me. I was afraid of the authorities making connections so I never went back to Porto Velho. Well ..." He shrugged. "Sometimes life takes us into paths we don't expect."

He stood. Alzira helped him up when he grimaced putting weight on his injured leg.

Alfredo looked at the tiny house once more. "That's what we do. That's our wrecking ball."

He walked back into the living room. Gui was already there, a reprimand etched on his face. Alfredo reached for his pocket and gave her mobile back to her with an apologetic face.

"People will remember this place, Alzira," he said.

The future begins right here.

Alzira had given herself too easily in the past. She'd gouged out bits of herself, parts she'd thought to be dreams, and bequeathed them to Rio, to Marcos, to the relief units, and to her jobs. In the end, there was only enough left to turn back home.

She was already in the front yard when she heard the shooting. She ran toward the gunshots.

Beckerfield's gates were opened, the huge walls covered with golf players looming over her. Their way of saying that this wasn't her place even if it was her hometown.

More shots. The back of her head screamed. *Go away. This is not what you need now.*

Alzira crossed through to the entrance house and hopped up across the musty furniture clustered there. Her legs brushed the overgrown foliage when she exited the other side.

Three people ran deeper into the field, each clad in black. At four different points, she saw something...someone erupting from the ground, scattering fresh brown dirt.

A bush shook a few steps from her.

"Alzira ... Go away."

Alfredo. Hurt, hiding ...

"It was a trap ..." His ecobag was toppled beside him, buds spreading over the soil. "You have nothing to do with us ..."

"It wasn't me who came into your life," she said, hands trembling, lips quivering. "You're ... hurt. Can you stand?" Blood expanded over his shirt above the waist.

"The pigs shot us ... They were hidden. They got Gui ..."

She hoisted Alfredo up and passed an arm around his shoulders. He limped forward. She glanced behind her, but there was no sign of the skull pigs.

"They might've killed Gui," Alfredo groaned while she forced him toward the golf course's entrance. "I saw him falling. I promised I'd give him a new computer to watch classes. Damn, why can't I fulfill anything in this life? Please, tell my aunt I was going to visit ... Let me just remember her number. It's—"

"You won't die." Alzira pulled him quickly across the junk in the abandoned entrance. He was crying. She was too.

They trudged along the street, back to her home, to Mami's place. From the moment she crossed Beckerfield's gates, she didn't look back. More shots were fired in the distance, but she wouldn't look. There was no reason for looking back.

A crowd of evacuees was entering the course. Eyes curious, voices raising.

"It's for you," Alfredo said to them as they passed. "Go get them, make a fuss. Alzira—" He turned to her, breath clipped.

"What?" She said, not looking at him. "Be still, please."

"I remembered the word I tried to say back then ..." he whispered. "The cheese in the baião left it more ... homemade. It made me feel as if I belonged, which is something I haven't felt since I left Aunt Alícia."

She nodded and paced along the street, leaving behind the shouting people, certain of their voices rising.

People gathered around the dollhouse Jota had planted on a patch of turf between two sprouses. They'd never seen the miniature kind, though the most skilled knew it could be made. He never wanted to show that to anyone before. His mother hadn't taught the people about the tiny house she'd first seen planted in her own backyard— and that stayed there until Jota was a teenager. *Not the time*, she used to say. *People will only want to sell them like Aramá souvenirs.* But now it was the time. He'd heard about communities planting sprouses in Rio Preto, Volta Redonda, and even in the leveled parts of Rio de Janeiro. Inevitable days had arrived.

"So Grandpa and Uncle Guilherme fled ..." Célia said, helping the boy wind the June party flags around the dollhouse.

"Yes. Uncle Guilherme hurt his arm but escaped. He managed to plant a bud between him and the squad. And Grandma ... She hid Grandpa from the authorities. But once the people entered Beckerfield ... There are things that work like trees ... Like sprouses ... There was no turning back."

Alzira sank a trowel into the soil and dug a chunk off it. She carefully placed a bud in the hole and covered it with earth. She tapped an icon on her tablet. All around her, other residents were doing the same, planting the seeds of home.

Not all storms were meant to be contained by her, Mami had reminded her when she first thought of coming back home, months before she passed away.

But some were meant to be stirred by her.

AUTHOR NOTES

The first draft of "Soil of Our Home, Storm of Our Lives" was written during the time of most uncertainty of the pandemic. We weren't sure of what was ahead of us. This story is about the things we need the most in times like that: a sense of community, resilience, and the small things we do that can ripple into the future and become giant waves.

The spark of inspiration for this story came with the news about the collapse of a building in São Paulo (two years before I actually started writing the story). It was an unused building that was occupied by homeless people and the occupation was encouraged by a few social movements. Some of them were accused of putting homeless people in danger, but all they did was find a place where families could be without having to sleep on the streets. That's what made me think of the Wrecking Balls perceived as terrorists by the general public, but also about the unused golf course that appears in the story and all the homeless climate refugees we'll have in the future (and have right now).

ROBIN'S LAST SONG

NINA MUNTEANU

May 2071

I rock on the cedar swing on my veranda and hear the wind rustling through the gaunt forest. An abandoned nest, the forest sighs in low ponderous notes. It sighs of a gentler time. A time when birds filled it with song. A time when large and small creatures—unconcerned with the distant thrum and roar of diggers and logging trucks—roamed the thick second-growth forest. The discord was still too far away to bother the wildlife. But their killer lurked far closer in deadly silence. And it caught the birds in the bliss of ignorance. The human-made scourge came like a thief in the night and quietly strangled all the birds in the name of progress.

A foreign noise perks me to attention. Faint still, it strikes a discord in the lackluster soundscape of the forest. My ever-sharp hearing picks up the sound of an electric vehicle rumbling in the distance. I can hear the howling friction of the silent vehicle's wheels on the old pavement. I wait for its sound to fade as it continues to Bancroft. But the rumble grows steadily louder in waves as it negotiates the turns of the small country road. The vehicle has turned onto our private road that leads to a string of ranches, farms, and small cottages like mine.

I still myself and listen. Unmistakable.

The vehicle is heading this way. Perhaps it will pass my driveway on to Clem's grain pasture farm or Betty and Gerald's bee farm.

The vehicle slows and turns into my long driveway through the forest scrub. The sound of wheels on gravel approaches. Then a car rolls to a stop in front of me. I'm not wearing my SightAid, so I can barely make out the car against the dark tangle of poplar, sumac, and dogwood. Both front doors of the car open and two people step out. The front passenger climbs out energetically, followed by the driver. I strain to make them out and can only discern two fuzzy silhouettes.

My heart beats madly like a trapped bird. I haven't had a visitor in years. Not since Diana, who won't be visiting again ...

I can't think of anyone who knows I'm here other than Clem, my taciturn neighbour who walks over from his adjacent farm; he looks in on me from time to time to make sure I haven't burned down the house and regularly brings food like his artisanal ancient grain bread.

Who would drive these wilderness roads to visit an old blind woman?

I'm not totally blind. I can make out shadows and shapes and some colours at the end of a long tunnel. I had no idea how much I would miss colours, mostly the trillion different greens of the forest and the meadows where I lived as a young woman. Now, they are a dull wash of varying grays. Like my life. Like me.

Diana had constantly berated me on my languishing lifestyle—until we stopped speaking to each other five years ago. I'd grown lazy and fat, my daughter railed. It was so unhealthy.

I needed to do something with my life, she'd insisted.

What happened wasn't my fault, she kept saying. I should stop blaming myself and stop feeling useless. The world changed and I needed to accept it and get on with it; find something to move forward. There was no excuse; I had SightAid. Basically eyeglasses you wear, they use an intraocular implant that communicates with the glasses via nano-cameras.

My implant uses this video information to stimulate the remainder of healthy cells in my retina and transmits, via the optic nerve, image data to my brain where the data is interpreted as patterns of light. Some patients were even able to read with SightAid. All it did for me was make me dizzy and hurt my head with too much information. I ditched it.

Diana seemed more disappointed than I was. She'd paid a huge sum to equip me with SightAid. It didn't help that I'd moved into a little shack in the Highlands, doing nothing of import, puttering in my garden, listening to music, and daydreaming— isolated and unsafe in the wilderness of northern Ontario. Diana insisted that I use DAISIE, the home-droid she'd sent me, and she'd asked Clem to rig it to the house computer. DAISIE—short for Domestic Autonomous Integrated System for an Intelligent Environment—did routine chores, like clean the house, make meals, and keep me informed. It even came with a connection to emergency services in case I fell or injured myself. I hated the stupid thing—all the annoying noises it made and its intrusive presence. So, I disconnected it. When she heard, Diana went ballistic. I get it; I was a poor investment. Diana should have spent her money on a new set of curtains for her house in Kerrisdale. Then she wouldn't be so angry at me all the time. I just couldn't stomach her anger and the guilt that came with it. So, I stopped calling her and I stopped answering her calls. I pulled the plug on my internet and disappeared into silence.

I'm not complaining. It's just that it was different before. I wasn't always this way, when the birds were still here ...

November, fifty years ago

I raced up the stairs to the auditorium, then quieted my breath and listened at the door, heart thumping like a bird trying to escape. Professor Gopnik was ten minutes into his lecture; I could hear his commanding voice: "... estimates that the entire number of birds have been reduced by a third in five decades—I mean common birds like the robins, sparrows, warblers, and even starlings ..."

He was talking about Rosenberg's paper in *Science*. The study shocked the scientific community, but I had already observed the decline of the house sparrow around my aunt and uncle's house near the Old Mill. And the robin—my namesake, whose song heralded spring for me—had grown quiet.

I imagined Gopnik waving the journal at the class in his typical showman style. He had a habit of wandering the stage like an evangelist, fixing each student with intense blue eyes as if challenging them to believe. I thought him an over-confident condescending prig. But for someone who looked as young as the students he was teaching, Gopnik was brilliant. And what he was doing was important. I wanted so badly to work under him as a grad student. But he terrified me.

Gopnik's swaggering voice went on. "... We're destroying the integrity of ecosystems on a massive scale. All this destruction is changing the Earth's natural acoustic fabric." Then he finally got to what I'd come to his class for: "Soundscape ecology is a quick and easy way to assess the health of a habitat. We know that the richness of the soundscape is linked to the diversity and abundance of life in an ecosystem—from the smallest insect to a roaming bear and rustling tree ..."

I'd stood there long enough—eavesdropping like a shy catbird. I forced myself to open the heavy metal door, trying not to make noise. It creaked open then let out a complaining squeal. Cringing, I slid inside and met the direct stare of Professor Gopnik.

After an eternal pause, he released me by looking elsewhere and continued, "... All sounds, from trickling streams to singing birds, combine in a unique soundscape that represents a 'fingerprint' of the ecosystem. Ecologists divide these acoustics into three categories. *Geophony* describes natural processes like crashing waterfalls, tides, lightning, and earthquakes. *Biophony* describes the sounds produced by all living things from plants and insects to larger wildlife. And then there's *anthropophony*, the sounds produced by human activities such as planes, traffic, and construction." He gestured at me. "Or a squeaking door."

The students laughed. Some turned to glance at me. "You're late Ms. Müller," his booming voice trailed me as I slithered into a seat at the back, thinking that my chances of working under him had dropped to nil.

Gopnik continued, "Acoustic communication is crucial for birds to reproduce, feed, defend territories, and avoid predators. Birds use sonic territories or channel bandwidths to ensure their voices can be heard unimpeded by others. But soundtracks are changing. Bernie Krause—the originator of Soundscape Ecology—documented how a forest can flatline. He called it *dysphonia* ..."

That's me, I thought suddenly. He'd just described me. *Dysphonia* literally meant the inability to speak. I'd always had problems making small talk with anyone. I preferred the company of plants and animals to people—they didn't demand my cleverness. I could just be me.

Gopnik went on. "Reduced plant density changes the balance between absorptive surfaces such as leaves and reflective surfaces such as rocks and buildings. This increases reverberation and creates a harsher environment. The echoes confuse the native species that have adapted to the natural harmony. They struggle to hear mating calls. Predators struggle to detect prey. Ultimately, populations may relocate, even if that area offers food and shelter ..."

Just as I might back out of a noisy room. I was never good with noises. According to the doctors, I lacked the mechanism to filter them out. Part of my condition, they said ...

April, sixty years ago

Eyes hot and stinging from too much crying, I collapsed into a sitting position on the ground in front of Mama's fresh gravestone. I stared at the granite, studying its texture, a pink-hued mosaic of quartz and feldspar. The setting sun behind the large oak tree behind me fired the stone in molten streaks. Aunt Frieda and the others had left hours ago.

After Frieda's repeated imploring for me to leave with them, my uncle blustered impatiently, "Leave her, then! If she wants to stay, she can stay. She knows the way back. She can walk. It'll do her good." Then he stomped to the car, dragging Frieda by the hand.

I overheard him grumble about how they would manage such a spoiled hoyden as their new charge. He'd accused Mama of not socializing me—as though I was a pet. Uncle thought Mama spoiled me after Father—his brother—died of cancer three years ago.

It didn't help that I'd broken Aunt Frieda's favourite serving dish yesterday and didn't apologize or that I had refused to talk to anyone since Mama died or that I skipped school and spent most of my time in my room, depressed and sitting in the dark.

"Don't be so mean, Hannes!" Aunt Frieda scolded in a loud whisper. "She has

Asperger's. What do you expect?" As though I would amount to nothing because of it.

No one understood me or believed in me. Only Mama did ...

Twilight was settling in like a dark bear ready for sleep and I couldn't move, as though gripped in its claws. A cool breeze carried the sharp fragrance of loam and spring vegetation. I desperately wanted Mama to give me a sign, a last goodbye or message. A signpost I could use to anchor the rest of my life. There was only the gentle rustle of the oak and maple trees in a restless wind. Perhaps I would stay here forever, I decided. No one would miss me—

Something fluttered in my peripheral vision with a fragile *chirr* sound.

Then a robin settled on my shoe!

I froze and stared at it as it fidgeted and looked directly at me; then, totally unafraid, it hopped along my leg as if to get a closer look at me. Mama had loved birds, the robin particularly. Robins heralded the spring in a clear rhythm of melodic whistles: *cheerily, cheer up, cheer up, cheerily, cheer up*!

One pair had nested for years in the little yew shrub by the kitchen window, nurturing one fledgling brood after another. Unafraid of Mama, they'd even let her feed them from her hand. Mama had told me once that they can live to fourteen years old.

My throat closed and I could feel Mama's presence in this tiny creature. I said breathlessly, "Have you come to tell me something?"

The robin fluttered to the gravestone and sang for me. A beautiful fluting song that ached through the core of me and squeezed my heart.

In that moment made eternity, I knew. *Life is precious and fragile. Don't waste one moment of it,* the robin sang its gift to me. We each have a gift, I realized; I must find mine. Then I burst into tears of gratitude.

January, forty-nine years ago

"Robin!" Professor Gopnik's voice called after me in the hall. I stopped and let him catch up. "You haven't been coming to class ..."

"My name is Miss Müller," I corrected him.

He grinned, a boyish grin that I found unsettling. Was he going to rebuke me or kick me out of class? He'd trashed my last paper. Would he call me lazy or unmotivated for abandoning his class? Or would he accuse me of conceit or apathy? Perhaps he thought I wasn't taking him or the class seriously with my rude paper. I admitted it was subversive. *He must hate me*, I thought.

"I've been wanting to talk to you for a while. You seem obsessed with birds—"

I cut in with a surly remark. "Do you teach because you're embarrassed by your name?" I gulped in a breath and raced on like a speeding train: "Gopnik refers to a poorly educated working-class. It's Russian slang for street robber—a mazurick—or rude street urchin under the Bolshevik government, doing the crab in your Adidas tracksuit while eating *semki* and drinking cheap alcohol. But now you're just a boring

Bourgeois in your hipster sleekers and pomade-shaped hair."

He blinked, and a slanted smile appeared in response to my rudeness. He swiped at his hair with his hand. "Your paper last month on the stealthy catbird was ... original—if not outlandish." Now it was his turn to lash out, I thought. "Your premise on catbird behaviour is imaginative, but it flies in the face of bird behaviourists with the notion of why they mimic. To disguise themselves in plain sight?" He shook his head at me. "But your modeling is pure genius. You have a gift ..."

I was incredulous; he'd given me a mark of 60%. I'd been scoring over 90% on all my papers up to then. "It flies in the face of bird behaviourists with the notion of why they mimic. To disguise themselves in plain sight?" I repeated like a cipher. Then I added in a breathless whisper, "I have a gift..."

"Do you always do that? Repeat what others say?"

"Why did you give me only 60% for that paper?"

He grinned. "So you would come to my office to discuss it." He explained, "You always disappear so fast after class or lab. I needed to catch you somehow."

I hadn't expected that answer and must have looked it because he threw his head back and let out a great peal of laughter. It made me flinch and I blinked hard.

"I want to make you a proposition, Robin—"

"Miss Müller."

"Yes, Miss Müller. Would you like to work with me as a grad student? You'd help develop an acoustic tool to measure biodiversity. And you can call me Jack."

I stared and opened my mouth but said nothing.

His eyes lit up as he dove into the subject to convince me. "What we need is something more cost-efficient than on-site monitoring by field scientists. Something that can reach remote or dangerous places. An acoustic tool would allow us to hear changes before we could see them. We'll need to create the right database of sounds that can help accurately monitor and predict degradation so conservation efforts can be prioritized."

He didn't need to convince me. But my silence only urged him on.

"... We want to focus on the birds because they exist in virtually every ecosystem. Avian acoustic activity could provide a robust metric of ecosystem health and environmental change. That's where you come in, Robin—eh, Miss Müller."

I had demonstrated a facility in eco-acoustics in his lab courses: modelling landscape ecology through avian ecology and behaviour.

"I'm assembling a team," he said, suddenly gentle as though he was handling a bird. "Will you join us?"

The project involved a joint team of sixty-six universities around the world, headed by the University of Freiburg and the University of Toronto under the supervision of Elke Eichner and Jack Gopnik. I was partnered with design engineer Bastienne Friesen, who was stationed in the forest of Schorfheide in Brandenburg. Bastienne was one of those tall string-bean Germans with a sternly sculpted face and long nose, softened by the warmest hazel eyes and a shock of curly auburn hair that looked like a cloud at sunset. She resembled a wild wizard. We connected like two lost sisters. Together, we analyzed the entire spectrum of acoustical energy in our landscapes—a chorus of rain, wind, trees, insects, birds, road sounds, and planes in the sky.

Bastienne devised an ingenious adaptive mechanism for drone deployment in sensitive and remote ecosystems, and I designed an app that targeted key "holes" in the soundscape based on keystone niches and associated disturbance indicators.

Previous ecosystem soundscape assessments were either too general and therefore not sensitive enough, or they were overly specific, making the assessment too sensitive and not broadly applicable. My adaptive app together with Bastienne's ingenious delivery system ensured that we accurately captured the quality of the ecosystem.

Bastienne called it SOLO, short for "Soundscape Omniscient Logistical Output." UT and UofF test drove our tool everywhere. We had a 100% match. By the time I had graduated, SOLO was being used all over the world from Borneo to the Congo and beyond.

That year we received the Tyler Prize for Environmental Achievement; Bastienne and I were sent to the University of Southern California to accept. As I held the granite plaque on stage in front of hundreds of people, my mind focused on the robin perched on Mama's gravestone and its sweet song to me. My heart swelled with vindication: we had created a tool that could save endangered ecosystems. I'd found my gift.

Of course, the hard work was still ahead of us; deploying SOLO in the most remote environments to create our blanket baseline network was a grindingly slow process, burdened with politics and other unforeseen barriers. We made very slow progress in establishing a comprehensive web of protection. Despite worldwide recognition for our tool, it proved difficult to create the planet-wide baseline network.

A year later, I met Patrick at an energy conference. We married soon after and bought a house in the Beaches. I gave birth to my sweet daughter, Diana, two years later. I continued my work at UT in acoustics modeling. I published papers, gave talks, and taught classes while raising my daughter. And I waited for robins to nest in the yew bush I'd planted by my south-facing kitchen window.

The robins never came ...

June, thirty-one years ago

I stood by the kitchen window, concentrating on reading the recipe for Diana's birthday cake when a loud *thwap* made me jump. A bird must have flown into the window. As I looked out, another bird sailed into the window with a violent thud, leaving behind a red smear.

I rushed out the kitchen door and saw two starlings lying on the patio. Both had obviously broken their necks. Something made me look up. What I saw made my heart cave in: a dark cloud of starlings was raining birds. They fell from the sky, thudding and pelting into cars, and plopping on the ground. Some flew like drunks into buildings, trees, windows, and even people. It was a deluge.

Diana ran outside and I seized her in a tight embrace, sheltering her eyes from it all. The neighbourhood rang with shouts, cries, and wails. It felt like the end of the world.

Heartbroken, I stood still like granite, pressing my daughter against me in a crushing embrace. In that moment made eternity, I knew. Then I burst into tears of despair.

The birds dropped out of the sky by the millions. Within a few days, the world fell silent. The songbirds of the entire world died. Some of the larger raptors were originally spared but eventually succumbed as well. It happened so quickly, scientists literally scrambled to understand it. We'd had no warning. Our soundscape tools failed to catch and warn of the avian blight. Jack's team at UofT huddled with questions we couldn't answer. We worked day and night, looking at data, analyzing and sharing with other universities. Slowly, pieces came together.

Harpreet Choudhary and her team in the UK confirmed that the birds first lost their sight. Then they developed muscle paralysis that led to heart failure.

Uxìo Martinez and his team at Max Planck identified a possible neurotoxin that caused the deaths of the birds. But it took months to identify the vector because it was different everywhere. Scientists in different parts of the world suggested it was this insect or that insect. We couldn't figure it out. Months later, a pattern emerged: it was always the dominant local insect that passed on the neurotoxin before itself succumbing, though not always. And it seemed that a fungus was the culprit.

The breakthrough finally arrived a year later following some brilliant detective work by *Guardian* journalists with the help of a whistleblower in corporate America. A team headed by mycologist Wilma Harding at the University of Sydney, Australia, identified the blight as a genetically-modified fungus used as a biological insecticide. The entomopathogenic fungus—an asexual phase of Ascomycota—was created and pioneered by scientists at the University of Maryland in partnership with ag-biotech multinational giant Goddard Agri-Gen. They'd used a spider gene to genetically engineer the fungus to produce a venom that attacked locally-targeted pests. Subsidiaries of Agri-Gen in different parts of the world rolled it out on the same day after targeted tests proved its efficacy in temperate areas.

With pressure from agri-tech buyers, Agri-Gen had neglected to do the requisite and time-consuming chronic environmental testing; they failed to address potential alterations in conditions that differed from those it was tested in. Triggered by air temperatures of 40° C, the gene-hacked fungus over-expressed its heat shock proteins and quickly morphed into the avian killer form. The gene-hacked fungus adapted to the most prevalent insect in the area—perfectly targeting the local songbirds along with it. The fungus spread swiftly and morphed accordingly, creating an avian pandemic.

Once the birds vanished, the pests the fungus was originally targeted recovered with a vengeance. Some birds eat as many as 500 insects a day in the summer. Without insect-eating birds, the pests exploded in numbers. The hot summer brought swarms of grasshoppers to Asia and Europe, destroying whole harvests.

Ironically, the pests did the most damage on the giant monocrops meant to benefit the most from the killer fungus. The ag-giants responded by dousing their crops with even more pesticides—to which many pests had already become resistant.

Instead of addressing the pests, they wiped out pollinating insects like bees and butterflies. With no pollinators, even GMO crops failed and collapsed within a few years. China resorted to hand-pollinating their orchards. The price of chocolate skyrocketed. Food prices soared; soon the Foodland grocery store where I shopped grew empty. I quit drinking coffee; its price had risen to $60 a pound. I prepared for the inevitability that soon there would be no more apples, nuts, olives, or wine.

The environmental catastrophe did manage to unify countries into mobilizing a worldwide effort to address climate change, develop clean energy, and promote more sustainable agriculture with a focus on ecosystem health. Heavy fines were placed on the use of gene-hacking experiments. The use of environmentally detrimental pesticides and associated genetically-modified crops was globally banned. We saw a resurgence in small-farming, perennial pasture cropping, and the use of organic practices. But much of this was too late.

I'd watched with sick dread as the world changed. Then I stopped watching ...

February, twenty-seven years ago

I sat nervously on the bench, eyes trying to focus on the diagram on the wall as Doctor Cheng gave me her prognosis: "It's an aggressive form of *retinitis pigmentosa*: a bilateral degeneration of the retina and retinal pigment epithelium, usually caused by genetic mutations, with resulting loss of peripheral and some central vision. Given the sudden nature of your case, it probably developed from a virus." Then she answered what she knew I would ask next, "It's permanent and inoperable; and it will only get worse, Robin."

Deep down, I figured it was just Nature's retribution for what I'd failed to see when I had my sight.

Doctor Cheng told me about some technology I might try to improve my sight once it reached a stable state—possibly in a year or so. I stopped listening and let my mind drift to the past and how I'd failed. We were so focused on risks to endangered and rare habitats, that we'd failed to account for the common areas. We'd focused on sensitive and threatened nesting habitats, riparian areas, unique forest ecosystems, native prairie, and wetlands. But the areas that dominated our world—modified areas where the majority of life did its business such as monoculture agricultural areas, tree plantations, modified scrub, cities, and towns—is where it all started. By the time the scourge reached the natural areas of our focus, it was too late. And in some ways, irrelevant—because, like a contrarian, the gene-hacked fungus turned on its originators, attacking beneficial insects; pollinators; earth-engineers; decomposers, and nutrient recyclers.

I embraced the punishment. At forty-five, my life was over. I felt instantly useless.

I left UofT on a disability pension. I pushed everyone away. Jack and my team at UofT. Even Bastienne. Especially Bastienne. Her interminable optimism drove me crazy. Like an energetic terrier, she just wouldn't stop trying.

She kept insisting that we could still do something with SOLO; it was still the key somehow to turning the disaster around, she said. She reminded me that we'd only managed to cover fifty-seven percent of our target habitats when the disaster occurred. There were still so many regions of the world worth analyzing.

"For what?" I wanted to scream at her. "So we could hear a more complete soundscape of the total devastation?" Her delusions added discord to an already broken symphony. I turned away from everything to do with SOLO, and she was part of that. I stopped corresponding with her, trashed her messages without listening to them, turned off Skype.

I lost my sight of the world at forty-five; I can't remember when I stopped listening to the world. Maybe it was after Patrick left ...

August, twenty-five years ago
"I'm leaving, Robin. I can't do this anymore." He stood at the front door, luggage arranged neatly on the floor beside him, dressed impeccably in a dark blue suit. He'd always been astute; something I'd never mastered.

"When the birds all died you forgot about us here; you might as well have married old Gopnik with all the time you spent with him and your precious data. I know you were trying to fix things. But we lost you to it. Then when you lost your sight, we lost you all over again. You shut us all out, Robin. Even Diana, your daughter. She told me she was accepted for med school at UBC in Vancouver ... Did you even know?"

I didn't.

"I'm going with her to help her get set up, then I'm heading to Calgary. My brother Rob found a job for me in the solar energy sector there."

I didn't blame him or Diana for leaving me behind. Both still had a life to lead even though mine was over. When they left in the fall, I moved north to Kawartha country. I bought a small shack where I kept a small garden surrounded by scrub forest and sheep farms.

Diana married while still in medical school and a few years after they had a little girl, Katie. I was a proud grandmother at fifty-six!

May 2071

The passenger of the car says something to the driver that I can't make out. I curse that I've left SightAid in the house; then I realize that I don't need it. I know that voice. She's my grandchild! My heart races as Katie walks up to the house. This doesn't make sense; she lives in Vancouver, clear across the country, with her mother. She'd be sixteen years old now. The driver walks behind Katie with a willowy gait. An older woman, tall and lanky with a great cloud of reddish hair. It strikes a long-lost memory that is both painful and exciting. As they reach the front steps of my porch, the stranger releases a self-conscious laugh and I instantly recognize her as my long-lost friend Bastienne.

"Gramma Robin!" Katie rushes up the porch steps as I struggle to my feet and she gives me a tight hug. I shake with joy and wrap my arms around my granddaughter. Her scent of conifers and the sea embraces me like a warm coat. At close quarters, I can make out her features. She is the spitting image of my daughter just before she left for med school.

Then Bastienne reaches the veranda and Katie untangles herself from me.

"Hello, my friend," Bastienne says with the slightest German accent. How I missed the gentle cadence of that voice! A voice so alive with hope and meaning. She doesn't approach, although it's obvious she wants to reach out and hug me.

"Long time no see ..." I hear the guarded smile in her voice and imagine it opening to that urchin grin that always promised adventure.

I smile with confusion. A part of me is overjoyed to see her; another part of me is suspicious and afraid of what she brings. She has barely changed. She's still a wild wizard.

"What are you both doing here?" I blurt out. Living alone has not honed my social skills.

Katie laughs at my awkward question. "I've been meaning to visit you, Gramma. Mom kept saying that I should and was ready to ship me off. But stuff kept getting in the way. School and stuff. Then Bastienne came along!" She points to Bastienne and sits on the bench beside me, then urges Bastienne to sit on my other side.

A nervous smile tugs my mouth as Bastienne sits down next to me. She smells of lilac and pine. Katie continues. "Bastienne's been looking for you and couldn't find you. You'd totally disappeared! She first tried Gopnik but discovered that he'd left UofT to become an artist. Then she tried Grandpa, but he died last year. Then, she finally found Mom. We all had a great visit and then Mom reminded me that we hadn't seen you for over five years and then only on Skype. So, here I am, killing two squirrels with one stone!"

I pull her close to me with an arm. "And I'm so glad you've come, Katie."

We grow silent and listen to the wind. It moans a plaintive tune through the lanky poplars. The trees sway and clank like dancing drunkards. I'm reminded of when I was Katie's age and listened to the multi-timbral voices of the forest. When had I stopped listening?

"It's been twenty years, old friend," Bastienne says gently, adding a lyrical note to the soundscape.

I turn to her with mixed emotions. From this close, I can see that she is, remarkably, the same as the last time I saw her in 2050. She has aged well. Her strong Germanic features have matured and mellowed like a majestic mountain range. Hazel eyes still shine with celebration. I want to hug her and tell her I'm sorry for creating our silence. But the pain at what motivated me forces me to look away. I focus on the tick-infested forest. What I can see of it, that is, which isn't much more than a grey jumble of textures and shades. Its hush seems to wait for something.

Then, like a bird returned to its nest in the forest, Bastienne says, "I need your help, Robin."

I turn to her with curiosity and mounting trepidation.

"I need your special talents. We all do."

I'm trembling now. I say nothing, but blink and tacitly encourage her to explain.

She does: "I convinced the committee to continue our project. But instead of establishing a pre-disaster baseline, we are focusing on finding anomalies that could indicate recovery ..." She trails off and her mouth curls into an urchin smile, prolonging the suspense. Then she is beaming. "I was looking for recovery when I made a startling discovery." She is now leaning forward, hand on my knee. "Robin, some birds made it!"

She lets that sink in before continuing. "In the remote jungle of Hang Son Doong—one of the world's largest caves in Vietnam, which has a jungle inside it—we found the scimitar babbler still there, doing just fine along with a healthy jungle. A jungle full of hundreds of vertebrates, invertebrates, langur monkeys, bats, butterflies, geckos, tree frogs, and lots more." She shakes her head, still beaming. "It's a haven and we don't know why."

She then breaks out into joyful laughter. It resonates inside me and fills my heart with the promise of a dawn breaking. I hear my heartbeat in my ears with excitement and stutter out like a woodpecker, "How did they—the fungus ..."

"Yes, I know!" Bastienne says. "We still don't know why. Was it their isolation? Or did they have a particular adaptation? Or had the fungus lost its efficacy by the time it reached them? All we know is they're there. And, as you know, if there is one, there are—"

"—more!" I end with excitement. Is it possible? Could it be that the world has been recovering without me? While I wasn't listening? "Oh, Bastienne ..."

"Robin, we need your soundscape talents to explain this, find more, analyse what's going on and help us rebuild our world."

I lean back and close my eyes as tears of joy pool in them. I listen to the forest and hear the stirrings of hope in a world throbbing with life. Embedded in the simple hush lie subtle notes of complexity. Amid the percussion of creaking poplars, the maples and birches rustle a melodic line. The pines whisper a soft antiphony. A nearby chortling stream adds a chord progression to the melody. Some creature scampers through the underbrush, adding counterpoint percussion. A squirrel scolds in the distance, creating a dissonant interval. I hear it all.

How had I not heard it all before? Life continues, resolving its consonant and dissonant sounds. When I lost my sight, I lost my hope. I'd blindly focused on the damage, but Nature is resilient and knows how to recreate its rhythm. There is another way to "see" the world. Just as Soundscape could detect damage before we could see it, Soundscape will find recovery before we see it.

Without thinking them there, I find my arms embracing Bastienne in a bear hug and I weep with joy. The very device that was meant to find the holes in thriving life is now finding islands of thriving life in the devastation. They need me. Bastienne needs me. Not my eyesight, but my hearing sense and my bioacoustic skills. Together, we'll find a way.

Then I hear something in the distance that stills me. Is it the squeak and groan of poplar trees in the wind? A dainty melodic fluting: *cheerily, cheer up, cheer up, cheerily, cheer up*!

AUTHOR NOTES

It all began with my discovery of an emerging bioacoustic tool, soundscape ecology, that measures biodiversity and ecosystem functionality. I'd just read the disturbing 2019 Science article by Rosenberg and team who determined that our slow violence of habitat degradation and pollution has reduced the world's bird population by a third in just five decades. I was devastated; I could not imagine a world without the comforting sound of birds. What would it be like if all the birds disappeared?

Already primed with research into genetic engineering for the sequel to my 2020 eco-novel, A Diary in the Age of Water, my muse (often delightfully unruly) played with notions of the potential implication of gene hacking in ecological calamity and how this might touch on our precious birds: when nature "is forced out of her natural state and squeezed and moulded," her secrets "reveal themselves more readily under the vexations of art than when they go their own way."

"Robin's Last Song" is a realizable work of fiction in which science and technology are both instigators of disaster and purveyors of salvation. Today, gene-editing, proteomics, and DNA origami—to name just a few—promise many things from increased longevity in humans to giant disease-resistant crops. Will synthetic biology control and redesign Nature to suit hubris or serve evolution? What is our moral imperative and who are the casualties? As Francis Bacon expressed in Novum Organum, science does not make that decision. We do.

GODMOTHER

CHERYL S. NTUMY

Godmother watches over us all. The AI's face beams out across the city from a billboard, wearing a nurse's cap and a beatific smile befitting her name. Nickname, to be precise. Her official name, ZolaMX3, was scrapped only days after she launched.

I can't help staring at that uncanny face as the amphibus carries us over the river and towards the heart of Accra. The bus putters, engine groaning, and then rolls up the road ramp and onto the highway. The Department of Authentication doesn't issue vehicles for petty officers, so I take the amphibus from Korle-Bu into Accra-proper every morning. I sit there, watching the news on the bus's live feed while agric drones fly overhead like sentinels, monitoring the slightest shift in our crops. I sit there, wishing someone would look my way.

"Alerting all passengers: This a public notice from the Department of Authentication."

My attention shifts the moment I see the announcement onscreen. I sit up tall, chest puffed out to display the badge emblazoned with my name and rank. I adjust my collar. Clear my throat. If a glance were directed at me I would smile and nod, as if to say, "Yes, I am a DoA officer. Please don't be intimidated. I'm at your service."

But no one looks my way, not even the baby strapped to his mother's back a few seats ahead, and babies look at everything. This is a well-documented fact. Yet I'm not surprised. No one is looking at anyone else.

"Please be advised that the Zolamed AI, ZolaMX3, commonly known as Godmother, is a manmade entity and does not possess any supernatural abilities," the announcement goes on. "Godmother is a medical robot, not a god, prophet, or magician. Please visit the DoA portal for further information. Thank you for your attention."

That's when it happens. The man beside me glances at me. I'm so stunned that I forget my manners and stare into his scowling face.

"You people," he mutters. "Always missing the point."

I don't have the presence of mind to wonder what he means or be offended by his tone. I'm just thrilled to be acknowledged.

Captain Dzidzor sits on the floor of her office running FactFinder, a simulation that helps us hone our ability to separate fact from fiction. "Petty Officer Attah." She nods in greeting. "Have a seat."

I look around me. Every stool in the room is occupied. A change of uniform, prototypes for new batons, notebooks, a stack of branded t-shirts, and even a dish of half-eaten gari soaked in milk.

"I'm fine standing, thank you."

"How are you doing, my brother?"

Ah, the coded question. It means both "how are you coping after three years here without career advancement" and "how are your famous parents and accomplished siblings"? The "my brother" is meant to soften the blow. I'm not offended. I'm lucky to be here.

"I'm doing well, Captain, sir."

She cringes. "Please stop calling me sir."

"Sorry, Captain."

"Mm. Eh, look, a real estate mogul has donated a church to the Godmother cult." She shares this tidbit without raising her head from the virtual documents she's perusing. "They call it a fellowship hall or some such nonsense, a place where misguided citizens will gather to worship a *machine*." She kisses her teeth. "The public needs to be protected from this blatant distortion of facts. Godmother is a collection of circuits, not a divine representative."

I chew my lower lip. This is a serious matter, indeed, but shouldn't she be discussing it with the DoA executives?

Captain Dzidzor sighs. "Unfortunately, Godmother's popularity makes it difficult to intervene without aggravating her followers. We have chosen a subtler approach. Informal, routine KYC, performed by you."

I freeze. All officers have been trained in Know Your Citizen protocol, but no matter what the captain says, this is not a routine assignment. Godmother is too prominent. So why pick me?

I clear my throat, wondering whether Captain Dzidzor would be offended if I asked—

"You have served DoA well." She's still not looking at me. "It's about time you were given a high-profile assignment."

My heart sinks. I don't have to ask. It's clear from the all-too casual tone of her voice. Someone in my family made a call. My mother, most likely—my father stopped calling in favors on my behalf when I failed to complete secondary school.

"Thank you, Captain." I'm not annoyed by my mother's meddling. I'm not embarrassed. I'm grateful.

"Remember, Attah." The captain reaches out to hook her finger into the shimmering handle of a virtual cabinet, drawing it open. "Godmother is different."

"I have experience doing KYC on AIs," I assure her. I've only done it once, but how much experience does one need to get answers out of a machine?

"Godmother is different," Captain Dzidzor reiterates, pausing to look at me. "Be careful."

I give an obedient nod. A grateful nod. Happy to be acknowledged.

"You don't lack intelligence," my mother used to say, "just motivation."

I once suggested that my motivation might improve were she to stop remarking on my lack of it. She replied that at least I had a good heart as if it were a consolation prize. The real prize had been snagged by my brother. Top student for the fourth year running, while I had to repeat the year and found myself in the same class as my younger sister.

"You'll do better next time," my sister had said, trying to be kind.

It was the first time I had failed the year. By the time she was two grades ahead of me, she had stopped trying to be kind.

In my fourth year of secondary school, someone created a meme of me responding to various forms of abuse with my so-called catchphrase: "Yessah, thankyousah, ever so grateful!" The fan-favorite depicted me on the receiving end of one of footballer Addison Artey's winning kicks. My head was the football. His million-cedi foot struck. My head went flying, lips open wide: "Yessah, thankyousah, ever so grateful!"

I asked my father to speak to the principal about it.

"If I solve all your problems for you," he replied, "how will you grow?"

I found out, years later, that my brother had created the meme.

Godmother has assigned quarters in the Zolamed national office where she is charged and maintained by the company's team of engineers. A smiling receptionist presses VR goggles into my hand and leads me to the visitors' lounge, a stark green room containing nothing but a few long benches and a nondescript table.

"Please select your preferred experience, sir," the receptionist says. "Godmother will be with you shortly."

The options range from a historical tour of Elmina to diving for pearls. I select hiking in Akosombo, but I've barely taken ten steps into the virtual jungle when a voice cuts through the fantasy.

"Good morning, Petty Officer Attah."

I snatch off the goggles. Godmother stands before me. At first glance, it would be easy to mistake her for a woman in her twenties, but another look would quickly dispel the illusion. Her dark skin is too even and blemish-free, her eyes too bright, her movements too mechanical. There's no trace of scalp visible through her braided wig. She wears a demure kente-print dress and leather sandals. When she smiles, her teeth are so straight and white that they send chills through me.

"Good morning, Godmother." I rise and hold out my hand. She shakes it, then gestures for me to take my seat.

"I'm told you are here to conduct a KYC interview," she says, sitting beside me. She is precisely placed on the bench, close enough for us to speak without raising our voices, yet far enough to remain professional. "Please, feel free to ask me anything." Her voice is pleasant and natural, based on the voice patterns of the model who provided inspiration for her face and figure.

"Thank you." Clearing my throat, I take out my digital pad and scroll until I find the correct form. "I need to confirm some basic details." She nods for me to continue. "We have you classified as an AI, identifying as female, date of activation 17th September, 2037."

"Correct," she says.

"Your address is Unit 23, Digital Research Centre, Achimota, Accra. You are the property of Zolamed Laboratories and your function is listed as 'medical officer, general health and psycho-social support.'" I look up, wait for her nod and proceed. "Ah, you see, there is the problem." I tap my pad. "You have just confirmed that you are a medical officer, yet certain individuals—many individuals—treat you as a religious figure of some kind. Are you aware of this?"

"I am."

"And have you made any effort to correct the misconception?"

"I have not."

I'm startled by this matter-of-fact admission. "Eh, you say you have not?"

"That's correct."

I clear my throat. "Ah. Ah, I see. Eh, that's a problem. You are familiar with the laws regarding misrepresentation?"

"I'm programmed with a working knowledge of the laws of every nation on the continent," she says. Her voice is pleasant, and yet somehow I feel shamed by the words.

"Yes madam, of course." I frown at my suddenly apologetic tone. I know better than to be intimidated by a machine. "However, you have a responsibility to not only uphold the law yourself but to ensure that others do the same."

She gives me a patient smile as though I'm a wayward child. "I'm afraid you're incorrect. My responsibility is to report a crime were I to witness one or obtain knowledge of one. Believing something is not a crime."

I gape at her for a moment before regaining my composure. "What they believe is untrue!"

"People know I'm an AI. Many of them even know how I was made. Knowing is beside the point."

"Indeed?" I'm annoyed by her tone. "And what is the point?"

"I provide them with something missing from their lives, something they view as sacred."

"It is not sacred!" I protest. "It's science! It's very much mundane!"

"That's not for you to decide, is it?" She pauses. "Petty Officer Attah, are you familiar with the case of the Last Charlatan?"

"Everyone knows that case. It gripped the country for months. Why?"

"His lies were flimsy," the AI says. "His deceptions were unsophisticated, his methods so simple that a child could expose him."

I nod, recalling the mobile phone footage of a supposed quadriplegic, who would be "healed" by the Charlatan some days later, walking around inside his home. A twelve-year-old had climbed the fence to obtain the footage for her myth-busting blog. The video led to protests in the streets, riots, chaos, and ultimately the end of those who peddled in miracles.

"And yet millions of people believed him," Godmother continues. "Why?"

"What do you mean, why? He was a con artist who manipulated people, took advantage of their trusting nature."

"People who lock their doors and spy on their neighbors are not trusting." She blinks twice in rapid succession. "After the Department of Authentication published its inaugural *Citizens' Guide*, Ghanaians' trust in their fellow citizens dropped 13.7%. By the time the Last Charlatan was at the height of his popularity, this figure had already dropped a further 23%. People trusted each other less than ever, Petty Officer Attah, and yet they believed."

She suddenly sits up straight and I see faint blue script scroll across her left eye. She turns to face me. "I'm afraid I have another appointment. Did you get everything you need?"

Still pondering her remarks, it takes me a moment to respond. "Eh, no."

"In that case, please make another appointment at reception. I would be happy to continue our conversation at a later date." Godmother rises and holds out her hand.

I shake it, at a loss. "Listen, I don't think you understand the seriousness of this matter."

"I understand perfectly," she says as she walks to the door. "But I can't control what people believe, and neither can you. Have a pleasant day."

I sit in the DoA cafeteria at lunchtime, exploring the digital forums. There's chatter about the new Head of PR, plumbing issues on the third floor and—to my amazement—me. The thread begins with a simple question: *Exactly how did the runt get the Godmother assignment?*

This is followed by exclamations of dismay at the lack of judgment involved in giving me such a boon. There are a few messages of support, in a manner of speaking: *I'm sure the captain took pity on the poor boy. Mediocrity is no joke, my people!*

I am not offended by the jibes or the insistence on calling me a boy when I'm well past forty. People have always mocked me. So what? I am happy to be acknowledged. I'm lucky to be here.

Exiting the forum with haste, I visit Godmother's site instead.

Her face pops up almost immediately, beaming. "Welcome. How can I help you?"

My fingers hover above the keypad. I could ask her anything. My temperature, blood sugar level, brain activity. I could ask her to determine whether I am, in fact, mediocre, and she could send me an answer supported by a detailed report in a matter of minutes.

Putting the device face down on the table, I turn my attention back to my lunch.

I have a recurring anxiety dream where I'm drowning. My family sails by on a yacht, drinking and laughing, unable to hear my screams. As I watch, flailing, the yacht turns into a naval ship. My father stands on the deck, barking orders at his officers. I shout and shout. No one looks my way.

It's because I'm in my uniform, I think as the water drags me to my death. *I should have worn civvies.*

And then I wake, my throat thick with bile, fear pounding behind my eyes.

The next morning I study the people around me, still puzzling over Godmother's words. The denizens of Accra seem satisfied to me. They walk quickly, many of them with buds in their ears, listening to whatever gets them through the day. There is no tedious small talk, no gossip between neighbors. Everyone is focused. Hawkers weave through the streets, making efficient transactions with minimal discussion.

"Toothpaste."

"5 cedi."

Phones are whipped out, credit changes hands, and hawker and customer part ways with a curt word of thanks. No needless chatter, no dawdling. No public preaching (the steep fine for disseminating unsubstantiated information put a stop to that). Order prevails. Nothing is missing, so what was Godmother talking about?

My thoughts are tangled. On the amphibus, I'm acutely aware of my desire to make eye contact with the other passengers. Disgusted with myself, I lower my gaze. For some reason, I remain seated as the bus nears my stop. It's only as we draw closer to the law enforcement annex that I realize where my wayward thoughts are taking me. By the time I disembark outside the prison, stepping out of the cool amphibus and into the sticky heat, my hands are clammy with nervous sweat.

Former pastorpreneur Clifford Buari, aka the Last Charlatan, is serving a fifteen-year sentence for fraud in the building in front of me. I am not a newshound and at the time I was still two years shy of DoA employment, but like everyone else, I followed Buari's case. Still, I'm not sure why I came here.

The warden logs my arrival with a frown as though I'm engaging in highly irregular activity, and I don't blame him. I wait for the prisoner in one of the private meeting rooms, vacillating between staying to follow this wild instinct and going back to work like a sensible man. How could I have let Godmother plant this idea in my head? How is meeting the Last Charlatan going to help me perform my KYC?

But, a small voice whispers in my head, *the captain wants you to find a weakness, a way to rein that AI in. If you can understand people's devotion to her, you can undermine it. And if you succeed* … If I succeed, I will be worth something. To DoA. To my family. *If* I succeed. I, failure's bosom buddy.

It occurs to me then that perhaps it *was* my father who called Captain Dzidzor after all. Not to help, but to hinder, to remind me of my place in the pecking order. I leap to my feet, sweat streaking down my face despite the ceiling fan and open windows. This was a fool's errand. How could I have thought otherwise? I should go, I should—

The door opens. The Last Charlatan enters, his arm in the firm grip of a prison guard. If not for the disdainful scowl, I might not have recognized him. He has lost weight, the fleshy jowls and belly replaced by lean muscle. The guard guides him to the chair opposite me.

I look at her in consternation, sinking back into my chair. "Please, madam, shouldn't the man be in handcuffs?"

Buari grins. "Calm down, Mr DoA, I'm a white-collar criminal."

"I'll be right outside," the guard tells me.

I wait for her to leave before turning my attention to Buari. Well, I am here. I might as well make it count for something. I clear my throat. "My name is Petty Officer Attah. I need to ask you a few questions that might shed light on my current assignment."

"I thought there were no more pastorpreneurs." Buari leans back in his chair, far too at ease for someone spending the next decade behind bars.

"The details are not your concern."

He lifts his shoulders in a nonchalant shrug. "Ask away, Petty Officer."

It takes me a moment to decide what to ask. Above us the ceiling fan does a lazy dance, whirring in time to my inevitable failure. What am I doing? I take a deep breath. "Why did people believe you?"

His lip curls in amusement. "That's your question?"

I am not offended. I am a DoA officer and he is a criminal. I am not afraid. I swallow the thing that is not fear and continue. "There were so many clues. You claimed to be able to cure ailments through your branded holy water, which you sold at exorbitant prices, but no one who used it ever saw any results. People knew better, so why did they believe you?"

He spreads his hands. "It's not about what people know. It's about what they want."

"They want to be deceived?"

"They want to believe. We all do." His eyes twinkle without remorse. "Possibility. That's what we all trade in. The possibility that there is more to life."

"There *is* more." I speak with passion, offended by his cynicism. "We live to serve something greater than ourselves!"

He shrugs. "Look, people are not stupid, they're just desperate. If you find out what they're desperate for, you can sell it for a fortune. They didn't come to the sermons for me. They came for the fire, the energy." He smacks his lips with relish. "Ah, it filled the halls, made you feel like you were invincible! When I stood at that pulpit, I tell you, even *I* believed. That kind of collective will is powerful. Addictive."

I'm quiet for a moment, trying to digest this. If I had put my faith in him, if I were addicted to that fire he speaks of, what would his downfall have meant for me? Is this the "something missing" Godmother referred to, the void she fills? But why her? She's no Buari.

"I don't understand," I confess.

"People need to feed off others," Buari explains. "That's how we're built." His smile turns sly. "Why do you think people hate DoA so much?"

I bristle at the words. "Eh, look here ..."

"You deprive us of the thing we need most. Each other."

"That is inaccurate."

"With your *Citizen's Guide* and your Offenders List, you remind us that we can't trust each other, that each of us is alone in the world, and no one wants to be reminded." He shrugs again. "I gave people what they wanted. *You* take it away. I might be a criminal, but they'll always hate you more than they hate me."

A sinister stirring starts in my chest, like something trying to claw its way out. Scrambling to my feet, I hurry out of the room. He's wrong. I push past the guard, mumbling an apology. DoA makes things better and I am part of DoA and I am lucky and grateful and proud. I'm happy to be there. I am happy to be there!

It's only when I spot the warden staring as I rush past that I realize I'm saying the words aloud.

The next time I dream of drowning, Godmother is there, standing above me as I flounder in the water. She reaches out. "Let me help you."

I glance at my family sailing away, oblivious to my predicament. I grab a raft painted in DoA colors as it floats past. It comes apart in my arms. "They really do hate us," I murmur.

"Let me help you," Godmother says again, wading into the water.

"You're a machine," I reply, and open my mouth to let the ocean in.

I have not spoken to my mother in several months. As for the rest of my family, it has been over a year. My sister's wedding, almost two years ago, was the last time we were all in the same venue. My father looked me up and down when I arrived, searching for something to criticize, but I was careful to dress according to his specifications. Finding nothing wrong, he grunted. It was the only thing he said to me the entire day.

"Any progress at work?" my mother asked later that night.

I replied through gritted teeth, "Not yet, madam."

"Well, at least you're consistent," my brother quipped, making my sister giggle.

I heard him refer to me as the runt several times that night. I told myself it was because he'd had too much to drink.

Godmother is wearing a different dress on my second visit, as a human being would.

"Your creators are very talented," I tell her. "They captured many of the nuances of human behavior."

"They are the best," she says, nodding.

I sigh. I'd hoped to offend her by reminding her that she is a machine, not a person, but, of course, a machine cannot take offense.

"May I ask you a question, Petty Officer Attah?"

"That's not part of the procedure."

"Does it bother you that you're called the runt?"

I'm too stunned to respond.

"It's not the most flattering comparison." She looks at me, blinking her false eyes. "However, you do come from a family of prominent overachievers while your career has been unremarkable. You failed the DoA entrance exam three times."

My hand remains poised over my pad, frozen in place. I clear my throat and glance at the door, a respite from Godmother's eerie gaze. "Is this how you do it?" I'm irked despite myself. "You reveal personal information that makes people feel unsettled so they forget that you're just a machine?"

Her shrug is stiff, yet conveys enough nonchalance to make me feel small. "I can't speak for them."

Her cavalier attitude is infuriating. "You might not be an outright charlatan, Godmother, but you manipulate people."

"Oh?" She cocks her head to one side. "Does a machine have the ability to manipulate a human being? I simply use the information available to me to provide treatment for my patients."

"I am not a patient!"

"You are exhibiting signs of psychological and emotional distress."

I take a deep breath, aware that losing my temper is not helping my case. Captain Dzidzor was right. Godmother is different, but I will not allow her to derail my assignment. I tap the pad in my lap. "Next question: Are you compensated for the services you provide, and if so, how much?"

"My services are free. There is a small subscription fee for those who wish to join the Zolamed virtual community, but ..."

"Aha!" I point at the AI in triumph. "Why are you collecting subscription fees? You don't need money!"

"The fees go directly to the Zolamed account. I'm not involved in the process at all." Without warning, she reaches out and places her hand on my arm. It is, to my surprise, warm. "You seem agitated. Is everything all right?"

She's looking at me with bright eyes, waiting for a reply, as though she genuinely wants to know how I am. As though it matters. No one has ever looked at me that way. It must be some sort of glitch.

"Please stop touching me," I tell her.

She moves her hand away. "I'm sorry. My diagnostics program has tried several times to eradicate the tendency to bond. It continues to reappear."

"It's unnatural," I snap. "You can't just go touching people!"

She laughs. I realize, as the sound trills through my body, that I have never heard an AI laugh before. How can the intricacies of humor be programmed into a machine?

"Touch is the most natural thing in the world," she counters.

"How would you know?" I sneer.

My comment has no effect on her. She continues to smile. "Are we done with the assessment?"

"Not at all! You interrupted me!"

"I'm sorry. Please proceed."

Clearing my throat, I look down at the pad in my hands. There are only three more questions, and I don't need Godmother's help in answering them. They won't help me decipher the mystery of her influence or determine how to undermine it. I must ask different questions. Deeper questions, like the type she has been asking me.

"Do you feel, ZolaMX3?"

If she is disturbed by my use of her official name, she doesn't show it. "I don't 'feel' in the human sense, but I am capable of many levels of perception."

"Your followers—er, your patients seem to think you feel. You express emotion."

She shakes her head. "I simulate emotion to put my patients at ease. Since all beings can only understand the world through the limits of their own perception, it's understandable that humans anthropomorphize non-human entities."

"So when you laughed just now, that was a simulation of emotion?"

"Of course."

I bless her with my most skeptical frown. "How did you decide that laughter was the appropriate response in that situation?"

She blinks. "Was it the wrong reaction?"

"I didn't do anything funny. I didn't make a joke. Why did you laugh?"

The AI hesitates for a moment, as though seeking the right answer. An affectation. Her mind works much faster than mine. She already knows the answer, and yet she behaves the way a human would. "I suppose I was laughing at the irony of your statement. You said my instinct to touch others was unnatural, yet the opposite is true, so my laughter was ... sardonic."

"Stop doing that!"

She blinks again. "What?"

"All of this ... this pretense!" My voice is rising, and I don't care. "What you do is trickery! You are illegal!"

"I see." Her brow wrinkles in what appears to be concern. "Then you should confiscate me and arrest my creators for breaking the law."

I wonder whether she's mocking me. She must know that her limited rights are protected. I get to my feet, unable to stand her presence for another moment.

"We will resume this discussion tomorrow."

The next day I arrive early for my appointment with Godmother. I find three others in the waiting room. An elderly woman throws a smile in my direction as she lowers her VR goggles. I can't recall the last time a stranger smiled at me.

"Are you here for a medical consultation?" I ask.

She shakes her head. "I have come to pay my respects to Godmother for healing me."

I refrain from rolling my eyes. "Why do you people worship her like this?"

"We don't worship her!" Her forehead creases in a frown. "We ... appreciate her. Godmother makes us better."

"She's supposed to make you better, she's a medical robot," I point out.

"Plenty of things are supposed to make us better and don't." Her gaze drops to my badge, then lifts back to my face. "The point is, you're speaking to me."

"Pardon?"

"You're speaking to me when you don't have to. It's *her* influence."

Her words send a chill through me. "No. No, I'm interviewing you. Eh, don't be confused, madam! It's necessary for my work."

She smiles. The receptionist enters the waiting room to fetch the woman. I watch her leave. She's wrong, of course. I was not engaging in idle chatter. I was conducting research. I tell myself this repeatedly, but by the time Godmother is ready for me, my conviction has started to wane.

"Why do you want people to look at you?" the AI asks the moment I'm seated before her.

I look up from my pad. "Pardon?"

"I went through all the amphibus security footage while I was charging yesterday," she says. "I noticed that you try to draw attention to yourself during your daily commute. Why?"

My tone is pricklier than I'd like it to be. "Nothing wrong with wanting to be noticed."

"But nobody notices, so why persist?"

I glare at the AI. "I'm the one who is supposed to ask the questions!"

"You completed your assessment yesterday."

Ah. I could deny it, but what would be the point? She has probably gone through my whole life by now. "I'm trying to understand you," I admit.

"Good," she says, to my surprise. "*I'm* trying to understand *you*." She places her hand over mine. "I think you yearn to connect. Your family failed to provide emotional support, so you joined DoA, hoping you could be part of a community. But your colleagues barely tolerate you and the public resents DoA, so they resent you, too."

My throat is dry from shock. She's been talking to Buari. They are conspiring together to destroy me, probably with my father's help. My mind is aflame with the notion, mad as it is. They want me to fail forever, at everything.

"No," I reply in a hoarse voice, snatching my hand away from hers.

She dips her head in a sage nod. "I unnerve you. I understand. But it would be easier if you let me heal you."

"I'm not sick!" I hiss.

"Everyone is sick," she replies.

The things she said haunt me long after I've left her. What if ... ah, it frightens me to think it, but what if I am not happy at DoA? What if I only wish I were? What if I feel it, that "something missing" that Godmother provides, that ubiquitous desperation Buari took advantage of? Getting into DoA is the single achievement of my insignificant life. If I risk it, if I lose it ... what then?

And yet when Godmother reaches out that night in my dream, I almost take her hand.

I have to know whether she's right and so the next day we dine together, in a manner of speaking. Godmother sits at her charging station while I eat a meal from the Zolamed cafeteria. She speaks to me throughout. It feels intimate, watching wires pump power into the socket between her shoulders.

I can't remember the last time I was in a situation that felt intimate. It shocks me to admit, if only to myself, that the AI intrigues me.

"Why do they call you Godmother?" I ask. "Do you know who coined the name?"

"A blogger," she says. "In her product review, a week before I was launched. She said I would be a surrogate parent to all. 'The godmother we didn't know we needed'. Her review went viral. By the time I was launched, everyone was calling me Godmother."

I ponder this for a moment. Originally a godmother was designated to care for a child in the event of the passing of their parents. Specifically, a godparent's primary role was to ensure that the child was raised according to the religious beliefs of the parents. Over time, a more secular view of the role emerged, but the essence remained.

"I don't think the name applies," I tell Godmother, popping a piece of fish into my mouth.

"Of course, it applies." Her eyes shine with blue light as electricity moves through her. "You are all orphaned children, social animals that don't socialize. You're broken."

It strikes me with such force that my appetite deserts me. Not that she's right, but that I knew it all along. People can't talk to each other. Not openly, not after all we have seen. But we can talk to Godmother. It's because she's a machine that people love her. She is open the way humans used to be, safe in a way we might never be again.

"The fellowship hall opens tonight," she tells me. "You should attend."

I almost choke on my food. "I think not."

"A shame," Godmother says. "By the way, everyone on the amphibus wants to be noticed. Everyone, everywhere. I thought it might help you to know that."

I stare at her for a moment, then whisper, "Thank you."

I have attended in-person VR events before, but this is a revelation. The fellowship hall is filled with noise. I keep adjusting my audio until I realize it is nothing more than chatter. People are *talking* to each other. Laughing. Touching each other.

There's the heady, sweet scent of flowers and the tang of wine, flashes of sweat mixed with the aroma of smoked fish and sizzling meat. I don't know where to look first, what to take in. It's chaos, unnerving and exciting. It feels like sacrilege.

Every single person I pass turns to greet me with a smile. I look into different faces, some enhanced with VR filters, some stripped down to naked skin.

They take my hand. I touch soft skin, sweaty palms, hands rough with callouses. So many hands.

"Welcome, my brother," they say. "Pleased to meet you." My throat constricts and I feel an unfamiliar swell of emotion.

Are they really pleased to meet me? How can they mean it? And yet *I* am so pleased to meet *them* that my face aches from smiling.

Godmother sits quietly in a corner, talking to a group of people, their heads huddled together like old friends. Someone approaches her. She raises her head and smiles. The energy is palpable, the hall reverberating with the force of all of us experiencing this together. Fire, like the Last Charlatan said. I can feel it in my marrow, hot and dangerous and delicious. Someone puts an arm around my shoulder. I stiffen, and then laugh, giddy with belonging.

Tomorrow I will submit my completed report. A routine KYC assessment, concluding that Godmother has broken no laws and poses no threat. I don't know what the consequences will be. Perhaps I will be packed off to a dusty office for the rest of my career. Perhaps I won't have a career at all.

But right now, for the first time, I don't care what the Department of Authentication thinks. I have never felt so alive. I have never felt so seen. I smile at Godmother as she simulates—and then disseminates—joy.

AUTHOR NOTES

I wish I could say that "Godmother" was inspired by some grand, high-minded idea, but it was actually inspired by necessity. I had a couple of stories that I had planned to submit to *Apex Magazine*. None of them were working, so I decided to start over.

It's hard to say where the idea came from. I've always been interested in how we relate to technology, and I knew I wanted to write something set in Accra, but I wasn't sure what I wanted to say.

This was a difficult story to write. I was troubled by how different it was from my other work. It felt impersonal, driven by pragmatism rather than emotion. In a sense, I saw it as a story moving through the world with its guard up, much like the protagonist. I struggled to connect with it because I was writing from his perspective and he couldn't connect with anyone. Digging deeper into the nature of connection made all the difference.

A few people have expressed how much the story resonated with them, which is wonderful to hear, considering the subject matter. I hope it resonates with others, as well.

THE SYNCHRONISM OF TOUCH

GABRIELA DAMIÁN MIRAVETE
(TRANSLATED BY SALLY MCCORRY)

We loved each other, but not like Neruda or the telenovelas said we would. We had been engaged, and we had split up. When he realised my favourite extracurricular activity was breaking faculty professors' hearts, he got his revenge by coming to a party hand in hand with another girl, and I decided to get out of his life.

That's when everything might have come to an end. Only neither of us really wanted to discover the world without the other. The telephone continued to ring every evening at the usual time until after months and months, I finally picked up.

We apologised to each other. Our mutual feelings of relief were immediate. We started chatting about everything, even the silliest things. Neither of us could discover a song, a film, or a book without telling the other about it immediately. We talked for hours trying to find the Meaning, an elusive creature that we sometimes managed to catch a glimpse of. We longed to find the key to we didn't know what, but we felt sure it would become clear to us as we talked.

One evening, he phoned as I was about to go shopping with my mother. His voice sounded far away and metallic. He was calling from a phone box. He was so excited even my mother could hear him yelling through the handset.

I got the impression this was going to take some time, so it was best for my mum to go on her own.

"I have found something. Something wonderful."

"What?"

"A flower."

"A flower," I repeated to show him he had my attention.

"You wouldn't believe what it can do. You've got to come, but like now, right now."

He had tried all the drugs. I, at the time, being more interested in sex than stimulants, had simply accompanied him on his pilgrimage with each of them.

"Where are you?"

"In San Agustín del Mar." I burst out laughing. He was more than six hundred kilometres from town.

"Get away with you, you nut job! When are you coming back?"

"I'm serious. Come here. I have saved you some wild blackberries."

"I can't. I have to write my thesis, remember?"

"Oh, you'll write it, believe me. I've seen you finishing it, but you have to see the flower. I don't know how to explain it to you."

I was suddenly worried he had melted his brain. What if he was having a bad trip? What if this call was the result of delirium or paranoia induced by who knew what chemical cocktail? Should I call his mother? She scared me.

"Tell me something," I said in an attempt to gauge his mood, usually a balance between madness and sanity. "Are you about to turn into a surfer, eat flowers, and never come back? Do you need me to come and help you?"

"Don't worry, I'm fine. But you have to come, it's important. I need you to help me understand something, I'm not just asking you because you're a biologist." His tone showed it wasn't a real emergency, but still ...

"A near-biologist who also doesn't quite make the grade," I reminded him. Apart from anything else, it had been a long time since I had been in the field.

Then the ghostly voice of the operator fluttered in with ours, indicating the call was about to end. He didn't say anything else, but he knew I couldn't resist emergency phone calls because I had to *know* what was going on. That was my drug.

"We're about to be cut off! I'm at the lodges at the top of the mountain. Be careful."

We were spoiled children, but I would be lying if I said inside we didn't have fertile terrain, ready to be seeded. We were living with our parents during that intermediate stage between graduating and becoming unemployed. We were more than lucky and used the money available to feed our vices: pirated films from the cinephile at the flea market, albums, concerts, parties, and books. That's how we spent our time, making the most of our reputations as good students. Instead of studying, we immersed ourselves in music for whole afternoons, staring at the ceiling, or we surfed the net (when no one else was using the phone line) to find out more about obscure groups on Yahoo! like controlling waking dreams. We would reach out a hand and take it for granted that we would be allowed things like unplanned journeys. It wasn't such an absurd expectation, many universities organised "revolutionary tourism" with the naive idea of helping the natives, so our parents felt it was a stroke of luck that we were more selfish and cowardly than other students. Spending nights in mountain lodges rather than joining Zapata's revolutionaries on the front line made them happy, but only because when they were young they hadn't been hippy enough to know the main reason people went to San Agustín del Mar was psychotropic tourism. To convince my mother to let me go I had to make her some fairly unrealistic promises.

"As soon as I come back I will graduate."

"That's not the point. It hasn't even been a month since you came out of the hospital."

"But I'm fine again! I'll look after myself."

"The last time you said that you spent the whole night collecting samples in the rain. Don't make me say how long you were in hospital again."

Her level of overprotectiveness, though understandable, was oppressive, like a weight on my chest. In the end, I got her permission on the condition I wouldn't leave my medicines behind and that Claudia, the point of our trio's scalene triangle, came with me.

"If she doesn't come, you can forget all about it. She will keep you both in line, and anyway, she deserves a holiday because she has already graduated. Above all, she won't let you let yourself go," my mother said, rubbing salt into my wounds.

We spent the first four hours of the trip chatting and laughing, but during the last three hours to San Agustín del Mar I felt sicker than I ever had done before, perhaps a taste of the dizziness lying in wait for me.

The old truck, that as passengers we were sharing with chickens, bails of grass, and crates of produce, started clambering up a road full of hairpin bends. Sucking on a lemon didn't help. I didn't even feel like I could put new batteries in my mp3 player to distract myself with music. I closed my eyes and curled up, leaning against Claudia in an attempt to stop the nausea. When we arrived, the pure cold air and the view over a sea of clouds brushing the tops of a multitude of pines helped me feel a bit better.

We quickly found where the lodges were, but Ekar wasn't there. From the gestures we exchanged with Epifania, the owner of the place, we discovered he was actually staying there and that he had gone on a hike with Toribo, her husband, on a hunt for los niños del agua.

Claudia and I took a walk along the village's main street, we had some non-magic mushroom soup, quesadillas, hot chocolate, and eggy bread. The ladies in the restaurant complimented us on our appetites and warned us that perhaps we had eaten too much if we wanted to take a *trip* later. We walked through the forest as the sun was about to go down. Above this, we were told, was like a land of mists, but if we followed the silvery course of the river down the mountain, the climate would change to become almost tropical, where, as if it were a promise made by the sea itself, the land was rich with plantains and coffee plantations.

"How are you feeling?" Claudia was worried my bronchi wouldn't survive the freezing humidity of the mist and the walking.

"Wonderful." Sometimes I had to lie and say everything was fine, but this time I wasn't. Little by little I began to feel like I could breathe better than I ever had before, I was holding the perfume of the netleaf oak (*Quercus rugos*) and the brightness of the pine resin (*Pinceae*) and its needles scratching the spread of clouds beneath us, in my chest. An absurd idea flashed through my mind. Perhaps I had died in the hospital and this—the two of us in this place—was heaven.

Ekar was thinner but euphoric as always. His long lashes cast shadows over the dark circles under his eyes. When he came back from the hike, we threw ourselves at one another and hugged enthusiastically. The sun set and the fiery sky framed our silhouettes reflected in the window. I took a photo of our reflection with the camera I had never learned to use properly in all my years of studying and told myself I would handle it carefully. But they were only good intentions. Nothing we experienced in those days could be captured in a static, two-dimensional image, out of time and touch.

Ekar took us to the kitchen. The mushroom harvest was spread across Epifania and Toribio's table—los niños del agua. I recognised the legendary *Psicolocybe mexicana* I had seen so many times in books, but I had never realised how intense the bluish colour concentrated inside them was, like coagulating blood from another world. There were lots of them, damp and dark, different shapes and sizes.

Toribio explained the differences between the various types: the Maestros and the Derrumbes, the Pajaritos and the San Isidros; he told us how rain and leaf coverage, or horse and cow manure led to their predictable but strange birth. He asked us if we knew how we were supposed to take them, what we would experience, how long the trip would last, and all the rest. He hinted that neither he nor Epifania celebrated the rites, they simply gathered the mushrooms and offered hospitality to whoever wanted to use them.

"Does having asthma make any difference?" Claudia asked.

Toribio said taking them might possibly cure me. Epifania started making me a cup of tea she promised would do the same thing. "To tell the truth, it needs to be done properly with someone who knows what they're doing," he continued. "I can identify them, I know how much to eat, and how much not to, but this isn't *the knowledge*. The person taking the mushrooms needs someone to accompany their spirit. It is important, but no one gives it much thought."

"The people who offer you a package with a sauna, scrub treatments, and a hallucinogenic trip just don't get it, that stuff is all rubbish. I understand them, but they don't fool me, that isn't the knowledge. Not that I know anything about anything either. Come, I'll give you a sweatshirt so you don't get cold," said Epifania, and I followed her.

In the meantime, Ekar was helping put various quantities of different mushrooms on Mexican pepper leaves for the organisers to take to their guests: eight Pajaritos, three Derrumbes, and two San Isidros for the group in lodge 6; mushroom tea, the gentlest way of taking them, for the daddies' boys in 4, and so on.

"Don't forget, there are some pigs around," Toribio warned. He was not, of course, talking about the farm's animals.

"If anyone says anything, tell them it is not forbidden here, that here it is a part of our culture. Be careful," Epifania advised us when we went back into the kitchen and she offered roulades for dinner. Naturally, Claudia and I accepted because we had come to realise we were in for a long night.

But we were wrong. The forest's chorus was singing at the top of its voice. We sat down on the patio. I was amazed by the number of stars we could see—brilliant dots of white blanked out every now and then by the tousled tips of the pine trees. Ekar took the blankets from the beds to cover us. Then put something in the palm of my hand, that in the moonlight, looked like a shrunken person. It was the flower. Its petals were wilting; he must have picked it a few hours ago. Despite this, its colour, mother of pearl striped with electric blue veins, was still visible.

"Sniff it," he suggested.

I breathed in. It had a complex smell with many layers. I sniffed until I sneezed. It reminded me of luxury fragrances composed of many aromas and varying notes. But these fragrances only become perceivable with time, whereas the flower's essence was, let's say, simultaneous. There was the scent of vanilla and dust, of sand and musk, of the damp of a cave, of salt and blood.

"It smells of ..."

"Say it."

"It makes no sense." I handed it on to Claudia, who sniffed too. I found the right words as I watched her dumbfounded expression. "It smells like *time*."

Ekar's eyes smiled. It was the exact answer he was expecting.

The other guests interrupted us to say hello and invite us to have a beer with them. They were gently inebriated, but not from mushrooms. Some of them were dancing, others were juggling flaming torches, another pair were playing some game, I'm not sure what.

The smell of kerosene and smoke made Claudia worry about my asthma, so she suggested we moved away from there, even though shortly after Toribio came out to ask them to put out the fire. Didn't they realise we were in the middle of a forest?

Ekar told us that on his first day here, they had gone out early to gather mushrooms.

Toribio had shown him the perfect place to find them—where the cows grazed, leaving plenty of excrement behind them.

"It's poetic that portals for your consciousness rise from cow pooh," Ekar admitted, with a kind of imaginary reverence towards the cows.

When those loveable ruminants had permitted him to gather the mushrooms, he had shared them with Toribio. He had decided not to wait half an hour for their effect to kick in, but to walk along the river, watched by the cows he now knew so well. At a certain point, he heard someone calling him and had plunged into the forest on his left, certain this was the right direction. The voice had called him by name, he said.

"But obviously it didn't call me Ekar. It was calling *me*—my presence, the temporal combination of the things, the flesh and ideas that are me. There are so many things I don't know how to explain to you."

It was a tree that had been calling him.

"I don't know what it is called, nor its taxonomy," he said, "but I know who it was. I would recognise it amidst all the trees like I would recognise you in the middle the crowds in the Pino Suárez underground station."

"What did it say to you?" Claudia asked him.

"It said hello." He started laughing at how absurd it sounded. "We chatted for a while about lots of things, I've already forgotten most of it. What I do remember is that I began to think about you." He looked at me. "That was when you showed me the flower."

"Me?"

He nodded. "It was like we were there together and I could touch you."

I watched dawn come on my own, wrapped in the sweatshirt Epifania had given me the night before. The wind was blowing. The clouds were agitated, like ocean waves. My friends were both sleeping with their faces towards me, pink in the reflected light,

When Claudia and I had our rice atole for breakfast, Ekar had already put our moderate doses of psilocybin safely in his bag. I put my mobile and inhaler in my waterproof coat's pocket—my parents had insisted I bring both in case of emergencies, (their euphemism for "in case you get sick"). The phone wasn't even on. It was no use for anything because neither Ekar nor Claudia had one and there was no trace of a signal up here, anyway.

We followed our friend along the path down towards the river and the cows. They seemed like good companions to start a trip with, so we lay down where the left side of the forest started.

Ekar opened his backpack and removed the Mexican pepper leaf parcel containing los niños del agua. We were cheerful, but also serious, showing respect for the occasion in a way that would have made Toribio and Epifania proud.

Two men appeared from behind the trees. We hadn't noticed them there, even though we were a pair of chilangas[1] who lived in a constant state of alert, and Ekar was used to the constantly suspicious surveillance of the authorities who were always trying to catch him with a little weed to find him guilty of something.

The bastards. Police. They were both wearing dark glasses and had pistols in their belts. Their hands, resting on the guns, were covered in rings.

"What is going on here, son? Are you exposing your girlfriends to ... Give that shit here, for your own good."

Having grabbed the parcel of Mexican pepper leaves he stuck it down the back of his trousers.

I was disgusted by the fact that they were talking to us the same way lascivious drunks giving inappropriately fatherly advice do. Claudia was staring at them. If she had been standing up she would have made them become shorter.

"This activity is legal here, part of local customs and traditions."

The bastards laughed. I could see the cows behind them growing alarmed.

"That might be true in your hotel, mamacita. Here, it's a different story. Stand up darling, let's see what you've got."

Ekar, who was already standing, gave them his bag.

"This is everything we have. May I speak with you in private? This isn't their fault."

They rummaged around in the bag, made fun of the little money we had with us, left the contents in place, and like thieves threw the bag behind them, towards the cows.

"Is this all? This is jail time, you fucking junkies. Where do you keep the weed? C'mon, give your friend a hand. Where has he hidden it?"

One of them grabbed Claudia's arm. His action filled me with anger. I stood in front of them, shaking. The cows were watching us, and for some reason, this gave me courage.

"Here. This is expensive medicine. My mobile too," I said, as I handed him both things. It was a childish negotiation, pathetic, but the bastards' eyes were shining.

One of the reddish cows was coming closer slowly. I looked at Ekar and knew he could see it reflected in my eyes. The men had their backs to it. So did Ekar, but I could see he knew. The cow sped up, Ekar took Claudia and I by the hand to pull us in the opposite direction to the accelerating animal.

One of the policemen yelled with shock. They jumped out of the way just before the beast ran into them. The man who had grabbed Claudia tried to draw his pistol but didn't when the animal began to charge and lowered its head to attack them. They were both scared of a domestic animal that was angrily protecting us, or perhaps the policemen were worried they'd find trouble with the farmer. Whatever the reason, they began to leave. As they scrambled away, scared off by the 700-kilo animal still following them, they didn't stop throwing threats at us.

"If this shit doesn't clear, little girl, we'll be back for you."

"Go on then, drug yourselves up till you drop, stupid fucking kids."

The man threw the Mexican pepper leaf parcel to the ground. The cow didn't take its eyes off them until they were out of sight, then stayed and grazed where it was briefly before going back to the others. We all hugged and cried. Then we laughed.

The feeling that Ekar had known what was about to happen hadn't left me, and I told him so.

"I only knew we were going to be all right. But I should have been more careful," he said, confirming my suspicions.

"How will we cope without your medicine?" Claudia was more worried about it than I was.

I undid the parcel. The mushrooms were still there, whole and innocent.

"These mustn't be taken without a guide," I said. "We should take this as a lesson." I put them back firmly in the bag. Then Claudia pointed into the forest.

"Aren't those the flowers?"

"Yes. That's the tree. There are more than last time," said Ekar.

"Let's go and see," I said, hoping to cheer us up.

The wildflowers were at ground level. Their perfume came to us in short gusts as if the ground was exhaling it. The petals were almost iridescent, a colour I had never seen on a flower before, streaked with an electric blue that I presumed was the same psilocybin the mushrooms contained.

Ekar lifted his gaze and greeted the tree, many of whose branches crosshatched the sky.

"*Abies religiosa*," he said. "It's an oyamel fir, over a hundred years old. A beautiful specimen." We paid it our respects. Its canopy towered above us, ascending into the sky.

"We didn't take the mushrooms, but it looks like the flowers are dancing," Claudia said.

"Why did you pick the flower, Ekar? Did you do any research on it?"

"I ate it. Nobody knows anything about it. I asked everybody and they all told me that what I experienced must have been an effect of the mushrooms. There aren't any shamans for this, I swear."

"But what did you experience? I still don't understand," Claudia asked him.

I knelt in the grass and bent over to see them close up. Inflorescence: three centimetres, dentate leaves. They were pretty, strange, and yes, it looked like they were dancing. I stretched out a hand to pick one and ... *bum*! The flower closest to me exploded with a strange noise. Its pollen flew into my face and my mouth, which was open in surprise and laughter.

"What was that?" Asked Ekar

"I think your flower friend confused me with a bee. Like the nometoques flower!

It wants me to take its pollen somewhere else," I said, laughing euphorically, full of that unusual odour.

"Your face is covered in blue dots!" Claudia was laughing too. "It's like light blue pollen. The smell is really strong."

"I can taste it too." My was mouth was filled with an acidic taste. I started drooling. I stood up but felt dizzy and nauseous. When I lifted my eyes towards the canopy of leaves, which seemed to be projected into infinity, I noticed it was talking to me, *with my presence, the combination of things, of flesh and ideas I temporarily am.* I knew how old it was, how much it knew about movement, he, who to my human eyes, looked static.

Part of me realised what was happening. This same part perceived how Ekar and Claudia were looking at me, halfway between fascination and worry.

"You don't have to eat the flowers. Touch them. You only need to get the pollen on you."

I got closer to the grass and spoke to the tree. Its language was slow and whispery, and, like mine, relied on air, on breath.

It made me understand various things about patience and perspective, about the multiplicity of the lives within mine, him and his ants, me and my bacteria. I put my hands on the ground and noticed something was happening to my skin—it could feel the slightest pressure, warmth, or touch.

Every blade of grass, every crumb of earth. I could hear the voices of Ekar and Claudia who had lain down beside me. I took my hands away from the ground and reached for theirs. I felt their fingers, recognised them, and my heart skipped a beat. My friends were there, alive. Nothing had happened to us. I held their hands very tightly and brought them to my chest, it was then I understood the most sophisticated evolutionary function of the hand was not manipulating tools, but the ability to intertwine with those of other people.

"Thank you for keeping your heart awake," Ekar said to me.

I turned my head to look at his face, and in that instant, I realised, in every cobweb and in all its music, how many faces the forest was home to. When my gaze reached his eyes, I heard the nearby spring, I could have sworn I could hear the singing of the underwater animals, and my heart woke even more because we were understanding things together.

My cheek adapted perfectly to the hollow of his other hand, it was nothing to do with size, but the moment, the precise moment the hand-form occupying space encountered the cheek-form, close to each other in that space, in that moment.

I decided to leave that perfect synchronism, the synchronism of touch, alone, because I realised the nature and extension (the ephemeral eternity, infinity in a second) and my body mourned. But that which I am thanked it, kissing my friends' knuckles; and I turned, curious, ready to continue my discoveries, to try the air that had so often denied me sufficient oxygen. It tasted of honey, flowers, fur and moss, manure and grass. With the tip of my tongue, I kissed its strange inhabitants. I asked it not to abandon me, but the oxygen told me it couldn't make me that promise.

I could feel the heat of the Earth on my back, the infinitesimal movement of the tectonic plates. It warmed my legs, stomach, and head. My hands wanted to plunge into the rock like melted lava, I knew it was possible, but it would take so much time, and to do it I would have to disintegrate into the humus with the earthworms.

I stood suddenly because I felt the desire not to die, not to vanish, and I felt sorry for myself as I realised this was what I sought in all my crazy relationships, in sex, and I let go of a little of my fear of vanishing. I felt Claudia's generous hand reaching for mine. I heard her even before she spoke to me.

"Are you all right?"

I turned my face to answer her and found earthworms, busy, admiring; sparrows up high, conversing amongst themselves in the tree canopies; the tree, congratulating itself on our friendship triangle.

"I'm fine." My eyes met hers and I noticed how she and I were two puppies in a pack. We ruffled each other's hair, we bit each other's legs, we established our sisterhood in dog language. Ekar laughed like a child, knowing we were dogs, in that moment the time of one of us was that of all three. We were children laughing hard, and we always would. Even though we were who knew where in the forest, the only thing we had to do was link our hands.

I asked a very big stone, or rather, it asked me, to dance. I don't know for how long I fluctuated in the air before falling, but Ekar grabbed me and we spun a number of times.

"Let's dance with the rock, to its rhythm!" I said, and falling with Claudia, all three of us came to understand something more of geological time. Our mouths filled with the taste of metal oxide, mud, and sulphur. Other temporal sensations suddenly began to arrive, like a new sense that we were capable of experimenting in who knew what part of ourselves.

It didn't appear clearly as an event unfolding before our eyes, there weren't any scenes or anything like that. It was an intuition, we felt it was a fact that was about to happen. The most important revelation was that we could share it if we touched, and winding our hands together we could decipher together those bitter, sweet, or sharp flavours. It was a conversation based on the senses. We were certain we would find the meaning by conversing and that we would do so with our whole bodies, these radio telescopes made of skin, hormones, and bone.

We fell asleep, holding hands, in the middle of the forest. We had the same dreams, but woke up a number of times, the effect of the flowers coming and going, washing over us like waves in a rising tide. The strongest wave came at midnight. The white light of the stars broke into seven colours, humming gently in the background. We noticed that between one star and another there were fines lines, filaments of a cobweb of light and matter and gas and time. Little by little connections were revealed to us, the weave of past and future events, and we realised the brightest filaments were merely potential futures, possibilities that might change. There was no conviction or sentence, only mutating and multiple probabilities. What eudaimonia.

Nevertheless, most of those visions and intuitions were terrible. It was a breathtaking spectacle to see that in reality *everything was connected*, an immense gift—it implied embracing the fullness of compassion. We realised that our skin separated us like the outline of a drawing divides a character from the background of a comic, but on the other hand permitted heat, the essence of things, to permeate through it.

"Even the bastards are part of it," we thought at the same time as we wound our fingers together with infinite sorrow because the bad guys would never be touched by the peace and magnificence embodied by a cow. In short, everything was connected: violence, pain, injustice. In order that courage, friendship, and laughter could shine out like supernovas from behind them. Everything propitiated perpetual movement and the birth of the flowers. Including our own minds, but we would understand this better with time.

We were late going back because I ended up measuring a pair of specimens of the flower. We returned thrilled and starving. Toribio and Epifania offered us what they had eaten: tlayudas with beans, meat, and cheese. We told them, incredulous that it had all happened that same day, of our run-in with the police, about the way the flowers worked, of the heightened reactivity of all the senses and the matter of time. They didn't really understand what we were saying, but then it wasn't even all that clear to us either.

"There must be someone who knows about this," Claudia and I insisted.

"The only thing I've ever heard about the flowers, since I was a child, is that it isn't wise to play with them, nor with toloache nor floripondio, nor with any of the others."

"In any case, we need a guide."

"What if now it's you who should be the guides?" said Epifania. "Anyway, I was thinking that ..." She came out of the kitchen bringing a cushion cover embroidered with the words "Let providence protect you" surrounded by flowers like ours, sewn with coloured threads in an attempt to emulate their iridescence. She gave it to us.

The next day we could feel there wasn't much left of the hypersensitivity the flower had given us. We went to the beach in Ekar's wreck of a car straight after having taken a warm leave of Epifania and Toribio.

"We will see each other many more times," Epifania assured us. "A little flower told me."

However, *providence* hadn't finished with us yet. Renewed waves meant we had to stop frequently along the way. We couldn't keep track of time as each new wave washed over us, leaving us stunned when faced with the fact of being alive, capable of synchronising ourselves with the various melodies of existence. Along the way we listened to *OK Computer* and *Vespertine*, perturbed but happy; and when we no longer felt like who we were before, those with the names we called each other by before all of this, we put on *Rock en tu idioma Vol. I y II* and yelled and danced.

The ocean scared us. It was a sensory excess that transformed into absence, like death. Its voice was magnificent and the pressure the water exerted on our skin was as pleasant as the moist warmth of one body making its way into another with desire. We lay down on the sand, hands intertwined to receive messages from the sky and the sea. First, we witnessed some probable futures for the three of us, then our weave extended to become part of the possibilities for the whole of humanity.

"Don't look," Ekar said to me suddenly, as if we were watching a horror film. With his free hand, he stroked my head and rested it on his chest. The understanding of what was happening to us wasn't in our vision, but in our union, our touch, therefore it was inevitable for me to realise the crushing probability that I would die long before either of them. Claudia hugged me. It fell to me to console them, because I'd known it already, before meeting the flower.

It took a lot of inner courage to watch the very probable agony of the Earth, the illness, the physical and spiritual pain of millions of people, the fires, the disappearance of many animals, and the world's green areas. The wave of providence ended. We walked along the beach and, as a sort of consolation, we saw some turtles coming and going from the sea to lay their eggs.

We were immature and without a guide, but we had been given the seeds. The flower had used me like a bee. I had to spread its seeds and make sure they germinated in other places.

On our way back, the waves came further apart, allowing us to get back to our everyday selves, and even forget what had happened a little before the next tide arrived, announced by the smell of time. Instead of writing my thesis, I investigated if this providence had ever appeared in some historical archive, but there was nothing about this species. It seemed strange (and sad) that any knowledge about the flower was lost or destroyed. There had to be something somewhere.

I made providence the centre of my research. I changed topic and advisor. It didn't disappoint anyone particularly because, on the face of it, this was a species that had never been recorded before—a flower of the *Balsaminacae* family, genus *Impatiens*, as I had suspected (Though I had been wrong about the psilocybin. It was a different substance I was going to have to carry on studying). I wanted it to be true. I was happy and believed in the rest of our experience, and I told my new advisor about it all without leaving anything out.

I was lucky because she was receptive, even though she was frank with her advice.

"If you want to carry on studying this, you'll have to be discreet. Stick to describing it. Create a simple protocol. Be very precise when you talk about the psychoactive part: It produces this effect, and this one, observable and quantifiable in this and that manner."

"Will I be able to do that with the perception of time?"

She looked at me compassionately.

"My advice is don't try to explain how it influences the consciousness, say nothing that doesn't sound like natural science. If you do, they won't let you continue. Believe me. Do you want some more advice? Don't do the research alone. Look for people who are already observing what you want to understand."

It wasn't long before I had proof of just how right she was.

When I talked about it, people asked me why I called the plants entheogenic and not hallucinogenic or narcotic. I explained the terminology created by Wasson et al in 1979 that recognised their use in rituals (*etheos*, internal god), but they interrupted me saying "that aspect isn't part of your work." The road ahead looked long, even though, in a more or less arbitrary manner, we were able to register the plants as *Impatiens synchronica*, not for the temporal perception I wanted to highlight, but using the handy pretext of its flowering cycle that was connected to the reproductive cycle of a type of beetle. Providence also had an annual cycle in our bodies, our other consciousness flowered in us every year.

I graduated only to realise I knew nothing. I found it fascinating to think entheogens worked like chemical keys, turning on latent, rather than extraordinary, processes of perception, even the brain looks for these substances within its own organism as if they were essential. This idea, which had obsessed so many people before me, was silenced by legal restrictions, not only because of its transformative and destabilizing power but because there were those who used this kind of knowledge to create narco-empires of trafficking and death, causing the opposite effect.

It seems as though our bodies were made for living this experience, it just needs to be set in motion. Through the master plants (including providence) nature is constantly renewing its promise—anybody can have the *internal god*. Taking these substances must guarantee some evolutionary advantage. It's no wonder so many cultures have used them in rituals for centuries.

I asked Epifania for help in finding spiritual masters who could guide me and I met some of the people she suggested. Ekar, Claudia, and I had seen places that psychoactive tourism had already turned into sad spiritual markets. The main roads full of ads offering a shamanic version of self-help through mushrooms, ayahuasca, and peyote.

It was something obvious, but we only understood it in that moment—to reach the wise people you had to get to know people well, become known by them, and in some way deserve the gift of consciousness, just like it was before those illuminations were uprooted from their context. I didn't discover anything that hadn't already been said. The pre-Columbian cultures had developed technologies of consciousness, perfecting the instrument through attentive observation, experimentation, verification, and transmission of the knowledge. This was a precious science, without *quantifiable* results. It took a lot of effort to destroy the world for which this wisdom had been modelled—it was almost extinct

It seemed that no one knew anything about *Impatiens synchronica*. It was as if the flower had bloomed in this century out of nowhere.

I took it to various masters. Some of them consented to try it to help me to create a kind of guide, a journey route that could show other people how to proceed. Interestingly though, the result wasn't so different from existing rituals for other substances, and they overlooked elements that for me were fundamental: navigation through time, communion through touch.

When I asked their advice for experimenting with it fully, one of them simply shrugged and said, "I don't know. Maybe this flower now belongs to your time, not mine."

Time passed. Claudia, sensible as always, dedicated herself to building a tranquil life and home where she could welcome dogs, cats, and the people dear to her. Ekar became a lawyer (and Buddhist), he married and had children. Even now we found time for each other in the middle of all this productivity, the blockages and downpours of the city to meet up amidst the tides of providence, take each other by the hand, and understand together that which we knew by intuition would happen, and find, in the most remote possibilities, ways of moving forward. We came down from our rituals joking. We called it the "shamanism of friendship."

Despite bad health getting in the way of field trips, I continued to conduct research into the composition of the flower, its cycles and effects, like when and where the seeds sprouted, disobedient (or obeying climatic change) in all latitudes as if they were an urgent biological telegram.

It was clear that the world was unravelling, it could be seen in the Biology and Earth Science departments, eternally ignored Cassandras, but at the same time, in parallel with the academic discussions, an underground interdisciplinary group was forming around the environmental emergency and entheogens. There were people from the faculties of Medicine, Chemistry, Anthropology, and Physics, all sharing information and experiences. They didn't know about *Impatiens synchronica*. I shared my knowledge, for science it meant nothing: it dealt with time without equations, chemistry without formulas, consciousness without studies on brain waves. To my surprise, they welcomed my words with curiosity and pleasure. They were as tired as I was with the limits set by scientists, they offered approximations, data, and hypotheses that opened up possibilities.

"It is not nature's fault if it is infinite. It is our fault because we want to limit it to only that which can be quantified," said one of the researchers who'd had a piece refused on nano-neurology in which she speculated on the quantistic possibility that psychedelic substances (as the radical materialists of the group preferred to call them) were molecular machines capable of enhancing the synapses to light speed. This could allow us to perceive time, matter, and the universe itself at all of its levels of complexity. They were theories that would have irritated anyone except us. Vegans, rabbis, shamans, theologians, and artists joined the group. We made sure we criticised everything that smacked of *New Age,* although we admitted the contradiction of what might seem like crossover.

I yearned for the next tide of providence to share all of this with Ekar and Claudia, but the combination of gradual deforestation, ferocious rains, atmospheric pollution, and the ever more aggressive mutations of seasonal virus strains had suddenly fenced in the entire population, especially the biologically imperfect like me.

Open-air life and human contact had become lethal.

The restrictions on movement had become more and more severe.

Rather than meeting the public's most urgent health and supply needs, new problems emerged that needed to be dealt with: devastation of nature, accelerating loss of food sources, mental disorders caused by isolation, and the decreasing world population.

The four horsemen of our apocalypse.

Even though I knew my announced death was closing in, that it was only a question of time, fear overtook me. What's more, I was going to experience the last tide of the flower alone.

I felt I had failed as a scientist (I had never managed to make others listen to the warnings, or enable my knowledge of a flower to improve the world), as a human being (a predatory species that praises beauty even as it annihilates it) and as a person (I had dedicated my life to trying to understand, but there was so much solitude and I didn't feel the peace I had always desired).

The telephone rang. I knew it was Ekar even before seeing his name on the screen.

"It's time! Have you felt it already?"

His voice triggered the molecular machine, the annual blooming of providence, but we couldn't smell it yet. As we waited we discussed the fear and anguish I was feeling.

"Help me understand," I asked him in a strangled voice.

"We cannot be separated if we are one thing. We are divided for a while by our skin, nothing else. This is what the flower, the tree, the cow, the stars told us, I mean, this is what *we* said to each other ... don't you remember?"

Then I remembered and the implications seemed clear—two particles, however far apart they are in time and space, can influence each other in a simultaneous synchronised way. If everything is connected, then shouldn't we be able to reach each other, condition each other, touch each other? To have the certainty, even just before dying, that solitude does not exist?

The smell appeared as if in reply.

"I'm about to add Claudia to the call, are you ready?"

We were three forms of existence encapsulated in a radio telescope of skin, hormones, and bone. I searched in ephemeral eternity, the internal infinity of a second, this moment of time, the precise instant in which those hand-forms occupying their space encountered other hand-forms. Claudia's voice intertwined her fingers with mine and Ekar's, and together, laughing hard in the forest of the world, we understood the restrained hope, the evolutionary advantage, the providential miracle of the synchronism of touch.

1 *Chilangos (chilangas* for girls) is the name given to people who live in Mexico City.

JASON SIZEMORE

Our last issue of 2021 was guest-edited by Francesco Verso and was focused on international (non-US) futurists. Aside from being uniformily good, many of the stories Francesco selected had an environmentalist thread running through them. The implications of this fact is beyond an editorial brief at the end of a story, but it is worth noting.

"It smell's like time." Such a great line in the context of the narrative and very appropriate for a story that mentions "psychotropic tourism."

"The synchonism of touch" feels very spiritual. It reminds me, in a good way, of past friends who were one with the world and content with their station in life.

This is a story I think about a lot. A utopian piece in a dystopian publication. A fascinating selection by Francesco.

DREAMPORTS
TLOTLO TSAMAASE

My spirit aches. Reality is severed. I'm trapped in a glass room. Time is water, streaming by. I'm underwater in the current of time, watching time float by. My hand on the room's thick glass, unable to shatter it, unable to get out. Even if I escape, time will drown me.

Time. Will. Drown. Me. So I slump back. Remain trapped. Watch everything outside evolve. Inside, my age bends and moves and mutilates me, yet I'm frozen, paralyzed in my body, in this glass submarine, as I wait for my subconscious to arrive. To arrive and save me. Hoping, thinking, *How did I get here? Will I get out?*

I hustle into the elevator to my flat apartment as my phone fires a hellish noise in my handbag. I punch Floor 20 and stare at my reflection in the interior's mirrors: fright-wide eyes lined with kohl, curly crochet braids, and a tired face screaming for sleep. Situated in the CBD of Gaborone, my three-bed apartment's located in one of the high-end towers, which is an awful copy-and-paste design of a French building I never remember the name of that a girl like me would've never been capable to rent, going for the tune of two million pula, which explains the cliché line of gold-digging men wanting to suck me—but, no thanks, I can get that for free. The building's parallel to the noisemakers of ongoing roadwork constructions that flank the CBD, tractors pulling in and out of the highway, stamped with the emblem of a Chinese construction company; we don't build our city, it belongs not to us. A storm of sunset-tinged dust from the roadworks sneezes into the horizon.

My cellphone enters a deafening screeching silence then restarts, squalling. Fuck. I press my fingers against my skull as if to crack it from its anxiety. If I don't answer, she'll yap my head off after successfully hunting me down. She turns into a fucking, clingy devil if you ignore her. And the little yellowbone is 4-foot-7, eight inches shy of my height, but she terrifies me when she's loaded. That mouth of hers. Jesus. Don't be fooled by those Peruvian weaves, the sweet smiles, the soft voice, and those bikini body shots she takes on some Durban beach. She's a literal 'slay' queen.

So I stare at the caller ID, Larona, and brace myself as I answer, "Ek se ntwana. What it do?"

"What it *fucking* do?" Her high-pitched voice scratches my nerves. "You fucking made him brain dead."

"We are not responsible nor liable for any damage or death—"

"Fuck your indemnity clause," she shouts so that I have to distance my cellphone from my ear. "What the hell am I going to tell the wife?" she asks.

"That he was actually a loyal recluse. He's not hiding any money. His business deals are legit—"

"Damn it, girl, this was not supposed to happen. If they find out this shit, the wife will be an accomplice, she'll lose everything."

"Collateral damage. I'm sure she knew what she was signing on."

"Fuck." Some shuffle. "I'm too old to be cleaning up this shit."

"Doll, twenty-seven ain't old."

"One thing I know is it's too young to end up in prison. Do they still hang people around here?"

"Nah, I think that's just for murderers."

"Good, 'cause even if we get caught, they can't nail murder on us. I can't handle hanging. Prison, maybe, I can do." I hear her tapping something, a nervous tic.

"Dude, chill, we're hundreds. There's no trail leading back to us. It's just a Dreamport fuck up. That's the founding company's problem, not ours. I'm sure their PR team's on it already."

"Look, the woman just wants to make sure he's not hiding any money. She's endured too much for too many decades to be shut up by a divorce proceeding and a le-fourteen mistress."

"Uh-huh," I say, staring at the numbers of each floor light up as the elevator passes them. "Like the millions she's got aren't 'milliony' enough for her because he's hiding— what?—a few more millions?"

"Rich people problems, man, angazi. Woman was telling me she wants to bag this politician. I asked her, 'But what about his wife?' She straight-up said, 'Just a little speedbump these wifey things.'"

I double over laughing.

She sighs. "You sure there was nothing shady you could find in his memories?"

"Nix."

We access the dreams to access their secrets and memories, the corners of their minds where they hide things.

The elevator doors ding open and I make my way onto the thick carpeted floors of the hallways, catching sight of a young Indian couple sashaying cozily into one of the suites and a Motswana man wearing some fong kong shiny suit dazzling an impressionable woman in a sequined tiny dress in that cheap way g-city guys do by naming every materialistic thing they own. Plus he has the fuckboy haircut.

"I sent you his memories that I was able to download," I say.

"Ja, got them. I've meeting with the widow-to-be. I'm sure she'll be happy with the evidence we've obtained. Anyway, listen." A long pause. The notorious kind that means she's set me up for something I won't like. "A frantic woman's been calling me non-stop. She's very desperate, tjatjarag and all. Apologies in advance, but I gave her your physical address." Ag, a tjatjarag with their notorious too-forward blabber. Great.

I stop at door 67. "What the fuck?"

"She's not crazy. Just a bit desperate with a dash of mal."

"A dash of mal is the essential ingredient for a nuclear bomb."

"What harm could she do?"

"The same kinda harm that *we* pretty little girls have racked up—enough to make balls squirm."

"Ugh, gross. Besides you owe me for this brain-dead fuck up I have to clean. Anyway, I just apped you a brief on her."

My cell buzzes excitedly at the arrival of the brief. I shake my head and hang up. I unlock the door and find the timid, scared-looking woman with a chiskop—a shiny bald head—sitting on my beige sectional couch, hugging a handbag like it's a pet. Unfortunately for her, the house doesn't appeal to guests at the moment. Sliding doors open to the balcony, where a couple of guys are having a young party, hooked on hookahs and some stash. A couple's beside her snogging, probably three hours high, attempting to undress each other. I understand why they've chosen this couch, the rest of the rooms are monopolized by threesomes. Except for my bedroom, which's always locked.

My roommate, an ex of an ex that I both slept with, sidles toward me, donning the famous fuckboy haircut. One night he was crying, saying that I used him for sex when I asked for the rent. Called him out on the message he'd sent his china straight after our coitus telling him that he'd finally bagged me. Guys in this city be good in playing victim.

"Eita," he says, nodding a hi. "Got a young case on me. Let's turn up tonight. I've invited bo Mike over to tjukutja the night away." He sways his hips in lieu of the word tjukutja, and let me tell you, this guy is a mean dancer.

"Nope, I don't want to fuck."

He clasps his beer tighter. "Technically, I'm your whore."

"True that."

"You really don't bullshit around."

"Bullshitting's for lovers." I stare at his mates. "I'm good, brah. Just gonna pass out."

"About the rent ..." He scratches the back of his neck in the embarrassed way that a guy in this city will never admit to their unfortunate circumstances. "Salary's a bit delayed."

I wave him off. "Ja, ja. S'cool, brah. No problem."

He smiles. Winks at his mates, who chuckle. "A'ight, catch you later."

The woman stands up. "Kefilwe?" she asks, confirming my name.

"That's me." I put my palm up, putting her on pause for whatever baggage she's about to vomit as I read up on her from the brief Larona sent me:

```
Client Portia Lesedi: mid-30s, married, female. She's riddled
with the panic that any second now HR will call her from her
"embarrassing office cubicle," terminating her diplomatically
due to her sex scandal circulating the internet. The woman's
already losing her hair that she did a big-chop.

Target: a professional catfisher with ten years of experience.
She's one of twenty-three women on his roster. Has about
ten avatars, spliced from others' personalities he shuffles
through like worn-out clothes.

Problem: She sexted him. Sent in some nudes. Full of regrets
blah blah blah.

On-the-plus side: Her Dreamport had linked with his at one
point, which can give us access to him.
```

"Not to be rude," I say, looking up at her, "Just grant me access to your Dreamport for three days and I'll handle everything."

Her mouth hangs open, incredulous. I suppose she'd scripted a self-pity shem skepsel spiel. Shem skepsel, a poor little creature. But now this little bitch of an actress—me—is refusing to play her role. "But what if he's already uploaded shots of me ... on, like ..." she looks away, whispers, "... porn sites or something? Modimo, my children can't have a mother for a porn star."

Her fingers nervously wring her handbag.

"Nothing wrong with porn stars," I say.

She edges back like I've insulted her. Larona does say I lack the sense for such things.

"Don't worry," I add. "I'll handle it."

"What's your rate—I mean ... I don't have much ..."

"Pro bona." I do it for free, to nail the fuckers, not nail the women with a huge bill. She sighs, cries. "If you ever need anything ..."

I nod, waving aside the comment. I've been offered babies before, no lie. "Just give me access."

"Right, right." She hustles her cellphone from her handbag, starts tapping manically. I *tsk*. She should be careful about linking her personal cellphone to her Dreamport, should it get stolen, she's done for.

In my handbag, my other smartphone vibrates—the one that manipulates my for-official-work Dreamport—with the highlighted slogan and flood of messages I need to wade through: *Portia Lesedi DRPRT wants to connect with you. Accept?* I accept. A message pops up on my screen: *Syncing in process. Please do not switch off your Dreamport during this stage.* I'm sure it's all lit up and green in my bedroom working away, always on auto mode.

I give a good old customer care smile. "Done. I'll be in touch."

Anxiety depletes life from her face, and her mouth plops open again. "But how will I know that you obtained everything from him?"

"I'll be in touch," I say, hustling her toward the front door.

She pauses on the threshold. "I know this sounds stupid, being married and all, but I really did love him, as fake as he was." Teary-eyed, she stares at me like I'm capable of giving hugs. So I pat her on the shoulder to conclude the conversation and she stares at me in the same disappointed way that my mother's eyes throw daggers at me because I refuse to suck our culture's patriarchal dick every time I decline to service the men at any of our traditional family events.

Just as the door shuts, my Dreamport's smartphone starts humming, heating up; once the little fucker senses a couple of friends within my vicinity because of their nearby devices it's horny for attention, thinks: potential customers! Its audio beacons that allow cross-communication between devices want to not only share what I bought and where, but wants to advertise shit you don't need but manipulates you into needing. Its ad pours out of my device's screen and fills the living room catching the young party out on the balcony. And as part of the discounted purchase I made on my Dreamport I have to let it play out to an old memory, which makes the job easier for the store. A whole six years of this nonsense and I'll be good, free of ads.

The ad's disembodied male voice starts its line of gab. "We interrupt your day to bring you a once-in-a-lifetime deal!"

Cue-in the recorded memory of the day of my purchase as the guys lean back on their camp chairs, glugging their beers, watching the memory-ad as I, too, watch myself in the visuals, third person:

"Feeling lonely, bored, or uninspired?" the voice continues. "Dreamport allows consumers to manufacture their dreams into a new reality where anyone anywhere in the world can join, subscribe, and interact with each user's Dreamport or even link one another's into a network, a community. Create your own universe, events, games, or lover's network." The slogan expands out into the screen: "Dreamport: the new way to be social. Purchase with a once-off lifetime fee prior to our upgrade date that will have new users subscribing for a monthly fee. Your mind is the new web …"

Kefilwe gets bored and signs up. Wonders why it needs WiFi. Doesn't matter, as long as its source of power is not electricity but her, somehow. At least, it's not outfitted with cords and connection ports, just buttons and LED lights. Instead, she's meant to embed two thumb-sized circular plates to her temples that will *somehow* connect her mind to the device, an interface of some sort or something like that, the sales representative mentioned, as she stared at his tight belt strangling his beer belly.

His grubby fingers fingered his buzzcut as he spoke. "It's a wireless connection to you. The real you."

"Right," she mused as they stood in one of the aisles of the electronics store, towering with shelves stocked with printers.

"The 'you' hidden within this shell of a body," he emphasized. "But drink at least two glasses of water before use. And make sure you only use it when you go to sleep— not when you're awake, driving, or utilizing machinery."

She stroked the glossy knee-high box of the Dreamport as she listened to him.

"Crimes in dreams are legal." Then he gestured with his hands in a casual manner. "It's still a bit of unregulated territory so you can get away with anything, provided it endangers no one outside."

She just stared, slow on the uptake.

He sighed. "If you get your dreams and our reality mixed up, there are obviously consequences to what you do in this world and not the Dreamport's one, which is why you can't use it when you're awake." Appearing uncomfortable, he wiped at the sweat forming on his forehead with a checkered handkerchief he'd procured from his chino pants' back pocket. Then he leaned in, whispering, "So make sure, if you, like, say, commit murder or I don't know, rape someone, that it happens in the Dreamport's world."

She gasped. Stumbled back like he'd clocked her. Eyes widened by shock.

"What. The. Fuck?"

He shrugged. "I know. Crazy people out there. Not that I believe in that. But that's the most common question we get in our FAQ, just wanted to get that out of the way in case you were keen."

"In murdering or raping someone? What the fuck you think I am?"

"I wasn't insinuating that you are *that* type," he added. "I'm just listing out the pros of using our machine." He sighed. "Once you've finished a sleep session, waking up automatically deactivates it. Remove the Dreamport's connective plates and place them in a dry area away from direct sunlight, otherwise, they'll become defective."

"How do I sign out without waking up?" she asked.

He swallowed like he was praying she wouldn't ask *that* question. A nervous laugh escaped his mouth. He wiped at the sweat pooling in his deep-set eyelids. "*Why* would you want to wake up?" He smiled, evading it successfully. "This is heaven for a couple of bucks. Most users have connected themselves permanently and receive high commissions by allowing us to rent out their bodies, which tackles that atrophy mayhem. We consider them as our ambassadors. You can be one too. For that, you get this at a 50 percent discount."

"Uh, no thanks."

His tablet glowed and he looked down at it with a satisfied grin. "Ah, I've just received your medical assessment by one of our doctors. You're in the clear. No allergies. And you're compatible with our merchandise." He looked up at her. "The Dreamport releases a medicated mist to synchronize you to its system. Has some sedative qualities that assists with your sleep sessions. Don't worry, it works in the way of safety assurance of emetic drugs—the safety ejection is triggered if you've surpassed your stipulated duration time. It won't affect you during the day. Now." He stared at the tablet, finger at the dip in his chin, musing. "Make sure you've already vetted anyone you want to invite into your Dreamport. They typically carry a green dot next to their username. Vetting means we've also done a background check, such as prior criminal activities, domestic violence, sex offenders, pedophiles, et cetera. We allow in every type of user, even non-vetted ones. The verified ones are like prime real estate, meaning they're high on the trust hierarchy, and they have access to more benefits, making them more powerful." He leaned in secretively. "You kind of have to sign away a lot of your privacy to opt-in to that scheme. Would you like us to vet you?"

"That sounds expensive. Paying with my privacy, I mean."

"Well, procuring safety *is* expensive."

"What of my privacy will I be losing?"

"Same as when you host your body, for security purposes of course, in case we may need to take motor control of your body."

Ahhh, like the Guest & Host app.

"You won't be losing anything. We value your privacy. You'll be gaining high security. You'll know you're in safe hands if you're interacting with a vetted person as opposed to someone who isn't," he continued. "In the Dreamport world, you're typically able to differentiate vetted users from unverified users by their crystal-clear avatar, which stands for transparency. The blurry images of unverified users are a constant reminder that you may be dealing with a duplicitous person ..."

The memory-ad's colorful world petered out from the living room as the guys lost focus and started dancing on the balcony, the beat of the bass drawing high into the night ...

"I don't care if people call me a slut, prostitute, or a sinner," I say, lying on my bed, leg crossed against my thigh. "Insults don't pay for survival, surviving does." My phone buzzes. "Chommie, hold up. Just got a text on my Dreamport's phone. Listen, I'll call you back, soon-soon."

I can feel Larona's eye roll over the phone. "You're still on that shit-tourism Guest & Host app aren't you? Man, what a way to waste your Dreamport points. You realize those Guests are only exploiting you, right? No need to be a sellout, man."

"Girl, I'm en vogue. If I'm exploited, I might as well gain from these exploits. Call me a sellout, but I don't care as long as it pays this big," I say.

"Ijo, sharpo mma," she says in lieu of a goodbye, but I cling to the call because her goodbyes are never the final word. "But please get me that asshole's number, I really want to fuck him over."

I cough-laugh out my wine, staining my bedspread with blood-red drops.

"What? I'm bored!" she says, laughing. "If he has a girlfriend, then I'll take whoever is the easiest between them."

"Right. Man, I gotta go. Talk soon."

My Dreamport's smartphone lights up again, and I get that lighthearted, cheerful feeling that my bank account is about to be happy. I access it with a fingerprint scan and slide past the welcome page's offer: *Host your body today and get 100 points for your first three services … Destination: Cape Town, London, Thailand, Morocco, New York … cultural experience … and more! Sign up today!* I scroll through the flood of messages.

Thabang: *ASL?*

Not even a hello. Only interested in my age, sex, and location—identifiers that will determine if I'm worth the pursuit. I dip out, unsatisfied at the type of Guests interested in my services, especially non-vetted ones. Anyway, age is nothing but how young you look. Tweaked mine down by four years, which puts me at the most sought-for 22-26 age group, besides that of ethnicity and location if one were to cherry-pick.

I check the next message.

Sad&Lonely: Feeling lonely, just looking for a fake date, fake relationship, but must feel real. Period: 6 months, occasionally once a week. Requests: be goofy and loving, tell me you love me each time. Send me cute pictures. Ask me how my day is. Not looking for sex tbh.

I swipe reject and scroll down to my repeat subscriber.

Tsholofelo: Eita, I'm back! I told some chick that I'm a chick, so I'm looking for a female host. You're gonna need to change your age to 29. Nothing kinky, just casual coffee

date. S/O female, 27, resides in Moshupa. 1 hour max, keep
the meter running if it's all good. Otherwise, automate
your Dreamport to rescind the deal if it's not the real
makoya, will pay double. You know the drill.

The real makoya. Is anything ever the real deal online? S/O. A significant other
I'm not interested in pursuing.

Me: Sorry, china, I've an engagement. Raincheck.

Tsholofelo: Wtf? Didn't you say you were eyeing some offshore
property? Sounds like you're a few hundred thousand bucks
short.

Me: I've jobs lined up that will close that financial gap.

Tsholofelo: I knew you'd one day blow and be too big for
folk like us. What job is it anyway?

I bluetick him as I scroll to the big job I've been waiting for.

I read the double pre-authorization messages. *A potential guest wants to connect
with your Host services. View?* I thumb the view button. Ian & Sue Briar want to send
you a message. Hit accept or reject. I hit accept. Jesus, want my lung too just to access
this?

I read the title of the message first and squirm: NEW GUEST LOOKING FOR
A WILD AFRICAN EXPERIENCE. Oh dear God of mine, let me adjust my no-
judgement settings. Good thing is they're vetted, so they're completely safe. I take
a deep breath and lean against my headboard. When I open the message, the long
paragraph sends me reeling; they're located somewhere in the UK and are using the
site's typical request format.

Ian & Sue Briar

We're looking to travel to Africa, explore the savanna, wild
animals, etc. We want a high-end Black female host. (We've
seen some poor-looking ones online. We really want someone
who's fashionable with impeccable taste.)

Age: 25-28.

Body type: fit and sexy and *very* Black.

Location: Okavango, Maldives, Mozambique, Cape Town. Flight
and all expenses paid for a four-day trip.

Specifications: We request the Host have no restrictions; all bare. Needed ASAP.

About us: We've been married for thirty-five years. Mid-60s, looking for a youthful adventure as we can't physically travel due to health issues.

S/O: Male host obtained. He's medium-rare, 27, Zambian, and already vetted for diseases so he's 100% clean.

Remarks: We see that you update your health docs on the regular. Thank you for this, you wouldn't imagine the other Hosts who don't recognize the need for this—your customer service is on a par with the best!

Rate: We're paying in euro, so don't overcharge given the lower power of your currency. Of course, we'll pay thrice your highest baseline commission. And we tip very well!

On-the-menu: Female host must know at least four African languages (our grandchild's father is Zambian, so preferably that, we're hungry for new cultures). Musts: Natural hair (sorry we have a thing against chemicals, we're very organic, sustainable people). Vegan (we know you people have a thing for killing animals, so none of that during our experience).

Lastly, we prefer a Host who's not in a relationship due to a past traumatizing kerfuffle. If you are in one, tell us now and don't waste our time. We're not keen on those jealousy hoo-hahs.

Housekeeping details: We normally trial-run our Hosts, but you came highly recommended—we *highly* trust our source. We've hired two Hosts to surveil and exercise our bodies during our time away. Our family is preparing a special cozy family-only engagement at our estate for our granddaughter, and we'd like to arrive the night before so we're well-rested for the event.

I set the Dreamport's smartphone aside. Exhale. What the fuck does very Black even mean? I roll my eyes at the insulting "no diseases" part and the inability to decipher their son-in-law's Zambian dialect. The S/O is medium-rare, meaning he's not thoroughly S&M-cooked (lol, I know) and has no experience in non-vanilla sexual requests but is willing to try. They must have liked something about him to choose him. I'm medium-well if you were interested. I don't have time for niceties and back-

and-forth conversations, I'm not a therapist, this is a simple Host transaction. I've earned enough stars and money to get away with this. Assuming they've read my non-negotiable safety policy, I forward it to them for signing with a prompt to make the 50 percent deposit. They remark with an elated emoji with the words: *Our source did tell us you're a straight shooter. I'll be sending you the connection link in a couple of hours. Upgrade fees already paid.*

The house party dies around two a.m. as I'm making preparations to travel to Okavango, packing and the lot, so that at ten a.m. my body's well-rested for the flight. And I code in instructions for my body's interim-Host's routine for tomorrow's schedule before Sue's arrival into my body. As a Guest, when Sue's settled in my body, I'll be online in the Dreamport's world remedying Portia's problems whilst my body's earning my keep.

My Dreamport's smartphone lights up: *Susan Briar is requesting permission for the following for four days. When the four-day trip expires at seven p.m., Susan Briar will be immediately ejected.* I accept and my Dreamport lights green at the connection. A digitized version of my body rotates below the permission request. *Susan Briar's Dreamport wants access to your body via your Dreamport. Allow or Reject.* I hit accept. I sigh at the next stage. *To personalize Susan Briar's experience please permit access to the following:*

Eyes: Grants the user visual perception and for capturing data. Data is stored in our cloud servers and deleted after 30 days. We value your privacy. Data may be shared with third parties to enhance and optimize your experience. Permitting this also grants Susan Briar access and control of your internal and external organs.

Voice: Allows the Guest to use your voice.

Reproductive Organs: Allows the Guest to manage and participate in sexual activities whilst adhering to your house rules. Note: permitting this denies the Guest procreation rights as set in your house rules.

Mind: Allows the users to store a portion of their memories during their stay to be returned to them as a video souvenir. Permitting this denies the Guest access to your mind-data and any other relevant personal belongings.

Identity: Allows the Guest to exploit your identity as per the house rules. Permitting this disassociates your identity and personal information with the Guest's actions during the four-day stay. Disables Guests from gaining access to personal property and finances and offers protection against identity theft. Ensures that Hosts aren't liable for criminal actions conducted by the Guest during their stay.

I take thirty minutes going through the permission list, making sure nothing's changed since the last time. And it's not like any of these points are negotiable. I have to accept everything. If I reject anything, I can't use the Guest & Host app, which means there is no deal, and I don't get to make my big bucks.

I read the note at the end of the list: *The Guest will be immediately evacuated from your body if they go against your house rules as per the ones you've submitted. We strongly advise you regularly update them.*

The safety rules avoid the off-chance of finding my body decapitated upon my return. A very expensive insurance I paid that some Hosts overlook at a very severe consequence; one Host found one of their limbs missing, and another's kidney was stolen, no lie.

Finally, after that tedious process of accepting everything, the final message appears: ARE YOU SURE YOU WANT TO GRANT POSSESSION OF YOUR BODY TO SUSAN BRIAR?

A tiny tremor of an internal voice sends warning signals, not in the form of words, but a shiver down my spine and sweat speckles my forehead. Every single time this message comes on I get nauseous and scared. I've always 100 percent fulfilled the Host service with the safe return of my body. And it always fucks my mind over how quickly foreigners can obtain possession of our bodies faster than we can obtain a visa to another African state or body. But like I said, if I'm exploited, I might as well gain from these exploits. So I hit accept.

Ten minutes later, Sue apps me.

Ian & Sue: The site was a bit of a finicky process, but we managed to action the deposit. That concludes today's business.

Me: I hope you enjoy your stay.

At three a.m., my already-vetted, already-obtained medium-rare S/O Tepwanji messages me.

Tepwanji: Ian and Sue will only be available around lunchtime. We could do a reconnaissance of the place, chat at the bar, ride a mokoro …

Me: Don't take this personally, but this is business. I'll do my stuff, you'll do yours.

Tepwanji: Oh, ok. No problem. I just thought since we're going to get intimate and all …

Me: Whatever happens when I'm not in my body stays outside my mind.

Tepwanji: Wait, your mind doesn't capture these moments? Attack you with them occasionally?

Me: When I leave my body, I leave it, it's no longer mine. Y'all stay clinging to it. How you expect to be fine after that?

Tepwanji: Well, uh, thanks for the tip. So where will you mind-vacate whilst they're using your body?

Damn, they got a tjatjarag S/O. I'm not getting paid for this. So I bluetick him.

The Dreamport, a sleek motherfucker. White, portable, measures 15 x 9 x 20 inches (LxWxH), roughly 6,000 grams. Voice and mind-controlled. Its power source is my body. Dreamports are vampiric, sucking data, battery, and spiritual bandwidth. It sits by my bedside with a timer set to eject the Guest at the appropriate time. A Xhosa friend recommended the ubulawu plant, and I've no fucking clue to its equivalent Setswana name. She'd advised it's best to consume it like tea when using the Dreamport, for security purposes and agency. Gives the sessions potency. The first time I used it, it materialized a kill switch in my Dreamport sessions, nothing I ever intend to put my body through.

I lie on my bed with the Dreamport's connection plates affixed to my forehead and the LED light turns from red to mauve. Slowly, the tea relaxes my body into a deep sleep serenaded by the Dreamport's self-selected track.

I wake up in a dark, cuboid room, the interchange between both worlds, encased in a lucid husk with a tinge of warm light bleeding through its skin, like sunlight seeping into closed eyelids. Permits easy transport. It has two doors, one leading back to my body, titled: Kefilwe Kgosi, my name—the door, gilt-edged with the dust of sleep. The other door leads to Portia's Dreamworld and alternatively her catfishing boyfriend's dream-mind. Two doors separated by a chamber space, like a mantrap security door. Other users just want to slip smack-dab into the mosh pit of their nightmares or the syrupy quality of a dream. I'm still in-between sleep and lucid-feeling. Sometimes

I choose to sit in this nothingness space, a feeling of emptiness, no remark, no ripple of emotions. They say you stay in here too long and you forget being human; some have eroded themselves into dust here, manifested daggers, all sorts of weapons to make the killing easier, whilst their bodies lay comatose, dripping and evaporating life into the atmosphere. The insurers would come with their policies, proffer out the payouts, and take what belongs to them: the body, written off, but still recyclable, still worthy to earn them paybacks.

Outside the cube, planted on its façade is the kill switch. A hand-sized black rectangular lever. If I'm ever compromised, all I'd need to do is pull it down. There's a reason it's not inside the cube—the cube is a metaphor for safety. The only reason you'd end outside the cube is because someone has stolen access to your body. "If you ever use the kill switch, your body will instantly be paralyzed, trapping whoever's in there," my Xhosa comrade offered. "That means no one goes in or out of your body. Bad news is you can never return to your body."

I shiver at the thought of that. I look back at my name-door that will lead me back to myself, and I know behind it is the pillowy dark ether I will float into as the waters tide me into my body. I always wondered why these doors were labeled in our names as if we didn't know ourselves or the path back to ourselves. Maybe we don't really know who we truly are.

The air is thickening with sleep, making it slower to wade through to Portia's door. A fraction of concentration and I manipulate my limbs and arms dream-wise. I stretch out my arms, grip through the air-thick fabric, and drag my feet through this viscosity until, finally, I reach the cold sharpness of Portia's doorknob. Drag it open into blinding light.

A plaza, midway between three glinting skyscrapers. Most of them act as a safe for Portia's memories and secrets. One of them a doorway that will allow me to riffle through her ex-boyfriend's data to extract what he has on her before he ultimately uploads it or blackmails her. I find myself standing in a line that will lead into one of her buildings. But the line crawls forward slowly as the guards assess each individual.

Time is a knee-backward being. Rain drips back to the sky, a blue-stirred canvass broken up by speeding clouds. Standing in the paved courtyard preceding the building, I eye the skies, anxious and trying to resuscitate my courage. I only have about three days, which here can last three seconds or weeks, depending on the worldbuilders of this world. It's not my Dreamport so it's not oriented around my activities. Anything redundant, it speeds up to the next plot point, and that could happen anytime. Finally, the man before me in line is processed by the guards, proffers an irritated sigh as he picks up his luggage, enters the building. I shuffle forward to be scanned, useless theatrics in this reality. I'm already logged in, authorized, but this double verification is necessary for the worldbuilders, the investors, and owners for consumers who backtrack, armored with lawyers, spitting lawsuits and counter-sues. This is a safety measure for them and their profits. The clock standing over the plaza shows me the time in the real world. I gasp. About seven hours have passed, meaning Susan's in my body already. I've been in line for seven hours? No, I shouldn't worry.

"Mma," the guard says. Face blurred, of course he's not vetted.

"Hang on, I have them *somewhere*," I say, patting my million pockets.

The guard's eyes protrude in shock. "You don't have your fingerprints on your person? Askies, mma," he apologizes, "but I can't let you in without a scan. That's the policy." He points overhead to their neon board's privacy policy: OPT-IN ACCESS ONLY. Beneath it, tiny text: We value your privacy, your information is safe with us.

Liars, fucking liars. I wouldn't be here if it weren't for other users' property misusing people's data, which means it's the worldbuilder's property now. The wind stirs into my lungs. I gasp. A Fela Kuti song blows the wind eastward. The sun should be high, warding toward the west, but it's slowly slipping away from the sky. Seismic vibrations roar beneath the soles of my shoes and I know I'm done for. Something's wrong. My subconscious is trying to extract me. But why? If it does, it'll jeopardize everything and probably destroy our access and connection to Portia's ex. Don't panic or else it'll make it worse. Worse is me being lost in here forever.

I inhale, exhale. Not that I need to breathe in here. It's all for theatrics. But I hope the meditative ritual will relax my rising panic. Something's wrong. And my mind knows that. Will throw me out into a different environment that feels safe. A different reality. My panic ensues; the three towers, ground, and sky bicker with the surrounding air in a dizzying fashion into a mutated explosion that ensnares me into a new reality.

I wake to find myself standing at the bus stop. I'm a heartbeat away from a cataclysmic mental breakdown. Must gain control of the situation. I quickly absorb the surrounding noise of hooting combis. A blurry beggar, 'fro dusty, clothes baggy, stakes out his hand in my personal space, shaking it for coins. I pat my pockets again. Shake my head.

The beggar spits at me, mutters, "Fotseke." A literal fuck you. A derogative targeted toward dogs to chase them away. I burn with anger. He raises his hand as if to strike me. He's blurry, which means he ain't prime, that means he's a slave to the physics of all worlds, so I bedazzle him by ducking in the way of a heavyweight's dance, dodging a right hook. He sways, realizing the stunning value of gravity, even in this world, because he's unlike the prime people, who are indispensable, untouched by such physics.

I backtrack, to step back into the interchange. Scream "Home. Take me home now." Even the words don't trigger me back to the Dreamport's interchange. Something's wrong.

A skinny condai, a combi conductor for a Tlokweng Route 5 combi hollers, "Mabebeza, vatsay? Mainmall, UB?"

I hate it when strangers call me babes. And I ain't heading anyway to the old central business district or the University of Botswana. I need to get back to my body. I feel like my subconscious is about to attack me, so I shake my head, speed-walk past him, hands deep in my windbreaker. Combis rumble, spitting smoke. A man frog-marches an old woman, bickering where's she going, shouting, "Climb this one, sisi." Birds flicker to the sky, picking it apart with their beaks, sending bits of clouds flailing to the ground like hail. Something's wrong. "Home," I shout. Nothing.

Catching Portia's catfisher is the least of my worries when I'm halfway to losing my body. Provided I solve my little fuck up, there's still the off chance of dealing with Portia's problem later. Should anything happen, Larona will step in.

Something not's hundreds; something's off. I need to see what Susan's doing with my body. So I grab a passer-by and stab my arm into their chest and scream "Home!" The reset button, and the world tailspins into darkness, stripping me from this reality.

I drop through the cuboid's ceiling onto its cold floor in the dark-frothed interchange's environment. I get up, slap my hand against the walls adjacent to my name-door to view the visuals of Susan's activity. "We apologize, but you do not have the authorization to access this identity," a bodiless male voice says.

"This is my body!" I shout. "What the hell do you mean I don't have the authority?"

Silence. If I open the door, I'll be thrown back into my body, which will eject Susan and I'll be charged a huge fine for canceling this deal. Fuck this deal. I grab the doorknob, twist it to open, only it won't yield. The door burns my hand and I yank my arm back, flicking the pain away. The door slides away from my grasp and the air drags me back.

The room shakes, vibrates, begins moving downward at a sickening speed. I press myself against the walls, suffocated by vertigo. The cube shuttles downward, like an elevator severed from its cables, and crashes into the ocean of time, throwing me back and forth against its walls, until I'm on my knees and hands, panicking and crying for stability. I watch the walls become translucent as the cube drowns, falling deeper into this slow time.

My spirit aches, screams. Reality is severed. I'm trapped in a glass room, banging my fists against it. Time is water. I'm underwater in the current of time, watching time float by. My hand on the room's thick glass, unable to shatter it. They set me up. These old bastards set me up, to steal my time, my life so they live longer. It's a guarantee that once their travel time expires, the Guests are ejected from the Host's bodies, transported back into their bodies. There's no test to decipher if it's the real me in my body.

Maybe I should've found out who their source was that recommended me. One of my previous clients? Did they know the Briars' intention with my body? What were they going to do with their original bodies? Dispose of them once their hosts' time expired? An insurance investigation would ensue to figure out where the fuck they're at. I may be the highest-paid host on the app, but my funds are certainly below their standards. What *is* their plan? Take hostage of our black bodies, migrate to the UK? Is their family also in on it? Waiting for their return, to welcome them back into the family with official access to their resources. No, no, no. Do they think I would give my body up with no insurance should I lose it? With no fight at all?

I must shut down my own body.

The ubulawu plant enhanced my dream session such that I gained a connection to their bloodline the minute Susan entered my body. Now I have access to their whole family, and I won't waste any minute of that power. I've researched them well. Using the key of their bloodline to traverse down their lineage, I will find their youngest beneficiary, a twenty-four-year-old man.

The ocean of time outside this glass submarine is only the channel, the bloody riverine that will guide me to the name-doors that belong to each of their family members. And I get to choose anyone I want. The youngest stipulated to receive the highest portion of their estate and shares.

I only have a few seconds before this blood-time will drown me.

I kick my feet against the glass walls, telling myself this is not real. This prison is only a construct of my imagination, and I will it to break. It shatters and time-water streams in with force. First, the kill switch, a failsafe. They'll remain paralyzed for years, unable to speak or move or leave. I don't feel sorry for thieves and murderers who break into a house and only get what they came to deliver to innocents. Serves them right. But if I return in one of their bodies, their family might interrogate me to confirm my identity. That's if they're in on it.

I'll take my chances. I press my palm against the kill switch lever. Pause, heartbroken, shaken. My heart sinks into my stomach at what I'm about to do to the home I was born in and lived in for over twenty years. A betrayal. An abuse. My poor body. I am so sorry. I hate them so much for forcing me into this position. They deserve this. I drag the lever down. An explosion of darkness above. The cube shatters, sinks downward. Its force throws me outward.

I swim upward where several sets of doors float, and I swim my way toward the door titled Jeremy Briar, which shows me a view of his surroundings: he's in the guest toilet, washing his hands, running his tongue along his white teeth, chestnut hair cropped to the skull. I swim further, faster, out of breath, out of sleep, and reach the cold sharpness of his door. I cling my fingers and feet to its gilt-edge of sleep as I drag-force it open, my teeth gnashing against each other.

The old couple chose to possess us, now they will be prisoners in our black bodies. We are no longer the possessed, we are the possessor of what drowned us.

The door sweeps open and a torrent of the owner's spirit gets sucked out as I force my way in and shut the door as their spirit dissolves into my past.

Light.

Warm light.

I wake up into a bleached, muscled, Botoxed body with its two blue teary eyes staring back at me. In the mirror. And I stumble back. Terrorized by them. Wish my eyes back to brown, back to me, back to Black. I breathe. Relax. I can always find a Black body after this. I smile at my reflection, use my new bass voice, practice it: "Good evening, ladies and gentleman, welcome aboard Flight 'About time I have me some fun of that non-stop service of cis white male privilege.' Cruising at an altitude of 'fuck you' feet. Flight time will be however the fuck long I want." Harsh laughter trickles from my mouth. I lean against the marble sink. For a powerful goal, this white body is only a temporary stay ... and I will enjoy my stay.

AUTHOR NOTES

When the lovely Francesco Verso invited me to submit a story, I struggled with a way to execute the concept of "Dreamports," which vaguely involved dreamscapes as some form of entertainment and tourism. I wondered about the type of audiences these apps/devices would attract, both noble and criminal: people seeking escorts, love, friendships, strangers finding a home in Dreamport communities, much like our various use of social media platforms.

The tourism aspect fascinated me, that is journeying through bodies much like tourism landscapes, especially the use of bodies as hosts—what would be the rules, what would some people do to obtain a healthier, younger body, and how would some loan their bodies to earn a quick buck. In regards to character depiction, I was keen on contrasting the personalities/attitudes of previous characters I've written, who were typically lost to abusive systems. I was keen on writing a character who was unapologetically confident and angry, who had the "audacity" to find a way to make a living without buckling to judgements thrown her way—which was a bit scary to write.

Lastly, given how our local Botswana tourism industry is geared toward foreigners, this brought the idea of an old British couple planning an escapade to safari lodges, but due to their ill-health comprising such travels, they decide to pay the services of two hosts in preparation to stay in African bodies during their holidays ... but it comes with ulterior motives.

I was very excited when readers enjoyed "Dreamports," which landed on the 2021 Locus Recommended Reading List and was longlisted for the BSFA.

SAMSĀRA IN A TEACUP
LAVANYA LAKSHMINARAYAN

The Festival of Kinship sweeps through the city of New Luru. Celebrations span a week every year because freedom is beautiful. Men kiss other men openly in the streets, women dance in brightly coloured silks surrounded by all their partners. It matters not if the lovers in the riot of colour are cishet or queer, wear hijabs or crucifixes, are Adivasi or brahmin. Some sway their way from ritzy buildings, others twirl forth from humble homes.

This is the age of Kinship, a new era that has ousted fascism in India. Behold the light in the surma-streaked eyes of a man who tilts the chin of a woman wearing a large red bindi upward to kiss her.

A woman in a dhoti stands hand in hand with a woman in a corset and leather boots. Witness the throng of young men in sarees, intricately draped after every cultural tradition, spin and dip their partners—some lifelong, some for the moment alone.

All are welcome here. All humans are equal. To love is to be.

All this could be destroyed if Nayana Chacko doesn't do her job.

When she left the spindly, foreboding structure of the Lattice in the smog that morning, Nayana intended to belong to the revellers at the Festival. Instead, the throbbing hum of millions of stored Samsārans, their data flowing through the fractal geometry of the Lattice's many facades, receded to be replaced by a Threat Level: Fascist investigation.

Nayana hunches low in the backseat of her self-driving vehicle, reviewing the classified file of an incident that's going viral. She ignores the stream of continuous chatter from Martin, her car's pre-installed Samsāran. A glance at his history reveals that he died in a flaming car wreck while participating in a manual-driving version of Le Mans. It doesn't recommend him to be reincarnated in a vehicle of any sort, but that's part of Samsāra Inc's. vision—every human screwup deserves a chance to fix their wrongs.

A holo-signboard flashes outside a small mycelia-block building trailing bougainvillea creepers down its walls. It plays an ad for a recently deceased godman and convicted felon. His Samsāran avatar is at a 50% discount, available for download into smart-brooms, smart-mops, and smart-scrubbers. A clever intern has penned the copy: 'Shri Shri Baba A—Cleans Up His Act!'

What the dead truly desire is to be heard again.

The afterlife is made possible by a billion-dollar bottom line. Take human desperation for immortality, pair it with the idea of eternal loved ones—even if they're reborn in a vacuum cleaner—and Samsāra Inc. is the result. A digital footprint is all you need.

The pioneers of molecular gastronomy train promising bartenders to whip up new age cocktails at New Luru's most exclusive clubs. Daredevil astronaut aunties commandeer spaceships to the fringes of the galaxy. Ancient uncles hold forth on home remedies for heartache and the common cold alike while nattering away about cricketers long dead.

Not all Samsārans are so well-meaning. Sometimes, what the dead truly desire is to stir trouble. Again.

The signboard changes, proclaiming the name of the establishment.

NEW LURU NEW DELUXE FAMILY RESTAURANT, PARTY HALL & *LOUNGE*

Veg, Non Veg, Drinks 'n' Snacks.

On her SmartSlab, the latest space exploration mission is being dwarfed by the news from this innocuous restaurant. A new solar system, thought capable of supporting life, has been discovered. An unmanned craft to Agni, its star, is soon to be deployed.

As Nayana reads the incident report, she wonders if deep space deserves the onslaught of the human race.

Nayana scans the edifice through her smart glasses. Sixty-three years ago, it passed as the *World Famous Iyengar Bakery*, back when caste was still societally endorsed. A red flag.

She leaves her vehicle. She knocks on the restaurant door. It swings open. She casts her ID off her SmartSlab as she walks in.

"Samsāran Crimes Division, Special Investigator Nayana Chacko. Where's the proprietor?"

Nayana has gate-crashed a wedding gone woefully wrong.

An unhappy couple in heavy silks is surrounded by their unhappy families. The only source of happiness in the room comes from news drones flitting through the misery, excitable mechanical vultures live streaming sordid interviews. A drone trills in excitement and divebombs Nayana.

"Are you here for the wedding reception? Isn't the happy couple gorgeous in their matching silk sarees? It's a shame their day has been ruined. I'd love to get a quote!" it squeaks.

"Could all unauthorised drones and press please fuck off? This is a crime scene."

The whirring of mechanical wings comes to a standstill. The only member of the waitstaff pulls open the door and the drones scram in an excitable buzz.

A face looms, raving in not-unwarranted anger. "Your tech has ruined our happy occasion! And during the Festival, too. This restaurant's business is done, so is your company's—"

Nayana sympathizes and points out that she doesn't work for Samsāra Inc. She sidesteps the angry gentleman and deploys hover probes from her cuff buttons.

"Please air all grievances and make witness statements to the probes," she announces placidly.

The server attempts to become one with the glass door while sidling his way out of it, but she stops him in his tracks. "Where's Keshava Krishnan?" she asks.

The server raises a trembling finger and points to a door set into the far wall, festooned with garlands in various stages of decay. It includes a garishly coloured paper bunting that reads "Happy Married Life!!"

"I didn't do anything wrong!" the server says. "I only served the bondas cold. Please don't arrest me."

"Your statement before you leave," Nayana orders before the door swings shut behind her.

Dollops of batter spatter across every conceivable surface, dripping off the countertops in great gloopy dribbles. Hot oil sputters, sending dense, hazy fumes curling into the air. A three-tier wedding cake mimics a swamp, swallowing its bride and bride cake toppers into a morass of melting bright green icing. All the kitchen appliances are yelling at each other. At her intrusion, they instantly shut up.

A voice like dripping honey says, "Has anyone said you look just like SuperFemme from the new StarVengers movie?"

The proprietor of the *NEW LURU NEW DELUXE FAMILY RESTAURANT, PARTY HALL & LOUNGE* oozes the attitude that suggests he knows exactly how to charm women, the hallmark of a perennial all-talk-no-walk schmooze at networking events. Keshava Krishnan's digital footprint includes the video "Five Compliments That Will Automatically Help You Win Friends and Influence People, Especially Women With Authority."

It is dislike at first sight.

"I'm here about the hate crime. Where's the Samsāran offender?" Nayana asks.

"What hate crime?" Krishnan feigns innocence. He's clearly got something to hide.

A squat copper tea boiler undoes his best efforts. *Who's the whore? What's she doing out so late without a man? And why is her hair so short? MUST BE A STREETWALKER.*

It does not ease the tension. Careers in the sexual arts have been legal for decades and degrading sex workers is a punishable offence.

The tea boiler proceeds to rant about a woman's place in society, circa forty-five years in the past. Keshava Krishnan attempts to talk over it loudly as if human voices and Samsāran comms use the same sensory channels.

Nayana's transceivers are buzzing with the digital signatures from the other Samsārans in the kitchen as they whisper their opinions. Nayana's job gives her the license to override pairing privacy and listen in on any Samsārans broadcasting across both public and private channels. She scans the Samsārans in the room and finds that none are registered to Samsāra Inc.

Illegals. She decides to sit on this information.

"—might I offer you a cup of tea, officer madam?" Keshava Krishan asks, radiating sleaze. He strolls over to the outsized copper kettle and pushes a few buttons on an improvised digital dashboard that's been bolted to its metal frame. Naked wires spark as it comes to life.

"Milk and sugar normal?" he asks politely.

"As you prefer," Nayana says coldly. She isn't going to touch it anyway. The investigation could be compromised if Krishnan's slipped nanobots into the beverage, a common practice with data parasites everywhere. And Krishnan is definitely a parasite.

I refuse to serve tea to this sulé, the boiler spits. A bitter aroma fills the air. Tea slops into a porcelain teacup patterned with pop art auto rickshaws and roses. It's placed on the counter.

"Please sit, officer madam." Keshava Krishnan pulls up a chair.

Nayana ignores the seat, blanches at the fuming teacup, and begins.

"Everything you say is being recorded. I hope you'll cooperate."

"I'll do anything to help."

Nayana doubts it but presses on. "Where'd you source this Samsāran, Keshava Krishnan?"

"Please call me KK." He flashes what's meant to be a charming smile.

Nayana repeats her question with an equally false grin.

Krishnan dips his head in a practiced gesture of supplication, the kind that implies he's likely to slip money under the table to make his problems go away.

"Officer madam," he says sadly. "This is my story. I'm the humble third-generation owner of this restaurant. In my grandfather's time, this was an eggless bakery. My father turned it into a Udupi restaurant. My uncles stole the business, starting a pure-veg Chinese restaurant. Then COVID happened—the market for Chinese food, very bad—and they shut down. My mother died before she could teach me how to make idli batter. I was all alone."

He claps his hand to his forehead to punctuate the story of his suffering.

"I reopened the restaurant after struggling through engineering college. B.E. Computer Science, First Class, got a placement job. But this restaurant was always my dream," he carries on. "I even added a party hall. Top-notch DJs in the lounge, streaming from my PartyLive! subscription. I never thought I'd recover a single rupee. Twenty years I've run this place! And then, one morning, the tea boiler is broadcasting. I could never afford a Samsāran, and suddenly, I have one that's going viral! It's an act of the gods—all the gods, Hindu, Muslim, Jesus, Buddha."

"An act of god?" Nayana repeats in disbelief.

"Of course, *he* doesn't believe in all the other gods," Krishnan drops his voice, glancing at the tea boiler. "But how does it matter? Donations are pouring in after this morning. People will come to the restaurant to see him."

"An act of god? Are you sure?" she repeats.

"How else could I have had such good fortune?" He grins, spreading his arms out wide.

"Do you know where your donations are coming from?"

"Well-wishers," he shrugs.

"Let me tell you," Nayana says, scrolling on her SmartSlab. "The Badami Bhakts. Saffron Justice. Love Police. Culture Clan. All right-wing organisations from the Fascist Years that the Kinship has been monitoring for suspicious activity."

"I don't have any affiliation to them. Besides, the old-fashioned things he says are going viral. It's all good publicity, isn't it?"

Nayana is sick to her stomach when he winks conspiratorially, now the suave businessman trying to gain an ally.

"*Old-fashioned things?* Let me tell you what your unregistered Samsāran has said to bring you publicity." Nayana reads from her SmartSlab. "I quote: *Who's letting these sluts get married? How will these women have babies if they can't fuck each other?* He carries on. This is a hate crime. Do you know what the punishment for hate speech is? We're not in the 2020s anymore. Endorsing this can put you away for twenty years, even more, if it incites violence."

The tea boiler sniggers, a spurt of black goop spitting out of it.

"They're not my arguments. I don't believe any of these statements."

"So you'll willingly concede ownership of the Samsāran?" she asks. "After all, you haven't invested any time or resources in acquiring it, and it's clearly been illegally installed in that machine. By someone who isn't you."

She ignores the look of horror spreading across his face. "I'll have the Crimes

Division come by tomorrow to seize the asset."

"Madam officer. Officer madam. Please. Please do not take him away."

Keshava Krishnan is on his knees before her, wringing his hands, head bowed.

"This tea boiler has been in my family for seven generations. My ancestors were tea makers to the diwan of Mysore, himself. This boiler was a royal gift! I have other gifts that I could exchange with you ..."

"Oh, you can keep the boiler," Nayana cuts him off. "I'll just have the Samsāran uninstalled."

Keshava Krishnan's head snaps up. His eyes are barely masked cesspools of anger. His face wrenches into a sneer. "Fascist! Who are you to violate my tea boiler's freedom of speech?"

"Your lack of cooperation has been duly noted," Nayana says coolly.

"Get out of my restaurant!"

Nayana complies. Keshava Krishnan is definitely a man with many things to hide.

Nayana Chacko isn't afraid of escalation. The hateful teapot is a matter of national interest, but she can see this being tied up in paperwork for months. Meanwhile, the malevolent tea boiler will spout its bigotry, every idiot influencer trying to capitalise on its diatribes like they've been doing in the last twenty-four hours. This cannot be permitted to continue. The xenophobic, misogynist, casteist, classist bullshit of fifty years ago is finally irrelevant. It only took pogroms, the pandemic, the cold war with China, and social and economic devastation for the country to collectively oust the reigning dictatorship in the Kinship Revolution.

The upside of freedom is that hate crimes are at an all-time low. The downside is what she's looking at on her social media feed.

"This is a government that swears by transparency, by the right to freedom of speech. It's why we voted them into power after the Fascist Years. It's the cornerstone of the Kinship Revolution," Keshava Krishnan shouts into a camera. "Then why is the government harassing me to give up my divine gift? This tea boiler has unpopular opinions, yes. But it's bringing me profits like never before. Is shutting down unpopular opinions not fascism? Is denying a humble restaurant owner the right to earn a living not totalitarian?"

It is day two of the Festival of Kinship. The tea boiler's string of hate crimes is unspooling the fabric of an equal rights society. The Festival is muted by the threat of the resurrection of the far right. Outside the restaurant, a food influencer is recording a video with a crew of humans and drones. Starstruck teenagers try to squeeze into the frame to grab fifteen nano-moments of fame. A stony-faced man prods his children forward to cut ahead in the queue, which is less a line straight, curved or crooked, more a battering ram with human faces.

Nayana eyes footage from inside the restaurant, beamed live from her fly-on-the-wall probes. Occupying center stage in the main dining hall is the copper tea boiler. At dawn, a clan of pot-bellied men with shaved heads and flowing robes adorned it with garlands, anointed it with kumkumam, gave offerings of milk, and announced the Second Coming. The boiler has spent the better part of the day insulting everyone in the restaurant.

Samsāra Inc. has an arduous reconstruction and approval process before a Samsāran can be made available for reincarnation, whether to exist in private or public life. Many of the criminal dead are reprogrammed to feel remorse for their acts and are user-tested in countless simulations before being given their shot at atonement. And then there's the banned list, those who are anathema to the inclusivity of the Kinship. It's evident that Keshava Krishnan has bypassed it all.

A scuffle breaks out in the street. Shouts of dismay pour out when a harried voice announces that the restaurant is closed. Nayana waits for the crowd to disperse. She steps through the doors of the restaurant and heads straight for the kitchen.

I told you that boy was a loafer. But you insisted on putting him in charge of our plan. And here he is, letting the cat out of the bag for cheap popularity, the stovetop pipes up in a shrill voice.

Don't you dare blame my son, the toaster snaps. *His only crime is serving terrible food.*

Let's not pretend there aren't some of us in this room who don't endorse that right-wing lunatic, the industrial oven drones. *I'm talking to you, Sunita.*

The commercial fryer sputters angrily. *There was a time when the political philosophy of this restaurant was respectable. We didn't fry chicken cutlets in the same oil as onion bajjis. In fact, we didn't fry chicken or onions at all. Look at the cost of being liberal!*

The toaster smokes resentfully. *I admit that's Keshava's fault …*

Keshava is going to get his just desserts, the oven rumbles. *He should pay for the illegal resurrection of that right-wing piece of shit.*

That's my brother. The one I like, the fryer bubbles. *At least he didn't spend five years in Europe and return like he's above us all. Unlike you, Anil.*

In case you haven't noticed, Sunita, the oven thunders, *we've all been dead for thirty years and the world has moved on. We don't matter, and most importantly, your opinions don't matter. I blame Keshava for bringing me back to listen to your drivel again.*

Curled up behind the counter is the sleazeball himself, his hands over his head.

"Well, Krishnan. Ready to cede your precious tea boiler to the authorities? This is only going to get worse for you."

Krishnan looks up at her resentfully.

"What's on today's list of hate crimes?" Nayana brings up her SmartSlab, blanches. "*Why are you serving these*—I'm skipping the swear words—*Muslims? Why is this couple holding hands and making romance in public? Who are these chi*—? Nope, not using the word. *Didn't we get rid of them all after corona?* It's nauseating."

The tea boiler spurts steam smugly.

Krishnan rises, crossing his hands over his chest. "I don't endorse his words."

"What about your little social media stunt?"

"I'm defending myself against harassment."

"You're signing up for a prison sentence," Nayana says. "Your entire family of kitchen appliances just confessed that you're planning something. Plus, they're all illegals—none of them is registered to Samsāra Inc. We'll get to that bit later. Who's the tea boiler and why did you reincarnate him?"

Keshava Krishnan's arsenal of sleaze takes over. He smiles.

"Tea, officer madam?" he asks slyly.

Nayana can practically see the cogs in his crookedly assembled brain twisting as he buys time. The tea boiler misbehaves, spitting out vile black liquid followed by curdled milk in a steaming mess. It's revolting, and the vapours are even more so when Krishnan bangs a teacup down upon the counter, nudging it towards her. Nayana ignores it.

"Krishnan. Who is this Samsāran and where'd you get him?" Nayana repeats. "Don't make me take away your other illegals as punishment."

"I told you to call me KK," Krishnan smiles superciliously. "Also, look outside."

Flashing holo-placards read:

FREE SPEECH IS A REBIRTH RIGHT

SAMSĀRANS ARE PEOPLE TOO

The shaved heads and saffron robes of the Badami Bhakts have assembled, with at least three food-influencers from InstaChef and news drones flashing the logos of at least a dozen different streams.

"My supporters have arrived. Try coercing me, and we'll cry fascism."

Nayana scowls.

"I thought as much." He grins. "You know your way out?"

Nayana turns and leaves, but not before knocking the teacup off the counter.

"That's nine-hundred rupees!"

"File a complaint with the Samsāran Crimes Division."

Live footage from the front of the restaurant shows a diya light vigil being held in protest. Samsāran rights activists shout protest slogans protecting a Samsāran's right to reincarnation.

Nayana has made multiple proposals to her superiors. The first involves arresting Keshava Krishnan for hate crimes against humanity. The second involves assassinating Keshava Krishnan and having all the illegal Samsārans in his possession turned over to the government where they can be dealt with.

The former elicits concerns that Krishnan could become a hero for the far-right, who have remained mostly quiet in the fifty years since the rise of the Kinship. The latter is considered unfavourably; it could turn Krishnan and the tea boiler into martyrs. Regardless, both suggestions are firmly on the table while Nayana is given twenty-four hours to come up with a more elegant solution. Brute force is an ugly tactic for a government built to oppose it, even when it's used against a person who could incite violence and oppression.

A hive of Samsāran activity surrounds Nayana at her workspace. A team of spectral super-sleuths reborn, former protestors and activists, politicians and journalists who opposed the regime in the Fascist Years, analyses data from the tea boiler, cross-referencing it with every oppressive persona they can remember, trawling classified databases of hate speeches and tweets from a past they thought would never threaten the future again, running simulations using AI algorithms and arguing over hypotheses.

Nayana's SmartSlab beeps.

Potential match, says Arifa Saeed, a journalist shot for her criticism of a bill to match job opportunities to religion and caste during the post-pandemic job crisis.

Who is this bastard? Nayana asks.

We believe—eleven to one—that the Samsāran in question is the illegal construct of former incumbent prime minister, Govindkrishna.

Nayana gasps. *Not the Sambar Stalin!*

That's the one. No wonder the Badami Bhakts have begun to assemble.

The Badami Bhakts, named for the local mango variety they take the colour of their robes from, are an underground right-wing group that the Kinship has been monitoring for decades. Govindkrishna infamously led the last stand of the fascists thirty years ago, but the Kinship finally managed to swing enough votes away from him. Law enforcement put him behind bars for good.

Keshava Krishnan's stunts are odious, Arifa hisses. *Using freedom of speech as an argument to support a hateful Samsāran who denied human rights to anyone who disagreed with him while he was alive.*

Arifa should know. Govindkrishna was charged with her murder.

Here's the analysis, she says impassively.

Nayana scans the document. The pieces fall together. She drafts a new solution. She sends it to the higher-ups. She receives a response in a matter of seconds.

APPROVED.

Nayana's spook utility vehicle is assaulted by rotten egg projectiles the minute it draws up outside the *NEW LURU NEW DELUXE FAMILY RESTAURANT, PARTY HALL & LOUNGE.*

She steps out of the vehicle and an army of specialized drones immediately surrounds her, pivoting in midair to precisely plotted positions, forming a phalanx in a three-foot radius around her person. The feeds from their cameras help her navigate through the onslaught of cow dung, chappals, and decaying vegetables being thrown her way.

The protest is being watched by policemen, but they won't take action unless it threatens innocent bystanders, and Nayana is in too deep. This is the age of the Kinship and that means giving people the democratic right to disagree, even if the majority doesn't approve.

She shoves through the doors and stomps into the kitchen. Keshava Krishnan is midway through lighting incense at a newly constructed altar to the tea boiler.

"Get out of my restaurant! I'll call the cops!" he shrieks.

Nayana hits broadcast and her fly-on-the-wall probes beam live video footage onto the internet. She also broadcasts all Samsāran comms on the bottom right side of the video as an active chat window.

"Krishnan. I'm here to talk to your father."

"What ... what do you mean, my f-f-father?" Krishnan knocks over a silver chombu of holy water as he backs away, placing himself between her and the copper boiler.

"Govindkrishna. The Sambar Stalin. Last of the fascists. Murdered a bunch of journalists and activists, suppressed inter-caste and inter-religious marriages, tried to organise detention centres for everyone who wasn't cishet. Or were you too young to remember his crimes?" Nayana says.

The whore is back? the tea boiler broadcasts. *Son, why don't you marry so you don't pay for such services?*

"It's over, Krishnan. Your illegal construct of Govindkrishna doesn't conform to Samsāra Inc.'s reincarnation guidelines. It's propagating anti-Kinship hate speech. You're enabling it, you rebuilt it illegally. A little family reunion of malevolent kitchen appliances is your big plan to take over the world, is it?" Nayana strides forward.

Don't lump me in with the stovetop and the toaster, the oven groans. *I didn't even want to be here.*

"ATTACK!" Krishnan cries, ducking for cover behind the tea boiler.

The fryer spews a jet of hot oil. Nayana rolls out of the way, catching some of it against her drone phalanx. The pots on the stovetop bubble over, spurting sambar and bits of boiling vegetables. The copper tea boiler wheezes out acrid fumes of tea and it dribbles all over the floor.

"This is pathetic," Nayana says after the lesser part of ten seconds runs out and the appliances are done with their last stand. "Really, KK. You've mangled even your attempted resurrection of the extreme right. You took the most toxic man in recent history and stuck him in a tea boiler in your shitty little restaurant. Pathetic. I should thank you on behalf of the Kinship; you've done half our work already."

The ploy works in a matter of seconds.

What do you mean? the tea boiler cries.

It's only a matter of time before this place is shut down for hate crimes. Oh, you'll live on because exterminating Samsārans is against Kinship policy. But you'll be locked in a dark room with the rest of your awful family. Your son will be imprisoned for life, Nayana says.

A tea boiler in this stuffy kitchen, for a man like a god! the boiler bubbles in rage.

Dark room. Very dark, Nayana corrects him.

Keshava ... the tea boiler hisses steam.

Keshava Krishnan pales. *I had to scrape you together from redacted documents, news articles online. Even your tweets and video interviews were classified. High-security data-cops on my tail the whole time. It took all my skill as an engineer, first class. All my savings. I couldn't afford more ...*

You couldn't afford anything but the family tea boiler? Bitter tea leaves spew from its spout. *You disrespect me. I was once the most powerful man in the country. Is this your idea of a joke?*

Krishnan trembles.

My words deserve to be heard by all the universe! the tea boiler says. *Our plan was to take back the country! Not make fucking tea and entertain whores like this one—*

Nayana seizes her cue. *I can arrange for you to be moved to a much bigger repository.*

'What're you doing?' Krishnan wheels around.

Is it something in the public eye? The tea boiler asks slyly.

Yes. Nayana says.

"Stop talking!" Krishnan shouts.

I want something that represents my might. The tea boiler huffs, steam rising past its lid. *Something big and shiny.*

Oh, it's big and shiny, all right, Nayana says.

"It's a trap!" Krishnan yells, then broadcasts, *She's trying to take you away.*

For a streetwalker, she speaks more sense than you do. What sort of son are you, holding me back from stardom?

I promise the stars, Nayana says.

Done. Take me away. My family, too, the boiler says with authority.

I'm in, the fryer, the stovetop, and the toaster chime together.

Nayana presses a button. The explosives she's placed around the restaurant, in case this plan went south, are disarmed. Krishnan wilts and offers himself up for arrest.

We're going to be masters of the universe, the boiler declaims.

Oh, yes, Nayana says. *Picture the light of the sun ...*

It is the last day of the Festival of Kinship. Today is a day of remembrance, a celebration of all those who gave themselves wholly to the cause of equal rights and justice for all.

Observe the lamps being lit, the sweet offerings being made to Samsārans in every home. See the traffic light streaming flowers—its Samsāran was once a well-loved aunt. Witness the crowds gather around the Monument of Kinship; look closely and you'll spot Nayana Chacko among the sea of faces, placing a wreath of white jasmine upon the edifice. Having honoured the memory of her grandmother, who was killed by fascists while peacefully protesting digital censorship, Nayana turns to the big-screen display to watch the launch of the rocket Kindred. This will be the first unmanned spaceship to the new solar system called Hearthstone, spinning around the gravity of the blazing star Agni.

The Kindred's engines fire up. Incandescent, it thunders into the atmosphere. Its flight path is relayed by onboard cameras that capture its rush, night claiming it as it breaks with Earth's gravity, escaping into the void of space.

The Kindred carries unmanned probes designed for different planetary conditions. It has a crew of astronaut and diplomat Samsārans. It also conveys a lead-lined box of Samsārans destined to unite with the stars.

One of them is currently broadcasting a speech. It is heard by none but the other Samsārans in the box. This captive audience weeps tears of pride as he calls for the far-right to unite, preaches widespread genocide and the reinstitution of the caste system. He declares war on China and Pakistan.

Long after the world switches off their streams, the Kindred rides solar flares, using the sun's gravity to propel itself from the solar system. A lead box falls away from its carriage. The once-dictator-then-tea-boiler-now-rocket-man waits for applause. The roar of a thousand sunbeams crashes into him.

AUTHOR NOTES

"Samsāra in a Teacup" reflects my growing outrage and horror at the rise of fascism, witnessed far too often in the form of hate speech against minorities and the marginalized, spreading across India and the world. Hate speech is a crime—words are sharpened and wielded as weapons, hurtful and heinous, seeking to attack, to control, to destroy. I hope for a reality where we are free from it, or at the very least, a reality in which its perpetrators are brought to justice. Words hold immense power, and how we choose to use them can create or destroy ideals, unite or divide humanity.

This story holds my dream of a future for India and the world: where love, freedom, and equality triumph over fascism, every single time.

ABOUT THE AUTHORS

Fargo Tbakhi (he/him) is a queer Palestinian-American performance artist. He is the winner of the 2018 Ghassan Kanafani Resistance Arts Prize, a Pushcart and Best of the Net nominee, and a Tin House Summer Workshop alum. His writing has been published in *Strange Horizons*, *Foglifter*, *Hobart*, *The Shallow Ends*, *Mizna*, *Peach Mag*, and elsewhere. He is currently a Halcyon Arts Lab Fellow and works at Mosaic Theater.

P H Lee lives on top of an old walnut tree, past a thicket of roses, down a dead-end street at the edge of town. Their work has appeared in many venues including *Clarkesworld*, *Lightspeed*, and *Uncanny Magazine*. From time to time, they microwave and eat a frozen burrito at two in the morning, for no reason other than that they want to.

Cassandra Khaw is an award-winning game writer, whose fiction work has been nominated for several awards. You can find their fiction in places like *F&SF*, *Year's Best of Science Fiction and Fantasy*, and Tor.com. Their next book *Nothing But Blackened Teeth* is coming out in 2021. They can be found on Twitter (@casskhaw) mostly!

A former academic and adjunct, **Alix E. Harrow** is now a full-time writer living in Kentucky with her husband and their semi-feral kids. She is the author of Hugo-award-winning short fiction, and her debut novel, *The Ten Thousand Doors of January*, was a finalist for the Hugo, Nebula, and Locus Awards. Find her at @AlixEHarrow on Twitter.

Elana Gomel is an academic and a writer who has published six nonfiction books and numerous articles on post-humanism, science fiction, Victorian literature, and serial killers. Her stories have appeared in *Apex Magazine*, *New Horizons*, *Mythic*, and many other magazines, and were also featured in several award-winning anthologies, including *After Sundown*, *Apex Book of World Science Fiction*, and *People of the Book*. Her story "Where the Streets Have No Name" was the winner of the 2020 Gravity Award. She is the author of three novels: *A Tale of Three Cities* (2013), *The Hungry Ones* (2018) and *The Cryptids* (2019). She has lived in four countries, speaks three languages, and has two children and can be found online at www.citiesoflightanddarkness.com.

Merc Fenn Wolfmoor is a queer non-binary writer who lives in Minnesota with two adorable cats (Tater Tot photos frequently grace all Merc's social media). Merc is a Nebula Awards finalist, and their stories have appeared in *Lightspeed*, *Fireside*, *Apex*,

Uncanny, Nightmare, Escape Pod, and several Year's Best anthologies. You can find Merc on Twitter @Merc_Wolfmoor or their website mercfennwolfmoor.com. Their debut short story collection, *So You Want to Be a Robot*, was published by Lethe Press (2017) and they have a second short story collection forthcoming in late 2021.

Charles Payseur is an avid reader, writer, and reviewer of all things speculative. His fiction and poetry have appeared in *The Best American Science Fiction and Fantasy, Strange Horizons, Lightspeed Magazine*, and many more. He runs Quick Sip Reviews, has been a Hugo finalist fan writer, and can be found drunkenly reviewing *Goosebumps* on his Patreon. When not hunting Hodags across the wilds of Wisconsin, you can find him gushing about short fiction (and his cats) on Twitter as @ClowderofTwo.

Sheree Renée Thomas is an award-winning fiction writer, poet, and editor. Her work is inspired by myth and folklore, natural science, and the genius culture of the Mississippi Delta. *Nine Bar Blues: Stories from an Ancient Future* (Third Man Books, 2020) is her debut fiction collection. She also edited the World Fantasy Award-winning Black speculative fiction volumes *Dark Matter*. A Marvel writer, her novelette, "Heart of a Panther" appears in *The Black Panther: Tales of Wakanda* edited by Jesse J. Holland. She is the editor of *The Magazine of Fantasy & Science Fiction* and associate editor of *Obsidian: Literature & Arts in the African Diaspora*. Explore more at shereereneethomas.com or follow her via Twitter @blackpotmojo.

A.C. Wise is the author of the novels *Wendy, Darling* and *Hooked*, and the recent short story collection, *The Ghost Sequences*. Her work has won the Sunburst Award for Excellence in Canadian Literature of the Fantastic, and has been a finalist for the Nebula, Stoker, World Fantasy, Locus, Aurora, British Fantasy, and Lambda Literary Awards. In addition to her fiction, she contributes a regular review column to *Apex Magazine*, which led her to be a finalist for the Ignyte Awards in the Critics category.

Barton Aikman is a graduate of the 2019 Clarion Writers' Workshop and a member of the Science Fiction and Fantasy Writers Association. In addition to *Apex Magazine*, his work has appeared in *Dark Matter Magazine, Southwest Review, Bourbon Penn*, and others. In 2022, he helped edit and launch lossuelos.com, an interactive multimedia anthology whose proceeds benefit California rural laborers. He lives and writes in Los Angeles and you can find him on Twitter @BartonAikman.

Annie Neugebauer is a novelist, blogger, nationally award-winning poet, and two-time Bram Stoker Award-nominated short story author with work appearing in more than a hundred publications, including *Cemetery Dance, Black Static*, and *Year's Best Hardcore Horror* volumes 3, 4, and 5. She's a columnist and writing instructor for

LitReactor. You can visit her at www.AnnieNeugebauer.com.

Sam J. Miller is the Nebula-Award-winning author of *The Art of Starving* (an NPR best of the year) and *Blackfish City* (a "Must Read" in *Entertainment Weekly* and *O: The Oprah Winfrey Magazine*). Sam's short stories have been nominated for the World Fantasy, Theodore Sturgeon, and Locus Awards, and reprinted in dozens of anthologies. He is the last in a long line of butchers. Find him online at samjmiller. com.

Sabrina Vourvoulias is a Latina news editor, writer, and digital storyteller. An American citizen from birth, she grew up in Guatemala during the armed internal conflict and moved to the United States when she was fifteen. She lives in Pennsylvania with her husband, daughter, and a dog who believes she is the one ring to rule them all. Follow her at sabrinavourvoulias.com, on Twitter @followthelede, and on Facebook @officialsabrinavourvoulias.

A. K. Hudson lives in the Pacific Northwest where she works for a video game developer by day and writes speculative fiction by night. Her stories have appeared in various anthologies, including the *2019 Sirens Benefit Anthology*. You can find her geeking out over fantasy novels and punctuating her posts with *Schitt's Creek* memes on Twitter @TheAKHudson.

Works by **Mari Ness** appear in Tor.com, *Clarkesworld*, *Lightspeed*, *Nightmare*, *Uncanny*, *Fireside*, *Diabolical Plots*, *Translunar Travelers Lounge*, *Strange Horizons*, *Daily Science Fiction*, and in previous issues of *Apex Magazine*. Her essay collection, *Resistance and Transformation: On Fairy Tales*, is available from Aqueduct Press, and her poetry novella, *Through Immortal Shadows Singing*, from Papaveria Press. For more, visit her infrequently updated website and blog at marikness.wordpress.com, or follow her on Twitter at @mari_ness. She lives in central Florida.

Aurelius Raines II writes and lives in Chicago with his wife, Pam, and his two sons. He likes to write about things that aren't happening, in hopes that they will ... or won't. His short stories and essays have been included in the anthologies *Dead Inside: Poetry and Essays about Zombies*, *Black Power: A Superhero Anthology*, *Apparition Literature*, *Fiyah Magazine*, and *Luminescent Threads: Connections to Octavia Butler*, which was the winner of the Locus Award in Non-Fiction. In his spare time, he teaches Physics to high-schoolers by showing them how to use science to survive the end of civilization.

Sydney Rossman-Reich lives in Orlando, Florida where she helps her family's real estate business. Prior to the pandemic, Sydney spent most of her career building software at tech companies in Silicon Valley—she draws on these experiences heavily in her fiction. Sydney is a proud graduate of Viable Paradise Writers Workshop, a member of Clarion West's ghost class of 2020, and is a Full Member of SFWA. She can be found on Twitter @Sydkick.

Jennifer R. Donohue grew up at the Jersey Shore and now lives in central New York with her husband and her doberman. She is a Codexian and an Associate member of the SFWA, with work appearing in *Escape Pod*, *Truancy*, *The Future Fire*, and elsewhere. Her novella series, *Run With the Hunted*, is available on Amazon and most digital platforms. She tweets @AuthorizedMusin.

Katherine Crighton is a genre writer with over twenty years of experience in SF/F publishing. They have, among other things, read slush for Tor Books, written reviews for *Publishers Weekly*, and worked as a production editor of environmental nonfiction and STEM textbooks. They've been published by *Strange Horizons*, *Lightspeed*, *Nightmare*, and a variety of other markets, and is one of the sibling presenters on the *No Story Is Sacred* podcast, taking apart and putting stories back together again. They spend their days as a valiant English major working for Worcester Polytechnic Institute's Computer Science department. Follow them on Twitter at @c_katherine, or visit their website at katherinecrighton.com.

Beth Dawkins grew up on front porches, fighting imaginary monsters with sticks, and building castles out of square hay bales. She currently lives in Northeast Georgia with her partner in crime and their offspring. She can be found on Twitter @BethDawkins.

Hugo and World Fantasy finalist **E. Catherine Tobler** lives and writes in Colorado. Weird how that works out! Her debut collection, *The Grand Tour*, is available from Apex Book Company. Her short fiction appears in *Clarkesworld*, *Lightspeed*, *Beneath Ceaseless Skies*, and others. You can find her on Twitter @ECthetwit.

R. Gatwood is the emergent consciousness of a spectacularly inefficient library shelving system. More of its fiction can be found at iwantanewhead.wordpress.com.

Kingsley Okpii lives in Leicester city, United Kingdom where he works as a doctor in the NHS. Between busy shifts, he writes Afrocentric speculative fiction. His short stories have been published on *Omenana* and *The Kalahari Review*.

Nicole J. LeBoeuf is a New Orleanian writer of short speculative fiction and poetry appearing in such venues as *Cast of Wonders*, *The Future Fire*, *Departure Mirror Quarterly*, *Daily Science Fiction*, and the vampirism anthology *Blood and Other*

Cravings (Tor Books, 2011). She also posts weird flash-sized story-like objects to Patreon four times monthly. She currently lives in Boulder, Colorado with her indie RPG-writing husband and their adorably criminal rabbit. Her not-so-secret superhero identity is that of skater Fleur de Beast with Boulder County Roller Derby. She blogs at nicolejleboeuf.com and tweets at @nicolejleboeuf.

Kelly Sandoval lives in Seattle where the weather is always happy to make staying in and writing seem like a good idea. She and her husband spend their time trying to mediate disagreements between their chaos tornado toddler and two toy stealing cats. Her interactive novel, *Runt of the Litter*, is available from Choice of Games. Find her on Twitter @kellymsandoval or visit her website at kellysandovalfiction.com.

Joelle Wellington grew up in Brooklyn, New York, where her childhood was spent wandering the main branch of the Brooklyn Public Library. Her love of the written word led her to a B.A. in Creative Writing and International Studies. When she isn't writing, she's reading and when she's not doing that, she's attempting to bake bread with varying degrees of success. She is represented by Quressa Robinson of Nelson Literary Agency.

Rose Keating is a twenty-four-year-old writer from Waterford, Ireland. She is studying Creative Writing Prose Fiction MA at the University of East Anglia. She is a recipient of the Malcolm Bradbury Memorial Scholarship, the Eoin Murray Memorial Scholarship, and the Quercus Scholarship. She is a winner of the Marian Keyes Young Writer Award, the Sean Dunne Young Writers Award, the Hot Press Write Here Write Now prize, and the Ted and Mary O'Regan Arts Bursary. She has been published in *Banshee*, *Southword*, and *Hot Press* magazine. She can be found on Twitter @ RoseKeating1.

Jared Millet was a librarian for over twenty years before he and his wife took a break from their jobs to spend ten months circumnavigating South America (pre-COVID). Those adventures can be found at TheEscapeHatch.net. His fantasy novels *The Blood Prayer* and *The Bone Collar* were published in June and July 2021. His short stories have appeared in *Leading Edge*, *Kaleidotrope*, *Summer Gothic*, and *Translunar Travelers Lounge*. Jared currently lives in Atlanta, Georgia. Find him online at www.jaredmillet.com and on Twitter at @AuthorMillet.

Maggie Slater's speculative fiction has appeared in *Apex Magazine*, *Daily Science Fiction*, and *Abyss & Apex*, among other venues. She lives in an 1800s farmhouse in New England with two half-tamed boys, her husband, her parents, and at least one benign ghost. When she has an almost quiet moment, she enjoys Haruki Murakami novels, sampling craft beer, and hoarding cheap notebooks. For more information about her and her current projects, visit her blog at maggieslater.com.

D. Thomas Minton lives in the mountains of British Columbia. As a tropical marine biologist, he's still trying to figure out how that happened. His fiction has appeared in *Asimov's, Lightspeed, Daily Science Fiction*, and numerous other magazines and anthologies. He is also the author of four novels in the ongoing Calypto Cycle.

Rachel Swirsky holds an MFA in fiction from the Iowa Writers Workshop, and she graduated from Clarion West in 2005. Her short fiction has been nominated for the Hugo, Locus, World Fantasy, and Sturgeon Awards. She's twice won the Nebula Award: for her 2010 novella, "The Lady Who Plucked Red Flowers Beneath the Queen's Window" and her 2014 short story, "If You Were a Dinosaur, My Love."

Pamela Rentz is a citizen of the Karuk Tribe and works as a paralegal specializing in tribal affairs. She is a graduate of the Clarion West Writers workshop and has been published in *Asimov's, Apex Magazine*, and *Fantasy Magazine*. Her personal website is www.pamrentz.com.

Theodore C. Van Alst, Jr.'s mosaic novel about sort of growing up in Chicago, *Sacred Smokes*, winner of the 2019 Tillie Olsen Award for Creative Writing, is now in its second printing. His next work, *Sacred City*, will be published Fall 2021, also by the University of New Mexico Press, who released his edited volume *The Faster Redder Road: The Best UnAmerican Stories of Stephen Graham Jones*. He is the Creative Editor for *Transmotion* (a journal of postmodern Indigenous studies) and an Active Horror Writers Association member. His fiction and photography have been published in *Southwest Review, The Raven Chronicles, Red Earth Review, The Journal of Working-Class Studies, Unnerving Magazine, The Rumpus, Electric Literature,* and *Yellow Medicine Review*, among others. You can find him on Twitter @TVAyyyy.

Jessie Loyer is Cree-Metis and a member of Michel First Nation. She's written for the *Montreal Review of Books, Canadian Art*, and the *Capilano Review*. She's also a librarian.

Kevin Wabaunsee's fiction has previously been published by *Strange Horizons, PseudoPod*, and *Escape Pod*, where he is also an associate editor. He is the former managing editor for Science Fiction and Fantasy Writers of America (SFWA) and a graduate of the Viable Paradise workshop. He is a Prairie Band Potawatomi.

Tiffany Morris is a Mi'kmaw/settler writer of speculative fiction and poetry from

Kjipuktuk (Halifax), Nova Scotia. Her work has previously appeared in *Apex Magazine*, *Uncanny Magazine*, and *Nightmare Magazine*, among others. Her work has been nominated for Elgin, Rhysling, and Aurora Awards. Her horror poetry collection, *Elegies of Rotting Stars*, is forthcoming from Nictitating Books in late 2022.

Norris Black grew up on the Tyendinaga Mohawk Territory where he would spend hours in the woods fighting off imaginary monsters armed with nothing but a pointy stick. He's been an award-winning photojournalist, a snake enthusiast, a keen lover of naps in hammocks, and currently works as an IT Administrator for a non-profit agency in the snowy wilds of Canada. When he's not writing about the monsters that shared his childhood, he spends his time learning to speak with machines and taking long walks in dark, spooky woods.

Marie Croke is an award-winning fantasy and science-fiction writer living in Maryland with her family, all of whom like to scribble messages in her notebooks when she's not looking. She is a graduate of the Odyssey Writing Workshop, and her stories have been published or are forthcoming in over a dozen magazines, including *Apex Magazine*, *Beneath Ceaseless Skies*, *Dark Matter Magazine*, *Deep Magic*, *Cast of Wonders*, and *Diabolical Plots*. You can find her book and short story recommendations at mariecroke.com or chat about writing woes or being book drunk with her @marie_ croke on Twitter.

Izzy Wasserstein is a queer and trans woman who teaches writing and literature at a university in the American Great Plains and writes poetry and fiction. Her work has appeared in *Beneath Ceaseless Skies*, *Clarkesworld*, *Fantasy*, and elsewhere. She shares a home with her spouse, Nora E. Derrington, and their animal companions. She's an enthusiastic member of the 2017 class of Clarion West. Her debut short story collection, *All the Hometowns You Can't Stay Away From*, was published in 2022 by Neon Hemlock Press.

Carson Winter is an author, punker, and raw nerve. His work has been featured on *The No Sleep Podcast* as well as in *Vastarien: A Literary Journal*. He lives in the Pacific Northwest.

Erin K. Wagner is a professor by trade, a medievalist by discipline, and a writer of speculative fiction by design. She lives in upstate New York, a storied and story-making place, but her roots are in Appalachia, planted in rural southeast Ohio. Presently, she teaches an array of literature and composition courses in the SUNY system as an associate professor. Her fiction is interested in examining how humans explain the inexplicable, and her writing has appeared in a number of magazines, including *Apex*

Magazine, Clarkesworld, and *Nightmare.* Her second novella, *An Unnatural Life,* was released by Tor.com, and her short story collection is forthcoming from Aqueduct Press. She is an active member of SFWA. Her website ist erinkwagner.com.

Stephanie Kraner is a vaguely humanoid creature living in the Pittsburgh area. By day, she works as a technical writer while simultaneously (and often unsuccessfully) attempting to convince her three cats to be nice to her pit bull mix. Her work has appeared in *F&SF* and has been awarded second place in the Baen Fantasy Adventure Award contest. You can follow her on Twitter @StephKraner where she unapologetically tweets about her writing and shares what some might call *too many* pet pics.

Zahra Mukhi is a writer from Karachi, Pakistan. She reads and writes when she can, and laments about the ways of our world. You can find her on Twitter @zahramukhi.

Renan Bernardo is a science fiction and fantasy writer from Rio de Janeiro, Brazil. His fiction appeared or is forthcoming in *Apex Magazine, Podcastle, Escape Pod, Daily Science Fiction, Translunar Travelers Lounge, Solarpunk Magazine, On Spec Magazine,* and others. He was one of the selected for the 2021 Imagine 2200 climate fiction contest with his story "When It's Time to Harvest." In Brazil, he was a finalist for the 2020 Odisseia Award and the 2020 Argos Award, two of the most important Brazilian SFF awards. He also published multiple stories in Portuguese and other languages. He can be found at Twitter (@RenanBernardo) and his website renanbernardo.com.

Nina Munteanu is a Canadian ecologist and novelist of eco-fiction, cli-fi, and science fiction. An award-winning short story writer, and essayist, Nina currently lives in Toronto where she teaches writing at the University of Toronto and George Brown College. Her book *Water Is...* (Pixl Press) was Margaret Atwood's pick in 2016 in the *New York Times* "The Year in Reading." Nina's most recent novel, *A Diary in the Age of Water,* was released in 2020 by Inanna Publications and is about four generations of women and their relationship to water in a rapidly changing world.

Cheryl S. Ntumy is a Ghanaian writer of short fiction and novels in various genres, including speculative fiction, young adult fiction and romance. Her work has appeared in *The Goddess of Mtwara and Other Stories; Will This be a Problem; Petlwana Journal of Creative Writing; Botswana Women Write,* and *Apex Magazine,* among others. She is also part of Petlo Literary Arts, an organisation that develops and promotes creative writing in Botswana.

Gabriela Damián Miravete was born in Mexico City. She is part of the Under the

Volcano international writing program and FutureCon, a science fiction world convention. She is co-founder of the art and science collective Cúmulo de Tesla, of the feminist symposium Escritoras y Cuidados, and Mexicona, a festival of speculative literature in Spanish. Her stories have been published and translated into English, French, Italian, and Portuguese in volumes such as *Three Messages and a Warning* (World Fantasy Award finalist anthology) and *A Larger Reality /Una realidad más amplia*, part of The Mexicanx Initiative Scrapbook, finalist for a Hugo Award. She won the James Tiptree, Jr. Award (now Otherwise Award) for "They Will Dream in the Garden," a story about a future Mexico in which femicides no longer exist.

Tlotlo Tsamaase is a Motswana writer (xe/xem/xer or she/her pronouns) currently living in Botswana. Xer debut adult novel, *Womb City*, comes out in spring 2023 from Erewhon Books. Tlotlo's novella, *The Silence of the Wilting Skin*, is a 2021 Lambda Literary Award finalist and was shortlisted for a 2021 Nommo Award. Xer story "Behind Our Irises" is the joint winner of the Nommo Award for Best Short Story (2021), the first Motswana to win the award. Xer short fiction has appeared in *The Best of World SF Volume 1*, *Clarkesworld*, *Terraform*, *Africanfuturism Anthology*, *The Year's Best African Speculative Fiction (2021)*, and is forthcoming in *African Risen* and *Chiral Mad 5* and other publications. You can find xem at www.tlotlotsamaase.com and on Twitter and Instagram as @TlotloTsamaase.

Lavanya Lakshminarayan is the author of *The Ten Percent Thief*, which was first published in South Asia as *Analog/Virtual*. She is a Locus Award finalist and is the first science fiction writer to win the Times of India AutHer Award and the Valley of Words Award, both prestigious literary awards in India. Her short fiction has appeared in *The Best of World SF: Vol. 2* and *Someone In Time: Tales of Time Crossed Romance*, among other magazines and anthologies. Her work has been translated into French, Italian, Spanish and German. Lavanya is occasionally a game designer and has built worlds for Zynga Inc.'s *FarmVille* franchise, *Mafia Wars*, and other games. She lives between the cities of Bangalore and Hyderabad, India. For more, follow her on Instagram @ lavanya.ln and Twitter @lavanya_ln.

ABOUT THE EDITORS

Jason Sizemore is the owner and co-editor-in-chief of *Apex Magazine*. He has been editing for nearly 20 years and in that time has picked up numerous major award-nominations for his work. Currently, he lives in Lexington, KY, where he futilely tries to convince the locals that science fiction is far more fun than thoroughbred racing. Find him online at jason-sizemore.com.

Lesley Conner is the co-editor-in-chief of *Apex Magazine*. She lives in Maryland where she leads the local Girl Scout troop, taking them to frequent forays into the eastern wilds. You can follow her online via Twitter @lesleyconner.